Acclaim for A. S. BYATT's

BABEL TOWER

"*Babel Tower* is fat, compelling, full of narrative invention, multivalent in its structure, and is a luscious and fascinating book."

—*Houston Chronicle*

"Extraordinarily ambitious, even admirable.... Byatt's ... prodigious imagination and literary skills will keep the . . . reader happily engaged."

—*Philadelphia Inquirer*

"*Babel Tower* is ... brilliant and rich, employing such a virtuoso range of narrative styles and character voices."   —*San Jose Mercury News*

"This is a book only Byatt could write: the humor mingled with a dark, suspenseful foreboding; the deconstruction of great novels intertwined with romance and jealousy. And happily, it's long enough that even the most compulsive reader won't finish it in a day."

—*Charlotte Observer*

"[Byatt is] a riveting storyteller who grants her own wish, making her readers care about the people in her book. The many stories twine together with ingenious thoroughness."   —*Newsday*

"Byatt's writing is extravagant and sensual, and even her most outrageous characters seem entirely real. A feast of a book."

—*Town & Country*

"It is all rich and often exhilarating. Byatt writes with a fierce intelligence and a sharply observant eye. Her characters are described with rare acuity and precision."   —*Orlando Sentinel*

"*Babel Tower*'s ... ability to sustain narrative bite while refusing to cave in to the nastiness it probes pushes Byatt to the forefront of active English language novelists. Here is a book for those willing to be angered, jolted and, possibly, enriched."   —*St. Louis Post-Dispatch*

"For intelligence and observation, Byatt has few peers."

—*Hartford Courant*

A. S. BYATT
BABEL TOWER

A. S. Byatt is the author of *Possession*, winner of the Booker Prize and a national bestseller. Her two novels that lead up to *Babel Tower*, tracing the fortunes of Frederica and her family through the 1950s, are *The Virgin in the Garden* and *Still Life*, and her other fiction includes *The Shadow of the Sun, The Game, Angels & Insects*, and two collections of shorter works, *Sugar and Other Stories* and *The Matisse Stories*. She has also published three volumes of critical work, of which *Passions of the Mind* is the most recent. She has taught English and American literature at University College, London, and is a distinguished critic and reviewer. She lives in London.

VINTAGE

INTERNATIONAL

BABEL TOWER

BABEL TOWER

A. S. BYATT

VINTAGE INTERNATIONAL

VINTAGE BOOKS

A DIVISION OF RANDOM HOUSE, INC.

NEW YORK

FIRST VINTAGE INTERNATIONAL EDITION, JULY 1997

Grateful acknowledgment is made to the following for permission to reprint previ-
ously published material: Harcourt Brace & Company and Faber and Faber Limited:
Excerpt from "Burnt Norton" in *Four Quartets* by T. S. Eliot. Copyright © 1943 by
T. S. Eliot and renewed 1971 by Esme Valerie Eliot. Rights throughout the world
excluding the United States are controlled by Faber and Faber Limited. Reprinted
by permission of Harcourt Brace & Company and Faber and Faber Limited.
Houghton Mifflin Company and HarperCollins Publishers Ltd.: Excerpt from *The
Hobbit* by J. R. R. Tolkien. Copyright © 1966 by J. R. R. Tolkien. Rights outside the
United States are controlled by HarperCollins Publishers Ltd., London. All rights
reserved. Reprinted by permission of Houghton Mifflin Company and Harper-
Collins Publishers Ltd. Alfred A. Knopf, Inc.: Three lines from "Peter Quince at the
Clavier," from *Collected Poems* by Wallace Stevens. Copyright © 1923 and renewed
1951 by Wallace Stevens. Reprinted by permission of Alfred A. Knopf, Inc. *The
Observer*: Article by Maurice Richardson from the May 8, 1966, issue of *The
Observer*. Copyright © 1966 by The Observer. Reprinted by permission. Random
House, Inc.: Eight lines from "Death's Echo" and twenty lines from "Circe," from
W. H. Auden: Collected Poems by W. H. Auden. "Death's Echo" copyright © 1936 by
W. H. Auden. "Circe" copyright © 1969 by W. H. Auden. Reprinted by permission
of Random House, Inc. Ronin Publishing: Copyright 1990P: Timothy Leary, from
Politics of Ecstasy by Timothy Leary, Ph. D. Permission to reprint herein given by
Ronin Publishing, Inc., Berkeley, CA. University Press of New England: Excerpt
from *Life Against Death* by Norman O. Brown. Copyright © 1959 by Wesleyan
University. Reprinted by permission of University Press of New England.

The Library of Congress has cataloged the Random House edition as follows:
Byatt, A. S. (Antonia Susan)
Babel Tower / A. S. Byatt—1st ed.
p. cm.
ISBN 0-679-40513-5
1. Married women—England—London—Fiction. 2. Trials (Obscenity)—England—Fiction.
3. Family violence—England—Fiction. 4. Young women—England—Fiction.
5. Divorce—England—Fiction. I. Title.
PR6052.Y2B33 1996b
823'.914—dc20   95-53210
Vintage ISBN: 0-679-73680-8

Printed in the United States of America
10 9 8 7 6 5 4 3 2

For David Royle

A NOTE FOR AMERICAN READERS

The Profumo scandal and the Moors Murders were important public events which helped to define the moral atmosphere of "swinging London" and the "permissive society" in England in the 1960s. Other important events were the prosecution and acquittal of the publishers of *Lady Chatterley's Lover* in 1960 and the prosecution and conviction of the publishers of *Last Exit to Brooklyn* in 1967. The *Last Exit* decision was reversed on appeal. I have taken some legal details from that trial, particularly the unusual decision by the judge to hear the defence witnesses before those for the prosecution, and also the fact that it was tape-recorded in full on behalf of the publishers, who later used their transcript to prepare the appeal.

John Profumo was Secretary of State for War in Harold Macmillan's government. In 1963 there were rumours that he had slept with a prostitute, Christine Keeler, who had also slept with a Soviet naval attaché, Eugene Ivanov. National security was thought to be threatened by this. Profumo made a personal statement to the House of Commons in March, denying the allegations, but resigned in June, confessing that his statement had been a lie. Also in June Christine Keeler and another young woman, Marilyn (Mandy) Rice-Davis, were involved in the trial of Dr. Stephen Ward, osteopath and artist, who was convicted in August of living on their immoral earnings, but killed himself on the day of the verdict. The trial made public figures of the two composed and attractive young women, and aroused a swarm of rumours of sleaze and corruption in high places, which contributed to the fall of the Conservative government. Lord Denning, an eminent judge, wrote a report on the "Profumo Affair" dealing solemnly with, among other things, rumours that a government minister had attended sadistic orgies at Stephen Ward's house in "a black leather mask which laces up at the back," and that there were parties where "the man who serves dinner is nearly naked except for a small square lace apron round his waist such as a waitress might wear."

Ian Brady was found guilty in 1966 of the murders of Edward Evans, Lesley Ann Downey, and John Kilbride. Myra Hindley was found guilty of murdering Evans and Downey, not guilty of murdering Kilbride, but guilty of abetting Brady in that murder. The murders were particularly horrific because they seemed to have been committed for the pleasure of murdering. Brady did have the works of de Sade, amongst others, in his library. The victims were buried on the Moors, and Hindley later confessed that further victims were still hidden there. Both Brady and Hindley are still in prison.

Her Telepathic-Station transmits thought-waves
the second-rate, the bored, the disappointed,
and any of us when tired or uneasy
    are tuned to receive.

So, though unlisted in atlas or phone-book,
Her Garden is easy to find. In no time
one reaches the gate over which is written
    large: MAKE LOVE NOT WAR

. . .

She does not brutalise Her victims (beasts could
bite or bolt), She simplifies them to flowers,
sessile fatalists who don't mind and only
    can talk to themselves.

All but a privileged Few, the elite She
guides to Her secret citadel, the Tower
where a laugh is forbidden and DO HARM AS
    THOU WILT is the Law.

Dear little not-so-innocents, beware of
Old Grandmother Spider; rump Her endearments.
She's not quite as nice as She looks, nor you quite
    as tough as you think.

                W. H. Auden, "Circe"

La Nature n'a qu'une voix, dîtes-vous, qui parle à tous les hommes.
Pourquoi donc que ces hommes pensent différemment? Tout, d'après cela, devait être
unanime et d'accord, et cet accord ne sera jamais pour l'anthropophagie.

                Mme. de Sade, Letter to her husband

I fear we are not getting rid of God because we still believe in grammar.

                Nietzsche

BABEL TOWER

It might begin:

The thrush has his anvil or altar on one fallen stone in a heap,
gold and grey, roughly squared and shaped, hot in the sun and
mossy in the shade. The massive rubble is in a clearing on a high hill.
Below is the canopy of the forest. There is a spring, of course, and a
little river flowing from it.

The thrush appears to be listening to the earth. In fact he is looking, with his sideways stare, for his secret prey in the grass, in the
fallen leaves. He stabs, he pierces, he carries the shell with its soft centre to his stone. He lifts the shell, he cracks it down. He repeats. He
repeats. He extracts the bruised flesh, he sips, he juggles, he swallows.
His throat ripples. He sings. His song is liquid syllables, short cries,
serial trills. His feathers gleam, creamy and brown-spotted. He repeats. He repeats.

Characters are carved on the stones. Maybe runes, maybe cuneiform,
maybe ideograms of a bird's eye or a creature walking, or pricking
spears and hatchets. Here are broken alphabets, α and ∞, C and T,
A and G. Round the stones are the broken shells, helical whorls like
empty ears in which no hammer beats on no anvil. They nestle. Their
sound is brittle. Their lips are pure white (*Helix hortensis*) and shining
black (*Helix nemoralis*). They are striped and coiled, gold, rose, chalk,
umber; they rattle together as the quick bird steps among them. In the
stones are the coiled remains of their congeners, millions of years old.

The thrush sings his limited lovely notes. He stands on the stone,
which we call his anvil or altar, and repeats his song. Why does his
song give us such pleasure?

I

❧❧❧❧❧

Or it might begin with Hugh Pink, walking in Laidley Woods in Herefordshire in the autumn of 1964. The woods are mostly virgin woodland, crowded between mountainsides, but Hugh Pink is walking along an avenue of ancient yews, stretched darkly over hills and across valleys.

His thoughts buzz round him like a cloud of insects, of varying colours, sizes and liveliness. He thinks about the poem he is writing, a rich red honeycomb of a poem about a pomegranate, and he thinks about how to make a living. He does not like teaching in schools, but that is how he has recently made some sort of living, and he reconstructs the smells of chalk and ink and boys, the noise of corridors and tumult, amongst the dark trees. The wood floor smells pungent and rotting. He thinks of Rupert Parrott, the publisher, who might pay him to read manuscripts. He does not think he will pay much, but it might be enough. He thinks of the blooded pink jelly of pomegranates, of the word "pomegranate," round and spicy. He thinks of Persephone and is moved by the automatic power of the myth and then repelled by caution. The myth is too big, too easy, too much for his pomegranate. He must be oblique. Why is there this necessity, now, to be oblique? He thinks of Persephone as he used to imagine her when he was a boy, a young white girl in a dark cavern, before a black table, with a gold plate containing a heap of seeds. He had supposed the six seeds she ate were dry seeds, when he was a boy and had never seen a pomegranate. Her head is bowed, her hair is pale gold. She knows she should not eat, and eats. Why? It is not a question you can ask. The story compels her to eat. As he thinks, his eyes take in the woods, brambles and saplings, flaming spindle-berries and gleaming holly leaves. He thinks that he will remember Persephone and holly, and suddenly sees that the soft quadruple rosy seed of the spindle is not unlike the packed seeds of the pomegranate. He thinks about spindles, touches on Sleeping Beauty and her pricked finger, goes back to Persephone, dreaming girls who have eaten forbidden bloody seeds. Not the poem he is writing. His poem is about fruit flesh. His feet make a regular rhythm on fallen needles and the blanket of soft decay. He will remember the trees for the images in his mind's eye, and the images for the trees. The brain does all sorts of work, Hugh Pink thinks. Why does it do this sort so well, so luxuriously?

At the end of the ride, when he comes to it, is a stile. Beyond the stile are rough fields and hedges. On the other side of the stile are a woman and a child, standing quietly. The woman is wearing country clothes, jodhpurs, boots, a hacking jacket. She has a green headsquare knotted under her chin, in the style of the Queen and her royal sister. She leans on the fence, without putting her weight on it, looking into the wood. The child, partly obscured by the steps of the stile, appears to be clinging to the leg of the woman, both of whose arms are on the top bar of the fence.

They do not move as Hugh Pink approaches. He decides to strike off himself, into a shady path on his left. Then she calls his name.

"Hugh Pink? Hugh Pink. Hugh—"

He does not recognise her. She is in the wrong clothes, in the wrong place, at the wrong time. She is helping the child on to the stile. Her movements are brisk and awkward, and this reminds him. The child stands on the top step, balancing with one hand on her shoulder.

"Frederica—" says Hugh Pink.

He is about to add her old surname, and stops. He knows she is married. He remembers the buzz of furious gossip and chatter at the time of this marriage. Someone nobody *knew*, they had said, they had complained, none of her old friends, a stranger, a dark horse. No one was invited to the wedding, none of her university lovers or gossips, they had found out purely by chance, she had suddenly vanished, or so they told each other, with variants, with embellishments. It was put about that this man kept her more or less locked up, more or less incommunicado, in a moated grange, would you believe, in the country, in outer darkness. There had been something else, some disaster, a death, a death in the family, more or less at the same time, which was said to have changed Frederica, utterly changed her, they said. She is very changed, everyone was saying, you would hardly know her. Hugh was on his way to Madrid at this time, trying to see if poetry and making a living could be done in that city. He had once been in love with Frederica, and in Madrid had fallen in love with a silent Swedish girl. Also he had liked Frederica, but had lost her, had lost touch, because love always came before and confounded liking, which is regrettable. His memories of Frederica are confused by memories of his own embarrassment and memories of Sigrid, and of that embarrassment.

It is true that she is changed. She is dressed for hunting. But she no longer looks like a huntress.

"Frederica," says Hugh Pink.

"This is Leo," says Frederica. "My son."

The boy's look, inside his blue hood, is unsmiling. He has Frederica's red hair, two or three shades darker. He has large dark brown eyes, under heavy dark brows.

"This is Hugh Pink. One of my old friends."

Leo continues to stare at Hugh, at the wood. He does not speak.

Or it might begin in the crypt of St. Simeon's Church, not far from King's Cross, at the same time on the same day.

Daniel Orton sits on a slowly rotating black chair, constrained by a twisted telephone wire. Round and back. His ear is hot with electric words that filter through the black shell he holds to his head. He listens, frowning.

"I say I'm completely shut in you know I say I say I say I don't get up off my butt and go out of this room any more I can't seem to get up the force I ought to try it's silly really but what's the point I say I say I say I say if I did get out there they'd all stomp on me I'd be underfoot in no time it isn't *safe* I say I say I say are you there are you listening do you give a damn is there anyone at all on the end of this line I say I say."

"Yes, there's someone. Tell me where you want to go. Tell me why you're afraid to go out."

"I don't need to go nowhere no one needs me there's no need that's why oh what's the point? Are you still *there*?"

"I'm here."

The crypt is dark and solid. There are three telephones, set round the base of a pillar, in plywood cubicles soundproofed with a honeycomb of egg-boxes. The other two telephones are unmanned. There is a small blue-and-white jug of anemones in Daniel's cubicle. Two are open, a white and a dark crimson with a centre full of soft black spikes and black powder. There are unopened blue and red ones, bright inside colours hidden under fur, steel-blue and soft pink-grey, above the ruffs of leaves. Over each telephone is a text, done in good amateur calligraphy. Daniel's says:

So likewise ye, except ye utter by the tongue words easy to be understood, how shall it be known what is spoken? For ye shall speak into the air.
There are, it may be, so many kinds of voices in the world, and none of them is without signification.
Therefore if I know not the meaning of the voice, I shall be unto him that speaketh a barbarian, and he that speaketh shall be a barbarian unto me. I Corinthians 14:9–11.

The second phone rings. Daniel has to decide to disengage from the first caller. Someone else should be there, but even saints can be tardy.

"Help me."

"If I can."

"Help me."

"I hope I can."

"I've done wrong."

"Tell me, I'll listen."

Silence.

"I'm here simply to listen. You can tell me anything. That's what I'm for."

"I can't. I don't think I can. I made a mistake, I'm sorry, I'll go."

"Don't go. It might help you to tell me."

He is a man playing a hooked creature in the dark depths on a long dark line. It gasps and twists.

"I had to get out, you see. I had to get out. I thought *I had to get out.* Every day that was what I thought."

"Many of us do."

"But we don't—but we don't—do what I did."

"Tell me. I'll simply listen."

"I've not told anybody. Not for a whole year, a whole year is probably what it is, I've lost count. It might kill me to tell anyone, I might just be—nothing, I am nothing."

"No. You are not nothing. Tell me how you got out."

"I was making the kiddies' tea. They were lovely kids, they were—"

Tears, hectic gulps.

"Your own kids?"

"Yes." In a whisper. "I was just making bread and butter. I had this big knife. This sharp big knife."

Daniel's spine stiffens. He has taught himself not to make imaginary faces or places for the voices; that has led to errors; he unmakes a cramped kitchen, a tight-lipped face.

"And?" he says.

"I don't know what come over me. I stood and just looked at everything, the bread, and the butter, and the cooker, and the dirty dishes, and that knife, and I just became *someone else*."

"And?"

"And I put down the knife, and I didn't say anything, I just went and got my coat and my handbag, I didn't even say, 'I'm just going out for a minute or two,' I just went out of the front door quietly and shut it behind me. And I went on walking a long time. And. And I never went back. The little one was in his high-chair. He might have fallen over or anything might have happened. I just never went back."

"Did you get in touch after? With your husband? Do you have a husband?"

"I did, yes. I do have a husband, I suppose. I didn't get in touch. No. I couldn't. You see I couldn't."

"Do you want me to help you to get in touch?"

"No." Quickly. "No, no, no, no, no. I'd die, I'd die. I've done wrong. I've done terrible wrong."

"Yes," says Daniel. "But I wouldn't say it couldn't be helped."

"I've said it now. Thank you. I think I'll go now."

"I think I can help, I think you need help—"

"I don't know. I've done wrong. I'll go."

St. Simeon's is not in use as a parish church. It stands in a grimy courtyard, and has a heavy, square mediaeval tower, now surrounded by a bristling cage of scaffolding. The old church was enlarged in the eighteenth century and again in the nineteenth century, and was partly demolished by bombing in the Second World War. The Victorian nave was always too high and gaunt for its width, and this effect is emphasised by the fact that it has been only partly rebuilt, inside its old shell. It once had gaudy nineteenth-century stained glass, of no particular merit, depicting Noah's Ark and the story of the Flood on one side, and the stories of the raising of Lazarus, the appearance of the risen Christ at Emmaus and the tongues of fire descending at Whitsuntide, on the other. All these windows were sucked in by bomb blasts, leaving heaps of brilliant blackened fragments strewn in the aisles. A devout glazier in the congregation undertook to rebuild the windows, after the war, using the broken lights, but he was not able, or even willing, to reconstitute the narratives as they had been. What he made was a coloured mosaic of purple and gold constellations, of rivers of grass green and blood red, of hummocks of burned amber and clouded, smoke-stained, once-clear glass. It was too sad, he told the Vicar, to put the pictures together all smashed, with gaping holes. He thought it should all be bright and cheerful, and added modern glass here and there, making something abstract yet suggestive, with faces of giraffes and peacocks and leopards staring at odd angles out of red drapery, with white wings divided by sea blue and sky blue, angels and antediluvian storks and doves mingling with pentecostal flames. The peaks of Mount Ararat balance on a heap of smoky rubble, amongst which are planks of the Ark at all angles. Dead Lazarus's bound jaw has survived and one of his stiff white hands; both make a kind of wheel with the hand breaking bread at Emmaus and a hammering Ark-builder's hand. Parts of the primal rainbow flash amongst blue-and-white wave-crests.

Virginia (Ginnie) Greenhill clatters down on high heels. She explains about late buses and bad-tempered queues. No problem, says Daniel. She offers him tea, shortbread, comfort. She has a sweet face, round, with round glasses resting on round pink cheeks and a mouth arched upwards. She settles in her own armchair—hers does not spin—and spreads out an expanse of complicated Fair Isle, oatmeal and emerald. Her needles click. Daniel is drowsy. His telephone rings.

"Remember there is no God."

"So you have said before."

"And because there is no God, do as thou wilt shall be the whole of the law."

"So you have also said before."

"If you knew what that meant. If you really knew. You would not sound so complacent."

"I hope that is not how I sound."

"You sound stolid, you sound blinkered, you sound one-dimensional."

"You never let me say much, to sound anything."

"You are not supposed to mind that. You are supposed to listen to what I have to say to you."

"I do listen."

"I abuse you. You don't respond. I can hear you turning your other cheek. You are a Christian parson or person. I waste your time. You waste your own time, since there is no God. *Homo homini deus est, homo homini lupus est* and you are the dog in the fable with his neck worn bare by the dog-collar, wouldn't you agree?"

"You want me to dislike you," says Daniel, carefully.

"You do dislike me. I can hear it in your voice. I have heard it before. I tell you that God is dead, and you dislike me."

"I listen to you, God or no God."

"And you haven't once told me I must be very unhappy, which is very clever of you, since I am not."

"I am reserving judgement," says Daniel grimly.

"So just, so restrained, not a fool."

"The fool hath said in his heart, there is no God."

"So I am a fool?"

"No. I just said that, because it seemed to fit. I couldn't resist it. Count it unsaid, if you like."

"*Do* you wear a dog-collar?"

"Under a thick jumper. Like many these days."

"Bonhomie. Anomie. I waste your time. I *am* a waste of time. I occupy your line with God when other fools stuffed with Seconal or dripping gore may be trying to get through."

"Just so."

"They are nothing, if there is no God."

"I'll be the judge of that."

"It is my calling to call you and tell you there is no God. One day you will hear me, and understand what I say."

"You don't know what I understand. You are making me up."

"I've riled you. You will learn—slowly, because you aren't very bright—I go on until I have riled you, because it is your *job*, your calling, not to be riled, but in the end I can rile you. Aren't you going to ask me why I need to rile you?"

"No. I can ask myself. And I'm too riled. Satisfied?"

"You think I am childish. I am not."

"I'm no expert in childishness."

"Ah, you *are* riled. I'll go. Until next time."

"As you will," says Daniel, who is indeed riled.

10

"Steelwire," says Ginny Greenhill. She has given this name to the death-of-god-monger, because of his voice, a clear BBC twang, a produced voice, plangent and metallic.

"Steelwire," says Daniel. "He says he wants to *rile* me and he does. I can't work out why he goes on calling."

"He won't usually talk to me. It's you he likes. He just tells me there is no God and rings off. I say, yes dear, or something inane, and he rings off. I've no idea if he's upset, or malicious, or what. Down here, I suppose, we are likely to over-react, to suspect someone who merely wants to *rile* you, of being desperate, even if he isn't. We see the underside of the world, I suppose."

Her needles tap. Her voice is comfortable, like honey and toast. She is in her fifties, and unmarried. She does not invite questions about her private life. She once managed a corset shop, Daniel knows, and now lives perhaps off a small private income and a pension. She is a devout Christian and finds Steelwire harder to take than masturbators in phone-booths.

Canon Holly comes down the stairs as Ginnie Greenhill answers another call.

"No, we're here to help, *whatever* the problem, you *might* shock me of course, but I do doubt it—"

Canon Holly takes the third chair and watches Daniel write in the log.

4.15–4.45. Steelwire. There is no God, as usual. Daniel.

"Any idea what he's up to?" The Canon inserts a cigarette into a cracked amber holder and puffs smoke towards Daniel. He moves around in a cloud of smoke-scent, like a bloater.

"No," says Daniel. "Same message, same style. He set out to irritate, and did. It's possible he's really upset because there's no God, or God is dead."

"Theological despair as a motive for suicide."

"It's been known."

"Indeed."

"But I think he's too gabby to be suicidal. I wonder what he does all day and night. He rings at all times."

"Time will reveal," says the Canon.

"It doesn't always," says Daniel, who has had one or two nasty experiences, hearing desperate voices subside into meaningless babble and the burring of an empty telephone, or rise more and more shrilly before the sudden severing of the link across the air.

Or it might begin with the beginning of the book that was to cause so much trouble, but was then only scribbled heaps of notes, and a swarm of scenes, imagined and re-imagined.

Chapter I   *Of the Foundation of Babbletower*

When the blissful dawn of the Revolution had darkened to the red light of Terror, when the paving-stones of the city shifted on flesh and oozed blood in their interstices, when the streaming blade rose and fell busily all day and the thick sweet smell of butchery flared in all men's nostrils, a small band of free spirits left the City separately, at night, in haste and secrecy. They wore various well-studied disguises, and had made their preparations well in advance, sending supplies secretly and ordering horses and carriages to be made ready at lonely farms, by those they could trust—for there was trust in some, even in those dark days. When they were gathered in the farmyard they seemed a ramshackle crew of rusty surgeons and filthy beggars, stolid peasants and milkmaids. In the farmyard those who seemed to be the leaders, or at least in charge of the plan of action, described the coming journey, across plains and through forests, always skirting large towns and villages, as far as the border of the land, where they would cross into a neighbouring mountainous country and make their way to the hidden valley, beyond the white-capped fangs of the mountains, where one of their number, Culvert, had a sequestered property, La Tour Bruyarde, which could be reached only across a narrow wooden bridge between two lines of peaks, across a dark and lifeless chasm.

They must travel fast, and circumspectly, never trusting anyone they met on the road, save certain helpers at posting stages, and in certain lonely inns and hamlets, who could be recognised by certain secret signs, a blue flower at a certain angle in the hatband, an eagle feather in a tuft of cock feathers. If they all came safely to their destination—as it was most vigorously to be hoped they would—they would be able to set up their own small society in true freedom, far from rhetoric, fanaticism and Terror.

So they travelled, through a press of dangers and menaces which will not be recounted here, but left to the imagination, for this story concerns itself not with the troubled world they left behind, but with the new world they meant so hopefully to build, if not for all men, since that hope had failed, then for these select few.

They did not all arrive. Two young men were caught by the military and pressed into the Army, from which they had much ado to escape a year later. One old man was knifed by an older woman as he rested in his sweat in a ditch and closed his eyes for sheer weariness. Three young women were caught and raped by a rabble of peasants, though they were well disguised as pox-ridden crones. When their young, smooth flesh was discovered under their artfully tattered clothing, they were raped again for their deceitfulness, and again for their sweetness and softness, and yet again, upon compulsion, so that they no longer had force to beg for mercy or tears to run down their blubbered cheeks, and then again, and so they died, of suffocation, of fear, of despair, who knows, or who knows if they thought it a merciful release. Their fate was never known by those more fortunate who came to the hidden tower, though rumours of it were rife on the roads. But in those days, so many were undone, these deaths were not remarkable.

The group who gathered on the crest of Mount Clytie, before making the crossing on the wooden bridge, might fairly have been thought remarkable. They were mud-stained and dishevelled, thinner after the privations of their journey, but full of vigour, their blood beating fiercely with renewed hope. They could not see La Tour Bruyarde (only one of the names of the place) from where they stood, but they were assured by their leader that once across the bridge and over the last natural bastion, they would behold a possible site for an earthly Paradise, a plain watered by swift streams and meandering brooks, in which was a wooded Mount or Mound on which stood their new home, on a site where his own family, throughout the ages, had always had a fortress-retreat.

This leader, though of noble birth, went by the name of Culvert, since it was a condition of their society that their names should be newly chosen, to signify relinquishment of the old world, and new beginnings in the new. His chief companion was the Lady Roseace. They were a beautiful pair, in the first strength of confident manhood and womanhood. Culvert was above the common height, broad-shouldered but lithe; he wore his hair, which was black and gleaming, longer than was fashionable, and it fell in great negligent tresses on his shoulders. His face was strong and smiling, with a full red mouth, both firm and sensuous, and dark eyes under decisive brows. Roseace was slender but full-breasted, and pressed her saddle with firm but ample buttocks. Her hair was also worn freely over her shoulders, though she had only considered it safe to release it from her hood since they came to the summit of Mount Clytie, and she now tossed her head a little from sheer pleasure at the breezy clarity of the air and the empty spaces of rock, snow and green vegetation spread below her. Her face was thoughtful and imperious, her lips firmly arched and her winged brows drawn in a habitual questioning frown. She had in her young life been destined by her parents for an uncongenial husband, and by the Revolutionary Powers for denunciation, summary trial and rapid execution, but she had escaped both parents and gaolers with equal resourcefulness and ruthlessness. On the day when this narrative begins her golden hair was curling and tangled and her skin lightly veiled with a powdering of dust, amongst which glistened diamond drops of sweat.

Other members of the assembled company were the young Narcisse, pale, gentle and hardly more than a boy, full of tremulous self-doubt and sudden starts of eagerness; the careful Fabian, who had shared Culvert's student freedoms and had been a voice of caution in his wilder enterprises; and an older man, who called himself Turdus Cantor, and was wrapped in a heavy cloak, appearing to find the mountain air, even in the fresh sunlight, chill. Fabian's brave wife, Mavis, was there, and with them were their three children, newly named Florian, Florizel and Felicitas. More children had set out, two families with their own young and orphaned cousins, but these were not expected to reach the bridge for a few days, since their journey was necessarily slower. Three younger women, clustered together and speaking in low voices, were the raven-haired Mariamne and the palely glimmering twin girls, Coelia and Cynthia. There were also the servants in charge of carts and pack animals—of these, who were appointed to become companions with the rest, once their destination was reached, more will be told at a later date.

Culvert looked around him, and laughed, and said:

"So far we have come, through risk and dread, and now we shall enter into the possession of our own lives and our own ways of living. La Tour Bruyarde, where you will be received, had lapsed into disuse in my grandfather's time. Its stones were plundered for the walls of barns and chapels, its halls were empty and the vines were creeping through the broken windows. But much work has been done, many suites and chambers have been restored, the necessary offices are in order, although as you will soon see, the building work will continue above our heads, to make all more secure and harmonious.

"All of you, I think, know something of my plans in making our retreat here. I wish our new lives to be an experiment in freedom—freedom in large things, in education, in government of our society, in shared labour, in the life of the mind and the life of the passions. Attention will be paid to things that may appear to be lesser things—art, dress, food, the decoration of our living quarters, the cultivation of our plants and trees. These will all be debated amongst us and made new in ways now only partly to be imagined, as we live our passionate and reasonable lives with goodwill. Petty restrictions will be done away with. New combinations will be instituted. Those who desire one thing greatly shall be satisfied, and so shall those who wish to flutter like butterflies from flower to flower.

"When we and our fellow labourers have crossed this bridge, and when Damian and Samuel have waited here another seven days in hope of the wagon with the children, and other straggling companions, we shall take axes and cut the supports away from the bridge, which will render us unassailable from this direction, from where our danger comes."

"Will it," asked Fabian, "render us also unable to escape from this valley?"

"We hope no one will ever wish to escape. But also of course no one should be prevented—we are designing a community of entire freedom—and to the south there are narrow passes through the mountains and ways in which, with difficulties no greater than we have just faced, anyone might come out. But I hope we shall all be living in such pleasure, and delight, and mutual usefulness, that such wishes would be far indeed from your thoughts."

"Far indeed," said Roseace, smiling, and spurring on her horse to be the first to set foot on the bridge. So they passed over in safety, some averting their eyes from the giddy chasm below, in which a sullen torrent roared over sharp black basalt, dimmed by stream and spray, forever out of reach of the direct warmth of the sun. Fabian clasped his young son to his breast so that the boy should not look down, but the boy's sister gazed about her in all directions fearless and

15

laughing. And so, talking animatedly of the haven they were so soon to see and enter, the company entered the rocky defile which would open on the Valley of Faisans. 🐚

Frederica seems set on coming into the wood, where Hugh is, rather than inviting him over to her side. She hands the boy into Hugh's hands and comes down quickly herself, rejecting assistance. She is as thin as ever, her sharp face still bony.

They wander along the paths between the trees. They do not know how to talk to each other. Once they met daily and discussed everything, Plato, the tanks in Budapest, Mallarmé, Suez, metre. This makes it harder, not easier, to ask for narratives of the six years that have passed. They mention old friends. Alan is teaching art history at the Samuel Palmer School of Art, Hugh says. He thinks he is also writing a few articles. He travels to Italy. Tony is doing rather well as a freelance journalist. He even does some television. Hugh himself is still writing, yes, he is still writing, it is the poetry that matters, he tells Frederica, who makes an affirmative noise, nodding her scarfed head, staring down at beech mast. He makes his living teaching, he says, but he would like not to. A publisher has offered him some reading, but it would only be for a pittance. Poets can only expect pittances, says Hugh Pink to Frederica, who makes the same, slightly suffocated, affirmative noise. She does not ask about Raphael Faber, whose poetry-reading group they once both attended. Hugh tells her that Raphael's poem "Lübeck Bells" has been published. He says it is much admired by those who can see what it is.

"I know," says Frederica.

"Do you still see Raphael?" asks Hugh innocently. Hugh was in love with Frederica and Frederica was in love with Raphael, but that was in what seems to him in this wood another country, another time, his youth, which is already gone.

"Oh no," says Frederica. "I've lost touch with everyone from that time."

"You were writing for *Vogue*," says Hugh, who had found that almost as odd as this manifestation in jodhpurs and jacket. Frederica was intellectually stylish but hardly part of the world of consumer delights and chic gossip.

"I did for a bit. Before I married."

Hugh waits. He waits for an account of Frederica's marriage.

16

She says, "My sister was killed. I don't know if you knew. And I married Nigel not long after, and Leo was born, and I was quite ill, for a bit. You don't realise at first, Hugh, what a death is going to do to you."

Hugh asks about the death. He did not know Frederica's sister, who was older than Frederica, had also been at Cambridge, he believed, but had lived in Yorkshire, where Frederica came from. He could not remember Frederica talking much about a sister. She had always seemed to be a kind of solitary, one-off creature, fierce and striving.

Frederica tells him about her sister's death. He realises that this narrative is practised, this is the way she has found it convenient—possible—to tell it. Her sister, she says, was married to a vicar and had two small children. And the cat brought in a bird, a sparrow, which took refuge under the refrigerator, and her sister had pulled it out and reached under it, and the fridge was not properly earthed. She was very young, says Frederica. Afterwards, she says wryly, we all suffered from shock. Shock waves, she says grimly. Waves and waves of shock. How terrible, says Hugh Pink, prevented from imagining by Frederica's matter-of-fact tone.

"And Nigel looked after me. I'd never needed looking after before, but Nigel looked after me."

"I didn't know Nigel."

"He was around. He wasn't *at* Cambridge, he just visited. His name's Reiver, the family have a house, an old house, Bran House, just over those fields, those are their fields, over that stile."

They walk on. The boy holds Frederica's hand. He shuffles dead leaves with quick kicks.

"Look, Leo," says Frederica. "Conkers. Over there."

One or two gleam, polished ruddy-brown, through split spiked green balls lined with creamy-white. They lie in a drift of chestnut leaves, in a hollow.

"Go and get them," says Frederica. "We always used to be so excited when we found any. We didn't often, local boys had always combed the ground first. They threw stones at the branches, to bring them down. They were a great event. Every year. I never used to make holes and fight with them. Boys did, but I just kept them until they were dull and shrivelled, and then I threw them out. Every year."

The boy pulls at Frederica's hand. He will not gather the conkers without her. He pulls, and she follows, picking them up amongst the dead leaves and offering them to him—"humbly" is the word that comes to Hugh Pink.

Hugh says to Leo, "Do you like to put strings through them?"

The boy does not answer.

"He's like his father," says Frederica. "He doesn't talk much."

"*You* don't," says the boy. "*You* don't talk much."

"When your mother and I were friends, before," says Hugh Pink, "when we were younger, she never stopped talking."

Frederica straightens herself jerkily and begins to walk again, leaving the other two amongst the conkers. Hugh's foot uncovers a monster, a solid glistening globe, bursting its cape. He offers it to Leo, who hands him Frederica's offerings, in order to inspect this. Hugh says, "I've got a little bag here I had sandwiches in. You could put them all in there, to carry them."

"I could," says Leo. "Thanks."

He drops the chestnuts solemnly into Hugh's bag, hands it back to Hugh, and puts up his hand to be held. Hugh takes it. He cannot think of anything else to say. Leo says, "Come to tea in my house, now."

"Your mummy hasn't asked me."

"Come to tea."

They catch up with Frederica.

"This man," says Leo. "This man is coming to tea, in my house."

"That would be nice," says Frederica. "Come to tea, Hugh. It isn't far."

Once this is agreed, the boy suddenly appears to feel free to run about, and begins to make little journeys into the undergrowth, pocketing feathers, shells, and a tuft of fur. Hugh says, "You've done a lot of living, Frederica. Real things have happened to you."

"Having things happen to you and living" says Frederica. She begins again. "They aren't the same thing. I suppose they must be the same thing. I used to be so sure about living. I wanted."

The sentence has no object and no end, apparently.

They climb the stile, and cross into the afternoon fields, where a heavy white horse is grazing, where a bird is singing in a thorn bush, where Hugh trips on a molehill and rights himself. He has a feeling he can't find words for, although it is to do with his poetry. It is a feeling he thinks of as the *English* feeling, though in fact it may be simply a human feeling about death. It is a brief knowledge of his own temporary body, all the soft slippery dark organs, all the minute interlocking bones, all the snaking, fizzing, prickling veins and nerves. It is the knowledge that he is *inside* this skin, and it is intensely pleasurable because it always goes with a sense of the huge sweep and intricacy and age of what is *outside* hair, skin, eyeballs, nostrils, lips and the helix of the ear. It is the irrational pleasure of a creature in the fact that its surroundings were there long before its own appearance, and will be there long after. It was not a possible pleasure, Hugh thinks, before he had lived a certain time, before the repeated crossings of local earth, in his case England, had become part of the form of the soft pale mass in his skull, part of the active knowledge of his sight and smell and taste. You cannot have this particular pleasure in living, Hugh tells himself, before you have begun to know you are dying. He thinks it tends to come in this sort of landscape—bitten grass, exposed stones, bush, tree, hill, horizon—because generations of his ancestors, thousands and millions of years before towns and cities, and still after, have had this sense in this sort of place. The cells remember it, Hugh thinks. Every inch of this turf has absorbed, he supposes, knuckle-bones and heart-strings, fur and nails, blood and lymph. There are equally strong feelings in cities, which also turn the mind like whirlpools, but not this one, which is essentially green, and blue, and grey. The thing which can flash into the brain a memory of *this* thing is the repeated reading of words which, like turf and stones, are part of the matter of the mind: the Immortality Ode, say, the Nightingale, Shakespeare's sonnets. There again the pleasure of the sense of one's own vanishing briefness—Hugh stumbles—is part of the pleasure in the durable words.

Sometimes he fears this feeling is no longer general, that few in his world would recognise it, and those who did would be suspicious, would call it stock response, silly pastoral. But still the smell of the earth, the moving lips of the horse in the grass, the tree's black twigs on the grey air, move him, living and dying.

He says none of this. He picks himself up and walks onwards. He watches Frederica's son, trudging sturdily across the pasture. He tries to remember what it was like to be so small, to have the sense that years are very nearly infinite, other seasons unimaginably far away, as they would be to a man on a planet that took half a lifetime to circle its sun.

Beyond the next gate, over the brow of the meadow, is Bran House. Hugh Pink sees that it does indeed have a moat, not metaphorical, behind which is a high encircling wall, inside which are a tiled roof and Tudor chimney pots. The wall is both blank and beautiful, made of old, soft red bricks, crumbling here and there, encrusted with mosses and lichens, stonecrop and houseleeks, ivy-leaved toadflax and wild snapdragons. Branches—fruit trees, a cedar in the distance—rear above the wall.

"How beautiful," says Hugh.

"It is," says Frederica.

"What a place for Leo to grow up," says Hugh, still thinking of his "English" feeling.

"I know," says Frederica. "I know it is a wonderful place."

"We go in through the orchard," says the child, running on ahead. Round a corner is a humped wooden bridge, over the moat, and a door in the wall.

As they go through the trees, Hugh says, "I never thought of you as the mistress of a country house."

"Nor did I," says Frederica.

"Only connect," says Hugh vaguely, thinking of Margaret Schlegel at Howards End. The phrase itself produces a renewed wash or swoop of English feeling.

"*Don't say that,*" says Frederica, sounding more like the woman he once knew than she has done all afternoon. Leo is busy wiping his boots on a bootscraper. A door opens, and a woman appears, middle-aged, in woollen stockings and tongued brogues, who takes him in, an arm around his shoulder, telling him it is tea-time.

"This is Pippy Mammott," says Frederica. "Pippy, this is my friend Hugh Pink. We were at university together. Leo invited him to tea."

"I'll put out more cups," says Pippy Mammott. She strides off, holding Leo's hand. Hugh and Frederica cross a tiled hall, past a turning square staircase, into a drawing-room, with window-seats and comfy sofas.

"They'll bring tea," says Frederica. "They'll bring Leo. Nigel isn't here. He's working, I suppose. He works for his uncle's shipping business, he goes off for days or weeks and comes back."

"And you," says Hugh. "What do you do?"

"What does it look as though I do?"

"I don't know, Frederica. When I last saw you you were all flaming and ferocious. You were going to be the first woman Fellow of King's and have your own TV programme and write something—in some new form—"

They have not sat down. Frederica is staring out of the window. Two women come into the room and are introduced to Hugh as Olive and Rosalind Reiver, Nigel's sisters. The tea is brought on a trolley, and handed about by Pippy Mammott. Olive and Rosalind sit side by side on a sofa covered with pink and silver-green blowsy blooms printed on linen. They are square, dark women, with strong bones, and shadows on their upper lips. They wear comfortable jumpers, one oatmeal, one olive, tweed skirts and opaque stockings over strong, shapely legs. Their eyes are like Leo's, large, dark and lustrous, under heavy dark brows. They ask Hugh Pink all the questions Frederica has not asked. What does he do, where does he live, is he married, doesn't he love their beautiful part of the country, how can he bear to live in a city with the stench and the crowds and the machines, would he like to see the grounds, the home farm? Hugh says he is on a walking holiday and is a long way from his next stopping place. Olive and Rosalind say they can run him over in no time in the Land Rover, and Hugh says, no, that is not the point of a walking-tour, and he must be on his way soon, now, before the light goes. They accept this without demur. They say he is very right to stick to his project, they approve of that, they say, there is no way as good as walking to see the real country. Pippy Mammott hands out scones, slices of cake, tea, more tea. The boy ferries between his mother and his aunts, showing things first to one, then the other. Pippy Mammott takes his hand and says it is time to go, now. Leo says, "I want to stay here," but is led away. "Say good-bye to Mr. Pink," says Pippy Mammott. "Good-bye," says the boy, not bashfully.

Hugh decides he ought to go. It is true about the light and he feels he ought to go. Frederica sees him to the door, and then walks out with him down the long drive to the front gate, to set him on his way.

"Do you come to London, ever?"

"Not really. I used to. It didn't work out."

"You should come and see us all. Alan and Tony. Me. We miss you."

"You could write. You could write about poetry."

"Try and come. You seem to have lots of help—"

"It isn't *help*."

She stands awkwardly, helpless. He wonders if he can kiss her. He doesn't exactly want to. Her old restless energy is in abeyance and

21

with it her sexual sharpness. He puts his arms rather suddenly round her and brushes his face with hers. She flinches and stiffens and then hugs him fiercely.

"I'm glad you were there in that wood. *You will keep in touch,* Hugh—"

"Of course," says Hugh.

The telephone babbles and quacks and purrs. Ginnie Greenhill tells, "Sex is so much a matter of how you feel about *yourself.* Oh, I know there are ideas about what is *normally* attractive, normal proportions as you put it, of course, yes, I do know—"

Babble, quack, purr, babble, a series of plosives inside the black shell.

"No, I'm not underestimating repulsion, of course it exists, it would be silly to underestimate it. But on the other hand there's such a *variety* of people around, such curiosity and goodwill—"

Canon Holly examines Daniel's log.

3.00–3.30. Woman who dare not go out of her room. No name, London voice, said she will call again. Daniel.

3.30–4.05. Unnamed caller, left home and children on impulse a year ago, she says. Northern voice. "I have done wrong." Reacted strongly against suggestion we might get in touch with family. Daniel.

4.15–4.45. Steelwire. There is no God, as usual. Daniel.

Canon Holly lights another cigarette. He is in his late fifties, handsome in a lean, long-faced, lined way, like a well-bred horse, with deepset eyes and long strong teeth, nicotine-stained. He is interested in Steelwire but has never picked up one of his calls. He himself is an expert on God. He has written a successful and controversial book called *Within God Without God* and has been seen on the television, supporting the Bishop of Woolwich and *Honest to God. Within God Without God* argues in a riddling and witty way that to lose the comfortable Old Man Up There, or for that matter the Friend of Little Children wandering amiably in the pastures beyond the stars, was to discover a Force which made all men Incarnate Words, Incarnate Souls, as Christ had shown. Godwithin, the Canon wrote, had not made us fearfully and wonderfully as a craftsman might pinch and poke a ball of inanimate dirt or clay. He made us much more fearfully and wonderfully because He was the inherent Intelligence in the first protozoa clinging together in the primal broth, because He had grown with us and still grew with us, He grew and divided in every cell of our growing and dividing body from egg to fertile parents. He was and is as Dylan Thomas has so beautifully put it, "the force that through the green fuse drives the flower."

Daniel is not sure how far Canon Holly's theological position differs from atheism or pantheism. He himself is temperamentally no theologian, only an instinctively religious man who is no longer sure what that word, "religious," means. He suspects also that his own position does not differ from that of Canon Holly. He sees that the Canon's thought works in a Christian framework of prayer, biblical references, ritual and theology, and that these things are part of the Canon's liveliness, his personal history, his self. Daniel is a watchful man. He thinks the Canon would shrivel if he were obliged to follow his own reasoning, his own metaphors, outside the walls, so to speak, of the Church, the singing, the ritual, the imposed duties. Daniel thinks also that he himself would *not* shrivel. Perhaps, given his very shaky assent to almost all the doctrines of his Church, he ought to go and live and work outside it. He stays, partly, because he needs the impersonality of the absolute requirement of virtue. He needs to be required, for instance, to be patient with Steelwire. This kind of work—without the impersonal sanction—becomes something different, more self-indulgent, something unnatural and perhaps unwholesome.

Within the walls, Canon Holly's sense of God working in all his cells like yeast gives him a bounding energy, at once touching and irritating. He is a founder-member of a group called Psychoanalysts in Christ, and has written a second book, *Our Passions Christ's Passion,* on sexuality and religion, drawing extensively on Freud and Jung, anthropologists and religious historians, William Blake, William James, St. Teresa of Avila, and St. John of the Cross. This book has had an even greater success than *Within God Without God* and has raised questions amongst the Church hierarchy, who wisely diverted him, along with Daniel, who was then recovering from a kind of breakdown, to the counselling centre, combined with a branch of the Listeners, in St. Simeon's. Canon Holly loves the work, he loves the callers, he loves Daniel and Ginnie and all the others. He listens to the incoming calls with an open-mouthed total attention, alert, shining-eyed, every sinew straining to leap into help, participation, communion. It is the sort of enthusiasm of which the Listeners have to be shrewdly suspicious. But it works. Daniel sees it at work, he hears the Canon's slightly husky voice urge on the hesitant:

"Go on, you needn't be afraid. Tell me, *tell me,* I cannot be shocked, I do assure you." Daniel sees that help is given and received. But he would not bring his own problems to Canon Holly. He would sooner set them out before Ginnie Greenhill's bland smile and comfortable nod. Ginnie Greenhill does not *need,* as far as he can see, to be told anyone's troubles, and yet she comes to listen. He has no idea why she does. He has not asked. He believes that a certain distance between them makes their work easier.

Ginnie Greenhill puts down the telephone with a little sigh.

"Another masturbator?" enquires Canon Holly.

"Not exactly. I didn't like this one. He's taken to following a girl from his work everywhere she goes. He says he's full right up of her, he's bursting with her, he doesn't sleep for the idea of her. He wants her to notice him but he knows he repels her."

"Does he?" asks Canon Holly.

"I could answer, How do I know? Judging from my own reactions I'd say I imagine he *does,* yes. People usually do if they think they do, don't they? You get more mistakes in the other direction. Though I remember one man who came here after *weeks* of going on about his awfulness and he was a big handsome brute who only needed to lose a few pounds and hold his head up. Odd how people see themselves."

"You handled him well," says the Canon, savouring the handling. "Real warmth, no false promises."

He brings out a letter from the Bishop in answer to an idea of his own for a sexual therapy workshop in St. Simeon's. Problems could be pooled, and professional advice given to unprofessional helpers. Ginnie Greenhill makes tea for all of them, and observes that in her view a money-management workshop would be just as helpful to a large number of callers.

"To listen to you, Ginnie dear," says the Canon, "one would think you were a frightful prude, ready to shy away from the first hint of bodily passion or misery. And one would be quite wrong, because I've *heard* you dispensing perfect acceptance and common sense to the most hurting and hurtful people."

Ginnie's knitting needles tap rhythmically. She bends her head over her wool. She says, "I do think, Canon, that the modern Church does somehow seem to be about sex, that does seem to be what it *cares* about, if I may say so."

The Canon is bright with glee. He lights another cigarette and sucks greedily.

"The Church has *always* been about sex, dear, that's what the problem is. Religion has always been about sex. Mostly about denying sex and rooting it out, and people who are trained to deny something and root it out become obsessed with it, it becomes unnaturally monstrous, that's why current moves to be more *accepting* and *celebratory* about our sexuality are so *exciting*—we may work *with* this force and not *against* it—"

"I thought," says Ginnie Greenhill, "that religion was about God, and about death. About how to live with the idea of death, that's what I thought it was."

And death too, the Canon begins on a run, what is death but part of sex, the germ cell is immortal but the sexually divided individual is doomed, it is sex that brought death into the world . . .

The telephone rings. The Canon leans forward.

"This is the Listeners. Can I help you?

"Yes, he's here. I'll fetch him. One moment. Don't go away."

He hands the receiver to Daniel, his hand cupped over the mouthpiece, holding in wisps of bitter smoke. "One of yours."

"Yes. This is Daniel. Who is that?"

"This is Ruth. Do you remember me, I used to come to the Young Christians, with Jacqueline, when you were up here, in Yorkshire?"

He has a vision of her, pale oval clear-cut face, heavy-lidded eyes, the long solid plait of pale hair falling between her shoulders.

"Of course I remember you. Can I help?"

"I rang to say I think you ought to come. Mary's had an accident, she's unconscious in Calverley Hospital. Her grandmother's with her, she's by the bed. I work in the Children's Ward, I think you know that, I said I'd find you."

Daniel is without words. He sees dancing mounds and hollows of egg-boxes humping like earthquakes.

"Are you there, Daniel?"

"Yes." His mouth is dry. "What happened to her?"

"She has a head injury. She was found in the playground. Some other little girl may have run into her, we don't know, she couldn't have fallen off anything, from where she was.

"Are you there, Daniel?"

He cannot speak. Ruth's little voice, as used as his own to dispensing comfort, says, "She'll almost certainly be all right, the wound's in the front of the head, not the back, and that's good. The skull's stronger there. But I thought you'd want to know, you'd want to be here."

"Yes," says Daniel. "Yes of course. I'll come right away. I'll get a train and come straight there, tell them all I'll come straight there. Thank you, Ruth."

"She's in the best place," says the far-away voice. "She'll be cared for as well as possible, you know."

"I know. I'll see you soon."

He puts down the phone and sits staring into the cubicle, a heavy man, shaking.

"Can we help?" says Canon Holly.

"My child's been hurt. In Yorkshire. I've got to go."

"You need hot sweet tea," says Ginnie. "Which you shall have. And the Canon will get King's Cross about trains, won't you? Do you know what happened, Daniel?"

"No. They don't seem to know. She was found in the playground. I must go."

The Canon has dialled and is listening to the burring tone.

"How old is she?"

"Eight," says Daniel.

He never talks about his children, and Holly and Ginnie never ask. They know his wife was killed accidentally and that he has children in Yorkshire, living with grandparents. He visits them, they know that, but he does not talk about these visits. Ginnie brings more tea and sweet biscuits—sugar for shock is one of their stocks-in-trade. The Canon suddenly begins to write down train times. At least, Ginnie says, Daniel has only a few minutes' walk to King's Cross, he can buy a toothbrush somewhere on the way. She asks practically about the child's state.

"She's not conscious. They say she'll almost certainly be all right, I expect they mean that, they'd be careful what they say, wouldn't they?"

"They would have to, yes."

"She's only a little thing," says Daniel.

But he cannot see Mary's face, conscious or unconscious. He sees Stephanie, his wife, lying on the kitchen floor, with her lip pulled back over damp teeth. This is who he is, the man who looked at that

26

face. This is what she is, a terrible face; this sight persists in his brain. This is her after-life. He is hunted through his waking life by that face, he has developed the cunning of a hunted creature who twists and darts to avoid anything in the passages of the brain that might trigger, might switch on, that remembered face. There are words, there are innocent, pleasant memories, there are smells, there are whole people, whom he avoids with ferocity in case they call up that dead face. He even paints his dreams with black ink, he clamps his dreaming head with a vice of will, he never slips into dreaming that face and waking with the memory.

He has told himself that survivors, like himself, quite commonly feel they are dangerous to others, to other survivors. He does indeed feel that he is dangerous to Will and Mary, his children, though that is not the whole story, is not the whole reason why they are in Yorkshire and he is here in St. Simeon's, under the tower.

And now it is as though he has hurled a rock at his small daughter, or pushed her from a high place.

"There's a train in fourteen minutes," says Canon Holly, "and another in an hour and fourteen minutes. You can't make it in fourteen minutes."

"I can try," says Daniel. "I can run."

He sets off up the steps.

La Tour Bruyarde must have been almost invulnerable in its great days, long ago. As the company approached it across the plain and the mountain meadows that surrounded it, they saw how thick and frowning was its outer wall, crumbled and breached in many places, here rising proudly, there lying in a dense arrested fall of mossy blocks crusted on the hillside. Men could be seen on the ramparts and in the clefts, repairing the structure. They wore brightly coloured singlets, cerise, royal blue, scarlet, which gave their labours an appearance of cheerfulness. The Lady Roseace imagined she heard them singing, that a faint hum of musical noise was borne to them on the air.

Within the confine of the wall could be seen not one but many towers, and of all shapes and sizes, as though this citadel had been put up at random over the ages, all made of the same stone hewn from the same mountainside, but otherwise startling in their variety, square and conical, simply stolid and highly decorated, with turrets, with slate cones, with small lancet windows glinting like eyes, with galleries and turrets, with encrustations of ivy and other creeping lifeforms. Many of these turrets appeared to be either unfinished or partly demolished, it was not always easy to say which, and the bright patches of colour of the workers' vests could be seen moving along these high ledges and opened rooftops. As they rode up the causeway which ascended the Mount or Mound a thin sound of cheering and welcome could be heard from high above them, and fruit and flowers were jubilantly thrown under their advancing feet.

They rode in between two great gate-towers, not, as the Lady Roseace had prefigured it to herself, into a central courtyard, but into a kind of dark tunnel, between walls which might be the sides of buildings or might be solid rocks, and which wound its way onward into the dark bowels of the place, lit occasionally by shafts of light in the gloom from high loopholes, and occasionally, at the darkest points, by lanterns hanging on smoke-blackened hooks from the stone. When they finally emerged they were in a well-like confine, with layer upon layer of dwellings towering above them, one corridor upon another, a Baroque balcony abutting a Gothic cloister, a series of classical windows, in elegantly diminishing proportions as they rose higher, under an unfinished thatched roof that might have suited a mediaeval byre. Some of the windows shone with myriad coloured lights, and some were gaping sockets with cracked arches. The sky was far, far away, it seemed to the Lady Roseace at that moment of arrival, and an intense blue, as the sky is when it is far, far away, scratched and scribbled on by the fingers and teeth, the stumps and domed skulls of the roofline.

The Living Quarters

Culvert led the Lady Roseace into the living quarters prepared for her. They travelled along many passages, through many doors and arches, up many flights of stairs and down almost as many, it seemed, so that she was quite amazed by their intricacy. Her door was hidden behind an embroidered hanging on a wall in a long gallery. She could not see what was depicted on the hanging, for the light was flickering and fitful, but had the impression of many heaped limbs energetically writhing, of spherical breasts pointing skywards and of watermelons, it seemed, bursting open on greensward.

Inside, all was rosy light. At first the Lady Roseace believed that she was in an internal chamber bathed in firelight, and then she saw that she was in a boudoir whose elegant windows were covered with a veil of translucent rosy silk, through which the sunlight poured. The room was sparsely furnished—there was an inlaid escritoire in rosewood, and a prie-dieu in the same wood upholstered in rose-coloured velvet, the most softly comfortable kneeling place possible to imagine. The rest of the furnishings were in a more oriental style, low divans, inlaid with ivory, spread with silk cushions of every size and shape, soft silken carpets woven with Persian roses and pinks and crimson-tipped daisies, huge soft floating daybeds, inviting languor, and hung with what appeared in that light to be flesh-coloured sealskins and cashmere shawls and rosy fox-furs. She ran through into the bed-chamber, which had a high huge bed like a galleon, hung about with richly embroidered silken curtains and floating with muslins and nets. Everywhere on little tables and chests were fantastically luminous bottles and flasks, breathing soft perfumes of flowers and musks. A body—many bodies—might vanish entirely in the soft cushionings and quiltings of that secret bed.

The Lady Roseace walked from room to room, exclaiming and touching, fingering silks and ivories, tortoise-shells and lustres, satins and furs and feathers. When she drew back the silk curtain from the window and let in the daylight, the rosy fire died away in many of the fabrics and artefacts, revealing a new subtlety of snow-whites and creams and ivories, of northern furs and southern bones and tusks, of silvery threadwork and palest gold silk quilting.

A close inspection would reveal, in time, that this richness was a light covering over stony coldness and crumbling, that the flagstones were stained and chipped, and the walls flaking away. But they were covered for now with bravely stiff tapestries and draperies, all white and rose-red in honour of the Lady Roseace. There was a most exquisite depiction, all in reds and whites, roses and flesh tints, of the chaste Diana bathing under snowy branches by a silver spring, and of the lovely young Actaeon, part ruddy youth, part milk-white stag, and all laced and interlaced with gouts of brilliant crimson blood, which dripped also from the bright white teeth of the pale hounds, as they reached elegantly for his extended, panting throat . . .

The Coming of the Children

Towards mid-afternoon on the third day the company were gathered on a great balcony, drinking and discussing what was next to be done towards increasing the pleasure and fruitfulness of their life together. Serving men and women poured foaming ale and crimson and golden wine, constantly replenishing beakers and glasses. It had been decided that there should be no more servants and masters—decided, that was, by the masters, for the servants had not as yet been informed or consulted about this project—but no agreement had been reached about the time and manner of this great change in the relations of the population of the Tower. All that was agreed was that it should be debated fully when the whole company was gathered together and what had been set in motion could be deemed to be truly begun.

The Lady Roseace and Culvert, Turdus Cantor and Narcisse were all looking out over the meadows and the plain when the keen-eyed Narcisse detected a movement amongst the trees at the rim of the bowl of the valley. From that height what emerged from the dark woody shadows appeared at first to be a slow worm attended by dancing ants, but as it made its slow way across the meadows it could be seen to be a series of covered carts and carriages, attended by pricking outriders, and as it came still nearer, all could see that there were three great covered wagons, each drawn by two bullocks, and, as they came nearer still, that the bullocks were fantastically decked with garlands and the tips of their horns were gilded. A cry went up from the courtyards below, "The children, the children are coming," and the company waited to glimpse them from above as they paced towards the gatehouse, before hurrying down flight after flight of staircases to greet them in the inner fastness where their journey ended.

From above, no one could be seen in the swaying wagons, save their drivers, all of whom were cowled in heavy hooded cloaks, and carried stubby whips with long lashes, such as were usual in that country to urge on the blundering slow creatures. And indeed the labouring white flanks were blooded here and there, were scored by encouraging strokes, which appeared to have no effect on the steady, deliberate pace of the flower-decked beasts. There was trouble enough getting these ungainly vehicles through the passages to the centre, if it was the centre, of the Tower, and strange stifled sounds, pitiful lowings and nervous bellowings reached the ears of the company before the carts finally emerged into the dark courtyard.

And then the joyful moment, so eagerly awaited, was there. From every side, the coverings of the carts were pushed back, rolled up, burst open, and the small faces and the soft hair, the bright eyes and the tender fists of the children were seen. Some were sleepy, stretching their little limbs to rouse from the abandonment of sleep. Some were alert and mischievous, smiling eagerly at the adventures to be undertaken. Some were more timid, hanging their heads bashfully, flickering their silky lashes on their plump cheeks. Some were whimpering—there are always some who whimper in any group of children; no group of children, however generally cheerful and playful, but has some little whimperers among them—but these were quickly silenced in the general excitement as the children were welcomed and lifted down from the sides of the wagons on to the flagstones of their new abode. They were handed from loving arms to loving arms, they were softly kissed and their little clothes tenderly set to rights, and there was much laughter and general cheerfulness in the shadow of the high roofs.

The drivers too of the wagons were urged to come down from their perches and join the throng. This they did, pushing back their hoods from their dusty faces, coiling the lashes of their whips and tucking them away. The first was an old friend of all, Merkurius, lithe and muscular, with a fine face like a knife and a quizzical smile that quivered the gutstrings of Cynthia and Coelia. There was great rejoicing at the safe arrival of Merkurius, for rumours had been rife that he had been cut off by troops, that he had been taken naked as he made love to a whore in a city brothel, that he had died on the scaffold as a secret substitute for his great friend Armin, that he had drowned in an attempt to swim across a river in full spate. The fantasies of the company had been most fearfully exercised by all these contradictory reports. The sensitive, Narcisse as well as Cynthia and Coelia, had undergone drowning and decapitation, naked apprehension and coitus interruptus, the chase, the flight, the whipping branches, the strangling thickets. Indeed the only consolation for these sensitive souls had been the plethoric variety of these narrations, which could not all be true, so might all be false, as they were now joyfully proved to be.

The second driver had a round red face like a burning flower, and jet-black cropped hair like one a week or two away from escaping from prison or the army. It was only when this personage threw back the cloak with a rich, round peal of laughter that it could be seen that the cloak concealed a billowy female body, that this jovial gaol-bird was the Lady Paeony, heroine of many amorous adventures, and of more anecdotes of intrigue, false and true. Culvert and Roseace hastened to embrace this solid person, who gave her whip a last crack in the courtyard and declared that all her little charges had been golden-good and deserved sweetmeats, that they had been quiet as mice as they passed the pickets, and sung as sweetly as larks, to her great delectation, as they crossed the mountain meadows, and that she loved them all, she could crush them in her arms for love and happiness.

And now the third driver came forward, and pushed back his cowl slowly and deliberately and revealed a grizzled head and a grizzled beard, and a leathery skin wrinkling round pale-blue eyes. There was a hush in the courtyard, and a thrill of whispering ran through the company, for no one knew him, and all enquired of others, if they did, or had seen him before.

And the Lady Roseace said, quick as a flash and unthinking, "This man smells of blood."

And the man took a step or two forward, fingering his whip and perhaps smiling a little amongst his beard, and perhaps not—different impressions were formed by different persons.

"Who are you?" said Culvert.

"You know me well enough, by name at least, and some of you by more than name," said the man. "To my sorrow," he added, but not in a sorrowful tone.

"If it were not impossible," said Fabian thoughtfully, "I should say your name was Grim, that you are Colonel Grim of the National Army."

"I have been Colonel in the National Army," said Grim, "and Colonel in the Royal Army before that, and a professional soldier all my life. And now I am here, and wish to join you, if you will have me."

At this acknowledgement, a great murmuring and even hissing began amongst the people gathered round the carts, and several people repeated what Roseace had said, "This man smells of blood."

And Colonel Grim stood there easily amongst them all, looking from faces of hatred to faces of fear, and said, "That I smell of blood is true. I smell myself daily and the smell disgusts me. I have had enough of blood. The gutters of the city are running with blood, there are flecks of blood in the loaves of bread, blood feeds the roots of the apple trees where stinking dead men hang among the apples. You may not believe me now, but a killer by trade who has had enough of blood is a good founding member for a community based on kindness and freedom, as yours is to be."

"How can that be?" cried Coelia. "We know what you have done, we have heard the stories, the tortures, the punishments, the killing, the killing—how can such a creature be a fit companion for the gentle and the harmonious?"

"We should rather kill him," cried a young man, "we should put him to the sword for the sufferings of our families and our friends; we should cement our social bonds with his foul blood."

Colonel Grim said, "A man of blood can smell bloodthirstiness in any household, any society, any family. It is my business to smell bloodthirstiness. I am a wolf who can detect a rogue sheepdog, Monsieur Culvert. I am an instrument of control and have been an instrument of terror, and I can tell you much of the nature of control, and terror, and control by terror, which you do not now think you need to know. But it is what all men need to know, you will find, even if you expel or kill me. I bear the mark of Cain in your household, Monsieur Culvert. I have red hands, and most of you, all of you it may be, have not. But Cain was marked so that the children of Adam should not harm him. A man is not only the history of his deeds, I suppose, according to your philosophy, if not to that of my previous masters. You owe it to me to see how I can live peaceably."

"I do not understand how you have come here," said Culvert, frowning.

"I persuaded Merkurius and the Lady Paeony that I was another, that I was your old friend Vertumnus, who died, I am sad to have to tell you, in the oubliettes of the Tower. I had forged letters from yourself with which I convinced them. You must not blame them, sir. I am a sufficiently clever man."

"He will bring the national armies in his train," said Mavis.

"And how should that be?" asked Grim. "And why should I come, thus openly and alone, saying who I am, and leaving my fate to you, if the armies were following in secret. No, if I wished, I could have had the armies here to greet you. But I did not wish—your hopes are mine, my good friends—I hope you will be my good friends. The armies will not bother you here, and I am no longer Colonel Grim, but plain Grim, grey and grizzled and making a new start in the evening of his days, if you will have me."

"Turn him away," said the Lady Roseace, wrinkling her nostrils.

But Culvert said, "What he says is just. He may stay, until any of us detect him casting any baleful influence on our family. For all men are capable of change and redemption, as he says, though he must be watched, to see whether he says so with guile, or with honest intention."

So they all went into the citadel together, discussing the day's events.

33

II

❧❧❧❧❧

Frederica reads to Leo. Inside his green and white room, which was Nigel's room, with its Beatrix Potter frieze, she sits on the edge of his fluffy eiderdown and reads to him about the Hobbit, setting out on his adventure. The curtains are drawn against the dark; they are lit by a bedside lamp inside a creamy glass shade, a creamy light.

"At first they passed through hobbit-lands," Frederica tells him, "a wide respectable country inhabited by decent folk, with good roads, an inn or two, and now and then a dwarf or a farmer ambling by on business. Then they came to lands where people spoke strangely and sang songs Bilbo had never heard before. Now they had gone on far into the Lone-lands, where there were no people left, no inns, and the roads grew steadily worse. Not far ahead were dreary hills, rising higher and higher, dark with trees. On some of them were old castles with an evil look, as if they had been built by wicked people. Everything seemed gloomy, for the weather that day had taken a nasty turn."

"A bit frightening," says Leo.

"A bit, yes," says Frederica, who believes there is pleasure in fear.

"Only a bit," says Leo.

"It gets more frightening later. More exciting."

"Go on reading."

"It was after tea-time; it was pouring with rain, and had been all day; his hood was dripping into his eyes, his cloak was full of water; the pony was tired and stumbled on stones; the others were too grumpy to talk."

"Poor pony. We don't let Sooty get too tired, do we? We look after him. He doesn't mind a bit of rain, Auntie Olive says. He's a tough little thing, Auntie Olive says."

"Yes, he is. Very tough. Shall I go on?"

"Go on."

" 'I wish I was at home in my nice hole by the fire, with the kettle just beginning to sing,' thought Bilbo. It was not the last time that he wished that!"

Leo rubs his eyes. He pushes his little fists into his eye-sockets and winds them energetically, so that Frederica's own eyeballs wince sympathetically.

"Be careful, Leo. You'll hurt your eyes."

"I won't. Those are *my* eyes. I don't hurt them. They itch."

"You're sleepy."

"I'm *not*. Go on reading."

"Still the dwarves jogged on," says Frederica, "never turning round or taking any notice of the Hobbit." Leo has settled into his bed: his head is in the hollow of his pillow, his cheek on his hand. She looks at him with appalled love. She knows every hair on his head, every inch of his body, every word, she thinks, of his vocabulary, even though he is constantly proving her wrong. And he has ruined her life, she thinks, for inside the new docile Frederica the old Frederica still has her histrionic passion-fits. I would walk out tomorrow if it were not for Leo, she tells herself hundreds of times each day, with contempt and puzzlement. She looks at his red hair, such a beautiful red, richer than hers, with the shine of those chestnuts he gathered with Hugh Pink. He is a very male child. He has strong shoulders and an aggressive jut to his chin. She is surprised by her passion for his small body as she was surprised by her passion for his father's, which it will no doubt grow to resemble; she thinks of Leo always as his father's child. She loves to see him straddle Sooty, his small legs at odds with the heavy straps and buckles and irons of the stirrups, his head, in its black velvet helmet, too important for his body, like a beetle, like a goblin. But Leo on Sooty is his father's son, in his father's world, where she doesn't belong, and isn't welcome. Nor does she want to belong or be welcome, she tells herself, with her usual mixture of honesty and fury, she has made a terrible mistake. Her voice goes on peacefully, dry and lively, telling about dwarves and wizard, Hobbit and trolls, things going bump in the dark, terror and mayhem, and Leo shudders agreeably. Inside her head she goes over and over what she has done, how she could have done it, how it cannot be undone, how she can live. Only connect, she thinks contemptuously, only connect, the prose and the passion, the beast and the monk. It can't be done and isn't worth doing, she thinks on a long repetitive whine, she has been here so often before. She thinks of Mr. Wilcox in *Howards End*, thinks of him with hatred, that stuffed man, that painted scarecrow. Margaret Schlegel was a fool in ways Forster had no idea of, because he wasn't a woman, because he supposed connecting was desirable, because he had no idea what it meant.

" 'Dawn take you all and be stone to you!' said a voice that sounded like William's. But it wasn't. For just at that moment the light came over the hill, and there was a mighty twitter in the branches. William never spoke for he stood turned to stone as he stooped—"

The door opens. Mother and son look up, and there is the man, the father, his return, as usual, unannounced. The sleepy boy is awake in a flash and sits up to be embraced. Nigel Reiver hugs his son and puts his arm round his wife. His cheek is cold from the outdoors—he has come straight up, he is even a little breathless, he is eager to see his family. He is a dark man in a dark suit, a soft armour, with the blue shadow of a dark beard on his solid cheek.

"Don't stop," he says. "Go on reading, I'll listen, it's my absolutely favourite book, *The Hobbit*."

"It's a bit frightening," says Leo. "Only a bit. Mummy says it gets more exciting than this, even more."

"Oh, it does," says the dark man, stretching himself on the bed beside his son, both heads on the pillow, looking up at Frederica, perched on the edge with the book.

He has nothing at all to do with Mr. Wilcox.

There is something to do with sex, which he is good at, and which Forster perhaps wanted Mr. Wilcox to be good at, but couldn't quite imagine, couldn't give life to.

The two pairs of dark eyes watch Frederica.

The room is full of slumberous warmth and watchful sharpness.

"And there they stand to this day, all alone, unless the birds perch on them; for trolls, as you probably know, must be underground before dawn, or they go back to the stuff of the mountains they are made of, and never move again. That is what had happened to Bert and Tom and William."

"I meant to stop there, it's a good stopping place, and Leo was nearly asleep, weren't you?"

"I *wasn't,* I was waiting for my Daddy to come."

"No you weren't. We didn't know he was coming."

"I did. I knew *in my bones* he would come this evening, I *knew* and I was right. Go on reading."

"Go on," says the man, lying on his back like a knight on a tombstone, his shiny dark shoes overhanging the bedfoot. So she goes on, for they are all happy, to the discovery of the treasure in the cave, and the end of the chapter.

"Have you been a good boy?" asks Nigel. "What has happened while I was away?"

"A man came to see Mummy, he was a very nice man with a funny name, his name was Pink, he found us in the woods and we asked him to tea."

"That was nice," says Nigel smoothly. He kisses his son good night, and Frederica kisses him, and the light is put out, and the little boy stirs his blankets into a containing nest.

Pippy Mammott has made supper for them to eat by the fire. She has made supper Nigel likes, shepherd's pie and baked apples with honey and raisins. She does not eat with Nigel and Frederica, but she does come in and out whilst they eat, offering second helpings, which Nigel accepts, refilling wineglasses, solicitously asking them to be careful of the apples, which are piping hot—"As they should be," says Nigel, detaining her to be congratulated on both pie and apples. He and Frederica sit in large armchairs each side of the wood fire, and Pippy Mammott stands between them with her back to the flames, warming her bottom. She tells him what Leo has been doing and saying, how well he is learning to ride Sooty, what a dauntless little boy he is, how they had an unexpected visitor, a friend of Frederica's apparently passing by quite accidentally on a walking tour.

"That was nice," says Nigel, smoothly, again. When Pippy has gone away with the trolley and the debris of the meal, he says, as Frederica is expecting him to say, "Who is this Hugh Pink?"

"An old friend from Cambridge. He writes poetry. Rather good poetry, I think. He was in Madrid for a year or two, and now he's back."

"You didn't say he was coming."

"I didn't know. He was on a walking holiday. Leo and I happened to bump into him, we gave him tea—it was Leo who invited him to tea—not me—"

"Why didn't you, if he was your friend?"

"Well, I would have, I expect, I would have got round to it—"

"Funny he just turned up—"

"Not really. He'd no idea this was where we lived. He was just walking. In the woods, like Leo says."

"I expect it was nice for you, to see an old friend?"

Frederica looks up, to see what is meant by this placid query. She calculates her answer.

"Of course it was. I don't seem to have seen any of my old friends for a long time."

"You miss them," states Nigel, in the same placid voice.

"Naturally," says Frederica.

"You should invite them," says Nigel. "You should feel free to invite them. You should ask them to stay."

Frederica chooses, after a moment, not to answer this remark. She stares, frowning, into the fire. She says, as placidly as he has been talking, "Are you back for long this time?"

"Does that make any difference? Why don't you just invite them? Maybe I'll be here, maybe I won't. I don't suppose my presence will affect your reunion."

"I didn't mean that. I just wanted to know how long will you be here this time?"

"I don't know. A few days. A few weeks. Why does it matter?"

"It doesn't. I just want to *know.*"

"Well, I don't know myself. There may be phone calls. Things may come up."

Frederica, looking into the logs, sees in her mind's eye a woman stepping barefoot across a bed of cinders, trying to find a path between little smouldering hot places, ready to break out into flames.

"When you go back, I'd like to come with you."

"Why?"

"Well. We used to do a lot of things together. Dancing, you know, things in town. And I would like to see some old friends, it's true, I would. I'm thinking, I might look for another job. I need something to *do.*"

This sentence comes out more tense, less casual, than she meant it to be.

"I would have thought you had a lot of things to do. A child needs his mother near him. There is a great deal here to occupy anyone."

"Don't talk to me like that, Nigel. That isn't the sort of thing *you* can say to *me.* You knew what I was when you married me—you knew I was clever and independent and—and ambitious—you seemed to *like* that. God knows I had nothing *else* someone like you might be interested in, no money, no connections, I'm not *beautiful*—all I was was bright and you can't marry someone for their brains and their—resourcefulness—and then expect them to behave like—"

"Like—"

"Like the sort of girl you might have been expected to marry—*but didn't*—one who has always gone hunting and shooting and likes just *being* in the country."

"I don't see why any girl would marry if she can't put up with being a wife. And a mother. If a girl becomes a wife and a mother, she must expect a few changes, I should think. I would have understood if you hadn't wanted to take the step. I don't think I more than half expected you would when I asked you—but you did. I thought you were a resourceful sort of girl. And now all you do is whinge. You have a lovely boy like Leo, and you whinge. It's not very pleasant."

Frederica stands up and begins to pace.

"Nigel, please listen to me. Please listen. I don't see very much of *you*—you don't tell me very much about where you are or what you do—"

"It wouldn't be of any interest to you."

"That may be. I don't know. But I *have to have something to do.*"

"You were always a great one for reading."

"But reading was *work*—"

"I see. You don't do it if you don't have to."

"I don't mean that. You know I don't. I know I don't *need* to earn my living—don't need, that is, in terms of money, don't *need*—"

Her need is so terrible, she is almost in tears.

"We aren't enough for you, Leo and me."

"You aren't ever here. And Leo has all sorts of people besides me, he's *rich* in people, Pippy and Olive and Rosalind, they adore him. He doesn't live in a nuclear family. All your friends, you and all your friends, were brought up by nannies."

"You know why in my case. My mother bolted, you know that. Bolted when I was two, you know that, I've told you. I've told you often enough. She had no strength of character, no resources. I thought you could look after Leo and be resourceful. I told you that."

He is rueful, charming, and bullying.

"Please," says Frederica. "Please let me come to London with you and see someone about some work. I could get some reading for publishers, I'm sure I could, and do almost all the work at home with Leo. Or I could go back to university and do a doctorate—I could work on that partly at home—and then, when Leo grows up, I could be ready, I could do something."

"You could see your friends. All your friends are men. I noticed. I can't take you this time, I'm going straight on to Tunis, I have to see my uncle, it isn't possible."

The little smouldering places are flaming here and there, like gas jets. Frederica takes fire.

"Then I shall just go. I shall just get up and go, myself, by myself. You don't care about me, you only care about your house and yourself—"

"And Leo."

"And *yourself.* You can't see *me,* you've no idea who I am, I am someone, I *was* someone. I am someone, someone nobody ever sees any more—"

She is less sure of this, that she is someone, than she passionately sounds. No one in Bran House sees what she thinks of as Frederica, not Pippy, not Olive, not Rosalind, not Leo, not even Nigel.

"Cambridge spoils girls," says Nigel, to provoke. "It's a sort of hothouse. It gives them ideas."

"I want to go back there," says Frederica.

"No, you don't," says Nigel. "You're too old."

Frederica goes to the door. She has some vague idea of throwing clothes into a suitcase and beginning to walk away down the road, in the night. She does not know where a suitcase is, and she is aware that such a plan is absurd. She feels that someone as clever as she is *must* be able to think of a way out of a situation—not a situation, a *life*—she should never have got into. Her nerve-endings hurt, in her hands, in her teeth, in her spine. Nigel stands between her and the door. He says in a small voice, a small, sad, honey voice, "I'm sorry, Frederica. I love you. I only get angry because I love you. You are here because I do love you, Frederica."

He has learned what a surprising number of men never learn, the strategic importance of those words. He is not a verbal animal. Much of what he says, Frederica has noticed without yet thinking about it, is dictated by the glaze of language that slides over and obscures the surface of the world he moves in, a language that is quite sure what certain things are, a man, a woman, a girl, a mother, a duty. Language in this world is for keeping things safe in their places. You must be brave, this kind of language says, and ordinary panic-struck human beings hear the imperative and perform extraordinary feats of tearless, uncomplaining stolidity. You might think that those who handle this solid currency with its few words would be able to add those other simple ringing ones, "I love you, I love you." They have clear meanings in this world, and women everywhere wait for them as dogs wait for titbits and sustenance, panting and slavering. And yet these words are withheld, for the most part, whether because their utterance renders the speaker vulnerable to rejection, or whether emotion embarrasses, is not usually clear. It is not a question of class. Working men and businessmen and owners of country houses do not say, "I love you," and women in council flats and women in town houses say constantly, "He never says he loves me."

Nigel Reiver has never put this generalisation to himself as a proposition. But if he does not think about language, he does think, and has thought, about women, and has discovered the force of these words as troublers of wrath, promoters of indecision, softeners of eyeballs and mucous membranes. If you say "I love you" to a woman, it makes her wet, his body knows. He stands between fierce Frederica and the door and watches her mouth soften slightly, watches the blood in her neck, watches her fists unclench a very little.

He concentrates on her. He wants her. He wishes to keep her. He chose her for the mother of his child. At this moment she is all he can see, all his senses are alert for her next movement, of repulsion, of uncertainty, of reconciliation. He watches as a cat might watch a frozen rabbit that cannot now jump this way or that; will it gain strength, will it look away, will it bow its head with beating heart? He loves her, that is what love is. He moves nearer, he puts his hand and his weight on the door, so that she cannot pull it open, so that her body is between his body and the hard wood. He knows without needing to think that if she smells his skin, if she touches his greed for her, she can move two ways, she can scratch with hatred, with the will to break free, she can want him to touch her, as she has before, she can do both together, scratch and want, want and scratch. When his body is in range he changes the verb.

"I want you, Frederica."

He names her so that she knows what he wants is *her,* is Frederica, not a woman, not Woman, not mindless relief, but Frederica. This is the language of courtly love, by instinct.

Her face is hot with rage, her blood is fizzing in her nostrils and ears. She moves her head this way and that to avoid his kiss, like the ritual dancing movements of gulls and grebes. He moves his head in rhythm with hers, he kisses her neck, her ear, with closed lips. She thinks, I am desperate, she feels desire, she is angry that she feels desire, she suppresses it, it recurs, it is like being electrocuted in parts and in small bursts, it is painful.

"I want you, I love you. I want you" go the small words. She is ready to sink to the floor, she cannot run away and will not respond. So he takes hold of her and takes her upstairs. Propels, lifts, supports, embraces, the verbs could go on for longer than the journey takes. From the swinging door to the kitchen quarters Pippy Mammott watches them go, and then removes the plates. She has seen this before. Frederica looks drunk, Pippy thinks, perhaps she is, Pippy thinks, she would like to think Frederica is drunk. Frederica has got a grip on Nigel, Pippy thinks, contrary to the evidence of her eyes.

Afterwards, he lies with his eyes shut, one heavy arm gently holding her to him. Frederica's body is warm and happy. The skin of her belly is glowing red with use and relaxation and happiness. Inside, also, she can hear her blood coursing, she thinks of it as "hearing" though this word is inaccurate, it is not to do with her ears. She wonders lazily why she thinks of it as "hearing" and decides that it is to do with the thrumming of one's own blood one hears in a shell and calls the sound of the sea. Frederica thinks in words, not exactly during love-making, or fucking, or whatever word custom and nicety choose for that activity, but before and after. She thinks now, looking at Nigel's damp heavy eyelids, at the droop of his mouth as though it had slackened after pain, that she loves him because he takes her beyond words, effortlessly and with skill. She thinks of Blake, the lineaments of gratified desire, and moves her sharp nose along his shoulder, sniffing his sweat, which belongs to her, which she knows, which she *knows* with her body. She thinks of the elaborate conceit of Donne, the pure and eloquent blood that spoke in the cheeks of the dead woman. Frederica's busy mind, in her skull under her skin and the tangled red hair on the moist pillow, casts about for the accurate quotation.

42

Her pure and eloquent blood
Spoke in her cheekes, and so distinctly wrought,
That one might almost say, her body thought.

"Her body thought," thinks Frederica. "Eloquent blood." Nigel wouldn't understand a word of all that, if she were suddenly to start talking in the night about lineaments of gratified desire and eloquent blood. It is only that his body thinks. She chose him for that, she thinks, and everything else goes with it. It ought to be possible to connect, she thinks, it ought, only connect, she thinks, and has an image of herself like a mermaid combing not only her hair but the fibres of her brain into harmony and alignment with damp, rosy fingers. Nigel utters words of his secret, sleepy speech. "Mn," he says, "hmn? a-hmn," and other such syllables. She breathes in his scent, their two breaths mix on the pillow, he answers tentatively "hmn, hmn," and their feet and hands communicate.

Mary's bed is curtained off at the end of the long ward. It is evening, and quiet, apart from the steady whimpering of one small child, his face muffled in his pillow. Mary lies on her back, quite still, her white face lit by a green-shaded lamp clipped to the metal bars of her bedhead. Daniel sits beside her, still hot and sweating, too heavy for the spindly visitor's chair. He has been there an hour, but his heart is still hammering, his collar is tight. Winifred, the grandmother, sits on the other side of the bed, peacefully knitting. She knows how to keep still, as her daughter did too, Daniel remembers, wanting not to remember. Mary's eyes are closed. Her breaths are regular and shallow. There is a neat narrow bandage round her brow, like a Greek princess's fillet. Her skin is white and cool, and spattered with freckles like brown seeds. Her hair is silky above the bandage, red-gold, gold-red. Her mouth is slightly open: he can see her teeth, baby-teeth and half-grown woman's teeth, together.

She does not move. Daniel sweats. Winifred knits. She breathes. Daniel shifts on his small seat, touches her cheek with a finger, draws back. Winifred says, "She has not changed since I got here. So still."

"They said the doctor would come."

"I suppose he will. He's bound to. We just have to wait."

Her knitting needles move steadily. Daniel resumes his study of his daughter's face.

43

After some time Ruth comes in, bends over the still face, and flicks up the eyelids with practised fingers, one, two, and looks into the unseeing eyes. "Good," she says professionally. She lays a palm on Mary's brow and says again, "Good." She is grave and beautiful in a grape-purple uniform, belted with a wide black elastic belt, under a white apron, with a pocket full of scissors and other implements. Her long pale plait is doubled up under her cap, which has a starched crown and a frilled fantail, like a dove displaying. She puts her cool little hand over Daniel's heavy ones and he is quite sure that outside the hospital she would never have touched him, but this is her place. She asks if he would like tea, and he says no, and asks when the doctor will come. "Soon," says Ruth, "soon, there have been other emergencies, he is on his way." She slips away, on black, rubber-soled feet. Daniel says to Winifred, "Marcus was taken with her, at one point."

"He still sees her, I think," says Winifred. "He's not given to discussing his life with us. As you know."

Daniel thinks about Ruth, and about Marcus. None of his thoughts are fit to tell Winifred, so he lapses into silence.

When the doctor comes, he is already on one foot, ready to go again, as doctors always are. Daniel knows doctors. He has been a hospital chaplain. Indeed, he has been a hospital chaplain in this hospital, in this ward, and knows why doctors do not meet the eyes of those to whom he now belongs, the anxious, the waiting, the helpless. Those *human gestures* were his own job, then. The doctor says to Daniel and to Winifred that the X-rays have shown no obvious damage—no fracture—and the child's condition seems stable, so that all that can be done is to watch and wait. She must be monitored for possible effects of internal bleeding. Time is most likely to heal. He is very young, and very pink, the doctor. He holds up the X-ray photographs of Mary's head, directing the light through them, and suddenly Daniel sees his child under the shadowy, cavernous image of her own skull, the nasal pits, the hollow eye-sockets, what appear to be super-imposed layers of teeth and are suddenly seen to be the adult molars, buried in the jawbone, surging up under the rootless infant crowns. All in order, says the doctor, folding these images briskly away again.

Later still, it is the end of visiting hours, and Mary still has not moved. Ruth reappears and says that they ought to leave, now.

Winifred says she doesn't like to think of Mary being alone—waking alone, is how she puts it. She is folding her knitting as she speaks. Daniel says he will stay with his daughter.

"We'll look after her," says Ruth. "She'll be all right. We can get you in a moment, if—"

"I can sit here," says Daniel, "and upset nobody. I know, I've sat here in the past, from time to time, I know how to keep out of the way."

Winifred says, "Don't you want to see Will? He's with his grandfather—I expect he knows by now you are here—"

"Tomorrow," says Daniel. "Tomorrow, I'll see Will. Now, I'm staying here. In case she wakes."

He knows, and Winifred knows, that if Mary wakes, it will be Winifred she will look for. It is Winifred's *right* to be there when she wakes, he knows, he knows Winifred knows. But he repeats, "I want to stay. I know it can be managed, I remember. I want to stay with her."

"Of course," says Winifred. "When you've come so far. You can see Will tomorrow."

He listens vaguely for sharpness or irony and detects none: he is too taken up with his daughter. It is also true that he has come to love Winifred and knows that Winifred feels something like love for him. His own mother died not long after his wife, angry and rambling in a geriatric ward, and had never, that he could remember, felt out his feelings as Winifred is doing now. If she is being sharp and ironic, she is within her rights. He stands up—the shape of the seat is impressed into his buttocks—and shambles forward and hugs his mother-in-law. She is thinner and smaller than he remembered. He says, "Thank you. I do know, you—I do know *you*—I owe you, Winifred."

"You watch her," says Winifred. She cannot bring herself to say meaninglessly, She'll be all right, in case she is not, and so casts around for words. "I'll go and see to Bill and Will and come back tomorrow. You know you can ring us up any time, if—"

"Aye," says Daniel.

Ruth says, "There's a kind of folding bed you can put down by her. Try and get some sleep. I'll be round every fifteen minutes to check her pupils. I'll keep an eye on both of you."

Night comes early in children's wards. Night comes early, but not complete darkness—angled lamps here and there illuminate tangled hair, spread-eagled monkey-forms attached to tubing and pulleys, a passionate toddler snuffling hotly into a pillow. Ruth produces a toothbrush and a towel from a cupboard, and Daniel tidies himself in a carbolic-drenched lavatory. He pads back through the ward to his daughter. The walls are painted with cheerful pictures, mostly of sheep. The artist seems to have found sheep either fascinating, or easy, or both. Little Bo-Peep, in her hooped skirt and with her crook, stands under a large tree and peers one way, whilst behind her quite a large flock of multi-coloured sheep scamper and bound over a green hummock in the opposite direction, into a blue sky. They are composed mostly of squarish masses of circular brush strokes, out of which poke black ears, black faces and thin, stick-like black legs. Some attempt, not very successful, has been made to foreshorten the fleeing ones. The blue sky is full of solid sheepish clouds. Bo-Peep is drawn from the back, her face hidden by a bonnet, which suggests a failure of confidence in the artist. On the wall facing her, Mary with her little lamb is proceeding along a fence towards a small-windowed hut labelled SCHOOL. Mary is dressed in a crimson jumper and a green skirt. She wears a school beret on fluffy (sheep-like) blond curls, and carries a square brown satchel which seems to weigh nothing. There is something not quite right about the lamb. Perhaps its legs are too short, perhaps its face is too big for its body, perhaps its fixed smile is too human. Mary's face, on the other hand, is round and empty, apart from smily lips and round pale blue eyes. Some sheep are looking over the fence and staring down on the trotting lamb. Black faces, white faces, horned, woolly.

Daniel sits beside his daughter. The night flows past. Ruth comes from time to time and turns back the eyelids, with their reddish lashes. "Good," she says, "good," and whisks away again.

Mary's mouth is a little open. Her teeth are wet. Daniel thinks of Stephanie's dead face, suddenly, with the full violence of the unprepared—the staring eyes, the raised lip, the wet teeth. He feels—it is no exaggeration—his heart willing itself to stop beating, juddering in his body like an engine in trouble. He feels waves of nausea. He waits for the image to fade as he might wait for the touch of hot metal to stop throbbing. He waits till it is gone, the face in the mind's eye, and then puts out a heavy finger and closes his daughter's lip over her teeth. Her lip is warm, warm and soft. He remembers the energy of the bursting teeth in her bony jaw. He touches her cheek, her little shoulder, he takes hold, in the dark, of her cool hand, he says, "Mary—," he says again, "Mary—"

Mary wanders in dark blue caverns. She does not walk, she weaves, or floats, or flies, between muscular fanning trunks of huge plants, or veined rocks. It is dark blue, and there is purple, and slate-grey, and there is a kind of dark light in and on it, given off by the pillars, the boughs themselves. She weaves her way and pain runs beside her like a shining wire, it traces her intricate path, but it does not exactly touch her—its light hurts her if she shifts her attention in its direction, its edge, its razor-blade edge, its needle-point, its flames about to break—but she dances with it slowly, she moves as it moves, it moves as she moves, they bow together, they curve and recurve, they keep a distance, in which there is nothing at all, no blue light, nothing, no visible dark, nothing.

Ruth returns every half-hour. "Good," she says, peering under the eyelids. "Good." Daniel sits stolidly, holding his daughter's hand. Ruth says, "Try and get a little sleep."

"I don't want sleep."

"You need it. I don't think she'll wake now. They don't wake—in the deep night—on the whole. You'll find she'll wake with the daylight. Shall I bring you a cup of Ovaltine?"

"I'll come and get it. Thank you. I need to stretch my legs. I'm all pins and needles, I'm numb."

Ruth makes him a cup of Ovaltine in a little kitchen, and they sit by the night nurses' desk, their faces in shadow, the desk lit by a pool of contained light from a green-shaded desk lamp.

"We can see her from here," says Ruth. "It's designed so we can see everyone from here."

Daniel asks Ruth how she is, what she has been doing. He expects some placid, nondescript answer as she sits there, sipping tea, her pale oval face turned down. She says, "If it were not for my spiritual life, this place—this work—would be quite unbearable."

He remembers he is a clergyman. This both makes it incumbent on him to answer this remark seriously and provides a way to answer it chattily, which is not the way it was said.

"I remember you were a very regular member of the Young Christians. Do you still go to St. Bartholomew's?"

"Sometimes I do. It is not the same, of course, since Gideon and Clemency went away. The new vicar is not a very spiritual man. He goes through the motions. I shouldn't say that. How can one know another person's soul? But—anyway—he doesn't speak to *me*. I suppose you are still in touch with Gideon, now, where you are. He is doing such wonderful work."

"I'm afraid I live an odd life, very shut away, I don't see old friends," says Daniel blandly, his professional voice coming back to him. What he feels for Gideon Farrar, his ex-vicar, is hatred and contempt, which he tries to mitigate with some kind of charitable mental effort, from time to time.

"I belong to Gideon's flock, so to speak," says Ruth. "I am a Child of Joy. I can't get to many of the main meetings in London, you know, and York, I work such terrible hours here. But he has his Family Gatherings up here on the moors too—the movement has taken on such wonderful life—miracles happen, everyone is—is full of awareness and life. I wish he came more often himself, but Clemency comes, and other family heads, we are all constantly in touch—it is a great joy."

"I am very glad," says Daniel cautiously.

"I went into this work," says Ruth, "because I wanted to do some good, to help little children, the innocent who suffer. No one tells children's nurses, when they go into training, you know, that this is the *worst* kind of nursing—the worst. You might be glad when the old—slip away—but these little ones—and those who stay here—a long time—are even worse than those who die. You can't talk about it, of course. I can, to you, because you understand how it is changed—it seems different—if the suffering can be offered to Jesus, can be part of His suffering for us—now and then I really *feel* that, though I don't *understand* it, of course—but then, we do not have to understand—"

Another voice, ecstatic, confident, is speaking inside her placid, stolid, small notes. Daniel says, "I was hospital chaplain here, you know. I've worked here. Not like you, but I have seen what you're telling me."

"You must have been so *needed*," says Ruth. "So few understand or can hear—"

This is not how Daniel remembers it.

He goes back to his child, who has not moved. Ruth looks again into the unseeing eyes and repeats, "Good."

Mary wanders among gentian-dark currents, through the lips of caverns, down falls and along conduits. The inky world swells and

48

sways. There is a far, faint booming in the silence. Someone some-where feels nausea.

Daniel dozes uneasily on the truckle bed. He is below the level of Mary's sleeping form, lifted up above him. His springs creak and groan. She turns, she moves, she flings an arm wide, a small hand touches him. He calls Ruth, who says, "Good," and checks the pupils again. Dawn comes, and with the dawn the day shift, busy with trol-leys, with sponges, with thermometers. Ruth brings Daniel a cup of tea, and tells him she has to go now, but will be there in the evening. Daniel gulps the hot tea and feels it spread in his belly. Mary's lips move.

"Look," he says to Ruth. "Look there—look at her lips."

Mary is somewhere in a chalky cavernous mouth. She is being sucked up, blown up, she wishes to float and settle, like sediment, but the medium in which she is suspended is in turmoil, she will be ejected. Her grape-dark world, her gentian caverns, are shot with angry or-ange, she sees blood, she sees hot veils, she twists her head this way and that as pain takes hold of it. She sees flat, orange. She opens her eyes.

"Mary," he says. "Mary. There you are—"

She struggles furiously to sit up. She puts hot arms round his neck, she buries her face in his beard, he puts his nose to her living skin, her hot hair, the pulse in her thin neck. All her arms and legs are in tur-moil, she worms her way out of the sheets and propels her whole body against him, anyhow. Her arms close in a stranglehold round his neck.

"My daddy, my daddy," says Mary, and Daniel kisses her hair, and his eyes are hot.

"I'm sorry," says Mary, "I'm sick, I'm sorry," and Daniel holds a dish for her to vomit. It is all a miracle, her voice, her struggling quickness, the heaving of her small stomach, the sounds of her retch-ing, it is life, she is alive. Daniel wipes her mouth with his own clean handkerchief, he smooths her hair on her brow. He thinks, There are people who would always have known—if they were me, now—that she was alive, that she would wake. But I belong always to those who know she could not have done. He avoids, this time, calling up the dead face.

Mary is better. The family are at breakfast. Daniel is still in Yorkshire. Canon Holly has told him he has bloody got to stay there for the present, now he is there. His telephone is manned by a new volunteer, a successful trainee, just the ticket. Mary is at home, but not at school. She is resting. She cannot remember anything at all about how she came to be lying there, in the playground. She has said once, she seemed to be in a huge space and something was coming down very fast out of the sky—a big *bird,* says Mary uncertainly, a shiny dark bird . . .

They are all at breakfast. Bill Potter, Winifred, Daniel, Mary, and Will. They are no longer in the graceless house in Masters' Row where Bill spent his working life, and Winifred brought up her children, and then her small grandchildren. Bill is now sixty-seven and has been retired for two years. For five years before his retirement Winifred dreaded it daily. He was a man whose work was his life. When he was presented with his leaving presents—a small carving done by an ex-pupil, in granite, a recalcitrant material, of a group of stony sheep, the complete Oxford Dictionary and a very large book token—the headmaster, Mr. Thone, had said that to many, Bill Potter *was* Blesford Ride School, and there had been groans, whistles, cheers, tears, and a violent fit of clapping. Winifred had had a vision of Bill torn out of Blesford Ride like a live tooth with bleeding roots. Also, she feared for herself. Bill was a man to whom it was possible to be married only if he was mostly not there. He expanded like volatile gas, he roared, he flamed, he hammered. She had her own quiet ways, which depended on his absence.

Bill had revealed in his speech of thanks that he did not intend to stay in Masters' Row. He had the right to do so, for three years at least, and the school had supposed that he would help out, as his predecessors had, would mark exams, coach university entrants, detach himself bit by bit. It was characteristic of Bill that he had said nothing of his plans to anyone before this speech: there were those in the audience who thought he had made up his mind then and there, in the Hall, listening to the valedictory cheering.

"I do not intend," said Bill, "to stick around, getting cross at the way things are done, or contemplating my own mistakes. I am going off in search of beauty. You can laugh. Blesford Ride is a decent enough place, and its gardeners do a decent job, but nobody could call it beautiful. The only God in the Pantheon who has got any good looks to mention is Balder, and he's dead and gone. I'm going to buy a house up on the moors—I've got my eye on one—and it will be a seemly house, and a well-proportioned house—with a garden, which

I shall cultivate when I'm not busy—but I shall be busy, I intend to be *very busy,* those who are not alive are dead, I've always said, and I'm not dying, by no means."

He was almost in tears, Winifred saw, and one more time she forgave him for excluding her, for rushing at things. He had not asked her if she wanted to move, but she did not want to stay, and perhaps he had known that without needing to ask. She thought the idea of a moorland cottage was folly, and said so. Everyone knew that it was not a good idea to isolate oneself suddenly on retirement, and there were Will and Mary, then eight and six, to consider, what about their schooling, had Bill *thought?*

Bill had thought, it turned out. He had found an eighteenth-century grey stone house, in Freyasgarth, a village in a fold of the moors between Pickering and Goathland. Behind the house, with its climbing roses, white and gold, the garden stretched to a dry-stone wall, behind which grazed sheep, on the moorside. In the village was a primary school run by a head teacher called Margaret Godden, who was, Bill explained to Winifred, a *real* teacher, he had sat in on her classes, the woman had the essence of the matter in her. Miss Godden was large and blond and fortyish and smiling. She had a passion for imparting knowledge, and a patient perfectionism. There were only two other teachers, Mr. Hebble, who took the middle class, and Miss Chick, who took Reception. Mr. Hebble lived in the village, was married, and had four children in the school himself. Miss Chick lived next-door to Miss Godden, and was Miss Godden's pupil and *semblable,* also running to fat, and also a perfectionist. Winifred liked both teachers, and was overcome by the yellow and white roses. The inside of the house was graceful and solid; the kitchen had an Aga and a stone larder, there was an outhouse with an ancient pump. Winifred had a vision of living—as Bill had so suddenly said—with beautiful things. With subtle colours, and changing lights, and old wood, and yellow and white roses. She and Bill took to travelling to country auctions, buying chairs, tables, chests, a dresser—it became a shared passion; they talked to each other as in some ways they had never done. Winifred said, "It is like that game you play with yourself, travelling on the top of buses, looking in at windows, thinking, Who would I be if I lived *there,* what sort of life would I have in that house—"

"That's how I found it," said Bill. "From a bus, coming back from an extra-mural class. You always get that feeling most in the early evening—about houses—when there's still light in the sky but there's light inside, too—"

For a year or two Winifred had a not unpleasant feeling, sitting by an open fire in the evening, polishing an oval table, watering window-boxes, looking down from a wide landing to a stone-flagged hall, its wide step worn by centuries of the dead, going in and out, busy with other lives, that she was a kind of ghost on a kind of stage set, making the appropriate movements for the beauty of the place. And then it became more part of herself—the place where Will's knee had bled on the stone, the curtains she had sewn sitting in that window and hung in this one, white sprigged with lavender and broom yellow, blowing in when she opened the window. Most surprisingly, Bill does not roar in this house, he does not crowd, he is neither bored nor sulky, he is, as he said he was to be, *busy*. He has expanded his extra-mural teaching. He makes long journeys up and down the Yorkshire coast, he has classes in Scarborough and Whitby, Calverley and Pickering, talking away about D. H. Lawrence and George Eliot as though their lives depended on it. He has developed an interest in the old itinerant Methodists, who came and spoke fire in these very houses. He is writing a book. It is called, at different times, *English and the Community of Culture; Culture in the Community and English; English, Culture, Community*. He is away quite enough for Winifred's peace of mind, and when he comes home, he talks to her about where he has been, what has been said. Miss Godden, Mr. and Mrs. Hebble, Miss Chick, come to dinner, and so do various members of the staff of the University of North Yorkshire, who have bought weekend houses in the hill villages, who tramp past in seasoned boots and woolly socks and admire the roses.

They have breakfast in the kitchen looking directly out over the garden to the moors. Bill sits at one end of the table and Winifred at the other. Daniel and Mary are side by side, their two heads bent over bowls of porridge with spirals of treacle, melting gold into mealy-grey. On the other side of the table sits Will, who is now ten, a stocky, dark boy with black eyes under thick black brows. It is absurdly clear who his father is, and it is equally clear that he is not looking at his father, he is not talking to his father. He is eating rather fast and noisily, toast and boiled eggs, ready for school. Bill has unwisely embarked on a discussion of Will's schooling. He could sit the Scholarship Entrance to Blesford Ride, where, as Bill's grandson, he would pay much reduced fees, or he could go on to the local state schools and continue to live in Blithe House. Bill says, "Perhaps you would like to visit the school, Daniel, while you're here."

"It depends on Will," says Daniel.

"I shouldn't think there's much point," says Will. "Anyway, I want to go to Overbrow Comprehensive. Everyone else is. My friends."

"There are things to be said for and against comprehensive schools," says Bill sententiously. "And things to be said for and against the old establishment. Boys do *learn* something in the old place, and that matters."

"So they do in the comprehensive."

"I don't say they don't. Perhaps you and your father should go and look at it, together."

"You're the school expert, Grandpa. You come."

"We should at least discuss whether you are entered for the exam, Will," says Bill. He says to Daniel, "He's very bright, Will is, you must talk to his head teacher, she thinks very highly of him, very."

"We can't discuss it now," says Will. "I've got to go to school."

Daniel, who is not stupid, can see his son deliberating over whether to forbid him to talk to the head teacher, and is glad when Will draws back from the blow. Will pushes his chair back with a scrape, puts on his anorak, gathers up his heavy bookbag. Winifred hands him an apple, a shortbread, a flask. He kisses her on the cheek, includes Bill and Mary in a "good-bye" and nods curtly to Daniel. "See you," he mutters, "later." Both knit their black brows, tense and puzzled. Will goes.

Daniel looks down and sees Mary's wrist, her little fist closed round her busy spoon. Every movement of every muscle pleases him. Mary says, "Will wants to go to Overbrow with Keith and Micky and that girl with the funny hair." She thinks a little, and adds inconsequentially, "You won't go just yet, will you, Daddy? You've only just come. *I* wouldn't mind if you came to the school, I wouldn't."

"I can stay a bit longer," he tells her.

"A bit," she says. "A bit longer."

Two people are coming over the brow of the moor and making their way by sheep tracks down to the back gate. Winifred gets up to make more coffee. "It is Marcus and Jacqueline," she tells Daniel. "They have been up doing something or other with Jacqueline's snails. She's finishing a Ph.D on those snails. They get up at four o'clock to go and count them, and so on."

"She comes and talks to our class about snails," says Mary. "We have a *colony* of those snails we look after for her, we do real experiments, we see what they eat and what colour the babies are. We have a big snail book, we measure them, we write it all down, it's useful."

"If you think snails are useful," says Bill, not unamiably.

The figures are so small, it is at first only just possible to make out which is which. Both are wearing anoraks and rubber boots; it is damp, good snail weather; both are thin, and walk springingly. Daniel does not want to see Marcus. Marcus is Stephanie's brother, and was in the room when the sparrow fled under the refrigerator and the refrigerator struck. Daniel has never asked whether, if Marcus had shown more presence of mind, he could have saved her. He is afraid of his own rage. Marcus was in his house, in a state of complicated nervous withdrawal, all that year, upsetting Stephanie, invading privacy, *brooding*. A creature so nervous and futile, Daniel supposed, would be cast again into the stupor from which he was vaguely emerging. Marcus was part of his memory of his own terrible return to that house, a stick-like creature with a face like bad cheese, waxy and sweating, standing close, close to the refrigerator plug in the wall and shaking. Marcus was not, he decided then, a *possible* concern for himself. He could not help Marcus, because he was who he was. Neither of them could hope or expect he could help Marcus. Let him suffer, he saw he had thought, and now here is this young man, with the young woman, striding down the moorside and, he can hear, laughing as he comes to the gate in the garden wall. How can he laugh, says the demon that squats in Daniel. It is 1964, Daniel replies scrupulously. She died in 1958. We are all alive. Marcus is a young man. He has a degree now, Daniel does not know exactly in what; Winifred has just told him that Marcus has a doctorate, he is now Dr. Potter, he does some teaching at the North Yorkshire University and has just joined an important research team. We are all alive, Daniel tells himself again, knowing that he himself is not. Not exactly, not all, not. Mary tugs at his sweater. "Come and see the snails, come on."

Marcus and Jacqueline take off their coats and are given hot coffee and toast and bacon and eggs. These things are delicious after the hunting in the damp and dark, the peaty breath of the moorland air, the cold, the sunrise, the movement, all of which were also delicious. Jacqueline is monitoring two colonies of *Helix hortensis* and two of *Helix nemoralis,* studying the genetic changes in the populations, which can be read in the varied bands on the creatures' shells. She has brought back some snails for the captive colonies and NYU, and Mary exclaims over these—"Look at their lovely horns, look at their little mouths, they have *thousands* of teeth, Daddy, did you know, Jacqueline told me . . ."

Jacqueline has become a handsome young woman, with dark brown hair, worn long to the shoulders, with its own wiry curl. She has an outdoor skin, sunbrowned and supple, and bright brown eyes. In the old days, she used to come to the Young Christians, with Ruth. Daniel wonders if she too is a member of Gideon Farrar's Children of Joy. He tells her that Ruth has looked after Mary really well, and she replies that she doesn't know how Ruth can do that job, day after day, it is so hard. Her face is naturally smiling, even as she says this. Marcus says, "Hello, Daniel," and sits down to his breakfast. He says, "Hello, Mary, how is the head?" Mary says, "I still don't remember how I got hit, it's really funny not to know something—so important to *me*—*me* not to know." Marcus, who is now working on the neuroscience of the brain, and on memory particularly, agrees that it is interesting. "It might come back," he says. "You might remember without knowing you remember. And then one day, it will suddenly come clear, you will know."

Marcus does not want to see Daniel. Partly for Daniel's reasons. As Daniel remembers Marcus by the electric plug, Marcus remembers Daniel's face, Daniel coming in through the door, Daniel seeing *that*. Like Daniel, he supposed he himself could not survive the shock. That he did, he thinks, when he thinks of it, he owes to the care given to him by Jacqueline and Ruth. Ruth held his body, and waited until he could cry, and wiped his tears. Jacqueline, robustly, ruthlessly, required him to be interested in things not himself. She dragged him to lectures, which after a time he heard; she bombarded him with her own problems, which his curiously apt mathematical mind solved ingeniously without his emotions needing to uncoil from their shell; she made him go on field studies trips when he could hardly drag one foot after the other; she involved him in her own passion for what was beginning to be generally known as ecological studies. When in spite of his pain he found he was interested, Jacqueline made him know he was interested, made him see he was alive. He sat with her once in a cave in a storm up on Saddle Moor: it was a cave with stony walls and a roof of dark earth, through which poked wiry roots of things clinging to the surface somewhere above. They made their way through air and nosed back into earth. They hung and twisted, out of their elements. As the storm raged, water began to soak through into the cave, streaking the earth with dark rivulets, shining in sudden drops and splinter-shapes on the rock face, dripping down the blind roots. He often dreamed of those dark patches, those few bright drops. That was how it was. It was Jacqueline's tough exactitude that make him recognise that that was how it was, that the water was making its way in.

Marcus knows he is guilty of Stephanie's death. He does not know what to do with this knowledge. He knows that the one person—apart from the dead—whom he has mortally hurt is Daniel, though he knows also that irremediable harm has been done to Will and Mary, and, beyond them, to Bill and Winifred. He does not think of Frederica as someone wounded by what happened. He knows that for him to sink into grief and guilt will do no good, so he does not, but this does not help. He thinks Daniel should not have rushed abruptly off to London, and thinks he should not blame Daniel for things, but think of his own blame. At the same time, he does his work well, very well, and is interested in his colleagues. He lives, and somewhere else he stays, as Daniel does, but differently, in that terrible place with that terrible knowledge.

Bill opens his letters, which have just arrived. One, in a brown envelope, he leaves till last, and then laughs when he reads it. It is palely typed, on official writing paper. Bill says, "This is from Alexander Wedderburn. They have put him on a government committee to study the teaching of English. It is to be called the Steerforth Committee, after its chairman, who is Philip Steerforth, you know, the anthropologist; they wouldn't put an *English* specialist in charge of an English enquiry, not bloody likely. Our grammatical Vice-Chancellor is on the list, old Wijnnobel, I see, but not chairing it. Alexander was never more than a hit-and-miss teacher—well, he says as much here—he wants me to submit evidence to the committee because, he is kind enough to say, I am the best teacher he knows. He says he will be visiting schools and hopes to come by; he says he can pick the parts of the country he visits, and hopes to spend some time up here. I shall write to him about the wonders of Miss Godden's Top Class writing projects. I may well write some evidence for him. It won't do any good—I've never known one of these things *do any good*—but some good ideas, some sound principles, lying about in the Education Ministry, who knows?"

Daniel says he has seen Alexander, and Jacqueline asks if Alexander is writing any more plays. Nobody knows. Daniel asks Jacqueline about Christopher Cobb, the naturalist who runs the field station, and Jacqueline says he is away, at a pesticide conference in Leeds. Bill remarks that Cobb has become very vociferous about crop-spraying and seed-dressings, and Jacqueline says he has had to be, nobody understands what is being done to the earth. Only Marcus knows—and Marcus only partly—what happened to Jacqueline in 1961 and 1962, when they both began their research careers at NYU, Jacqueline working with a Dane called Luk Lysgaard-Peacock on the population genetics of snails, and he himself, at that stage, working on the mathematics of a model of consciousness with the mathematician Jacob Scrope, under the direction of the micro-biologist Abraham Calder-Fluss. Nineteen sixty-two, Marcus's second postgraduate year, was the year of the Cuban missile crisis. Marcus's generation, including Marcus, are haunted by nuclear fear, a millenarian anxiety that the ultimate weapon will be—hurled, deployed, unleashed?—leaving a world of winter and emptiness and sickness, a world imaginatively constituted by film of Hiroshima and Nagasaki, whose emblem is the upsurge of the mushroom cloud over Bikini atoll. When Cuba came, Jacob Scrope packed his books and clothes ready to depart for Ireland, out of range of a possible London bomb, or bomb on the Fylingdales Early Warning System, with its white globes resting on the moors. Marcus was rattled by Scrope's assessment of the risks, but Jacqueline was solidly unmoved—"They cannot be such *fools*," she said, "they are just male creatures puffing themselves up like gannets and geese, they will back down and look the other way, you'll see, *they've got to*, they're human." Her confidence came out of her own good sense, which had been Marcus's life-line, but he could not quite share it. In his experience, good sense was not so strong in human beings as people like Jacqueline supposed, as the society they lived in was built on supposing. In effect, like gannets or geese, Khrushchev and Kennedy deflated their swollen breasts and stepped aside. In the interim, Jacqueline had begun to notice that thrush-anvils where she and Christopher Cobb had counted shells were deserted, that eggs were not hatching in nest-boxes, that dead owls were appearing in barns and farmyards. In the spring of 1961, tens of thousands of birds were found dead in the British countryside. Cobb's activities began to include the delivery of boxes of tiny corpses to the laboratories of NYU for analysis, where they were found to contain mercury, benzene hexachloride, and other poisons. In 1963 Rachel Carson's *Silent Spring* was published in England, and Jacqueline gave a copy to Marcus. On the royal estate in Sandringham, Jacqueline told him, the dead birds included: pheasants, red-legged partridges, wood-pigeons and stock-doves, green-finches, chaffinches, blackbirds, song-thrushes, skylarks, moorhens, bramblings, tree sparrows, house-sparrows, jays, yellowhammers, hedge sparrows, carrion crows, hooded crows, goldfinches and sparrow hawks.

She said to Marcus, "We shall kill the planet. We are a species that *has gone wrong* somewhere. We shall kill everything."

"We've all been saying that about the Bomb. I think we probably shall kill everything."

"We shall kill everything because we're too intelligent, and not intelligent enough to control our own intelligence. Nobody *meant* to kill these birds—they were just trying to improve something else—the wheat, the potatoes, a lot of this is owing to *seed-dressings*—trying to make things grow. I think—I do think—we might learn not to be so aggressive, when it's not just another man or another *army* that's at stake. But I think we're just too *stupid* not to destroy the planet."

Marcus said, "Fallout changes genes. Chemical mutagens change genes. Something that has taken millions and millions of years to make forms that *work*—we can just destroy—or turn into monstrosities—in a twinkling."

Jacqueline said, "There's so little one person can do. Collect dead birds."

"Make sure the evidence is watertight. For politicians who are short-sighted and won't care."

They were young and healthy, they were full of the huge, energetic despair of the young and healthy confronted with rational fear. Their waking dreams were haunted by the idea of sumps, and desert wastes, and rotted tree trunks, and lifeless lakes where no birds sing. Every pleasurable walk on the moors, looking for snails, listening to larks climbing and plovers calling, was as surely accompanied by the vision of all this rotting and vanishing as their ancestors' ramblings might have been by the vision of hell-fire, red-hot pincers, and eternal thirst.

Daniel asks Bill, watching him tidy away his post, what news he has of Frederica.

"None," says her father. "She doesn't deign to communicate. If I didn't know her better I'd say she'd cast us off as vulgar relations, but

I do know her better—she was properly brought up, as far as *that* goes, she may be an intellectual snob but she's no social snob and *I absolutely refuse to believe* she married that man out of any desire to rise in the world of saddle-thumping bottoms and hunt balls. Now and then she sends a packet of snaps of the little boy. I notice she isn't on them. We've got lots of pictures of him *on his pony* and *boating on lakes*—"

"Nothing wrong with ponies—"

"You know very well what I mean, Daniel. Very well. She's bitten off more than she can chew. I can't say I liked him—that *Nigel*— when we did meet, and I can't say I'd choose to spend any more time in his company even if I was asked, which I won't be. No, no good will come of it. She's closed off from us, like Beauty and the Beast, like Gwendolen and Grandcourt, and one of these days she'll turn up with bag and baggage, I wouldn't be surprised. She's not a patient creature, our Frederica, she might have been knocked sideways, but she'll stand up again one of these days, and look around, and—"

"I don't see how you can state all that, Bill," says his wife. "You've no evidence for any of it. She may be very happy."

"Do you think so? Do you think so?"

"No. But I don't know. And there's the little boy."

"She's my daughter. I know her. Something got into her. Something was always getting into her. She needed someone like you, Daniel, someone like us."

Daniel says, "You wouldn't even come to my wedding, you monster. You made everyone's life a misery. You can't just say we're alike, now."

"Well, we are. That was a battle of like with like. This isn't. I should think the attraction of that *Nigel* was exactly that he wasn't like us, that he had nothing to do with us. Well, there are lots of people who have nothing to do with us who would make better husbands for Frederica is all I can say—"

"You don't *know*, Bill. You're just hurt," Winifred says.

"No, I'm not hurt. I've learned a few things. I've learned that if one of your daughters is dead, you just have to feel glad the other's *alive*, even if she won't come to see you, that's what. You get things in perspective. What's alive is alive, and kicking, I suppose. Frederica was always kicking. I've upset Daniel. I didn't mean to. I'll take myself off and write to Alexander. Daniel, you *know* how things are between us, don't pucker up."

"I know," says Daniel. "Give my best to Alexander. He's a good man."

Marcus says he must go, and Jacqueline goes with him. Daniel shakes Marcus's hand, which is no longer, he notices, limp like a dead fish. Marcus is a perfectly ordinary intellectual-looking thin young man, with longish pale brown hair, and glasses. Daniel asks Jacqueline if she still sees Gideon Farrar.

"No. I gave all that up. It suddenly seemed not to mean anything. I'm sorry."

"Don't say that. I never liked it, myself."

"It does Ruth good. And it does her *no good,* too, in some ways, I think."

"Indeed."

Mary goes to bed, for a regulation prescribed rest, and Daniel is left alone with Winifred, in the quiet kitchen of Bill's beautiful house. Winifred says, "Honestly, Bill is *too much.* He worries a lot about Frederica. He misses her—and then, with Stephanie gone—he feels it more, that she seems to have abandoned us. I hope you think it's funny that he's decided you're like him. I hope it doesn't seem a final insult."

"No, no. The fire's gone out in that chimney. We should shake hands. Anyway, it's half-time. It's our duty to acknowledge truths. Half-truths included."

"And Will will come round," says Winifred, who wants everything to be calm, to be good, to be well.

"Why should he? What I did to him—what I did—was wicked, was preposterous. Look at it coldly, look at it straight: a woman dies, a man is left with two kids, so he walks out one day and *just leaves them*—so they've lost two at a stroke—how can that be forgiven?"

"But you can't look at it coldly, Daniel—you have to see how it was *then*—you were half-mad, and were doing them no good—and you can't say we haven't looked after them well."

"I don't. You've done wonders. They are *safe* kids. They have a home. A family. I'm not a family. I know all that."

"And for Bill. It has been important to him to have Will—he *plays* with Will—he couldn't play with Marcus, you know—he was awful—these things can't be redeemed—but he has done well, and it makes him happy."

"I didn't abandon my kids to make Bill happy."

"I know that."

"Before I met her—Stephanie—I had this idea of my life. At the edge, just over the edge. Where people weren't managing. When we were married—I tried ordinary happiness—I were lucky, we were happy—some of the time—and both of us knew what a *chance* it was, what the odds were against it—and what we'd—abandoned for it—her work, her books, her friends—my—my need to live where it's dangerous. Yes, that's it. Where it's dangerous. And when she died—I were pushed back, into *that* world—as though I shouldn't have tried to hoist myself out of it into a sunny shelf, wi' her—but a life, wi'out her—I couldn't—I thought."

"Daniel. I know. Don't hurt yourself."

"There's more. *Then* I felt—I were dangerous to *them*—Will and Mary. That I could do them no good, that they'd got to be got away from what were happening to me—for their own good—I really thought that—"

"It may have been true."

"Yes, but now. But *now.* Now there's Marcus—looking like—like an ordinary being, *laughing* with that girl, Jacqueline—and here's me—with my son hating me—how can I tell you? The world's changed, and Will and Mary have changed—disaster is my job, Winifred, I know what—the living look like, as opposed to the walking dead. They're the living."

"And you're the walking dead."

"That's it. I'm not. Not exactly. Only some of the time. Only *really.* Hell. I can do what the living do, I can eat my breakfast, I can think how lovely Mary looks, eating hers, I can find Bill funny, going on about Frederica, I can *smile*—I've got out of that—that *clear black state*—you see the world through a veil of coal, you know—"

"I know."

"And now I don't. How can I go back to what I do in London and leave Mary, when she were so nearly dead, and I wasn't there? How can I let Will hate me so? I can tell you—it's still truer that I'm the walking dead than that I'm so to speak resurrected. I love the smell of your toast, but it's only because I remember it, not because I notice it. You know? I don't know if you know. I think almost all human beings walk about over the crust of some *pit* they know is yawning for them—almost everyone has things they'd rather not see in their mind's eye—*daren't* let their thoughts start up—I'm no different from anyone."

"You're different because you say it. Because you see it in other people. Because you look at it, and work with it, instead of sidling away or looking in another direction. Those people in London need someone. There aren't many around like you. You can't be all things to all men."

Every morning the company in La Tour Bruyarde were awoken by delightful sounds of pipes and cymbals and fresh young voices. The Lady Paeony had formed the children into an enthusiastic choir, who sang their *aubades* in corridors and court-yards. No one was irritated by these dulcet sounds, which were most carefully kept sweet and low, so that pillowed heads only turned and lifted to hear more clearly. The assembled company broke their fast to-gether in the Great Hall, and were served with bread freshly baked in the great ovens of the castle, with honey, and currant jellies, and little dishes of clotted cream and jugs of foaming milk from the cows who grazed on the grassy slopes below the fortress. The Lady Roseace had discovered the cowsheds, where the heavy gentle beasts were milked, and the dairy, where their milk was churned and sieved and skimmed and whipped, quite by accident, as she daily discovered new regions of their sequestered realm. She had cried out with delight upon en-tering the dairy thus unawares, and indeed from a rather dank and mouldering passage, which she had believed to be a shortcut to the la-trines. It was a place of order and beauty, cool and glimmering, with earthenware tiles on its floor, and many varieties of tiles on its walls and working surfaces, tiles darkly green and richest lapis-blue, tiles sprigged with forget-me-nots, and decorated with blue milkmaids on white glaze, with windmills and weathercocks and other innocent country creatures. A large young woman with round red forearms was patting butter, and another was pouring a great flood of sweet, warm, foaming milk into an earthenware pancheon. The Lady Roseace had wandered delightedly round this quiet place, touching cool surfaces, tasting cheeses with a pink finger, and had finally walked from the dairy down a flagged passage into a byre where a young man and a young woman were milking two creamy-golden cows, in that smell of straw and mild piss and animal heat which is unforgettable as rose gardens. She watched entranced as the ten fingers pressed and coaxed and squeezed and tickled and stripped, and the two large udders softly shuddered and contracted under the finger-tips, and the teats sprang and started, and the white liquid spurted and hissed into the pails. The young man's face was pressed into the hairy groin of the cow, and both were softly beaded with sweat.

The Lady Roseace thought no employment could be more delightful, and said as much to Culvert, when he came into her rosy boudoir that morning, as he always came, to discuss the day's doings. She asked him who the delicious people were who inhabited the dairy and the byre, and he replied that they were the dairymaids and the cowman, those who had always had charge of those places. Inspired by the idea of the skimmer, and the butter-pats, and perhaps also by the memory of the warm, fragrant flank of the cow, the Lady Roseace said that this was a trade she would like to learn, and that it was their intention, was it not, to abolish the status of servants and masters, so that ideally there should surely be no dairymaid and no cowman?

Indeed, that was so, replied Culvert, and no one was more conscious of the urgent need to proceed with that project than he himself. Indeed, since their arrival in the Tower, he had busied himself with the writing of a Memorandum which should form the basis for a discussion of the best way to set about the division of labour in the community and in the economic circumstances in which they found themselves. And he had found, he went on, abstractedly inserting his hand in its customary place between Roseace's full breasts, and playing elegantly with her right nipple, that the consideration of the division of labour had entailed the consideration of all sorts of diverse other things, such as the system of education that might prove most fruitful, and ideas about desirable modes of dress, and new forms of language. His brain was in a turmoil, protested Culvert, transferring his delicate fingering to the left nipple and leaving the right one straining upright. The Lady Roseace stared dreamily out of the window, and shuddered agreeably, and said again that she would like to work in the dairy, she was very attracted to the idea of the dairy. She said also, as she sank dreamily to her knees on the goatskin rugs, and felt Culvert parting her moist thighs with his hard hand, that perhaps he should discuss division of labour with the whole company before his complex Memorandum was entirely complete. Otherwise they might think, she said, her voice frilling and shivering with bliss as he opened her lower lips, that he believed himself to be the master and architect, and not only one of a free and equal society, as they had agreed, she said, getting out the word "agreed" before a long wordless moan of bliss overtook it.

Culvert addressed the assembled company in the place he called sometimes the Theatre of Tongues and sometimes, though less often, simply the Theatre of Speech. There were other theatres, as we shall see, the Theatre of Mime, for instance, the Theatre also of Cruelty, in other parts of the citadel. The Theatre of Tongues had once been a chapel, like some of the other theatres, the Theatre of Sacrifice, for instance, and there were of course also other chapels in the Tower, some of them disused, some of them no more than an anchorite's cell, some of them adapted to other purposes, garderobes maybe, or wine-stores, or places for the strict examination of souls and bodies. No count of the chapels had ever come up with exactly the same number as any other, and so it was also, with even more exorbitant margins of error, with the other rooms in that place.

The Theatre of Tongues was so called partly at least because in the gloom of its upper vaulting could still be seen an ancient frieze depicting tongues of flame, boiling upwards like pyres or faggots and descending also like crowns. The walls were crumbling and the fresco damaged. Some believed the tongues of flame to be part of a lively depiction of hell-fire, and their case was partly borne out by the presence of a soot-black demon over the south door, brandishing eight arms, each holding a wailing infant, with his mouth, full of gnashing white fangs, ready to ingest them. But others believed that the flames were the relics of a depiction of the Pentecostal descent of the Spirit, and explained the shadowy stick-like figures barely visible beneath the tongues as the Apostles waiting in the Upper Room. They too had visual proofs, of a kind, for there was a faded frieze of bishops' mitres that ran beneath all.

The Theatre of Tongues was still lit dimly by Gothic windows along its two flanking walls, but where the altar would have been a new stage had been constructed, with midnight-blue velvet curtains spangled with golden stars, and everything necessary to raise and lower stage-sets, plinths, thrones, plaster walls, and other such useful adjuncts. The seats in this building were carved, high-backed benches, pews you might have called them, if in a church, not a theatre. They were not uncomfortable but gave the company, perforce, the rigid attentive posture of a jury.

Culvert made an entry from the rear of the stage, looking modest and dynamic, as he knew well how to look. He was beautifully dressed in green breeches and white stockings, with a simple but intricately tied cravat, and his glistening hair tied back. He spoke fluently, with wit and passion, for an hour and a half at least, reading from time to time from his unfinished Memorandum when his ideas became too intricate.

The main matters he touched on are listed below, for the convenience of the present reader. The truly curious may find his theory of the human passions and velleities set out in exhaustive detail in Appendix A2 of the present work—though it must be stressed here that his ideas at the time of his appearance in the Theatre of Tongues were in a very early stage of their formulation, and had by no means even begun to resemble their final carbuncular multi-faceted brilliance or their intricately systematised web of correspondences and cross-referred psychopolitical acuities. Indeed at that time the genius of Culvert was only instinctively *reaching towards* his visionary understanding that a community of bodies and minds could be forged by the general will and the general confluence of desires into One Being acting simply for its own self-preservation and its own entire delectation. To this end he was to elaborate his understanding, his taxonomy, of the co-operal passions, great and small, of human creatures, of the ways to release their energies as flowers release sweet smells and puff out pollen, all natural as breathing and bleeding.

These are the substantive headings of Culvert's speech. Whilst he delivered it, the Lady Roseace, and not only she, took intense pleasure in observing the decision and flexibility of his upper lip, the energetic pulse in his white throat, the muscular swell of his buttocks in his shining breeches and, not least, as his rhetorical urgency increased, the harder and rounder pressure of his virile member in its satin casing. By the end of the speech the Lady Roseace was positively aching to touch and release him, and relieved herself in a wild frenzy of clapping.

1   The community must strive towards complete freedom for each and every member to live and express himself—or herself—to the utmost.

2   To this end all false distinctions of the corrupt world from which they had fled must be abolished. There must be no masters and no servants, no payment and no debt, but a common consent about the work to be done, the delights to be enjoyed, the just sharing of these, and the proper remuneration of all from the common fund of goods and talents. Professions must be abolished, along with privileges, all

must turn their hands to all that was possible, as their desires led them, for work desired to be done is work well done, and slave labour is always ill done.

3   "It will be found," Culvert said, "I believe, upon just reflection, that many of the evil distinctions and oppressions in our world come from institutions we have not dared to question. Most of us have already questioned and rejected the religions of our forefathers and compatriots, seeing to what evils they have led, but we have not sufficiently studied how those *unnatural* institutions—marriage, the family, the patriarchy, the pedagogic authoritarian relation between teacher and pupil—have also harmed our natural impulses and inclinations. I believe I may be able to demonstrate how much harm has been done to female affections, as well as to male vigour, by the institution of monogamy, as I believe I may be able to show that both rationally and emotionally a child may be stunted by being left only to the attentions of its progenitors, however amiable and well-meaning."

He discussed also:

4   How it might be possible to fit work to the natural inclinations of all—men, women, and children—as they varied from home to home and from age to age.

5   How a more beautiful and less restrictive form of dress might be devised, doing away with false modesty, which in the new order would be unnecessary, and with harmful bones and laces, unless there were those—as he believed there would be found to be—who took pleasure in the constraints of such things on the flesh.

6   How language might in the end need to be reforged and reinvented, for there were no words in the language for many of the pleasurable exercises and human relations he proposed, and such words as there were were pejorative and harsh, carrying with them associations from the old prohibitions and pruriences of priests, patriarchs, and pedagogues. "Language," cried Culvert, throwing open the damp cavern of his mouth, with its hot quivering tongue and gleaming teeth, "language is a bodily product, a product of our earliest intimacies and desires, from the babble of the infant at the breast to the impassioned discourse of the visionary who tries to speak what is yet unformulated and unshaped. We will remake language in our own images," cried Culvert, "with our own kissings and sippings will we

make new names for what we will do and be, for the relations between ourselves, and the relations between ourselves and the world."

7　He proposed also that the whole community should take part in various theatrical performances from time to time, and on a regular schedule to be mutually agreed. There should be dance, mime, music, debate, choral singing, gymnastic displays, tumbling, juggling—

"Sword swallowing and fire-breathing," interjected a voice from the hinder pews.

"Those too if there can be found amongst our number persons whose sensuality inclines towards the taste of cold steel, or the thrill of scorched gullets.

"There shall also be dramatic presentations, and not only of old plays about old things, the ambitions of kings and generals, the moanings of monogamous lovers, but of new plays about new social forms, new encounters, new desires, new resolutions of new conflicts. And after the plays there shall be debates concerning the meanings and the value and the excellence and demerits of the performances, and these debates shall be no less full of energy and passion than the plays themselves.

"Also I propose that we regularly meet for story-telling. There may be those among you who suppose story-telling to be primitive and childish, but I say that story-telling is the primal human converse, since we are the only animals who look before and after, referring to past events and wisdom, and envisaging the future in the light of these things. I propose that we tell each other, one by one, the true stories of our lives, and this with several ends in view, viz., the greater understanding and friendship this will bring about for each of the other, and equally the greater understanding these narratives will give of the true patterns of passions and desires that rule each of our lives. And when these passions and desires are in this way made manifest, the community will the more easily be able to see how these energies may be cunningly put to use for the common good and the common delight. And as the narrators become more skilled and trusting, and as the listeners become more subtle in questioning and probing, so shall the stories become more and more truthful, as hidden things, shameful secrets, desires suppressed with violence in the harsh old days, are brought out into a clear and reasonable, friendly, and accepting light and warmth. For it is also my belief that what is kept secret and separate festers in body and brain, to the detriment of the individual and the community.

Sunlight cures suppurating diseases of the skin, and friendly contemplation may cure many boils and carbuncles on the psyche.

"Later we may even wish to *enact* these stories together, to enact them even with beneficent and healing differences, restoring losses, fulfilling desperate needs, who knows? I should hope that the tale-telling may become the central, the sacramental activity, so to speak, of our union.

"But these are only thoughts, and only my thoughts. We must all think long and deeply as to how to proceed, and skilfully and quickly about the immediately pressing problems."

Not only the Lady Roseace, but all the assembled company, including the little children and infants who could not have understood a word, applauded vigorously after this speech. Various questions were raised, in a spirit of co-operation and enthusiasm. Turdus Cantor, for instance, asked whether the proposal for autobiographical narrations—which he believed might be both instructive and amusing—did not smack in some way of the confessional practices of the old Church, and might not be, as the confessional had been, manipulated by unscrupulous men to instil fear and obedience in the weak. To which Culvert replied that that might be so in a *secret* confessional, as the Church's was, but not in the frank and open and sympathetic group of loving supporters he envisaged.

The Lady Mavis, clutching her infant Florizel to her breast, asked how soon Culvert proposed to institute communal care of the young, and whether it would be done without further thought being given to providing for all the needs of the smallest members of the community, including mother's milk and the lalling of the maternal voice. For speaking of her own desires, she said, she felt a passionate need to feed and cradle and comfort her own infants, and so she was sure did every woman. To which Culvert replied that nothing would be done without full debate, and that her confessed proclivities seemed to suggest, *prima facie*, her suitability for employment in the nurseries, but that this too, would need looking into, considering also the passional needs of the infants themselves, and of other possible nurses and wetnurses.

As for Lady Mavis's naïve view that all women had a natural inclination to caring for infants, specifically their own infants, he had only to call on history to prove her wrong. He had only to refer to the habit of exposing unwanted infants, usually females, in jars outside the walls of civilised Athens, or the Chinese habit of regular infanticide of unwanted female young, whom they suffocated with affection, or punished too captiously.

A young woman called Dora, who was, or had until that moment been, a lady's maid—if indeed that moment was the moment of emancipation, or unshackling, or evolution desiderated by Culvert— this young woman asked, in a pretty and languid voice, which the Lady Roseace prevented herself from characterising as "insolent," whether her own natural passional need to live the life of a lady, and drink tea, and lie on a couch, and flirt with gentlemen, could now be put to good use, in the new order. Culvert answered this flippancy with a most beaming gravity, saying that he hoped that from now on, from time to time, to be regulated and ordered by the organism of the community, everyone who so desired might lie on a couch and sip tea, for these were not insignificant pleasures by any means. And that also flirting with gentlemen, fulfilling the desires of gentlemen, and indeed sharing mutual pleasures with them, would be part of the rights and duties of all women in the Tower. And that also productive work must be done, the community must be fed, agriculture, cooking and so on must happen, and those unable to carry out any duties in the fields or kitchens must find other ways of benefiting the common wealth. The questioner could hardly be employed as a whore in the new order, he supposed, for pleasuring should be by mutual consent and freely given—unless particular passions felt an irreducible need to be paid for their services—for he had noticed that to some, coins of the realm in the palm of the hand, or the stocking under the bed, were a greater delight than any number of ejaculations or embraces, and he was not yet firm in his own mind as to whether this proclivity would disappear in a harmonious world, or persist ineradicably. The young woman appeared to be taking some time to think out the im- plications of this last observation—her pretty brow was knit and her mouth pouted thoughtfully.

From the back of the theatre, in the shadows, the dark voice of Colonel Grim could be heard, breaking into the momentary silence.

"And who will be responsible for cleaning the latrines?"

A further silence ensued. Colonel Grim said, brisk and conversa- tional, "I ask again, who will be responsible for cleaning the latrines? And I offer you the observation that many previous attempts to found ideal societies or just commonwealths have foundered on just this question, which is not trivial but, if you will forgive a little wordplay, of *fundamental* importance."

No one could think of an answer to this question, though Narcisse proposed that the task be shared by the whole community, by rota, everyone working with a partner for so many days of the month or year. He added, with a graceful smile, that he would be only too happy himself to purchase his release from this duty with anything it might be in his power to offer anyone, after the institution of the new order. Merkurius said that the best way would be to find someone whose natural passion was ingenious invention, and who, with a system of pulleys and funnels, runnels and pumps, might perhaps make the latrines self-sufficient, might construct a self-perpetuating, self-evacuating, self-purifying system. Turdus Cantor said that if they were to work on the assumption that everyone had a set of passional inclinations that contributed to the good of a society, perhaps they should ask if anyone here had a passional inclination to the clearing of excrement. He had seen Bedlam lunatics happily at play with the substance, but he thought there were not yet any Bedlam lunatics amongst them. Culvert said that the persons in question might only have been restrained in Bedlam because their natural desire to handle turds was disapproved by society, and that such persons might indeed be usefully employed in latrines in a reasonable community. Another silence ensued which was broken by Marius, a twelve-year-old boy, who remarked that cleaning latrines could be a form of punishing offenders here, as in schools and military camps he had seen. The Lady Paeony said she hoped that no form of punishment would be thought desirable in the new world they intended to build, and the discussion moved away from Colonel Grim's question to the question of the desirability, or otherwise, of punishments and sanctions, which took up several sage, delightful and exhausting hours.

After the debate, Turdus Cantor said to Grim: "No answer was found to your question."

"No. And things are thereby already worse, for those who did clean the latrines will hardly continue to do so."

"Some leaders would have set an example by setting themselves at the head of the first rotating cohort of shit-shifters."

"That is not his style. But I believe he will find a solution to the shit-shifting. I do not think shit-shifting will be his downfall."

"Yet finding volunteers will not be easy."

"All men can be coerced into voluntary acts against their instincts. You will see."

"You are not sanguine about our success, Grim, I think."

"I do not say that. I say, I am not a young man, and if there is success, it will be so much delayed that I shall not live to see it. Whereas if there is failure at the outset, I shall be here, to take a hand. I can be relied upon for some things."

That evening, Culvert in his chamber was visited by Damian, who was, or who had been, his valet. Damian knocked as usual, discreetly and respectfully, and Culvert as usual answered negligently, "Come," and lay back on his couch with his booted legs extended. It was, or had been, Damian's duty to draw off these boots, kneeling solicitously at Culvert's side, and to carry them away, pushing his long arms into their warm sheaths, fingering and massaging the supple leather on to the tall boot-trees, before returning to tuck his master's toes into their embroidered velvet slippers. Around this minor ritual, over the years, master and man had arranged many solicitous little games. Sometimes, for instance, Damian would brush his lips over every inch of the damp silk stockings, one after the other. Sometimes he would strip them off gently, and kiss Culvert's beautiful naked feet, inserting his tongue precisely between every pair of toes, whilst the master lay back on the cushions with all sorts of smiles, voluntary and involuntary, playing over his sensuous lips. Damian was a thickset man, shorter than Culvert, and in all probability a few years older. He had a cap of very straight black hair, cut like a pudding-basin helmet, large, sad, deep-set dark eyes, and a luxuriant but well-dressed moustache, whose fronds aroused particularly delightful sensations in Culvert's toes, and not only his toes. Sometimes his attentions were spread upwards to the knees and the thighs, and sometimes he would respectfully unlace the breeches and nose and caress with his tongue the magnificent rod which sprang to view. He had a straight Norman nose, this Damian, with which he produced very particular shivers and frissons in Culvert's groin, and in the soft pouch which contained his balls. These games were for the most part wordless, and Damian had a very nice understanding of how far he might go—in the direction, that is, of the upwards exploration of his master's body, of which the full lips were the most sacred, most infrequently conceded treasure, and in the direction of vigorous manipulation or even attack. For there were certain days when the little ritual ended with the master spread-eagled naked among the cushions, and the man throwing himself upon him, with sinewy force, opening his own clothing as he did so, so that here and there skin met skin. If Damian, in these games misjudged the pressure

71

required, caused too much, or too little pain, the master would kick out with his considerable muscular power, and tumble the man to the ground. Once he had cracked Damian's collar-bone with one sharp, well-placed impact of the elegant white foot.

Tonight, Damian came into the room and stood loosely inside the door, all his muscles relaxed.

"Come, come," said Culvert, kindly enough.

"I do not know what I should do," said Damian.

Culvert lounged against his cushions. His face was particularly beautiful in the light of a candle in a golden-rose Venetian glass shade, which stood on a shelf above him. After a moment's thought he saw what Damian seemed to be thinking, and said lazily, "You must do what you want, now, of course. You must do what gives you pleasure."

He added, with a singularly sweet smile, swinging his foot from the edge of the couch, "Perhaps you should take my place here. When we have played that game, when you have taken the place of the master, and I have been your slave, that has made you happy, I think. I have given you satisfaction in that capacity, have I not? Perhaps tonight we should play that game?"

Damian stood in the shadow of the doorway, stolid and hunched.

"That game is over for ever. You must see that. We cannot play that game any more, monseigneur, or should I say 'my friend,' after what you said today in the Theatre of Tongues."

"But I said also, we must all do what gives us pleasure. We must find out the subtle secrets of what most pleases us, and perform the acts we desire to perform. What we have done together has pleased you, Damian, I think. Your sweat was the sweat of an excited man, and your sperm has spurted into these cushions in joy. There is no reason why this should cease. Come and lie down here, and I will take off your boots and your breeches, and lick your feet and blow into your maidenhair."

"You understand nothing, I see," said Damian steadily. "The pleasure I felt then was in the pleasure of my independent thoughts whilst my body, like my life, was at your command. My livelihood depended on being able to please you, in this as in other things, the preparation of cravats, the service of wine and sweetmeats, the ready presentation of whips and cigarillos. If I was able to discharge my seed on your body or your cushions, my lord, it was because inside my head I watched, like a voluptuous sultan, a scene in which you were bound, ankles to neck, with cords that cut your fine flesh, whilst black girls whipped you with bull pizzles. I could come at will at the imaginary sight of those imaginary runnels of blood, sir, my friend, and so I was able to fulfil my duty. Of which I am now absolved."

Culvert sat upright, and the shadows chased each other like clouds across his ivory brow.

"Perhaps," he said doubtfully, "that is how we should proceed. I cannot, I fear, provide black girls or bull pizzles, but cords there are in plenty, and perhaps you should bind and hurt me, and thus fulfil your desires."

"You still do not understand," said the other. "Those too were the desires of a servant, a bondsman, a *man* with a master. Those are the desires of a man whose desires are secret, not his own, at another's command. Now I am a free man, or so you seemed to say, and I must learn the desires of a free man. And what I desire is perhaps not to do with you at all, but to lie in the arms of the Lady Roseace, and hear her sweet voice call me my love, my heart's desire, my dear darling, and other such tendernesses of which I know nothing, and to feel her fair fingers touch me with fear, and gentleness, and tenderness. And perhaps that may never be, for I do not know that she could ever desire me, bound or free. Unreciprocated desires, my lord, my friend, may prove to be as troublesome as latrines in your new economy."

It was then that Culvert felt the first movement of the invention that was to bring so much pleasure and so much terror to La Tour Bruyarde. It came to him that these problems—the regrettable desuetude of his pleasant games with Damian, the problem of Damian's desire for the Lady Roseace, and whether she could return it, were susceptible to a solution involving Art, involving Narrative, involving Theatre, as he had dimly adumbrated it earlier in that long day. For if the members of the community no longer had fixed identities or functions, but were all in need of finding themselves in the new flux of their beings, then a way, the way, the best way, for this self-discovery might be enactment of what had been and what might be in the future, or in the imagination, before the company, for the benefit of all. And in the Theatre he and Damian could again be, box and cox, master and man, and in the Theatre Roseace could safely simulate or feel desire for Damian that might be unforthcoming or unapparent if the man presented himself, requiring it simply for his own good, at her chamber door.

But he was unready to propound this new scheme of the universal benefit, so instead he said to Damian, "I propose, then, since I feel myself in urgent need of release and relief, that we find some strictly equal and balanced way of pleasuring each other, so that we may both go our own ways and sleep soundly. I propose that we lie here, face to face, cock to cock, naked on this carpet and perform upon each other only those acts which are the mirror-image of what the other performs. A kiss for a kiss, a handle for a handle, and so to satisfaction, and this shall be a seal of the new equality and respect between us, whatever we may subsequently choose to do, or not to do. What do you say to this, my friend?"

"I say," said Damian, "that it is an elegant solution, and one I shall accept with the intention of taking direct and not mendacious pleasure in your embrace."

So they stripped, and lay down together, mouth to mouth, cock to cock, awkward as two virgin boys, and Damian kissed Culvert long and hard upon the forbidden lips, which at first flinched away, and then opened deliciously and returned the kiss with good measure. And so matters went on, a little awkwardly at first, but then with more heat and animation, spurred on in inventiveness by the artifice of every embrace being exactly reciprocated. The details I well leave you to imagine for yourselves, for I know your imaginations will prove more fertile of quick breaths and jissom than my pen and ink shadows of desire. But I can assure you that they came together to a most triumphant and arching climax, and cried out, both together, in honest delight in their shared exploit. And Culvert thought to himself the Commonwealth had commenced well and inventively, as he meant it to proceed. ❧

III

✂✂✂✂✂

Dear Frederica,

    You said you would like a letter, so I am writing one. It was so strange, seeing you in that wood, like a creature from another time, or another world, and with your beautiful son. It was a great shock to me to see him, because I had not even known of his existence, and this made me realise how far apart we had grown, which I am sorry about. I doubt if you ever knew how much you meant to me, and it is only since I saw you that I have come to realise just how much I miss your uncompromising intelligence and the sense I always had that you knew why reading and writing *mattered* in the world. We all thought we knew that, then, but that was why it was such an unreal, such an isolated, Paradisal time—that we should all be there *to read poetry,* that that was what we were *for.* I suppose if we had stayed on, this might have been possible to perpetuate—as Raphael has done—but I would feel uneasy about that, even if I were academically good enough, which I am not. I don't feel that I would be quite *real* if I spent the rest of my life inside the walls of a College—like Tennyson's soul in the Tower in "The Palace of Art"—although I do see that there is a perfectly tenable intellectual position from which this view is absurd. Raphael's life is a good, rich, exacting, complicated life—and just as *real* as the lives and deaths of his family in Auschwitz, though I completely see how, for him, *that* reality drains life from his own. Anyway, I think I will tell you a little about the reality I have made for myself—and its elements of unreality—and hope you will reply.

    The most important thing to me is still writing poetry. I say that first because often I don't do it for days and weeks together and I *do* spend long hours either teaching or reading for the Papagallo Press, which makes defining myself as a poet rather absurd, and sometimes depressing. Some of the time I tell everyone I meet "I am a poet" and the rest of the time I never mention it at all, I say, "I am a temporary teacher," or, "I have a part-time job in publishing." I've written one or two things I'm quite pleased with, but I know I don't have my own voice yet, and this worries me, since for a poet I'm no longer young, really. If I get up the courage, I'll send you the pomegranate poem I was working out in my head when we met, and you will think how strange it is that those images came out of your yew trees—tho' yewberries are not unlike miniature pomegranates—an image I couldn't fit in. All poems trail behind them images that are part of them but can't be fitted in. Everything connects to everything, despite you being so *furious* when I quoted "Only connect" about your present life.

Monday to Thursday lunchtime I do supply teaching. This varies enormously from school to school. Sometimes I have eager sixth-formers doing *The Winter's Tale* or *Hamlet* and sometimes I have kids of thirteen and fourteen who cannot keep still or quiet or speak in words of more than one syllable and who do from time to time *frighten* me. I have had a pair of scissors pushed into my ribs and spent a week or two with one eye closed up by a blow with the corner of the Bible. There is something peculiarly *horrible* about going back into the atmosphere of school, which I can't say I ever enjoyed or liked (an understatement) and despite the violence, the stupidity and the philistinism (all of wch. you might think of as "real"). School has its own closed, tower-of-ivory reality with its own rules and language quite as much as Cambridge colleges. I'm lucky I think because I didn't *expect* to find it rewarding or exciting—colleagues with high ideals about sharing D. H. Lawrence or Hardy with London teenagers inevitably come to grief—one colleague who spent hours of his own time compiling an anthology of writings about Fire for a group of teenage girls had his classroom set alight amongst witchy shrieks of glee. There is a lot of educational idealism around but I think *Lord of the Flies* got it triumphantly right, and find that most children think so too, in schools where I am allowed to teach it. I hope this doesn't mean I shall find my head on a sacrificial stake in the playground, on the analogy with my fiery colleague.

Every now and then I meet surprising children—there is a boy called Boris in my present comprehensive with a perfect *ear,* the poetic version of perfect pitch, who gives me great pleasure and *savours* Hamlet's throwaway rhythms— but I do not want to get attached to any of them, that would make me A Teacher, and I am not. I teach for the books I teach—what I have discovered in *Hamlet* over the last year in Stepney and Tooting Bec and Morden would stagger even you, Frederica. And if I am any good as a teacher it is because I care more about the books than about the kids and some of the kids respect that, and I have a knack of frightening them wch. I think you may be born with or not, so sometimes they listen. I think it's because they know I don't love them and don't care what they think of me. I thought I'd be a hopeless disciplinarian, but I'm not. I say, "Shut up," and sometimes *they do* and that gives me pleasure. Who would have thought it?

And then for a day and a half I work for Rupert Parrott. The Papagallo Press is an offshoot of Bowers and Eden, a kind of loss-making highbrow branch where Rupert does things he considers worthwhile—poetry, a few literary novels, even essays. He wants very much to start a monthly journal under the Papagallo imprint, and if he ever does there is a slim chance I may get to be the first editor. But old Gimson Bowers is not too keen, and he controls the lucrative bit of it, the textbooks and the religious books, these days. Bowers is making a lot of money out of a curious theological tome called *Within God Without God* which everyone seems to need. The Papagallo Press is in Elderflower Court, a Covent Garden cul-de-sac, and consists of two dingy offices up a rickety staircase and a basement full of packaging. I love it. I even love all the very bad poems that come in, and I have to send back, because it makes you see how much poetry matters, even to people with no ear, no vocabulary and no thoughts to put together. When the schoolkids say, "Wot's it *for*, then," I tell them about how people pick up the pen when their baby's born or their gran dies or they see a wind in a wood.

Perhaps I will try to describe Parrott. He's curly, and plump, and not very tall, and public school. Late 30s early 40s. He wears waistcoats, sometimes red or mustard-yellow wool, sometimes sort of brocaded. He has a sweet, pursed-up little mouth, and a slightly high-pitched voice, which makes everyone think he's more limited than he is, because he fits easily to a stereotype. But he's actually very bright, and can tell a hawk from a handsaw, and is doing good things. He likes my poetry, but he has reservations, which I accept and respect. I don't think you'll imagine him *right* from this description, but it'll do to start with—you must come and meet him.

I had better stop writing this long letter and go back to marking essays on *Goblin Market*. I have seen both Alan and Tony recently and told them I had seen you and they were delighted—they miss you, they say, and send their love, and hope, as I do, to see you soon. We were callow creatures then and you had so many of us half or altogether in love with you—but that was then—and now we are older and wiser, I suppose.

I think I will include my pomegranate poem, if I work up the courage. Perhaps I will dedicate it to you, if it finds a home. I wonder sometimes if it is still *possible* to write poems about Greek myths—are they not dead, should we not be thinking about quite other things now? But poems about the classrooms and bits of the quotidian seem just as conventional and just as dead-alive to my eye, to my mind, as Demeter and Persephone. Who have been

Powers, Frederica, for much longer than the 1944 Education Act, or Canon Holly and his Inside-Out God. I don't know what I'm saying. They don't *feel dead* though of course the poem—I see as I write—is about Death in that sense too. You will see it doesn't really have an end and that's because I still don't know why it got written—I'll let you know if I find out. Do write back now I've found you again.

Lots of love,
Hugh

Pomegranate

> *Puzzle-fruit, skinny globe, parchment-tough,*
> *Packed with jelly-cubes stained with*
> *Blood and brown water, containing*
> *Soot-black spheres like fine shot*
> *Containing orchards.*
>
> *Sherbet in the dark and black-skinned boys*
> *Bring moonsilver plates with melons*
> *Like crimson moons in snakeskins.*
> *Bring burst pomegranates and curled segments*
> *Of orange light with teardrops of tissue*
> *Fat with sweet juice. Bring silver pins*
> *For the seeds, and silver spoons*
> *For the sirops and goblets*
> *For blood-black wine. They sing*
> *Sweet and low in the dark, they sing*
> *Of deserts in moonlight.*
>
> *She sits in a silver chair*
> *His velvet-dark pupils*
> *Stare, take her in and in*
> *Do not reflect her. Such dark eyes*
> *Are not seen elsewhere. This dim light only*
> *Shines mildly, shines soft black*
> *Blue-white teeth smiling*
> *Between soft black lips.*
> *He is large, he is comely.*
> *His gaze is fixed on her.*

She sits in a silver chair.
Picks with pink fingers, listless.
For politesse eats a few seeds.
Pomegranate-taste is almost
No taste, and so surprising. She savours
The absence, she swallows
The dark little spheres in their jelly.
Her throat ripples. Her palate
Considers, remembers

The taste of earth and water, faintly sweet.

He smiles in his darkness.

In the air the old woman ramps.
She is angry, she is dry, there is no moisture in her.
Her breasts are leather, they are dry as her shoesoles.
She has whirlwind and salt in her skirts.
She tramps on, she peers in fissures where hair roots
Shrivel and fail to grip. Bony birds
Peep and cheep. Their eggs are husks
With no flesh in them, no coiled lizard
With damp down, no nubs
To spring into pinions. She stumps
Through dry fields, leaving cracked clay
And dust. She will make earth's surface dust
All dust. The old woman's anger
Is single and fearful. Dust blows
And drags in her skirts. She stirs it
With horrible pleasure, extracting
Damp from soil and bones and soft seeds

Pippy Mammott brings this letter to Frederica at breakfast in Bran House. They are all round the breakfast table, looking out over the lawn to the moat and the fields and the woods. Leo is eating a boiled egg with toast soldiers, Olive and Rosalind are eating bacon and egg and fresh mushrooms, which they are praising as they eat. Nigel is helping himself to more mushrooms from the hotplate on the sideboard when Pippy Mammott comes in with the post. She puts his letters by his plate, and gives two each to Rosalind and Olive and one to Frederica. Then she goes back to her porridge.

The letter is fat and Frederica does not at first recognise the handwriting; she only knows she knows it well. Then she sees what the letter is, and puts the folded poem beside her plate, and considers putting the whole letter away until later, to read in private. She looks up, and sees eyes on her, Pippy's eyes, Olive's eyes, so she unfolds the letter and starts to read, smiling to herself a little. Nigel, returning from the sideboard, sees this smile.

"You've got a long letter. Who's it from?"

"An old friend." She does not look up, she reads. Nigel opens his letters with an unused butter-knife, rip, slash, rip.

"A Cambridge friend?"

"Yes."

"A good friend, a particular friend?"

"Yes, yes. Let me read my letter, Nigel."

"It seems a particularly *juicy* letter. Tell us what you're grinning at."

"I'm not grinning. It's a description of teaching in London schools. Read your own letters, Nigel."

He gets up, and goes back to the sideboard. Olive says the mushrooms are moreish. Nigel ignores this diversionary move. He says, "Share it with us, the joke, Frederica."

"There isn't one. Let me finish my letter."

"It must be a love letter," says Nigel, silkily, standing behind her. "What's this you've put aside?"

"None of your business."

Nigel leans over and picks up the folded paper.

"A poem. Nothing to do with you."

"The young man who came to tea wrote poems," says Rosalind, mildly enough.

"The young man who came all the way from London to get lost in the Old Forest," says Nigel. "I wish I'd been here to meet him. I do really. What does he say now he's found you, Frederica?"

He leans forward, and snatches the letter. His movements are quick and clean; Frederica's grip is loosed and her letter lost before she can think. He gives a little jump like a fencer and is out of reach, with the table between them. He holds up the letter. He reads:

"Dear Frederica, You said you would like a letter so I am writing one. It was so strange, seeing you in that wood, like a creature from another time, or another world, and with your beautiful son."

He reads in a clipped, childish voice. He says, "Etcetera etcetera etcetera here it is. 'I doubt if you even knew how much you meant to me, and it is only since I saw you that I have come to realise just how much I miss your uncompromising intelligence blah blah blah.' "

Pippy Mammott says, "Don't be *naughty,* Nigel." There is no expectation in her voice of being heard, or heeded.

Frederica says, "Give me that letter."

Nigel goes on reading out sentences in a faintly silly voice. No one reacts, so after a time he gives up and finishes reading the letter to himself, frowning darkly. Then he opens the poem, and starts on that, with a new mocking edge:

> *"She sits in a silver chair*
> *Picks with pink fingers, listless.*
> *For politesse eats a few seeds."*

Frederica, rage rising in her, nevertheless notices that, even in the mock-sobbing voice he has now resorted to, he has put the stresses where they should be.

"What kind of nonsense is this?" he asks, bold and confident. "Why can't it say what it's about?"

"It does."

He reads a few more lines, again getting the stresses automatically right, and then gives up.

"Give me back my letter and my poem."

He cannot quite think what to say next or do next, and looks darkly about, threatening and ruffled. He is quite possibly about to give the papers back to Frederica when she says unwisely, "Where I come from, it is quite unforgivable to take away people's private papers."

"You aren't where you come from. You're here. Here I don't like you getting letters from soppy poets, here it isn't done to keep up with old boyfriends once you're married with a child."

"Your beautiful son," says Leo, in a musing voice, reminding them of his presence.

"Little boys aren't beautiful, dear," says Pippy Mammott. "A better word is 'handsome' or 'good-looking.' "

Leo repeats mulishly, "Like a creature from another time or another world and with your beautiful son, that's what it said. Like elves perhaps I thought or hobbits I think he means, you see, we surprised him, he was nice, I liked him."

Frederica, who has been working up to a roar of rage as full throated as ever her father uttered, stares dumbly.

Leo says, "I don't like you reading in that silly voice I don't like it. I myself asked him to tea, I *liked* him, I told you."

"It's easy to see he twisted *you* around his little finger," says Nigel, less dangerous already.

"I don't know what that means," says Leo. He looks from one of his parents to the other, trying to think what next to say or to perform to avert disaster.

Nigel says, "Here. Take your letter, then. I hope you mean to write a poem back."

"I can't write poems."

Frederica folds the violated letter, and watches Nigel eat his mushrooms. He stares down at his plate, black, black eyes under long black lashes. Such dark eyes / Are not seen elsewhere. I hate you, Frederica's head says, I hate you, I hate you, I should never have come here, I cannot *live* here, I have been a fool, a fool, a fool. She holds tight to her letter under the table and chews a little bread, thoughtfully, and thinks of Hugh and Frederica-then, another person. Frederica-then could tell immediately whether a man was or was not attractive to her, whether or not she could bear him to touch her. It had nothing to do with loving the same poems, or finding it easy to tell someone a grief, a success, an idea. There were men she felt potentially *connected to,* and men she did not. She thought about this for a moment, without understanding it. She liked, indeed she loved, Hugh Pink, *much* more than Nigel, she told herself crossly and in panic. But Nigel's body stirred hers as he angrily dissected mushrooms, and Hugh, whom she had been so pleased to see, gave her the pleasure of an old well-loved book, lost and found again. Not this appalling sense of connection, of being-to-do-with-*her,* which endures. Nigel munches mushrooms.

Hugh Pink's letter has changed Frederica's marriage. She is accustomed to telling herself her marriage is unhappy, but she is also accustomed to blaming herself for this. She made a wrong decision, she did not take account of the circumstances, wise little remarks of this kind she makes constantly to herself, mixed with more shapeless moanings of boredom or frustration. She does not blame Nigel yet for her unhappiness, although she is constantly angry at his long absences, and at his failure to see what she needs, by which she means *work,* not too well defined, but *work.* She is ready to explain that she loved him because he was different, but that this has not transformed her. She is still Frederica. She is ready to explain this, but the conversation never happens, for Nigel is not a talking man. She tells herself that she should have known this. Poor Frederica is so desirous of being responsible for her own fate. Human beings invented Original Sin because the alternative hypothesis was worse. Better to be at the centre of a universe whose terrors are all a direct result of our own failings, than to be helpless victims of random and largely malevolent forces. This is bad because I didn't think hard enough, says Frederica to herself. She is distressed by Nigel's letter-snatching, both because it is his first real act of aggression against her—not listening is not always aggression—and because it makes him look ridiculous. She is upset by how silly he looked, reciting Hugh Pink's words in that childish, finicking voice. She needs to love and want him, even if she does not like his friends, his family, his life. She likes him to look secret and dangerous. Not silly.

Hugh Pink's letter brings about other changes. Just when Nigel is for once at home and watchful, Frederica receives a spate of letters from old friends. These are unsolicited—she has written to no one—but she fears that Nigel may imagine they are all responses to desperate, or affectionate, messages from her. He watches her read them. He snatches no more, but he asks who they are from. She tells him. All your friends are men, he observes again, truthfully. Once he says, "You wouldn't like it if all my friends were women." "I wouldn't mind," says Frederica staunchly, but her imagination works for a moment on his absences, and she sees that she would mind. "It's just a peculiarity of my education," she says, placating. Nigel does not answer.

One letter is from Alan Melville.

Dearest Frederica,

Hugh Pink says you would like to hear from us, and told us all where you were. We all drank your health in the Lamb and Flag, Tony and Hugh and I, and one or two others. Hugh says you are living in a Country House, with woods and fields. I cannot see you doing this, but should like to, as I'm sure you do it very spectacularly, as you did everything. Do you have a collection of paintings in your house? I am thinking of writing a book on early Venetian art, and there are some surprising faces and places from those perpetual golden worlds hidden away in the corridors and the grey northern light of the English

House. I don't earn a living by this kind of thing, yet, so I teach—not in a school, like Hugh, but in the Samuel Palmer School of Art, in Covent Garden. I teach Art History to painters and potters and industrial designers and weavers who think they don't want to know about Giotto or Titian in case I make little dents in their Originality—they are all Sons of God, of course, even the most slavishly derivative. You would like to see this place, it would interest you.

Hugh isn't very good at describing buildings and people. He *noticed* some yew trees, a staircase, a ha-ha and some teacups but gave me no real idea of your surroundings or of you. He did mention your very beautiful son. Why didn't you send a card with a stork, or a silver basket of dragées? I am good at Country House sort of people nowadays—shall I come and see you?

Another is from Alan's close friend Tony Watson. In the old days, when they were room-mates, Frederica used to call them the chameleon and the fake, for Alan, a child of the Glasgow slums, had a blond, agile, classless social charm, and Tony, the progressively educated son of a distinguished Marxist man of letters, had a whole repertoire of working-class tastes and mannerisms, and an assiduously cultivated accent, part-Birmingham, part-Cockney. Tony's letter is longer than Alan's, and more affectionate, although it is Alan to whom Frederica feels more attached. It is with Alan that she has best negotiated real friendship, she considers, without any danger of falling into sexual abjection, instability or bullying. She has wondered from time to time if he is queer.

Dear Frederica [says Tony],

I gather you are in need of amusement. There is plenty here, what with the Election hotting up, and lots of dancing—twist, shout, shake, everyone's got dislocated spines or ankles, it's an epidemic. I wrote a piece on the Mod Clubs for the *Statesman*—you wd. appreciate my Leavisite analysis of the Lyrics of the Who—as you would appreciate my Italian trousers—tho' come to think of it, you never had any musical sense, and then again maybe you are twisting away somewhere in some swish night club and don't need me to report on the latest sounds. I wish we hadn't lost touch.

Seriously, though, the Election's the thing. I'm working hard in Belsize Park, leaflets, doorsteps, the lot. The atmosphere is electric—in *places,* honesty leads me to add—there are whole reaches of the Labour Party quite as staid and stuffy as the Shire Tories you seem madly to have decided to settle amongst. I shall have to rely on you to be the *agente provocateuse* of a one-woman Revolution amongst the bulls and the milk churns and the saddle-soap and all the braying. Tread carefully, Watson, you idiot. I go up and down promising a New Morality and a New Technology and no more nasty scandals with call-girls, trousersdown ministers, no Masked Men in frilly aprons with horsewhips, but good honest Liverpudlian economists and clean men in white overalls making *useful classless things* to bring about equality quicker and quicker (the washing-up machine as an agent of revolution goes down a treat on the North London doorstep, esp. to the larger part of the workers, i.e. women, trapped in unpaid sloggery and dirty dishwater).

I've got quite a bit of political reporting into the papers—two pieces in the *Mirror,* three in the *Statesman,* one in the *Manchester Guardian.* Witty breakdowns of long dull speeches, résumés of election meetings in unvisited places, that kind of thing—I'm making a name for myself, I think—but the real place to be these days is Television, you know—this is the first Election where it will play a major part—poor Lord Home (well, Sir Alec, but it sticks in my throat or ballpoint) has a face like a skull and ill-fitting teeth and you can see these trivial matters nailing down the coffin-lid tighter and tighter on every doorstep, which of course delights me, but I don't like the mindless malice. They call him Skullface and say he glares at them—like the Evil Eye. The TV's a Magic Box, Frederica, and its power is only just beginning to stir. I must get into it, I must get on it. Words are wonderful but *passé—that's where the power is,* girl, and I'm going there. Your heavy friend from the Socialist Club, Owen Griffiths, has got in on the Labour Party Press Relations, and can be seen from time to time grinning obsequiously on the silver screen—do you watch the box, my dear, or are you above such vulgar amusements in your pre-industrial Retreat? I'll say for Griffiths he's understood the essential thing, which is that the box is *small*—he's teaching people with the instincts and training of rabble-rousers to be urbane, and intimate, and say things quickly and not repetitively—a lot of them find it *so hard*—no Great Rally rhetoric for yr. fly Welsh boyo—he gets to tell the big nobs where they go wrong and what they do best—he'll go far, I predict—but I'm not sure how serious his *principles* are—

Hugh says you've produced a sprog. Difficult to imagine, frankly, but I suppose you handle it with your usual mix of frowning determination and *nerve.* I meet all sorts of people these days. Old friends were made slower and deeper. We love you, Frederica, come and visit us, come and play, come and *work* for Victory if you're allowed. (I suspect you're not. Now then, Watson, watch it!)

Do you remember *Comus*? Do you remember the brilliant person who organised *all* your admirers to come and see you perform—always resourcefully—a débacle? Well, the same extraordinary skill has set in motion a kind of leaflet-dropping-campaign amongst the cows, to show you're appreciated. Chin up, and imagine a big, hot kiss from

Tony

My dear Frederica,

It is not often I write a letter, but I gather one is in order. So here speaks a voice from the past, and I very much hope from the future, to say, *very* discreetly now you are a married lady of substance, do you remember a motorbike, and a quite *bloody* hotel in Scarborough, and my willingness to help out with your more esoteric problems? And a beach in the Camargue, and the terrace at Long Royston, and the smiles of a summer night, and your clear young voice (well, *I* remember your voice, *you* can only hear from inside your head, it is the one voice you *will never hear,* I can tell you professionally). "I will be still as stone, I will not bleed." The *timbre* of that voice is gone, inevitably, along with the lights in the trees, and I very much fear the renaissance of the Verse Drama, and will not come back, which is sad.

What are you doing? I am still riding two horses—both aimed at the stars—it cannot go on, I tell myself, I shall tumble in all my pink frills into the sawdust in the ring, to change the metaphor—I work as hard as two men, and have two lives. I have my lab. at North Yorkshire, in the Evolution Tower, where we are doing some very interesting work on the construction of vision, the perception of shapes, visual memory from birth, and that sort of thing. I see yr. brother from time to time, who is involved both with the microbiologists and the new neuroscientists, whose work of course impinges on my own psychological experiments on *active* brains—they think very highly of Marcus, do Abraham Calder-Fluss and Jacob Scrope, you will be glad to hear. Our idealistic Vice-Chancellor still holds to his vision that all Knowledge is One, and we do talk to each other across institutional boundaries, more than in most places of research. So I tell them that my Other Life—my secret, shameful flirtation with the magic Box—is really One with my serious analysis of how the human brain constructs and recognises faces and boxes, and they more or less buy it, because I do good work, and have good assistants.

I have been making one or two rather elegant little Arts programmes about art and perception, recently. Do you ever watch? You can hardly begin to imagine what *will* be possible to the screen—to the Box—of art and thought in the next ten or twenty years. We have a cultural instrument in our hands wch. can—which will—transfigure the way we see the world, and so the way we live, for good or ill. Probably for ill—knowing the deep human need for inertia, for ease, for non-thought, but the moment I write that, I see that the opposite is also true—it is human to *need* complexity, difficulty, thought, and

86

the Box provides it, in its way. This is a more serious conversation than we have ever had, do you realise—because I can't see you, I'm not distracted by your face and your presence, so I say what I think. Written culture, not Box Culture, sweet Frederica, soon to be relegated to museums and dusty book-shelves. I will tell you a secret—you can't think in language in the Box. It *has to be* thought with images, associations, quick flickerings of form. The public fear is that the Box will be used by powerful manipulators to control the Masses—like Huxley's Soma—but that's not what interests me. It *could* be done, but anyone ingenious enough to do it would get bored with wanting to—I mean the scientists, of course, not the politicians, who are simple souls. What interests me is that these new thought-forms will change the *molecules in our minds* and what they do and can or can't do—and Shakespeare, and Kant, and Goethe and even Wittgenstein will be just too creaky and hard to bother with—*for better for worse,* Frederica, I make no judgement.

I didn't mean to embark on all that. I meant to write a ponderously gallant letter to a vanished flame, and to say, come back to us, come and see us, come and *talk*. There's a pilot programme of a TV game guessing literary quotations being made—and as always, they're desperately short of any women who know any quotations—now you aren't a famous writer or any-thing but you *are* quick-witted and presentable and you know a hell of a lot of quotations—so if you find yourself in London for a bit—give me a ring, I know the producer.

I am told you have a son. What a responsibility. I'm not sure I shall ever be fit to undertake it.

Look after yourself. Write to me. Whilst language is still a valid means of communication.

My love and homage,
Wilkie

Dear Frederica,

I have only just learned that you have a son, so am writing belatedly to congratulate you, and hope you are happy—you vanished rather suddenly from our midst. I think of you often, and do hope you are happy.

As for me, I work in educational television, producing little scenes from various plays and analyses of them. It's not wholly satisfactory, because one never gets to grips with a complete play, and even as teaching it isn't satisfac-tory because I never see the children I am addressing, but it is a pleasant enough life, and my colleagues and the actors I meet are agreeable, and so it goes on. I am not writing at present, though I have one or two ideas, both for television plays and for the theatre.

The most interesting thing that has happened to me is an invitation to be part of a Government Enquiry into the teaching of Language. We have had our first Meeting—we are chaired by an anthropologist who seems reasonable enough so far, and are a mixed bag of well-meaning persons—teachers, linguists, writers, broadcasters, a forensic psychologist and a physicist. We have a heavy programme planned of visits to schools and colleges, and huge heaps of Evidence are already coming in to be studied with care. I have written to yr. father asking him to give his views. He is the best teacher I have ever worked with, or met, and his mixture of down-to-earth practicality and high ideals is what we need, I think. Professor Wijnnobel, the NYU Vice-Chancellor, is one of us, tho' he is not the Chairman—as he is a grammarian, it was felt he might be too *parti-pris* I suppose to weave conflicting views together.

It would make me happy to hear how you are, and your husband and son, of course, also. I think this letter may be rather stilted, but you will read it with yr. usual acumen.

All best wishes,

Alexander

Dear Frederica,

Forgive a word out of the blue, or black, after so long. I was recently in the north—you may have heard that Mary had an accident, quite a serious accident, but is now well and back at school and seemingly happy. Perhaps you didn't hear, as you seem to have lost touch, as I did. That is why I am writing to you. I have been talking to your father, and I think he would very much appreciate a word from you. That is clergyman-talk for he's hurt, he's upset, he wants to hear from you and is too proud to say so. I'm not good at writing letters, and certainly not to you, to whom writing is second nature. Your father did me the honour to tell me he thought we resembled each other (him and me)—there is only you in the world now who would see the full humour and irony of that, so I am telling you. I did *not* hit him with anything, but agreed with him with Christian mildness, for there's a bit of truth in it. But the one who is really like him is you, Frederica, and he knows that too, and is not getting any younger. Forgive me for saying so— put it down to professional habits of meddling for God's sake—but he has already lost one daughter. I don't know why I don't mention your mother— she's a more patient and secret soul—but it was him I talked to. Much to both our surprises.

You don't need my news. I am still working in the crypt. Holding people back from the edge—sounds melodramatic and often is—who might or might not be better if they just plunged over. It's a funny specialisation. It suits me, but I see people singing in the streets, and they look queer, which makes me realise I am.

Look after your beautiful son, Frederica. (I saw the pictures you sent them.) I didn't do well by my son, and I see already I shall regret it for the rest of my life. I expect we shall see each other again, and I hope I know you well enough to be right in thinking you'll forgive me for interfering—whether or not you do as I suggest. Clergyman-talk again. God bless you.

Love,

Daniel

Nigel watches Frederica open these letters, one after the other. As she reads them she looks up at him, and watches him watch her. She reads Alan's words, and Tony's, and Edmund Wilkie's, and Alexander's and Daniel's, with his still, dark silence charged with watchfulness at the other side of the table. There is autumn sunlight on the white tablecloth and the silver spoons, and the dark man watches intently. The letters bring with them vivid ghostly images of friends, Alan's quiet smile, Alexander's fading beauty, Tony's curly humour, the improbable conjunction of Daniel and her father. They remind her of herself as she was, argumentative, passionate, silly, clever. When she rereads them in private—which means her bathroom, which has a window scratched by trailing jasmine fronds and dotted with the advancing suckers of Virginia creeper—the life of the words, and the quick ghosts of the writers, bring with them the presence of the dark watcher. He is more real than they are. She knows his shoulder-blades and his belly, his throat and his dark cock. She thinks of his cock, reading Wilkie's letter, Alan's letter, Tony's letter, and she licks up tears. He is more real than they are, and she is less real than she was.

She does not know if she dare answer all these letters, and put all the answers in the Chinese bowl in the hall, from which the letters are taken. She writes answers, tears them up, and writes other answers, and tears them up. She is afraid. She arranges to go into Spessendborough on market day with Olive and Rosalind, and there she buys a heap of postcards, addresses them, and writes brief notes on all of them saying, "Wonderful to have your letter. Answer coming soon. F." She has no address for Daniel, but remembers the name of the church and addresses it to the crypt. Olive and Rosalind watch her post these pictures of hills and riverbanks, and summer fields. She fans out the postcards so they can see how little she has written. She does not know why she does this.

Nigel stays at Bran House for a long time. They have good days. They picnic in the hills with Leo, they show him the tracks of deer and badgers. They discuss Leo. Later, Frederica will not remember what they talked about. She remembers his hand on hers in bracken, and a kind of happiness, she remembers two lazy bodies stretched on rugs, and frantic secret mental activity in her own head. She puts off answering all the letters until he goes again, and he does not go.

The next letter he takes is an innocuous brown one, with a typed label, addressed to Mrs. Nigel Reiver. He reaches across as she is about to open it, and says, "Give me that." She gives it to him; he reads it, and hands it back; it is a routine invitation to a Commemoration Dinner at her old college in Cambridge. "Please indicate the names of any other Old Students you may wish to sit near."

"Why did you do that?" she asks him.

"I thought you might be planning something. I thought maybe you were going on with what you once said about going back to that place. I got it wrong." He does not add, I'm sorry, but it is grudgingly in the air.

"Perhaps I shall."

"I don't see how you could."

"I could if—if I really wanted to. I could go up and down. Some time there, some time here. With ingenuity. *You* come and go."

"That's one reason why you can't."

"You can't just *say* that. It isn't *fair.*"

"I don't see why. You made a commitment. You knew what you were doing."

"No one ever knows exactly what they are doing—"

"I thought you were so clever. You don't get married and just go on as though you hadn't."

"You don't change your nature overnight if you get married."

"Perhaps not. But you change, all the same. I don't want you to go off here or there as though Leo and I don't exist. You've no need."

"You *can't* think it's as simple as that."

"I don't see why not."

In the end he is summoned again. Uncle Hubert telephones from Tunis. Nigel prepares to set off for Amsterdam. Frederica finds herself, to her annoyance, hurt and upset that he is going. She does not really know if this is because she will miss him, or because she is angry that he has autonomy and she does not, or because he can leave her so cheerfully. Marriage has its emotions that are part of its elastic cage, that don't exactly belong to the individual people who happen to be *in* that marriage. She thinks, I won't ever be so silly as to get married again, and then thinks how silly that thought is. Since she is married.

She finds Nigel, in their bedroom, reading her letters. It is the day before he is to go. He is sitting on their bed, with Wilkie's letter in one hand, and Tony's in the other.

"I was just making sure," he says, with his gathered, energetic calm, "that you weren't up to anything."

Frederica stands still in the doorway.

"And am I?" she says, with the ridiculous heavy irony of such situations.

"I don't like your friends," he says. "I don't like these people."

"They weren't writing to *you*," says Frederica, studying his face.

"You are just a bitch, really," he says, in the same collected voice. "Just a silly bitch."

Frederica once had her father's capacity for rage. She stands for another moment in the door, tingling with anger in fingers and guts, and then begins to roar. She advances on Nigel and retrieves her letters—Daniel's is a little torn. She says what is always said in these scenes, that she will not be treated like this, that she will not stay another moment, that she is going, *now.* She opens wardrobes and flings clothes on the carpet. She finds an old suitcase and begins to throw things into it, weeping and screaming. Her letters, a nightdress, a toothbrush, a bra, a sweater; she can hardly see for tears; the things that *must* come, books, letters, are too heavy, are too many, the idea of their *weight* provokes a fresh spout of tears. "I'm going, I'm going, I'm not staying another minute," she screams, throwing things, any things, some black silk panties Nigel bought her that she has never worn, higgledy-piggledy into the suitcase. The release of adrenaline is a relief and an excitement. Nigel comes up behind her and takes hold of the red hair in the nape of her neck, and gives it a sharp professional twist. The pain is excruciating. Frederica hears various bones in her neck crack and shift. She thinks, "He has killed her," stops to marvel at the pronoun, and sees that she is still alive, in possession of her senses, and in pain.

"Silly bitch," says Nigel again, and gives her some sort of blow—with a knee? with the other elbow?—in the small of the back, again causing major pain with minimal effort. Frederica has never been in a physical fight. Her siblings were both almost uncannily gentle; her father's rages led to devastated furniture and burned books, but not to hurt flesh. Her schooling was respectable and her tongue caustic; she was not the sort of child to be victimised. This is new. Nigel's arm is across her face. He is breathing heavily. She opens her mouth and inhales hot cloth. Her tongue touches fuzz. She twists her head and her nose slides past cotton of shirt-cuff, and then skin, skin intimately known, skin acrid with anger. She sinks her teeth into it as best she can. She tastes blood. She cannot turn off some mocking self-censor in her brain that despises her, Frederica, for having to do such vulgar things.

"Bitch," says Nigel again, crashing his free fist into her ribs. Frederica is winded. She moves her head again from side to side, moans in pain and disbelief, grips with her teeth and more or less *chews,* producing rather a lot of blood, filling her mouth. "Bitches bite," she thinks in a suffocated way, and finds half a moment to wonder about vampires, as the blood runs between her teeth. Then she falls forward, limp, completely inert, dead meat. The oldest trick in the book, the commentating brain thinks. It works. Nigel lets go, stands up to look at the body, and Frederica kicks nastily at his legs with her full force, catching him off balance. He falls, half on the bed, half on the floor, and Frederica, counting the cost to her battered spine, stumbles to her own feet, and flings herself past him into the bathroom, locking the door.

There is a little pile of poetry books by the lavatory. Frederica likes to sit in there and learn things by heart, keeping something essential alive. There is Yeats, there is Mallarmé, there is Raphael Faber, there is a Shakespeare. Frederica sits on the lavatory lid and opens the Shakespeare. She finds she cannot see the words at all—the air is *simmering* and her sight seems veiled with a lucid poppy-scarlet. She licks blood meditatively from her lips and her teeth—salt, metal, and something else, she thinks, the taste of *life* and salt and metal. She is shaking too much to get up and rinse her mouth. Her teeth hurt, too. They are loose in their sockets. She sits there in a studious position, holding the Shakespeare, and breathes bathroom-air—body-smells, watery-smells, ghosts of perfume, a remote tang of bleach. Blood.

There is a silence. Then there is a shuffling. Nigel is moving about in the bedroom. She waits. There is a sudden explosion of terrible sound: he is battering the bathroom door with something heavy and howling imprecations. The door is solid. The house is solid. It is a house which once did not have many bathrooms, but those that have been added have solid doors. Frederica sits inside, holding Shakespeare, and says nothing. She cannot think what to do. She is a creature to whom impotence and indecision are painful. After this has gone on some time Frederica thinks of the other inhabitants of the house and wonders what they will think, what, if anything, they will do. She thinks Olive and Rosalind and Pippy Mammott will put their heads under the bedclothes and shut their ears. She thinks of Leo, which she has been trying not to do. Will he hear, will he be afraid, who will he blame? Now she feels both guilt, for the first time, and real hatred of Nigel, for the first time.

The barrage stops as suddenly as it started. She waits for a questing "Frederica?" but there is nothing. The door is so thick she cannot hear exactly what is happening out there. Shufflings, draggings, a crash. Silence. Silence. She looks at Shakespeare, and finds she has got him open at *Much Ado about Nothing*.

Benedick: I do love nothing in the world so well as you. Is not that strange?
Beatrice: As strange as the thing I know not. It were as possible for me to say I love nothing so well as you, but believe me not, and yet I lie not.

Frederica, skinny and freckled at twelve, Frederica angular and noisy at seventeen, Frederica surrounded by young men in Cambridge at twenty, has always had in her mind, as the image of love, this contented prosaic recognition of inevitability. What is love, what is love, is it just a dangerous *idea*? There is a kind of twang, and the room goes dark. There is also no line of light under the bathroom door. It is black, black. She cannot see Shakespeare or her own feet. It is the country, there are no street lamps, the window is black, too. She hears her own hot breath, and a drip of water, somewhere. Outside the bathroom door a thick voice asks, with desperate satisfaction, "And *now* what will you do?"

She doesn't answer.

"You can't stay in there for hours and read *now*, can you? Come out."

She cannot answer. She draws her knees up to her chin, enfolding Shakespeare in her body.

"I can wait. I can sit here and wait," says the voice.

She tiptoes to the door, and says through the keyhole, "You'll frighten Leo."

"And whose fault is that, you bitch, *who* wishes he'd never been born?"

There is a renewed battery on the door. Frederica retreats again. Her eyes have got used to the dark. The window is a small, smoky square, midnight-blue-black. She can see the shadows of the jasmine fronds and the creeper leaves. She can see a star or two, bright pin-holes behind the glass, stars without identity, isolated from the spread of the sky.

A long time passes in the dark. Frederica reflects on Daniel's letter, and his interesting revelation that Bill thinks that Bill and Daniel re-semble each other. She recognises the situation she is in, because all her childhood was passed amongst howls of rage, amongst tempests of invective and maudlin reconciliation. She thinks that she married Nigel at least in part because his composed silence appeared to be the opposite of Bill's wrath, and here she is, now as then, locked in the bathroom, waiting for the storm to subside. Stephanie too married Bill's opposite against Bill's wishes. And it is true what Daniel says, he resembles Bill. Fate comes up and hits you behind the head, Frederica thinks ruefully, probing her sore neck, her lumbar ganglion. *Mutatis mutandis*—Bill talked a lot, and did not hurt. Nigel repeated one word over and over, and hurt a great deal. Leo is an articulate child; perhaps he will not need to hurt people. At the thought of Leo, she begins to snivel again. Her mind puts it to her in a small way. "She is snivelling." A good, almost onomatopoeic word. Tears run down her nose.

"Can I come in, Frederica? I won't hurt you, I'm sorry. I won't hurt you."

If this were Bill, this would be the turning point. Anyway, she is tired out, and fatalistic. She creeps in the gloom and turns the key and retreats again. He comes in very slowly, feeling his way blindly along the wall. He has wrapped one of her cotton petticoats round his dam-aged hand, his left hand. He puts his other hand on her breast, hot on hot, heavy on pricking.

"You *are* a bitch, though," he says, his voice thick with indescrib-able things, but no longer aggressive. "Aren't you? A real bitch, I should have known. Look what you've done to my hand."

"I can't see. You ought to put the lights back on, whether you took out the fuse or interfered with the mains. In case—anyone else—wakes."

She is whispering.

"Come with me, then. I don't want you to do anything silly."

"I'm not in a state to."

"Come with me."

He puts his hand round her wrist. They negotiate the dark house, sidling along walls, padding across landings, taking courage on known staircases. The fusebox is in a kind of safe in the scullery. Nigel lets go of Frederica in order to be able to reach the master switch, which he pulls down with a kind of iron groan or twang. A streak of light appears in the doorway from a light left on in a dim corridor. There is no sound in the house. Nigel pats Frederica's buttocks, a man encouraging a mare. "There," he says.

They make their way more quickly back to their bedroom, lit as it was before only by table lamps and reading lights. It is a horrid scene. The bed is full of emptied bottles of Frederica's lotions and powders—mostly presents, since Frederica's favourite perfume is still Johnson's Baby Powder. The floor is scattered with broken chair legs. The broken chairs lie around like dead animals, amputated limbs in the air. The mirror is monstrously cracked. The curtains are bloodstained, and so, spectacularly, are the sheets and the bedspread. Frederica thinks of Wilkie's letter, reminding her of her unforgettable defloration, and speaks quickly, in case Nigel too is remembering this.

"It looks like the scene of a murder."

"It does look pretty bad." He seems rather proud, as well as moderately abashed.

"I'm not sleeping in here. I'm going to find somewhere else to sleep. Do you think we ought to clear all this up?"

"No. Why? *They* can, they're paid to clear up. Let's go somewhere else then. We could sleep in your old bed, where you used to stay. Where I came creeping in the night."

Frederica thinks of saying she wants to sleep alone. But she is tired and desperate for sleep, and afraid, more than she cares to admit to herself, so afraid that she is prepared, like many women at many times, to take comfort from the man she is afraid of. So they creep quietly along corridors to the guest room in which she used to sleep, and find the bed made up under a dust sheet, which Nigel pulls to the ground, leaving traces of blood in it. They make love. He is clever and gentle, and leaves the pillows bloodstained, she sees in the morning. The pain in her spine makes it hard for her to come, and once or twice she tries to give up, or to fake, but Nigel insists, he waits, he touches her most secret places, he sings his speechless song in her ear, and in the end, there it is, bliss, she comes, she cries out, her voice and her body shake, and Nigel says, "There you are. That's all right," meaningless phrases loaded with many meanings.

In the dark, lying with him, Frederica says, "You hurt me, badly."

"I could have killed you. I learned unarmed combat in the Commandos, doing my National Service. I could kill you any time, just like that, you would hardly notice."

Frederica cogitates.

"Are you saying I'm lucky you didn't kill me by accident?"

"Something like that. No, don't be silly. Just, I've been taught how to find where it hurts."

"And is that a warning or an apology?"

"Both, don't you think? I think it's better not to talk, talking makes it worse. Sleep on it, let it pass, you *liked* just now, what we did just now, didn't you, you were happy, weren't you?"

"Yes. But—"

"I said, don't talk. You are a talkative silly bitch, Frederica. Talking *hurts.*" He puts a hand, warm, hard, friendly, over the triangle between her legs. "Trust me. Go to sleep now."

The next day, there is a woman washing bloodstains from the wallpaper on the landing. Pippy Mammott is seen with a man in a van, who carries away the broken chairs. There are new sheets, the curtains are replaced, the depleted bottles restored to their places. Nigel goes away again. He kisses Frederica, and Leo, who wraps himself like a great squid around his neck. "Be good," he says to both of them. "I'll ring you. Be good."

Olive and Rosalind do not talk to Frederica. That is, conversation of a repetitive kind takes place at mealtimes, which take place regularly. Breakfast is quiet, lunch is administrative—"I think I need to go into Hereford for some stuff for the roses, and to get my hair cut, do you want to come?" Tea is rather more determinedly social, which means that the sisters and Pippy Mammott do try to talk to Frederica, which means in practice that they always all talk about Leo, who is always present for tea—lunch he sometimes, usually, has in the nursery. They discuss his achievements, his sayings, Sooty. They always end by saying he will get a big head if this goes on, and the child always puts his hands to the sides of his brow. The first time he did this, it was with genuine alarm because, Frederica could see, he feared his skull was swelling outwards, but now he does it for effect, because his aunts and Pippy Mammott always laugh so much. They sometimes also compare his doings with those of his father at his age. Tumbles are compared, also fear of the dark, "sharpness" and growth. In the early days there was some attempt to tell Frederica about Nigel's childhood, as though she was full of distress at having been shut out of this golden age, as though she needed, in order to be fully alive, to acquire their knowledge by proxy. This kind of talk happens rarely now, and nothing has succeeded it. Frederica wonders sometimes if Pippy was always there, if she was present during the growing up of Nigel, or if she has assimilated her knowledge from the house and its inhabitants. It would be simple to ask, but Frederica does not ask, just as no one in that house ever asks anything about Frederica's own past, her parents, her sister, her brother, her sister's children. She mentions these children from time to time by way of comparison with Leo—she plays the Leo conversations like a board game with herself, scoring increasing points for each repetition of certain clichés, and jackpots for a cliché that can be got to include Nigel, Marcus, Leo and Will in one banal generalisation. The sisters and Pippy know something is wrong with what observations she offers, but they do not know what, and do not, she supposes, greatly care.

She thinks they talk to each other quite differently when she is not there. Sometimes she hears a passionate buzz of talk behind a closed door, notes of urgency, notes of insistence, notes of pain, notes of laughter, none of which she ever hears face to face.

She does not want to know. She is not Olive's kind of person, nor Rosalind's, nor Pippy Mammott's. They let her know this, with no cruel intention, seeing no need for kindness, simply making certain things clear. She happens to be there, Nigel happens to want her, she is a necessary part of Leo's wonderful existence, the house is big, there is room for all of them, she doesn't say much, she is a bit feeble, really, a bit wet, they all go their own ways, and if she wants an errand done, or a doctor fetched, or a letter posted, they are only too ready to help. Only too happy to help. *Helping* her integrates her into the way of things. Helping her pleases Nigel and Leo. There is nothing she can do to help them. Except, possibly, keep out of the way, which indeed she does, though they don't wholly like the *manner* of her keeping out of the way.

In the early days of her marriage, she and Nigel treated the house as though it was a honeymoon retreat. They climbed the stairs hand in hand towards the bedroom, at all hours, coffee-time, noon, tea-time and evening. They touched each other, Frederica remembers, handing teacups, pouring wine. They passed the sisters, Pippy, on the stairs, and were unseen, as though they were not there. Frederica, alone and vulnerable, is now retrospectively embarrassed by this bad behaviour, or what she supposes was taken for bad behaviour, since nothing is, or was, said. Nigel is like a Pasha in his palace, she thinks, but cannot say. Leo is a male child in a harem. Leo will be sent away to school when he is eight or so. He will go to the school his father went to.

Frederica thinks she cannot bear Leo to be sent away to sleep in a dorm with boys. She has seen them cry. It is not good.

Frederica thinks that when Leo has gone, she can go.

Frederica thinks that when Leo is eight, she will be thirty-two and her life will be almost over.

She encounters Olive and Rosalind as one being, but they are not twins. Olive is older than Rosalind, but not by much, and both are older than Nigel, by five or six years, maybe seven—again, Frederica has not asked and is not told. This means they are well into their thirties, and must have thought about marriage themselves, though there is no sign of it. They are married to Bran House. They do not quarrel, they do not even have sisterly spats, which Frederica finds odd and baffling. She tells herself, without conviction, a long story in which they once fought to the death—over a man, over one of them's passionate desire to leave, to do something else, drive a rally car, nurse in a hospital, take a degree in poultry keeping, go on a Hellenic Cruise—Frederica's invention fails rapidly—and in her story, after this fight, they were both so battered and afraid that they agreed never to differ again. There is no evidence for this fantasy other than the tendency of their faces to set into masks of mild sullenness when they are unobserved. Like Nigel, they have large dark eyes sunk fairly deep under very definite, solid bars of dark brows. Nigel's beard is heavy and he shaves twice daily—the mussel-blue shadow from jaw to cheekbone, along the long face, is one of his attractions. All three have darkly shadowed upper lips. The hair on Olive and Rosalind's heads is neatly cut and solidly controlled. The rest of them is hairy—their tweeds, their handsome, dark-haired legs, their lips. It is not certain that they are unhappy because they look unhappy. Nigel can look intensely gloomy when he is most enjoying himself. It is the set of their faces. Leo has their solemn eyes in a much more volatile geometry.

They do have their own social life, in which they do not include Frederica. She has gone to one or two County Shows, and has enjoyed the drama of the jump-off, the smell of the horsehair and leather. She has learned to ride, which she does, in her way, enjoy— riding is the nearest she comes to being part of the alien world she thought would be full of surprises. She likes to ride with Nigel, she likes to canter over grassland with dew on it, she likes to see his neat body bent over the mane of the horse in front of her—*this* has an immediacy that excites her. She likes to strike out for the horizon. But riding with Olive and Rosalind is not like that. They like a companionable pottering trot, or they like to hunt, which Frederica will not attempt to do, for which they almost invisibly—What do *we* care what *you* think is right?—despise her. But riding friends come and go, other families come and go in Land Rovers. One woman, Peggy Gollisinger, an elegant nervous woman smelling overpoweringly of Ma Griffe, did try to make a friend of Frederica. She came once or twice and sat in the drawing-room with the new Mrs. Reiver, launching immediately into an intimate account of her husband's infidelities, soaking up gin and tonic like a hot bouquet reviving in water with aspirin. Then she fell asleep on the sofa, and Pippy Mammott showed in her chauffeur, who picked her up and carried her away. "That always happens, I'm afraid," said Pippy to Frederica. "There are those who just don't get out the gin, no matter what. She doesn't react too well to that treatment either. A lost soul, poor Peggy, I'm sad to say." Frederica wondered if she herself had been diagnosed as another potential lost soul.

Olive and Rosalind's most substantial friend, most frequently invited, most frequently invoked, is a woman a little younger than themselves, Alice English, petite, energetic, with a floppy mass of silvery-fair corkscrew curls, and a round face with a sharply pointed chin at the bottom of it, and widely spaced, very blue eyes in the top half. Alice is livelier than the Reiver sisters, and tells Frederica several times in the first weeks of their acquaintance, "We must be *great friends.*" Frederica comes to see that this is because Alice had hopes of Nigel, though she is far indeed from knowing whether these hopes had any justification.

Nigel has never mentioned Alice English, but this is no use as evidence in either direction. Alice English occasionally says with determined jauntiness, "I *know* Nigel thinks" this or that about things, such as the dangers of comprehensive education, or the wrongness of lying to the House, or the importance of an incorruptible judiciary, or the punishments to be inflicted on Communist spies. She comes round more frequently now the battle-lines for the election are drawn—she is something to do with the local Conservative Party Committee—and invokes Nigel's putative views more and more firmly and frequently. Frederica took a certain pleasure in Alice's earlier half-confessions. It is pleasant to be in possession of what someone else desires—or at the least reassuring to know that someone desires what you have got. But she cannot sympathise with this new bred-in-the-blood Tory Nigel who would, if he were there, be rousing the shire to fight in the back streets of Worcester for fear of letting in that nasty, sneaky little man Harold Wilson. Alice *knows* that Nigel thinks Wilson completely unprincipled, completely vicious, completely incompetent. Alice *knows* that Nigel thinks that Wilson wants to give everyone's hard-earned savings to scroungers who delight in milking the State to live in luxury in flats they pay next to nothing for, with cars parked outside, and tellys inside, oh yes. Alice even *knows* Nigel would want Frederica to come and help dissuade the shopkeepers from listening to that twisted man's blandishments. Nigel has never mentioned politics to Frederica. Frederica assumes he votes Tory—it is part of his illicit attraction, like Don Juan, like Byron, an ultimate, inadmissible *sinfulness.* She assumes he must know she can't and won't vote Tory, though lately she has begun to wonder. If he had ever said anything to her remotely resembling what Alice says she knows he thinks, Frederica might have thought twice about marrying him, for his class would have become—as Alice's is—aesthetically completely unacceptable. But he has appeared uninterested. And Frederica's Puritan upbringing has so far had a curious effect on her politics. For whereas both Bill and Winifred are wholehearted members of the Labour Party, by class origin, by instinct and by thoughtful conviction, they have brought up their daughter in that tolerant, non-conformist, cautiously sceptical tradition that requires you to look twice at everything, to look for the good and bad in everything. Bill has his fanaticisms, one of which is a fanatical rejection of fanaticism. So Frederica knows that her gut reaction against the Conservative Party is as questionable, on the face of it, as a gut reaction against homosexuals or Negroes. Homosexuals, Negroes, and Conservative Ladies are human beings, Frederica knows, and believes. Nevertheless when Alice English says, "You *must* give a hand, Frederica, you must support our people," Frederica feels ill with instinctive loathing, and replies, in a voice much more her own than is usually heard in that house, "They are *not my people.*" She thinks. She says, "And I am very glad they are not, I have to say."

She goes upstairs. Treading heavily. Bang, bang. She closes her bedroom door. Bang. What use is any of it?

She looks for Tony's letter, to comfort her. She has not looked at her clutch of letters since she put them away; they are contaminated by rage and bloodshed, which would horrify the writers. She finds Tony's letter, idealistic and canny, and also finds Daniel's, with a momentary surge of guilt. He is right. She should write to Bill and Winifred. She cannot. She is afraid of reliving in any way the days of the death of Stephanie. She wishes with part of her that *everything* had ceased to exist with her sister, her past, her home, *everything,* for good memories are more painful than bad. The violent ending makes the whole story appalling; Stephanie's smile, Stephanie's wisdom, Stephanie's lazy peacefulness all become ghouls, phantoms, terrible shapeless figures flailing in empty air. What Daniel says is of course right. Bill has lost one daughter and should not therefore lose two.

She thinks she *will* write a real letter to Bill, not now, not quite yet. She looks for Edmund Wilkie's letter and cannot find it. She goes through everything again. It is not there. It was the most personal and the most surprising of the letters—for Wilkie is less her true friend than Hugh, or Alan, or Tony, never loved, as Alexander was. It was also the only sexy letter, the only real provocation to an unauthorised reader. She turns out her drawer—her sweater drawer—where the letters had been hidden. She goes through her desk. Nothing. She becomes very rapidly convinced that Nigel has taken Wilkie's letter. Wilkie's letter flares in her mind into something hugely important, the lost object sought in dreams whose discovery will put everything right. She sees the scenes it evoked: the bed full of blood in Scarborough, the Evolution Tower in NYU. Also she begins to relive the pain of the blow in the spine, the torn hair. She feels hatred. Frederica is a fierce woman, but hatred terrifies her. She thinks of Nigel as something dangerous and repulsive, and she feels herself degraded by these feelings, herself sickens her.

When it is night, she begins to search Nigel's secret places. She has never opened his drawers, never touched the heaps of paper he leaves lying around. His papers are papers which are inert and a little dusty, not touched with life, as her own are. Now she goes through a heap—on the top of a chest of drawers—a futile and silly thing to do, since he would hardly take Wilkie's letter and leave it lying around amongst bills and bank statements. She then goes through his sock drawer, an apple-tray of tidy black balls, his shirt drawer, his under-pants—so very neatly folded, so clean, so anonymous. She runs through the jackets in the wardrobe, looking inside envelopes crum-pled in inside pockets with NIGEL on the outside, scrupulously read-ing *nothing,* as though her own lack of prying might protect her from his. She puts things back where she found them, even a sealed con-dom tucked in a brown envelope. Inside his wardrobe are various locked cases and briefcases. She looks at these, and then, still possessed by the black swollen hatred, she goes back to where she found a cigar box full of little keys at the back of the underwear drawer. This has the appearance of a place where a tidy man puts keys to things which may be lost, vanished or forgotten, keys which may be useful if other keys are lost. Keys which are the male equivalent of the sewing-machine key, the old jewel-box key, the key to the five-year diary that got finished and thrown away in embarrassment. She takes the cigar box over to the deep wardrobe and tries various of the keys on vari-ous of the boxes and cases. One largish suitcase gives off, when opened with a very simple key, an odour of decay like ripe cheese. It turns out to contain a wad of clearly unwashed rugger clothing, in various colours—tangerine and black, a sumptuous purple and crim-son. There are socks with what she supposes to be ancient mud, liq-uid in the 1950s, even, caked dust since then—she has never known Nigel to play rugger. She locks it again quickly. The fitting of this key is encouraging, and so she persists through several failures, with a de-licious sense of committing an outrage, a justified outrage. She opens another case—a kind of document folder—and finds a mass of school photographs, Nigel at five, Nigel at nine, Nigel in boater and blazer, Nigel black-a-vised amongst rows of staring young men with starting eyes and solid, fleshy mouths. Then a very small, rather complicated, not at all flimsy key—a key which is not one of an endless series ran-domly distributed, but a special key, with a barrel and fierce little teeth, opens a large rather battered document box not unlike the box brandished by the Chancellor of the Exchequer on Budget Day.

She has not found Wilkie's letters. She has found a collection of magazines and photographs. "*You* know the kind of thing," one man might say to another, or one woman to another. And nod, with sophisticated understanding. So much flesh, so very stretched over such muscles, such globes, so much clean, silky, peachy *skin* with a high gloss on it. Such damp holes laid bare, such glistening prongs, such pearly teeth approaching, ingesting, such purple sprouting veins. Such things, such trusses, such tresses, such improbable contortions of such essentially incompressible rubbery flesh. Such glossy pouts, such gouts of blood, such tears, such fear, such good fun, a bit of all sorts. Such inventive angles, a clitoris, an anus, a glans, an uvula, a cascade of this or that or the other liquid or solid. One was called *My Bad Little Bedside Book*. And another *Naughty Girls Well and Truly Punished*. The human body is not infinitely various but it is much more various than the range of poses and postures and parts in these pictures. The human erotic imagination appears to have strictly limited matter to work on. Padlocks, chains, thongs, spikes, cages, boots—nothing much has changed since the mediaeval torture-chamber was furnished, apart from the invention of rubber, which has produced some odd embellishments and habits. If you had asked Frederica whether these things did harm, or whether they should be suppressed, she would have given you an orthodox answer, an answer soon to be orthodox in advice columns everywhere, no, they do good, they are simply amusing, if people like them, they're good. She is quite unprepared for the effect on her own body of *seeing* these exposed buttocks, these sow breasts, these globular mouths. She thinks quickly of herself, of her own pleasure in the dark—to what extent her response to the pictures is erotic—and she thinks, whilst he is . . . whilst I am . . . whilst we are . . . in his mind he sees . . . And she is sick, and knows you cannot unsee what you have seen, and that this is *of no importance* and that it has changed everything in the flickering half-light of her erotic imagination. It is like finding trunks of butchered limbs, she tells herself wildly, hands and feet under the floorboards, I cannot manage to pretend I haven't seen. One is attracted or repelled and I am repelled, and it is not as Freud says, that attraction underlies repulsion, as with certain ambiguous smells, which I *do* understand— no, all this, it is simply horribly *simple,* like fairground dollies, and degrading, however my good liberal mind tries to avoid that judgemental word, degrading, and dirty, for all the pink and orange spanking cleanness of that overblown flesh.

She thinks of making a bonfire, and this causes her to remember her father making a bonfire in her childhood of her carefully concealed cache of *Girls' Crystals*. Poor Bill, how would he compare this with the sickly narratives and *Schwärmerei* of the *Crystals*? She can't tell. Her own erotic imagination works after words, in the not-said; before she knew precisely what men and women did together she imagined Elizabeth Bennet and Darcy naked at last, she imagined Mr. Rochester, but what he brought was a comfortable enfolding containing excitement, and a look of love, of love of *her*, Jane-Frederica, Frederica-Jane, the beloved.

If you put your finger on one of these fat breasts, she says to herself, it would spring back at you like a balloon, with a kind of a whine and a kind of a *ping*.

She locks up the box and puts it back where she found it.

In her dressing-gown pocket she finds Wilkie's letter.

It is of course possible that it was not herself who put that letter there. She certainly has no memory of doing so.

Frederica goes into Spessendborough in the Land Rover with Olive, Rosalind, Pippy and Leo. She says she wants to come for the ride, which is partly true—she needs to get out of Bran House—but she also wants to make private telephone calls, she is not sure to whom; she is almost too cast down to be in need of Wilkie's sharpness. Spessendborough is a small market town, one end of which is taken up with covered cattle pens and stained concrete yards. The other end is pretty, with an inn—the Red Dragon—a wide High Street along which run old-fashioned shops, a baker, a butcher, a sweetshop, a haberdashery with thick wavery glass windows, and more modern shops, selling more old-fashioned things—local craft pottery, home-made jams and preserves, a chemist's with coloured bottles. There are side streets of red-brick Georgian houses, and streets beyond them of low cottages with little gardens full of flowers, polished brass knockers, and spick-and-span lace curtains. There are two cafés, the Spinning Wheel and the Copper Kettle, full of dark spindle-legged armchairs with Jacobean chintz cushions and slightly rocky tables, oval and round. For some reason the Reivers always go to the Spinning Wheel, and never to the Copper Kettle. They like to have cream teas in the Spinning Wheel, scones and raspberry jam and Cornish clotted cream. The teapots have knitted teacosies with fluted panels and woolly bows on top. Frederica waits until Pippy has lifted the teapot and then says she has forgotten something at the chemist's and will be back shortly. There is a phone box just beyond the chemist's, out of the sight-line of anyone in the Spinning Wheel.

She has a large collection of pennies, and sixpences, and shillings. She stands in the red box and deploys all these on top of the directories, which are torn and mangled. There is the usual smell—stale tobacco, faint urine, airless dustiness, Bakelite and stone. She picks up the receiver and dials the operator, to whom she recites—making her decision at the last moment—Alan Melville's number. In the distance she hears the bellow of a protesting cow. She waits and hears clickings and hummings and vacancy and burring, and then suddenly a clear Scots voice.

"Hullo. Hullo?"

"Alan?"

"Yes. Can I help?"

"Alan, it's me. Frederica."

"Frederica," he says, in a pleased voice. "What do I say after so long? Are you well? Where are you? Are you ringing for any particular reason?"

He was always, even when closest, rather agreeably courteous and detached.

"No. Yes. I needed someone to talk to. I was so glad to have your letter. I feel you're a long way away—in all sorts of ways, not only miles. It's lovely to hear your voice, it really is. Damn, the money's running out. Hang on. That's better. I've put in a shilling, that'll keep us going."

"Can I ring you back? Where is your phone box?"

"Spessendborough. No, it's OK. I've saved lots of change. I'm ringing from a phone box because—I'm ringing because—I feel I can talk more *freely*—"

"Frederica, you don't sound happy. Is something wrong?"

"No. Not exactly. No. I'm a bit lonely. That's what it is."

There is a tapping on the glass walls of the box. It is Leo, whose white nose is pressed against the pane, at the level of Frederica's knees. She looks round. They are all staring in at her from different sides, Olive and Rosalind and Pippy Mammott. They look rather severe, but when they see her looking, they wave and smile, encouragingly.

"I've got to go now, Alan."

"But you haven't *said* anything, darling, you haven't even begun."

"I've got to go. They're all round the box."

"Let them wait a bit."

"I *can't* talk to you with them watching. I can't. I'll go. Give my love to the others. Tell them their letters were—were—"

"Frederica. Can I ring you back?"

"No. Yes. I don't know. I'll try again."

"You sound really *bothered,* Frederica."

"I've got to go. I've got to go."

"Frederica—"

"Good-bye. Give my love to Tony and the others. Good-bye—"

They do not need to criticise, they do not need to ask whom she is calling, they do not need to say, "You said you were going to the chemist's, and we find you in a phone box," because all these things are perfectly clear to all of them, immediately. Frederica says, "I'm sorry to keep you waiting," and they say, "Not at all, you weren't, we just happened to come by," and so they all pile into the Land Rover, Frederica between Pippy and Olive, with Leo on Pippy's knees.

Frederica thinks, The idea that I am *trapped* here is an illusion. I could just get up and go, tomorrow, I could. If I just said "I'm going now," it is quite likely these three would be *glad of it,* that's how it is.

Leo says, "Your tea was cold. We just wondered where you were." He puts a small hand into hers, and grips. She is kept rigid by the solid bottoms of Olive and Pippy, pressing against hers.

Leo develops a passion for the story of Tommy Brock and Mr. Tod. Frederica tries to read him other things, *Thomas the Tank Engine,* more Hobbits, but night after night he insists on coming back to this rather unsavoury tale. He can recite large parts of it, and particularly enjoys the dénouement, when the fox believes he has killed the badger with a trap.

"I will bury that nasty person in the hole which he has dug. I will bring my bedding out, and dry it in the sun," said Mr. Tod.

"I will get soft soap, and monkey soap, and all sorts of soap; and soda and scrubbing brushes; and persian powder; and carbolic to remove the smell. I must have a disinfecting. Perhaps I may have to burn sulphur."

"What is sulphur, Mummy? What is persian powder?"

"Sulphur is yellow and has a disagreeable smell," says Frederica, whose style is infected by Beatrix Potter's own idiom. "Matches have sulphur in them, and fireworks, and so does the smell of bad eggs, which you probably don't know—eggs don't seem to go bad these days. It's a nasty smell."

"Tommy Brock must have smelt *very* nasty if you need a bad-egg smell to get rid of his smell," says Leo. "What do you think he smelt of?"

"Like people's dirty feet when they haven't washed for *months*," says Frederica. "You probably don't know what that smells like, either."

"I've smelt Mr. Wigg's shirt when he's been gardening," says Leo. "What a *pong,* Daddy says, Mr. Wigg makes. Do you think Tommy Brock smelled like Mr. Wigg, Mummy?"

"*Much worse,* Leo. And you ought not to say people pong, it's an ugly word, and you might hurt their feelings."

"I like it. Pong. Pong. Ping-pong-ping-pong. Ping is like needles and pong is like Sooty's piles and pools."

"That's enough of pongs. Let's get on with the story."

"You haven't told me what persian powder is."

"I haven't, have I? That's because I don't know. I told you yesterday I didn't know."

"You could have *found out.*"

"I could. How was I to know you would want Tommy Brock and Mr. Tod for a fourth time running?"

"You could have known. I *love* Tommy Brock and Mr. Tod. We will have them tomorrow too. I love it when they do horrible things to each other. They are horrible people and they do horrible things and everything is *horrible* and the little rabbits are all safe after all. Only a bit frightened, they were, the little rabbits. Their mummy *wringed* her ears, she was worried. How do you wring your ears?"

"You can't, if you aren't a rabbit. Something like this."

Frederica puts her hands to her head and more or less wrings her red hair. Leo laughs shrilly—the story overexcites him.

"Go on reading, now. Go on." He prompts. "Mr. Tod opened the door . . ."

"Tommy Brock was sitting at Mr. Tod's kitchen table, pouring out tea from Mr. Tod's tea-pot into Mr. Tod's teacup. He was quite dry himself and grinning; and he threw the cup of scalding tea all over Mr. Tod."

Leo shrieks with laughter and rolls about on his pillows, damp-skinned and catching his breath. Frederica touches his hair, and then buries her face in his chest. He clutches at her hair and kicks, convulsed with laughter.

One day, a week or so later, they are all having tea, Olive, Rosalind, Pippy Mammott, Frederica and Leo, when the sound of wheels is heard on the gravel outside. Rosalind says, "That must be Alice," and

Pippy Mammott, her mouth full of fruit cake says, "Not Alice's car. Land Rover." "Not our Land Rover," says Olive. "No shuddering noise." "Don't recognise it," says Rosalind. Pippy goes to the window. "Three men," she says. "No one we know. Getting out. Coming to the door." "Conservative canvassers?" says Olive. Pippy has gone to the door. There is a male murmur, which ends distinctly with "Frederica." Frederica stands up and goes herself to the door. There is Pippy Mammott, and there on the flight of steps leading up to the front door, where they have no right to be, where in some sense they do not exist, are Tony and Alan and Hugh Pink. The Land Rover is new and shiny. Hugh says, "Good afternoon, Mrs. Mammott. We happened to be passing—"

"And thought we would look up our old friend Frederica," says Tony.

Alan says, "Frederica. We aren't intruding, I hope?"

Frederica is afraid she will cry. She runs down the steps and puts her arms round Alan's neck. He hugs her. Tony hugs her. Hugh Pink gives her a peck of a kiss on a cheek. Pippy Mammott stands in the doorway and observes these indiscriminate embraces.

"Tea?" says Frederica with a slightly hysterical laugh. "Would you like to come in for some tea?"

"That's what we *hoped* you would say," says Tony, advancing on Pippy Mammott. "So kind," he says, though Pippy Mammott's expression is not exactly kind. "We've come such a long way, tea is just what we want, isn't it, Alan, isn't it, Hugh?"

They come in, a body of energy, they look around themselves curiously, they advance on Olive and Rosalind and shake their hands.

"You found your way back, I see," says Olive to Hugh Pink.

"It wasn't difficult. We happened to be passing. We thought we'd look up Frederica. On the off chance."

"The tea's cold," says Pippy Mammott. "I'll make fresh."

She goes off with the trolley. Frederica performs introductions: Tony, Alan, Hugh, Olive, Rosalind, Leo.

Everyone sits down and considers everyone else, watchfully. Alan says one or two polite things to Olive and Rosalind about the architecture of Bran House, to which they reply briefly, at a loss.

Tony says, "And you, dearest Frederica, how are you keeping? What are you doing with yourself, tell us how things are?"

"I have Leo," says Frederica, and stops. "Tell me—*you tell me*—about everyone—about what you are doing—"

Tony says, "Everyone's got election fever."

Alan says, "I've got some lectures to do at the Tate, on Turner, I've suddenly got interested in Turner, romanticism was never my thing, but I've got interested—"

Hugh says, "I actually sold my pomegranate poem, the one I sent you, to the *New Statesman*. I've written quite a lot, there might be a book, almost. Can't call it 'Bells and Pomegranates,' that's spoken for, but I'm having a go at bells. No competition with 'Lübeck Bells,' of course. More of a relation of 'Mary, Mary, Quite Contrary.' "

"With silver bells and cockle shells," says Leo.

"*Exactly,*" says Hugh to Leo. "A garden full of shiny things—"

"But a silver nutmeg. *And* a golden pear."

"Your son is a poet, Frederica."

"He likes words," says Frederica.

"He could hardly not," says Tony, looking at the dark aunts on their sofa. They do not speak. Pippy Mammott returns with the trolley, and fresh tea. Tony eats three slices of fruit cake and Alan eats a sandwich with cucumber and Gentleman's Relish.

"And Wilkie?" says Frederica. "You must have seen Wilkie?"

"He's full of his television game. He's made a pilot, he says it's hilarious, literary knights and theatrical ladies getting everything *deliciously* wrong, mistaking Auden for Byron, he says, and Dickens for Oscar Wilde, and Shakespeare for C. S. Forester, he told us to tell you you've got to come and play, everyone is playing, even *Alexander* is playing, you have to come and play . . ."

"You'd leave them all standing at the starting post, Frederica," says Alan.

"No one wants to see *me,*" says Frederica.

"No, but you will make them want to. You always did."

They take the tea, and smile vaguely at the denizens of the house who offer it, they talk in a trio, lightly and brightly, they reminisce, they cross-refer, they are not impenetrably rude and private, but they speak Frederica's shop, Frederica's staple chatter and gossip and thoughts, for which she is dry and thirsty. She begins to speak. She tells Hugh why she loved his poem. She discusses Persephone in the dark with the fruit and seeds, and furious dry Demeter in the air. They quote lines at each other, Hugh and Frederica, companionably.

Leo says suddenly, "Picks with pink fingers, listless."

Hugh smiles at him. "I didn't know your mother had read it to you too."

"She didn't," says Leo. "Daddy did."

The two dark women narrow their mouths and look at each other. Frederica puts out a hand towards Leo. Hugh, thinking of his poem, notices none of this. He says, "Did he like it?"

"I don't think so," says Leo.

"Poetry isn't his—" begins Frederica.

"He likes hobbits," says Leo. "*I* liked it," he says kindly.

Alan Melville says, "I should very much like to take a walk in your woods, Frederica, if we may? Do you think we could go on a walk? Being from the grey north I don't know this country. It's very beautiful."

Frederica stands up. "Let's walk," she says. "Yes, that would be wonderful, just what I need, a walk, let's *walk*."

Alan says to Olive and Rosalind, "Would you like to come with us?"

"Well, that would be—" says Rosalind.

"No thank you," says Olive.

"No thank you," says Rosalind.

It is the first time Frederica has seen them disagree, Frederica thinks; then she thinks she *must* be exaggerating, she just feels she is herself again, dangerously happy and observant.

"We won't be long," she says, going into the hall, getting a jacket. "I don't suppose we'll be all that long and anyway it doesn't matter, does it?"

"I'm coming," says Leo. "Wait for me."

"Better not, dear," says Pippy Mammott. "You might miss your supper. Lovely Welsh rarebit, you like that, and treacle tart, you like that, too."

"I'll get my coat too," says Leo, making for the door.

"Your mummy doesn't want you," says Pippy Mammott. "She'd like to see her friends she hasn't seen. We will all just stay here quietly until she comes back. We'll play Happy Families. You like that."

"She *does* want me," says Leo. He stands stiffly, near tears, full of force, Bill Potter's grandson, Nigel Reiver's son, a small figure by the chimney-piece. "She *doesn't want to see them* without me. She doesn't."

Frederica stands and looks at him. She doesn't speak, but she does meet his eye. It is Tony Watson who says, "Where's this coat then?" and Alan who says to Pippy, "We'll take *very* good care of him, we'll bring him back in plenty of time for his supper."

Frederica holds his coat for him, and he shrugs himself into it. They set off through the orchard and across the meadows, with Leo at first swinging between Hugh and Alan, and then riding on Tony's strong shoulders, clutching his curly head, and pointing things out, things rapidly becoming invisible in the thickening autumn evening, a crow, a jump, a trough, a gate with dead stoats and magpies nailed to it.

Because he is there, nobody asks Frederica about her life. It occurs to Alan that the child, however small, has come out with precisely that intention, conscious or unconscious, of preventing Frederica from talking to her friends about her life. If there is a reflective pause in the conversation the boy rushes in, with lots of bright, showy, slightly shrill chatter, *in case*, Alan thinks, *in case*. The three friends accommodate themselves to the situation. They are real friends, they came to help as best they can. It is quite dark in the woods, the smoky light lingers after sunset.

They come back companionably, discussing words for twilight: dusk, gloaming, *crépuscule, Dämmerung*. Hugh quotes Heine—"Im Dämmergrau, in das Liebeland / Tief in den Busch hinein." Alan says to Frederica, as they prolong the walk by coming back to the front door round the outskirt of the moat, "You really do live in a moated grange."

"When Hugh came, he kept quoting 'Only connect.' I got quite cross, but he was right, of course."

"Did you connect?"

"Look, Alan, how can one say one thing is more *real* than another, here and London, people with their heads full of books and people with their heads full of figures? But I got a bit sick of all the Cambridge literary intensity. I am half sick of shadows, I said to myself, I will Connect, and found myself in a moated grange."

"Complete with Mrs. Danvers."

"Don't. You can do *awful damage* with inappropriate comparisons."

Leo says, "Im Dämmergrau in das Liebeland."

Hugh says, "You can twist your tongue round anything."

Alan takes Frederica's hand.

They come round the corner, across the bridge over the opaque green water, and crunch across the gravel. There is another car beside the Land Rover, a shimmering silver Triumph, not Nigel's green Aston Martin. On the top step, looking down from a height, are three men, one of whom, much the smallest, is Nigel. The other two are

111

both dressed in blazers and flannel trousers, formally informal. One has dark skin and a large curling white beard, elegantly trimmed. The other is bald, with horn-rimmed glasses. Alan drops Frederica's hand, and Tony lifts down Leo, who looks around him, and then makes a little rush across the gravel, and toils up the staircase to his father.

Frederica apologises for her friends, although she knows she should not. She introduces them, says they are old friends, explains that she had no idea they were in the neighbourhood. Whilst she says all this, falling over her words, Nigel and his companions remain stolidly in possession of the centre of the top step, in front of the door. He nods quickly and silently in the direction of Alan, Tony and Hugh, as they are introduced, neat, unsmiling, economical nods. He introduces his own companions, Govinder Shah and Gijsbert Pijnakker. Both these persons hold out their hands formally to Alan, Tony and Hugh, who have to take them on a slant, like courtiers.

"And my wife," says Nigel. "Delighted," says Shah. "So glad to meet you," says Pijnakker. Frederica has a sensation of being summed up and judged, by both at once, in different ways. Shah has soft full lips inside his beard, and deepset dark eyes, under curly white brows, with smile-lines set round them. He is wearing an Indian silk scarf inside an ivory silk shirt inside his dark blue blazer: it is flame and gold, with little flowers in crimson and black. Pijnakker is egg-shaped, a shining egg-head on a solid egg-body, neat and hairless. His shirt is striped butcher-blue and white, and he wears a navy scarf tied extremely neatly. Nigel is wearing a dark sweater and dark trousers. Alan, Tony and Hugh are all in corduroy jackets and trousers, over polo-necked sweaters. Nigel's friends make Frederica's friends look flimsy and insubstantial. Frederica's friends, on their own ground, might make Nigel's friends look pompous, but they are not on their own ground. The two groups might join and talk animatedly and fuse, but that is not going to happen. Nigel explains to Frederica's friends that he has important things to discuss with Pijnakker and Shah. He then offers the friends a drink, which they refuse, retreating towards their Land Rover. Tony says, "Why don't you lend us Frederica to have dinner with us in Spessendborough, whilst you talk?" There is an effort of pure will behind this casual invitation which everyone can feel. Nigel says, "Oh, I don't think so, I don't think she'd want to do that. We've only just arrived."

Frederica says, "You won't really need *me*, if you have things to discuss—"

She knows rationally that there is no reason why she should not say this.

She knows she will pay for saying it.

"We'll be around a bit," says Tony. "Staying in the Red Dragon. Perhaps we'll see you again."

"Perhaps," says Nigel. "Who knows?"

It is quite clear to everybody that he hopes never to see them again.

Frederica dines with Pijnakker, Shah and Nigel. She does not often meet Nigel's friends, and when she does, they do not much talk to her. Nigel's social life seems to be spent in a very male society, a society of clubs, bars, cigars and complicated intrigue. When he is at home, this world rings his moated grange invisibly, airy voices, guttural voices, suave voices, excitable voices, thick-cream voices, European voices, Asian voices, American voices, call him to the telephone, and he sits all evening, lying back in a leather armchair, talking to the wide world. Frederica supposes that if her friends had not come, she would not have been asked to sit through dinner with Pijnakker and Shah. On the rare occasions when people from out there do come to Bran House, she is somehow relegated to Leo's nursery supper, or Pippy Mammott puts her up something delicious on a tray by the fire. But tonight she sits through dinner and nobody has much to say to her. Pijnakker addresses her more or less in the third person, through Nigel. "Your lady wife is very comfortable here in the country," he says, including them both in a pleasant enough smile. "In Holland we have no such variety of landscape. It is all flat. Has your lady wife ever visited Holland, I wonder?" "No," says Frederica. "I should like to see the Rijksmuseum. I should like to see the Van Gogh paintings." "You must bring her, once, Reiver," says Pijnakker. "Rotterdam is not beautiful, but she would like Delft and Leiden, she would be interested in tulips." These are not words that interest Pijnakker, but his intentions are kindly. Shah says, "So you are interested in paintings, Mrs. Reiver." He, unlike Pijnakker, does look *at* Frederica. When her eyes meet his, he gives her a little private smile, which may or may not be automatic. He says, "I do admire your brown dress, Mrs. Reiver. It is *just* the brown for your lovely hair. What kind of pictures do you like particularly?"

Frederica is fond of the dress she has on, a jersey tube with a high neck and long thin sleeves in a dark brown, between coffee and chocolate. It makes the most of her long thin body, her long thin

113

arms. Dresses are becoming shorter. It makes the most also of her long thin legs. Govinder Shah is considering her small breasts inside this tube. His look is kindly, but Frederica knows he does not find her attractive. He believes strongly that she *wants* him to find her attractive, and so his eyes linger where they can, politely.

She says, "I don't know a lot about pictures, I'm afraid. I know quite a lot about Van Gogh. I have a great friend who wrote a play about him. Literature is my subject."

"I believe there have been many plays about Van Gogh," says Pijnakker. "People find him very interesting, he was religious and mad, very Dutch. He sold only one painting in his lifetime. I admire his persistence, to go on against such odds. What normal man would paint hundreds and thousands of pictures no one wanted to buy? I ask myself, did he *know* they would come to be wanted, or was it pure chance?"

"Hundreds of people make things nobody wants," says Shah. "But I agree with you also, there are those with the courage of their convictions who make things they know people *will* want, those who are ahead of their time. Some of these appear to be madmen, and some of them are. I believe Van Gogh's brother was a dealer. He may have seen more clearly that people would some day want those pictures. Or he may not. I believe he bought them all, stored them all. Maybe he was merely kind. Maybe he was merely exercising family loyalty."

"He too died mad," says Pijnakker. "The Dutch are much given to melancholy-madness. It is the grey rain on our coasts. That is why we voyage, to escape the grey rain and the melancholy-madness."

"Whereas we in the sub-continent," says Shah, "we voyage if we must to escape the extreme poverty and mess we have made of our daily lives. We have made a world in which enterprise is impossible, because we are not orderly beings, but lazy and corrupt beings, and if we have any enterprise we brave your grey rain and your melancholy-madness in order to earn our daily bread and if we are lucky some butter and jam and perhaps eventually foie gras and caviare to put on our bread. But we do not like your grey mists and your miserable cold wet winds, we get sunsick, we like to go back and forth and cannot."

All three men laugh at this speech, as though it says more than it appears to say.

"Happy the man," says Shah, "with an office in Rotterdam, and an office in London, and a house on a hill in Kashmir, and a villa in Antibes, and a yacht in the Mediterranean and an ocean-going boat too in the North Sea, a free man."

Pijnakker says, "Vincent Van Gogh was melancholy-mad in the south, too. The sun did him no good, I think. I like the sun myself, I am partial to a week or two in North Africa or Italy or southern France, I protect my eyes and my skin, and do not expose myself excessively."

"You are presenting yourself as a cautious and moderate person, Gijsbert."

"Only in some ways, Govinder. Only in some personal ways. I take risks when I must. You cannot do business without taking risks."

"That is so. The important thing is, to be clever about *which* risks."

They laugh again. Frederica in her brown tube, is not there, not for those two, not even as a pair of female eyes to observe their male liveliness, for they do not exactly see her as female. Nigel does. He watches her, as well as watching Shah and Pijnakker; he fills their glasses often and hers not at all. She thinks perhaps he is not speaking much because he is partly thinking about the appearance of Alan and Tony and Hugh. But perhaps he never speaks, she wonders. Even his telephone world consists mostly of listening, his head cocked on one side, his lips and brows thoughtful.

The three friends are eating steak and kidney pie in the Red Dragon. They started with tomato soup, and went on to the pie, which is really very good. The dining-room has low beams, which may or may not be old, and a bar at one end. There is also a real wood fire, in a chimney. A wood fire is a cheering thing.

Tony says, "She can't stay there, she'll go mad."

"You can't just *say* that," says Hugh. "She went there. Perhaps she really likes it. Perhaps she had a hankering for country life. I do, from time to time."

"Do you think she likes it?"

"No. No. I don't."

"*Why* did she go there?" says Tony, as though a good analytic explanation could immediately be produced.

Alan says, "I have noticed that all sorts of people, who are perfectly sensible when offering opinions about Shakespeare, or Claude Lorrain, or even Harold Wilson, simply go off their rockers when deciding about getting married. Tough people get pressured by weak people and vice versa. People marry their *ideas* of what they wanted. I know a girl whose ideal was a man with coal-black hair and she found one, and much good it did her. He is the most *boring* man and keeps a model railway in the attic. And then I've noticed people marry to spite their parents, or to repeat the mistakes or the successes of their parents, or quite often both. People marry to get away from their mothers, and hundreds of people marry one lover in order to get away from another, and what they're really thinking about isn't the one they *are* marrying but the one they aren't. Or they marry to spite someone who didn't want them."

"Or for money," says Tony.

"Or for money," says Alan. "I would have thought it was built into Frederica's scheme of things *not* to do that, but of course she might have been in revolt against her scheme of things, temporarily at least."

"She said she got married because her sister died," says Hugh. "That is, that isn't *exactly* what she said, but she intimated that that changed her, her sister dying, and she was changed."

"I don't see," says Tony, "how the death of a sister could turn you into a country lady; it seems an odd reaction, to say the least."

"You could imagine a scenario," says Alan, "where a completely new beginning in a completely new place—a new life . . . She couldn't be so *silly*."

"She was always silly," says Tony. "That was what made her bearable. Silly and clever at once, and so sure she was right, poor dear. There's a certain *Schadenfreude* in seeing her in this mess."

"No, there isn't," says Hugh. "It's just *awful*. And that amazing little boy. He wasn't going to let her say a word to us. He didn't."

"*That* is the daftest thing of all," says Tony. "*That* makes the whole mess irretrievable."

There is an element of enjoyment in Tony's contemplation of Frederica's predicament. Alan and Hugh are more perturbed, but also less disposed to interfere. Hugh says, "You can't *tell*, of course. The most surprising couples are happy in the most surprising ways."

Alan says, "You can tell. She's miserable. She's lost and miserable and ashamed."

Tony says, "Well. What are we going to do?"

"Can we do anything?"

The waitress brings lemon meringue pie.

Alan says, "We can't just leave her."

Hugh says, "I don't think we'll find it easy to see her again."

The firelight flickers. The pub is comfortable. They order coffee and whisky, and talk about Harold Wilson and Rupert Parrott. Outside a wind gets up, with rain in it.

Frederica goes to bed early, and Nigel goes into the study, with Pijnakker and Shah. Frederica lies and reads Durrell's *Justine,* which she has picked up because she thinks its narrative is strong enough to be gripping even in the state she is in. She thinks, I could just get up and go to Alexandria, and then she thinks that those who *will* go to Alexandria are in fact Pijnakker and Shah and Nigel Reiver. None of them would probably give more than ten minutes to Durrell's mannered prose but they would be more at home in his world than she would. She does not want Durrell's Alexandria in her bedroom and turns out the light. Lying rigid in the dark, willing sleep to come, shakes the brain and causes bone-ache. She puts the light on again and takes up Rilke. She is reading *The Sonnets to Orpheus* in bed in a side-by-side translation, to keep her mind exercised. This goes better. A little grammatical wrestling is wonderfully soothing, and she finds two lines which shiver her flesh and which she thinks she must show Hugh.

> Geht ihr zu Bette, so lasst auf dem Tische
> Brot nicht und Milch nicht: die Toten ziehts.—
>
> (If you go to bed, leave on the table
> No bread, no milk: they draw the Dead.)

And then she thinks she will find it hard to show Hugh anything again.

When Nigel comes to bed, late, late, she pretends to be asleep. He crashes around, putting on lights: a quantity of malt whisky has been consumed. Frederica lies like an angry needle along one edge of the bed. He gets in, switches off the light, and reaches for her with a heavy arm. She wriggles away. He pulls at her. She has a sudden vision of the buttocks and breasts and mouths in the briefcase. She slips out of bed like an eel, snatching up Rilke, and retreats into the bathroom.

She hears his voice, "What were you holding his hand for?"

She tries to remember. The Moated Grange. There is no answer. She thinks of slamming the door, restrains herself, shuts it very quietly, and waits.

Ist er ein Hiesiger? Nein, aus beiden
Reichen erwuchs seine weite Natur . . .

(Is he from this world? No, from both kingdoms
Sprang his wide nature . . .)

She waits for the explosion. It does not come. Nigel has gone to sleep. Whisky is beautiful, sleep is beautiful, silence is blissful. Frederica's eye-rims are sore with suppressed tears.

The next day is Sunday. Frederica breakfasts with Shah and Pijnakker, who then set off in the Triumph. She finds herself walking. Along landings, along staircases, through rooms, back. She thinks of going out for a walk, but thinks also that the friends might come. And indeed, at about ten, she hears the telephone. Pippy is there to answer it in the hall. Frederica is on the landing.

"Hullo? Oh yes. I don't know where she is at the moment, or what her plans are. I'll go and see."

Frederica begins to come downstairs.

Nigel comes out of the drawing-room, and nods to Pippy. Pippy says to the telephone, after a decent moment's rest, "I'm so sorry, I find she's busy all morning, I'm afraid that won't be possible."

The telephone speaks gallantly. Frederica comes down the stairs. Nigel nods again at Pippy, who says with a cluck of sympathy, "I'm so sorry, she can't come to the telephone, she's gone out."

And before Frederica can move, she has put the phone down.

Frederica says, "You could see I *wasn't* out, Pippy. What is this?"

Pippy looks at her, drops her gaze, and trots away. Frederica says to Nigel, "So I am not to go anywhere, ever?"

"Don't be ridiculous."

"I'm not being. You have just told a lie to my friends, to my *old friends,* you have said I wasn't there when I was."

"I'm sorry," says Nigel, with the flexibility that is always disarming. "I'm sorry, that was bad. I just can't stand those people."

"You don't know them."

"They don't like me, and I don't like them. And you are married to *me.*"

They stare at each other. Frederica says, "I am going to call them and say I am here."

"I don't want you to. I want you, just this once, to stay here, to please me. We'll go out with Leo. We'll go for a drive. It will be good for Leo to have both his parents."

" 'Just this once,' " says Frederica, picking on the operative phrase. "What do you mean, 'Just this once'? I *never* go anywhere, I *never* see anyone, I have no life, and when my friends come, you have the gall to say 'Just this once, don't go.' "

"You have to understand," says Nigel, "I don't feel sure of you. You aren't the sort of girl I was accustomed to. In a sort of a way I was a bit scared of you. I'm frightened you might find me boring, me and Leo, and want to go off, or something. You can understand that?"

"Oh yes," says Frederica. "I can understand that. But I can't live with it, any more. If you keep me shut up here because I might go off, I *will* go off, you can see that?"

"Leo—" says Nigel.

"Don't blackmail me with Leo. I am myself, as well as Leo's mother. *I want to see my friends.*"

"Just this once—" Nigel begins doggedly, and then laughs, sharp and unhappy. "Look, we'll start again, we'll go to London, I'll take you to Amsterdam with Pijnakker and you can look at your pictures, we'll go on a holiday—we could go to the West Indies—"

"I don't *want* to go to the West Indies, I want to go where I can talk about books—where I can *think*—I have to *think,* the way you have to do whatever you do do, with Pijnakker and Shah—"

"You can think here. It isn't thinking you want, it's men. You need lots of men."

"*No,* Nigel. I need—"

"He was holding your hand."

"Is that so terrible?"

"Yes. Yes, it is. To me, it is."

"I'm sorry. It wasn't anything. Leo was even there. They are just my friends."

"Just this once—stay with me. I'm sorry. Stay with me."

She stays, because she sees only too well that if she *does* attempt to telephone the Red Dragon, all that will result will be hideous embarrassment and violence. They go out in the car, Frederica and Leo and Nigel, and they have what might be called a good day. Both of them talk to Leo, who chatters to both of them. Leo does not mention

Alan and Tony and Hugh, though Frederica is waiting for him to do so. It is as though they had never come, never existed.

When they come back, Nigel says, "There, that was a good day."

Pippy carries Leo off to bed. She brings supper for Nigel and Frederica. She does not meet Frederica's eye. Frederica is tired. She has got through another day, and finds this consoling, until, when relaxation dribbles a livelier blood into her veins, she starts thinking again: Getting through another day, and another day, what sort of a life is that? "Most people's lives," some cynical Good Fairy mutters in her head. "Most people's lives." Frederica stabs carrots, savagely, with her fork. She thinks, Today is Sunday, they all have jobs, they will have gone home.

Rifts are closed, but also sprung open, in bedrooms. Frederica sees that Nigel has a scenario for this night, a scenario of long, subtle, complex love-making, of gentleness and closeness, of pleasure and loss of self and exhausted sleep. She tries, because she is tired, and because in some ways she is in despair, to school herself to accept this, because it is what he has to give, and because she needs sleep and unconsciousness, and because of Leo. She watches Nigel undress—he likes to sleep naked—and she thinks to herself that his body is more real to her than those of Tony and Alan and Hugh added together—and Alexander and Wilkie and Raphael Faber, she tells herself rather wildly. She even sits quietly on the edge of her side of the bed, in a white lawn nightdress with long sleeves and a yoke and collar, and wonders whether women in previous centuries would even recognise her despair, given that she does not want to go away and make love to Tony, Alan and Hugh, but merely to talk to them, merely to feel a little mental space for freedom. The bedroom is dark, and Nigel has drawn the curtains, which are dark red, a kind of damask, with red trees and red blooms on a red ground. When Frederica is alone she leaves the curtains open and sees stars or clouds. She imagines Alan and Tony and Hugh in a large room with white walls and pale blue curtains, with open windows blowing the blue curtains, and sunlight coming in. She hunches her shoulders and stares at her knees. The naked man pads, strutting a little, as naked men do, in and out of the bathroom, making tap noises, spitting noises, flushing noises. Frederica sits and waits, and thinks. She thinks, I am a woman, and thinks what a silly pretentious thought *that* is. She thinks, I thought that, because the kind of woman I am is not quite sure she *is* a woman, she likes to be reassured about that. I am a thin woman, a sharp woman, a wordy woman, not the sort of animal men think of at all when they think of a woman. Cambridge obscured this, temporarily, there were so few women, we were all treated as though we were real ones, like nurses in prisons, like secretaries in barracks.

The man carries his penis in front of him, neither erect nor quiescent, but stirring with life, but solidifying. He says, "Darling." He approaches the motionless woman and pulls at her nightdress, intending to lift it romantically over her head.

Frederica sees in her head, with total clarity, the succession of images in the locked case, the screwed-up bodies, the blown-up flesh, the carmines and roses, the slippery rubbery masses. She twists away, clutching her garment, and says, "It's no use. None of it is any use. You know as well as I do that this is over, that I can't stay, that it hasn't worked. Tomorrow I will put some things together and get a taxi or something from Spessendborough and just *go* in a civilised sort of way. And then we can be friends and it will not be so awful."

She had not expected to say any of this, and is uncomfortably aware that her tone is that of a nanny talking to a child. Nigel stops a moment, and then continues his advance. The penis has not shrunk, it has become an angry club, wavering in front of him. His face is flushed. He takes hold of Frederica's hair, pulls her head back on to the bed—she lets herself fall quickly, remembering the commando grips—pushes up the nightdress and takes her. He does not try to hurt her, he does not kiss or caress her. He bangs away, and explodes, and sits back on the floor, swaying slightly. Frederica says, in a thin voice, frightened and furious, "*That* has nothing to say to it. I am going to go, tomorrow."

"No," says Nigel. His eyes are full of tears. They run on to his cheeks. Frederica wipes her legs with the sheet and the nightdress.

"It isn't *me* you want," says Frederica. "You just want to hold on to what you've got, like all possessive males, you're like one of the stags when one of the females tries to trot off, you bellow and rush. It's nothing to do with *me*."

"How do you know? You don't know my thoughts, you don't know *much,* I often think. You don't notice much. How do you know what I feel?"

"I don't think I care any more what you feel. I'm going to go and sleep in that other room. Good night."

She goes into the spare bedroom and sits on the edge of the bed, in the dark, and shakes. She waits. She is not thinking, she is simply afraid. She waits. When she hears footsteps along the corridor, she gets behind the door. She is still shaking. Perhaps she will faint. The door opens violently and the man comes into the room. He stands, accustoming his eyes to the dark, and Frederica whips round the door, and runs along the corridor and down the stairs. She runs into the kitchen and out into the scullery, and pulls at bolts, and chains, and goes out into the quiet damp night. She goes on running, across the back yard, through a gate into the stable-yard. She listens. At first there is no sound of pursuit and then she hears a door open. That is all. He is not crashing. He is coming quietly. Frederica opens the door to the saddle-room, quietly, quietly, slips in and shuts it. She does not like to be shut in. She wants to be out in the air, to run all the way to London, but that is silly, she needs to be very clever. She gets behind a rack of saddles and waits. She thinks, when he opens the door, if he opens the door, this nightdress will shimmer. She finds a horseblanket, drapes it over a chair and crouches under. Every hiding place is also more dangerous, because she cannot run. She can hear her own blood, banging in her head and her heart. Her mouth is dry. She crouches.

After what seems a long time, the door is thrown open with a crash. She can hear him breathing. She sees his bare feet, and the bottoms of his pyjama trousers, striped blue and white. She breathes shallow, shallow, just enough air to keep alive. He says, "Frederica?" She keeps still. He walks in and looks around. She thinks he must have a hunting animal's instinct for warm flesh and breath, but he listens, and does not come towards her. He says, "I'll find you," and she can tell from his voice that he does not know she is there, not really, he is a bit embarrassed, for all his heaving rage, to be talking to an empty room. He goes out, leaving the door open. She still cannot hear his feet on the paving stones, which makes her feel hysterical. She hears a door, another further door, a sudden movement of a horse in a stall, the scrape of a metal shoe. She hears the second door close. Then for a long time she hears nothing. She crouches in the cold in her damp nightdress and says to herself, "Come on, you are clever, intelligence can be used for *anything*, what are you going to do?" But she can think of nothing at all, except going back into the house, and hiding, and waiting until morning, and running on to the road, once she has some sensible clothes—and the road is some two and a half miles away, and unfrequented—and hitching a lift. And there is Leo. How can she run away when he is awake?

After perhaps two hours, she comes out, and stretches her cramped body. There is silence. He will be waiting for her in the house. Perhaps, she thinks, it will all get out of hand and he will kill me with his commando tricks. She does not *really* think he will do that. No human being in full possession of life and thought *really* supposes they are about to die. She thinks if she can just manage to hide *in* the house until breakfast time—until light—

She flickers back barefoot and silent round the edge of the stable-yard, across the back yard, to the back door. The air is cold and damp. The sky is overcast. The door is locked and bolted. She stands on the doorstep and thinks what to do next. She feels curiously relaxed. She will have to be let in bedraggled and cold, at dawn, but what will that matter? She breathes a deep sigh.

"And *now* what will you do?" he says, behind her, stepping out of the house-corner. He has put on a shirt and a pair of plimsolls. He is holding an axe. Frederica screams at the sight of the axe, as he meant her to. It is not a very big axe, as axes go, a neat, portable, shining little axe.

"Don't be ridiculous," says Frederica, doubtfully.

"I'll get you," he says thickly and moves towards her.

Frederica runs.

She runs like fury, through the yards, into the orchard, across the orchard, out into the field. He runs after her. He runs better, but she is madder, she runs quite extraordinarily fast, her mouth is wide and fills with cold night air, and drags at it in great gulps. She runs across the field. He laughs, he stands at the top of the slope of the field as she is stumbling down it, he gives a great whoop of laughter, and throws the axe at her.

She ducks and twists. She cannot see, she will never know how good or bad his aim is or was meant to be. The flat of the axe catches her on her ribs and winds her. She and the axe fall together, its blade bites the flesh of her hip, cuts at her calf. The nightdress reddens very fast, with blood. Frederica lies on her side and stares dumbly at the grass, at a molehill, at the skyline, at the black and grey clouded sky. She is winded. Her eyes hurt. She feels blood and blood, her blood, great hot puddles of it. It has a finality. She stares.

He runs to her side, he kneels beside her. He is beside himself, he is crying, he tears up her nightdress and makes an efficient bandage to stanch the blood. He says, "I didn't mean it, I didn't mean it, you know I didn't mean it."

"What's mean?" says Frederica incoherently, and lapses into bliss-ful unconsciousness. She comes round in his arms: he is carrying her up the hillside, back into the house. She thinks, I might get some sleep.

He bandages her up very successfully. He straps her up in sticking plaster and lint, he swabs and stanches. He says, "They're only super-ficial cuts, you really don't need a doctor, I do know what I'm talk-ing about—"

"Because of the commandos."

"It comes in useful. I am *terribly sorry.* What can I say? I don't know how I . . . I do love you . . . I don't want to hurt you."

"That's not what it looks like."

"I know. Oh, God, *I'm sorry.* You have to understand—"

"I understand."

"I don't like the way you say that."

"You aren't meant to."

"Please, Frederica."

"Go away. I need sleep."

"You need sleep."

He goes away, obediently. She lies in her bed, and Pippy Mammott brings her breakfast. Pippy Mammott says, "I gather you fell over something in the night."

"Something like that."

"I'd be more careful, if I was you."

"What do you mean by that, Pippy?"

"What I say. I'd be more careful, rushing around in the night."

She pretends to be worse than she believes she is. This gives her a kind of space for manoeuvre, though she does not know *what* she will manoeuvre. Leo comes to see her, and strokes her face.

"Poor thing. You're ill."

"I fell over. I was silly."

"You'll get better, Daddy says so."

"I just need a lot of sleep, Leo, that's all, I need to keep very very still. I can't walk very well."

"Poor thing. Poor thing."

"Leo, don't cry. I'll get better. I promise."

He weeps and weeps. She sits up and holds him. All this is not good for him.

"Your face is all bashed, it's horrible, you must have had a *horrible* fall."

"It was. It was quite horrible. But I'm getting better, you can see. No harm done."

"No harm done," says Leo in a little voice. "No harm."

Nigel and Leo go out riding. Olive and Rosalind have gone out too, to help Alice English with her leaflets. Frederica does not know where Pippy is—she might be anywhere—but she is desperate. She gets up, puts on a pair of slacks and a sweater, and goes down the stairs. She can walk perfectly well, although it hurts to do so. She is bruised by the fall, as well as cut by the axe. She stands in the hall, thinking, and then opens the front door and sets out over the gravel. If Pippy is there and is going to stop her, it will be now. There is no sign of Pippy. She crosses the moat, at the bridge, and starts to walk down the drive. She has half an idea that if she can get as far as the road, she will flag down a passing motorist. She does get to the end of the drive, and sits down on a bit of wall, at the edge of the empty road, which is very empty. She hears a sound of bicycle wheels and a creaking chain. She stares at her feet. A voice says, "Frederica!" She jumps. She cries out. It is Hugh Pink, on a very large, very old bicycle. They look at each other.

"What on earth have you done to yourself?"

"Do I look awful?"

"You look horrible. Black and blue and yellow and scraped."

"I fell over."

Hugh puts his bicycle down in the roadside. He gets out a hand-kerchief and wipes his face.

"And how did you fall over, Frederica?"

"Well," says Frederica. "It was in the course of a marital dispute."

"Go on."

"I can't. I shall cry. I don't want to cry, I want to think what to do. Why are you still here?"

"I wanted to see you. To see if you were all right. We thought we were making things worse, and we thought we hadn't any right to interfere, and we thought—we were worried about you."

"Thank you," says Frederica gravely. They sit side by side. She says, "Where are the others?"

"In the woods, in case you came that way. We rang once or twice, but you weren't there, they said you couldn't speak."

"I was there."

"We knew you were. That's why we stayed. It seemed rather feeble just to keep patrolling, but you see it worked."

"It did. Here we are. They might come any minute. What am I going to do?"

"Come back to London with us?"

"How can I? What about Leo?"

"Well," says Hugh, "we could bring the Land Rover to the track in the wood, at night. Can you get out? We could be in London before they saw you'd gone. I suppose you can't just walk out yourself?"

"I can't drive."

"That's remiss of you. You'd better learn. I mean it, we could whisk you away tonight, if you want. You look as though you *ought* to be whisked away, if I may say so. I never took you for a masochist."

"I'm not."

There is a long silence. Hugh says, "I'm sorry. I expect I spoke out of turn. Forget it."

"No, you didn't. Of course you didn't. I ought to get out. I've made a terrible mess of my life. There's Leo."

"Bring Leo."

"How can I? He's a happy little boy, or would be, if I was happy, he has a good life, he's loved, he has his *ways*—I'm not the most—not the central—"

"No?"

"No. I don't think so. I can't bring a little boy who doesn't know anything about all this—in the middle of the night—"

"I'm not saying you're coming *for ever*, Frederica. Just offering a lift to get away and think. You can arrange for Leo later. To see him, to have him, I don't know, to make a better arrangement—just coming away with us now can't be the *end*, you know."

"No."

There is another long silence. Hugh says, "You can't be that good for him, the state you're in, now."

Wounds have their uses. Frederica stays in the spare bedroom, claiming that hers will rest better in solitude. She goes to bed early, undresses and gets into bed with a book. She has no idea what she will do: the idea of a midnight escape is in one way absurd, romantic, ridiculous, and in another appalling. For how can Leo be left? And yet, how can she will her own annihilation, what will she be to Leo, if she is not Frederica? Mummy. It is a word she hates. Why do the English have the same word for a swaddled corpse and cuddly maternity? She thinks for a moment of her sister, Stephanie, like and unlike, mummy in both senses, Frederica thinks grimly. Stephanie too married for sex. It seems improbable, looking at fat Daniel, but Frederica knows it to be true. There they were, the children of a passionate liberal intellectual, and one married the Church and one the Shires, and for what, for sex. She thinks Stephanie was happy. No one is wholly happy, but Stephanie loved Daniel and loved Will and Mary, there was no doubt of that. Stephanie had some capacity to will her own annihilation. Frederica thinks she perhaps married Nigel because Stephanie had married Daniel, and was dead, is dead, will be dead. Stephanie had stepped outside the Cambridge circle of talk and endless discriminations, moral and aesthetic; she had grasped at sensuous happiness. Like Lady Chatterley, walking into the woods to be annihilated, trailing little threads of quotations from Milton's blindness and Swinburne's pale Galilean and Keats's unravished bride of quietness, and Shakespeare's Proserpina, willing them all to go away, so as to lose herself and find herself in the body, in the spring. And that was our myth, Frederica thinks, carrying on her conversation with Hugh, in her head, that the body is truth. Lady Chatterley hated *words,* and Nigel has no words, and I cannot do without them.

I came here, because Stephanie's death annihilated me, at least temporarily, so I was able to live in my body.

Leo lived in my body, a temporary visitor, part, not part, separate now.

Not altogether.

Who matters to him, "Mummy" here, Frederica there, somewhere where Frederica *is* Frederica?

I always resented my own mother's passive quietness. It was not a life. It was what I do not want. It was what I did not want. It is what I have got.

Leo. I could *steal* Leo. But here he is someone, here everyone loves him, here he has a real life, even if I don't.

Leo would have a better life here.

If Leo met me, met Frederica, *somewhere else,* where Frederica was Frederica, at least there would be some truthfulness. He would be angry, but we would talk.

Do you *really* think that?

No. No. I think if I go I might never see him again. I think if I stay we may both be destroyed. I think that's melodramatic. I think, even if it's melodramatic, it's *true*. Melodrama happens. Axes are thrown. Commando tricks are used.

You're just trying to talk yourself into anger, Frederica. Or fear, enough to leave. You *want to leave,* that is what you want, *even if Leo stays,* but you would like to think you *ought* to leave, too, you would like permission.

You won't get it. Leo is your son. You must stay with him or go. You must choose.

"*Now* what will you do?" says the melodramatic sneering voice in her head.

She gets up and begins to dress. The house is dark, the voices are silent, the doors are closed. She is about to commit a crime. She packs nothing; she wants nothing of this life. She is still discussing with herself whether she should go as she goes down the stairs. But her body has taken charge and is creeping with efficient stealth, like a cat burglar, through the kitchens, out of the house.

It is a very misty night. Frederica sees great grey veils moving in the stable yard, in the yard lights. She stops to pick up a torch from the saddle-room, and then sets off cautious, quick, picking her way in shadows of walls, back where she so frantically ran, into the walled orchard. The mist is mobile: it swirls around, apple trees, cherry trees, bare now, are suddenly silhouetted against it, and then suddenly clear in the light of the moon against a patch of blue-black sky with stars sprinkled on it. There is quite a lot of wind, in sudden gusts. Twigs rattle and creak. She hears her heart in the soles of her feet. She stays at the edge of the orchard, where it is darkest, amongst gooseberry bushes and espaliered pears and apricots. She thinks she hears footsteps padding after her, and stops suddenly to listen, and hears nothing but silence. She is jumpy. A man might spring out with an axe, or a sword or a gun. Or just with quick, efficient, chopping hands. The moon, when it is now and then uncovered, is almost full. The sky is in turmoil. Ribbons and rags and heaps of vapour race and coil.

She hears another sound in the bushes, a kind of blundering sound, and stops dead, against the wall, crouching. She thinks perhaps it is a badger: there are badgers in the woods which have been known to come into the orchard, that human place between the house and the wild. There is another very small crunching, and then silence. Some creature, foraging.

She reaches the orchard door, and turns the key, and opens it. Beyond, the field is dark and clammy and open. Behind her there is a sudden rush of running feet and she swings round in fury and turns the blinding light of the torch towards her pursuer. "And what will you do *now*," she hears in her head. But there is no face in her torch-beam, only a flurry of sound and then arms clasping her damaged leg like a serpent coil tightening, strong, small arms, and a face buried in her wound and butting it.

"Leo. Let go. You're hurting my hurt. My love, let go."

"*No.*"

"I won't go anywhere. Come here."

There is a kind of exchange of grips in the dark. Frederica lifts her son, who clutches at every part of her as he rises, with wiry hands and almost prehensile feet. Then he is up, his arms in a stranglehold round her neck, his face driven into her collar-bone, the whole of his body glued to hers with furious determination. He is in his pyjamas. His feet are bare. His face is wet. His teeth are clenched.

"Leo. Leo."

He cannot speak. They stand there, then she sits down, the boy still knotted round her neck.

Many years later, somewhere on the Río Negro, an Indian called Nazareno will bring to Frederica a sloth he has detached from a tree. The sloth is covered with grey hairs and moves slowly, slowly, unable to move really, on the grass in front of the hotel in the clearing. She has three long crescent-shaped nails, and her bowed arms gesture feebly. She stares with round, dark, small, other eyes, without thought or expression. Frederica thinks the creature has a goitre on her neck, a swelling, and then sees it is not so: round the neck of the sloth is wound the child of the sloth, so tight that its lineaments can hardly be discerned, there are simply figures of eight in the strange grey fur and what might be a head lost in what might be a collar-bone. Frederica sees the strangeness of the sloth, and remembers suddenly with total clarity this moment at the gate of the orchard, when her son grips, grips, and tries to burrow back into her body. And she thinks, then, what she cannot think now, standing at the gate: That was the worst moment of my life. That was the worst.

Leo gets out, "I'm. Coming. With."

"It's all right. I'll take you back to bed. We'll go in."

"No. I'm. Coming."

"You don't understand."

"I'm tired," he says. "I'm tired of thinking and thinking what to do, I'm just *tired*. I want to come. You couldn't. You can't. Go without. You can't."

"Leo. Let go a bit. You're like the Old Man of the Sea. Strangling Sinbad."

"Go on," he says. "Go on. That's what he said, the Old Man."

And Frederica ceases to think at all, but sets off again, hurrying and limping, across the field, with the hot child clutched to her breast, clutching with hands and feet. And so, somehow or other, they get over the stile without his hold being relaxed, and set off through the wood, keeping to the ride between the yew trees. Frederica says from time to time, timidly, "Are you all right? Are you comfortable, my darling?" and he does not answer, only grips, heavy and sullen now, inert as if he were asleep, or dead, except that he grips. She sees the dark bulks of the tree trunks, and the clouds racing above the stiff and soughing branches, and she moves in pain, imagining another, younger Frederica, springing along for the joy of freedom. She will remember no man's body as she will remember this hot, angry, grasping boy: she will remember no pleasure of the flesh, and no pain, as she will remember the touch of these arms, the smell of this hair, the shudder of this effort of breath. Both of us know I meant to leave him, she thinks, as she stumbles on; this will be between us. Her grip on him is as tight as his on her: she can hear their two hearts thud, their breaths are mixed. And when Alan Melville steps out of the trees to meet her, his wavering torch lighting her path on the earth, he thinks for a moment of the lion in Stubb's absurd and wonderful picture of the great cat clawing for purchase on the shoulders of its white-maned mount and prey, he thinks of demons, before he sees what she is clutching, a small boy, at the end of his resources. Both woman and child have bared teeth and look not quite human.

"Hullo, Leo," says Alan, gravely. "Are you coming with us?"

The boy cannot answer.

Frederica says, "He took matters into his own hands. Can he come?"

"I don't think you can be separated," says Alan judiciously.

IV

⊱⊰⊱⊰⊱⊰⊱

. . . and it was also about that time, the time of the first flourish of the theatrical presentations in the Theatre of Tongues, but before the ceremonies instituted in the Lady Chapel and the Chapel of the Holy Innocents, that the Lady Roseace took to slipping away from La Tour Bruyarde to take solitary rides and rambles in the forest. She would have been hard put to it to explain why she did this, if asked, and thus sought a certain secrecy, in order to evade being asked, and perhaps also in order not to have to clarify to herself why she went. If challenged, she intended to say that her fancy chose solitary riding, as others' fancies or fantasies chose the actions and rituals now being acted out with much ruddiness of skin and much expenditure of hot pantings and licking of lips in the Theatre of Tongues. But she had a heartfelt wish not to be asked, for the desire of solitude—at least in others—was not a desire upon which Culvert smiled freely. There were still many discussions to be held on how to accommodate the incompatible desires of Damian, Culvert and the Lady Roseace. Culvert was hopeful of the outcome of these debates. The Lady Roseace, contrariwise, prided herself on being no man's creature. That was still in the springtime of the enterprise.

At that time it was also the springtime of the year, or just before. She still rode in a quilted jacket, but had laid aside her fur wraps and her furred hat, and went covered only in a light hood. She had discovered many wide rides, which, as they penetrated deeper under the cover of the trees, became little twisting paths which opened on pretty glades in some of which the first flowers were springing on the green turf, aconites and hellebores, primroses and shy violets. And she would dismount and wander distractedly amongst the dark trunks, seeing how

the bright little buds advanced each week, and appropriating these secret places in her mind, saying, My primroses are further on than I had
supposed, or, My thrush is making a great song and dance in my hazel
coppice. She began to think of herself as the dryad of those trees, tend-
ing them, though she did nothing but stare and smile and walk to and
fro. And she would get bolder and explore a little more and a little
more, extending her domain, savouring the scents and the singing in
the thickets, thinking sometimes of how she would pass the rest of her
days in La Tour Bruyarde and sometimes more vaguely of what might
be taking place in the world beyond the valley, in cities and harbours,
on roads and highways, along rivers and on the open sea. A hen pheas-
ant led a procession of little chicks across her path, and she bent to cup
one of the soft little things in her hands, but they cried out, cheeping,
and scattered and she followed, clutching her skirts and pushing back
brambles and thorny branches from her face, seeing the burnished
bronze of the female feathers flash amongst dead bracken, and so
going onwards, until she came to another clearing where the trees
were higher and blacker and not in bud, though they bore strange
fruit. The clearing was circular and the trees held out their black stiff
arms, and at their arms' length swung swaying and creaking things that
she took at first for suits of clothing, or scarecrows, and then saw
clearly to be the thing itself, human creatures whose faces were black,
whose eyes were plucked by beaks, whose bellies were swollen and
stank.

They turned and creaked, and the trees stood stiffly and rattled and
creaked. And a voice behind Roseace said, so that her heart stopped,
"The fruit of the forest, eh, my lady?"

Roseace turned, trembling with fear or outrage, and there close behind her was Colonel Grim, who must have crept up whilst she was
preoccupied with brambles, and come close, close, whilst she stared
at dead men.

"Et ego in Arcadia, is it not so, my lady? I am sorry if I gave you a
fright. May I escort you away from these danglers, back to your pastoral hiding place?"

"I did not hear you."

"That is natural. You were preoccupied and I am a trained tracker of
beasts and men. Allow me to hold back these branches for you."

"I came here to be alone."

"That is evident, and so you shall be. But it would be less than
chivalrous in me to leave you quite immediately, quite suddenly, after

you have had the shock of coming upon our fellow creatures in the state they are in."

"Who are they?"

"That I do not know. Such gatherings are alas not uncommon in these reaches of the forest. The usual explanation is that they are the victims of the Krebs, though the Krebs, like all bloody tribes, are made responsible for many foul things done by others."

"I do not know of the Krebs," said the Lady Roseace, standing stock-still and reluctant to turn back, for to turn back would be to touch in some way the bulky body of Colonel Grim. Like most if not all the inhabitants of La Tour Bruyarde, she felt a strong aversion to the idea of touching the Colonel. Whether or not he was aware of this, the Colonel took her by the arm and led her back through the branches to the previous clearing, where he invited her to sit on a mossy stump and recover her senses. The Lady Roseace had seen worse sights in the Revolutionary wars from which she had so decisively fled, and would have returned haughtily to her horse, if it were not for an uneasy sense that it would do her no good to make an enemy of Grim. So she sat, toying with her whip, and accepted a silver cannikin of aquavit from his flask.

"The Krebs," said Grim, "are a people, or tribe, who inhabit, or infest, the deep forests and the caves under the mountains. They are short and swarthy, and their bodies are hairy. They have an odour which is offensive to delicate nostrils, and an incomprehensible speech of grunts and spitting. They are not often seen—they hunt in packs, wearing furs and carrying leather bucklers. There is much dispute amongst the learned as to whether they are or are not human creatures. They have a reluctance to leave even their dead in human hands, with the result that we have been unable to examine even a corpse. No one has ever seen a female Krebs, unless it is that the two sexes are indistinguishable and fight side by side, fur-wrapped. They take no prisoners and destroy those who have seen them, it is said, either by blinding, or more often by the punishment of death. It is not good to have come even so close to their trails as to have seen those danglers, my lady. As far as I could see, the peculiar nooses of leather from which they dangle are the work of the Krebs, but I know—it is my business to know—that there are also roaming gangs of more ordinary villains and outlaws who imitate their styles, to safeguard, with fear, their own hiding places."

"You know a great deal," said the Lady Roseace.

"I patrol the bounds of Culvert's kingdom, my child," said the old soldier. "It is more vulnerable on this south side than he thinks, and the outside world has not ceased to exist because he has closed it off and turned away from it. I advise you to ride no more in these glades if you do not wish to become scattered bones and a skull picked clean."

He looked at her lovely face, with its full lips and wide, clear eyes suffused with sparkling liquid, and under the fine flesh of her face the Lady Roseace felt he saw her bone-cage, with staring sockets, dark nasal pits, and rattling pearly teeth in a gaunt jawbone. She bent her head in silence, and her interlocutor continued.

"And I should like to ask, if it is not impertinent, why you ride out so frequently into these woods, and always alone? It might be thought by prurient minds that you have assignations of some kind, but I have been your invisible companion on these wanderings from the first, and can vouch for your innocence of outside intrigues."

The Lady Roseace's breasts and throat were flooded with sudden heat as she answered, with her prepared answer:

"Culvert wishes to provide for the full exercise of all human passions, which he believes to be intrinsically valuable because they are human. And I have a newly discovered passion for solitude and secrecy, solitude, secrecy and wild nature, a not uncommon, indeed a banal, human passion, which I indulge. Or thought I indulged, until you revealed to me a moment ago that my solitude was an illusion, a most displeasing revelation."

"I could say I feared you might need sudden protection from the Krebs," Grim replied, seating himself on an adjacent stump and settling, it appeared, for a long conversation. "Or I could say I feared you were betraying the community, though that explanation does, I agree, lack plausibility. Or I could say, with truth, ma'am, that I have a long-standing passion for information, for knowing exactly the doings and comings and goings of everyone else. I have been a spy in my time, my lady, and it is an avocation that gives intense passional pleasure to men of my type. Here such passions can be freely acknowledged. Here they do no harm. If you take my advice, and wander no longer in these woods, you will never know from what horrors my inconvenient passion may have saved you."

The Lady Roseace compressed her lovely lips, for she saw both the sense and the chafing inconvenience of what he said.

"You take no pleasure in Culvert's popular discussions of pleasure?" the grim man asked, more conversationally. "I have noticed you are frequently absent from these delightful consortiums, into which the majority of our fellow citizens throw themselves with such passion."

"They repeat themselves somewhat tediously," replied the lady. "Their discussions are circular and rambling, and return again and again to the same assertions, which are not greatly elaborated from their first appearance. I agree with you that our fellow inhabitants do indeed take intense pleasure in these contests and concords of debate, but a passion for discussion, like the more usual female passion for gossip and scandal, appears to have been left out of my make-up. Indeed," she went on, interested enough in herself to forget her mistrust of her companion, "those aspects of my nature which caused me to seek this retreat, a desire for solitude, for retirement from the hurly-burly of meaningless, or alternatively dangerous, social activity, make me peculiarly unfitted for the incessant and almost feverish social activity which has, very naturally, it appears, sprung to life in our midst. I admire—I have always admired, even adored—the force, and charm, and powerful intelligence of Culvert. I see the logic of his endeavours to reform—or restore—human nature. But I am not prepared—not ready—not sufficiently convinced of the inevitability of his analysis— to submit myself to all his projects."

"I believe," said the Colonel, "that this morning's debate was to be on the pleasures and pains of micturition and evacuation, on the interest taken by certain persons, including some in our company, in the products thereof, liquids and solids both, and the relations, in the experience again of certain persons, of these processes with the intimate—or solitary—processes of love and desire. Do I have it pat?"

"More or less," said the lady, her mind straying to her own mild pleasures in these matters. A blush then spread over her whole body as she realised that if, as he said, the Colonel had been present unseen during all her wanderings, he must have seen her squatting amongst celandines and sighing with relief and delight as she loosed a streaming puddle into the mossy earth. Had he looked away, did he take pleasure in watching? She had held her skirts bunched high and had felt the balmy air circulating around those white and shapely buttocks, that warm and clinging slit which Culvert wished to offer on stage to the admiring gaze of the whole community. Had Grim seen her with pleasure, and if so, with what kind of pleasure? The idea of his secret eyes was more unpleasant, more interesting and more disturbing to the peace of her inner passages than Culvert's public project.

"If he can excite the community to excite themselves about these matters," the Colonel continued imperturbably, "he will have achieved a subtle political coup, and will be well on the way to solving his urgent housekeeping problem. For we positively must solve the problem of equitable shit-shifting, madame, companion, our very existence depends on it. I have seen fevers run riot in gaols and military camps with festering sanitation."

Roseace had no answer to this, so sat quietly, toying still with her whip.

"He must have foreseen," said the Colonel, "that point still to come when the discussion of the liberation of passions brings us to the liberation of those passions which take pleasure in the hurt of others. I do not speak of a manacle a little too tight, or a whipping that raises a man's member in protesting bliss, such things can be accommodated for our delectation and instruction, on stage or in the bedchambers and dungeons. No, I am curious about the point at which your Culvert will come to consider the pleasures felt by crowds in their Sunday best who watch the heads fall under the axe, or the lion's teeth sever the gladiator's jugular. Can he stage a public hanging and stop short of death? For he may find one suicide amongst us who will offer himself once—and once only—to those whose delight is to make meat of others. It may be that he can find more who have discovered, deliberately or inadvertently, the unsurpassable excitement of spending themselves, of dying in the poets' metaphysical sense, at the precise moment of giving up the ghost with the spurting seed, as the noose tightens, as those poor danglers must have done with no one to cut them down. A dangerous game, Madame Roseace, and still no real satisfaction to the meat-makers."

"Culvert would never countenance making one man happy at another's expense," retorted the lady, though she was inwardly troubled about adjustments of happiness to be made between herself, Culvert and Damian. "And your interest in bloodthirstiness, Colonel Grim, must stem from your own bloody nature, which you have acknowledged, and renounced, I believe."

"My pleasures, in part," he answered, "derive from the strategies of warfare, which have no place in our sealed and separate world, but may yet be needed to defend it. But I see that I have distressed you with my idle and perhaps wholly unfounded speculations, and I can assure you that I take no pleasure at all in torturing the imagination of the fairer and gentler sex. Shall we return to La Tour Bruyarde?"

"I am reluctant to do so," she answered, courteously enough. "The air is so balmy, the flowers and trees so soothing, despite the terrible fruit on the thorn trees in the next clearing. I feel well, out here, and would like to journey farther."

"I do counsel you most strongly not to do so," said he. "This is not a good place, not friendly to innocent humans, however it may wear a spring smile. Let me show you something, madame."

"I do not wish to go back to the danglers," said the lady, using the Colonel's word to disguise her nausea at the thought of them.

"There is no need, madame. Break off a twig from a thorn tree in this clearing—a young twig, not a dead one."

"Why should I?"

"Do it."

So she put out her hand and broke off a green twig, with tight, energetic little buds. And from the severed end came a slow dark gout of blood, a clot of thick blood like a liver-coloured slug humping its way free, and behind it gushed a freshet of red blood, which sprayed her habit with fine scarlet drops. She drew back in horror, crying out, brushing her hand against her skirt so that her fingers in turn were blooded. She begged the Colonel earnestly to tell her the reason and meaning of this phenomenon.

"I do not know for certain," he replied. "Various explanations have been put forth, all of them hypothetical, not to say, in certain cases, metaphysical. You will be aware, as a lady of culture, that the divine poet, Dante Alighieri, ascribes this phenomenon to the Wood of the Suicides in his journey through the Inferno, and the association of hanged men and this bloody sap persists also in the popular imagination in these parts. More vaguely, it is said that this is a place where so many men have been slaughtered, by the Krebs, or by others of their own kind, that the earth is drunk with blood and bonemeal; which bubbles up so prevalently that the trees cannot convert it to innocent green ichor, or phloem, or sap, but must regurgitate it in horror and disgust. And then there is a contrary legend, which asserts that the earth and the trees here hate men—like the Krebs, who are in some sense their foresters and *semblables*—and take pleasure in consuming the dead or the unwary who lie against their roots or under their shade. And there is also a tale, such as you will find all over the world, but without the attestation of bloody sap, that the trees are transfigured men and women, or maybe transfigured Krebs, that the Krebs may be trees that walk, or that these trees and the Krebs may bear the same relation to each other as do the caterpillar and the butterfly—men's ingenuity, and men's dreaming, make reasons for everything, as bees make honey, or trees make fruit. I only know that to me the place gives off a scent of hatred and pain. I am not welcome here. Nor are you."

The Lady Roseace shuddered with a primitive fear and disgust at these words, and allowed herself finally to be led back to her horse, and mounted by the Colonel.

They rode back over the plain to the Tower together; Roseace turned over many things in her mind. The sky was full of great full-bellied clouds, like flying clippers, like rolling drunkards, like racing steeds, fleeing before the wind. The Tower was above them, alternately in deep shadow, and bathed in brilliant golden light. It was not a shapely building, seen in this aspect. Its decaying ledges and terraces ran into one another, so that certain aspects appeared like a heap of rubble, or a rocky chaos, or an accidental heap. But under the sunlight, even from a distance, its inhabitants could be seen rushing zestfully about their business along couloirs and arcades, so that the huge mass pullulated with human life like an antheap. And the Lady Roseace, as she rode on, with the man of blood ambling quietly at her side, did not know if it was a longed-for home and haven, or voluntarily chosen In-pace, that is to say, dungeon. 🐚

"We are a Society for the Protection of Frederica," says Tony Watson.

"A Society for the Promotion of the Fortunes of Frederica," says Alan Melville.

They are meeting in Alexander Wedderburn's flat in Great Ormond Street, where, it had been agreed, she would be most comfortable and least likely to be immediately discovered. Alexander, surprised by various dawn telephone calls, has given up his bed to Frederica and her son, whom it is difficult to separate from her. His bed is large and comfortable. Frederica, after a fitful sleep, woke in it in one of his shirts and thought grimly of the irony of finally coming where she had for so many years hopelessly desired to be. She has even left two or three token smears of blood on Alexander's sheets, from the inflamed wound in her haunch. Alexander himself has passed a perfectly comfortable night in his spare bedroom, but he is apprehensive. The three friends have given him a colourful and alarming account of the vengeful and violent nature of Nigel, whom Tony, perhaps unfortunately, has labelled the Axeman.

Their discussion of the future is horribly complicated by the presence of Leo, who sits beside Frederica on Alexander's linen sofa and leans his body into hers, as though two could become one. Frederica looks ill. Tony says she must see a doctor. He is already thinking in terms of divorce: he thinks there must be a medical record of the wound, *now*, but cannot say so.

"It isn't too bad," says Frederica.

"It's bad enough," says Tony. "I can see you are in pain."

Alexander pours coffee for everyone from his blue coffee-pot. He remembers pouring coffee for Daniel Orton from this pot on his arrival in London after his flight from Blesford. He thinks: I am a person to whom people persist in coming for help, despite the fact that I am not helpful, I am not useful, I am not kind and concerned.

It is Hugh Pink who says directly to Frederica, "What do you want to do?"

Frederica puts an arm round Leo's head, an embrace which also half-muffles his ears.

"I can't go back. That's certain and might as well be said."

Leo's lips tighten. He does not speak.

"I need a place to be quiet, and think. I need work. I must be independent."

Everyone looks at Leo.

"We shall have to think it out step by step," says Frederica. "I need somewhere now where I can be with Leo. Later—Leo must think—"

"I do think," says Leo. "I want to come. You want me to come, you do. I know you do. You do want me to come."

"*Of course I do,*" says Frederica. "Only—"

She thinks of his pony, his settled journeys from kitchen and paddock, his little world. She thinks of starting her "career" with a small and anxious boy to look after.

"Only—" repeats Leo, his face quivering.

"Only nothing. We'll find somewhere. Something."

Alexander says, "I have an idea. It might even be a very good idea. What about Thomas Poole? He is living by himself—well, by himself with his children—in the Bloomsbury flat I used to lodge in. His wife left him. She went off with the actor, Paul Greenaway, who was Van Gogh in my play. He has two teenage boys and a girl who is about twelve, and a little boy, Simon, who is eight, who is bigger than Leo. He runs the Crabb Robinson Institute for Adult Education—he could almost certainly find some classes for Frederica to teach—it's a way of making part-time money that many women find helpful—he's got space in that huge flat—he might help out. No one would think of looking for anyone there."

"I liked him." Frederica remembers Poole, a colleague of Alexander and her father at Blesford Ride School. "He was good as Spenser in your play." Both Frederica and Alexander remember, and do not mention, Thomas Poole's affair with the beautiful Anthea Warburton, herself then, like Frederica, only a schoolgirl, which had ended in pregnancy, abortion, and grief. The grief, Frederica remembers, had seemed to be more Thomas Poole's. But appearances can be deceptive.

"If part-time teaching is a good thing," says Alan Melville, "I can find you a few hours immediately at the Samuel Palmer School. Now the artists have a degree course, they have to study things other than art, and we teach them literature. It's quite interesting."

"And I could ask Rupert Parrott about proof-reading and writing reports on books," says Hugh. "It's dog's-bodying, but it can be done at home. It's a way in, to that world."

"And there's Wilkie's television game," says Tony. "And you could try to get some reviewing. That isn't easy, but you could do it—"

"Work," says Frederica, "I need *work*."

"And then," says Tony. "We can think out the rest. What you will do. In the long run."

"We can," says Frederica.

Alexander, Frederica and Leo arrive at Thomas Poole's flat. This is a large, Edwardian mansion flat in Bloomsbury, on the sixth floor. Alexander lodged here in the late fifties when he was working on *The Yellow Chair.* Poole's wife, Elinor, left suddenly in 1961 to join Paul Greenaway, who was playing in a revival of *Pygmalion* in New York. The Pooles' four children, Chris, Jonathan, Lizzie and Simon were then fourteen, twelve, nine and five. They are now seventeen, fifteen, twelve and eight. The two elder boys are at Blesford Ride, where Alexander and Thomas met as teachers under Frederica's father. Alexander still thinks of them as little boys, but Chris is already working for university entrance. He asks after them as Poole shows them into his living-room, which was once Alexander's bedroom. It has a big, corner bay-window, out of which can be seen, like a rocket landed from another world, the discs, dishes, turrets and antennae sprouting from the column of the new Post Office Tower.

It is not possible to discuss Frederica's future in front of Leo, and it is still impossible, it seems, to detach Leo from Frederica's side. He sits beside her on a pale Swedish sofa and twists his hand into the fold of her skirt. A young Austrian woman appears, Waltraut Röhde, with brown curls, a sweet petal face and weightless bird-bones. Her smile is confidently shy. She tells them Lizzie is swimming, and Simon is in his room. She tells Leo she is bringing tea and chocolate torte. "Torte?" says Leo. "Keck," says Waltraut. "Cake. I made it. It is good."

Frederica looks round her. The walls are lined with books. She gives a little sigh. Thomas asks after her father; Frederica says she has not heard from him; Alexander says he has had several communications, because of the Steerforth Committee. "He is in his element," says Alexander. "He has his grandchildren, his house on the moors, his evening classes. We were all afraid for him, when his occupation was gone. And he is in his element."

Waltraut returns with a tray of teacups, and again with the chocolate torte. The chocolate torte attracts Simon Poole, who is a leggy boy with a delicate neck and shining straight brown hair flopping over his brow. He is shy, but courteous, and greets everyone. Waltraut tells Leo that Simon wishes to show him his railway. Simon agrees to this in a friendly mutter. Waltraut, whose English is more resourceful than her accent might suggest, tells Leo it has three separate tracks, a turntable, two stations and a Pullman coach. Simon says, "I'm making a new points system." Maybe because both Waltraut and Simon are so patently gentle and harmless, maybe because he is tired of gripping, maybe because the chocolate has soothed his brain, Leo allows himself to be led away. Frederica finds her hands are shaking. She tells the two friends in a rush that she can't talk in front of Leo, that she can't ever go back to Leo's father, that she must have work, she must start her life again, that she cannot think what should happen to Leo. "I can't go back, I can't keep him, I can't send him back. *I can't think,*" says Frederica to Thomas and Alexander, who look at her with concern and affection.

Thomas proposes, as Alexander had hoped, that Frederica should for the time being come to live in the flat. There is room, at least whilst the big boys are away at school. He, Waltraut and Frederica can look after Lizzie and Simon and Leo, and also do their own work. He can, in fact, offer her at least one evening class at the Crabb Robinson Institute, since one of his teachers is having a difficult pregnancy and has been ordered to rest. It is on "The Development of the Novel Form" or something like that. "I think I know you well enough to know you could make a go of it," says Thomas Poole, adding, perhaps unfortunately, "It must run in the blood, I should think."

"I always said I would never teach," says Frederica.

"We all said that," says Alexander.

"It is only a suggestion," says Poole.

Frederica looks round at the books.

"No," she says, "I'm not turning it down. I feel like Simon and Leo with that chocolate cake. Greed. Pure greed."

But her face, when she says that, does not, Alexander thinks, have quite the old rapacity.

Thomas asks Alexander how his work on the Steerforth Committee is going. Alexander says that he is absorbed by it and that everyone else appears to feel the same. They are worried that if there is a change of government at the Election, now imminent, they might be disbanded. He finds it interesting, he says, partly because he likes to watch the group at work as a group—the formation of alliances and conflicts, the little eddies of passion and incomprehension. The committee is very thorough: he has visited, or will visit, schools in villages and city centres, prosperous suburbs and agricultural fens, schools for infants and schools for teenagers. Anyone's idea of teaching and learning, he says, looking for confirmation at Poole's thoughtful face and Frederica's drawn one, comes from his own early experience of being taught. "And I suppose we all thought life was somewhere else, not in the classroom, that was the essence of it." He remembers, he summons up, a pervasive smell of trapped boredom, of brown linoleum and dusty windows, of slow, slow-ticking clocks and scratches and splutters of intransigent ink. And within this sea of brown air and chalky ennui a few moments of vision: a theorem coming out just so, a chorus ending from Euripides, Hamlet saying "Words, words, words." He can still catch that feeling, he says, on the visits to secondary schools. But in the primary schools there has been nothing less than an explosion of a *new* sense of what children are and can do. He has a sense sometimes, he says, that he and his fellows are like Alice, travelling in a brighter world Underground or through the Looking Glass. He has seen such things—such brilliant paper forests hung with poems and painted birds, such cardboard towers, such purposive hurrying and constructing and experimenting . . . He has talked to the experts in language acquisition and learning psychology on the committee and now knows that small children are miracle-workers of sentence-construction *ex nihilo,* and that once we understand this we need not drill, or force . . .

"It is all very exciting, certainly," says Thomas. "But there may be sufferers for all this ferment of activity. Simon, for instance, my own son, Simon. I think he's a natural quiet boy in a corner. But they are always saying he doesn't *relate* to other children . . ."

"He seems a bright boy, to me," says Alexander guardedly.

"I think so. But maybe he is emotionally disturbed, more than I think. I've tried to compensate for his mother's absence—"

Alexander's crest falls. He is almost sure that Simon, Simon Vincent Poole, is his son, and not Thomas Poole's son. Simon's mother, Elinor, was also almost sure, and took some pleasure, at the time of Simon's birth, in explaining to Alexander the exact degree of her almost-certainty. Since then, Simon's existence has been a constant preoccupation of Alexander's. When Simon was very small, and Elinor was still at home with the children, Alexander experienced him as a threatening problem, an extension of Elinor's emotional raids on his peace, which were alternately seductive and more or less sneering. He feared for his friendship with Thomas, which mattered to him, and which he had managed to sustain. Then, after Elinor's departure, he had had a bad few months *thinking,* as a moral conundrum, about Simon's hypothetical position, with a father who was not his father, and a mother departed. He had not experienced any wish to get to know Simon. He did not like small children. Simon was in a family, with his own siblings (or half-siblings) and a settled existence. Any claim of Alexander's was in a sense ludicrous, since it was a claim based on a moment of pleasure and the accident of genes. If genes were an accident. He avoided meeting Simon.

The major problem was Thomas. Alexander has not the slightest idea whether Thomas Poole knows, or suspects, any of this difficult history. He does not see how Thomas can know, and continue his amiable trust in Alexander. He does not see how he cannot know, given Elinor's fits of emotional teasing and taunting, which appear to be part of her nature. He thinks that if Thomas *did* suspect that Simon was Alexander's son, his present behaviour would be exactly as it is, if he could sustain it. And so every conversation between the two friends is ambiguous, for Thomas either is, or is not, partly trying to needle and wound Alexander with his obsessive accounts of Simon's problems and his assertions of his, Thomas's, Simon's father's, single-handed and single-minded care for the boy.

Things have taken another turn since the Steerforth Committee began to sit. For Alexander is now able to imagine eight-year-old boys. He has seen what they write, he has discussed what they feel and know. He would like to speak to Simon. And dare not. Sex is a short thing, thinks Alexander, looking at Frederica, whom he once desired, who once desired him, and its consequences are long.

Leo and Simon come back into the room.

"We are going to stay here for a bit," Frederica tells Leo. "With Waltraut and Simon. Will that be all right?"

"I think so," says Leo.

Alexander looks at Simon. His nose has no real form yet, but his mouth, his mouth surely . . . Thomas Poole puts an arm round the boy and draws him close.

"OK, Simon?" says Thomas.

Simon rests his brow on Thomas's shoulder.

"OK," says Simon. "I don't mind."

Much later that evening, Thomas Poole and Frederica sit together, on either side of the hearth. Poole remembers the Frederica of the play, awkward, incandescent, full of ambition. He has made an appointment for her to see his doctor, and cannot bear to see her so damaged. He says none of this. He says, "I like your Leo."

Frederica frowns and gulps.

"So do I. He is . . . I would have left him. But he came, he *would come*—"

"If you had left him, you would have gone back?"

"Would I? I suppose I would. It's like still being attached by a rope, by a cord, that stretches for ever. I can't bear to go back. Not only because—because things have gone wrong. Because I shouldn't have gone there." She looks round. "There's a room that's called the library, but there isn't a book in the house that anyone *reads,* except children's books, of course."

"Why did you go there?" asks Thomas, quietly, neutrally.

Frederica looks round at the books.

"It's like my parents' home here, the same things matter. And I wanted to get out of that, then. When Alexander was talking about his education, that was how I remember my childhood—*brown air,* he said, that's how it felt, stifling. I thought people were *really living* somewhere else, not just doing everything at second hand. Well, that was part of the reason. There was Stephanie. She made all the past, all my world—a way into death. And then there was Nigel. He *was* more alive than—nice, clever, second-hand Cambridge people. I thought he was the opposite of everything—so *faded,* so—so *discussy* and not *doing*—but he wasn't really. I was a total fool. It would be simply a ghastly lesson, if it wasn't for Leo."

"A child needs his mother," says Thomas Poole. "Conventional wisdom. But true, as I know to my cost."

Frederica says, "There, he has everything. He has two devoted aunts and a kind of super-nanny, he has a pony, and a house with a moat, and stables, and an orchard and the earth—don't tell me all these are simply material things, for they aren't, he loves them, he belongs there—I don't, I only love them out of the glamour they have because they *aren't* what I am or want—but he—I ought not to take him away."

"You didn't, as I understand it. He came."

"How can he know *anything* about how we should have to live, how can he make any sort of anything anyone can call a *decision*—he just *came*—he probably supposes if we're together we shall go back to-gether—"

"He may suppose that. Has he said that?"

Frederica considers. "No. But children don't say what they really think, almost ever, do they? They can't say what they hope, in case it's gone, like a flash, if anyone truly says no."

"Nevertheless, he is a clever boy, and he came. And children need their mother."

"Nigel might let *me* go without too much terrible fighting. I don't know anything about divorce; I'll think that out next. But he'll never let *him* go, and he'll be right not to, a child needs two parents, and Nigel loves Leo—"

"Then, in time, a *modus vivendi*—"

"I don't think so. He's like my father. An absolute master of the will. No, he won't let me go and see Leo at all, I know that, inside myself. I don't want to *use* Leo, in a battle of wills—"

"Nothing you have said leads me to suppose you have any idea of the sort. You love Leo. Leo came. Take it gently. Your instinct was right. A boy needs his mother. I don't know why Elinor left as she did. That is, I can see she was in love, and all that sort of thing, and perhaps she wanted a different sort of life, that's understandable, too. But to leave like that—to go out one evening—when I was teaching—and leave a note with the baby-sitter—and simply never—never voluntarily—speak to any of us again. She took *nothing*, not a photograph, not any of their writing. Can you understand that?"

"In a way. It may have been the only way. To be able to go at all."

"But she cannot have imagined—or let herself imagine—them, the next morning—in a month—in a year—"

Thomas Poole is full of passion. He is reliving the next morning, the next month, the next year.

Frederica says, "She can't have permitted herself to imagine—"

Thomas says, "A child needs—"

Frederica begins to weep, hoarsely, desperately, racked by great sobs. Thomas puts an arm round her. The door opens. It is Leo. He looks at Thomas to see if Thomas is responsible for the tears, works out that he is not, and launches himself, like a bolt, into Frederica's lap.

"Don't," he says. "Don't, don't, don't."

Frederica obediently dries her tears.

"I don't know what you'll make of him," Hugh Pink says, more than once, on the way to see Rupert Parrott at Bowers and Eden. "He isn't quite what he appears to be."

Frederica is getting into her stride. Bookshops. Vegetable litter from the market. Election posters. London. Life. She is wearing a kind of shift dress in a sacking-like cloth, with a black bow at the neck, cut just above the knee. I shall have to get my hair cut, she thinks, looking keenly at the passers-by. Will it work, has it enough weight, my hair?

"You keep saying that," she says to Hugh. "As though he's a magician. Or shady."

"No, no, it's nothing like that. On the contrary. It's just that he appears to be so *typical* of something, and isn't quite. You'll see."

It is Hugh's day off supply teaching. He is giving it up to take Frederica to meet Parrott, who might give her some manuscripts to read. This is kind of him, as he needs that sort of work himself, in order to write his poetry. He has become obsessed with Orpheus, is reading

Rilke, is afraid that this is banal and is overwhelmed by the vision of the dead head still singing. He tries lines in his own head:

> The dead
> Head
>   Eddies, is held
> Briefly by a crag, the blood
> Reddens the river briefly
> Becomes watery, water
>   The song
>   Runs on
> The dead eyes
> Are wet with the water

"Do *you* like him?" says Frederica.

"Parrott? Oh yes. Very much." He thinks. "He's religious. That's what you don't see at first."

"Is that bad?"

"No, why should it be? Just surprising." The poem is no good, it sounds *soft,* it should be cut and clear but running on.

Number 2, Elderflower Court, does not feel quite safe on its joists. It is a tall, thin house, which is in fact joined back to back to other tall, thin houses, by makeshift doors in walls and bridging corridors across shafts of dim courtyard. The entrance hall is minute, and contains a school-mistressy table in oak and two armchairs with dusty padded seats and oak arms. There is a rather faded display of books, front-on, on a shelf in the wall. *Within God Without God* and *Our Passions Christ's Passion* by Adelbert Holly. *Within God Without God* has a kind of Op Art black-and-white spiral, swirling into a vanishing black hole which is also the O in Holly. *Our Passions Christ's Passion* has the same spiral, in blood-red and a flaming orange. They are elegant, and evidence of energy.

Inside a cubby-hole opening out of the entrance hall is a lift, with a creaking iron trellis door, and a jerking, whining, ramshackle method of hoisting itself. Frederica and Hugh go up to the fourth floor and, almost ducking, travel round three sides of an uneven rectangle in dusty corridors painted bottle-green. Parrott's office is in what must once, in Dickensian times, have been a servant's attic. It has a sloping mansard ceiling and is painted in a colour resembling tobacco-stained onion skin. The floor is heaped with dusty books; there are shelves of dusty books; there is a desk piled high with dusty paper, on which are two photographs, a posed bride in veil and train, and a row of smiling babies in suits with frilly collars.

Rupert Parrott is a small man, with a lot of tight dark reddish-blond curls, which are kept from being a mop only by rigorous training with scissors. His face and body show the same effects of discipline. He should be plump-cheeked but is not, quite. He should have a double chin, but it is barely perceptible, and the little paunch which should be beneath his lilac shirt and his pink-and-silver-spotted purple tie is also not really there, though the eye stubbornly tries to sketch it in. His mouth is, as Hugh has told Frederica, round, a little puckered, with soft lips drawn in. His eyes are blue and his nose nondescript. His voice has a public school drawl, which, with the impression of now-you-see-it-now-you-don't fleshiness, should make him seem slow. But the overall impression is of quickness, of energy, of an ease perturbed only by his own need to get going.

Hugh introduces Frederica and explains her urgent need for work. Parrott asks her what her interests are, and she replies that they are rather narrowly literary, but that she is quick at learning and interested in everything, really. Parrott says that they pay a number of readers, almost all of them women, to work their way through the slush heap—that is, the unsolicited manuscripts that arrive in dozens every morning.

"We pay them, I say, but *not very much,*" says Parrott, looking at Frederica, "because we haven't got very much, and because there are so many intelligent women sitting at home with children, desperate for bits of work to do, you see."

"I see," says Frederica.

"The firm in the past," says Parrott, "has concentrated on politics, standard thirties left-wing politics, Fabian analyses of leisure, that sort of thing. It was me that persuaded Gimson Bowers that religion could be a big seller. He's an old-style socialist, takes a simplistic line, religion's not true, it's nonsense, why bother. I said I thought there *was* an interest, a definite interest—the established Church is in a sort of ferment, look at *Honest to God,* a quiet SCM pamphlet by a quiet bishop, a national bestseller, and *what a furore.* And there's much more extreme stuff than the Bishop of Woolwich, much sexier, *literally*— sex and religion, both in the Church, and amongst all these new youth cultures. Death of God theology, exciting stuff. Charisma.

Studies of charisma. The breaking up of our moral structure as we know it. All the trouble about Christine Keeler and Profumo and the Establishment—it's all cracking up, the *conventional visions* we were happy to live by even if we didn't believe them. And now it isn't possible, and people want to read about it all, they want to know what to think. We're moving into a period of moral ferment, moral re-alignment, fruitful chaos, people want to know what's going on.

"I thought of a series called something like *Touchstones of Modern Thought*. I really need a word like 'beacons,' but you can't call anything beacons because it sounds like primary-school readers. And perhaps beacons are out of date anyway; they sound Napoleonic and we want to be in the white heat of spiritual energy, so to speak. Torches? Spearheads?"

"Arrows of desire," says Hugh. "Or warheads."

"Burning issues," says Frederica.

Rupert Parrott considers this.

"*Al*most," he says. "Not bad. Burning Issues in Religion. Burning Issues in Psychiatry. Burning Issues in Sociology. It isn't quite right."

"Burning Issues in Witchcraft," says Hugh.

"Don't mock. Witchcraft is a real issue. It's on the increase. There's a lot of interest in *wicca,* the Old Religion. I don't share it—I'm tied up in Christianity—but readers do. They write in. It's a serious interest."

He hands Frederica a book with a cover depicting a cross-legged prisoner in a padded cell in a dunce's cap.

LANGUAGE OUR STRAITJACKET
BY ELVET GANDER

Frederica opens the book. All the pages are blank.

"It's a dummy," says Parrott. "Though he'd like that joke, that you opened up his anti-language book and found pure, pristine white space. He's another of my discoveries. I discovered Canon Holly, I personally discovered Canon Holly, and I had the idea of writing to Gander, after I heard him talk at the Round House on the anti-psychiatry movement—very powerful stuff, the idea that it is the psychiatric institutions themselves that are disabling, that if we label people as schizophrenic and psychotic we *reify* these descriptions, we make people into madmen by calling them that. We published his first book, *Am I My Brother's Keeper?,* you may have seen that, it had a considerable *succès d'estime* and sold a lot of copies."

Frederica studies the jacket. Elvet Gander is apparently a gnome-like person with deepset eyes, a long, thin nose, a curly mouth, not much hair and a deep suntan, though that may be the effect of the photograph, in which he is cut off at the waist, but is clearly sitting in a high, winged, throne-like chair, although he is wearing an open-necked shirt. The jacket copy says that *Language Our Straitjacket* is part of a whole new intellectual movement which questions the constricting forms of our civilisation, and asks if they may even be a function of our language, of the printed word more especially. It quotes Marshall McLuhan:

"A state of collective awareness may have been the preverbal condition of men. Language as the technology of human extension, whose powers of division and separation we know so well, may have been the 'Tower of Babel' by which men sought to scale the highest heavens. Today computers hold out the promise of a means of instant translation of any code or language into any other code or language. The computer, in short, promises by technology a Pentecostal condition of universal understanding and unity.

"Elvet Gander," the jacket copy concludes, "accepts McLuhan's premise that language divides, but questions his hope that Pentecostal understanding will be found in technology, or primarily in technology. He has his own daring ideas about how such understanding may be re-created and renewed."

"Interesting," says Frederica.

"You must go and hear him speak," says Parrott. "He is charismatic. Truly charismatic."

"Charismatic" is a word he savours.

He finds four manuscripts from the slush heap for Frederica to read, all novels, one neatly typed with large spacing, one messily typed and dog-eared, one a single-spaced carbon and one handwritten. The neatly typed one is *The Voyage of the Silver Ship* by Richmond Bly. The dog-eared one is *Mad Dogs and Englishmen* by Bob Gully. The carbon is *A Thing Apart* by Margot Cherry. The handwritten one is *Daily Bread* by Phyllis K. Pratt and has an attached letter. "I am sorry to send you my book in a handwritten state. There is in fact a typewriter in this house, but it is not in a state that will produce anything more legible than my manuscript. I hope you will be able to read it, and look forward to hearing your opinion of it."

Frederica agrees to write brief reports on all these works. As they go home, Hugh says, "It would be better, really, to *write* a novel, Frederica."

150

She looks stricken.

"I know. I don't have any ideas. I've been educated out of it. Have you noticed people who write novels never studied English literature? They did philosophy, or classics, or history . . . or nothing. Even thinking of it brings on a kind of panic. The only kind of novel I could write is the sensitive-student-at-Cambridge kind of stuff I know enough to flinch at and *despise*—"

(Oh, but the bliss of talking about books, all the same, and not about houses, and things, and possessions.)

She is limping along at great speed. Her limp is more pronounced. Hugh says, "Does your leg hurt?"

"Yes. It won't heal. Thomas is sending me to his doctor."

Frederica sits down in the evening in the Bloomsbury flat—in fact, at the same desk at which Alexander wrote *The Yellow Chair*—and begins work on these manuscripts. She reads. She cooks supper with Thomas Poole, and she, Lizzie, Leo, Simon and Thomas eat stuffed pancakes and fruit salad (Waltraut is at her English class). Leo is more relaxed: Simon is a kindly boy, and has taken him under his wing. Alan Melville telephones: tomorrow he has arranged an interview for her at the Samuel Palmer School. There are two part-time courses to be taught, on metaphysical poetry and the nineteenth-century novel.

Frederica takes pleasure in writing her reports on the four novels.

The Voyage of the Silver Ship by Richmond Bly

The plot of this work, if it can be called a plot, concerns the determination of a group of misfits and magical beings to rediscover the land of their origins, Eled-Durad-Or, which is believed to be the home of ancestral beings able to live for ever, to communicate without speech, and to change the material world by the power of thought. The world in which the group live (Bonodor) has been enslaved by a dark Enchanter (Miltan) who has covered it with disfiguring mills (nineteenth-century mills, to judge from the architecture), tall chimneys and fastnesses with drawbridges, fire-throwers etc. operated by grinding technology. On the outskirts of the industrial wasteland are a few stunted woods and some sooty rivers. The friends are summoned by mysterious messages to a gathering at a hill of dust and ashes. They are mostly known by descriptions: the Tattered Man, the Hairy One, the Brownie, the Fool, the Half-Man (who is also half-goat), the Stone Spirit and Frog. This last is suspected throughout of being an emissary of the Enemy but turns out to be a sacrificial hero, whose grisly death in a stone doorway prevents the door from closing and makes it possible for the rest of the crew to enter Eled-Durad-Or.

It is hard to differentiate between these beings, since they all speak in the same high style and find much—possibly most—of their experience inept for putting into words, e.g.:

"Then was the Fool carried away into another sphere, where his spirit moved amongst the dark roots of the world like a blind being, and his whole body communicated with unutterable powers, so that he was nigh fainting because of his extreme apprehensions."

Many "adventures" are embarked on. There is a good scene where the crew are being hunted across an almost non-visionary i.e. almost concrete moorland by a pack of black dogs with red glittering eyes, and there is also a good scene, when, having managed to find the mooring place of the Silver Ship, they embark on the Utmost Sea and are becalmed amongst ice-floes and are attacked by a pod, or posse, or herd of dangerous narwhals which advance in gleaming and serried ranks, waving their horny lances. Mr. Bly is possibly more at home with herds of inarticulate creatures than with thinking human, or semi-human beings, or Frogs. There is little, even no, sexual interest in this tale. All the women (or female spirits) are inhabitants of, or visitants from, Eled-Durad-Or and are tall silvery figures with very beautiful belts who raise their arms frequently in interesting gestures I feel resemble the Dalcroze movements executed by Ursula and Gudrun by the lakeside in *Women in Love*. But nothing ever really *happens* to any of these characters. Every threat, even the great Borg on the Ice Mountain, dissolves into a visionary experience of the ineffable, and causes most of the characters to make long rhapsodic speeches. These could almost, but not quite, be scanned as blank verse, which makes them unpleasant to the inner ear.

This story obviously has ambitions to be like Tolkien—because of genuine admiration, I should guess, and not out of a desire to emulate his sales. But it entirely lacks his narrative urgency, physical weather, real earth. It also lacks his merry humour, which might be thought to be a good thing, but is not, I assure you. The story also has all sorts of echoes (unintentional, I imagine) of *The Wizard of Oz*. It is a curiously vacant work, whose driving force appears paradoxically to be the desire to create and people an imaginary world.

Mad Dogs and Englishmen by Bob Gully

I cannot believe there is not already a book with this title. If I were asked to imagine one, I might imagine this one, in a gloomy mood. It is, I suppose, a picaresque narrative and describes the adventures of a sour-tempered Englishman in his twenties called Johnny Hipp who is hitch-hiking his way round the south of France. He is being relentlessly pursued by an unfortunate girl from his home town (Preston, Lancs.) called Deanna, who has hairy legs, spots, mild halitosis, dirndl skirts, greasy hair and a wart on her chin which is the object of some would-be Joycean paragraphs of execration. From Deanna's handbag Johnny Hipp occasionally steals wads of currency. ("She does nothing to earn it and gets no pleasure from it and doesn't need it, whereas I am in urgent need, and know how to get pleasure from life with only a minimum of dough.") These thefts appear to be his only means of support, since he appears never to have worked, or done anything at all except bumming around and autostop. He is fed and housed by beautiful French and Italian women who stop their sports cars and take him up, apparently deducing from his unsavoury external appearance the rigour and dimensions of his "todger." They come in several colours, "silky raven," "shimmering platinum," "flaming *rousse,*" but have identical globular breasts, honey-pots, and sweet-smelling pubic hair. He tends to leave them because he has seen an even better one out of the window of a restaurant or Ferrari waiting at a petrol station.

There is a lot of food in this novel—mountainous cassoulets, wonderfully glistening aïolis, "brandad de morrue" (sic), "boullabaise" (sic) and so on. The meals are only a prelude to ravenous couplings, however, and the food is nothing beside the drink—mostly beer, oddly, considering the surrounding vineyards. But Johnny Hipp is also not averse to Pernod, Martini, white port, muscat, vin rosé (*faute de mieux*), cognac, armagnac, crème de menthe, Cointreau, Chartreuse and so on, all of which he regurgitates along with the food wherever convenient (or inconvenient). I have not done a page count but I think it is a damned close-run thing between copulation and vomiting. Any satire or irony is buried too deep beneath a sickly affection for Johnny Hipp and his stamina to be discerned. There is little dialogue. ("There was no need for mere words. I threw myself upon her and she opened wetly and the dialogue of bodies, disrupted by some mumblings and gruntings from my out-of-synch gut, began its rhythmic wallop.")

Johnny Hipp's own appearance is probably, to a dispassionate outsider, at least as repulsive as Deanna's is to him. He spends a lot of time lingering on the smells of his crotch, armpits and toenails, on his dirt-encrusted underwear, his filthy shoes, his stained shirts, his beard-stubble, as though these were all evidence of some goat-like virility mixed with honesty and lack of affectation which attract women as honey attracts flies (one of his own comparisons).

His geography is insecure. He would need a jet plane to get from Cannes to Nîmes in the time he allots to the journey; Vence is nowhere near Montpellier as far as I can remember, and much of the Camargue is not open to road-users.

The book, as you might suppose, ends exactly where it began, with Johnny Hipp, blear-eyed, hungover, belching and full of self-admiration waiting outside the gate of Aigues-Mortes (as he is when the book opens) to be picked up. Anyone in his senses (or her senses) would drive past quickly.

A Thing Apart by Margot Cherry

This novel is the history of a sensitive young working-class girl called Laura (she would not be called Laura if she were working class, and I suspect she is anyway lower-middle-class which everyone finds the least interesting origin, though it is what very many, perhaps most? people are). Laura gets a scholarship to Oxford to read English, and falls in love with a young man called Sebastian, who does not fall in love with her, and may even be in love with his best friend Hugh; they were at school together, in the army together, and are now very brilliantly reading English together, and acting at OUDS.

Laura spends several chapters agonising over whether or not to go to bed with various young men, and spends various *nuits blanches* with one or another. Her virginity is finally taken, not by Sebastian, but by Hugh (who is naturally smaller, stronger, more muscular, less dreamy than his willowy friend). We have here the beginning of a faintly interesting triangular relationship, of which Margot Cherry makes nothing, as she is interested in diagnosing who is "in love" with whom. Some narrative satisfaction might be gained if we were told whether Laura married Sebastian or Hugh or no one or someone else altogether, but we are not told: Oxford days come to an end, and everything is vague and shadowy and in the air.

This is the sort of novel every young woman at university reading English imagines she can write—though most ["most of us" Frederica writes honestly, and then crosses it out in the interest of impartiality and objectivity]—most don't have the stamina or determination actually to write all these hundreds of pages. There is something peculiarly touching about the details of daily life that Margot Cherry includes, even if her characters are stereotypes and sticks. She describes the bathtubs in Somerville College, water running down her arms when she punts, college gardens, electric kettles, coffee bars, the Bodleian library, as though these things had never been seen or described before. This has a curious effect on the reader, for they have in fact been described *so often* that they have a kind of banal mythic force, into which Margot Cherry's pale narrative drives suckers, and soaks up a kind of energy. This applies also, to a certain extent, to the emotions of the books, the empty *longing,* the clumsy negotiation of sexual decisions. I think on balance Margot Cherry can write, and might write well if she had something to write about.

And why is not Oxford, and young love, and Shakespeare *something,* I do ask myself. Because it fills me with a kind of nausea I suspect would not be peculiar to me. It is déjà vu in its youth and newness. It is a reason why sensitive young women should refrain from writing sensitive young novels about Oxbridge. All the same, having done these pages, she might do something else?

Daily Bread by Phyllis K. Pratt

This novel opens with a woman making bread. It describes the action of the living yeast, and the dough, which is beaten down and swells up. It describes the patience of waiting for dough to prove, it describes buns and loaves and hot cross buns in the oven.

The heroine of this book is a clergyman's wife in a Warwickshire village, who has thirteen children and is obsessed with bread-making. Her name is Peggy Crump. Her husband is the Reverend Evelyn Crump. She met him when they were both volunteers in refugee camps, and was converted to Christianity by the strength of his faith and its obvious useful life in the world. He was not advanced as he hoped—he is very irascible when not labouring in extreme situations—and they are now living in genteel near poverty in a backwater. Various incidents (a death from leukaemia, a pompous bishop, capital punishment, a vision of "*delightful emptiness*") cause Peggy to lose her faith in God, but Evelyn forces her to continue "as if" and indeed with all those children she has little choice.

The drama of this novel—and although it appears at first to be a storm in a teacup, it is a real drama—occurs when Evelyn himself has a dark night of the soul, and has a vision of the devil, who tells him a) that he himself, the devil, is a fiction and b) that Christianity is also a fiction, and that Evelyn must learn to live without fiction, in the world of death.

This vision reduces Evelyn to extremes of pessimism, sleep-walking, self-starvation, histrionic riddling sermonising and deliberately incompetent suicide bids. Peggy tells him, as he told her, that he should live "as if" and when he tells her that a consecrated priest can do no such thing, although it is quite all right for a housewife to do so, she attacks him, after premeditation, with a bread-knife, and there is a great deal of blood everywhere.

This novel is not a tragedy, and not a melodrama, but a peculiarly poised black comedy. There is a most wonderful comic jumble sale (an image of cosmic and social disorder and pointlessness), some sanely and rigorously observed teenagers, a sweet curate, a pugnacious donkey, a menacing baby and all sorts of other good things.

The book turns on the image of bread, in a completely satisfying way. The bulging life and expanding energy of Peggy's bread is contrasted with the communion wafer which is no longer the Host for the body of the Lord. It is almost (but not quite, not *tidily*, symbolic) as though the yeast cells were the true God, sustaining everything. The metaphor threads its way through the text, bobbing up in cucumber sandwiches, brioches at the bishop's palace, mould and penicillin.

I think you should read this book and consider it carefully. It made me laugh and it made my hair stand on end. Also, it made me feel that the English language can *say* things, deep, funny, difficult things—something in which I was beginning to lose faith after reading the other three books.

When Frederica has finished writing these reports she feels a kind of complicated glee. It has many components: she has enjoyed the act of writing, of watching language run black out of the end of her pen; this has in turn made her feel that she is herself again, and has made her body real to her, because her mind is alive. And then there is the idea of money, however little, money earned, which is independence. And then there is pleasure, not only in Phyllis K. Pratt's handwritten bombshell, but also in the industry of Bly, Gully and Cherry, who have felt writing to be important enough to sit down day after day or night after night and invent imagined worlds as though it mattered. And this pleasure in turn makes her feel more tolerant towards Olive and Rosalind and Pippy Mammott, now they are no longer the bounds of her world—because of them she recognises Peggy Crump's imprisonment with a strong savouring, whereas Margot Cherry's Laura seems infinitely far away.

Thomas Poole knocks at her door and tells her supper is ready. He has cooked it: it is gammon and spinach and béchamel. Frederica tries to describe to him her pleasure in writing the reports. She says, "I love having something to do I *can do.* And I love it that all these people have done all this work even if it's hopeless. Is that silly?"

"Oh no," says Poole. "Pleasure in use of energy, I know that so well. Like when a rather stolid boy at school would suddenly write twelve pages instead of one, and you saw his mind was *going.* It was enough."

"I must *work,*" says Frederica. "It kills you, unused energy, it turns against you."

She thinks of the yeast.

"I like to see you smiling," says Poole. He hesitates. "I am so glad you have come here. It seems odd, when I remember you—such a cross girl, such a wayward girl, such a puzzle to your father. And now a woman, with Leo, and here."

Frederica smiles with a little constraint, pleased and bothered by the word "woman."

They have a good supper together. They talk about Phyllis K. Pratt, and Elvet Gander, and about why sensitive young women should not write novels. They do not talk about Nigel. But soon they must.

Bill Potter is rewriting his lecture on *Mansfield Park.* He has been giving extra-mural classes on *Mansfield Park* now for thirty years, not every year, but most, and he always rewrites his lecture, partly out of courtesy to the new students, who deserve more than stale repetition, partly because his relations with this secret and sad text change constantly and slowly, like a man's relations with his own family. He is thinking about Sir Thomas Bertram, who paid insufficient attention to his daughters' moral upbringing, but is able to make a satisfactory substitute family from his wife's sister's son and daughters, the Prices. He thinks with love of his grandchildren who live with him.

Outside, the village is quiet. A car purrs in the distance, expands its roar, and does not pass, but stops. The door bell sounds. Bill supposes Winifred will answer, but she appears not to be there. It rings again, and he goes to open the door.

It takes him a moment to recognise his son-in-law, Nigel Reiver. He sees a stocky man in a scarlet polo neck and a tweed jacket over cavalry twill trousers. Nigel sees a gnome-like old man, with a few strands of flyaway grey-and-ginger hair and sharp, faded blue eyes.

"I want to speak to Frederica."

"Well, you've come to the wrong place. She isn't here."

"I think she is. I've come instead of using the telephone, because I worked out you'd say she wasn't there, or she might not want to speak to me. I have to speak to her."

"Young man, you have written yourself a story in your head that bears no relation to fact. I didn't know she wasn't with you until you just told me. I'm sorry she hasn't come here, if she's seen fit to go away, but she hasn't."

"I don't believe you," says Nigel. Bill sees he is what he thinks of as "all worked up." "I'm coming in, to look for her. She's got to talk to me. And I want Leo."

"I can't help you," says Bill. "And if I could, I wouldn't. What sort of a life are you making her lead?"

"A very comfortable life," says Nigel. "Would you mind getting out of the way? I'm coming in, to look for my wife and son."

"I don't tell lies," says Bill. "They aren't here."

He tries to shut the door. Nigel's face works. He pushes the door open with such force that Bill's head is crushed against the rough wall behind it. Bill, grazed, bleeding and dizzy, falls to his knees in the hall before Nigel, who immediately puts his arms round him, murmuring frantic and inarticulate apologies, touching the grazed scalp with horrified fingers. They stagger, in a kind of embrace, into the kitchen, where Nigel, curiously efficient, finds a clean tea-towel and begins to bathe his father-in-law's head.

Bill says, with quavering sharpness, "Look about you. Do you see any sign of them? Go through the house if you must, now you've forced your way in. You won't find them."

Nigel is indeed staring round the kitchen, almost *smelling,* it appears, for traces of the lost. He does make a dash into the hall, at this invitation, and Bill hears him crashing doors on the upper landings. Blood trickles into Bill's eyes. Nigel reappears, carrying a green, full-skirted dress.

"This is hers."

"It is. It's been here since she went off to be married. Cast-off. We've got a cupboardful. Think if you've seen her in it."

"I'll take it."

"As you please. Shouldn't think she wants to see it again."

"I'm sorry I hurt you."

"It's easy to be sorry after the event," says Bill, and stops short. It is a sentence often said to Bill by others. He looks more closely at Nigel, and dabs blood with a dirty handkerchief from his brows.

158

"No—use mine—it's clean," says Nigel. He sits down on a stool, at the corner of the table, next to Bill.

"She ran away in the night. With Leo. I hadn't been too nice to her. I'm going to be better. I get, I get carried away. *You know*," says Nigel, recognising that Bill, *mutatis mutandis,* does in a way, know. Bill does not reply. He dabs busily with Nigel's handkerchief.

"I was sure she'd have come up here. That's what women do. They go back to their mothers. I waited a bit—I was so furious, I felt I needed to calm down and think—I thought it out."

"Frederica doesn't do what 'most women' do."

"I don't know how to start finding her friends. I'll kill them. I'll kill them all—"

"She won't thank you for *that*."

"I love her. She knows I love her. And how can she have taken Leo? He was happy. He had a happy time. He'll be all bewildered and upset. Children need homes, and routines. He *belongs in my house.* She can't just take him from me, in the middle of the night, with no discussion, no warning, no message, no—"

"You don't appear to be very good at *discussion,*" says Bill.

Nigel glowers at him.

"I'll go now." He looks anxious. "Will you be all right? Should I stay till someone comes? Do you feel faint?"

"No," says Bill, who does feel faint. "I shall be very glad if you do go. Now, if you will."

"Will you let me know if you hear—if they are all right, if they need money or anything, if—"

"I will do as Frederica wishes," says Bill. "As you should know."

Marcus, coming home for lunch, sees a man outside his house arranging a green party-dress like a fainted woman in the back seat of a green Aston Martin. He watches it drive off, skilful but far too fast, back through the village.

The General Election finally comes on October 15th. Frederica and Thomas Poole watch the results together on the television, along with Hugh and Alan, who have no televisions, and Alexander, who has taken to dropping in more frequently since the arrival of Frederica and Leo. Poole himself is a literary man not naturally inclined to want a television in his house—he fears it as self-indulgence, he is puritanically inclined to regard it as a waste of time. But he has been talked into it by his children, who claim to be social pariahs at school because they cannot discuss *Batman* and *Top of the Pops*. Tony Watson is in Huyton for Harold Wilson's count; he is writing an in-depth analysis of the effects of television on elections, and is full of exasperated admiration for Wilson's ability to adjust his television appearances, his shape, his message, to what the opinion polls tell him. The election is very close, and it is not clear until the next afternoon that the Labour Party has in fact achieved an effective overall majority of five. The friends eat chilli con carne and drink a great deal of red wine. Frederica thinks often, but does not speak, of Olive and Rosalind and Pippy Mammott watching with bated breaths the fluctuations in the fate of "our people" as the balance sways. They are the enemy; the Conservative Government is somehow involved in sleaze and failure and ridicule, in the prancing of Christine Keeler and Mandy Rice-Davies, in a huge gap between public and private fronts, in deceit and humiliation. She is ready to like Wilson, suddenly seen at midnight waving his arms wildly, in the crowded hall at Huyton. He has trebled his majority. He kisses his wife for the cameras. Behind him can be seen the large, gleeful face of Owen Williams.

"He wanted to marry me," Frederica announces. "I wonder what would have happened if I—"

"I should think it would have been horrible," says Alan, placidly. "He's wedded to his politics, you'd have had to be a Hostess, you'd have hated it."

Hugh says, uncharacteristically sharply, "It was just Cambridge. Everybody felt they had to snap up somebody. A lot of misery was caused, a lot of silly misery. There were too few women, everyone was silly."

Frederica is vaguely hurt. Harold Wilson beams manically at the camera. It is at this point still quite possible that he has lost the election.

Alexander says, "If he wins, I wonder if he will disband my committee. I was beginning to think we were doing something useful. We have become, so to speak, bonded. We are a Group, I am interested. I want to go on. We're visiting primary schools all next week. Like Brobdingnagians. I'm learning things."

Nobody has any thoughts to offer on this. They separate in the small hours, mildly drunk, mildly contented. Thomas and Frederica see them out at the door of the flat, like a married couple. Thomas puts an arm round Frederica's shoulder. She does not break free, but does not respond to the gesture.

"Do you think Hugh Pink is in love with you?" Thomas asks Frederica.

"No," she says. "He was once, I think, but as he says, everyone was in love with everyone, especially women. We thought we were special and we were only scarce."

"Were you in love with him?"

"Oh no. I was in love with Raphael Faber. Or with the idea of Raphael Faber. The unattainable, you know, the teacher, the tabu, the monastic. I could *feel* a lot and nothing happened. It's far away."

"You've changed," says Thomas Poole. He thinks a moment, and then pulls her towards him and kisses the top of her hair, softly. He releases her.

"Good night. Sleep well."

"And you. Tomorrow we shall be in the new white-hot technological world. Or not."

They are.

On the steps of the Samuel Palmer School of Art and Craft, the word "portal" comes into Frederica's mind, seeming odd and bristling, as words do when they detach themselves and insist. The School does indeed have an imposing portal, which has a whole paragraph to itself in Pevsner's architectural guide to London. It is a long stone building which takes up the whole of one side of Lucy Square, which is next to Queen's Square beyond Russell Square and Southampton Row. The front is adorned with bas-reliefs by Eric Gill and the portal, reached by a flight of wide, shallow steps, is set deep in a round stone arch, at either side of which stand Adam and Eve, life-size, also carved by Gill, both holding apples and both smiling as though the Fall were a matter of little or no consequence. The arch above them is composed of serried ranks of flying figures, though whether these are angels, genii or fairies is not wholly clear. The handles of the two heavy dark doors are brass castings of a sphinx and a mermaid, both with golden breasts rubbed bright by constant touching.

"Portal," says Frederica to Alan Melville. "This qualifies as a portal. It's a queer word, portal."

"'Beauty is momentary in the mind—/The fitful tracing of a portal;/But in the flesh it is immortal,'" says Alan, grasping the brass breast of the sphinx.

"I may have been thinking of Lady Chatterley quoting Swinburne," says Frederica. "She goes on about 'Pale beyond porch and portal' and how she has to go through them. Something to do with Proserpina coming up from the earth."

They are in the building, which is, and is not, like any teaching in-stitution. There are long corridors and staircases—all solid and stony, made to endure—and a faint whiff of the institutional smell of polish and disinfectant. But the corridors are also lined with paintings, bright abstracts, Pop portraits of singers and filmstars, Blake-like clouds of flying bodies, collages of masks. And the smell of disinfectant is drowned by the smells of the work itself—oil, turpentine, putty, hot metal. Alan is telling her about Liberal Studies.

"I always said I would never teach," says Frederica. "But it will be nice to be working with you."

The Head of Liberal Studies has a panelled office, with bright colour-spattered linen curtains (made by the textiles students). He offers Frederica coffee in a tomato-red cup (made by the ceramics students) and looks through her CV, which she and Thomas Poole have ex-pertly put together. He is a large and handsome man, with what Frederica's mother would have called a sweet face, bright blue eyes, great wings of groomed black-and-white-streaked hair, and a soft, smiling mouth. He is wearing a blue corduroy suit and a red knitted silk tie. Round the room, three deep, are paintings and prints with beautifully lettered verses and quotations underneath them, all of which Frederica sees are from Blake. An abstract of splashes: "Exu-berance is Beauty." A rather childlike face on a blue starry ground: "He whose face gives no light, shall never become a star." Trees, a huge collage: "A fool sees not the same tree that a wise man sees." An eye: "One thought fills immensity." "The tygers of wrath are wiser than the horses of instruction." There is also a large, Piranesi-derived etching, with the verse

> Such are Cathedron's golden Halls in the City of Golgonooza.
> And Los's Furnaces howl loud, living, self-moving, lamenting
> With fury and despair, and they stretch from South to North
> Thro' all the Four Points. Lo! The Labourers at the Furnaces
> Rintrah and Palambron, Theotormon and Bromion, loud lab'ring
> With the innumerable multitudes of Golgonooza round the Anvils of Death!

"Golgonooza" is a word that has always annoyed Frederica. It is infant-babble, not true language-forging. It is unintentionally comic. The Head of Liberal Studies murmurs "Impressive" as he reads the CV, and looks up to see her studying the varied images.

"I make Blake the centre of my teaching here. He is the greatest English poet and the greatest English painter. He draws the mind out of itself. The students find him inspirational. Over the years I have made this collection of their tributes to his genius—as you can see, the styles are diverse, but the source is One. I like to employ creative people. Do you write yourself, Miss Potter?"

(Frederica has decided to return to her maiden name.)

"No, I'm afraid not. Studying English literature knocks the desire out of you. But it might be different here—where everyone is making things."

"There is a special atmosphere. I try to write myself. I think if one is entrusted with the minds of creative people one should at least try to create oneself, don't you think?"

"Oh, yes."

"I have been inspired by the Prophetic Books."

Frederica, unguarded, begins, "I could never stomach the Prophetic Books because the language is ugly—whereas the Songs of Innocence—"

He smiles forgivingly. "I think you will find upon closer attention that the language does have a beauty all of its own, a peculiar beauty. A *free* beauty—free, as he said, of the monotonous Cadence—the *bondage*—the fetters of rhyme and blank verse. 'Poetry Fetter'd Fetters the Human Race.' You need an ear made new. It is visionary—the vision of Albion and the Druids as the foundation and source for the Hebrew religion—"

"It's an interesting myth," says Frederica, trying to read the dedication of a rather wistful water-colour of the invisible worm in the heart of the Rose.

"Or truth, or true myth," he says smilingly, as she deciphers the dedication.

"To Richmond Bly, who taught me to understand the infinite nature of Desire, with admiration and love from Marigold Topping."

Frederica whitens momentarily as her gleeful dissection of *The Voyage of the Silver Ship* rises in total recall to her mind. She swallows nervously. Richmond Bly does not notice. He is offering Frederica a year's part-time employment, on probation, and an office in which to see students and write lectures. Alan will take her to see it.

Up, up, up. The solid, shallow-stepped staircase hugs the wall of the Samuel Palmer School. It is wide—large objects are regularly carried up and down it. It has an elegant wrought-iron balustrade and its steps are worn in the centres, reminding Frederica of external processional staircases for monks. The staircase is dark, but at the top are the studios, roofed with glass, full of light. Alan takes Frederica through these, to the end of the building, past flashes of colour, past pools of dark and light, in the smell of oil and acrylic and turpentine and spirits. In the last airy space, in the centre, stands a strange object, surrounded by a swarm of students in black, tight clothes, and two men in jeans with what seem to be projectors of some kind. The object is a huge flask, or retort, or diving bell, with rounded sides rising to a kind of funnel into which one of the projectors appears to be pouring coloured light. As Frederica watches, this light changes from red-gold to cyan blue, and then to indigo, and then to acid yellow, and then to rose-pink. The walls of the retort or cask are painted matt black with variegated shapes and sizes of portholes out of which shimmer ribbons and flashes of changing coloured light. The light has a thick, liquid quality. The students are armed with black cardboard tubes, or periscopes, and drawing pads, and are peering in where they can, some crouched at low portholes, some perched on high stools. The operations are being directed by a burly man with not much hair, in a paint-streaked and unravelling mariner's sweater in oiled wool. Alan introduces this person, who seems to know and like Alan, as Desmond Bull, who is a painter, in charge of the Foundation Year. "This is Frederica Reiver—Potter—" says Alan. "She's going to teach literature."

"Good luck to her," says Desmond Bull.

"Can I look at what you are doing?"

"Please. Go up to the top, the view's best from there. Matthew here invented these coloured lights—he's got all sorts of oils inside jars and frames—it's a kind of instructive colour-happening. Come up this ladder."

Frederica climbs up, and peers in. The diving bell appears to be full of liquid light, but it is only air, somehow dense with colour. The background colour changes and is traversed by shoals of green spots, or golden streaks or waving lines of crimson and emerald. So delightful, so mesmerising, is the play of energy, light and colour that it takes Frederica some time to see that something is coiled below the imaginary depths, a wavering trousse of hair, or seaweed, a smooth succession of stones, or limbs, hard to fix, hard to discern, as it shifts from gold to green to sky blue.

"Is it a sculpture?" she asks, delighted, and is answered by a vo
from the depths, plangent and twanging. "No. It is a living creature.
The Human Form Divine, precisely. Any movement is illusory. I am
a professional."

"You can come out now," says Desmond Bull. "Coffee-break time."

Frederica retreats from the brim of the flask. Whoever is inside
gives a little jump, and clasps the edge of the tank with long greyish
fingers, distinctly grey, once out of the coloured light, though
whether intrinsically grey or by contrast is hard to say. A head then
appears above the rim, a head long, long, with a long, fine nose,
hooded eyes and a thin mouth, a head clothed and veiled in long,
iron-grey hair, dead-straight, smooth, long, iron-grey hair that cloaks
the shoulders and bust as they rise, so that it is impossible to see
whether this is a man or a woman. A long, grey leg, sinewy and thin,
is then hoist over the edge of its prison, also cloaked in the long, grey
threads, and then the strange figure, all blue-grey in the daylight, is
perched briefly on the edge, jumps down, and advances towards
Frederica on tall, thin legs moving amongst its tent of hair. Frederica's
eyes focus on the genitals, which a swing of the hair-curtain, accidental or deliberate, reveals to be male, rather small, clouded by iron-
grey pubic hair. The creature holds out a bony hand.

"Jude," he says.

"Frederica," says Frederica, registering a not very nice smell, a
smell of fish, of old frying pans, of rancid oils.

"A very ancient, fish-like smell," says Jude, in his high-pitched,
cultivated voice. Frederica feels a frisson of distaste, and catches him
looking at her, waiting for just such a frisson. When he has noted it,
he turns away, and moves towards the folding chair by the studio
heater, three roses of red elements on a metal stalk. He extends his
grey hands into the red light, turns a thin grey shank in the rose. The
skin on his ribs, the skin on his buttocks, hangs in sculpted folds, not
flapping, but folded, like the plated armour of a rhinoceros. Students
bring him coffee in plastic cups and offer him biscuits, which he refuses. A whole group gather at his feet.

Alan takes Frederica into her little office, which is a partitioned-off
corner of the high studio, still under the studio lights, and with a
white table and a good anglepoise, not a desk. The chair is pink
moulded plastic, with hands, feet, and a microcephalic head for her
own head to rest against, its long-lashed eyelids closed, its red mouth
pursed to kiss.

"Who was *that*?" says Frederica to Alan.

"Jude. Jude Mason. Not his real name, I suspect. He's a bit of a mystery man, a bit of a poseur. No one knows where he lives or where he comes from. He doesn't say much, but occasionally he lectures the students on Nietzsche. They like him. They listen to him. He turns up for some sessions and asks for modelling work, and then he vanishes, and then he returns. Art school models are hard to come by, and he's reliable."

"He looks like Gollum. Or Blake's Nebuchadnezzar only thinner."

"He's not very pro-Blake. He gets into arguments with Richmond Bly's Blake-clique or -claque. He prefers Nietzsche."

"Which reminds me of something awful." Frederica recounts the story of *The Voyage of the Silver Ship*. She cannot resist making it funny. It is funny, funny and sad. She says, "When I saw the mills of Golgonooza I knew. I should have listened to you telling me his *name,* but I obviously couldn't bear to hear it. What can I *do*?"

"Keep very quiet," says Alan. "Tell nobody else, no matter how tempting—you always talked too much, my dear, and I'm glad to see it coming back to you, but resist, resist. Forget the Silver Ship and all who sail in her."

"You never talk too much," says Frederica, turning her attention to her friend. All the way through Cambridge, she would ask herself, and occasionally him, who he loved, what he loved, and never came up with an answer. He is neat, and fair, and kindly, and she is sure of his friendship, and sure she does not know him. She likes this state of affairs.

"What is it like," she asks him, beglamourised by her surroundings, by the other-side-of-the-mirror world beyond the portals. "What is it like, teaching art history to artists?"

"Horrible," says Alan. "They think the dead are dead, and irrelevant to their own problems, or worse, threatening to their *originality.* Well, not all of them. Most. You'll see. It's quite testing. It tests your own reasons for caring about Raphael. Or Giotto, or Piero della Francesca. But they tend to vote with their feet, so you don't always have the pleasure of arguing the toss with them. That's one thing. Another is that places like this are run on the energies of part-timers, paid low rates for piece-work. If they don't come, you've got no class, no course and *no money.*"

"All the same," says Frederica. "It's alive, here."

166

V

❧❧❧❧❧

Alexander's fears that the new Labour Government might disband
the Steerforth Committee prove to be unnecessary. What happens is
that two new members are added, to give it a more popular aspect.
Like all committees, this one is a mixture of the relevant Great and
Good from some perennial Civil Service list, and judiciously balanced professionals in its field. The original list was as follows:

Professor Sir Philip Steerforth	Chairman, holder of a personal Chair in Anthropology in Glasgow University
Professor Gerard Wijnnobel	Vice-Chancellor of the University of North Yorkshire, grammarian and polymath
Dr. Naomi Lurie	Reader in English at Oxford, author of *Various Traditions of Meditational Verse* (1955) and of *Dissociated Sensibility, Myth or History?* (1960)
Alexander Wedderburn	Playwright, Producer, BBC Educational Television
Malcolm Friend	Journalist and broadcaster
Hans Richter	Physicist, now employed by Eurobore Oil Company
Arthur Beaver	Head of Child Development, Institute of Education, Chester University
Emily (Milly) Perfitt	Children's book writer
Auriol Worth	Headmistress, St. Clare's School for Girls, Dorking

167

Guy Croom	Headmaster, Botton Grammar School, Derbyshire
Alex Swinburn	Head of English, Goldengrove Comprehensive School, Croydon
Louis Roussel	Psychologist
Walter Priest	Devonshire LEA English adviser
Walter Bishop	Acting Head, Conisborough Teacher Training College

To these the new government had added:

| Mickey Impey | Liverpool poet and performer |
| Roger Magog | Freelance writer and teacher, author of twenty-seven books, including *The Sacramental Calling* (1956), an account of the transformation of a secondary modern school English group after being encouraged to write "freely" |

There are also Civil Servants in attendance: Aubrey Wace, the Secretary of the Committee, and his assistant, Agatha Mond.

The brief of the committee is to make recommendations for the teaching of English language in both primary and secondary schools. This brief included attention to areas where small wars are raging: the teaching of reading—sound or sight?; the usefulness or harm of teaching grammar; freedom of expression against correctness and conformity to rules. In his preliminary speech to the committee, sitting uneasy and inhibited round a board table in the Ministry of Education, Philip Steerforth said:

"Language and children are two things we might say previous generations in our culture took for granted. We have made both problematic, and made them objects of intense study. Between us we bring to bear a formidable array of expertise and talent in both fields, that is, child development and education, and the study of the nature and behaviour of language itself. We must be philosophically rigorous, and w̲e̲ ̲ ̲ ̲lso be intensely *practical;* otherwise we shall be sitting here in ̲ ̲ ̲ ̲enty years, for both subjects are young, are in transition and ̲ ̲ ̲ ̲ur work may be *helpful* but cannot hope to be definitive. Let us also remember that we are, many of us, parents, and consult our hopes and fears and understandings from that source."

The work of the committee is divided into two kinds: the gathering of evidence and consultation with teachers, and the debates in the Ministry. There is also the evidence, which pours in by the sackful, passionately written pleas for grammar, for the abolition of grammar, for learning poetry, for learning nothing ever again "by rote," for "look and say," for sonics, for mixed-ability teaching, for remedial teaching, for the gifted child, for the non–native speaker. There is a brief moment when Alexander surveys this mass of passionate paper like a cool human observer, knowing that he is about to become part of it, that he is about to join the battle and the battlefield.

He does not wholly know why he agreed to join the committee. Partly, he was flattered to be asked. Partly, he is interested in language; it is the medium of what he still thinks of as his art. Partly, his art is not going well. He wants to write differently, and does not know how. There is a new life in the theatre, and it is not one that bears any relation to the lyrical richness of his one great success, the 1953 verse-drama, *Astraea*. The new theatre is based on Artaud's Theatre of Cruelty. It believes, not in measured verse, but in "shattering language in order to shatter life." It is a theatre of blood, of screams, of bodily extremity. It is iconoclastic in a mannered way. Glenda Jackson has appeared as Christine Keeler, stripped, bathed, and ritually clothed as a convict to the recitation of the words of the Keeler court case. She has then appeared, to the same chanted words, as Jacqueline Kennedy, preparing herself for the funeral of the President. This has been followed by *The Persecution and Assassination of Marat as Performed by the Inmates of Charenton under the Direction of the Marquis de Sade.*

Alexander, the man, was moved and appalled by the production, by the writhings and moanings and ritual head-bangings of the impersonators of the insane: by the concatenation of the artist-Marquis and the tormented revolutionary, by Jackson again, a wildly erotic Charlotte Corday beating de Sade with her long hair. He also feels that *it is not good* to release such violence as spectacle. And beyond that, secretly, he thinks "childish." But what is "childish"? The child is wiser than the man, in the thought of this time. He is old, he is out of date, he once believed in contemplation, in singing rhythms, in thinking things out, and all this is swept away by this new bleeding, and howling. It may sound bathetic to say that he joined the committee also to observe the drama of the politics of groups, but it is so; there may be an idea there.

The consultation process is wide-ranging. The committee is too large to crowd into any classroom or staffroom, so it divides itself into platoons, which make local forays, north, south, east and west, visiting schools in Wales and the Fens, in Cumberland and Dumfriesshire, in Devon and in Belfast. Alexander manages to attach himself to a group which is to be based for two nights in York, and will visit primary schools in Leeds and Freyasgarth, grammar schools and comprehensive schools in Calverley and Northallerton. He has chosen this group partly because it will enable him to see Bill Potter, whose grandchildren's primary school, at Alexander's suggestion, is one of the chosen ones. He has also chosen it because it will be organised and accompanied by Agatha Mond, the young Principal from the Ministry of Education.

The rest of the group are Professor Wijnnobel, Hans Richter, Louis Roussel, Auriol Worth and the two new members, Mickey Impey and Roger Magog.

Alexander manages to travel from London to York with Agatha Mond. She is a darkly beautiful woman, around thirty, he thinks. She says little, and keeps her head down, studying the papers in front of her. Her hair is long and straight and worn in a loose bun. Her eyelashes are long and black. Her hands are fine. She is perhaps a little thin, and looks perhaps a little sad and withdrawn. She is Alexander's type; he recognises her; a woman reluctantly self-sufficient with a secret anxiety, or fear, under her cool look. All the women he has loved have been like this, quick dark women with potential passion. Except Frederica. He does not like to think about the very brief period when Frederica enforced love from him. He sits opposite Agatha Mond and watches her arrange her papers, as the London suburbs go past, and the edge of the Midlands. He fetches her a cup of coffee and observes that early rising is tiring. He asks if she has far to come.

"I live in Kennington. It isn't too bad. I get claustrophobic in the Tube."

"I can walk to King's Cross. I am fortunate. I live alone."

"I live with my daughter," says Agatha, answering his question precisely. "She is four. I have to make arrangements for her when I go on these visits, and of course I worry about her. She has just started at a local nursery school."

"Her father?" says Alexander, who has already observed that there is no wedding ring.

"She has no father," says Agatha Mond. She does not elaborate. After a moment she says, "Careers for women are not easy in this country. One of the odder and more humane provisions of the British Civil Service is that women may have up to three illegitimate children, with maternity leave, and no questions asked. It is unexpected. And useful."

"Indeed. But your life must be very strenuous."

"It is not easy. But it is quite manageable. I am very fortunate to have this job."

They ride on in companionable silence. Alexander says, "What are our new recruits like?"

"You must form your own judgement. Mickey Impey did begin a degree course at Liverpool, but dropped out. He performs at the Cavern and the teachers and children get very excited to hear he is coming. They ask for him to recite his poetry. I suppose no harm can come of that."

"And Magog?"

"Don't ask. He writes to the department every week, with new ideas for educational initiatives. When this committee was first mooted, he wrote suggesting himself as an obvious member. Civil servants react badly to that kind of thing. He may be quite all right. He just seemed—overwhelming. But it was not felt that we could—at the present juncture—resist any suggestion of the new Minister. It was thought better to absorb him."

"Now you look very official."

"I love the impersonal verbs. 'It was not felt.' So useful."

"Elegant and stuffy."

"Exactly."

"I don't think you are stuffy."

"Oh, I have to be. I have to be. Actually, I like it."

When they get to Doncaster, he says, "It must be very interesting for you, to do this work, with a four-year-old child."

"I talk to her like a watermill. I hear so much about the need to talk, and *how* to talk. I exhaust her with talking." She laughs, and then

171

frowns. "I love her too much, because I'm on my own. I try not to talk about her but I think about her all the time."

Alexander thinks of saying: I have a son who thinks he is another man's son. But he does not say it. He thinks: Here is someone to whom I might say it, one day. But maybe she thinks I am an old buffer, a has-been. Maybe she is being kind to me. He has never had to worry about this before.

Just before York, she says, "I've been wanting to tell you. I once acted in a production of *Astraea*. It was OUDS, at Oxford. I was doing research at the time. I was Bess Throckmorton. I married Walter Raleigh. I loved it."

"When it was first put on," says Alexander, "I was in love with the woman who played Bess Throckmorton."

She too was his type, dark, secret, smouldering.

"I fell in love with Edmund Spenser, but it came to nothing," says Agatha Mond. "Short and sweet, a midsummer's night."

They are at York. They step out into the station. Alexander takes Agatha's bag. As they get into the taxi, he says, "What is your daughter's name?"

"Saskia. She doesn't look like her, like Rembrandt's Saskia. She looks like me. But I always think of Saskia as *complete*, somehow. It's a name of good omen."

They are becoming friends, Alexander feels. He is alive. Yes, he is alive.

Their first visit is to the Star Primary School in a Leeds suburb. They are driven there from the Dean Court Hotel in York. Alexander is not able to sit next to Agatha Mond, who is having a serious discussion in the front seat with Professor Wijnnobel about the grammar evidence. Wijnnobel is too tall to fit comfortably into a minibus seat: he stoops, and inclines his large face gravely. Hans Richter sits behind Alexander, who is one of the few people he talks voluntarily to. He wears a business suit, and has well-cut grizzled grey hair and a neat, unremarkable face, with glasses. Louis Roussel sits at the back of the bus, away from Wijnnobel, to whom he is ideologically opposed. He is a little man, dark and birdlike, energetic and short-tempered. The two new members sit apart from each other and everyone else, as new members usually do. Roger Magog looks suspiciously around at the others, sussing them out, summing them up, at once self-conscious about their probable attitudes to him, and vaguely believing that his scrutinising self is invisible. Alexander wonders how he himself knows all this. Magog wears a shabby off-white polo neck under a shapeless tweed jacket, the garments of a slightly passé authenticity. His thinning hair is pale red, and his fat curly beard is dark russet.

The Liverpool poet is very pretty, with a mane of buttercup-coloured curls, a sweet full mouth, and huge innocent blue eyes. He is wearing a collarless jacket over a bright blue shirt that intensifies his eyes. He has been very pleasant to everyone so far, helping the women up the bus step, standing aside for the older men. The other woman is Auriol Worth, the headmistress, dressed like a headmistress in a good-looking navy suit and white shirt. Her face is precise and professionally observant. She is about fifty. She looks so like a headmistress that it is hard to make anything of her. She says to Alexander, of the poet, as they wait on the pavement, "If I had that one in my class I'd keep a special eye on him."

The Star Primary School is called the Star because of its revolutionary architecture. The committee has come to see it because it is new and exciting. It is wholly glass-walled, and is built in the shape of a star. It is wholly open-plan: the children gather in little, impromptu-looking groups, in one or another arm of the star, bringing with them their brightly coloured bean bags, their plastic stools, their little tables. They are grouped not by age, nor by subject, but by some sort of self-directed choice of activity. A group is making coiled clay pots. Older children are helping younger ones. A group is pouring and measuring water to and from a series of plastic containers, solemnly measuring and recording the heights of the contents. Little ones are pouring. Older ones are measuring. Still older ones are making a graph of the measurements. In another arm of the star children are watching snails climb the walls of a glass tank and are drawing the horns, the mouth, the foot. Small people dart busily and loudly from open space to open space, calling out, "We *urgently* need a wooden spoon," or "Mandy's gone and done it *again*." Someone is playing the recorder in one star-tip, and someone near her is banging a drum. Because there are no classroom or corridor walls the children's work is on display on easels and noticeboards in the centre. There is a display of portraits of "My Family," and a table with the children's weekly newspapers displayed. There is a book corner in one aisle with a round bookcase, a lot of cushions, and a casual heap of books beside them. There is a lot of noise. It is, on the whole, purposive noise, shrill, variegated, busy, but loud. Alexander—like many of the older members of the committee—is moved by the contrast with his own schooldays. These little children, brightly clothed, free-moving, are different beings from the cowed, subservient, watchful little boy he remembers as himself. One inevitable effect on all the committee members who are not professional teachers, and even on those, like Alexander, who were and are not, is fear, the old cold terror of the school building, of power, of authority, of judgement. In places like this, that is gone. A little girl appears with a piece of bobbin knitting; she says, "Excuse me, I think I've dropped a stitch, it's all gone funny, like moth-holes, I wonder if you could put it right." He takes her darning needle, he prods at the wool. She expects his help as her right. He notes the analogy "like moth-holes."

All the same, he has the beginnings of a headache, from the noise. Where are the corners where a child such as he was might hide, might crouch and read? There are no hiding places. It is all open, all group life.

Auriol Worth is talking to the headmaster, an enthusiastic young man, young for a headmaster, who is able to talk to her quite coherently about the degree to which the children select their activities and the degree to which he suggests and complicates them, whilst keeping up a running conversation with passing children and teachers, like a juggler with a stream of green and orange balls, never confusing them. "I think you're bored with clay, Cilla, I think you should go and join in Miss Morrissey's group, which is talking and writing about amphibians. Everyone always thinks they want to do clay, but actually you need to do a *lot* of things in a day.

"Never mind, Heather. I expect Mr. Dinsdale thought you were upsetting the others. If you come to me at break I'll explain how to measure squares and then you won't feel left out.

"We try to let them dictate the pace and the interest, Miss Worth, but of course we must have things difficult enough to attract and occupy the ablest."

"And what about peer-pressure *not* to attempt the difficult?"

"Ah, there we have to be cunning. We have to disguise the difficulty."

"So you don't encourage ambition, as such."

"We disapprove of competitiveness. We like co-operation. Everyone has his or her talent, which we try to foster."

"And you are not flat on your face with exhaustion at the end of the day?"

"Often." He laughs. "But it's worth it."

Roger Magog is studying the project on "My Family." He says to Roussel, who is passing, "How significant that all these mothers appear to be angry. 'My Mum screming.' 'My Mummy shouted at me.' All these little children draw their mothers with a big, open mouth and a stick body. Only her screaming mouth matters."

"Little children have a very simple scheme of human beings in their drawings," says Roussel. "They learn bodies and hands and faces later. The older children have parents with bodies."

"My dad has a big stik," says Magog. "My dad has a Big ball. He threw the big ball hard at me. It hurt."

"It probably did," says Roussel.

"Sticks and balls and dads," says Magog. "How direct, how innocent, how clear. And the mums screaming. The modern family. Sad."

"Not necessarily."

"Oppressive. 'Go to bed, says Mum. I wont I say I wont. You will says my mum is ther no pease. I hate bed. I want to stay up all nite.' "

"Interesting," says Wijnnobel behind him, "that *e* on nite. The child knows how to elongate the vowel, even in a misspelling."

Alexander is trying to find a group of children who will be doing what Simon Poole might at this moment be doing. He finds a writing group with a young teacher. They have their "newsbooks" and their personal dictionaries, which they carry about in little cotton bags, since there are no desks. They write and talk and take their work to the teacher, who gives them long words for their dictionaries. Alexander asks the teacher what they read, and is shown bright cards with large pictures and a line or two of text. "I read them poems," she says. "I read them Spike Milligan and of course I read them Mickey Impey's *Naughty Poems for Bad Boys and Girls*, they love that. It's great he's actually here."

"Do they learn the poems?"

"Oh no. That would take the pleasure out of them. Learning by rote is very destructive, we know that now, they must *discover* things. Some learn things almost by accident, but we'd never *make* them. They don't learn tables, either, we draw number-squares and they *discover* the relations. That way, it stays in the mind."

"But they learn the alphabet," says Alexander, looking at the dictionaries.

"Oh no. Not as such. Not *by rote*. They sort of assimilate it."

"So how do they find their way round their dictionaries?"

"I show them. Until they know it."

"I used to love chanting the alphabet. Backwards and forwards both. And tables. And French verbs. A sort of pleasure. Like dancing."

The young woman shudders expressively.

Mickey Impey is asked to say one of his poems. The children come out of the arms of the star. He sends two to fetch some big boxes, so he can stand up above them, so they can see. He is a natural showman. He says:

"Children are always being told, come here, go there, do this, do that. They can't help it, they have to. What they get told makes no sense to them, they know what they really want, but the Tellers don't know and don't care, do they, they just go on fixing the world to make it comfortable for themselves, to keep children quiet and nice and sweet and *good*. So I wrote some poems for *bad* children. The one I'm going to read is about some children who go off to a secret country where there are no pushers-around and find all sorts of strange creatures who want to help them take charge of their own lives. Here it is."

The poem was long. The peroration went:

> *And the Blue Blebs*
> *And the Yellow Yetis*
> *And the Purple Prongs*
> *And the Green Groaners*
> *And the Redundant Reds*
> *And the Great Grey Grunters*
> *And the Picky Pink Pixies*
> *And the Orange Owls*
> *With the horrible Yorubas*
> *And the loathsome Lapps*
> *Come when he whistles*
> *When Mickey the Mad Imp whistles*
> *And they strangle the Grandmas*
> *They annihilate the Aunties*
> *They top-and-tail the Teachers*

And truss them in twenties
And trepann them and toast them
And toss them to tigers
Who howl with delight
And dance all the night
In the burning bright light
Of the fire they have made
Of school-uniforms and books and pens and inks, and desks and chairs and
  blackboards and footballs and hockey sticks and chalk and dusters and
  chemistry kits and globes and bunsen burners
And they dance and they prance
They writhe and romance
And feed till they choke
On choc-ices and Coke.

"He is out of date in his equipment," murmurs Auriol Worth.

The children roar with applause. Mickey Impey organises them into a long dancing crocodile, and they prance serpentining round the school, chanting loudly after their Piper, whose energies show no signs of flagging, though one or two little ones begin to stumble and cry. Finally Agatha pulls at his arm, and tells him the group must move on: they have other schools to visit. He does not stop immediately: she has to trot alongside, explaining. His lovely face is sulky. He calls to the children, "Do you want to stop?"

"No," cry most. "Yes," cry a few.

"They want to go on," says Mickey Impey.

"Well, they can't," says Agatha, tartly. The rest of the committee group behind her.

"You see," says Mickey Impey, turning to the children as he leaves, "they don't care what you want, they don't *really* let you do as you please, it's all a trick, when they tell you you're free to choose."

A wavering scream, from some of the children, as though he were a pop star, answers this.

The Aneurin Bevan Comprehensive School in Calverley is not a shiny-bright new place like the Star Primary School. It was once the Archbishop Temple Grammar School and the Leeds Road Secondary Modern, and is now one institution on two sites. The old Grammar School is panelled and dark and echoing. The old Secondary Modern is square and shapeless, with pre-fabricated classrooms in its playground, a smell of inadequate sanitation, and exotic salty-looking fungus or chemical rash sprouting on its heating conduits. In this school there is a vigorous discussion of the problems and blessings of mixed-ability teaching. The committee are taken to a fourth-form improvised play, which centres on a family conflict between the women who make Sunday lunch and the men who want to go out to the pub and to football. Parts have been given to the less articulate to make them more articulate, with some success—one girl cries suddenly into the hall:

"And must I spend all my days like this, the same thing time after time, shopping and cooking and waiting till what I have cooked is cold and greasy, week after week after week, and then washing it up and saying it doesn't matter when you come home smelly and sick, smelly and sick, is this what it is to be a human being?"

This eloquence causes her subsequently to blush bright scarlet, and deeply embarrasses her male co-actors, who can only say, "Oh come on," and "It's not so bad as that," and "Women do go on." Magog is delighted with this moment, and congratulates the teacher on bringing out the girl's inner conflicts. The teacher replies that that girl's father is a vicar, and teetotal, and some imagination has gone into her performance. Alexander is bored. He remembers that school is 90 percent boredom. For the good and the bad student alike. Youth is boring, but this is not to be admitted.

The headmaster of the Aneurin Bevan School too is a tryer and an innovator. He has a school council and runs regular school debates in the hall of the old Grammar School. He has staged a debate in honour of the committee.

"This house believes that no good is done by the teaching of English grammar."

There is a hidden agenda to this: the headmaster himself, a geographer by profession, remembers his English language lessons as a boy, the parsing of sentences, the location of dependent clauses, as a form of intense torture, an exercise baffling and pointless. The school week is short, this man reasons, the school year is short, school days in toto are short, and clause analysis is a cruel waste of time. It is probable that most of his colleagues share both his feeling and his opinions. It is probable that most of the children do. Learning English grammar, even to passionate readers, is peculiarly repugnant and somehow *unnatural*.

The headmaster introduces the committee to the school.

"We have the honour to have amongst us a very distinguished group of people who are studying the very question we are debating today. We have Professor Wijnnobel, a distinguished grammarian, we have Alexander Wedderburn, a playwright whose rich language has entranced many of you, we have a young and popular poet, Mickey Impey. We have a scientist, a psychologist and an educational writer, all of whom will bring their own wisdom to the debate. I want them to see that the boys and girls in this school have thought carefully about this subject and I also want them to see that we are in the habit of debating issues that concern us, putting clearly points of view we may or may not agree with, and *listening to what is said by others.*"

The debate is lively. The proposer, a pink-cheeked, darkly handsome sixth-form boy, argues that we all learn to speak grammatically without being taught, that we can understand poems, newspapers, political speeches and each other without always working out what is a noun or a verb, let alone a subordinate noun clause or a subjunctive. When we learn other languages we might need a small grasp of such terminology, but that is the place to learn it.

The opposer, an intense plump girl, argues essentially that grammar is like the names of chemicals or parts of the body. We need to know about the circulation of the blood and the valves of the heart. Language is part of us: it is natural to want to understand it.

The seconder of the proposal destroys this argument. You might die if no one understood your blood or your heart. You would go right on talking if no one told you what a noun or a verb was.

The seconder of the opposer is a nervous boy with downcast eyes and argues that no one will get a job, or pass an exam, if they don't speak and write properly. Rules are there to make life better. People may not like rules but they wouldn't like life without them. Knowing the rules gives everyone an equal chance.

The debate is good. A surprising number of children take part. They are well prepared, with points written out on little cards, which they read. It is quite clear where the passions of these children lie: the anecdotal comments are all one way, the meaninglessness, the injustice, the silliness of particular grammatical problems, the *waste of time*. Such supporters of grammar as there are are rather decorous and dutiful, perhaps even selected by teachers and briefed to support it. "It helps us to write in a more interesting way." "It helps us to see what we really mean."

There is an overwhelming vote against grammar. Wijnnobel congratulates the headmaster on the articulacy of his students. Mickey Impey, who has been wriggling in his seat throughout the debate and occasionally putting his feet up on the back of the chair in front of him (Hans Richter's), suddenly plucks at the headmaster's sleeve.

"Can I say something to these kids? I've listened to them, now I'd like to talk to them. Do you object?"

"I told you," says Auriol Worth to Alexander. "If I had him in my class, I'd watch him."

"Ought we to stop him?"

"Probably. But fortunately it isn't our place."

"Go ahead," says the headmaster to Mickey Impey.

"Listen, you kids. My name is Mickey Impey, I'm a poet. I've listened to what you've been saying and some of it was good, real good stuff, but really you're all herded along by all this way of talking you think is so clever, Mr. Chairman, Ladies and Gentlemen, and all that junk. Listen to me, don't let them brainwash you. Listen to me, think freedom, think *creativity,* think vision. They make you sit there and study all this stuff about Einstein and relativity and so on. You don't need any of that. There was one great man who understood it all—*William Blake.* He saw that if you look at the world properly your imagination inhabits infinity. He understood infinity. Listen to this, it blows your mind.

> *How do you know but ev'ry bird that cuts the airy way,*
> *Is an immense world of delight, clos'd by your senses five?*

Or

> *One thought fills immensity.*

Or

Energy is the only life, and is from the Body; and Reason is the bound or outward circumference of Energy. Energy is Eternal Delight.

Those who restrain desire, do so, because theirs is weak enough to be restrained, and the restrainer, or reason, usurps its place and governs the unwilling.

"You should be thinking about *this,* about how to use your own energy, about how to see Infinity, not all the stuff they teach you. When

I was at school, no one told me anything like this, so I am telling you."

Some smile. Some titter. Some applaud. Some shuffle, embarrassed. The audience is not one. Those who have spoken are anxious to have their speaking praised. There is always the perennial fear of looking silly which runs in groups of the young. In other places, at other times, Mickey Impey can overcome that fear, can harness and use it, but here his speech goes off at half-cock. Both Mickey Impey and the headmaster are aware of this. The headmaster thanks Impey smoothly "for the message you have decided to share with us," and Impey sits down, frowning.

Alexander says to Wijnnobel, "*Why* do they so hate grammar?"

"It is something we must try to understand. It is a phenomenon we must analyse. Of course, the grammar of which they are complaining is hopelessly out of date, it is Latinate, it has nothing to do with modern thinking. But I do not think that is at the root of the problem. Perhaps a reluctance of the brain to contemplate its own operations."

This last sentence appears at first to Alexander to have nothing at all to do with the teaching of clause analysis. Nevertheless, it is interesting.

Mickey Impey is absent that night at dinner in the Dean Court Hotel. So is Wijnnobel, who has gone back to his university. It is Magog who asks Agatha Mond whether anything can be done about the behaviour of Mickey Impey. A professional *enfant terrible* himself, he does not like terrible behaviour in other, especially younger, men. Agatha replies diplomatically that she is sure that the chairman or the secretary will have a word with Impey about correct behaviour in committee members. In her experience, such problems are usually solved by the unruly member either conforming to the group customs or leaving. She is looking pretty, even beautiful, in a dark red dress which brushes her knees. Her legs are long and thin. She is one of the perhaps 10 percent of women who truly look good in such short skirts. Alexander goes up the stairs behind her and reflects that all the same, it is odd when Civil Servants wear dresses that reveal the movements of their bottoms and the backs of their knees, like schoolgirls, or female commanders of cartoon spaceships. He says, "Do you *really* think our Young Turk will conform or quit?"

"He may well quit. He may get bored. My view is that he will quit. I don't at all want to upset our political masters by complaining about him. He adds a bit of variety. He'll get bored, don't worry." She adds,

"Moreover, he is an excellent group irritant, like the grit in a pearl. He will make the rest of the group cohere, and work together."

He resists the impulse to put a fatherly arm round her shoulder.

The next day is their visit to Freyasgarth. Alexander takes time out in the morning to walk up the road to see Bill Potter, who is expecting him. He is surprised to see Bill's bruised and broken face and asks if he has had a fall.

"No. I haven't. I'm not an old man falling over my own feet yet. I had my head smashed between the door and the wall by a cross young man. My son-in-law. He wanted Frederica. Wouldn't believe she wasn't here. Wouldn't believe I didn't know where she was. Apparently she's done a bolt, taking the boy. I await developments. Never a dull day. I'd be glad if I did know where she was. She needs protection."

"I know where she is," says Alexander, after some thought. "She's being looked after. Sensibly."

"If you see her," says Bill, "tell her we'd be glad to hear from her. Tell her I haven't got so long left on this earth. A daughter's a daughter. She'll come to understand that. Tell her. Oh, I don't know what. You'd better not tell me where she is. In case that lout comes back and tortures the information out of me. He's capable. He'd cry over his handiwork after—he was very spry with damp cloths—but he's got a temper."

"I'll tell her. She's lying low."

"Most sensible thing she's done so far. Though if she'd had *any* sense at all, she wouldn't be in this mess. She should have married a kind man, like Daniel."

"You wouldn't let Daniel in your house."

"No. Well. I've come round. It was his Christianity I objected to, not him, and I've come to the conclusion he's no more a Christian than I am."

"You're a thorough old Puritan preacher, and always were."

Bill smiles at Alexander.

"One of the very few benefits of growing old," he says, "is finding out who's gone along with you, who it is you really share your memories with. We know each other pretty well."

"We do," says Alexander.

Bill has twice said he is old, since Alexander came. He looks older. The battered skin is healing slowly, and is thin as onion skin. The

bruises are huge. The blood in them is black. His smile is unintentionally gruesome. Alexander smiles back with love.

Alexander rejoins the committee in Freyasgarth School. They are listening to Miss Godden, the headmistress, telling a fairy tale, *The
Great Green Worm,* to the middle class, the seven- to eight-year-olds.
The school is made of the local grey stone and is large and simple, a
space divided by two movable partitions, dating from the 1930s. The
children sit in rows behind long desks, the younger ones at the front,
the older ones at the back. The committee sit at the very back. They
are not comfortable. Those with small enough bottoms—Agatha
Mond, the poet, Roussel, even Hans Richter in his suit—are on infant chairs. Wijnnobel is enthroned high on Miss Godden's shabby
desk-chair. Miss Worth and Mr. Magog share a small gym bench, on
which they make room for Alexander.

"The Green Worm gave a long hiss (that is a serpentine way of
sighing) and without reply, plunged beneath the waves. What a loathsome monster, said the princess to herself; he has greenish wings, and
his body is all sorts of changing colours—he has ivory claws and his
head is covered with a mane of ugly fronds. I really would rather die
than owe my life to that creature."

Miss Godden's voice is quiet. She lingers on the more enticing
words: serpentine, hiss, fronds. The children are still. They listen.
They do not shuffle. She expects them not to and they do not. She
writes up on the blackboard a series of synonyms: *snake, serpent,
dragon, worm,* and gets the children to add other words they know:
viper, adder, python, grass-snake, slow-worm ("A legless lizard, you know,
children, not a real snake, a creature that evolved legs and then decided to do without them"), *boa constrictor, cobra, Nag* (one child has
read Rikki-Tikki-Tavi), *puff-adder, black mamba, rattlesnake.* This leads
to a brief discussion of the difference between synonyms and scientific names designed to differentiate clearly between species and varieties. They talk about the "feel" of words, what is different in *worm* (a
"fat, thick, *slow* word," says one red-haired girl) and *snake* ("a kind of
quick-sliding but *cutting* word," says the same girl) and *serpent* ("a kind
of fairy-thing, or demon out of the Bible," says the girl). They talk
about why people don't like snakes and why in stories people are
often changed into them. Alexander looks at the girl. She has soft
red-gold hair and large dark eyes, and freckles, a soft scattering and
speckling of pale coffee on cream. Her brow is wide, her mouth is

wide and soft. He knows her, he can read her genes in her face, in her skin, in her lips, even in the movements of attention of her head. She is Stephanie's child, and also Daniel's child, Mary; she carries Bill's flyaway redness and Winifred's old–gold slowness, an alertness that is Frederica (but also dead Stephanie), a slow stare of thought that is her father. She was born within a week of Simon Vincent Poole. Alexander thinks of the boy. He is himself, he has his life ahead of him. Does it matter if he carries Thomas Poole's genes or mine? To Alexander, it does. He wants to *know* Simon. He looks at Mary. He thinks of Agatha Mond's Saskia, who "has no father."

"At the end of these lessons," says Miss Godden, "we always read the page of the dictionary with our word on it—*worm* today, or *snake,* you may choose, Mary Orton, since you have been thinking so hard, which. We look to see all the words there are that none of us know, even me. We think about how many words there are, and what a lot we can do with them."

Wijnnobel nods his head. The poet does not attempt to address this class, partly perhaps because he recognises another charismatic presence in this stout, story-telling middle-aged teacher, partly because he appears to be genuinely interested in the story and the word-game.

He gathers his forces, however, at school dinner. This is eaten at long tables constructed of the bench-desks, and served from large aluminium cans by overalled dinner ladies. The committee sit at the teachers' table, and are served with a sort of lamb stew, some very watery reconstituted peas, some mashed potatoes grey in colour and containing pebbles of solid starch.

Mickey Impey says very loudly, "This stuff is *muck*. Nobody ought to be asked to eat *muck* like this muck. Kids ought not and we ought not, and I *won't eat this muck*." Alexander can see him thinking: it crosses his mind to incite all the children to throw around, or symbolically refuse, their food. Some are eating busily: some are making listless gestures with their forks. It is not nice food, and it is not completely inedible. He would rather not eat his own, but is embarrassed by the poet into making an effort. The poet stands up and scrapes the whole of his plate into the can of hot water in which the dirty cutlery is soaking. He says, "There must be a pub in this village. Anyone for a sandwich?" Nobody answers. He stalks out. Agatha is right. The rest of the committee becomes markedly more cordial towards each other.

The committee meets to discuss these and other visits. They sit round a long table in a drab room in the Ministry of Education, which is to be transformed into the Department of Education and Science. They sit on the whole in little professional groups: academics with academics, teachers with teachers, writers and journalists uneasily with each other, no one next to the sweet-faced poet, who sits drawing cartoons on his notepad. Later, these groups will splinter and reconstruct themselves. Alexander sits opposite the chairman, Philip Steerforth, the secretariat, and the other academics, Wijnnobel, Naomi Lurie, Arthur Beaver. He sits there not to catch the chairman's eye but in order to be able to look at Agatha Mond. He does not see himself as part of this group, but as an individual, an observer, present almost by mistake. Other people, as they have done throughout his life, see him as understanding and gentle: a force for cohesion. Auriol Worth and Roger Magog are sitting one on each side of him.

Agatha has written clear reports on the visits they have made. Arthur Beaver, who was not present on the visits, remarks that the Star Primary School and Freyasgarth represent opposing ideas of primary education. He is interested to know if the visiting party has formed any views about their relative merits.

Hans Richter says that it is autumn. He says he says this because in summer the Star School, which appears to be so airy and light, will become intolerably hot, and both teachers and children will be simmering with discomfort. He says architects often ignore people.

Alexander says that that school contains no private places.

Magog says most schools do not contain private places. He asks Hans Richter if his observation is a metaphor.

Richter says no, it is a physical observation. But that mental states flow from physical states, and that when the children are too hot, they will learn less well.

Steerforth recalls his committee from architecture to the teaching of language.

Auriol Worth says that both primary schools were good schools; that the children in them were learning and were happy. She says that unfortunately, perhaps, the good teaching depended in both cases on individual teachers. The headmaster of the Star School had eyes in the back of his head and an unusually good organisational brain. Another head in his place might well, with the same principles, preside over aimlessness and chaos. Equally, Miss Godden was a teacher capable of holding the attention of several age and ability groups at once, and exercising their minds. But a teacher less gifted and inventive could simply lose their attention.

Arthur Beaver says that the committee's report must contain a chapter on the activity of the teacher; the language teaching depends on the ability, and indeed the philosophy, of the teacher.

Magog says that what strikes him is the hatred of grammar demonstrated by the debate at the comprehensive school. It appears that no amount of good teaching can make grammar other than repulsive to the vast majority of kids and probably teachers. When he was a boy—

(All the committee members, all through the committee's deliberations, refer in a certain tone to when they were a boy, or a girl. They trail clouds of past life, glorious or cramped, through the dusty official room. Alexander watches them. He imagines the boy Magog was: fat, thick-kneed, curly, sulky, aggressive, never the *best* boy at anything in the class, always near the best.)

—when he was a boy, grammar was experienced as a trap set to catch you out, as a series of gates in a maze for rats, as an instrument of absolute power and punishment by teachers, as a series of nasty interruptions to any creative flow your writing might get up, as oppression, in short.

He says it doesn't seem to have got much better. He says he is sympathetic to the abolitionists. What that boy said in the debate is true. We speak grammatically without learning grammar.

Naomi Lurie says that without grammar no child can unravel the sentences of Milton, or Donne.

Walter Bishop says most kids will never read Milton or Donne. There is no reason why they should suffer parsing and clause analysis for the sake of the few privileged ones who will. They need to be able to write a job application. To read a government form.

Guy Croom says that human beings, like it or not, need rules. No community can operate without a few simple rules according to which it conducts its business. He is not in favour of new educational methods which attempt to promote discovery at the expense of learning a few facts. He thinks children are being cheated by being made to *discover* all sorts of things they could actually simply learn about and then go on to discover more interesting things. Rules facilitate. Rules create order, and without order is no creativity. The poor little children who didn't know the alphabet are wasting *hours* looking through their dictionaries at random. There is a pleasure in learning ordered rules which seems now to be despised. He thinks no one can cope with the world who hasn't internalised a few simple rules of mathematics. He thinks that football and tennis and games of cards would be intensely boring without rules. Anyone who has a child, he says, who has tried to make up a new card game as it went along, and has been subjected to the *total boredom* of the *ad hoc* and the random, will know that the need for rules is a deep human need.

The poet says, "That's what the Fascists said." He says, "If you *make* people learn old poems they hate them. You should let them just find them. You should perhaps prohibit them, outlaw them. Then they'd be hungry for poems."

The chairman asks Wijnnobel what he feels about rules.

Wijnnobel says that he does not think it is helpful to draw an analogy between the rules devised for political or social control of group behaviour and the forms of the structure of language which can be observed and described in all societies. He says, rather carefully, that he believes in the teaching of the forms of language, because if we have no words to describe the structure of our thoughts, we are unable to analyse their nature and their limitations. Nietzsche, he says, claimed that all Western philosophy studies variations on the same problems in recurring circles because all ideas are "unconsciously dominated and directed by simple grammatical functions" which are in the end, Nietzsche also says, *physiological*. This is not the same as saying that philosophical problems are "only language": it is a claim that *what we can think* is a function of our linguistic competence. He himself—unlike some others in the room—is of the opinion that the grammatical forms and structures we use are innate, are part of the structure of our brains informed by our genes, and that the extraordinary subtlety and reach of human intelligence—*and* its limitations, its recurrent worrying at insoluble "problems"—are a function of this innate order. He also believes that studying this order is hard, and contemplating it is repugnant to many. But if we do not teach words to describe the structure of language, we have no means to consider the structure of thought. This is not a defence, he adds, of the ornate Latinate grammatical exercises now taught, which should be scrapped.

Magog says he agrees with this, and that the rules of grammar desired by Mr. Croom do indeed often turn into petty rules of social oppression and alienation. He believes that the relations between teachers and children are what is wrong. When he was teaching, he got the confidence of his children, he persuaded them to write more and more truthfully, more and more passionately, about the conflicts in their family life—their hopes and desires—as he has recorded in his book *True Life Stories* (an ironic reference to the Agony Aunt magazines, as he is sure he has no need to tell this distinguished gathering)—"and the vocabulary and complexity *and punch,* Mr. Chairman, *and punch* increased with the truthfulness—"

"And after," says Auriol Worth. "After you had stopped teaching these children, whom you had encouraged to speak in this way—to reveal things—I have read your book—afterwards, what happened to them? How long did you stay with them, after you had inspired them to write about abuse and hatred and tension?"

"I was there for a full *two terms.* Before I—before I sold my book. They were strengthened by facing their conflicts."

"A teacher is not a psychoanalyst."

"I have had a lot of flak from people like you, who do nothing much for those *in their care*—"

"I teach them, Mr. Magog. I teach them to read, to write, to think. I teach them *to look outside themselves.* I respect my position. And theirs."

"You are simply an authoritarian—"

"All authority," says Miss Worth sadly, "nowadays, seems to be wrong."

Arthur Beaver says that the present lively exchange of views exemplifies some of the problems he wants to put to the committee about the philosophy of teaching. Martin Buber, he says, claims that the teacher in past times had an accepted authority derived from his culture. He was, in a fine phrase, "the ambassador of history, to this intruder, the child." And the sickness of this system, which intensified as the cultural authority crumbled and was called in question, was a "will to power" which could become domineering and cruel as it became more uncertainly individual. The contrary fault Buber called "Eros," the degeneration of authority into an idealised reciprocity and affection, of a professional relationship into a personal one. Which is not sustainable between all teachers and all children, for it depends on honesty and durability, and all teachers *do not feel* genuine affection for all children, nor do their pseudo-parental relations endure beyond the inevitable parting at the year-end. It is a kind of buddy-buddy relation, which some people believe to be part of child-centred education.

"I see what you are saying," says Magog. "But I can assure you I felt *real love* for every child in my class. *Real love.*"

He glares about the table. Alexander believes him. He also knows that there are charismatic teachers who do occasionally inspire by love.

"For two terms," says Auriol Worth, acid, headmistressy. "You felt real love for two terms. You translated the love into your written words, and you made their private pains public."

"With *every care*—"

"I am sure. Every care the reading public and the law could expect."

A line of division, a set of terms, are set up. The committee will divide, will see its own divisions, in terms of Eros and *Wille zur Macht*, the buddy and the boss. Alexander is fascinated.

After the meeting there is sherry. Alexander moves to the side of Agatha Mond and helps her to hand round glasses. The scientist, Hans Richter, taps Professor Wijnnobel on the shoulder.

"I liked what you said. About order. About describing thought. If *that* is what we are doing, this whole undertaking looks quite different. I thought I was just here to see if science teachers could be got to explain themselves a bit better, in better English, and so on. But what you said changes everything. You said something very fine about the limitations of our thought.

"I am convinced," he continues calmly, as though he were discussing the structure of salts, "that there are intelligences in the universe of which our own are only a very small sub-set."

Gerard Wijnnobel is startled. He has a momentary vision of huge angelic heads, spanning the visible heavens, of an order of serried wings, at once feathered and glassy, at once living forms and geometrically intricate patterns.

He inclines his great head and strokes his thick moustache.

"As to that," he says, "I do not know how we could have any evidence of that. As a two-dimensional paper man could not see or address a three-dimensional clay or flesh man."

"But he could intuit his presence. As we intuit the possibility of solutions to problems before we solve them."

"Or fail to solve them," says Wijnnobel.

"We intuit probable failures, also."

"It is certain that we cannot imagine the languages of such intelligences."

"I shall apply my own intelligence to the language we have. It is more interesting than I supposed."

"Indeed," says Wijnnobel.

VI

Gerard Wijnnobel sits in his official car and thinks about language. He thinks about order and disorder, about form and chaos. He has thought about these things all his life, always with a sensation of an impossible endeavour. His thought is a raft of parallel planks on a darkly swelling sea, it is a most beautiful cone of light around which is the formless, or maybe only invisible and unmapped, dark. He is Hans Richter's paper man, floating on his two-dimensional kite on currents of air, of force, he cannot describe or explore.

He grew up in Leiden, the son of a Protestant theologian, a Calvinist who puzzled, who agonized, daily over the exact relations between virtue, predestination and the words of the one Book. He is not wholly and purely of Dutch Calvinist descent: his mother's father was half-Jewish, a child of a Talmudic scholar and a Dutch Catholic lady who had come to believe that the Church was guilty of terrible cruelty to the Jews, which had come from a misreading and misuse of the Scriptures. Gerard Wijnnobel's grandfather, in his turn, had become obsessed with the language of the Book. He had set out on a doomed attempt, part mystical, part historical, part exegetical, to find the traces of the Ur-language, the original speech of God, spoken by Adam in Eden, and indeed by God, the Word Himself, when He called the universe into being out of chaos, simply by naming it. In the days before Babel, before God punished the human race for its presumption in raising its winding structure towards Heaven by dividing its tongues, by setting confusion amongst its speech—in the days before Babel, the occult tradition went, words had been things and things had been words, they had been *one,* as a man and his shadow perhaps are one, or a man's mind and his brain. Afterwards, after the fall of the tower, language and the world had not coincided, and the languages of men had become opaque, secret, enfolded in an incomprehensible and un-pierceable skin of idiosyncrasies. After the fall of the aspiring tower (almost all mythologies held), the original, divine, single speech had been shattered like a smashed crystal, into seventy-two pieces, or into a number which was a multiple of seventy-two. Various words and let-ters could be read as splinters of this original sphere—each Hebrew letter, each word, each grammatical form. Kabbalists, Hermetics, Ha-sidic students of the Torah and the Talmud tried to reconstitute the Old Speech, the *Ursprache,* from these lost fragments. Gerard Wijnno-bel's grandfather spent his days on the search for this ancient order, oc-casionally disputing with his grave Calvinist son-in-law over whether or not the Tongues of Flame which descended on the apostles in the upper room at Pentecost had caused them to be able to speak, amongst the unknown tongues in which they babbled, a version, a fragmentary part, of the original Tongue. The fact that Kees Wijnnobel believed that Joachim Steen was doomed to burn in eternal flames after Judge-ment did not prevent him from finding his linguistic speculations in-teresting. Kees Wijnnobel was not convinced that the original Tongue had been Hebrew. He thought it was something more natural, more intrinsically part of the nature of things, a tongue in which there were words for *lion, lamb, apple, snake, tree, good, evil* which wholly contained and corresponded to *all* their power and meaning. Elephant spoke ele-phant, earwig spoke earwig.

The young Gerard Wijnnobel listened and watched. He listened, watched, was revolted, and revolted. The lesson he drew, quite clearly from his father's Bible commentaries, and more reluctantly—for aes-thetic reasons—from the speculations of his grandfather, was that it is possible for human beings *to spend the whole of their lives on nonsense.* And not only that, but that perhaps also there was a trap, a quirk, a temptation *in the nature of language itself* that led people, that induced them, to spend the whole of their lives on nonsense. He discovered Nietzsche, who preached against Christianity and its forms with all the delicious fervour and energy of a Christian hell-fire preacher con-verted, and Nietzsche said, "I fear we are not getting rid of God be-cause we still believe in grammar." Theo-logy, the language of God, grammar, the forms of theology.

Gerard Wijnnobel became a mathematician. He became a mathe-matician in order to contemplate order and to renounce the mess of language. He worked on the Fibonacci numbers, which describe, among other things, the spiral of the cochlea in the inner ear and the principle that curls the ramshorn, the ammonites, certain snails, certain arrangements of branches around tree trunks. He withdrew into pure form, as though he saw only the relations of quadrilaterals, lengths, and primary colours of Mondrian, when once he had seen the forms of light made and recorded by Vermeer with an image of a rectangular coloured window and the enlightened solid body of a reading, or thinking, or pouring woman.

Perhaps because he came to England in the war and thus had to speak and teach and ultimately think in another language, which, however well mastered, was not his own, the Wijnnobel of the 1940s and 1950s turned his attention back from the forms of mathematics to the forms of language, to grammar. He became interested in Roman Jakobson's theories of "distinctive features" of all languages, in Saussure, who saw language as analogous to a chess game in which words were arbitrary signs to which certain formal functions were assigned, and most recently in Noam Chomsky's claim to have demonstrated that there was a deep universal structure of language, a universal grammar, innate in all human brains, not learned, any more than the beat of the heart or the focus of the eye is learned, not modified by society or experience, but part of human biological identity, capable of constructing the hum and buzz and thought patterns of innumerable tongues. As beavers are born knowing how to make dams, and as spiders are born with the ability to make webs, so human beings are born with the ability to speak and think in grammatical forms. Chomsky's generative grammar, Chomsky's transformational descriptions, still in 1964 new and uncompromising, are mathematical in their exactness and depend on the use of algorithms and mathematical structures for their understanding. Gerard Wijnnobel is convinced intellectually that Chomsky is right: that the human brain is born with a capacity to generate and transform language—that this is innate, not absorbed into some empty bucket or inscribed on some tabula rasa, but there in the folds of the cortex, the dendrites and synapses and axons of the neurones in the brain. The theories, both of learning and of language, that preceded this one are more interested in the way the mind is formed and shaped by society, or by learning, or by random events. To believe that linguistic competence is both innate and unalterable, in the present world, smacks of determinism, smacks of predestinarianism, and of more unpleasant things, a suggestion that heredity, not environment, differentiates between men. Many of the men Wijnnobel meets find that suggestion morally repugnant, exactly as he found his father's ideas repugnant. There is much talk, in his world, of language as either a crystalline, immutable structure, or as order-from-chaos, a flame-like structure that holds its changing shape in the winds of its environment. Aesthetically, Gerard Wijnnobel would like to believe in the flame, in the shifting, variable, changing form. Intellectually, he believes in the crystal. Intuitively, also, he believes in the crystal. Chomsky's descriptions of the human capacity to construct language fit his own sense of his own uses of it.

He believes too, that in some distant future the neuroscientists, the geneticists, the students of the matter of the mind, may find out the forms of language in the forest of the dendrites, in the links of the synapses. The genes are aperiodic crystals, dictating, to the matter they control, the structures, the forms, the substances that matter shall become. Somewhere in the future the understanding of their invariable form may lead to the understanding of the web of grammar and its invariable deep structure. Or so Wijnnobel believes. None of this is exactly helpful with the problem of what to teach to small and not-so-small children, with which the committee is engaged.

VII

❧❧❧❧❧

Thomas Poole sends Frederica to see his doctor, a cheerful fat man in
Bloomsbury Square. The ménage in the flat, after two months, has
taken on some aspects of a marriage. There is equable discussion of
shopping lists, of the feelings and friendships of Lizzie, Simon and
Leo, also of books, of the novels on Frederica's new course, which
takes place in a school called Our Lady of the Sorrows, and of ways
to dovetail this teaching with the teaching at the Art School. Leo is
quiet. He asks sometimes if they will go "back"—he does not say
"home"; children can use language with great care. He says, "They
will miss me," and specifies, "Sooty will miss me." He watches Frederica for signs of intention, and Frederica attempts to convey settled
calm, temporary certainty, trust.

Frederica's wound is healing badly. It festers, it re-opens, it is the
wrong sort of shiny pink, there is pus.

Thomas Poole puts a hand on Frederica's shoulder as she leaves.

"Courage," he says. "These things take time."

Frederica turns her face to him. He will kiss her; it seems natural.
Leo appears in a doorway, and Frederica shrinks into herself, briefly
putting up a hand to ward off a non-existent blow.

"I'm sorry," says Thomas Poole, easily.

"No need," says Frederica.

The fat doctor, whose name is Limass, probes and palpates and dresses
the wound. He says, with his cheerful manner, "This is a nasty one,
this is a mess, the way it hit you was bad luck."

Frederica says, "There is something else."

"Tell me."

"Something is wrong with my—with my vagina, with all that area. It is very painful. There are what I think you would call pustules. And a sort of crust."

She is precise. She is shamed. She is in pain.

The doctor ceases to smile, does a cursory examination, writes out a chit, and tells her she must attend the Middlesex Hospital clinic for sexually transmitted diseases. Frederica, feeling automatically guilty, because she has gambled sexually in her time and has survived, drops her head.

"When did you last have intercourse?" asks the doctor.

"With my husband. Only with him, since I got married." As this fact establishes itself, guilt is transformed to rage. A vision of the contents of the case in the wardrobe flashes across Frederica's inner eye. She moves her uncomfortable thighs together and feels pain, irritation, discomfort, separate feelings, that accompany all her movements as she walks.

"I see," says the doctor. "You do not seem to have married very wisely."

And Frederica feels a perverse desire to defend Nigel against this easy judgement, even though her own rage does not abate. Or perhaps it is only to defend herself, for having chosen unwisely. She says, "Things turn out different from what you expect."

"They do. Now you trot along to the Middlesex and get analysed before you get any worse. And keep off sex."

"I can't imagine ever wanting—any such thing—again."

"You'll be surprised," says the doctor, with cheery resignation.

"Hullo," says the plangent voice, affable and unpleasant. "Daniel the parson-person, Daniel the Vicarious, Daniel the Representative of a dead preaching-man. Are you well?"

"Little you care. Yes, I'm well. And yourself?"

"I am battered and bruised, my friend, bleeding in invisible places. Last night I went to preach my message, as I make it my duty to do—a man needs to make himself a pretty fantasy of a duty to inhabit human society every now and then, and I thought a modicum of human society was in order, a taste of the honey of human intercourse, sweet Daniel, invisible Daniel—I *yearned* weakly, dear Vicarious, to improve at least one person's understanding. So off I went to my local to preach my little preachment. I told them:

"Woe to all lovers who cannot surmount pity!

"Thus spoke the Devil to me once: 'Even God has his Hell: it is his love for man.'

"And lately heard him say these words: 'God is dead; God has died of his pity for man.'

"So be warned against pity: *thence* shall yet come a heavy cloud for man!

"But mark too this saying: All great love is above pity: for it wants to create—to create what is loved!

" 'I offer myself to my love, and *my neighbour as myself*'—that is the language of all creators.

"All creators however are hard.

"Thus spoke Zarathustra."

"It's better in German, but I don't suppose your education included the language of the ex-enemy, O parson-person, you don't sound like a man of great European culture.

"So I cast these pearls before the locals in my local and they took me by the hair and by the seat of my trousers and inflicted much local damage on my person with their boots, sweet Daniel, their boots and a bicycle chain and a broken pint glass, you would e'en have wept to see it, were you human, which I do often doubt, for you are so unsweet to me, so heel-dragging in the matter of soothing my sores as your dead Master bids you to, for I am the afflicted, O parson, O person, I am your work whether you like me or not, if I understand you rightly.

"Are you asleep, O Yorkshireman? Could you not watch with me one little hour?"

"I am *not* asleep. I am watching with you. You ought to talk to Canon Holly. He reads Nietzsche. He does Death-of-God theology. It sounds to me as though you and Canon Holly could have a fine debate. I am sorry you got bashed, but you do seem, if I may say so, to have asked for it. Indeed, I quite often feel like bashing you myself, if I ever set eyes on you."

"Ah, my sweet friend, my dear Judge come to judgement, at last a moment's true understanding, a moment of *rapport,* worked for incessantly since I began to infiltrate my voice into the passages of your reluctant and unready earhole. I do most deeply, my temporary love, desire to be bashed, as you put it, to be bashed to smithereens and shards and molecules and *pulp* and *broth,* and if you are ready to oblige me I will manifest myself. In the alleys of Smithfield I sought you and I found you not, among hatchets and saws I perceived you not, I turned aside the red robes of justice and saw fearful implements of torture and belabouring but my sweet Daniel, my chastiser in surplice and soutane, I found *not,* although my fessae ached for him, also my lower gut and my labile tongue . . ."

"Listen, you. I do not want to chastise you. Or anyone. I don't wear a surplice or a soutane if you happen to like those things, I wear *boring cords* and a *jumper,* so come off it. Shall I get Canon Holly to talk to you about Nietzsche and the Death of God?"

"There is so much more pleasure in talking about those things to someone who can't bear to contemplate them—so much more skill and difficulty to overcome for the proselytising Prophet. Talking to your Canon sounds like preaching to the converted, a doddle, with no kick to it."

There is a noise in the stairwell of the crypt. Heavy feet descend the spiral stair, quick, sure, hurrying. Behind Daniel, Ginnie Greenhill rises to her feet, holding her knitting needles defensively before her.

A voice, sharp, deep, well-bred. "Is Daniel Orton here? I was told to look for him down here."

"He's working. On the whole we don't see clients down here; there is a sitting-room *upstairs,* where you can have tea."

"I'm not a client, you silly woman. I've got to see him urgently. It's private."

"I don't know—"

"I can hear shouting," says Steelwire's tremolo. "You are distracted. I shall lie down and lick my poor wounds. Think of me licking them, my reluctant friend. Think of a tongue-tip touching blood."

"There is nothing worse," says Daniel, "than people trying to stir your imagination with what doesn't stir it."

"Ah, you are *touché,* I can hear it. How can you be a Christian person and not be stirred by the flow of blood, the *taste of blood,* my dear reluctant friend?"

"Is *that* Daniel Orton?"

"You can see he's talking."

"A moment of your time, Mr. Orton."

"How exciting," says Steelwire as Daniel replaces the receiver. Daniel turns to consider his visitor. A dark, heavily built man, his own height, with well-cut hair, a suit, a silk tie, a blueing chin. Heavy brows, a heavy frown.

Daniel puts out his hand. "Can I help?"

"I think you are hiding my wife from me. I've been looking for her, and I think it might be you who's hiding her. I want her back."

"We don't betray professional confidences—"

"You don't know me. We're related, not really, but in a way. I'm Nigel Reiver. My wife's Frederica. I've not met you but I know about you. You married my wife's sister, who died. I know about you. I think she might have come to you. It's been two months now, and I've been looking, but I've had trouble finding you, too. I've thought it out, she would have come to you, of course. You wrote to her, I saw the letter. I don't want to hurt you, or her, I just want her back. And my son. He ought to be with me. His life is with me. So please, tell me where she is. Tell me where she is. I don't want to hurt her, *I want her back.*"

"I don't know where she is. I didn't know she'd gone."

"I don't believe you. You *must know where she is.*"

"I don't." Daniel adds, unfortunately, "Which looks like a good thing."

Nigel Reiver steps back and punches Daniel in the face. Daniel staggers, and puts up an arm to protect his head. Ginnie Greenhill presses a panic button which starts up a loud angry bell, at earth level above them. They are frequently attacked by clients and have discovered that this bell is enough to deter most of them from further violence. There is also an understanding with the local police that if they hear it sound, they will "look in" to make sure all is well. In this case, the loud noise seems to have a maddening effect. Nigel takes another lunge at Daniel and lands a sideways blow on his ear. There is a sound of ripping inside Nigel's expensively built suit. Daniel thinks briefly of Steelwire, who would be sorry to miss the crunch of bone on skin, the red wet flow of blood. He tries to be a sort of pacifist, but it is not good for people to get away with hurting other people. He advances on his brother-in-law and takes a grip on the knot of his tie.

"Listen, you. I don't tell lies. If I say I don't know where she is, then I don't know where she is. You'd better try to understand that, it'll save time."

He wants to hurt Nigel. His blood drips from his swelling nose on to Nigel's nice shirt. Nigel thinks. Nigel brings up his right hand and slaps Daniel very hard across the untouched ear. Daniel understands that this is all he can do. He *must* strike out. He is overwrought. The bell jangles and howls. A policeman appears at the head of the staircase. Daniel, a little breathless, says it is all all right, thank you, there has been a misunderstanding.

"If you're sure, Mr. Orton," says the policeman.

"A complete misunderstanding," says Daniel.

The two men glare at each other. Nigel makes a conciliatory effort. "I know about your wife. I know how hard you took that. My wife has gone off with my son. I *want them.*"

Daniel sees the dead face, unprepared, unexpecting. His mind reddens. He plunges forward and hits Nigel in the mouth. More blood splashes and drips.

"Christ!" says Nigel thickly. "I'm sorry. I said that wrong. What a godawful mess. Can we sit down?"

"If you insist."

"I told you, I'm sorry, I know I said that wrong, I was trying to— trying to—you know what—and I made it worse. Look, I was the one who comforted Frederica. I held her while she cried. Don't hit me again, I'm just saying—you and I—we know each other and we don't. I know it's private. She cried and cried in my arms, Frederica. I want her back."

He is saying, says Daniel's red mind, that he married Frederica because of *that,* because of Stephanie. He looks at the floor. He scowls. They both scowl. Ginnie Greenhill notes a fleeting resemblance: dark men like dark bulls.

"I'm stepping in deeper, trying to make it better," says Nigel. "Have a hanky, I carry several. They're clean."

Daniel mops blood.

"OK. I accept you don't know where she is. Where can I go? I ought to go after those sodding friends of hers with the Land Rover but I can't remember their sodding names. I *just wanted them out* of my house and out they went. Now I want them, I don't know where to start. I want my boy. He's my boy, he's my blood, *I love him.* A father can love a boy, a father should be with a boy—and a boy with his father. That's true isn't it?"

Daniel drops his head. His son is in Yorkshire. Nigel's son is with Frederica, about whose maternal instincts Daniel, even Daniel, does not feel automatically hopeful. He has never wholly liked Frederica. Part of him does not even want to think of her crying for Stephanie. Who was his. Who was his.

"Every day," says Nigel, "I think, today she'll get in touch. And she doesn't."

"I'll look around. I don't say I'll find her, I don't say I've any idea where to start either. I'll try and give her the message. To get in touch. Then it's up to her."

"I went up to Yorkshire. I smashed the old man's head in a door. I didn't mean to. I've got a temper. I don't mean anything by it."

Daniel laughs.

"What's funny?"

"That's what he always said himself. He didn't mean anything by it. I do advise trying to get her back by peaceful means."

"I love her," says Nigel.

"Love," says Daniel. His work has given him a professional horror of the word. He says to Nigel, guiding him up the stairs, "You've ruined my professional life. You've bashed in both my ears. All I can hear is humming and interference and random noise. Horrible. My work is listening."

"It's funny work. I expect it gets you down. Other people's agonies, nothing you can *do*?"

"It does, a bit. It does."

"How the other half live," says Nigel, emerging. He gives Daniel a card. "In case you hear anything."

"I told you, my ears are out of action."

They part.

"Our great Projector," said Colonel Grim to his almost-crony Turdus Cantor, "is to turn his attention to those tender young sucklings in our midst, to the children whose pretty babble enlivens our dark corridors and sweetly disturbs our contemplations."

"He has none himself," said Turdus Cantor. "None that he acknowledges, none that are known of."

"That has never prevented an enthusiast from pronouncing on the subject. And you must consider, Turdus, my friend, that we were all children once, we are all experts on that state."

"And what we propose for others we derive from our own fears and hopes in that distant time. And so the race goes on."

"But Culvert, save his soul, means to make a new race of children and a new race of men to follow."

"He may do good. Men—and women—love him. They will listen for hours together to his speaking. They would not listen so to you or to me. They would not do as we asked."

"In the old days, which are departed, they did as I ordered."

"But, my dear Grim, the bad old days are departed, indeed."

"And if a man promises happiness, and it is not forthcoming, the people may hate him."

"Or if he has taught them wisdom, they may understand, nevertheless."

"Have you ever known that?"

"No. But hope is a pleasant human failing. Let us go and hear our Projector's blueprint for the liberation of the babes at the breast."

The Theatre of Tongues was crowded to hear Culvert speak on the education of their children. The children themselves, of whom there were perhaps fifty or sixty in the Tower, were not present at this oration, for various ladies had voluntarily taken upon themselves to teach the little creatures the skills of the old civilisation, to wit, reading, writing, figuring, languages, dead and alive, sewing, plain and ornamental, drawing and painting, singing, dancing, playing on flutes, fiddles, tambourines and glockenspiel, making paper carnations, cooking little cakes, observing such humble creatures as spiders, lizards, flies, cockroaches, earthworms and mice; also the growth of beans and mustard seeds. All this activity was admittedly unplanned and haphazard but it kept the little people quiet, and satisfied their driving and exhausting curiosity and activity in what were felt to be reasonable, innocuous ways. But it was known that Culvert had proposals more rational, more profound and more searching for the employment of their long days. ("Who does not remember how long, long are the days of childhood, how the minutes creep, creep, and the hours and the days sink and sough like heavy velvet, and the months are unimaginably far, like other planets, like stars in the black, with dark dust between now and the now to come, perhaps to come?")

I will not give Culvert's speech in *toto*, for although I can assure you that it was most charismatically delivered, that his audience swayed to his periods and parentheses like pink-eyed rats before a cobra, like the faithful at the feet of an inspired preacher, the truth is that on paper it is quite possible that the magnetic quality would be lacking from this oration, as is so often the case with spoken enchantments reduced to flickerings of black ink. And then, he had done so much work, had burned so much midnight oil, with Damian and Roseace bringing him sirops and stimulants, sweets and salts, that his thinking and speaking ran into diverticulated pockets of matter, like those pockets that develop in an overstimulated gut, and retain festering irritants. For he had thoughts on play, and thoughts on the learning of speech and reading, thoughts, most recondite, on the order and organisation of the secret sensual life of infants, which in his view should be uncovered and made public, thoughts on punishment (ah, such finely graded, such delicately apposite, such generously imagined thoughts on punishment), thoughts on group life, thoughts on solitude, thoughts on corruption and so on and so on, thoughts on stubbornness and thoughts on readiness to please, that to recount them all would take more time than any sane reader in this fallen and trivial world would accord me. So I will somewhat brutally summarise his sayings, in order to speed my narration. It is true that the purity and beauty of his ideas were not wholly incarnate in their subsequent application, but I believe they may nevertheless shine through. He meant *well*, he meant *well*, Culvert, and maybe few of us can have a better encomium.

Because the children were not present, many of the women of the Tower were not present, because they were "caring" for the children, as they believed.

But Mavis, wife of Fabian, mother of Florian, Florizel, and the little Felicitas, was present, because she clung greatly to her little children, and feared that Culvert meant to sever their ties.

And Roseace and Damian were there too, and could not keep their hands from each other's body. Culvert had been astonished by the success of his theatrical device where Roseace out of good feeling enacted before the community, in the Theatre of Masks, a passion for Damian's body, which Damian desired her to have and which in daily life she could not feel. And so, as I told you, wearing a sweet-smiling mask and a dishevelled wig, she had submitted in public to the passionate advances of Damian, who had chosen a warrior mask, a stern heroic mask, and achieved his desires to cries of encouragement and pleasure from the audience. But since that time Roseace's flesh ached and yearned for Damian—and he, only a little less, for her—and so they coupled in Culvert's bedroom as he wrote, separated to bring him sustenance, and then coupled again.

This, Culvert believed, was a good result of his intentions.

He had concluded, for himself, that Roseace's breasts were crumpled in texture and that Damian's buttocks were overweening and absurd.

He had proved that a formal enactment of a feeling may lead to that feeling.

He had never noticed that Roseace simpered.

I am about to deflect myself from the summary of Culvert's speech with a vicarious plunge into the pleasurable communion of Damian and Roseace. But I will reserve that for the sweetmeat to follow the meat of his discourse.

A Child, said Culvert, was born to a Woman, and some Man was usually known to have been implicated in the seeding of that Child, though there was less certainty about which Man than many desired to have.

In the corrupt world from which we have fled, he said, this Child was then reared in a Family, made up of a Man, a Woman, and such brothers, half-brothers and female children as were gathered into that group. The social structures of the Society they had fled, to wit, monarchies, the Christian religion, places of education and so on, were all made in imitation of that Family. They were structures of authority, of persecution, of narrow loyalties, of hierarchy, of exclusive and narrow affections and privileges, all of which led to oppression, irrationality and the sense of private property and personal greed.

In their new world, in the Tower, all men would be equal and would care equally for all men. There would be no marriage, no family, and the children of the community would all be the children of every member. Thus envy and favouritism would be abolished. All suckling mothers would give milk indifferently to all suckling children; all would feed equally well or ill, and thus no one would hurt any other.

In order to achieve this, all the children in the Tower would be removed to the new Dormitories which he had had constructed in the last few weeks (even using outside hired labour so as the more rapidly to begin the new order and to abolish the Family). The new Dormitories were constructed in one wing to his own design. In them were cots and cushions, great beds and narrow beds, curtains and coverlets of all kinds of rich and bright colours, for he had observed that children required the stimulation of various colours and textures. Lights, too, he had made, that would shine all night, for he had observed that children were afraid of the dark. And in places these cast shadows, for he had observed that children liked to be frightened by grotesque shadows, and in others they did not, for some children were harmed by fear. And he had observed that some children desired to sleep in heaps like young puppies, and some were of a more solitary nature, and desired to sleep alone, and he had made ample provision for both.

"And if one child desires to heap itself with another who desires solitude, what then?" asked Turdus Cantor.

The children will learn to regulate their own society, explained Culvert. They will learn to respect each other's desires and to offer kindnesses reciprocally. As our society becomes more harmonious, so this will become more natural to them. Grasping and bullying are products of the Family and the Establishment. These will be replaced by reasonable groups, founded on well-established desires.

He went on to education. Children, he said, would learn at their own speed, what they pleased, as they pleased. We should not impose on them early restrictive vices to deform and twist their minds, such as blind, uncomprehending repetition of verses or numbers, such as the laws of perspective or moral saws and sayings. All should be true discovery, all questions should be answered at the time when it was urgent to a child's mind to have an answer, and not otherwise. Books they should have in plenty—their nature to be agreed by the whole community—and adults should always hold themselves in readiness to teach, both how to read and how to understand the contents. For a child, said Culvert, may want to read for fifteen hours together and then not again for a week or two, and it is my belief that those fifteen hours are worth months of forced attention.

Also, he said (remember, I summarise), it is my deep belief that we, who call ourselves adults, grown-ups, reasonable beings, have much to learn from very small children. For we perceive, if we watch attentively, that very small children are full of delighted activity and exploration which we, narrow and shunted, repress in them with smacking and pursing our lips, and threatening with vile things, with castration, with blindness, with dwarfism, with the Fires of Hell. Small children are natural beings, they explode from their mother's wombs full of natural energies and powers which we pervert and suppress. Consider the natural propensity of little girls to raise their skirts and display their round bellies and little bottoms to men and women. Should we not stroke and admire and cherish what they so innocently offer? Consider the natural propensity of both sexes to seek the pleasures dormant in their little organs, in their soft small tails and their hidden sweet beads of flesh. Should we, as now, terrify and hurt them by howling and thundering, or should we not rather smile and play with them? If left to play in innocence, what might they not become, what might they not learn, and in turn teach us, of refinements of pleasure, of ecstasies of perception, of courtesies and reciprocities undreamed?

At this point Culvert's discourse became visionary in its intensity, and hard for some of his more pedestrian or earth-bound companions to follow. For he appeared to be advocating a new kind of school, or theatre (theatre and school, and also church, were part of each other in the forms of his thought), or ritual, even, in which the men and women would set themselves to learn by imitation from babes and sucklings, in which all would be innocently naked on the stage together, and innocently explore all flesh, mature and nubile and milky-new, all apertures, all lips, all teeth, all recesses, all flowings of milk and blood, of seed and sweat, of saliva and tears, of sibilants and labiles, for was not the babbling and lalling of our infant selves and our infant teachers a beginning of language more sweet, more full of promise, than the austere croakings and scratchings and hummings and hawings we had in our fallen state made of it. Oh, cried Culvert, to a great ecstatic sigh of most of his listeners, if we might again approximate our sensibilities to the moment of our birth and learn all afresh, as we shall forge new, freed sensual apparatus and new, unimagined powers of sympathy and pleasure, so shall we forge a new true language, a language of love and playfulness and truth without innuendo or inadequacy or lameness, a language like a sword, a language as immediate as the triumphal song of the seed from the cock, a language before shame and beyond shuffling embarrassment—a new universal speech.

He said also that he had observed that children did not evince the same disgust at the excrement of the human race as was shown by the more squeamish adults, a disgust which had led to the diminishing usefulness of the latrines in the Tower. This disgust might be a distortion of the sensibility induced by our cramped education, but it might also be natural, a natural development. He felt that the childish pleasure in dirt and mess should be set to use, and proposed to found juvenile Troops of cleaners, who should gallop in and out of the Tower with their own little handcarts and ponycarts containing tubs of the offending matter, to the sound of bugles and pipes. He had devised a uniform for these Troops—a subtle olive hessian with scarlet braid at every conceivable juncture—which he now displayed to the assembled company, who applauded courteously.

His ideas on punishment, which are germane to much of what I am to tell, although they were first propounded here, were in a state of some incoherence, and I will save discussion of them for a later point. He would like, he said, to proclaim that there should be no more punishment or chastisement anywhere in their reasonable passional world. But things were not so perfect, not yet, it was hard to see . . . On the whole, he said, it was better for adults never to punish children, whose little peccadilloes should be corrected by their peers, in an atmosphere of tolerance and laughter.

At this point the Lady Mavis asked if she might speak. Culvert had marked this lady as his opposer. She was tall and brown and spoke slowly: she and Fabian, her partner, for husbands there were now not, spoke often together and agreed on almost all things, as though they thought each other's thoughts, and communicated sans language. And this state of doubleness, as though they were two trees that had grown together, was highly regarded in the old state, before the Revolution, but was now regarded with suspicion by the people of the Tower, as though she set herself up to have other ideals from them. And although many had availed themselves of the new freedoms, so that sweet orgies of four, or twelve, or twenty took place every night in the little side-chapels and minor dungeons, although more and more were putting themselves forward to act out their desires in the Theatre of Pain and the Theatre of Tongues, no other member had so far approached Fabian or Mavis. And these two had in the early days of escape been all smiles and friendliness; the Lady Mavis had created many gay fêtes champêtres for children and adults, with delicious breads and cakes made by her hands, with sweet lemonades, with barley water and fruit fools decorated with cherries and angelica. But now that the pleasures of most were more frenetic and fiercer, these simple feasts were almost shunned, or attracted only the very old and the very young. And on the Lady Mavis's wide brow the shadow of a frown had replaced the wrinkling smile of welcome. One night she and Fabian had discussed, in their stony chamber, the advisability of entertaining other lovers. "It might amuse you," the Lady Mavis had said to Fabian, who had replied, "If I closed my eyes, my dear, and imagined that pink Pastorella or creamy Chloris was in fact your own lithe brown self, with the little scars and the laughing-lines and the secret folds I know so well, I might be able to go through with it, but in truth I doubt it. And it would be a blow *against* freedom of desire to indulge in variety for fear of social disapproval. For such conventional prescription of behaviour is what we fled. And if we desire only each other, whom we know and trust, that too should be possible to accommodate in freedom."

"He may make us act on his stage," said the Lady Mavis.

"I think not," said Fabian. "This is not a monarchy and he is not a king. *All of us* are to do as we please. Let those act who discover themselves by acting."

"He will say, we do not know ourselves," said Mavis.

"And we will demonstrate that we do," said Fabian.

He will hate us, thought the lady, but had not the courage to speak it aloud. Fabian however, heard her thought. And his face too, bore a slight frown.

Culvert had spent time analysing the predominant passions of his people, and writing them down in a table of affinities and oppositions, linked by many little arrows and symbols of swords and crosses, cocks and bulls and open mouths. A truly harmonious world, he concluded provisionally, would need about five times as many citizens to make sure that every possible desire was present and reciprocated. Since the Tower would not accommodate these extra persons and passions, those present in fact must be made to double up, so to speak, to "try out" passions which did not come to them naturally. If a man had a desire to pick off the scabs of another, and no passionate scabbed skin could be found, someone must simulate this passion in the Theatre of Pain and perhaps even learn to feel delight in it.

He had the Lady Mavis picked out as a simple type, the female whose sole purpose was her need to give suck. She was a woman, Culvert's diagnostic pronounced, whose whole sensuous being was concentrated in her big brown nipples and their dark aureoles, whose only delight in life was the drag of infant suction, the love-bites of toothless gums, the steady suck of tiny lips and the kneading of little fingers in her fat round flesh. Since their coming to La Tour Bruyarde she had assumed the freedom of unlacing her clothes and presenting the bursting globes of her breast at every opportunity to her infant's mouth, without shame, which was of course desirable, for shame was abolished. A percipient reader might suppose that the Projector would designate such a person as wet nurse to the whole dormitory of infants, and consider her well placed and useful. But the truth must be told: something in Culvert was disgusted by the sight of these breasts, and of the milk dribbling from the infant lips as it gushed too plentifully forth. He felt a desire, as he saw her placidly feeding her child, to run at her with his hands, or even with a weapon, to pierce or bruise those assertive rounds, to mix hot blood with the pallid milk, to slice, to sever . . . He did not, as a good analyst of desires should have done, consider the whence, the wherefore and the possible satisfaction of his desire to hurt the Lady Mavis. He had not reached that stage in his development which was the deep contemplation of the natural human urge to hurt, to harm, to pierce, to open, to bruise, to stab, to strangle. No, the unregenerate Culvert turned his attention away from his loathing of the Lady Mavis's mammary display, and tried to be rational, to think in the interests of the community. She was not much use, this lady, in terms of reciprocated new delights, for no one appeared to desire her, perhaps because all were repelled by her insistent maternity. He thought she must learn to partake in the polymorphous and manifold pleasures of the flesh, for the good of the greater number. In his secret soul he began to devise a scenario for the transfiguration and opening of this austere lady. In the interim he replied, a little testily, that of course she might speak. And he felt a touch of nausea for he knew in advance what she would say, and how it should be countered.

So the Lady Mavis stood up, holding against her breast her little son, Florizel, and said in her milky voice that it was possible to dispute the wisdom of separating small infants from their mothers who had given birth to them. For a child's body grows for a time inside a woman's body, and after it is severed from the umbilical cord, it is still part of her, in that it cannot stand or walk alone for a year or more, and in that its natural economy, its bodily well-being, is dependent on the milk she provides and the care she takes to teach it skills and keep it from harm.

"I do not argue," said the Lady Mavis, "that there is any God who designed or created us so, but I do argue for Nature, for everywhere in the natural world we see such particular bonds and such particular care. Even the female Alligator, who was once thought to be an unnatural and even cannibalistic Parent, has been observed to shelter her tiny offspring in the horrid cavern of her jaw, so that they run in for safety between her terrible teeth. And she does not indiscriminately shelter all such soft helpless amphibians, but only her own, the issue of her own eggs, which she knows and recognises."

"And if this is so," repeated Culvert with patient contempt, "do we not see what evils spring from this partiality, this hotbed of egotism and privilege, this nest of demanding love which holds back the adventurous child from exploring the outer world? It is not only in brute fact, but over and over in analogy, that Mothers have smothered their sleeping infants by rolling over their heavy bulks on their defenceless sleeping faces. No, let us, with a system of checks, balances, reinforcements, subtle affections, extend from each of us to all the others those thrustings and heats of 'maternal' affection, so that all may feel love for all, and the world expand in harmony, for none will compete for what is proffered to all, no orphan child will cry for the breast, no overindulged sprig struggle to evade the strangling maternal clasp—we shall all be one, and one will be all. All will feel *enough* of this mothering-passion, *all*, men, women, castrates and children, and none will emit or endure *too much*."

And they all cried out, Culvert was in the right, nothing would be taken from Mavis's children if they were removed from her exclusive company, but much would be given *as well as* what they had.

And while the company were exploring the new Dormitories, which were opened by the Lady Paeony, who cut a pink ribbon with a pair of scissors, Colonel Grim and Turdus Cantor made their way to the battlements and looked out over the plain. And the company exclaimed over the ingenious sleeping accommodation, the huge circular cushioned beds, decorated with embroideries of lambs in the fields playing sweetly with lion cubs and spotted leopards. And Colonel Grim said to Turdus Cantor, "I see a troop of horsemen approaching. Where is our watch?" And Turdus Cantor said, "Your eyes are better than mine, I see nothing. I am not sure we have a watch, for there is not always a Companion who desires to stand at the post since no one ever comes."

And the company exclaimed over the pretty cupboards for playthings and chamberpots and clothing, all decorated with painted butterflies and smiling lizards.

And Colonel Grim said, "I see a banner with a bleeding tree. The Krebs are riding across the valley in full daylight. They do not usually travel by day. I think you should hurry down and alert Culvert and the others, for it may be they mean to attack us. For there is no way out of the valley to the north now the bridge is cut."

The company had no armed guard and no organised defence for the Tower, which would in fact be difficult, even for a large force, to break into, once the great gates were closed and the bridge down. But everyone bustled to and fro, like insects disturbed in a nest, and found out what swords, pistols, pitchforks, muskets, spits, carving knives and so forth could be brought to bear, as the company of the Krebs approached closer—for Colonel Grim's clear eyes had seen well, they were indeed the Krebs, riding fast and furiously, about a hundred strong, and chanting as they came, in a language no one could interpret.

Their horses were low and ugly, with rough black hair and starting manes; they galloped close to the ground, in a cloud of dust, surprisingly fast. The faces of the riders could not be seen, for they all wore flat leather helmets, with a kind of leather prow projecting over their noses. They wore also black leather jerkins, supple and polished, matt here, glistening there, and leather breeches, also black, so the whole troupe was a moving, singing black shadow, above which sparkled a cloud of silver spear-points on black spears, like monstrous metal midges. Their shoulders were very broad, and their arms very long, but their torsos were squat and their waists narrow, and their bow legs, wrapped round the bellies of their horses, short.

The people of the Tower stood behind their battlements, brandishing their ramshackle collection of weapons, men, women, and a few children. The Lady Paeony declared it was a pity they had not had time to prepare boiling oil, and the Lady Coelia said they had precious little oil to spare, and would be hard put to it if the Krebs took it into their heads to encamp below the Tower and lay siege to it. And when the Krebs came nearer they began to blow great horns, great ramshorns, and circle around before the closed gates.

Then Culvert called down from the battlements, "Do you come here in peace?"

And a high, grinding voice, unaccustomed to the tongue of the Tower, answered thickly, "Neither in peace nor in war. We bring you a thing."

"It is a trick," said Narcisse. "They wish to make us open the door."

"We wish to exchange this thing for things you have. For wine and flour and sugar to make a feast. It is our feast day."

"Show us your thing," cried Culvert.

"You must come down and see," said the Krebs.

"It is a trap," said Narcisse.

"I think not," said Colonel Grim. "It is true that periodically they have great feasts, and like to season their sour beer and their rootcakes with our more refined provisions. Let us go down, Culvert, and see their thing. Fabian will stand over the bridge with a musket, and Narcisse with another, to cover our sally, and we will see this thing."

"We have enough flour and wine for ourselves, and none to spare," said the Lady Paeony.

"And how much shall we have if the Krebs take a dislike to us and camp there to starve us out?"

So Culvert and Colonel Grim went to the mouth of the bridge, and told the Krebs to show their thing to be exchanged.

And they brought a great leather sack, tied with leather ropes.

"Open it up," said Colonel Grim. "So we may barter."

And the Krebs opened the mouth of the sack, and kicked the sack several times, two of them, with their small, sharp, booted feet.

And out crawled a man. He came out with difficulty, his long grey hair matted with blood, his face a mask of blood, his arms bound, and his ankles, so that he could only slide like a snake out of the mouth of the bag. He was gagged too, with a leather strap between his teeth.

"He is a friend of yours," said the Krebs. "Or so he said when we took him."

When they turned their faces up to speak they could be seen to be covered with dark hair, fat faces with mouths lost in the hair, and small glittering black eyes.

"We cannot see him for blood," said Culvert. "Let us see him."

"He is a friend of yours, he says," repeated the Krebs. "If you will not acknowledge him, we will kill him for spying. As you please. Also we will take his ransom as your food parties arrive, for we know where they are and when they will come. But our feast is now, and we would like wine now."

"Stand him up, and untie him," said Culvert.

So the Krebs undid the leathery knots, and helped the man roughly to his feet, jostling him, and leaving his hands tied.

He was a tall man, in a long black cloak. His eyes shone dark in his bloody face.

"Can you see me, Culvert?" he said. "Through all this muck and mire? I am not a gift you would have chosen, but I would be grateful if you would accept me, for the alternatives are not pleasant."

His voice, though racked by pain, was dry and precise.

And Culvert laughed.

"You are right," he said. "You are a gift I would never have chosen, for you and I shall never agree to the world's end. But I can do no other but accept you, old enemy, for I will not have your death on my head."

And no one had any knowledge of the stranger, save Culvert. But they found out food enough, and drink enough, to satisfy the Krebs, and the stranger walked painfully but proudly across the bridge into the Tower. And Culvert said to the assembled people:

"Let me make known to you my old childhood playmate and student companion, Samson Origen. Let me say also, in front of him, as he stands there covered in blood and dust, that he comes as the serpent into our Paradise, for he is the world's great nay-sayer, and there is nothing in the world on which he and I agree. There is no human being worse fitted for our project, or more opposed to our aims, and so we must welcome him with tender loving care and overwhelm him with sweet reason, and seduce him with reasonable pleasures, or he will have us all shivering and chastising ourselves in monastic cells, not because that is our secret delight, but because we must have no delight under the moon. Is it not so, old enemy? Do I misrepresent you?"

"I will keep quiet," said Samson Origen, "for the present, I promise you."

And then he fainted away on the cobbles where he stood, and further philosophical dispute had to be postponed.

Frederica stands on a small platform at one end of a large studio, lit from above. She is dressed in a short black woollen dress and a knitted jacket in black, as long as the dress. Her hair is loose and long: her sharp face looks out from between its curtains. The students sit in chairs with swinging notepad arms, the men in dark jeans, the women in shirts and smocks mostly in dark, fruity colours, slightly acid. They have pale lips and eyes made up like sinister dolls, with long lashes and a bruised look. They are professional waifs. Some are taking notes and some are doodling. Frederica is speaking passionately about paper lanterns on a dark lake, primroses and ruddy sea with crabs, white storks and turquoise sky, and the great sinister cuttlefish "that stared straight from the heart of the light." Everything for

213

Lawrence, she says, is loaded with *meaning*. She describes the shattered circle of the reflected moon. She talks of the white flowers of evil, the *fleurs du mal,* floating on the sea of death. She is teaching a ten-week course on "The Modern Novel." Art students read with difficulty; choose some *short books,* said Richmond Bly. She has chosen *Death in Venice, La Nausée, The Castle,* all of which are still to come. She has begun with Lawrence and Forster because that was where, in Cambridge, she ended. "The novel is the one bright book of life," said Lawrence, and Lawrence was the point of perfection towards which the novel had been heading, it appeared then. Men asked her if she was "a Lawrentian woman." The sixties are slowly gathering speed, and the sixties do not find Lawrence daring: he has been admitted to the Establishment with the Lady Chatterley trial in 1961. Daring is *Naked Lunch,* is Allen Ginsberg, is Artaud. Frederica by a pure trick of time feels *involved* in *Women in Love,* which is a book about which she feels a fierce ambivalence (it is powerful, it is ridiculous, it is profound, it is wilfully fantastic). Its existence is part of the way she sees the world. It matters to her that these students should see it.

She does not yet know them very well. Later, she will distinguish; potters notice different things from textile designers, painters use language more flamboyantly and more loosely than graphic designers, sculptors are either silent or voluble, industrial designers dislike the culture of the book, jewellers are fey, theatre designers read as though books were blueprints for structures of images. At this early stage, she is a little afraid of them. She is there presenting herself as a *literary critic,* and these students are *artists.* Instinctively, she does not offer them critical categories or moral judgements. She tries to seduce them into seeing that books are complicated formal structures. For they do not like books for the most part. For them, brightness and meaning are elsewhere, are in the studio, in the pub, in bed.

A novel, *Women in Love,* for instance, she says, is made of a long thread of language, like knitting, thicker and thinner in patches. It is made in the head and has to be remade in the head by whoever reads it, who will always remake it differently. It is made of people whose fates are more interesting to its maker than those of his friends or lovers—but who are also an attempt to understand his friends and lovers probably. The people are made of language, but this is not all they are. A novel is also made of *ideas* that connect all the people like another layer of interwoven knitting—*Women in Love* is a novel about decadence, about love of death, about thanatos as opposed to

214

eros. The ideas are made out of language but that is not all they are. This novel is made of visual images—the lanterns, the moon, the white flowers—which you might think were like painted images, but they are not, for they have to be *unseen visible images* to be powerful. They are made out of language but that is not all they are. We must all imagine the broken moon, and she takes her power from *all our imaginings* and their sameness and their difference. She is trying to make the painters and sculptors see how a novel is a work of art and is not a painting. She is trying to understand something herself. A young woman smiles at her: a young man in glasses writes furiously. They are listening. *The group is listening.* She has them: the knitting is a fishnet.

At the other end of the studio, on another platform, another group of students is arranged, less formally, lying on the ground, squatting on the floor, round the model, Jude Mason, who has been reading to them from what appears to be a blood-red ledger. He is partly dressed: below his spare haunches he is naked: he sits on the edge of the platform, his knees drawn up amongst his long grey veil of hair, his balls poised on the dust between his dirty feet. He wears a dirty velvet jacket in a faded speedwell blue, a skirted jacket, from the turn of the seventeenth and eighteenth centuries in style, with filthy lace cuffs and a kind of jabot or cravat. Under this jacket, and beneath the cravat, he is unclothed, his body lean like dark metal. He calls out now, in a sawing voice, "You should teach them Nietzsche. Man in a little skiff on the raging sea of Maya, of illusion, supported by the *principium individuationis.*"

Frederica is angry. The thread of the class attention is broken. Anything she can say will sound school-mistressy or piqued. So will silence. She says, "I am talking about Lawrence."

"I know. I can hear. Bits of it are not uninteresting. The knitting idea is not at all bad, writing does resemble that despised art. Continue. We may yet join your circle."

Frederica stares angrily at him. All imagined retorts sound petulant. He smiles, a self-satisfied, *smart* smile on his drawn, sinewy face.

"Because it is knitting, I should be glad if you wouldn't break the thread of my argument."

"*Argument,* is it? Happy those who earn their daily bread by arguing, as opposed to displaying their flesh and blood for study. I will hear your argument."

This too is a nice provocation: it requires Frederica either to invite him into her class, or to speak up to be heard and interrupted, or to speak low, conspiratorial, so that he cannot hear. The best would be to invite him. But she does not want him. She does not like him. She does not like his look, his smell, or his sawing voice. He is disruption in person. She decides to continue. She opposes herself to him. She wills the attention of her group, the fringes of which turn their heads to see what Jude will do.

"At the centre of *Women in Love*," says Frederica, "is a mystery, an emptiness. The two women are wonderful both as real women making decisions about love, about sex, about the future, and as myths, as mythic beings willing life or death. But what are we to make of Birkin, who in many ways is Lawrence, in many ways is the central consciousness of the whole tale? We are told, and mostly forget, that he is *an Inspector of Schools*. Indeed, at one moment, we actually see him inspecting a school, when he discusses with Ursula the sexuality of the hazel catkins. But mostly we do not believe in him as an Inspector of Schools. He has the entrée both to the upper-class society of Nottinghamshire and to the Bohemian artistic world in London. There is no reason why this should be so. It feels wrong."

"Matthew Arnold," says the sawing voice, "was an Inspector of Schools."

"Also the author of innumerable books and poems," says Frederica, this time managing to contain and include Jude's contribution. "And part of a cultural dynasty. I was going to go on to say, we experience Birkin, if not as Lawrence's *alter ego* (though he is best when most absurdly insisting on his maleness, for which Lawrence intelligently and complicitly *mocks* him)—if Birkin is not Lawrence's *alter ego,* he is the presence of the *author of the book*. And *Women in Love* is not, is trying very hard not to be, *A Portrait of the Artist*. Lawrence may have said, "The novel is the highest form of human expression yet attained"—which you are in a better position to question than most people are—but I think he felt a kind of sickliness in writing novels about writing novels about writing novels."

"*Tout existe pour aboutir à un livre,*" speaks the Chorus. Frederica gives him a theatrical nod of complicity, covering rage, and goes on again.

"He was in the tradition of realism in which George Eliot wrote of the travails of Lydgate and the moral defeat of Dorothea. He wasn't an aesthete, he didn't want to be. But he was pushed towards it. Because *Women in Love* is a novel about experiencing the world as art—

good art or bad art. It came at the time of the First World War and the trenches, but it does not look directly at those, it is about the forms of vision and the forms of thought."

"And sex."

"And sex. Seen as part of art. But Birkin is not an artist, because Lawrence felt a distaste for writing with his nose in his navel. He wanted to write about death and Europe. And there is an emptiness, a lack of solidity, *because Birkin is not writing a book* when in fact we experience him as though he is. As there would have been an emptiness—a disappointment—if *all he was doing was writing a book*—when Lawrence wants to talk about everything, all life, *not books.*"

She stares at the students fiercely. They stare back. They are all listening. She does not know if she has put it properly this time. It is a question that obsesses her: the unreality of Birkin, Inspector of Schools, who sees the world as a book he isn't writing.

Jude says, "You know what Nietzsche said. He said, 'Only as an aesthetic product can the world be justified to all eternity.' He says *we are all art works* of 'the veritable creator,' 'although our consciousness of our own significance does scarcely exceed the consciousness a painted soldier might have of the battle in which he takes part.' "

"That's a red herring. I don't believe in your 'veritable creator.' "

"No. But maybe your David Herbert does or did, maybe his Birkin does or did or will. I'm afraid you're snarled up in your own narrow little utilitarian roots."

Frederica is about to reply angrily when there is a disturbance at the other end of the studio, and two people come in. The first is Desmond Bull, who says, "Here she is. The class must be finished or almost finished. All these kids must move on."

Behind Desmond Bull is Daniel Orton. His face is an interesting mess, his eyes lost in black bruised pits, his lips split, his nose crimson and florid.

"I've come to tell you," says Daniel, "that your husband is looking for you."

Frederica scrambles off the platform, and embraces him. The students begin to pack up.

"He found me," says Daniel, mildly enjoying the drama of his own appearance. "I hope he can't find you."

Desmond Bull fetches a chair. Daniel and Frederica sit down. Things rush through their minds. Stephanie, William, Mary, Leo.

"He went to see your father, too."

217

Frederica laughs. "I hope he didn't turn *him* black and blue."

Daniel says, "Don't laugh. He did. He slammed a door on his head. Your father took it calmer than I would. He let him go off with your dress."

"My *dress*?"

"Your dancing dress, your dad said."

Frederica does not like the idea of Bill hurt. Of Bill vulnerable.

"Help me, Daniel," she says, putting out a hand to touch his sleeve. Behind her she senses a whiff of rancid grease, of sour sweat, of fish.

"A Daniel come to judgement," says Jude. "I do believe I have found you at last, my own, my sweet, my only friend, and in the flesh, in the splendidly substantial and generously *abundant* flesh which I hadn't envisaged in all its perfection. Will you acknowledge this thing of darkness, my invisible Master?"

"Oh sod," says Daniel, alarmed out of his manners. "Steelwire." He repeats, "Oh sod."

"Steelwire?" says Jude. "An expletive I do not know."

"What we write in the book at work when we hear your nasty voice," says Daniel. "Descriptive, sort of."

"Is it flattering? Am I flattered? On the whole, yes. It is not bad. A little fame, a pseudonym. Steelwire. It isn't good, either. My name is Jude Mason. It was not, and now is. I am my own progenitor. In my own way. Will everything else be an anti-climax?"

"Probably," says Daniel. "You should start ringing someone else. I've got to talk to Frederica, now. Seriously."

"We shall meet again. I am glad to have seen you. You have an un-expected beauty, parson-person, you do not glitter or gleam but you have a sort of *light* in you. I hope my own appearance was not too dis-appointing."

Daniel stares gloomily from his chair. His eyes meet Jude's en-crusted navel and travel down, across his limp grey member, towards his thin knees.

"You smell like an alley-cat," he says.

"I know several. Resourceful beasts, my friends. Do you know, I was present in the aether when meat was made of our friend's cheeks and ears?" he says to Frederica.

"Go away," says Frederica. "Please. I've got to think. You can talk to Daniel after."

"No he can't. I'm going. You and I can go somewhere and talk and then I'm going."

Frederica and Daniel talk in a coffee bar. It is a good coffee bar for talking in; it has booths, around Formica tables. Muzak plays. Frederica, who has been avoiding Daniel, who has not attempted to see him or answer his letter, is almost overwhelmed by her happiness in seeing him, by his reality and solidity. Tears rise in her eyes and run over: she puts out a hand amongst the coffee stains and Daniel grips it.

"It's not that your letter wasn't right. It was that I couldn't cope. I have been *such a fool* and now I'm scared. I wouldn't be *so* scared if it wasn't for Leo. I can't do right, for him."

"Tell me."

She tells him. The whole sorry story, the attraction of strangeness, the trap of the country house, the horror of being "a married woman" ("I thought I would still be *myself*, Daniel, and wasn't"), the mistake and the wonder of Leo, the guilt, the guilt, the Conservative canvassers, the friends, the anger, the blood, the axe. She does not tell him about the Bluebeard cupboard or about her visits to the Middlesex Clinic for sexually transmitted diseases.

Daniel listens well. It is his job, and he knows Frederica. She tells him hysterically that *he is real,* tears dripping down her sharp nose.

He says, "He told me he comforted you when she was killed."

"He did. That is true."

They stare at each other.

"It's not really *unusual,*" says Daniel, referring to the pain of grief and memory. "It's all over the place, everybody's got something. It doesn't make it any easier."

Frederica is grateful he is prepared to share any part of his pain with her. She grips his hand on the table.

"What will you do?" he asks her. "Get a divorce?"

"I must. There's Leo. It won't be easy."

"You need a good lawyer. I know one or two—it goes with the job. I'll give you a name and a number. You'd best get on wi' it, get some peace at the end. Where are you living?"

"With Thomas Poole. It works beautifully. He has an *au pair* and we all share the baby-sitting. Leo is not a baby. You must come and see him."

"I should like that. I work long hours, but I should like that. And I wonder—should we all go back to Yorkshire for Christmas? They'd be glad to see you—you know the reasons, beyond that you're their child and in trouble. And I'd like Leo to meet Will and Mary. It's not quite right that they don't know each other. Blood's thicker."

"Not so much these days. I'll think. I'm scared. I want to lick my wounds, I don't want to *discuss* things, the idiotic things I've done."

"You won't need to. Come with me."

They discuss Jude, briefly. Daniel describes his gadfly phone calls. Frederica expresses distaste. So does Daniel.

"He wants us to dislike him," says Daniel.

"Then we will," says Frederica. "We will dislike him *intensely,* if that's what he wants."

Frederica's extra-mural class is not in the Crabb Robinson Institute, but in an old elementary school, in Islington, a Catholic school, red, ugly, with a basement canteen serving ham and cheese buns, doughnuts and potato crisps, watery coffee and tannin-tanned tea, a school which has the beautiful and mysterious name Our Lady of the Sorrows. Frederica's course at Our Lady of the Sorrows has the workmanlike title "Post-War British Fiction." There is one full-length book on that subject, by an American, which states that post-war British fiction is about rebellious working-class lads from the provinces asserting themselves and finding a voice where once they were mute. It says that this subject is entirely new. Frederica questions this view: has the author of this work never read Lawrence, never read Arnold Bennett? She reads this book and takes a certain aesthetic pleasure in the critical attempt to make interesting what is (compared with Lawrence and Bennett) intrinsically *not very interesting,* except that everything is interesting *if you take a run at it,* she tells herself, I will get myself interested in Amis and Wain and Braine and all those others. I will also teach *Lord of the Flies* and Iris Murdoch. I am myself a provincial person become self-conscious but I cannot like the world of these novels. Lawrence was greedy for knowledge, for learning, he was interested in natural history and cultural history, he felt people should get out of mining villages. These people mostly sneer at such things. They have chips on their shoulders. I will say why this depresses me.

Her first extra-mural class resembles an Ionesco play. "If there are fewer than seven students," said Thomas Poole, "the class may have to close. It is pure luck whether people come or not, especially in your area. It is pure luck whether they stay, to some extent. If they don't, the class will be closed."

The class is on the top of the school, up four flights of steep red stone stairs, with an uncompromising metal railing. When Frederica goes into the room, clutching an introductory talk—"Some Trends in Modern British Writing"—she is greeted by the sight of about fifteen people squatting in an uncomfortable circle on small chairs, made for gnomes, for people Leo's size. There are two youngish men in dark suits, a middle-aged couple, a very pretty girl and a stretched-skinned woman who was once beautiful, a small man in a very clean forget-me-not-blue jumper over a tightly knotted green tie, a severe-looking woman, a large comfortable woman, an elderly man in a tweed jacket, and a nun. Frederica stares at this uncomfortable ring of unrelated faces.

"They can't expect you to sit like that," she says.

The nun says, "It has been known. Sometimes the only available chairs are infant chairs. I knew a woman who got down and her bones set into that position, and she had to be carried home bent up like a ladder, most unfortunate."

"My astronomy class," says the elderly man, "has more or less acceptable chairs."

"I think," says the blue jersey, "we should do a raid on other classrooms, Miss Potter, and quickly, and decisively."

The faces, variegated adult faces, with none of the homogeneity of the art student groups, look up at Frederica in a circle, assessing her, assessing the situation. One of the women has amazing blue-and-silver eyelids. One of the men has pince-nez:

"Do you know *where* to raid?" Frederica asks the blue jumper.

"Two floors down, double classroom, nothing in it *pro tem*."

"We shall get into trouble," says the large lady.

"We are all grown-ups," says Frederica.

They organise themselves. They find an empty classroom full of junior chairs, small but tolerable. One of the suits hands them to the other, who hands them to a chain of helpers on the stairs. In ten minutes the group is resettled, the discarded infant chairs stacked neatly at the back of the room. Frederica gives her talk. She is nervous; she has no idea who these people are, or why they are there, strangers who have walked in from the London streets, from a day's work, or perhaps a day's housekeeping, strangers who perhaps want to know about Post-War British Fiction because they want to write it, or perhaps because they are in need of dinner-party conversation, or perhaps because they desperately need to meet someone, anyone, and find

Post-War British Fiction a convenient background noise to accompany these meetings, or perhaps because they have to get out of a house they are shut in, or want to change themselves in some definable or undefinable way.

At that first meeting the group is not a group, and it is only ignorance of their names and natures that prevents Frederica from coming to the conclusion that they are too heterogeneous to form a group. She takes the register:

Rosemary Bell (a dark, thin, pretty woman who is a hospital almoner)

Dorothy Brittain (the large woman, an editorial assistant on *A Woman's Place* magazine)

Amanda Harvill (a beautiful woman, tanned, lined, well over forty, without profession)

Humphrey Maggs (the speedwell-blue jersey, who turns out to work as a clerk in Social Security)

Godfrey and Audrey Mortimer (a retired married couple)

Ronald Moxon (a taxi-driver)

George Murphy (a stockbroker)

Ibrahim Mustafa (a research student)

Lina Nussbaum (an unemployed receptionist)

John Ottokar (a computer programmer)

Sister Perpetua (nun and teacher)

Alice Somerville (retired Civil Servant)

Ghislaine Todd (a young psychoanalyst)

Una Winterson (housewife, mother of four children)

She is new at teaching; she has always said she would never teach; and teaching is in her blood. As she talks, she scans the rows. The two men in city suits sit together at the back (later they will separate). One is dark and one is blond. The dark one meets her eye with a slightly aggressive smile. The blond one stares down at his knees. The married pair smile encouragement. The large lady listens best; she manages to convey an awareness of the rhythms of the structure of Frederica's argument. Amanda Harvill's painted eyelids go up and down, up and down: it is not clear that her listening look *is* listening. Ronald Moxon and Lina Nussbaum fidget and shift. Lina Nussbaum, under a huge frizz of hennaed curls, fidgets worst, and makes a popping sound with her mouth. Sister Perpetua and Humphrey Maggs, accomplished listeners, sit side by side, respectful and thoughtful, and do not move a muscle. Frederica scans them all for signs of interest and rejection. She weaves a web of attention—a mention of Kafka caused a quick movement of interest in Ghislaine Todd; when his name comes back, Frederica meets the other woman's eye. Bit by bit, apart from Lina Nussbaum's popping, and possibly the downward stare of the blond John Ottokar, all the attention is somehow woven together. The questions are at first slow: a kindly one from Audrey Mortimer, a professional one from Humphrey Maggs, who has clearly already read all the proposed Post-War British Novels, a challenging one from Dorothy Brittain, designed to make the atmosphere more electric, a somewhat mischievous one from George Murphy, who has noticed an inconsistency in Frederica's brief account of the Welfare State. They are all talking to Frederica, not to each other. Frederica refers a tentative remark of Rosemary Bell back to the truculent Mr. Murphy, and for a moment the two exchange embryonic views on the effects of the Welfare State on the British people and on Post-War British Fiction. Threads are being knotted. The group walks down to the canteen and eats and drinks, measuring each other, asking "What do you do?" and "What do you think of C. P. Snow?" and "Did you see the *Marat-Sade*?" No one speaks to the nun, who appears unconcerned by her solitude, sipping tea. Frederica looks at them all with an incredulous excitement. She thinks of Olive and Rosalind and Pippy Mammott, of the orchard and the moat. At her elbow, Una Winterson, a quiet, fair woman, inquires socially if Frederica is married, if she has children. Frederica does not want to have that conversation; she turns round in irritation and sees a soft face stretched with anxiety. "I have four: they take up so much time; this is the first time I've come out on my own for thirteen years. I started a degree in classics once, but I got married in the middle and Mike (my husband) thought it wasn't worth going on. I do hope I haven't lost the ability to think. I do sometimes wonder if I have. I don't think I should ever have the courage to talk aloud in class, you know, that's why this coffee-break is such a good idea. If the coffee was only nicer."

Later, like all groups, this class will develop its closeness and splits, its inner circles and its scapegoats, its ritual lines of alliance and alignment, of opposition and passionate disagreement. Frederica is new to already sensed that the group must come together, and that ▢▢▢ ▢mething to do with her own position, standing up in front ▢▢▢ ▢d speaking for an hour and then, after food and drink, lis-▢, ▢▢king sure.

The adult students are unlike the professional students. They desire knowledge and they come from what they think of as the real world, of work, above all, but also of things lived through, marriage, birth, death, success, failure, which are all phantasms to young students trying to find their shapes in the pages of books. The adults are inclined to measure the books against life and find them wanting. "It made me laugh like a drain," says the taxi-driver of the burning of the blankets in *Lucky Jim,* "but I'm buggered if I can see why I should spend time *talking* about it." George Murphy, the stockbroker, asks with a mocking belligerence why novels are about so little of the world: "the kitchen, forgive me, the *media, academe,* the novel. Just think a minute," he says, "what is going on out there, multi-national companies, people getting killed in very new ways in Vietnam, the discovery of the DNA, men in space, and the novel doesn't seem to have any idea about any of them. Why should I bother?"

"Why do you? Why do you come?"

He smiles. "I joined a class to find out how to mend my Lambretta. And for another ten shillings I could have another class. So here I am."

"Why do you stay?"

"Oh, I like to think a bit about life and death and sex. I expect we'll get on to those things."

Frederica gives a lecture about halfway through the term on "Nostalgia for Tolstoi." She takes her texts from Iris Murdoch and Doris Lessing, both of whom express a sharp dissatisfaction with fragmentary modern forms, and consequent moral simplicities and simplifications. The adults, who tend to talk about characters in books as though they were people whose fates were real, important and interesting, seize on this lecture and attack Frederica. Why, they say, can they not read Tolstoi? Why not read, says Dorothy Brittain, Tolstoi and Dostoevski, George Eliot and Thomas Mann, *Madame Bovary* and Proust? It is agreed that next term this will happen. Frederica does not know, yet, what this decision will do to her.

Frederica sits in the common-room at the Samuel Palmer School with her good friend Alan Melville. She tells him about the extra-mural class and Nostalgia for Tolstoi. She says, "It is funny how the tensions in all groups are sexual, whatever else they are." Alan looks her up and down, and says in his quietly amused Scottish voice, "You seem to be thriving on it. You are beginning to look like the Frederica I remember. Are they all in love with you?"

"There is one very beautiful one, but he never speaks."

"I didn't ask if you were in love with them. That way does no good. You must realise, they will all be in love with you, because of the nature of groups, and you mustn't take it personally."

"We go out in a group now, to the pub, after. At first only a few went, a kind of *inner group,* and then they asked me, and I try to include *all the others,* not just the kind of lively and intense ones."

"A good instinct. You are a born teacher."

"I am not. This is temporary. I am getting back my ambition but I've no idea what to *do* with it. But *I will do such things*—"

They laugh. Frederica thinks what a pure pleasure it is to have a friend who is a man. She looks at his clear-cut fair face and feels full of love for him: he is very attractive, sex is in him, and she has the good sense not to be attracted, for she knows, without knowing how she knows it, that to be Alan's friend is a durable delight, and to be his lover would be a disaster. And how does she know that, and in what unspoken reservations, in what reticence, in what brief sad silences, does she diagnose disaster? She says, "I do love you, Alan."

"I need to be loved. Come to my lecture on Vermeer, after coffee. I have written a wonderful lecture on Vermeer, and I would be glad of your presence."

The painter, Desmond Bull, comes up behind them. He too is a Scot, a craggy-looking Scot with gingery eyebrows like furry caterpillars, a heavy, bristling jaw, sharp blue eyes and diminishing fine red-gold hair in a *faute-de-mieux* tonsure. His chest hair, inside his very open shirt, is abundant and curly and fiery. He wears a matted and unravelling cardigan whose original colour is almost impossible to distinguish: it may have been some sort of blue.

"I shall come, Alan, I shall come and see your slides of Vermeer. You can count me in."

"I'm thinking of applying for a full-time job at Sotheby's," says Alan, apparently irrelevantly.

"You'd be richer. And you wouldn't find *Rituals* in your classrooms."

"Rituals?" says Frederica.

"Happenings. *Old-fashioned* Happenings, organised by Bly. The Calling-Down of Powers. Sub-Golden-Dawn. Most amusing. Here is the man himself."

Richmond Bly approaches smilingly, bearing an exquisite Japanese ceramic cup of some sort of herbal tea. The common-room is a kind of heterogeneous repository of works by students—a zebra-striped sofa, a scarlet plastic bench, a few very comfortable Bauhaus leather-and-steel chairs. The walls are hung with paintings, chosen very fairly from amongst the current student trends: two brilliant hard-edged abstract acrylic paintings; a large soft grey abstract whirl; a painting of stick-like figures in a sombre green park, owing something to Lowry, something to Seurat, something to Nolde; a mystical image of floating figures in conical hats. There is also a reproduction of Linnell's portrait of the mildly agricultural Samuel Palmer, and two of Palmer's prints of sheep, clouds, trees, dark, light, linear insistence and the mystery of space and vanishing behind the lines. The coffee-pots are variable: a silver one, hand-beaten in the jewellery department, with an extravagant rose agate knob, and an austere and functional steel one from Industrial Design, which does not pour very well. All the cups are different, heavy stoneware, thinnest porcelain, comic monkey-heads, lop-sided cabbage-forms, perfect globes of rosy glaze.

"I hear good reports of your classes," says Bly to Frederica. "The students like them."

"I'm glad."

"I am told you are working for a publisher."

"I read for one, in the evenings, yes. Mostly rubbish."

"I am looking for a publisher. I have written a book. A rather *unusual* book, I flatter myself, and such things are, sad to say, hard to place. I wonder if you would care to read it—"

Frederica says she would be honoured. She adds that she does not know *much* about publishing—almost nothing—her opinion is not of much worth—

"You must by now have some inkling of what goes on in the commercial mind. You know the story of J.R.R. Tolkien. His publisher wanted to reject *The Lord of the Rings* and it was published as a profit-sharing venture—to please the Professor—who is now *very rich*. The commercial mind fails to understand the public hunger for the stories of romance and mystery."

"I'm sure that's true," says Frederica, staring at the glass table in front of her, under which Bly's feet are twisting round and round each other in an energy of enthusiasm.

"My lecture is in ten minutes," says Alan. "I must see to my slides."

"You must *take the register,*" says Bly. "These students *cannot have their degrees* without attending art-historical courses. It is a rule."

"I know," says Alan.

In the lecture theatre, he sets up his slides. Desmond Bull and Frederica sit together under the projector. The time for the beginning of the lecture comes, and goes, and ten more minutes go past, and no one comes. At the end of this time, the door opens, and admits Jude Mason, fully clothed in his dirty blue velvet frock coat and a pair of extremely tight midnight-blue velvet trousers. He does not look at them or speak to them, but sits in the front row, as far as possible from Alan, Desmond Bull and Frederica, meticulously swinging out and arranging the flaps of his coat, folding his hands and bowing his head, as though in church.

"As I expected," says Alan.

"We are here," says Bull. "You can show us Vermeer."

"I never went to lectures at eleven in Cambridge," says Frederica practically. "They destroyed the whole morning's work."

"Nor did I," says Alan, who is writing an extremely neat column of Os in his class register.

"There's a movement amongst them," says Bull. "They really believe the past is dangerous, is a kind of death. They think it destroys their originality. They think academic talk is anti-art. But mostly they believe in making a rupture, making a revolt, making a new world."

"Vermeer is not my idea of an oppressor," says Frederica.

"Perhaps I am," says Alan. "I tell them I think he solved problems quietly in the corners of his paintings that they take whole pretentious blown-up canvases to explore, and went on, and solved more, and then more—"

"The size is part of the point," says Bull.

"I do know that. I do understand that. It doesn't interest me *much*—"

The sawing voice says from the front row, "Why are we waiting?"

The paintings, or not the paintings, but light shadows of them, thin skins of colour transfused and transfixed by the stream of light, appear

227

on the screen. A woman pouring eternal creamy-white milk from a jug, in a plane of light, a woman weighing gold dust, intent faces closed on their own meditation, knowing somehow, Frederica thinks, that this moment of concentration is to stretch out into eternity, or at least, into an unhuman stretch of time. The geometry of maps, of carpets, of the panes of glass in half-open windows, mediating light, mediated by light. The *View of Delft,* with the yellow patch of roof and the perfect spherical bubbles of light on the wet sides of the ships. A meditation intense, quiet, concentrated and apparently without any touch of anger, or hurt, or aggression. Alan shows how certain lights are made in the *camera obscura.* He does what his own new light-beam, his own lenses, can do, and shows Frederica and Desmond Bull what Vermeer could never have seen, a painted blush, a poised mouth, hairs, the light on a wet eyeball so close that they are resolved into flickering movements of a lost brush in paint now fixed. And then he draws back, and there is a woman, in a room, playing a spinet, weighing gold dust, pouring milk.

When Alan has finished, the sawing voice says, "You could weep, couldn't you?"

It is not clear how this is meant to be taken. Therefore it is not answered. Bull says, "Painters complain, art historians complain, that everyone these days only sees transparencies, which are the colours of light, not the colours of pigment. And so they get the wrong ideas, they see *wrong,* these people say. I say, this is new, it exists, we see all this light—we can learn from it—we could even learn to paint things *to be transparent*—"

Alan says, "They talk about slashing Rembrandts and Vermeers because young painters don't get enough attention. Such *anger*—"

"Just Oedipal," says Frederica. "Possibly."

"Oedipus felt guilty, my dear. These people feel they are waging a holy war. The young against the old and the dead."

"They will grow old themselves," says Frederica, who throughout the increasing youthfulness of the sixties fails to understand how the professionally young fail to understand that they will grow old.

"They may not," says the sawing voice. "They are working up magics to stop time. They are making timeless moments, they are reversing its direction."

The woman pours the milk from her jug. The jug will never empty, her careful wrist will never lift.

"And do you think," says Jude Mason, "that in another thousand years, or two hundred, not to be overweening, my own stringy limbs and my not-very-clean face will shine off screens in theatres in times to come?"

"I should think," says Bull, "that all your images are made in materials with built-in obsolescence, if you want to know."

"Writing is safer," says Jude Mason, "if you want to perpetuate yourself. I am writing a book."

"*Everyone* is writing a book," says Frederica, thinking rather hysterically of Richmond Bly.

Frederica is aware that Desmond Bull finds her attractive. This is not particularly flattering since it is clear that he also finds a good half of the women students attractive, and possibly some of the teachers. But it does stir a flicker of new-old life in her, a kind of readiness. He wanders into her little office, where she is sitting screened off from the Foundation studio, where the students are still experimenting with Jude's grey flesh in an alembic of light.

"Would you like to come and look at the work, one lunchtime? I've got a studio in Clerkenwell, we could go in my van."

"I ought to go home and see my son. I do try to get home for lunch."

"It wouldn't take long. You'd like it. Your son's got all your life."

"I ought not."

"But you will."

She goes with him. He buys a French loaf and a packet of salami and a bottle of Valpolicella and they get into the van. Frederica knows that this is something he does often and often. Only the woman changes. She does not mind this. She likes Bull: she likes the way he knits his brow when thinking. Shut in the van with him, with a faint odour of garlic struggling with a strong smell of exhaust and an even stronger smell of turpentine and white spirit emanating from Desmond Bull, she thinks drily that painters must be at a disadvantage as far as pheromones go. Bull's smile, his strong body, his quick hands are attractive, but the smells are certainly not. She sits upright beside him and discusses Jude Mason.

"Nobody knows where he lives," says Bull. "He picks up his letters from a poste restante in Soho. You might say he was pathetic, tho' he's got a perfect right to his own style, dirt and all—but he isn't, quite, he's got a sort of integrity. Richmond Bly thinks he's mad."

"*I* think Richmond Bly's mad."

Frederica bites back the story of *The Silver Ship*.

"Madder than Blake. Silly-mad. I agree."

The studio is two large rooms built over a warehouse, and is entered up an iron ladder. The smell of paint thinner intensifies, killing the last of Frederica's hunger. The rooms are very large, but the living space is very small, since both rooms are walled in with large canvases on stretchers, several deep. In the centre of each room is a double mattress, with rumpled pillows and a bright Scandinavian blanket. On the floor of one of the studios is a Baby Belling and an electric kettle. In the other is a very small fridge.

"Sit down, make yourself comfortable. It's very basic. You can have a party, or an intimate cuddle, in here. I call these two rooms the Divided Self of Desmond Bull. On your left, modern art post-Rauschenberg. On your right, the Scottish European, the guilty painterly painter. Where would you like to be?"

"How can I tell, if all I can see is the backs?"

"You want me to turn them?"

"That's what I came for, isn't it?"

Desmond Bull pulls the cork and gives Frederica a plastic cup of red wine. It is not very nice red wine. It is sour. He puts an arm round her shoulder.

"Oh, I dunno," he says. "Come and look at my etchings and all that. Why don't we sit down and have a bit of a chat, and so on, and a drink, and then think about the work?"

He puts a hand on her breast. Frederica puts a friendly hand on his hand. Somewhere inside her, her body tries to respond. This arouses a series of protesting tugs of pain and misery in her inflamed interior. Desmond Bull gives her a warm and turpentiney kiss. Frederica says, "I'm a bit off all this at the moment. Just at the moment, it won't go. And I want to see the work. I did come to see the work."

Bull is momentarily disconcerted. Frederica thinks with amusement that he would be much less worried to show her his naked body than these hidden images. And that the idea of sex, of possible sex, has turned her into *a girl, the girl* (at the moment) in his eyes, whereas when they talk, she is someone. He says, "Well, where shall we start?" and then, "It's a bit private, you see, all this. I do it to sell it, but I do it all by myself here, it's a kind of frenzy, I do it *by myself,* and then it has to be looked at, it has to go out and be public." He says, "I'm a bit of a schizophrenic." It is a very fashionable word. But when he turns the canvases round, Frederica sees what he means.

In the left-hand studio, the work is made by someone in the grip of the idea that art is everything and that everything can be seen as art. There is a sense in which it is a junk shop. One work is made of hundreds and hundreds of electric wires, stripped, coiled, layers thick like thick impasto, and all colours, woven red and black fat wires, heavy-duty blue plastic wires, orange, brown, green, acid yellow, like nests, like tangles, like barbed-wire fences, like cartoon roses. Another is rows of pebbles. "One from every garden of every house in my mother's street. Each pebble represents *a* suburban garden. This one is fat and green. That one is rather thin and sort of russet. They are in rows like the houses they come from." He pauses. "The woman who goes with that stodgy grey one wears curlers and has cancer. The one with that quartzy one is a dishy blonde who comes out on her doorstep in a dressing gown."

"How am I supposed to see all that?"

"You can't. But once I tell you, you know it, don't you, you can't unknow it. You can look at the subtle colours of the pebbles, see, the *variety of the colours*—I love this blood-coloured one with blue flecks, the lady who goes with that wears desperate, sad, broken high-heeled yellow shoes and keeps swaggering and staggering. Each of the pebbles has a number, that's the number of the house."

"Which is your mother?"

"That's the right question, you see, do I or don't I distinguish her in that row of pebbles? Which is my mother?"

"Forty-two is dried melon seeds. All the rest are stones. Ergo, forty-two is your mother."

"She's got cancer, too. Of the ovaries. She's shrivelling. I told you, these things are sort of private."

"It's a row of *stones*—" Frederica struggles. "Can it mean anything to me without your talking?"

Desmond Bull is turning things round, bringing colours and forms and objects into the studio, further reducing its open space. He exhibits a gaudy and strangely pleasing collage of flowered shirts, pressed very flat, blue with yellow daisies, pink with red poppies, orange with purple hibiscus.

"You can go out of your mind with looking at these colour combinations," he says. "Shop windows scream at you. You know?"

He turns more. Black canvases, white canvases, some shiny and uniform, some with the black and white smeared over colour, which stares faintly through, a hairstreak of crimson here, a veiled patch of delicious apple green there, yellow ochre under a black stain, indigo under smoke.

"Rauschenberg erased de Koonings, he just painted over them. On the principle that there was art lying around all over the world, and that there was talent all over, you just make what you need, what you see now. These are all erasures of my own work. There are old paintings of mine struggling around under the black and white. I can remember what some of them are—that one was a rather good Cubist self-portrait, that one I think was a Bonnard-ish sort of a window into a garden that wouldn't give up being derivative—yes, look, there's a bit of apple blossom under the black—"

"Did you erase them because you liked them or because you didn't?"

"Both. Both. Paintings I was too fond of and ones that I rather loathed."

"It's all very *theoretical*."

"It is. It's passionate too, that's what gets me, that's why I do it. It comes out of a sort of idea about art—being *everything*—and *everything being art*—and this is a bit like taking LSD—all the world begins to explode and implode with glittery *meaning*. I'm sorry you won't come to bed with me. It breaks the tension."

"That's a good reason for sex."

Frederica is still baffled by her own relation to the mysterious/ordinary pebbles.

"The thing about the pebbles is, they are no good to me without me being inside your head. All I can do with them, is get *my own* row of pebbles. Or whatever. Shirts, or a collage of chocolate papers, you know?"

"You won't forget my pebbles."

"I won't," says Frederica, almost irritated by this fact. "Of course I won't." And she never does.

"If people *give* you pebbles," says Bull, "it's no good. And for pebbles read anything. I had a girlfriend who always turned up with bags full of shirts she thought I might like. I made a collage once of her offerings—one for each fuck—but it was a half-hearted affair."

When the bottle of wine is drunk, and another, found in the bedclothes, has been opened, Desmond Bull moves into the second studio. This time he does not speak; he moves from wall to wall, humping the canvases and grunting, and offering no more comment than "a painting of masks," "another painting of masks," "another painting of masks," "a painting of masks on fire."

Frederica too does not speak. She does not know enough about paintings to comment on the paint, or even to think accurately about it. She has been in the Art School long enough not to try to convert it into narrative, although the masked figures half-invite this. They are very unsettling; they are articulated skeletons, or studio-articulated lay figures wearing masks that are full of extremely articulated expressions of horror, delight, the rictus of sexual bliss, the smirk of flirtation, the disintegrating template of age, and are at the same time purely flat, purely patterns of well-laid patches of paint, related planes, or a band of dark floating seed-shapes that read suddenly, in another light, as dark hollow eyes in the light, on the paint, in the painted light. Some of the colours are sombre and brilliant, reds, flames, golds, Veronese blues. And some are pale, bluish pinks on thick chalky white, candle-wax colours with touches of transparent blood-pink, and here and there a yellow hand, and here and there a sky-blue foot.

"It's about the impossibility of figurative painting," says Bull.

"About what it feels like to *be* a human body in an abstract world," says Frederica, cleverly, catching his thought.

"I hadn't put it quite that way. I like that. Have some more wine."

"I like the pinks."

"That's Ensor. His pinks are staggering. I'm still learning. You might say the masks are Ensor—but the masks are mine too, they aren't his, his kind of grisly carnival isn't what I'm doing, mine's about Greek tragedy too, about *coming from behind a front.*"

"As though the erased paintings were trying to talk," says Frederica, inspired. He looks at her very sharply.

"Something like that. You're a clever girl. One of these days, when you're not off it, you must come back and we'll have a good long *friendly* fuck, if you understand that."

Can one fuck erased paintings? Frederica thinks giddily. And is a naked prancing man a mask for a brain and a pair of eyes watching and watching and trying to make sense?

"I ought to get back to my son," she says. "I'm glad I saw the work."

Back in the Bloomsbury flat Leo is sitting companionably with Thomas Poole and Simon. He does not run to greet her, but this is a form of punishment; his averted eyes are full of trouble and punishing anger. Thomas Poole, too, looks at Frederica as though she were a desirable woman. He says, "Mr. Parrott rang. And Hugh Pink. You are in demand. And Tony Watson, who thinks he has talked the *New Statesman* into letting you review some books."

"Good. I'm tired."

"I'll bring you a cup of coffee. Sit down and I'll bring you a coffee."

He stands up. She feels guilty. She should have been home hours ago. Thomas Poole touches her hair on his way out to the kitchen. Leo says, "Sometimes you can hate people quite a lot."

"Who? Who do you hate?"

He does not answer. After a bit, he says, "I hate not knowing where people are. I like it when people are where I know where they are. At Bran House, I knew where everyone was."

"I don't go for long. I always come back. I'm earning our living."

"We once *had* a living."

Frederica cannot speak. He creeps to her side, and puts his arms round her waist.

"Never mind," he says, as she might have said.

She bends her head to his. She smells his hair. She has no choices. She imagines suddenly a film in which a sagacious dog travelled hundreds of miles, back along the scent, or the magnetic field, which pulled from what it knew and loved. This hair she could distinguish in a room piled high with other heads. This note she would hear through all others. This person is the centre. It is not what she would have chosen but it is a fact, it is a truth stronger than other truths. It is a love so violent that it is almost its opposite.

"We hate people when we love them," she says. "Sometimes."

VIII

Frederica, Leo and Daniel travel north for Christmas, sitting together on the crowded train like the nuclear family they are not. Thomas Poole is hurt that Frederica and Leo have not stayed to make a family Christmas in the Bloomsbury flat: Christmas is a time when some-body is always hurt. Both Frederica and Daniel are afraid of going back into the family from which Stephanie is absent. Frederica is also aware of having behaved badly to her parents, who do not know Leo. They are fetched to Freyasgarth from Calverley station by Marcus, who says little but seems calm, which was not always the case. As they drive out along the moorland roads Frederica's heart lifts: it is grey, it is dark, it is windswept, it is the north from which she comes.

She is taken aback by the beauty of the new house. It is Winifred, not Bill, who meets her on the doorstep, a Winifred smiling with un-questioning delight and weeping a little—"*Frederica,* Leo," touching both with a warmth that in the earlier days would have been reserve and holding back. Frederica finds that she too is weeping. Leo clings to her leg and watches. Behind Winifred is Mary, who runs at Daniel, and is lifted in his arms. Behind Mary is Bill, smaller than Frederica remembers him, paler and less fiery, waiting to see what his daughter will do. Frederica rushes forward and kisses him too. Marcus carries suitcases to pretty bedrooms looking out on moorland. They are all vaguely aware that Frederica's return from her long sulk or evasion is and is not the restoration of the lost daughter. Stephanie will not re-turn. Winifred embraces Daniel. Bill shakes his hand. Exclaiming with pleasure, sniffing with emotion, the family moves into the living room, which is in the dark of a winter afternoon, except for a tall Christmas tree, shining with multicoloured lights, red, blue, green, gold, white, and decorated, by Winifred and Mary, with the magical golden wire hexagons and polyhedrons made eleven years ago by Marcus for Stephanie's Christmas tree.

Next to the Christmas tree stands Daniel's son, Will, who is ten, with Daniel's dark hair and watchful dark eyes. He stares at his father with angry intensity, and flinches when Daniel approaches to hug or kiss him. Daniel retreats. Frederica says, "You remember me, Will?"

"More or less," says Will, sounding absurdly like Daniel.

Winifred fetches tea on a trolley. There is tea in her wedding-present silver teapot, there are sandwiches of potted meat and egg and cress, there are hot mince pies and a huge Christmas cake. "We made it together," Mary tells Daniel. "Grandma and Will and I made it, we stirred and stirred, we made it *months* ago and left it to *mature*; it's full of brandy and lovely spices. And yesterday we iced it and decorated it for you all to come. We piped everyone's initial round the edge— Marcus helped us put the proportions right—*B* and *W* and *F* and *M* and *D* and *W* again and *M* and *L* for Leo—with silver balls round the letters, and roses decorating them, and then in the middle we made the moors in snow—we put the Fylingdales Early Warning System in the middle because Will wanted it, though it's a funny thing—and snowy trees, and here is a frozen lake—and there is a beck and some crags—Jacqueline says we oughtn't to have the Fylingdales balls but Marcus says it's all right, they're there—they look lovely in icing sugar and we can *eat them up*—"

Daniel says the cake is beautiful, which it is. Winifred says, unnecessarily, that it's a *secular* cake, and Mary says quickly that they are all going to the Carol Service in the church in the village tomorrow on Christmas Eve. "It isn't midnight, it's for the *family*, the teachers at my school go, we sing, I'm good at singing, everyone's going. Except Grandpa, of course."

At teatime Jacqueline Winwar comes with presents for the family to be put under the tree. She is accompanied by the geneticist with whom she works on her snail populations, Dr. Luk Lysgaard-Peacock, half-Danish, half-Yorkshire, with a square-cut jutting gold-red beard, gold-red hair and dark blue eyes under deep eyebrows. Frederica has never paid much attention to Marcus's young friend Jacqueline, whom she always thinks of as one of two, Ruth and Jacqueline, the blonde and the brown, Marcus's religious friends, Gideon Farrar's Young People. She remembers Jacqueline as a nice brown leggy girl with long bunches of hair and owlish glasses. What she now sees is a wiry young woman, about twenty-six years old, who moves quickly and neatly, and has a poised and watchful oval face under a cap of shining brown hair, variable browns, all blending and changing in the light. She has clear dark brown eyes behind black-framed glasses. Will goes and stands next to her. Mary kisses her and so does Winifred. Marcus says "Jacquie," with real pleasure, and is also pleased to see Luk Lysgaard-Peacock. Daniel asks about the snails and Luk says they are hibernating. Frederica watches as they all sit and chat easily. She sees Jacqueline look at Marcus, and then sees Luk Lysgaard-Peacock look at Jacqueline, both with that look that betrays a particular interest, not proprietorial but simply more alive, more alert. She watches Winifred hurry to give Jacqueline tea, mince pies, cake, information about carols. She thinks: My mother would like her for a daughter. She thinks: But it was the *other* one Marcus liked, a much more fey and boring person. The nurse, he liked the nurse, she remembers. She looks at her brother. He is talking to Luk Lysgaard-Peacock. She hears the word "engram," she hears the words "molecular memory," she hears the names Scrope, Lyon Bowman, Calder-Fluss. Jacqueline says, "There has to be something wrong with the planaria experiments, I cannot believe memory is carried that way."

"We could try and repeat the experiment," says Lysgaard-Peacock.

"I'd like to get up something with snails," says Jacqueline. "They have large neurones. You could do something interesting on the chemistry of memory."

Frederica watches Marcus. No, he is not sexually interested in this nut-brown intelligent person. Or does not appear to be—who has ever been able to say what Marcus wanted? Whereas from time to time Jacqueline gives a quick look in his direction. And Luk Lysgaard-Peacock gives a sharp look in hers. Frederica thinks about sex and is quite unaware that she is hearing the first discussion of what will be a scientific advance, an important piece of research.

She thinks: Families pull together and fly apart. Now, I am pleased and excited to see all these faces which resemble mine and each other. But by the end of the holiday we may all feel trapped and impinged on and diminished.

There is a sound of wheels stopping with a whine and a scream. The door bell sounds. Winifred opens the door and stands, puzzled. On the doorstep, in a navy overcoat, shoulders squared, is Nigel Reiver.

"I am hoping," he says, "to find my wife and child. I have brought their presents and thought—since it is Christmas—they might speak to me at least. I have come a long way."

"Come in," says Winifred, uncertainly. It is indeed Christmas; he is the husband and father; hospitality requires that he should be let in; Winifred knows nothing of him or of what has happened.

"Wait—" he says, and fetches from the car two large cardboard boxes, wrapped in Christmas paper, striped in midnight blue and silver, with shiny rosettes of blue and silver paper ribbons.

Frederica stands up in the room with the Christmas tree and moves to stand in the doorway, so that he cannot cross the threshold into the lighted group inside. He puts down his two large boxes, and stands easily there, meeting her eye, ready to move quickly. There is his real face, the dark, dark look, the intentness that always stirs her.

"I did think," he says, "it might be sensible to talk, just to talk. I do think you might at least let me know what you think is happening. I do think I have a right to say Happy Christmas to my son. Don't you?"

The real wrong, Frederica thinks, was hers, was done by her in marrying him when she did not wholly want to, when she could not go through with it. This knowledge makes her tentative, uncertain.

"I don't know," she says, barring the door. "It's no good. It's no good."

"I don't want to impose myself on you if you don't want me," says Nigel. "I won't stay long, though I've come a long way. I want two things: to see my son and give him a Christmas present, and to have a *sensible* discussion with you about where we go from here, even if it's only to arrange a time and place to have a discussion. That's all. I think I have a right to that, I do think so."

Leo appears at Frederica's side. He is white, and staring. He looks from one to the other. Nigel holds out his arms. Leo looks at Frederica, who nods—what? Permission? Understanding? He walks past her, and is lifted in his father's arms. Nigel buries his nose in the bright hair whose scent is the centre of Frederica's existence. There are tears in Nigel's eyes.

"I've missed you," he says to Leo. Leo twists his hand in his father's collar. He looks back at Frederica with Nigel's black eyes in her own sharp white face. She is ready to die, to lose consciousness.

"*Take your coat off,*" says Leo.

"Come in," says Frederica, moving with stone legs, out of the doorway. "Come and meet the family. It is Christmas."

She introduces him. "My father you know. My mother, my brother, Marcus, my brother-in-law, Daniel, Will, Mary, this is a friend, Jacqueline, and a friend, Dr. Lysgaard-Peacock."

"I'll go now," says Luk Lysgaard-Peacock.

"No—" says Frederica. "There is no need for anyone to go. Nigel has just come with presents, he isn't staying, no one must move."

Her voice is sharp. It makes people want to move, and begs them not to. They do not move. Lysgaard-Peacock and Jacqueline do not move. Winifred takes Nigel's coat, and brings him tea and cake. Leo sits on his knee, with an arm round his neck. Bill and Nigel nod at each other with a curious respect: Nigel then nods at Daniel, who smiles and frowns together. No one speaks, so Nigel says, "I brought presents for Frederica and Leo. Perhaps they should open them, since I won't be staying. Perhaps," he says, looking at Will, "you could fetch the two boxes in the corridor."

Will does as he is asked. Nigel tells his son to open his box. Still in the same fiercely cosy voice he tells Will to help Leo. Will helps. The box is opened. A Hornby electric train is revealed, a beautiful thing, a Flying Scotsman engine, carriages, trucks, rails, turntable, station, signals, points.

"He's too little," says Will. He stares almost angrily at Nigel.

"I'm not," says Leo. He clasps the engine to his chest. "I'm not too little. This is *mine*."

"I think you could help him set it up and understand it," says Nigel to Will. "He's not too little if someone works it with him, shows him the ropes, sets it up." He smiles his warm secret smile at Will. "I'll be glad if you'll set it up for him. I'd like to do it myself— all fathers like to play trains at Christmas—but I shan't be here. But you will."

He has somehow acquired a little more territory. He turns to Frederica.

"Won't you open yours?"

"I'll put it under the tree with the others and open it later, on Christmas Day."

"Now," says Nigel. "I may have to take it back, I need to know now if it is what you want."

Nothing, she wants to cry, I want nothing. Leo says, "Open it. I want to see. Open."

Will carries the parcel across. Frederica pulls listlessly at the blue rosette, at the wrapping paper. Leo climbs down from Nigel's knee and comes to help. The shiny paper rustles. There is a large, solid, cardboard box. There is silver-and-pink tissue. There is a dress. It is dark charcoal grey with a high neck and long tight cuffs, woven with red silk braid and embroidery, very rich, very plain. It is a long tunic that goes over a short, slightly flaring skirt. It looks like, it is, Courrèges. Frederica, like most women with red hair, does not wear red, but there is one red, a clear dark vermilion, that brings out the fire in her hair and the gold in her dusting of freckles. This is that red. No one knows what to say. Winifred is wearing a heavy green polo neck and a tweed skirt; Jacqueline is wearing a dark brown double-knit jumper over fawn cord trousers: Frederica herself is in jeans and a checked flannel shirt. Leo says, "Put it on."

"I can change it, or get it altered," says Nigel.

"Put it on! Put it on!" says Leo. "Now. I say, now!"

And Frederica, who has been holding the lid of the box, ready to replace it, suddenly puts it down, picks up the dress, and walks out of the room to put it on.

"I thought," says Nigel to Winifred, "there must be a pub near here, where I could stay—"

"Our bedrooms are full," says Winifred foolishly.

"Completely full," says Bill. "No room at the inn, I'm afraid. None."

Frederica comes back wearing the dress. In its honour she has put on black tights and carefully dressed her hair in a chignon. She is beautiful. Frederica is never beautiful, though often alive with attractive energy, but just for the moment, in the Courrèges dress, she is wholly beautiful, it is the word. The dress fits almost too perfectly: her small high breasts sit neat and elegant inside its beautiful seams; her thin wrists, her narrow waist, her long thin hips, are beautiful where the silk-lined cloth skims past them, making them look like necessary forms in relation to each other. It is a strange style, formal, tailored, severe, ending so far above the knee that the brevity of the skirt should be childish, a gym-slip, a dolly-dress, but is not. Frederica's long thin legs are set off by it; another inch on her thighs would spoil its up-and-down simple complexity. She stands there. Luk Lysgaard-Peacock says, "Beautiful," and Nigel looks sharply at him.

"I can't take it," says Frederica. Every precise inch of it is a betrayal of carnal knowledge, of Nigel's certainty of the nature of her body, of how it works, how it moves, how it is.

"And everyone always says men can't shop for women," says Nigel, as though she had not spoken. "They can if they put their mind to it, of course they can. When I saw that red, I thought, That's the one, it's a risk, but it'll work. And it does. You have to admit it *does something for you,* Frederica. You've got to keep it—no strings—whatever you—whatever we—decide. I want you to have it. It's *yours.* No one else could wear it like that. Leo likes it, don't you?"

"I like it," says Leo.

Winifred makes a new pot of tea for her son-in-law whom she does not know. Leo sits on his knee. Frederica stands there, incongruous and beautiful. The dress isolates her from the company, as though she were in cellophane wrapping. She looks at Nigel with reluctant admiration: there are things he knows how to do. He discusses with Winifred the possibility of local pubs. Luk Lysgaard-Peacock thinks of recommending the Giant Man at Barrowby and then looks at Frederica and does not speak. Leo says, "You might possibly sleep here with us, possibly you might."

"I don't think so," says Nigel, with the same reasonable ease. "Not just now, I don't think that could be managed."

A clock strikes in the village. Mary says, "We shall miss the carol service, we *must go.*"

"Count me out," says Bill.

"We already did," says Mary. "But Daddy will come, and Grandma, and Will, and Jacqueline and Dr. Lysgaard-Peacock, will you come?"

"Why not?" looking at Jacqueline.

"And Marcus will come with *them,* and what about you?" says Mary, looking doubtfully first at Frederica and then at Leo and Nigel.

"Last year we went to carols," says Leo.

"So we did," says Nigel. "In Spessendborough. It was lovely, wasn't it? I love carols. They connect you to your ancestors. Mine are all buried in Spessendborough."

"We don't run to *ancestors,*" says Bill.

"Everyone has ancestors," says Luk Lysgaard-Peacock, looking at the faces with a geneticist's eye.

"Come to the carols," says Leo to Nigel. He turns to his mother in her dress. "You come."

"I'll change this dress."

"*No.* Come in the dress."

Frederica changes her dress.

They put on their coats, all except Bill, and walk through Freyasgarth to St. Cuthbert's Church, where in the candlelight they sing the old songs: "O Come, All Ye Faithful," "Unto Us a Boy Is Born," "Lullay My Liking," "We Three Kings," "It Came upon the Midnight Clear," "The Holly and the Ivy." Leo stands between his parents, holding both hands from time to time, separating them and connecting them. Daniel stands between Will and Mary. The singing is not much, but there are one or two sweet high voices in the stone, and Luk Lysgaard-Peacock has a clear, unafraid, pleasant tenor. Mary, alone of the Potter stock, can sing, and does, clear and small. Frederica thinks of years of being *trapped* in school singing. And now she is a grown woman, autonomous, and *trapped* by her own nature—her own acts and choices.

Winifred weeps for her daughter Stephanie.

Will cannot weep for his mother.

Nigel's bass is occasionally off-key, but a useful augmentary din.

Daniel thinks of the child in the straw. He thinks of his son, who has a brief life in front of him, and of Mary's son, who was most cruelly killed, long ago. He thinks of the face he does not think of and manages to avert his attention from it in time, by concentrating on song. "The holly bears a berry, As red as any blood, And Mary bore sweet Jesus Christ, To do poor sinners good."

Back in the house, there is a move to leave Nigel and Frederica alone to talk. Frederica does not want this, but everyone nevertheless disappears: Luk and Jacqueline to their own families, Bill to his study, Marcus and Winifred to wrap presents, Daniel and his family to wash up. Nigel and Frederica and Leo sit together in the sitting-room in the evening dark. There is a wood fire.

"We never lived in a beautiful house," says Frederica, wondering.

"Listen," says Nigel. "Come back to our house—not for Christmas, I can see you're here—but come back *for a visit,* say Boxing Day, say the day after—there's the Meet—we could talk a bit and think things out. Sooty is dying to see Leo, and so are Pippy and Auntie Olive and Auntie Rosalind—they are *very sad* at spending Christmas without him, when families ought to be together—"

"This is mine—"

"And I found you, because I knew you'd be here, because *families are important*. So I know you know they are, so I know you know Leo ought to see his."

"I want to see Sooty," says Leo. He says, "I want to see him every day." He says, "Let's go back and just see him, Mummy?"

"I can't," says Frederica.

"Only for a few days. You can bear us for a few days."

"I can't. I mustn't. I can't come."

She cannot, in front of Leo, cry out that she is sorry, she made a hideous mistake, she should never have married, and now they must all suffer for it.

Nigel says, "Well, let Leo come. Let me take him back to see Pippy and Sooty and the aunts. We love him, he's ours, it will be his house, I have a right to see my son."

Frederica bows her head. She thinks she knows that if Leo goes back to Bran House she will never see him again, unless, of course, she too goes back. And she is afraid of going back, physically as well as emotionally. She cannot go there again. It is quite reasonable for Nigel to want to see, to entertain, his son—she believes a child needs two parents, she believes, in principle, in civilised sharing. She also fears, with a sick, exhausted part of her, that Leo may be happier in the end at Bran House, where his life will have a form to which he has been brought up, a form that is his inheritance, on one side. And then she thinks of him being sent away, a little boy, to boarding school, as Nigel was. And then she remembers the clinging body of the boy on the run through the woods.

"I don't know if that would work," she says weakly. She may be being hysterical. Leo could go for a fortnight and come back. He *might* come back.

She is sure in her bones that he would not.

"What do you think, Leo?" says Nigel. "Do you want to come with me?"

"It isn't fair," says Frederica. "How can you make him choose?"

"*You* made him choose," says Nigel with sudden violence. "*You* took him off against his will, against my will, without a word, with your shoddy *friends* in a vulgar way—"

"He *came*—"

"Ah. So *he* came. So in that case you were prepared to leave him then. So you can let him come back now. Bran House is *where he belongs*. So are you coming, Leo?"

"Not without Mummy."

"Just for a week or two, with or without Mummy. If you can persuade her to come, so much the better—if not—"

"You *can't do this to Leo*. Let him go to his grandmother now, let's talk this out without him."

"Leo. Are you coming? Come with me. Come home."

"Listen, Nigel. I *can't ever come back,* I should never have come in the first place, and so far it's *all my fault* because of that. *All*. I think we should get a quiet divorce and think things out *quietly*. As for Leo, he *chose to come with me* and he is with me. Later, when we have a—an official arrangement—"

"There won't be one. If you think I'm going to give you the pleasure of divorcing, you can think again. You are my wife and my son's mother as far as I'm concerned. I don't go back on my word."

"I'm not ever coming back. You know that, really."

"Leo! You come. Now. Get your train, and come."

"Leo—go and find Grandma. I'll try and explain to—to your father—"

"Bitch!" says Nigel. He walks up to Frederica and grabs her shoulders. Frederica flinches and struggles. "Bitch!" says Nigel. "Manipulative bitch." He flicks her about the face with his palm. "Don't you *dare*—" he says, thick with sudden rage. Leo begins to scream. He screams and screams. Everyone appears. Daniel goes up to Frederica, and Nigel lets go. Leo runs to Winifred.

Bill says, "It looks as though you'd better get going."

"It's nothing," says Nigel.

"It isn't nothing," says Frederica.

"Come on," says Daniel, and takes Frederica and Leo away, holding both their hands. Bill continues to glare at his second son-in-law.

"I don't say who's right and who's wrong," says Bill, "for I don't know, and no one's perfect. I do say, you'd better get going, until Frederica says she wants to see you. We are her flesh and blood."

"Leo is *my* flesh and blood."

"We know that. But now isn't the moment. Please go. Christmas statistically breaks up thousands more marriages than it sustains, they say. Try again later. *Please go.*"

Nigel is about to say something belligerent, notices Bill's scars from his last visit, desists, and goes, slamming the door.

Perhaps because Nigel has united them, the family take pleasure in one another's company on Christmas Day. Winifred and Mary have made the house pretty, as the house in Masters' Row was never made pretty. Christmas dinner is traditional and tastes good; the turkey is well cooked, the bread sauce bland and spicy together, the stuffing full of herbs and interest. Frederica and Bill talk animatedly about her next term's novel course. She talks to her father about talking to adults, and about teaching *Women in Love.* They discuss the problem of Birkin, who is a teacher, not a writer.

Bill says, "You can go away from Lawrence and get in a frightful rage with him—a *silly* man, even at times a *bad* man—and pompous— and then you come back and open the book and there's the language, and the vision, *shining* at you, with authority, whatever that is."

"I didn't understand about teaching. I thought it was *dry.* But it isn't. It makes things more real—another world, that is also this world—more real in *this* world—you can't say things like that."

"*That* is what is missing from old Birkin, Frederica. He doesn't have a way of doing that."

"And next term," says Frederica. "*Madame Bovary, The Idiot, Middlemarch, The Castle, Anna Karenina,* I think *Mansfield Park,* perhaps *La Nausée*—"

Life, she wants to say, though it is books she is talking about, and her life, her angry husband, who has a Bluebeard's cupboard full of rubbery pink flesh and has been taught silent slaughter, her life is simmering away elsewhere. She smiles at her father, and imagines his life differently, a class in Scarborough reading *Bleak House,* a class in Calverley coming to grips with *Paradise Lost.* She imagines him imagining dinosaurs striding through the foggy London streets and angels shining in the distance through the trees of the Garden.

In the afternoon she helps Will and Leo to put the train together. The three of them make a good team: Frederica helps Leo unobtrusively, so that he knows the train is his, and can fit the pieces without Will becoming impatient or snatching. At the same time she asks Will's advice, which he gives. Daniel watches them. He offers help, once, but Will snatches the piece of rail from his hands and fits it somewhere quite different. Daniel thinks that there is nothing motherly, even so, about Frederica. She is thin, she is quick, she is nervous: the two boys treat her neither as an adult nor as an equal but as something in between. Leo treats her almost as a prisoner, putting out a small imperious hand to pull her back if she strays too far away. He remembers Stephanie saying that no one *played* in their childhood, and sees that it is a process to which Frederica is applying her intelligence, that does not come naturally to her.

His son, he thinks, will never forgive him. His son, like him, is single-minded. He himself loved one person, and now she is gone, he survives best without feelings of his own. Will intuits this, feels abandoned, and does not forgive. Daniel can foresee a time when they will both regret being so set in themselves, when it might be too late, but he can do nothing. He cannot get through to Will, because they both are as they are. Mary, on the other hand, requires love of him, expects it, creates it where it seemed impossible. He goes off to look for her.

"You ought to talk to your father," says Frederica to Will.

"I don't really want to," says Will.

"Probably you do and don't," says Frederica. "Most people are like that, with fathers."

"I more don't. He went away, just like that. I'm all right without him."

"He was broken up—" says Frederica, as she might to an adult. "He was just broken up, he couldn't go on, they were too close, he and she, he took it worse than other people might. You must *try to understand*. You are very like him. Something in you must understand."

"It almost doesn't matter what I *understand*," says Will. "I can't be different. I was broken up too. You know."

"I know."

Leo clambers up Frederica, and puts his arms like a vice round her neck. Will watches. Frederica almost pushes Leo away, and then holds him tight. Will says, "I get on as best I can."

"I see," says Frederica, across her son's hair. Will puts in the last piece of rail, completing the circuit.

"Now the power source," he says. "And the engine. Will it go? Will the points work?"

"Let Leo push the switch."

"Come on, Leo."

The train receives its power and begins its rush round the miniature landscape, into a tunnel, through a station, past a platform. Leo switches it on, off, on, off.

"Don't blow it up," says Will. "Gently. Try the turntable."

The two heads bend over the rail. Daniel comes back.

"My father drove an engine," he says to Will. "Your grandfather."

Frederica sees Will think about getting up and going away. He moves the points, instead, rushing the train behind a sofa.

"Will has made an amazing track," says Frederica.

The little train rushes powerfully round, and round, and round.

The good temper persists into Boxing Day. Some of the party are invited to drinks that evening in Matthew Crowe's wing of his Elizabethan house at Long Royston, the rest of which now belongs to the University of North Yorkshire. Alexander Wedderburn has spent Christmas with Crowe, and will be there. It is a long drive from Freyasgarth, but Frederica, Bill and Marcus set out in Bill's car, with Marcus driving. Daniel stays with his children, with Winifred, and Leo.

Crowe serves champagne in his panelled study, under his painting of the flayed Marsyas. He is older: his rubicund face is more hectic, his hair sparser, he has shrunk. Frederica has put on the Courrèges dress, telling herself that she has brought nothing else suitable, telling herself also that by an effort of will she can make it hers, and shear it of its associations with Nigel. Today, too, she looks beautiful.

The room is full of people. Some of them Frederica recognises: there is Alexander, talking to the Vice-Chancellor, Gerard Wijnnobel. There is Edmund Wilkie, dark and rapid, fatter than he was, talking to the philosopher Vincent Hodgkiss, and a slight dark man who turns, and is Raphael Faber. Frederica feels the slight shock human beings feel on seeing a lover, a beloved, unexpectedly. He looks quickly at her, and away. He must be staying with Hodgkiss, his old friend. Crowe takes Bill away to talk to Wijnnobel and Alexander, who are talking about the Steerforth Committee and the teaching of English. Frederica follows: she is unready for Raphael. Alexander puts an arm round her shoulder and asks if she is well. The discussion resumes. The committee, it appears, has become divided into two camps, not so much about the English language as about teaching methods. Alexander describes these camps, following Arthur Beaver's distinction, as those of Eros and the *Wille zur Macht*. Those who believe in love and freedom, and those who believe in rules and authority. Grammar, Wijnnobel says, has somehow become involved in this because of the confusion between rules prescribed by tho[se] and rules or laws discovered in what might be called na[tural] old argument, with a new twist. He is at ease, as far as ease. Bill says the secret of good teaching is to know thos[e] to care more about what is being taught. Frederica has a sudden memory of Jude Mason interrupting her Lawrence lecture with Nietzsche. "Only as an aesthetic product can the world be justified to all eternity." She begins an anecdote.

"I am trying to teach D. H. Lawrence to a group of art students who don't believe they need to know about the past, don't believe they *ought* to know about the past, and I am constantly interrupted by a kind of naked grey-skinned androgynous model with a sawing voice and long grey hair who recites bits of Nietzsche—"

They laugh. They talk about teaching.

Marcus finds some of his colleagues. Professor Sir Abraham Calder-Fluss is there, a small man with rough white hair and a neat white moustache. He is a biochemist who has worked on protein synthesis in pigeon brain-cells and has a cautious interest in the new disciplines of neuroscience. With him are Jacob Scrope, whose field is artificial intelligence, and Lyon Bowman, who does delicate physiological work on the structure of the cells of the brain, the dendrites, the synapses, the axons, the glia. Scrope is handsome in a carved way, like a mediaeval monk, with a long lined face and cropped hair: Bowman is shorter, and fleshy, with a red mouth and dark curls. Marcus's research, tentatively entitled "The Computer as a Model for the Activity of the Brain," is being conducted under the supervision of Scrope, who is constructing primitive computers with different algorithms to mimic the processes of perception and learning. Marcus does not wholly like Scrope, but he does like Bowman and is both moved and repelled by the Golgi-stained slices of brain tissue with which Bowman works, the complicated branching forest of nerve cells, the spaces. He likes the mathematical work and is good at it, but he is not wholly sure whether what he is doing is what he wants to do. Wilkie is interested in Scrope's computer models, which can be related to his own work on perceptual scanning and the recognition of forms. How much information, he has been finding out, does the eye need before it can say: This is a tree, this is a face. He has been studying illusions: the brain seems to fill in spaces in its own blind spot, left blank in a pattern, like a tablecloth, with more of the same, with *imaginary, hypothetical* tablecloth.

The scientists discuss memory, the chemistry of thought, the mechanics of vision.

The teachers discuss the political connotations of requiring, or permitting, children to learn poems, mathematical tables, the alphabet.

Matthew Crowe detaches Frederica from the teaching group, and takes her over to talk to the Dean of Languages, Professor Jurg Müller, and the English Professor, Colin Rennie, who is a Scot, and whose subject of study is the novels of Walter Scott. This group is attached to the group containing Hodgkiss and Raphael Faber. Crowe says to Frederica, "I involve myself as best I may in the University which is growing up round me. I try to follow Gerard Wijnnobel's Renaissance ideals and mix the arts and the sciences in some idea of Learning or Thought, but you see how they divide, how they discuss amongst themselves. And then over there is a sociology teacher, Brenda Pincher, and all the wives, they make their own group and talk about whatever women talk about, no doubt. It can't be clothes, their clothes are uniformly horrible, don't you think, whereas you are resplendent. If it isn't an impertinence, which it is, how did you come to be able to afford *that* dress, my dear? I heard you were married, you must have made a very splendid marriage to have that dress."

"I made a disastrous marriage, it has all gone wrong, I am in despair, the dress was a propitiatory present which I shouldn't have put on, because I won't be propitiated, but it was all I had—or perhaps I couldn't resist it. Are you satisfied?"

"No. I want to know *everything*. But later. Look out of my window. See the towers encroaching on my Elizabethan paradise. The Language Tower. The Evolution Tower. The Mathematics Tower. The Social Studies or Social Sciences Tower—they are quarrelling about the name—which isn't finished. They haven't built all the layers of connecting walkways yet. I believe it will look like a beehive."

Müller and Rennie do not want to talk to Frederica. They are having an amicable argument about Lukács's view that Scott is the major European novelist among the British. Müller has written on Nietzsche, Freud, Mann and the end of European cultural continuity. Rennie has written on Scott, Goethe, Balzac and George Eliot. They are heavyweights. They suppose a young woman in a Courrèges dress is a bore. They move closer together and turn their shoulders. Raphael greets Frederica, and asks if she remembers Vincent Hodgkiss. Hodgkiss is not physically memorable; he always appears different, when met again. Frederica smiles at him. Raphael says, "And how is marriage suiting you, Frederica? You appear to be blooming."

"Blooming" is not a word she would have expected from this precise, secret person. It carries a note of hostility, she feels, which is undeserved and irrelevant.

"Marriage is not suiting me. I turn out to be bad at it."

"I see," says Raphael.

There is a silence whilst Frederica thinks about Raphael, whose lectures she attended, at whose feet she sat, whom she loved, in terms of Eros and *Wille zur Macht*. He, like Crowe, for different reasons, seems smaller, as though a light has gone out. It is fearful, the realisation that we no longer love what we desperately loved and desired. It is a kind of death, and also, Frederica sees, a lightness, a beginning of freedom. This face, this intent face, is just a face.

"We were discussing our host's painting of Marsyas," says Vincent Hodgkiss. "Raphael does not see how he could live with it. Raphael thinks he should burn it. Ceremoniously."

Frederica feels a perverse desire to defend the picture, which has always given her a frisson of terror, disgust, and then pleasure of some kind. She looks at it, the faun bound to the tree, his pelt at his feet, his lips drawn back from his pointed teeth, his whole body glistening dark red with the gouts of blood that are about to burst forth into fountains. His anatomy is lovingly accurate; his bloody muscles fold over his shoulder-blades and belly.

"It is about art. And pain—"

"I know *that*," says Raphael, as though her simplicity is contemptible. "But it is wrong. It is bad."

"Very fashionable," says Hodgkiss. "Have you seen the *Marat-Sade*? Through the howls of the mad and the victims and the executioners, the new world, the new truth."

"Don't be silly," says Raphael, putting down his friend with the same impatient contempt he showed Frederica. "All that is simply disgusting, *Schadenfreude*, something in ourselves we should recognise and look away from. I do not say we do not need to know it. I say we should not indulge bad imaginings."

"It's powerful," Frederica persists.

Raphael smiles sweetly at her.

"It's something that shouldn't be seen. Simply. I shall go and look out of the window at the nice abstract humanitarian towers."

He goes. Hodgkiss lingers a moment, and then wanders over to join Wijnnobel, who has approached the scientists, thus linking the scientific and the language-teaching groups. They are discussing the search for the elusive engram, the trace of a vision, a touch, a voice, a thought, left, where? In a body, to be recalled. The idea of the "molecules of memory" is currently exciting both biochemists and artificial-intelligence workers. Abraham Calder-Fluss explains for Hodgkiss's benefit. "The idea is that it is possible that learned information, as well as genetic coded information, might be retained in and transmitted by very large molecules, such as the DNA and the RNA. And this idea received reinforcement from the immunological study of proteins, since antibodies recognise intruders into organisms, remember them, encode the information in some way, and prepare themselves to resist subsequent invaders. So we wonder, in turn, if the roots of our own memories, the structure of our own consciousness, are to be found in these amazing macromolecules."

Wijnnobel asks what kind of research can be done. Lyon Bowman describes the work of James McConnell, editor of the *Worm-Runners' Digest,* who has trained planaria, flatworms, simple organisms, to avoid bright light, which they associate with electric shock.

"And then he chops up the trained beasties and feeds them to a group of naïve beasties, who absorb their molecules and, he claims, their learning with them—because the cannibals also avoid light, and the control naïve worms rush gaily towards it. I find it hard to credit, myself. What fear of the butcher, what desire for grass pastures, should I not have absorbed from my steak and kidney?"

Hodgkiss says, "The question is, whether the word 'information' means the same in all cases, that of immunology, that of the DNA, that of the mind of the scientist building a computer, or whether you are all thinking by analogy, which is dangerous. I am not enough of a scientist to answer my own question."

Marcus looks quickly at him: he has put his finger on something Marcus has felt to be wrong in all this without having the linguistic interest to sort it out.

Bowman says, "There are physiological changes—very rapid ones—in growing brains—which later cease to happen. I should look *there.*"

Marcus has a momentary sense of the shape of what he wants to know, wants to find out. He feels it as a shape in his own brain, an embryonic form of an idea which cannot be formed in words, or even in a diagram, though it is tantalisingly close to one, it is a sort of a *form* of a thought-not-thought. How does he know it is there at all? Also it is to do with Bowman's work, not Scrope's, but he knows that, before he knows what "it" is that he is looking for. And yet, when he finds it, it will feel like recognition, he thinks, not cognition, not a line scratched on a pale, blank, even *tabula rasa.* He thinks of his brain. He thinks of it as long, powerful feathers curled in a skull shape, layer in layer. He thinks of this wordless thinking as preening, smoothing, until all the little hooks and eyes connect and the surface is glossy and brilliant. He does not know if this analogy is useful or misleading or both at once. He has begun to know enough about science to know that scientific thought moves along in such metaphors and analogies, which it must both use and suspect. He thinks it would be interesting to talk to Hodgkiss. He continues to stand quiet and silent, looking attentive. Calder-Fluss talks about Schrödinger's intuition in the 1940s that genes were crystals—"and there are the aperiodic crystals of the DNA in the double helix. And this raised, in Schrödinger's mind, the idea that life, organic life, feeds on both order—the aperiodic crystals—and also disorder—random atomic vibrations and collisions. And then we begin to see that the *whole universe* might be an information system—of messages flowing through crystals amongst parasitic noise—and human thought then becomes a way of transmitting order between parts of the universe—of *informing* it—"

Their thoughts are interrupted by a crashing noise and a disorderly scuffle at the other end of the room, where the women, the wives, are gathered, quietly discussing, according to Crowe's hypothesis, washing machines and clothes. Frederica is now part of this group, which consists also of Mrs. Bowman, dark and solid in a printed silk dress, Mrs. Scrope, a faded blonde in a little black dress, Mrs. Rennie, a large woman, Mrs. Müller, an awkward woman, Lady Calder-Fluss, a small, sharp, watchful woman, and a tall, square figure, in a burgundy shot-silk cocktail dress with a square-cut low neck, who is Lady Wijnnobel. She has square-cut dark hair with a fringe, large mixed-coloured eyes, a gold bracelet, a cigarette, and a glass of orange juice. Frederica is the only woman in the group who is not surprised to see her. Everyone else has known that the Vice-Chancellor is married, and that his wife never appears in public. She is vaguely rumoured to be "ill," and it is understood that she is never asked after. There is a rumour that she is a Bertha Rochester, mad and shut away. But here she is, in the flesh, contributing nothing to the discussion, staring at the carpet or occasionally at the Marsyas, rocking slightly as though her feet are uncomfortable in the medium-high heels she wears.

The women are discussing, not clothes, not washing machines, but depression. They describe the fear of waking up and the difficulty of getting up, the long days that rush by and the long days that drag, listening to the clock, to the radio, and the washing. They discuss the Calverley doctor, and whether or not he will prescribe pills, and whether or not pills will help, and whether or not one ought to *take* pills, and how bad it is to be bad-tempered with children, and a common feeling that children are like fat jugs into which their life is being poured, like rushing electrical vehicles for which they, the women, provide energy which is not entirely re-generated, like young healthy carnivores (says Fleur Bowman with a smile) who consume the maternal flesh with the Weetabix and Alphabet Pasta in a smiling and automatic way. They say they blamed their mothers for being depressed and that they are now depressed. Brenda Pincher asks, can they not *work,* and they begin a long choral account of the ways in which they have tried this—a bit of typing one did get, one evening class Mrs. Rennie taught, but the baby-sitter never came; Lady Calder-Fluss surprisingly confesses that she wanted to go back to scientific research, to do a Ph.D., but her husband thought it better not.

The sociologist, Brenda Pincher, does not contribute to this discussion, or conversation, or sharing. She listens intently: she is underdressed in brown wool, and has longish pale hair. She does speak, however, to ask Frederica who she is, and what she does. Frederica says she is separated from her husband, and trying to make a living by teaching and writing reports for publishers, and, she hopes, other things. She says it is difficult to look after her son and work. Lady Wijnnobel says, "Your husband should provide for you so that you need not work."

"I don't want to take money from him, not for myself anyway. And I like to work, I need to work, I need to think."

"Did you have the same ideas about work before the birth of your son?" asks the sociologist.

"You should not have had a child," says Lady Wijnnobel, "if you are not prepared to care for him."

She sounds extremely angry: her voice is thick, her face a dark red.

"I can't care for him if I'm *not myself,*" says Frederica.

"You were not created to care for *yourself,*" retorts Lady Wijnnobel, swaying on her heels and looking at the ground. "He who loses his soul shall save it."

Frederica in turn becomes angry.

"I don't think you know enough about me to know what I should do with my life."

"I can see you are not a good woman," says Lady Wijnnobel very loudly.

Frederica finds that her hand is working away in her pocket, to push off her wedding ring. She looks round at the women, who look at the ground with unhappy fixed smiles, all except Brenda Pincher, who asks, in an impersonal sort of voice, "How do you know she is not good, Lady Wijnnobel?"

"I can see round her head a flame of wickedness. She desires to destroy her man and her son," says Lady Wijnnobel, with thick decisiveness. "These things can be seen, if you have an eye to see them."

"I'm sorry," says Frederica. "I'll go away."

"You will stay where you are told to stay," says Lady Wijnnobel, "and listen to what I have to say to you."

Camilla Scrope runs and pulls at the Vice-Chancellor's sleeve, as his wife advances angrily on Frederica, her hand raised, to scratch, to grip, to hold back; it is not clear.

"Eva!" says Gerard Wijnnobel.

"I must speak my mind."

"No, my dear, you must not. You must say you are sorry, and come home now. Now, Eva. Say you are sorry."

He puts his arm round his wife and leads her away.

Mrs. Rennie says, "I knew we ought not to be talking about depression. I knew I'd been told she'd been inside Cedar Mount. I knew I ought to *stop* talking about depression and so the only remarks I could think of were about that."

"I think she'd been drinking," says Mrs. Müller.

"Heavily," says Lady Calder-Fluss. "I noticed. It is a great pity."

Nobody speaks directly to Frederica, who feels that she is somehow branded as "not a good woman" even though something is clearly very wrong with Eva Wijnnobel.

She manages to push off her wedding ring, at last, and thinks of Frodo Baggins, the Hobbit, pushing off his ring of invisibility.

Brenda Pincher says to her, drawing her aside, "And how did you react to all that?"

"Oh, with automatic guilt. I am not a good woman. She saw it. How would *you* react?"

"Much the same, I expect."

She wanders away. Frederica considers her: she is one of the university teachers, an insider, not an outsider, but there she is, relegated to the other halves, the spouses, the merely social appendages. She wonders idly what she is working on, and, as Alexander comes to look for her, forgets Brenda Pincher.

Brenda Pincher retires to Matthew Crowe's panelled lavatory, where she opens her shoulder-bag and takes out a tape-recorder, of which she changes the tape. She has embarked on an interesting research project on the lives and conversational preoccupations of university wives, which she will extend to a larger one, she thinks, on the motherhood and married lives of educated women, in due course. She collects their speech habits, their sentences, their regrets, their hopes, their circular discussions, their pregnant silences, as Lyon Bowman collects patterns of dendrites and glia. She will write a book, in the early 1970s, called *Hen-parties,* which will be a huge bestseller and change many lives, including her own. Now, she wonders whether it would be ethical to erase Lady Wijnnobel's outburst, and knows it would, and cannot do it, out of aesthetic attachment to the disproportionate rage, the moral fury from nowhere. Though she herself does not find the rich redhead in the expensive dress likeable, by any means. Arrogance is recognisable on first sight. She thinks she is *someone,* thinks Brenda Pincher with unfocused distaste, slotting in another tape.

IX

The winter, closing in on the mountains around La Tour Bruyarde, brought on a certain lassitude and disaffection among the inhabitants. Icy draughts whistled and flapped along the twisting corridors and through the great halls, under the doors of stone-walled chambers and down the vertiginous stairs in the turrets and cellars. They huddled in wool and fur and the new pleasures of the flesh seemed less rosy and enticing. The Lady Roseace's face developed a porcelain pallor and her red lips were tinged with blue, cyclamens rather than clove-sweet pinks. The folk still gathered daily to hear the inspiring confessions of the storytellers of the day, to devise playful chastisings and subtle recompenses for pains inflicted and endured, but these occasions too were infected by cold and damp, and many desired not to strive but to sleep, or to go south to the sun and the bright ocean.

Culvert took to walking from room to room in the Tower, always finding a door he had never before opened, a cupboard whose contents were unknown, a glory-hole that breathed decay or a new loft full of hanging bats and thick-twisted cobwebs.

He went also from chapel to chapel, making an inventory of the images of human life therein, the dim limbs and bursting eyes on walls and reredos, the carved, twisted bodies, the empty stares of angels. When he had first come, in the full flush of his zeal for human reason and human passional energies, he had caused many such votive objects to be taken down and carried away, with the object of repainting the walls with lovelier fancies, tributes to beauty of form and freedom of desire, to the joys of copulation and the delights of orgiastic eating, truths, he had said to the other inhabitants, to replace repressive lies and dark imaginings. But now, in the winter, and in the first itching of his first moment of doubt or boredom, he came to ask himself how these images came to be there, what need had created them, to what sick string in the human heart they vibrated.

"Our Projector has discovered Religion," said Turdus Cantor to Colonel Grim, as they stood in furred gowns on a balcony, watching the solitary promenade of their companion deep below them.

"He inveighed most mightily against it," said Colonel Grim, "in his fiery youth. Priests, he said, were poisoners, poisoners of minds and persecutors of young and tender instincts."

"One extreme of passion may become its opposite," said Samson Origen, who was standing at a little distance, unseen in a dark hood. "Hatred may become love. Only a studied indifference can maintain its nature steadily."

"We shall see changes, then?" said Turdus Cantor.

"Our Projector is curious to dissect and galvanise human nature," said Colonel Grim. "Religion is an intrinsic part of human nature."

"I have travelled much," said Samson Origen, "and have met with no society without a religion."

"And you yourself," asked Colonel Grim, "do you hold by any faith, or follow any rite, or pray to any God?"

"I do not. It is natural to human creatures to seek illusion, to tell tales, to make up powers. I make an unnatural effort: I stare into the dark, and abstain from imagination. It is a destructive way, and the rewards are meagre. But I am compelled to it by my nature."

Meanwhile Culvert went from the Mary Chapel to the empty shrine of the Bleeding Heart, and deciphered, candle in hand, the Stations of the Cross in many styles by many artists, from the workmanlike and earthy to the thrilling and rococo. He was, he believed, a reasonable being, a student of happiness and a not-inconsiderable analyst of human nature. It had been his deep belief that the stories of religion were mere lies foisted on a credulous public by fat power-loving priests, bishops and cardinals, and he believed he understood the roots of the desire for power, the desire to control human desires and human hearts. He had been drawn in his rebellious youth to the gay and anarchic tales of Grecian deities, lustful, cruel and capricious, and had been wont to say that their captiousness could never exceed that of a baleful Deity who could complacently equate the slow torture of one man, and that his own son, indeed, his own self in some arcane sense, with the remission of payment for all the centuries of all the evil done by all the torturers of all human tribes and families. But now in the dark days Culvert was revising his understanding, which he now deemed to have been too facile, too youthfully energetic. He wandered from flagellation to flagellation, from bleeding, handcuffed, naked figure to bleeding, handcuffed, naked figure and asked himself to what deep lust in universal human nature these sights corresponded. He did not believe it was so easy as barter of guilt for white-washed innocence, blood spilt for a new infantile freedom of action. No, no, he thought, we desire to see the infliction of pain in order to contemplate its mystery and to stiffen our courage and dread for our day of need, when we shall know it in truth. And then he thought, This too is a superficial understanding. For we take pleasure, if we are truthful, in the observance of the infliction of pain, in the thrill of the knife slitting the nostril, the nates, the veins in the wrists, the anal rose, in the heavy descent of the axe-blade through hair and skin, through gristle and muscle and sinews, through red flesh and spurting blood and pearly bone and soft red-brown bone marrow. And then he thought, This too, is not all, for we are pleased to imagine, to anticipate, the start of our own blood in fresh wounds, the heat of the sheet of it running along thigh and breastbone, the sting, the smart, the lively writhing of the nerve-ends, this we desire, if truth were told. We envy the meek figure with his bruised shanks and his bloody face, we envy him a knowledge we have not.

And so he pursued his quest, from particular to particular constructing the universal. There on ancient cracked boards were Germanic sufferers with snarling agonised lips, with black gouts of blood in hair matted with thorns and oozings, with lacerated ribcages dripping darkly, with grim, foundering buttocks and knees and calves spattered with thick dark strokes of pain. There by contrast were sweet Italian innocents all prettily crimsoned on ivory and snow and linen, skins laced with trickles and seepings like bright ribbons, down sweetly complacent faces; there were ecstatic Baroque brothers of these initiates, rolling hot eyes to the complicit Sky, panting with red tongues, spreading the cockles of armpit and groin to the gaze and lash of the torturers, who were grave-faced and detached, or greedy and corpulent, or troll-like and toothless, or snarling and canine, or dull and beastly, but always satisfied, always taking satisfaction from the bliss of blood or a job well done. As the artist took pleasure, Culvert told himself, pulling his fur robe tighter with a thrill of horrified pleasure in response, pleasure in the infinity of ways of representing the red lips of a wound or the tender bruised mound of a whip-welt. Is this, the analyst of human nature asked himself, the worship of Death or the worship of Beauty and Pleasure? And he answered himself, to his own satisfaction, The one is the other, and a kind of dark delight invaded his whole frame with a shivering heat, freezing and burning.

So he went on his way, musing on the cruelties of religion, or the religion of cruelty, and came to a winding stair which went down and down, smelling of mouldering growths and old wet stones, down, along, round, down, and his candle flame swayed and bowed and stank in the shadows. And at the foot of the stair was a round door in the stone, which opened with a great key, opened easily, for the wards of the lock were well-oiled, although it appeared forgotten. And inside the door was a Lady Chapel, which, although it appeared to be in the bowels of the earth, was lit fitfully through a stained-glass window, depicting a throned woman in rich blue robes, wearing a golden crown and a sweet smile, with a wheel of seven great swords stuck in her heart and a great apron of blood welling from her wounds to her breast and her lap, and running in tongues of crimson down her blue gown to the flowered mead she sat on. And on the left wall was a great painting of a woman white as stone, and staring, bearing on her knee the bruised and broken body of her son, a foul thing with gaping mouth and dislocated shoulders, with swollen ribs and trailing, piteous pierced hands and feet. And this image was framed in flowers, red roses, white lilies, blue irises, the only colour, where all else was stony and shadowed and veined with grey. And on the right was a painting, tenderly done, of a young girl bending her head over a new-born babe cradled against her naked breast, and the babe was swaddled tight in bandages, and had tight-closed bruised eyes and a mottled, purpled skin, a clammy skin it seemed, as the new-born and the newly-dead have, both.

And before all these women, all these three women, these Mothers of Pain, were row upon row of little lights bravely burning, which, when Culvert considered them closely, could be seen to be helical snail shells full of oil with burning wicks in the oil.

And the pews in the chapel were piled high with old bedding straw, for it was now a storage chamber, and the walls were lined with bales of hay, and in the centre of the chapel, before the altar, was an old woman on a three-legged stool, spinning thread by the light of three fat wax candles, standing in ornate church-silver candle-sticks. She had a face like a nutcracker, the old biddy, and a watery, crazed eye and an empty socket of stitched skin next to it, and a mumbling mouth, fallen in, and knobbed, gnarled fingers like twigs, with sore red tips like bright buds. And Culvert had given orders (or suggestions, for the inhabitants were in theory free to reject his instructions) that the members of the community should wear bright, clear colours to signify the new order, but here was this old crone in a black scarf and a black stuff gown, just as the peasants of his childhood had been, and those of his father's childhood, and his grandfather's. And she was spinning a thread that combined scarlet and white, in a fancy twist.

She greeted him familiarly, "Good day, young master."

"Good day," said he, puzzled.

"You don't know me," said she, "and I could take offence at that, for I was your nursemaid once, your little mouth guzzled and sucked at these dry breasts, and before that I was there at your coming into the world, I was the *sage femme* who presided, the midwife who saved you, drawing you all bloody and reluctant out of your sweet mother's bleeding cunt, and slapping life into your backside with one hand, whilst you dangled from your little ankles from my other hand and mewed and howled.

"My name is Griva," said she, somewhat huffily since he showed still no sign of knowing her.

And it seemed to him that he remembered a sweet smell of her laundered undergarments on a sunny day, but he could not swear to it. He felt in his pockets for something to give her and came upon only a wizened little apple, which he looked at, perplexed, until she took it from him, saying, "Thank you," and bit into it fiercely, so that the juice spurted on her chin.

"And what are you doing in the bowels of the Tower?" she asked him, chewing with her toothless gums.

He sat down on the end of a pew, amongst the dusty hay.

"I am thinking," he said, "about religion, and what it means, and about the human tendency to need its practices. I am not thinking very well."

"Thinking," said she, "will not get you far, in that context, my sweeting. What do you think, my nurseling, where do your musings lead you?"

"To ceremonial," said he. "To rites performed. To the question Why? and the deep question Why in truth? For it is my observation that all peoples observe certain festivals, to wit, the turn of the year, the feast of the dead, the return to life and such matters. I remember the blessing of the fields, a pretty ceremony, and the candles for the dead souls, all flickering and gleaming."

"I could tell you much," said she, "of the Carnival as it was held in the halls of this house in the days of your forefathers, of the dancing there was, and feasting, and mumming, and ceremonies there were performed."

"Tell me," said he, "for this is what I was in search of. And chance led me to you and your memories."

"Chance," said she, "or something by another name, strong too, chance's sister."

So they sat together in the half-dark, the winter-dark, candlelit and waxy-smelling, and she told him of the old Feast of Misrule at the turn of the year in the Old Hall of the Tower. Of how a Lord of Misrule, the Babu, was chosen from amongst the grooms or footmen—"Sometimes he was a bit lacking, as they say, bats in his belfry, and sometimes he was chosen because he was above himself, an uppity being, a pompous nob, a puffed-up capon, and in the first case, your fool would give out silly orders, as it might be, to wash all the ladies' faces in winelees, or to make pies of live blackbirds, or to dress the hall with bulls' pizzles and pigs' bladders, and no matter what it was, it had to be done, for he was the Lord, but only for a day, only for a poor day. But the uppity lordlings whose come-uppance was near, they was more savage, my young nurseling, for they knew what was coming to them and they made sure their pains were paid and their election got its quittance in advance so to speak, so there were roastings and whippings of other young lordlings in plenty, ordered by the Lord of the Day, there was trousers pulled off and spankings performed—and more ingenious punishments, and hangings and danglings and spittings and pokings that would take me a month to retail to you—"

"I should be delighted to hear them—"

"And so you shall, my lovely, and so you shall. But in all cases, whether the Lord of the Day, the Babu, was fool or knave, at the end of it certain things happened as sure as night follows day or death follows life. And these things were: the birth of the new Sun out of the fat body of the Babu—who ate beans and other flatulent things to bloat his belly. And the topsy-turvying of all folk, so that the menfolk danced in skirts and bodices and the ladies had the freedom of trousers and hunting-jackets, and at the end all danced and chased in masks all around the stairs and halls of the Tower, beginning at nightfall of the Shortest Day and ending at the first light which finished the Longest Night and brought the New Year, who was a bloodied babe in the skirts of the Babu.

"And the Yule Log came in—which had been smouldering away for a whole year under the hearth, and the boar's head came in with it, with spiced apples in its snout, dripping with fat, and the Great Pie came in, which was made of snails and pigs' tails in a great spiralling savoury tower, topped with a pastry bird to finish. And they lit the fire in the hearth from the old log, and put in the new, and danced in the light of the flames, and they roasted more snails on its crest in great iron pails, dropping the hot oil into the shells so you could hear the creatures wince and sigh and screech as best they could. The peasants, you know, my nurseling, roast a tower of live cats over the great fire at the year's end, but this was not done in the Tower, for the ladies were squeamish. Indeed in the later days of the Tower they made the little snails from chestnut flour and marzipan but those were soft, sweet parodies of what should be, for there is spirit-life in snails, my dearie, and marzipan is a stolid substitute for succulent flesh."

"Why snails, old woman?" asked Culvert, not because he believed the old creature knew the answer, for it was his opinion that the peasants of modern times did many things of which the original sense was lost in the antiquity of inherited practices. But he thought also that these stunted folk with their repetitive lives might have preserved some wisdom of the earth, some harmonious chord between them and the original Nature in which men and beasts and plants all participated, which might be apparent to a keen intelligence. And the idea was coming to him that their practices, reintroduced, might make in his community a new life of the blood, more subtle and profound as a source of energy than cool-headed local reasonings.

"What spirit-life is in snails?" he asked old Griva, leaning towards her in the half-dark, in the scent of her unclean black garments and the apple-juice of her eating.

"Men say they go between us and those who sleep under the earth," said the old woman. "They weep continuously for the dead, their trails are bright with their tears, they go on their bellies like Him who was punished in the garden, but they are not evil beings, but wanderers, between this world and the next. For the fattest ones are always found in the graveyards—and those we do not pick, or only the naughty boys, in secret—and they hang on fennel, the plant of the dead, and taste of it too, when they are stewed or roasted. They are creatures of the night, making moony trails by starlight, but they are creatures of the Sun too, for when he goes to bed early, they go to their long sleep, and pull a horny window over their shelly, spirally houses. And when he returns, they return from their deathly sleep, their flesh stirs and out they come, cold creatures seeking the warm. They go between, you see, my dear boy, they go between earth and sky, they go between fire and water, they can play the king and the queen too, and their children are like glass and pearls. And when we have sucked them from their hiding place we make little lamps of their dead shells, for that they live in the dark and yet come into the light—they make silvery light with their weeping pathways in life, and hot fiery light in death. They are neither fish nor flesh nor fowl, and so magical, as things undecided are magical, because they are not fixed."

"This year," said Culvert, "we shall hold Carnival again in the Tower. We shall make beautiful costumes, and fantastic masks, and there shall be a rite of the new Sun, we shall welcome the new Sun in our blood, we shall have a Babu and a Woman Clothed with the Sun, and be beasts and men. And I shall send people out to collect snails, old woman, and you shall instruct our cooks in the making of the Great Pie."

"I am already spinning scarlet and white wool for your robes," said the old woman.

"And how did you know that I myself would be the Woman Clothed with the Sun?"

"I knew," said the old woman, shaking her head, whether with grief, or palsy, or grim humour, Culvert could by no means see. "As I know you will prick your finger if you play with my distaff as you are doing."

"Nonsense," said he, wielding the distaff and tangling the thread. "I have an insatiable desire to know how things function in this world."

And he pricked his finger, as she had foretold.

And she took his bloodied finger and put it in her own mouth, and her old, brown, wrinkled lips closed softly on his flesh, and her tongue licked his rough skin and sucked sweetly on his blood. And as his blood ran into the wet saliva and apple-juice on her tongue he remembered everything, his nose up against the warm bag of her breast, the scent of her milk, his little fists kneading her like sweet pastry, the hot swaddling bands between his legs. And tears ran down his cheeks, for the onward flow of time, for the crumpling and drying of flesh and blood, for the singularity of a man shut in his skin as time sucked the marrow from his bones.

"It is odd," said Colonel Grim, "that there should be such a preponderance of scarlet in the costumes or robes for the coming Carnival. Our honoured leader's *name* is evergreen, but his taste runs to flames and blood."

"You should not be surprised at that," said Samson Origen. "For soldiers have always loved to be brilliantly clothed when they parade about, and you yourself have worn a scarlet coat and a scarlet cloak with gilded buttons."

"I have heard it said," said Grim, "that the coats were red so that the blood of wounds should be hidden. But I give that small credence, for our small-clothes were white as driven snow, and there are also green soldiers, like holly trees, and black soldiers, to hide in the night. No, we were red to strike fear of our bloody-mindedness into the enemy, and brassy to glint like the hot sun as we advanced. How we loved our uniforms, and how tender we were to what lay under them."

"Judges are scarlet," observed Turdus Cantor, "and cardinals too have arrogated to themselves that rich colour."

"Also the Whore of Babylon," said Samson Origen. "The original Scarlet Woman on her scarlet beast, swallowing the stars."

"Though our sins be as scarlet," observed Turdus Cantor, "they shall be washed white in the blood of the Lamb. Who is himself woolly-white, with bleaching blood, a paradoxical beast."

"A man in a uniform," said Samson Origen, "or a man in a robe, for they are the same things, is not a man, but a cipher, but a function, but a walking idea; his clothes walk and speak for him. And undercover, who knows who he is, or what he does."

Culvert, all alive with enthusiasm, joined their group and begged that they all take parts in the coming Rite or Play for the New Year on the

Shortest Day. Colonel Grim, he said, was to be the *sage femme*, or Wise-woman, or Midwife to the New Year, and was to wear a specially de-signed gilded mask and a great coif. And Turdus Cantor was wanted as godparent to the New Year, and he would be clad as an old beldame with a black mask and white woolly hair. And the Lady Roseace would be godfather to his godmother and their names were to be Logos and Ananke, and they were to sing sweetly together at the birth.

"Sweet singing is beyond me," said Turdus Cantor. "My old voice is cracked."

"Then you shall have pan-pipes," said Culvert. "And there will be gongs, and cymbals, and clanging bells, and zithers and flutes."

"And what do you hope to bring about with all this?" asked Sam-son Origen.

And Culvert told him how he hoped to make the rhythm of the people's blood hum to the rhythm of the turning earth and light the fire of the new Sun in all their hearts. And Culvert told Samson Ori-gen that he desired him to be a Pythoness in the Rite and wear a dou-ble mask facing backwards and forwards. And Samson Origen said he would not play, he would not take part, he would neither dance, speak, sing nor mum. "I will watch," said Samson Origen, adding "as long as one man watches and only watches, what you have is art, and intelligent, as opposed to religion, and terrible."

"I do not want you to watch," said Culvert.

Their eyes locked.

"But you do not want to make me act against my will," said Sam-son Origen. "And my will is to watch, my pleasure is in watching and only in watching. I believe in detachment, Culvert, in the solitary strong mind, as you know. I have seen the Krebs dance for the new Sun, and it is not pretty and not instructive."

"Tell me how they dance," said Culvert, and his eyes glittered.

So Samson Origen, in an even tone, in quietly polished sentences, sipping his hot wine with cinnamon, told his three companions of the great seasonal feasts of the Krebs, of the building of fires and the binding of prisoners, of the brewing of fermented milk with sour barley and pigs' blood, of the drumming of the women, of their wailing voices and averted faces, of the great horns belling and coughing and sounding, of the gongs and the cymbals, the castanets and the tambourines, the bladders and the rattles, and of the long, snaking lines of dancers, all moving as one, stamping with flat feet, rolling their oiled buttocks, faster and faster, of the frightened beasts who were driven into the circle round the fire and torn apart slowly by fingernails and teeth, living haunch from haunch, rib from rib, gut from bloody gut, until the Krebs were clothed in bloody hides and crowned with bleeding horns, or with the heads of wolf or wild-cat, bear-cub or hind, wild ass or mongoose. And the fire would burn brighter and brighter and sputter with fat from the roasting crea-tures, and then the prisoners would be brought in, and meet the same fate as the beasts, ripped apart and roasted, licked and tasted. And Samson Origen told of the election of the King of the Day who must lord it over all, and was carried on their black shoulders on a wooden throne in the firelight, and crowned with jewels and fed on wine and honey, whose hands and feet were kissed and slavered over, whose rich robes were embroidered in scarlet and golden silks. And he told how, when the sun came over the dark hills at the edge of the plain, this King was whipped, and roasted and torn to fragments and devoured. Samson Origen told this tale coldly, marshalling his facts, but he saw Culvert's eyes bright and wet, and saw the hot rheum in Turdus Cantor's old eyes. Those of Colonel Grim were dry as his own, he saw, and the pulses in his neck and brow were steady as ever.

"And do the Krebs have a God," asked Culvert, "in whose name they roast and consume this unfortunate being?"

"They do," said Samson Origen. "But they may not speak his name, under pain of death, and I do not know it. But the names of his masks are legion: there is a black horse, and a flaming fire, a great worm and a white kid, all of which at different times they dance for and dress themselves to simulate."

"Have you seen this thing?" asked Culvert.

"I have," said Samson Origen. "I watched, endeavouring to feel neither fear nor excitement."

"And did you observe the face of the King of the Day? Did he show fear?"

"He showed smiling vacancy, whether from extreme fear or be-cause he was drugged and unaware, I do not know."

"Or happy, perhaps, in the mystery."

"I think not. You may entertain that idea, but I think not."

. . . So the feasting and dancing, the japes and the singing, went faster and hotter and more lusty. Up and down the staircases and along the corridors they danced, in great human eels, yet not human, for there were bears and boars, horned goats and silly sheep, cunning cats and sly foxes, ravening wolves and hooded crows prancing there, with sweaty human legs and tails, often enough, and little or nothing else, save that the women wore gourds and codpieces and the men wore apple-stuffed breasts, and swishing skirts. And all over the Tower were the brave little snail-lights. And there was no Babo, but at the head of the table was Culvert in the scarlet robes of a priestess, with long, blond curls on his head, and a red mouth and painted fingers. And beside him was the Pope, or Priest, or Bishop, mitred and with a gilded mask, and Colonel Grim, clothed as a beldame, and Roseace and Turdus Cantor as Logos and Ananke, she in a black, studious suit with a silver hawk-mask, and he in many-coloured female robes, with the face of a snake in gold and green. And when the Longest Night was drawing to its thickest, the Yule Log was ignited with great ceremony, and huge trays of snails were put to roast on it, and boiling oil was dripped into their cavities, so that hundreds of tiny boneless bodies writhed and winced and boiled together. And when dawn approached, the ceremony began on the high dais. It was a long and tedious ceremony, for Culvert had not yet got the knack of ceremonies, and did not understand that a mass of men must move, and exult, and engage and if necessary suffer and scream together and as one, if a ceremony is to weld a people. He wished, their Projector, to be all things to all men, Scapegoat and Whore, Mother and Father, Life and Death, Punished and Punisher, and, as will be subsequently clear in this narrative, his folk were not whole-heartedly implicated in his symbolic strutting and groaning, nor were they exempt from that modern saturnalian emotion which is most destructive of religio-aesthetic passion, embarrassed laughter.

He had devised a ceremony in which his eyes were bound, his robes were parted and his posterior fiercely whipped by the officiating Pope, or Priest, or Bishop, to whom he gave a stack of white willow wands and urged her to ruddy them truly and not in jest, for real and not faked blood was required to flow in their new world. Now the Pope under the flammiform cornute mitre was none other than the Lady Mavis, who was quite as reluctant as Samson Origen to perform any role in the Carnival rites, but had not that gentleman's cold blood, or his certainty of rectitude. And Culvert had overridden her demurrings and diffidences with accusations that she was not prepared to sacrifice her private desires for the general life. And when she retorted that it had not been part of the project to enforce people to submit their individual beings to the general will, but to har-

267

monise both equally, he accused her of equivocation and bad faith. It was clear, he said, that she hankered for old orders, for bourgeois fustiness and the servile respect of servants, for hypocrisies and respectabilities and niceties that had been swept away by openness and truth. It was true also, said he, that she inclined still towards the vices induced by that stultifying and crippling institution, the Family. Truly, said Culvert to the Lady Mavis, it appeared to him that perhaps she should consider returning to the world outside. And she thought of the burned and salted fields of her home, of the gibbets and the death cells, of the roving bands of hungry soldiers, and wept bitterly. She thought also of her vision of *fêtes champêtres* and beribboned hats under sheltering trees, and wept more strongly. And she was afraid, for her history had taught her that fear was reasonable and appropriate, and she said she would play a small part. And her child too, the little Felicitas, Culvert insisted, should play a part, she should be the New Year, the Birth of the Sun, a candle to light the whole community to brighter days. Her terror pleased him, for she had always in the past looked at him with a kindly, indulgent, critical look, as though he might grow into a good man in some distant future when he should have discarded certain follies. It pleased him to make her the instrument of his ritual chastisement, for she would hate in principle to see any man whipped for any reason, and yet she would desire, in part, to whip himself for his treatment of her, and yet, too, she would hate that in herself.

And so it proved, for the hand that was raised to whip the white (if pimpled) posterior of the Whore trembled greatly, and fell lightly. Lay on, said Culvert between his teeth, or it will go ill with you. Lay on, said Colonel Grim, in his character of *sage femme*, lay on lustily or you will never be free, and you may reasonably do, dear lady, what both of you desire you to do. Lay on, said the Lady Roseace, laughing behind her hawk-mask, let him see what a Fury a woman can be, when aroused to righteous wrath.

So the Pope laid on, softly, hesitatingly, and then, as Culvert's blood began to blossom, more and more furiously, cutting his backside into a trellis of weals, and continuing even when Culvert's frenzy of pleasure and pain had reached its sighing, sinking climax, so that Reason and Ananke had to pull her back from her task. And then she sat down on the stage, her head nodding under her mitre, and howled like a beaten child. And Reason and Ananke brought great tubs of red winelees, and poured them over Culvert's scarlet posterior, so that the stage was a sea of blood and wine. And out into this red liquid, between the straddled legs, crept a naked child, with a candle, the little Felicitas, who had been cowering under the throne in the stink and turbulence and juices, and now did as she was told, a blood-red naked child, holding aloft a lighted candle, and quite unable to control her bitter weeping. And the people murmured, because both Pope and New Year were so miserable and howling. And Culvert rose in his robes, suddenly deflated, and his eyes darted daggers. And one pair of hands, Samson Origen's, clapped twice, softly. And outside, over the woods, the watchmen saw the first red slip of the new sun, for Culvert's timing had been impeccable.

Tales have been told earlier in this narrative of the delicate and indelicate doings in the Dormitories devised by Culvert. That wise man's conception of childhood was, it is to be feared, somewhat idealistic in its paradisal vision, for he saw the small human creatures in those vaulted sleeping places as rays of pure energy, as beings made of pure, warm, uncorrupted flesh and instincts full of creative kindness, of high inventiveness, of playful spontaneity when not thwarted, perverted and deformed by sick adult inhibitions—prohibitions sprouted from a sick society with stunted desires. It is true that the playfulness, spontaneity and inventiveness of the Lattermen, as the heads of the latrine corps were called, had flourished exceedingly amongst the beds and couches in the juvenile Harem. "To the free judgement of their peers," Culvert had said, "the community would trust the correction of the little peccadilloes, the omissions and hesitancies, of the youthful aspirants to freedom, for they would best know what was appropriate, and how to weigh the offence against the atonement, which might be a small thing, a brief abstention from chocolate, or perhaps a small service, the cleaning of another child's shoes."

What punishments the Lattermen devised in the dark hours has been told, as far as I dare tell. Jojo, Adolphus, Capo and the Grinner have been duly celebrated for the sweet humiliations, the atmosphere of apprehension, the wonderful arbitrariness they devised, so that boys and girls could be induced to punish themselves with sickly fears, and obsessive dreads, not knowing when the jolly mockery might begin, or the process of accusation be set in motion, day or night. For these bright boys were as adept at invading the essence of the closed grey soft matter in the young skull, or the bloody rhythm of the little heart, as they were at invading the beds, and mouths, and bottoms, of the little sleeping figures. And on the day after the Rite of the Solstice they pronounced themselves most dissatisfied with the behaviour of the child Felicitas, and that on two counts; first, that she had *shown herself off* in taking a central rôle in the Rite, she had *sucked up* and abased herself in order to procure this putting of herself on view, all naked with her silly candle. And secondly, that having displayed her meagre little body in this ostentatious way, she had *wept like a baby* and spoiled the whole jolly occasion; she had mightily *let everyone down*.

So they stood the little thing in the middle of the Dormitory, and pulled off her nightgown, and laughed at her nakedness. They wore the pretty masks they had all pranced in during the Carnival, Owls and Pussycats, Tadpoles and Newts, toothy Rabbits and snouty Bears, and pushy little Lambs, and they danced round her, pointing and poking and criticising her little belly and thighs and her trembling little knees. And then Jojo pronounced that she would not be punished *now* for her misdemeanours, but would be given time to think, and reflect, and that the judges would come when they were ready, and do to her what they would do, though they would not say now what it would be.

So they all turned away from her, and giggled together, and the little thing took up her nightdress and crept away to a cot in a corner where she often lay curled like a desperate snail in its shell. And Jojo came after her and snatched at the garment, saying she had wanted to be naked, and naked she should be. So she crawled in under her blanket, and her teeth clattered together like knitting needles, and this noise annoyed Adolphus, who took hold of her jaw and clattered it up and down in good earnest, whilst the others laughed.

And during the night, Felicitas could be heard sobbing and wailing, although these sounds were partly stifled by her pillow and blanket. But Jojo and Adolphus and Capo could not, they declared, sleep in this racket, so they rose up, and took the child from the cot, and put her on her head in the broom cupboard and turned the key. See if you can howl arsy-versy, they told her through the door, but she did not answer, for she could not.

And in the morning the door was opened by her brother Florian when everyone had gone to breakfast, chattering and laughing together. And the child fell out of the cupboard, rigid as a board, and cold as a stone to touch. She was not dead, Florian found, putting his cheek to her grey lips, which breathed a little warmth on his own warm skin. So he wrapped her in a blanket, and nursed her, and lulled her, and after a time she began to shiver, and the blood began to flow through her limbs, and she got to her feet. And she said, "B-b-b-b-b," and "C-c-c-c," but no other word. Nor did she ever again speak word, but crept silently about the Tower, always hugging the wall, for she would not stand freely, and would meet no one's eye, and drooled from the corner of her mouth.

And Florian asked himself whether he should speak to any member of the community about what had happened to his little sister. He saw it would be best to say nothing, for his own sake, and did indeed keep silence for some little time. But one day, finding his mother weeping over her silent child, he could not help himself, and told how it had come about, all of it, only he would give no names. And the Lady Mavis wept bitterly when she heard him, and could not think what was best to do. It might be thought, she should have spoken of the matter openly in the Council of the community, and sought justice for her child. But she judged it best to make peace, for the children were children she had risked her life to save from the soldiers of the Revolution, and she believed they were only children, and had done more harm than they knew. So she asked Jojo and Adolphus and Capo to come to her room, and there she said that no good was done by accusations or retribution; it was part of her creed that no eye should be plucked or tooth extracted in rage or cold vindictiveness. We must love each other, however hard it is, said the Lady Mavis to the meekly downcast boys. Who replied that she was quite right, and also quite wrong to suppose they had harmed her child, who had over-reacted to her rôle as the New Year. Someone, they said, had tittle-tattled, and told lies, but, as she herself had said, forgiveness was of the essence of community living and loving, and they would forgive, naturally.

And the next day, at breakfast, Florian was not to be found. A search was instituted, after twelve hours or so, when it was deemed by the community to be urgent, but the Tower was vast, and the pits and wells and glory-holes and oubliettes so many, and the moat so deep and the ramparts so high that no sign was ever seen again of the foolhardy boy, neither hair, nor bone, nor drop of blood, nor sweet smile.

After the disappearance of Florian, and the unavailing search of the Tower, the Lady Mavis became silent and withdrawn, although she still continued to perform tasks in the community, to peel potatoes, to mend torn clothing, to cook the little cakes, the spiced pastries or mirlitons, which she made better than anyone. She asked to be excused from her duties in the nurseries, and this withdrawal was felt to be graceful and natural, despite the general desire to do away with the feelings of partial maternity which gave rise to it.

But after some little time, the members of the community all received pretty little notes bidding them to a feast in the paved courtyard at the summit of the White Tower, or the Pierced Tower (it went by both names, which referred to the colour of its stone, and the ornamental aspect of its architecture, with many ogive and lanceolate windows). The pretty little notes referred to a *fête champêtre*, which was not so inapposite as it may sound, for the summit of the Tower, surrounded by crumbling battlements, had long been overgrown with tufted carpets of self-sown wild grasses, tenacious barren fig trees and gaudy ragwort, snapdragons and dandelions. And although there was a general opinion that my Lady Mavis's *fêtes champêtres* were now a little tame, a little *passée*, there was also pity for her in the community, and most of them mounted the cracked stairs at the appointed time, jostling each other on the turns, laughing and greedy for the good fare they confidently expected.

It could be seen that the Lady Mavis had prepared her little feast with some care, building a small canopy of red and black silk against the decaying battlements, and setting out on a long damask-covered table beneath it tasty dishes, flagons of pink bubbling wine and garlands of holly, with leaves like needles and berries red as blood. And she herself wore a snow-white robe under a scarlet overdress, with a garland of the holly shining in her hair.

Now the people quickly perceived that with great ingenuity the feast had been laid out on the table in the form of a Man or possibly of a Woman, for the Lady Mavis, in her old-fashioned modesty, had wreathed the joining of the legs in further holly, beneath which sugared figs could be seen nestling, and the breasts were, as we shall see, ambiguous. Now this human feast seemed on first sight like a giant gingerbread man, such as the Witch offered to Hansel and Gretel to entice them into her cottage, a great form composed of smaller forms, custards and tartlets, marzipan sweetmeats and blancmanges, jellies and syllabubs, mincemeats and flummeries, fools and darioles, mirlitons and millefeuilles. Its head was crowned with a circlet of tarts, of cockscombs, and the flesh of its body was all veined and contoured and dimpling, made of peaches and cream here, and slices of quince there, blueberry veinings and blackcurrant flushes. The face was whipped cream and meringue with rosepetal pies for cheeks and huge lips plump and red with apple cheeks and cranberry froth opening on an oval tart of baked larks' tongues, surrounded by sugared almond teeth. The eyes had sloeberry tartlets for pupils, and greengage jelly for the iris, flecked with vanilla, and white syllabub slicked round that, fringed with lashes of burned spun sugar. The Sweet Human had long red shining nails, on its fingers and toes, made of pointed tartlets glazed with scarlet redcurrant jelly, from which dripped pendant tarts like gouts of blood, also glazed scarlet. The breasts of this confected Being were low circling mounds of pink marzipan sweetmeats, with a castle of chocolate truffles for nipples: they were the breasts of a young girl or nubile boy, sweet to touch, sweet to taste. The navel was a deep custard tart amongst the peaches and cream, with a spiral swirl of *crème pâtissière* inside it. The sweetmeat body was, so to speak, naked except for a necklace of round red tarts of currants in scarlet jelly, and a line of these ran also, like Pantaloon's buttons, from chin to belly to crotch, and a further line also dissected this line at the waist, bonds or quarterings of glistening vermilion. "Like flies drowned in blood," said Jojo to Adolphus, of these round tarts, licking his lips.

Between the breasts of the Human Cake was a large shield-shaped exterior heart, composed of a phalanx of tiny, blood-red, heart-shaped tarts. Into the triangle which pierced darkly down between the plump red shoulders of the plump red heart was pushed a dark, triangular slice of cake, like a blade, covered with what appeared to be soot.

The Lady Mavis watched and smiled as the happy horde dismembered and savoured the Baked Human. She remarked smilingly to Culvert that in the early days of their planning of their escape, the dark days of hiding, and mutual trust, and danger, they had imagined a society where sweet things were freely prepared for all comers, where everyone could eat cake, and spiced tartlets, who desired them. Culvert, who had a sweet tooth, bit into a mirliton and reminisced about how he planned to replace wars in the New Order with great contests of gastrosophy, with tournaments of pastry-cookery, with intense trials of skill in the construction of raised pies, or "melting moments" or "bouchées à la Reine" or frangipani, or succotash, or meringues glacées.

And when the limbs of the Cake-Man were scattered and despoiled, when the sweetness had been sucked from its navel and the chocolate nipples had melted succulently in various mouths, when its face and its heart were tattered and disfigured with gaping holes, the Lady Mavis climbed on to the battlement steps, and stood dark against the sky, with the winter wind ruffling the silk canopy at her side, and lifting her somewhat dishevelled hair.

"I have a few words to say," said this Lady, "if you will grant me a few precious moments, before you resume your nibblings and savourings and sippings, which I hope are satisfying as I meant them to be. And my few words consist of a question, and after that, if I have no answer, of a statement."

"She is like the schoolmistress confronting the naughty boys," said Jojo to Adolphus. "But we have no such silly authority here; here are no teachers and no pupils, but freedom."

"My question," said the Lady Mavis, "to which I fear I may have no answer, is Where is my son Florian? For I do not believe that no one knows what became of him. I believe there are those among you who could say, if they chose. And if he is alive, I wish to succour him, to release him, to embrace him, and if he is dead, to weep for him and to bury him decently. This is not much to ask."

The Lady Roseace, flushed with pain, said, "You know well that we have searched everywhere, and for days. We could not have been more diligent if he were our own child—which indeed he was—for we are all part of each other. We have left no stone unturned; we have dragged the moat; we have combed the woods."

"And opened every cupboard," said Jojo, with an air of grave concern. "He was not shut in any cupboard in the castle: we made it our business to investigate every cupboard, every coal-hole, every store-room."

"He was a self-willed little boy," said Adolphus. "He could have wandered into the pig-pen, or the abattoir, or fallen into a well, or been carried off by wolves. He did not listen to advice. I do not think you will see him again."

"We must not lose hope," said Culvert, without conviction.

"In the old days," said Colonel Grim, "I would have known how to find out what had happened. But my old methods are not part of our new world."

"And must never be again," said the Lady Paeony, with scorn. "How many innocents have not confessed to unreal evils on your rack?"

"Just so," said Colonel Grim. "We shall never, I believe, see the bottom of this matter."

"That is the conclusion I too have come to," said the Lady Mavis. "And now, I have a few other things to say."

And she went to the table, and took up the triangular sooty segment of the sugar heart of the Human-Sweetmeat, which had been left untouched on the table. She bit into this, and climbed back to her station beside the battlements, tasting its black taste on her tongue, ingesting its shadowy substance.

"We are told by antiquaries," said she, "that in ancient Babylon, in the chamber at the top of the ziggurat which was reserved for the activities of the God Baal, he came sometimes to sleep with the priestess, and sometimes to share a feast at a giant stone table, and sometimes, in difficult times, to demand a sacrifice. And there are many tales of what this sacrifice was—a red human heart, tastefully roasted, a whole human infant, the first-born, trussed and tossed into the flames of his altar fire. It is told that on his feast days a great cake was baked, and cut into small portions, one of which was blacked with the soot of the eternal Fire of his altar. The people took their cakes blindfold, and he who chose the black square was the Chosen One, devoted to the God. And for a time this Devoted One was fed and fattened, granted his desires of the flesh, sweet cakes and wine, sweet bedfellows and smoky opiates. And when his time came, he was led smiling to the fire, and the God was pleased, and did not wilfully torture or persecute the people for the following year, but let their corn and vines grow rich and their children spring up plump and healthy. We are told that the Krebs still build a Bale Fire and make their offerings, somewhere in the forest, a prisoner, a fool, a goat, a beloved son—the tales vary. And in the religion we have renounced, too, the god-man made himself bread and wine, drank the bitter cup and offered his body to dismemberment, to save the people from pain. He sacrificed himself to himself, as we were all taught.

"We are not gods, we are rational beings in pursuit of happiness. We have no gods, to judge or to comfort, to afflict us or to take away pain. All we are is ourselves, and we have discovered in ourselves in these latter days deep-rooted desires to hurt and to be hurt, ancient instincts of immolation and oblation. I have thought much, over these last weeks, about the desire to hurt. In the farmyard, the sight of blood on a wounded bird, a broken wing, a lame foot, arouses the fat fit hens, the young cockerels and the growing chicks to a frenzy of plucking and pecking. They will peck to death a beast which is injured; they will strip its breast bare of plumage, and expose pimpled purple skin, and then blood, and then bone. This is usual, this is not unnatural in these witless feathered things.

"I do not think there is any god to whom I may sacrifice in order to demand the restoration of my son. I do not believe in vengeance—it is part of the old ways, which we have abjured. Whatever may have happened to my sweet son's eyes and his growing teeth, I ask for no other mother's son's eye or tooth in recompense. All we can punish is ourselves, and the stripped, ridiculous hen, if she could, would hasten her end, if she were rational. If I harbour the idea that my death might propitiate the spirit of cruelty that is abroad amongst you, I know that idea for the sentimentality it is. I should like to think that I can take with me," said she, climbing higher on the battlements, with the wind stronger in her hair and garments—"I should like to think that I can take with me the yeast of blood-lust and malice that is at work, that I could concentrate its energy in my body and extinguish it with my life. Because I go voluntarily, *no one else is guilty* of my death, I kill myself, and restore a kind of preliminary innocence. I mean the pain to stop with me, and the old innocence of flowers and sweetmeats to be restored for a time."

And she ascended another step to the battlements, and stood looking at them. And a strange, strangled sound was heard amongst the skirts of the ladies, and the little Felicitas struggled out and ran across the courtyard, and clambered up the steps, holding to her mother's skirts, and making the raw sounds of the voiceless. The Lady Mavis bent down and picked up her daughter, with tears streaming down her cheeks, and cradled her in her arms, kissing her.

"The child has saved the mother," said the Lady Roseace.

But the Lady Mavis turned again, and climbed, and stood for a moment high and free on the wall itself, crooning to the child in her arms, and then stepped out into the air, crooning and murmuring.

They all ran to the battlements. Culvert alone did not: he ran down. He had an idea of catching his old friend in his strong arms.

Jojo said to Adolphus, "She has decided finally to be a *vol-au-vent*. She is light."

She was light, and the Tower was high, and her skirts were voluminous. The air pressed under her skirts, and lifted her and played with her, like a sycamore seed, like a kite, eddying and spiralling. They could not hear if she was still singing to the child, but they could now hear the child screaming, a rough, shrill sound, as she took account of her slow descent to death.

Culvert was again defeated by his own Tower, whose corridors deceived and delayed. He hurtled and fell: he stood again and found he had run in a circle and was rising where he had been descending. He put his shoulder to a door and found it rusted in its hinges and locks; he ran on, opened another, almost stepped out himself into air.

So the Lady Mavis came down like a great bird, swaying in her skirts amongst the child's raucous cries and her own singing. But when she saw the tree-tops, where she might alight like a bird, or break her fall, she made various ungainly movements with her body, twisting and turning, and managed to project herself downwards head-first, her skirts tumbling around her face, her stately legs scissoring the air in their lace-edged drawers. And her head hit a sharp rock, like a snail dropped by a thrush, and burst apart as Culvert managed to rush across the moat from a side gate with a railed bridge. He was in time to pull the child Felicitas, unharmed, from her mother's twitching grip, and to wipe the blood and brains from her little face.

"She is wrong," said Turdus Cantor, "if she thinks she will terrify those who hurt her son out of their course."

"She will give them a taste for blood," said Colonel Grim. "And for spectacle. As we saw in the old world."

"Hers was an old illusion," said Samson Origen, "that self-punishment will shame the wicked. So many women hurt themselves, thinking their pain will hurt their persecutors, who take pleasure in it."

"And what do you make of her talk of sacrifice?" asked Turdus Cantor. "Her thinking on that matter was deeply confused and deluded, it seemed to me."

"All thinking on that matter is confused and deluded," said Colonel Grim. "But a little blood shed has always been wonderfully fortifying to the energies of judges and soldiers, kings and priests. All such like to seal their pacts with blood."

"Necessity is ineluctable," said Samson Origen. "A self-perpetuating mechanism. Our blood oils its cogs, whether we offer it up or not. Our intention matters not a jot. On the other hand, the absence of this lady is the removal both of an irritant and of a goad to persecution in our little world. It could calm our flushed blood. Or it could arouse further animosity against less vulnerable targets. Blood finds its own level, like water."

Frederica thinks of antechambers, and wonders why, since she is not in an antechamber, but in Arnold Begbie's office, sitting opposite Arnold Begbie, both in tan hide chairs with chrome frames. Begbie is a partner in Begbie, Merle and Schloss. They are on the ground floor of a Georgian house in Sunderland Square, which is, just, Bloomsbury. The room is mostly full of Begbie's large oak desk. Sunlight floods through the window, which is covered with an intricate steel mesh. Beyond are the spearheads of the iron fence of the residents' locked garden. Faint from the garden come voices of children, running and calling.

Frederica looks like a pantomime Maid Marian, in a short green suede dress, mesh tights, high crumpled suede boots. Arnold Begbie's suit is dark, his tie spattered regularly with blood-red dots. He has springing black hair in just-controlled surges. His eyes are black and his skin sultry, his bones—nose, chin, cheeks—jutting and pronounced. His voice is subdued and Scottish. He murmurs, writing, looking down.

"You are quite decided upon divorce."

The meshes make patterns on his blotter.

"I wouldn't have come if I wasn't."

"You know your own mind."

"I didn't mean to sound rude."

"You didn't. So many people come to me, to discuss divorce, when divorce is the last thing they want. Tell me about yourself, Mrs. Reiver, and about your husband."

Frederica gives what she thinks is a precise, dispassionate résumé of her marriage. She has thought out what to say and what not to say. She explains that she was left alone for very long periods, and that her husband opposed her return to any kind of work. She says that she saw no one, but that when her friends visited, her husband was unreasonably angry. She says unemphatically that he became violent. He attacked her, she says. He hurt her. She tried to run away, she says, and he threw an axe after her, wounding her. She is proud of the level, quiet, informative voice in which she says all this. Arnold Begbie writes. He says, "Is that all?"

"We are incompatible." A silly word. An undescriptive word. "It is all my fault. I should never have married him. I know I should not."

This she thinks every day. Mr. Begbie taps his pen on his strong teeth. Incompatibility and mistake, he tells her with practised gentleness, are not grounds for divorce. Grounds for divorce are desertion, cruelty, adultery, insanity and certain arcane and unacceptable practices he is sure they need not go into. It is possible that Frederica is in a position to petition for divorce on grounds of cruelty. Neglect, refusal to listen, can amount, in some cases, to cruelty. Physical violence is certainly cruelty, though the courts take into account the character and circumstances of the partners in deciding what the effects of one particular act of violence might be deemed to be. He imagines she is not used to being struck, or to having things thrown at her. No? Good. And she saw a doctor, perhaps, after the axe wound?

"Of course," says Frederica. "We told him I tripped and fell on some barbed wire."

"A pity. Would he have believed you?"

"I don't know. He stitched it. My London doctor dressed it. I told him how it happened."

"That, unfortunately, would be too late after the event to be very helpful. He might however be able to say that such a wound could not have been caused by barbed wire. The courts do not always look favourably on unsupported assertions of cruelty by the complainant. Did anyone else see the wound?"

"Several people. None of them were people it was any good *telling*—"

Arnold Begbie allows this matter to drop, and asks whether Frederica supposes her husband will contest a divorce, if she asks for one. Frederica says she believes he will: when last seen, she says, he was pressing her to return, and to return her son. He does not like to be thwarted or contradicted, she says. She adds that she knows that if she allowed her son to visit she would never see him again. The solicitor says that the courts may have views on the father's rights of access. Frederica says that she herself believes her child should see his father; that she would encourage this; that she knows in her bones that she would not see him again, if he went there, now. She may need to find evidence, says Arnold Begbie, to support the feeling in her bones in a court of law. Frederica's bones become briefly knobby and obtrusive in the seamless dry run of the language of the discussion: she has a sudden vision of them, quivering and bloody, inside her composed flesh and her green suede. Her bones are not evidence.

Arnold Begbie brings up the subject of adultery. Mrs. Reiver has not herself mentioned any suspicion of adultery. She has said that her husband was often absent for long periods. Has she ever imagined that he might be seeing other women, during those periods?

Frederica says she doesn't know, and hasn't thought about it. She says she believes her husband loves her and adds, flushing slightly, that as far as sex goes, they are happy, they are compatible. That silly word, again. She says her husband is a man who likes women. She hesitates. Arnold Begbie watches her hesitate. He prompts her. "You have remembered something."

"Not exactly," says Frederica. "But I have—I have a venereal infection." She is proud of the precise, unpleasant word. Because she is Frederica, having brought herself to say it, she thinks of irrelevant connotations, Shakespeare's hot Venus, panting for Adonis, Spenser's veiled Venus, medieval Venus, a regal being charioted by doves and accompanied by her winged son and his burning arrows. She shifts in her seat. She says, "There is no other way I could have caught it."

"No other person."

"That is what I said."

"A communicable venereal disease is evidence of adultery. You can produce evidence of that?"

"Yes."

The conversation continues. Frederica dredges her memory. It is agreed that Arnold Begbie will write to Nigel Reiver, saying that his wife intends to petition for divorce on grounds of cruelty, and see what response he gets. In the interim, Frederica must go home and write out an account of her marriage, as fully as possible, listing every example of anything that might be construed as cruelty, and anything she may recall which might be evidence of adultery. Arnold Begbie would like to know what Mrs. Reiver would say to an amicable meeting—in the presence of her solicitor—to discuss the questions of divorce, maintenance, custody, care and control of her child.

"I don't want him to know where I am living."

"That may be difficult. Where are you living?"

Frederica tells him. He says, "And Mr. Poole, in whose flat you are living. Do you hope to marry him, if you obtain a divorce?"

"No—" says Frederica. She says, "It is purely an arrangement—it isn't what you think—it is to share the looking after children—it isn't—"

She cannot tell if he believes her. He says, "If you petition for divorce, you are required to enter a statement asking the court's discretion with regard to your own adultery, if there has been any adultery. Your solicitor is required to bring this matter to your attention."

"There *hasn't*," says Frederica, with a strong sense of injury. "For one thing, as I told you, I've got this infection . . ." She stops in some confusion.

"And if you had not, you would be tempted."

"I'm not saying that. I don't think—"

"You don't think it is my business. But it is, Mrs. Reiver, it is. I cannot advise you to go on living with an unattached man—even in the presence of an *au pair* girl and several children—if your husband is likely to contest the divorce."

"I can't earn my living if I can't share the child care."

"You could ask your husband for maintenance for yourself, and your son."

"I won't *do* that. I want to earn my own living."

"I would not be emphatic about that if you hope to persuade the courts to allow you custody of your son."

"But my present arrangement—"

"Does not look good, frankly. I advise you to move. Unless you really wish to marry Mr. Poole. Do you think he wishes to marry you?"

Frederica, who has her complex anxieties on that point, is silent.

"Reflect on it, Mrs. Reiver," says Arnold Begbie. He smiles. "We shall find a way. Don't look so downhearted."

"I feel suddenly trapped."

"We shall find a way to free you, don't worry."

This is Frederica's first legal narrative. It is an official tale, told to a partial, official listener. Frederica selected its narrative elements; Arnold Begbie sorted, assessed, rearranged and added to them. It is only the beginning. There will be more. And more, and more.

Coming out of the offices, into the winter sun in the square, Frederica stops to peer through the railings at two blond children, a bigger girl, a smaller boy, riding tricycles on the gravel path round the grass. Two women are sitting with their backs to her on a bench. She can hear their conversation.

"They're all the same. I say, 'You say, "Don't nag." I wouldn't nag if you'd only ever *listen* to what I'm saying and remember it.' But he thinks it's beneath him, he thinks anything I say is bound to be trivial and somehow demeaning, he goes on thinking his *important* thoughts. I tell him, 'I don't want my brain cluttered with questions you can't be bothered to listen to or answer, I could think important thoughts if I didn't have to remember every trivial thing *for you*.' He doesn't care about cluttering my brain, his own's a plane of white frost, an infinite *tabula rasa,* on the personal plane, so to speak."

"I think they feel threatened," says the second woman. "He treats me as though I was a fussing hen, or his mother, who's stopping him doing what he wants, telling him grown-up things are *naughty,* slapping his fingers. I don't want to be his mother, I don't want to be *anybody's* mother as far as slapping people and stopping people goes. But you don't have much choice, if people are to eat and be kept clean. He laughs at me in an indulgent sort of way, but *like a little boy,* if I try to talk about any household thing, and off he goes to the pub. But he gets pretty mad if I do anything he doesn't like while he isn't looking."

"He says, 'Is there any?' or 'Where is the?' all the time. He comes in at any hour, and says 'Is there any food?' He stands there: 'Is there any bread?' He doesn't *look* for it. 'Where is the butter? Where are the matches?' Often he can see them. But I have to run up and down, fetching things. He needs that."

"You don't *have* to."

"It's quicker. More peace, in the end."

"What would happen if you didn't, if we didn't?"

"He might hit me. He might leave."

"Do you really think so?"

"Yes."

A sharp laugh. "So do I."

They are the chorus. All Frederica can see of them are two huge knitted hats, one black, one white, and two fake-fur coats, one orange, one shocking pink. Their voices are pleasant BBC voices, with humour in them. Their husbands are one indistinguishable He, and in the context of those husbands, these women are also one indivisible voice. This is the narrative of women talking, women watching children, talking. Owing to accidents of fate, or quirks of personality, Frederica has never really been part of groups of women talking. She was hated at school; her Cambridge friends are men; she cannot make common cause with Olive and Rosalind and Pippy. But she can recognise an archetypal, anonymous female narrative, and wonders

suddenly how this talk affects the relations between the w
the men they return to. Does the speaking of mocking criti
Cyril and Fred and Louis and Sebastian into He He He
they are seen again, does it strengthen opposition to Him
Him in laughter? She thinks this because she knows already, in a pale
and partial way, that the legal narrative she has just constructed has
changed several people: Nigel into the Husband, herself into the
Plaintiff, Thomas Poole into something he is and is not.

She finds this rather exciting, as an idea about the dynamics of
human behaviour.

She finds it frightening as a human experience of her own. She has
always thought her life was her own, and she was in charge of it. Even
when the axe hit her, she was filled with the rage of the hurt of *her*,
with the fury of her own intention to get out, to regain her freedom.

But this narrative is like a fishnet, a trap. It redefines her and so
changes her.

She thinks further, as she goes back to Thomas Poole's flat, about
antechambers. There are times in life, she thinks, when I am most
conscious of being myself, and these are all times of waiting: before
journeys, between the first and the worst birth pains, before exams,
before going on stage. Times when I was complete because something was about to happen, but was not happening. I have a life
which is a string of these moments of completeness, which I remember so clearly, although they are not important, they are nothing. I stand outside a door, and cannot imagine action that will
happen.

She cannot remember how it was before she married Nigel. She
cannot remember how she came to do so.

She is afraid of divorce, which will free her, as she was not enough
afraid of marriage, which trapped her.

I was not thinking, she concludes, thinking now, harshly, of her
then self. I was a fool. I gave him something that didn't exist, because
I wasn't thinking, a wife, like the simulacrum of Helen who went to
Troy whilst the real one did nothing in Egypt.

Why did I?

It was something I thought I had to do.

Why?

It is what people do do.

Why?

She sees in her mind's eye the heavy figure of Daniel, who married her sister. She sees her sister, her head on the café table, crying and laughing and saying she is happy.

I married Nigel because Stephanie married Daniel and died.

Nonsense.

Then, why?

The three friends stood outside the Chapel of Tongues, which was crowded with folk who had come to hear the new confessions of the young Narcisse, who stood before the derelict altar and recounted to them his early seduction by a hirsute nursemaid, and his subsequent enthralment of a flute-playing tutor. His lovely face was, as I have said, white as alabaster and ruddy as a rose, and his hair was black as ebony.

"These tyrants of our childhood," said he, "direct our young inclinations when we have neither force nor knowledge to resist. They teach us titillation, secrecy and control, and in turn become our victims when we learn their lessons too well, when we obtain in our turn power over their desires and their weaknesses. They teach us shame, and treachery, when all should be innocence and freedom. I have confessed before you how I betrayed my friend Hyacinth to the police because his love wearied me: I have confessed how I drove Amaryllis to despair with indifference and neglect. I have reflected much, and see that the creature I was was licked into shape—oh, most literally—by that great brutal nursemaid with her hairy lips and her shaggy breasts, in whose loathsome, suffocating, hot embrace I was so frequently and with such taunting endearments crushed. She made me desire what revolted me, and as she made me, so I am."

"He goes back and back," said Turdus Cantor. "He began with a man's guilt over the selling of Hyacinth, and called another meeting to say he had found its source in a schoolboy's betrayal of his friend's secret acts to save himself a whipping. Now he says the schoolboy is the son, so to speak, of the too-much tickled nurseling. He will go back and find treachery in the womb, mark me, and they will listen."

"He does not mention the pieces of silver he was paid for Hyacinth," said Colonel Grim. "It is all the body's desire and the perversion of desire. He might speak of the desire for silver amongst his elaborations on tweakings and pokings, lickings and twistings. Cool silver roundels that buy sweetmeats and men's lives, that represent indifferently *any* object of desire."

"And desire shall fail," said Samson Origen. "Our great Projector bids us clarify and examine our desires, acknowledge each dark wriggling thought and appetite, bring them into air and light, and make them clean, and healthy, and innocently wise. But I say that which is crooked cannot be made straight: and that which is wanting cannot be numbered."

"You are a man of few desires," said Turdus Cantor. "What is hard for many is easy for you."

"I have one deep desire," said Samson Origen. "I desire to be at that point when desire shall fail. I desire not to be. Fat Silenus, with grease and winelees oozing from every pore, told the King who caught him that the most desirable state was never to have been born, and the next best was to die soon, for that peace is true peace, which our young friend will not find, whatever he unearths in his memory or his imagination to confess, whatever burdens he unloads into the minds of others, whatever hurts he shares about and about. True wisdom is to stand silent, and neither to give nor to take, but to be still."

"You have not been so silent since you came amongst us," said Turdus Cantor. "You eat and drink. We profit from your conversation. We take pleasure in your company."

"Truly, the gabbing and optimistic atmosphere of this place has had its effect on me," answered Samson Origen. "And your two dry minds, my two friends, have almost made a dent in my resolve to have no attachments. But it cannot last long, as we three all see. The day of blood will come, desire shall be slaked, Culvert will see where he is going, and I shall look on." 🐚

Frederica and Alan Melville stand outside the Life Studio, under the glassy lights of the Samuel Palmer School. A group of students are gathered, sitting in a rough semi-circle on the floor, listening to these words, to which Frederica and Alan also listen, at some distance. The reader is Jude Mason, who holds a great heap of untidy typescript on his naked knees. He is wearing nothing but a shiny red dressing-gown which hangs open, revealing his iron-grey body. His face is buried in his long, long iron-grey hair, which is greasy and gleaming. His filthy feet grip the step of the dais on which he is sitting, almost prehensile.

"Here endeth the second lesson," he says, tossing back the curtains of hair. "All is vanity." He beckons to Frederica and Alan, who approach cautiously, entering the perimeter of his pungent smell.

"You no doubt think it is great vanity to read my opus to this captive audience," he says to Frederica, in his clear, sawing voice. "You are a literary person, and I have written a work of literature. But I dare not expect you to take an interest in it."

"I don't see why," says Frederica. "It surprised me. It excited me. I'd like to read it."

The gaunt face peers out between the hair, the deep eyes glittering.

"It's not a *nice* book, my dear. It's not a book for nice young women."

"Don't be pretentious. I don't care if it isn't nice. I said, it excited me."

"Books can hurt you."

"I know. If you don't want me to read it, that's OK. I'll go and get on with *Madame Bovary*."

"*That's* not a nice book. That's a mischievous work of despair. My nasty book has more hope in it than that cartload of clay."

He is over-excited by her interest, and unattractive in his over-excitement. Frederica finds herself staring at the defining limits of his taut belly, in order not to meet his eye.

"You didn't think I could write, confess it, you thought I was rubbish, talking rubbish."

"And if I did, you meant me to."

"You can read it. In *manus tuas*. Here." He prances towards her, on a wave of his odour, and thrusts the heap of paper into her hands. "I appoint you my *reader*. Greater love hath no man than this. Though it will require a modicum of love on your part, to go through all that *bumf*, oh, what a word, what a good word, bumf, bumf—I am overcome with over-excitement."

"Is this your only copy?"

"Are you hesitating? Do you regret your commitment? Shall I take it back?"

"Please, stop all that. I daren't be responsible for your only copy."

"You aren't. I sell my body, I purchase carbon paper. I write it all out by hand also, and primarily, I exude, I excrete, little black threads of meaning and bodily *anguish* along feinted lines on scholastic paper. I would not bring my only copy here in this plastic bag, do not think it. It is the child of my body, it is my only delight, I keep copies at my humble *home,* clones, versions. This is my *mundane* copy, fit for crushing with me if I go under a car. At home I have an immortal copy in many-coloured inks. Do not say many-coloured inks are derivative, I forestall you, I tell you freely it is a tribute to him, to Father Rolfe, to the great Baron Corvo, who taught me the bliss of scarlet and emerald inks."

Thomas Poole tells Frederica that an inspector is coming to her evening class. It is February and dark in the evenings. The class has held together, despite Christmas, and the dark days of the solstice. Thomas has told Frederica that it is important to make her students present papers to the class. They are reluctant, Frederica says, they are there voluntarily, why should she make them? If, indeed, she can make them. They like to hear *her,* her cleverness, her passion. She is afraid that they may bore each other. Thomas Poole says that the classes function as therapeutic groups, and that speaking out is part of the therapy. Frederica retorts that she is not a therapist, and that her students are not sick. They are intelligent people, who need to think hard and deep, and don't get the opportunity. She holds it against Poole, later, that he has used this word, "therapy." He persists. She will find that they are grateful to be made to speak, he says. Students, even adults, require you to be the authority that requires effort out of their lassitude and self-mistrust. If he is wrong, in Frederica's judgement, about therapy, he is right about authority. Frederica has learned to make the students speak, and she, and they, are excited by what they say. Nevertheless, the inspector has chosen a difficult day. The evening's presentation is on Kafka's *Castle.* Who would speak on *The Castle,* she asked the class, a month ago. She expected an enthusiastic offer from Ghislaine Todd, the psychoanalyst, who often refers to Kafka, but in fact the one who raises his hand is the quiet blond man in a suit, who never misses a class, and never speaks, except occasionally over coffee to the other suited man, the owner of the Lambretta, whose attendance has become spasmodic.

"Oh, good," said Frederica then. "Are you specially interested in Kafka?"

"Yes," said the blond man. Frederica waited. "Yes, I am," said the blond man.

And now he is about to speak. Thomas Poole and the inspector are in the back row of the circle, which is two rows deep. The lights are dismal. Someone is crunching a Polo mint. John Ottokar stands up, holding a neat white sheaf of papers. His face is classical, broad-browed, blue-eyed, quiet-mouthed, amiable. His hair is massed and thick.

"I think I remember at school being told you must never say 'I think,'" he begins. "But all I can do is say what I think, since there is no other reason for standing here. I am fortunate if you listen. No one in this book listened to K the Land Surveyor, except the official whose bed he invaded by accident, when he had the chance to speak, and he only fell asleep.

"I didn't really read before I came to this class. So I can't make the connections some of you make between this book and other books. This is the book of all the books we have read that has told me most about what it is to be a human being, although what it says is that to be a human being is almost nothing.

"What you notice at first is two things: the Land Surveyor who can't get himself accepted or recognised, and the Castle.

"He can see the Castle in the distance, but there is no way of getting there, or speaking to it.

"In the village, where he seems to have to stay, everything is full of human bodies and human emotions—sex, and competition, silly quarrels and status problems like hens in a barnyard.

"You might suppose the Castle would be fine, or imposing, or a fortress. But is isn't. It resembles the village, or a rock. Or an optical illusion. Kafka tells you several things about it, and the things give contradictory impressions, contradictory feelings. It is in the 'glittering air' in the white snow, it 'soars light and free.' It also resembles his home village he came from. 'It was only a wretched-looking town, a huddle of village houses, whose sole merit, if any, lay in being built of stone, but the plaster had long since flaked off and the stone seemed to be crumbling away.' Also there is a tower, 'graciously mantled with ivy, pierced by small windows that glittered in the sun, a somewhat maniacal glitter.' It is a *mad* tower. Kafka says it seems 'designed by the trembling or careless hand of a child . . . as if a melancholy-mad tenant . . . had burst through the roof.' What is this Castle? It's where he wants to go and can't go, it's the place *where he isn't now,* it's gracious and glittering and mad. Kafka's words don't hang together. Nor does the Castle.

"Life in the village is a muddle and a mess. Like the worst ideas any of us have of life in groups, groups like families or also people who work together, full of sudden hostilities and equally sudden warmth between people which isn't real, hasn't a reason. Everyone talks all the time. They gab and gabble, they explain and excuse themselves, they are shifty and evasive. It is all really power struggles at some level. You don't know if the Castle is different or the same, since you can't go there.

"Everything is like a dream, where you can grasp on to thinking processes or *complicated* human emotions, but only to be denied by the obtuseness of your own sleeping body. Or you are denied by unresponsiveness or *animosity* in the other creatures in the dream world.

"Kafka was a clerk who got pushed about by bureaucracies. He couldn't bring himself to get married. He writes about love and power in a world of struggling maggots and puppies and dreamy muddle. He could be writing about the survival of the fittest. But although the Castle officials are well fed, they're sleepy, too, they can't sit up and take notice, they *don't know what's going on*.

"That's the key to it, really, they don't know what's going on. They have language, but they can't think with it, they fuss about. They talk about love and influence but they mess those words up, they don't *mean* anything. And freedom, what is it? If you're sleepy to death you can't be free. The words of this book are all dilapidated like the Castle itself. When K tries to phone the Castle at the beginning, before he knows better, he hears a funny buzz in the telephone. 'It was like the hum of countless children's voices—but yet not a hum, the echo rather of voices singing at an infinite distance— blended by sheer impossibility into one high but resonant sound which vibrated on the ear as if it were trying to penetrate beyond mere hearing.'

"Children singing is like heaven, but the idea of them humming and buzzing is like the playground, where you can get hurt, where there's no order.

"All the people in this book are in a way no more than cross children. I'd like to discuss this idea more.

"Language gets you nowhere, society seems to be just a mad structure that has only one function—to keep *itself* going in an unthinking sort of way—not for any reason.

"I read another story by Kafka, 'The Penal Colony,' in which there is a terrible instrument of torture, which has a bed, on which the condemned man lies, gagged, and a Harrow, which writes his sentence on his body with needles, in his own blood, and kills him with writing. It is worked by an official who loves it. He keeps telling the other man, the explorer, that the condemned man *can't read* his sentence but *he can feel it in his body.* There isn't any order except this mad mechanical precision—and the torture machine, like the Castle—isn't so good close up, its cogs make a nasty noise, its felt gag is worn out with earlier tortures. K is a Land Surveyor but he can't get far enough out of the mess to survey. K thinks Barnabas the messenger is an Angel stepping in the blizzard, but he is 'really' only a boy in a dirty jerkin. The messages aren't messages. But Kafka can write in this *non*-language, like an angel, about there not being any angels, and nothing to survey. This is an inhuman book about being human. Or a human book about being inhuman. Or am I just playing with words?"

The discussion is heated. Ghislaine Todd, the psychoanalyst, and Rosemary Bell, the hospital almoner, have developed a running argument about the reasons for male fear of women in the early twentieth century. Todd sees K's impotence as a result of his demonisation of mother-figures, whilst Rosemary Bell sees it as a result of social oppression. Sister Perpetua observes that both these interpretations may relate to the disappearance of God, who was or is both Father and Authority, and whose Presence would make sense of the senseless Castle and the frantic earthly desires and struggles. Humphrey Maggs says Sister Perpetua may be right, but you can't make God exist just because it would make sense of things. Ibrahim Mustafa says that God does exist, and that Kafka knows it, whether he thinks he does or not. An argument develops about K's "assistants"—are they hostile siblings, or anarchic employees in a society without purpose, or perhaps the testicles beside the phallus. Or schizophrenic emanations from K's own damaged psyche, says John Ottokar, or the Id running away from the controls of the Ego and the Superego. He has never said so much before: Ghislaine Todd smiles at him warmly. The inspector is delighted. He makes notes.

Afterwards, they all go to the pub. The pub is called the Goat and Compasses and has a rather clever swinging sign with a Satanic albino goat wielding a compass rather in the manner of Blake's Urizen. It is a dark brown-leather-and-open-fireplace pub, with electric imitation coals; there are a lot of mock-vellum lampshades on mock-candles. They have their own very dark brown table in a deep dark corner, with high settle-like benches along two sides and several mock-mediaeval stools. A good half of the class always go there, and intense relationships are formed. The whole group offers advice on Una Winterson's marital problems, or listens to Humphrey Maggs's views on Harold Wilson, on capital punishment, on homosexuality, the concerns of the day. They do these things in the light of Madame Bovary, of Dostoevski's Idiot, of Proust. Frederica finds she does not want to sit near Thomas Poole, who has come with them and is deep in conversation with the battling Freudian and Marxist. She takes the opposite corner of the table, and finds herself sipping red wine next to John Ottokar. She tells him his paper was splendid. She says, "You never talked, before."

"I don't talk. I thought it was time."

"I don't really know what you do."

"I write computer programmes. For a shipping firm. I am a mathematician."

"George Murphy came to the class because of his Lambretta."

"I came to learn language. I've never used language. I grew up without it."

"I have a mathematical brother who's suspicious of language."

"My situation is complicated. I am an identical twin, and we were both mathematicians. We grew up speaking a kind of private language—almost a silent language—of signs and gestures. We closed everyone out. No one could reach us. We were like a child and a mirror that spoke to itself. I think it frightened us, but when we were frightened, it intensified—our need of each other. We didn't relate outwards. And at the same time, we were each other's prison."

"Did you have the same friends?"

"No friends, until we went to university. We tried to go to different universities, but that didn't work—we started in different places and ended up in the same one. We fought. We both wanted to work in artificial intelligence, and by then we both wanted the other to do something else. It was like being torn in two—being *half* and half. If we saw each other by accident, it was like seeing ourselves when we had thought we were invisible. I can't explain. Anyway. I had a hard time talking to people. Except in computer languages. Algo. Fortran. Cobol. But I saw it wasn't enough. I sat through meal after meal saying nothing. I met girls, and said nothing. Then I got my job."

"And your brother?"

"He went another way. I may tell you, some day, not now. We had problems. He found—a way of talking I don't like. I needed badly to learn language in a—detached?—way. Not *personal* language. You don't follow. I'm sorry."

"You use language with great assurance. Look at your Kafka paper. As you must know."

"I'm interested in whether you think if you don't speak. I felt like—like an ape learning, or Adam in the Bible, writing that paper, making myself think thoughts. I thought, Did I think all those things before I had to write them?"

"Did you?"

"Oh yes. But not in words. In shapes. In feelings. Those words, the word 'shape,' the word 'feeling' don't quite describe what I mean, what I thought."

He has an eloquence, Frederica thinks, which is aware of itself but innocent; he uses words well and with glee because they all appear to him new-minted. She says, "I'm glad you came here to learn language."

"Not only that," he says in a low voice. "I come for another reason."

Frederica looks at him.

"One that does and doesn't need words," he says. "*I want you,*" he says, quickly and quietly.

She is aware of the whole of him, blond smile, fierce intent eyes, his hands on the table, his legs and feet beneath it, near her own but not touching. She responds for a moment, in silence, with a fast flood of blood to her heart and her pale face. He smiles. She does not. He watches her trouble. He stands and walks away to fetch more drinks. He is a grown man, not a student; he is older than she is. The three words have changed everything: and nothing, for she has known, before, how things were. But now they are spoken.

On the way home, Thomas Poole congratulates her on her class. She is a born teacher, he tells her. The group has a life of its own. She remembers that he had used the word "therapy," and is angry. Books are not therapy, she thinks, they are understanding, they are thinking. She is still out of breath because of the fierce certainty of John Ottokar. She says, "My solicitor says I've got to move out, but I don't know where to go. He says I can't go on living with you and hope to get a divorce."

Thomas Poole says, "I had hoped you would stay permanently." His voice does not expect her to say she will.

"I can't," says Frederica, striding along in the dark. "I've got to find somewhere innocent and unexceptionable. I don't see how."

She asks Daniel if he knows where she can live. He does not. She asks Tony, Alan, Hugh Pink, who are also unable to help. It is Alexander, who found her her first refuge, who comes up with her second. He sends her to see Agatha Mond.

X

꧁꧂꧁꧂꧁꧂

Two people walk into Hamelin Square on a cold February day. Hamelin Square is not a square: it is a spoon-shaped cul-de-sac, in Kennington, in a part of London south of the river, where there are acres of buildings and no public green spaces that are not small, flat, and surrounded by wire fences. There are many wide, straight, dusty main roads, some of them lined with elegant Georgian rows of houses. There are many small tunnels and mazes of housing of every age, Georgian, Victorian, Edwardian, wartime prefabs in faded pinks and blues, and abutting these tiny homes are tall towers in monumental rectangular concrete, balcony above balcony, grey against the sky. Hamelin Square consists of early-nineteenth-century houses, with elegant long windows, decreasing in size for three floors, and basement areas reached by steps. These houses are quite pretty, in a slightly pinched way; diminished models of the grander Georgian houses on the roads. They are in an extraordinarily mixed state of repair. Some are gentrified, with bright white paint, window-boxes, brass door-knockers and pretty curtains. Some are crumbling, with dirty net curtains on sagging wires, and blistered paint. One or two are gay and incongruous in West Indian mixes of bright dark blues, plum pinks and acid greens. In the centre of the spoon-bowl is a patch of mud that is not a green, on which are two old car-seats, a rotting mattress, a new and bloodstained bright pink baby-doll nightdress.

The two people progress slowly. Frederica's natural aggressive stride is impeded by the slow progress of her companion. She is wearing a long black cloak-like coat over a knitted grey tunic, over green tights and high black boots. She is carrying a dull gold breast-plate and bossed shield, and looks a little like Britannia on the pennies, or the ghost of Britomart. Her companion is wearing corduroy trousers, a blue hooded jacket with silver fur, and a large gold helmet, whose plastic visor descends, imprisoning his head, every few steps, and has to be pushed up again. He is alternately brandishing and trailing a large gold plastic sword with a jewelled hilt, which is too large for him and impedes his progress further. If Frederica offers to carry the sword, he stands still, stubborn with fury, and strikes his head so that the visor falls yet again.

Frederica is a woman who goes everywhere in a rush, in a trajectory. This creeping progress is alien to her. So is the knot of love that winds her round the small figure of her son, so that she feels his steps in her feet, his small angry bones in her gut. She has not been able to work out how far she should consult him on the proposed house-moving. She remembers, she thinks, that at four her own head was whirling with adult thoughts and understanding, all wholly uncommunicated. She supposes Leo must be the same, but does not know. He is happy at Thomas Poole's. He likes Waltraut Röhde, he likes Simon. He has to move or Frederica cannot escape his father. Frederica does not know how anyone can go on bearing so much guilt, so much emotion to be organised and endured. She says, "We could stick the visor up temporarily with plasticine; then you could see."

"I might want it down, if an *enemy* approached."

"We could stick it up in the street, so you could walk faster."

"A street is where an *enemy* might be, I should think." He brandishes the sword, and stands, yet again, stock-still.

If this woman, in this house, doesn't love him, I shall hate her, thinks Frederica.

She has never really had a woman friend. Girls at school disliked her for being clever and she accepted this, as her due, both as a compliment and as a punishment. Cambridge meant men, to love and talk to.

They arrive at Number 42, at the point of the spoon. It is decorously done up: the door is new black paint, the windows are white, the bricks are repaired, there are no window-boxes. Frederica holds up the visor when they mount the steps. It falls again, when they ring the door bell. Agatha Mond sees them, as she opens the door, against the winter light, black-cloaked, gold-gleaming, helmeted and booted. "Come in," she says. "I've made tea."

Agatha lives on the top two floors of the house. The arrangement they are discussing is that Frederica and Leo should rent the basement and ground floor, for a low rent and some reciprocal baby-sitting. Agatha's part of the house is spotlessly clean. The curtains and sofa are rich, dark and bright with William Morris's Golden Lily; the walls are white and studded with prints and paintings, some abstract, some nineteenth-century, some Doré Dante illustrations, some of John Martin's images of Paradise, Chaos and Pandemonium with swarms of small bright angels like light-emitting bees. In the kitchen Matisse's Jazz prints sit also on a white wall, amongst earthenware jugs and bowls, Sabatier knives, a mixture of old blue-and-white plates on a dresser. In one corner is a playhouse, solidly built of wood and beautifully painted with crimson and white climbing roses and blue columbine. It does not occur to Frederica to think that this order is the result of a frantic morning's cleaning in her honour. She diagnoses the brown jar of graded wooden spoons, large and small, deep and flat; the clean tea-towels on scarlet hooks; the well-used but scrubbed chopping board; the glass jars full of coffee beans, cereals, tea, brown sugar, white sugar. Here is natural order, in which someone takes pleasure. There are two kitchen windows, and two blinds, emerald green and sky blue, which are happy together.

Agatha Mond gives Frederica tea in an old Spode cup and squeezes orange juice for Leo, to whom she also gives a large moon-like biscuit with a smiling face iced on it. For this, he consents to take off his helmet. As he does so, Saskia Mond, dark and wiry in a corduroy pinafore dress and a skinny blue jumper over scarlet tights, appears from her room. She and Leo stare unsmiling at each other and retreat to the sides of their respective mothers. The two women sit facing each other, neither on the sofa, both alone in hard armchairs, as far away from each other as possible.

I can't live here, Frederica thinks. I can't keep this up. I might just as well go now.

"When I bought the house," says Agatha Mond, "which I did very cheaply, because in those days none of these houses were done up, I always intended to share it. So I made two separate entities. There are two kitchens, two bathrooms, although it's so small. And then I've never quite felt I *could*—or that I had to—but I go away so much at the moment, with the committee—and Alexander said he thought you and I might get on . . ."

Her face is composed and severe. She addresses Frederica as though Frederica were a meeting. All her features are perfectly proportioned; her eyes are large and dark but not melting.

"Logically, I thought," says Agatha Mond, "that two women with the same interests—and with children the same age—could make a really sensible arrangement—as long as we thought it out—and built in safeguards for if we didn't like each other—and a reasonable set of rules so we don't start by annoying each other inadvertently. I never have shared—but I'm sure most sharing founders on silly little mis-understandings that could have been foreseen."

Frederica says she is sure that that is quite right.

"It would get harder and harder to discuss difficulties, once the ar-rangement was established," Agatha Mond persists.

Frederica thinks: She is actually very nervous. She is naturally man-aging. She is also afraid, for herself, for her daughter. I should perhaps just go. She looks up from her knees and catches Agatha's look di-rectly, and sees her own thoughts being read.

"Of course I am nervous," says Agatha. "It is our children who are involved as well as ourselves. But I am right, we would need rules. If you wanted to come."

"I must go *somewhere*," says Frederica. "I'm all right where I am, in a way, but it might prejudice my—attempt to get divorced. I think I should say—I don't have much income, but I don't want to earn it by baby-sitting. I will do my share, of course, but I must *work* or I'll die."

"Of course. That is understood. That is why we need to think it out."

There is a silence. Agatha offers to show Frederica the vacant half of the house. This consists of a ground floor—two rooms and a kitchen, and a basement, containing a bedroom and a kitchen. Every-thing is white, the new bath, the walls, the worksurfaces in the tiny kitchen, the table surrounded by pale wooden chairs. It is surgically anonymous; the floors are sanded and varnished wooden boards.

"I didn't want to impose my taste," says Agatha Mond. "One can hate other people's colours; life can be unbearable with other people's idea of cheerfulness or quietness, don't you think?

"I thought the two households would live separately altogether—apart perhaps from one meal a week, or a fortnight, to be decided; the two women would need to make the acquaintance of each other's children, to know them well. I have a visiting surrogate granny, for difficult evenings, who also irons and polishes; her services could be shared, by arrangement. There should be no feeling that either should ever invite the other to any dinner party or anything—and they would have to be extraordinarily careful about *borrowing* things—though I think arrangements could and should perhaps be made about the Hoover, perhaps only the Hoover . . ."

Her voice is full of doubt. Frederica stares around at the bare white walls, the sparkling white tiles. She has no home-making talents: she has never needed any.

Leo needs a home.

Agatha Mond's voice is full of efficient clarity, fear, and doubt. She is a Civil Servant, vulnerable through her child.

"Do you have parties?"

"Oh no. But that's because I don't like large parties. I'm quite sure, by arrangement . . ."

Frederica says, "I don't think it would work. I don't think I should come here. I don't think my way of life—"

She has no idea what her way of life is. Agatha Mond says, "I quite understand, I do understand—"

Both their voices are drowned by screaming from above. Both women, simultaneously, imagine both children torturing and being tortured. They turn and run, fast. They are young and agile.

Saskia, weeping violently and gesturing with pointy fingers, is dancing round the playhouse. Inside there is a blunted crashing and the fabric is swaying as though it is about to burst. Agatha says to Saskia, "Are you shut out?" and Frederica calls to Leo, "Are you shut in?" Saskia stops crying enough to gasp, "He's *stuck* in. I can't get him out." She then resumes her shrill wailing. Agatha kneels down. Leo is hopelessly entangled, his sword at an angle blocking the doorway, his visor jammed down, his head beating like a giant beetle against the window. Agatha persuades him to keep still. She moves the sword, patiently, inch by inch, manoeuvres the angry small body round it and extricates it. She shows Leo how to take off his helmet in the confined space and wriggle free. She extricates the helmet. The two children sit on their mothers and sob with damp red cheeks.

"I made a cake," says Agatha Mond, smiling now the danger of house-sharing has been averted. "We may as well eat it."

It is a very good cake. It is a golden cake, containing translucent vermilion glacé cherries, shaped into a Hansel and Gretel gingerbread house, thatched with chocolate icing, with blue-curtained windows in yellow brick walls, up which grow climbing flowers on spiralling green stems, surrounding an arched green door. It has barley-sugar twisted chimney-pots, quite Elizabethan, and two doves sitting on the roof. Leo and Saskia carry their slices into the playhouse, into which they both fit, leaving the armour outside the door. Frederica crosses the room to look at the pictures on each side of the chimney-breast. They are facsimiles of the contrary "Nurse's Song" and "Nurses Song" from Blake's *Songs of Innocence* and *Songs of Experience*. Innocence is on the left, the poem contained in the arms of a weeping willow, in a pink-and-gold sunset glow. The nurse sits at the base of the tree, perhaps sewing, perhaps writing. Beside her, two rose-coloured slender girls hold hands in an arch, under which, into the warm light, the rest of the circle are dancing.

> *When the voices of children are heard on the green*
> *And laughing is heard on the hill,*
> *My heart is at rest within my breast*
> *And everything else is still.*
>
> *"Then come home, my children, the sun is gone down*
> *"And the dews of night arise*
> *"Come, come, leave off play, and let us away*
> *"Till the morning appears in the skies."*
>
> *"No no let us play, for it is yet day*
> *"And we cannot go to sleep;*
> *"Besides, in the sky, the little birds fly*
> *"And the hills are all cover'd with sheep."*
>
> *"Well, well, go & play till the light fades away*
> *"And then go home to bed."*
> *The little ones leaped & shouted & laugh'd*
> *And all the hills ecchoed.*

On the right, Experience shows three figures in a doorway, a purple woman bending solicitously over a green-clad youth with long blond hair and a hand laid across his waist to emphasise, rather than conceal, his sex, which is faintly outlined in gold on his green breeches. Behind him a female figure of indeterminate age sits in the angle of the doorstep, head bowed. Vines heavy with grapes climb richly upwards, purple, gold and green, reaching out spiralling tendrils towards both woman and youth.

> When the voices of children are heard on the green
> And whisp'rings are in the dale,
> The days of my youth rise fresh in my mind,
> My face turns green and pale.
>
> Then come home, my children, the sun is gone down,
> And the dews of night arise;
> Your spring & your day, are wasted, in play,
> And your winter and night in disguise.

"I wish *I* had these pictures," says Frederica with abstract politeness.

"I wish I had them all. I love their doubleness. One thinks differently about the innocence of children once one has them. And about oneself, one's own childhood."

Frederica looks out of the window, at the mud and rubbish in the centre of Hamelin Square. Some children are chasing and dodging each other between the car-seats, three black, three white children, screaming. It is not possible to tell if they are playing or trying to hurt each other. She says, "At the Art School where I teach, my Head of Department is mad about Blake. He gives lectures on recovering the energies of childish innocence, polymorphous perversity and unrestrained desire."

"That crops up in our committee, too. We have members who talk about learning from the children, letting the children set the agenda, freeing the curriculum. Personally, I find it hard to sympathise with.

"When I was a child I was terrified of other children. They seemed to me like ravening tigers or stupid trolls who wanted to tie you down and poke you. I wanted to be a *real person,* which meant grown-up."

"So did I," says Frederica. "You understand slowly that you understand things that you can't *say* or *use* until you're—'a human being,' I used to say to myself—I felt I was a *person* inside a kind of silly mask and disguise, to whom people spoke in voices suitable for my silly face and silly clothes—*even other children*—"

"And then you wonder—is everyone else in a silly mask, or is it only me—"

"And you don't even know the answer, but you suspect it's only you—"

"And you wait to be a grown-up, or a real person, or a human being—you wait savagely in solitude, guarding your secrets and nursing your—hopes—possibilities—"

"And you find that everyone else, now you're a real person, is saying how much more authentic it is—how much more *free*—to be a polymorphously perverse child—"

"And you wonder if your own child thinks as you thought—"

"Because your child *is* innocent, there is a sense in which you know they *don't* know all the things you are so confident you knew all the time but didn't say—they can so easily be hurt."

"So easily. It's no good saying that childhood is like paradise. It's at least as much like hell. Whatever you do."

"Yet when we get the idea of Paradise"—says Frederica, looking away from Blake to the black Martin engraving of the angel Raphael, made of white light, advancing under black Romantic paradisal trees across a glade towards the softly luminous naked figures of our first Parents—"when we get that idea, it is a memory of a *first state*—we did *once*—when was it?—experience everything more brightly than now—"

They stop, almost out of breath. They smile at each other. Agatha Mond's face is brightened and lifted by her smile; it is less beautiful than it is in repose, more pointed.

"I've never had this conversation," says Frederica.

"Nor have I. More cake?"

A turmoil in the playhouse ends their talk.

Frederica has made a friend.

Three weeks later, Frederica and Leo move into the lower flat in 42 Hamelin Square.

Frederica goes to St. Simeon's to see Daniel. She is restless and lonely, and since Christmas the two have become more friendly than in the past. She stops in the vestry of the half-church, and considers the notices. There is a poster for Gideon Farrar's Children of Joy, "The Christian Embrace. It's Child's Play—the Mums and Dads Are Learning Fast," with a large photograph of a barefooted circle of people of all ages hugging each other and smiling ecstatically. There is a very small card in a corner, with a decorated border in green, red, and blue inks vaguely Gothic, richly elegant, which on inspection contains bleeding red-breasted pelicans and robins, and pointed-toothed bats and monkeys amongst its foliage. It contains a text in beautifully penned Gothic script.

There is a great ladder of religious cruelty with many rungs; but three of them are most important.

At one time one sacrificed human beings to one's god, perhaps precisely those humans one loved best, as in the sacrifice of the first-born.

Then in mankind's moral epoch, one sacrificed to one's god one's strongest instincts, one's "nature." The joy of *this* festival glitters in the cruel glance of the ascetic.

Finally, what was left? Did one not have to sacrifice everything comforting, holy, healing, all hope, all faith in a concealed harmony, in future bliss and justice? Did one not have to sacrifice God himself, and out of cruelty self-cruelty to oneself worship stone, stupidity, gravity, fate, nothingness?

To sacrifice God for nothingness—this paradoxical mystery of the final act of cruelty was reserved for the generation which even now arises: we all know something of this already.

Frederica stands and considers this text, which she cannot place, although it is vaguely familiar. Then she goes down the spiral staircase into the crypt.

Ginnie Greenhill is in her cubicle, listening to the squawk and splutter of the telephone. Her round shoulders, in an apple-green sweater, are tense: from time to time she nods attentively, staring at her egg-box walls.

Daniel is sitting in his own cubicle, reading. His large face is brooding.

From Canon Holly's little sanctum come animated voices. Coming into the crypt, Frederica is surprised to see Rupert Parrott, smoking a briar pipe, woolly-pated and rosy-faced, wearing a greenish tweed jacket and a mustard-coloured waistcoat. He is sitting on the Canon's swivelling chair, turning this way and that, gesticulating. The Canon, also smoking a pipe, and wearing a cassock, is buried in a decrepit leather armchair.

Daniel is pleased to see Frederica. He offers her tea, and goes to fill the kettle. Rupert Parrott swivels energetically and catches sight of her as he comes into view.

"Frederica! I am thinking of publishing a collection of your Reader's Reports. I laugh aloud. I didn't know you came here."

"I come to see Daniel." She sees Parrott coming to the conclusion that she is in Daniel's pastoral care. "He's my brother-in-law."

"You surprise me. I thought you were in training as a Listener."

"I've thought of it. I don't think I'd be any good. I'm not patient, and I'm not self-effacing."

"I'd like to be——" says Parrott, his pink cheeks pinker. "Of course I'm partly here as Adelbert's publisher. But I am interested in the work. The work is important. I'm thinking of publishing a book called *The Helpers,* which I'd like Adelbert to write. About individuals in the caring professions—a psychoanalyst, a psychiatrist, a probation officer, a Listener—and some of the newer leaders of encounter groups and things that are springing up——"

"Tea," says Daniel.

"Please," say Holly and Parrott. It has become a tea party. They chat. Ginnie Greenhill continues her passionate listening to the telephone's babble, in another world.

"Frederica does wonderful work for me, for a pittance," says Rupert Parrott. "I almost never publish anything she reports on, but I *do* appreciate her reporting."

"You did accept Phyllis Pratt's *Daily Bread,*" says Frederica. "I was glad about that, she could write. That would interest Daniel and Canon Holly, it's about a clergyman who loses his faith."

"She came to see me last week," says Parrott.

"What is she like?" says Frederica. "Tell."

"She is *very* large," says Parrott. "In a black broadcloth suit, with a priestlike hat, flat and black with a dull red ribbon. She came into my office and said, 'I have come to withdraw my book.' I said it was already in production, I said the cover was chosen—it has a wonderful cottage loaf on it and a great knife, a shiny knife—a bread-knife—I said we all loved the book. She said in a toneless sort of voice that it was an unpublishable book, not worthy, and she wanted it back. So I said it *was* worthy, and that I should be hurt—one always makes the mistake of supposing *large* people are kindly and concerned—and she repeated that she'd come to withdraw it, it wasn't worthy. She was being the immovable object and for some reason I felt I had to be the irresistible force. So I said she owed me an explanation, she'd wasted a lot of my time and money and emotion, and all that didn't matter, but I thought she was *really good*—I'd at last discovered a *really good* novelist—and as I said it, I saw I really thought it, and I became quite distressed, quite distressed on my own behalf. So she sat there, and repeated her two sentences, about withdrawing the book, and not being worthy. And something made me say, 'If you can honestly *assure* me that this is your own wish—that I should disrupt publication—that you are under no pressure—' And suddenly she was all water, her face dissolved, she said her husband had read the blurb we sent and felt it was all about him."

"Is it?" asks Frederica.

"Probably. How do I know? But I felt somehow furiously determined. So I lectured her on what she owed me—and how good it was—and she got hotter and hotter—steaming hot—and went off to think, she said. I don't know what she'll do. She didn't go into detail. I haven't stopped production. That book *matters to her,* I can sense. I couldn't work out what she was like."

"She can write."

"Oh yes."

"And the other book?" says Frederica. "All that typescript I gave you. *Babbletower.* Have you read it?"

"Oh yes," says Rupert Parrott. "Two or three times." He lowers his voice conspiratorially. "It's a dreadful risk. It could get any publisher into trouble. Even in these marginally more enlightened days. It's not a nice book."

"It sticks in the mind," says Frederica, testing.

"It does. It does stick in the mind."

"Has anyone else seen it?"

"No. I've been thinking about it."

There is a sound above them, and then a sound of feet coming down the stairs.

Black, shiny, cracked patent shoes. Very dirty speedwell-blue socks. Filthy skin between socks and trousers. Tight pin-striped trousers, silver stripe on matt black, calf-clinging, rising to a high waist and old dress-braces. A cloak of iron-grey hair. A velvet jacket, stained midnight blue, partly threadbare, an old white silk evening muffler, a long grey face under the grey hair, an aura, an odour of active staleness and decay.

"I had believed," says the plangent voice, "that you lived here immured and listened to the voices of which the air is so full, the wailing to which I have made my small contributions. I felt a certain inhibition about imposing my corporeal presence on this ghostly converse and so I came secretly and saw that others felt no such compunction, that there is a steady stream of distinctly solid fleshly visitors, of which I thought I might make one. I left a calling card, which was found acceptable, or not immediately torn up or cast into the flames. I wondered if I might be permitted to continue my theological debate with the judicious Daniel in judgement. And I see Frederica, taking tea. This resembles the under-earth hideout of the Lost Boys. Do I interrupt, should I leave, may I stay?"

Canon Holly says, "We welcome all comers. I recognise your voice. We are happy to see you. May I know your name? I am Adelbert Holly, over there is Virginia Greenhill—you have spoken to both of us—and this young man is a visitor, Rupert Parrott."

"I know that name," says Jude. "The arm of coincidence is long."

Frederica's mind has been racing. She does not know whether Rupert Parrott has made up his mind for or against *Babbletower*, but she is fairly sure that the sight and smell of Jude is not likely to influence him favourably. Jude's last remark, however, is decisive. She says, "This is Jude Mason. The author of *Babbletower*, which we were discussing."

"Ah," says Rupert Parrott. He looks at his feet, and twirls in his chair. Jude advances to the centre of the crypt. Rupert Parrott says, "Some of the tortures the little boys undergo in the Dormitories, in your book—"

"Far-fetched, you think? Improbably ingenious?"

"Not at all. Wholly convincing. Traditional, even. I wonder if you were at Swineburn School, perhaps?"

Jude stares; his face closes.

"I even seem to recognise some of the more unpleasant cupboards and places of water-torture. And a few very local slang terms. 'Fessy,' for instance. 'Bullapot.' 'Gullanging.' Were you there in the days of Claude Hautboys?"

Jude stands in his grimy finery and drops his head, so that his face is covered by a curtain of greasy hair. Then he lifts his head, parts the curtain, pushes it back over his shoulders, and says, "No mean French scholar, an excellent guide along the more recondite pathways of French decadence. Heavy-handed, though, and heavy in other ways, very heavy."

This adjective causes a rictus of mirthless laughter in Rupert Parrott's brownie-like face.

"Heavy," he concurs, nodding.

"I matriculated," says Jude, staring intently at Parrott, "and then put an end to it. I scarpered, I quit, I fled, I discharged myself, I disembogued, I ran away betwixt the dark and dawn and was no more seen in that place. Over the hills of Cumberland and far away I wandered, piping wild, feeding on swine-nuts, and so to Paris, a wandering scholar, where I found *protection* and a library."

"A good library," says Parrott.

"The best," says Jude. There is a silence. "May I hope that you found my offering acceptable?"

"A book for our times," says Rupert Parrott. "Strong meat."

"I am a vegetarian," says Jude. "A butcher only in the imagination." It is as though they are speaking in code.

"You realise that this book runs the risk of prosecution? Even after *Lady Chatterley*."

"I had not considered the matter. I wrote what I had to write. *Lady Chatterley* is a vulgar and improbable book."

"And *Babbletower*—"

"Is all around us," says Jude, casting an arrogant stare around the egg-boxes, telephones and battered chairs amongst the fanning pillars of the crypt.

"It is a challenge," says Parrott. "A challenge I must say I feel I have to accept."

He is worked up. He is sweating slightly around his crinkled hairline.

Daniel recognises the tension in his voice. Daniel spent a long night talking Rupert Parrott out of cutting his wrists, some time ago. He remembers, though he tries not to, a Parrott obsessed by self-disgust and moral despair, a Parrott who finally arrived, tear-smeared and shaking, in St. Simeon's in the small hours, to be consoled by Daniel and subsequently invigorated by Canon Holly's calm acceptance of his secret self, his hidden desires, his ambiguities and equivocations. Daniel told him human beings were infinitely diverse, but Holly commanded him to love his own difference, to admit his dark side into the circle of his fuller Self. And so *Our Passions Christ's Passion* found a publisher and Rupert Parrott became a visiting helper of the Listeners. He is wary of Daniel, whom he does not love but does trust. Daniel can see both why Parrott feels he must publish Jude's book, and why this will not be easy for him, if the book does get into trouble. Daniel knows nothing about book-trouble. But he knows, he thinks, a real suicide risk from a counterfeit or mimic.

"We should drink to this venture," says Canon Holly, producing a bottle of Hungarian Bull's Blood, fashionable at that time. Slugs of Bull's Blood are poured into various unbreakable tumblers, and they drink, including Ginny Greenhill, whose caller has abruptly rung off in mid-sentence, interrupted by despair, a visitor, embarrassment, collapse, she cannot say. Frederica proposes the toast:

"To *Babbletower!*"

They drink.

Frederica sits in the basement in Hamelin Square. She tries to write, and cannot. The paper is blank in front of her. It is early evening. The flat still smells faintly of new paint. She is looking at the area wall through the slats of a buttercup-yellow Venetian blind, which casts a ghostly gold and violet-grey shadowed lattice, or grid, on the white expanse of the paper. She has a new writing table in pale pine-wood and a deep blue plastic chair on chrome legs.

She is surrounded by writing and cannot write. Tony Watson has shown some of her reports for Bowers and Eden to the new literary editor of *Spyglass,* a cultural weekly founded by a minor member of Bloomsbury, surviving with a precarious circulation and a disproportionate reputation for wit and influence. Frederica is now part of a rotating team of four novel columnists, and is therefore surrounded with cardboard boxes of hardback novels. She can review four or even five of these at once, giving the most important perhaps two hundred fifty words and the least a thirty-word sentence. She has learned, the hard way, what you can and can't say in two hundred fifty words. You cannot summarise a plot in that space: you can only hint, at an atmosphere, at an analogy (Amis-territory, Murdochian moral intricacy, Sparkian wit and *bizarrerie,* Storey-north, Snow-corridors). However often they may tell you you should not use adjectives, here you have no choice; adjectives must substitute for discrimination and for narrative: *shocking, flat, murky, torpid, energetic, ferocious, intricate, gripping.* Clichés have become clichés because they are concise, useful and evocative (more adjectives) but Frederica has her standards. She eschews both *vivid* and *vibrant,* both *brilliant, hilarious, maxi* and *mini.* From feeling like an ugly sister clamping a bleeding foot into a glass slipper, she has come to enjoy picking her way precisely through the possibilities. She plays fair. Any really waspish sentence must be balanced by one purely descriptive. Every week two or three novelists write in with at least a thousand indignant words pointing out what she has *not* said. The column makes a substantial addition to her income, more through the sale of suitcases of rejected books than for the words themselves. For every book she reviews, she reads and sells perhaps twenty. She knows a great deal about how not to write a novel.

On the other side of her desk is a heap of books for the novel class. She is constructing a lecture on love and marriage in *Howards End* and *Women in Love*. She has written:

"Margaret Schlegel's credo is 'only connect' but she has to admit failure. Rupert Birkin spends most of *Women in Love* vilifying 'connection' and expressing intemperate suspicion of and antagonism to the word 'love.' But he ends in a mystical vision of oneness and connectedness, beyond language.

"Both writers, both novels, assert an antagonism between 'the machine age' and human passion. Both, in this sense, are pastoral, implying that love was fuller, or easier, or more natural in some primitive, Edenic past, before 'society' became complex, or work mechanised.

"Why?"

She thinks she might abandon her empty page for the lecture, but knows she ought not. This thing must be written. "Just write down everything you think relevant, every example of behaviour you object to, find unacceptable," said Arnold Begbie. "And then I'll formalise it. I'll write it up."

She feels nauseous. She has made three or four attempts. She has written:

> He hit me.
> My husband hit me.
> Nigel hit me.

This last heavily crossed out.

> He struck me with the side of his hand, intending to hurt.
> He is trained to hurt.
> He pointed this out.

She has changed the word "struck" to the word "hit." She has a vague idea that this piece of writing should be bare, unemotive, scrupulously neutral, whatever that might mean. "Struck" carries a stronger emotional charge.

> When I locked myself in the lavatory, he turned off the house electricity, to leave me in the dark.

Does this act, which was indeed frightening and humiliating, class as cruelty, or as petty comedy?

> I was frightened. Afraid. Alarmed.

All crossed out.

> When I tried to run away, he threw an axe after me.
> He has had military training. He meant to hit me.

Is Frederica's opinion on this evidence or not evidence? Is it even her opinion? She remembers the smell of the soil in the night, the wriggling horizon, a sound of rushing wings, which was probably only in her head. She does not remember the impact of the blow. She remembers the later seeping and oozing of the wound, the changing colours of the bruising.

> Nigel's horrified face.
> He is not a monster.

The wound hurts her memory less than the refusal, both angry and bland—and how can one man be both at once?—to allow her to *work*. Than the assumption that it was a question of allowing. Though it was. She does not think either Mr. Begbie or the Divorce Court will be interested in these reflections. She writes:

> He steadfastly refused to allow me to discuss my undertaking any work of any kind, though I married on the assumption that I would do so. He claimed to admire my intelligence and independence.

Claimed to? Did he? What do those words *mean*?

> He shut my father's head in a door.
> He attacked my brother-in-law, who is a clergyman.

The document is nauseating because it is the skeleton of a document that could truly plead, that could make its reader weep for pity and laugh grimly at human folly.

The document is nauseating because it is a lie. It recounts true facts, for a valid purpose—to get Frederica out of a marriage that has become a trap—but it recounts these things one-sidedly, in inappropriate (inappropriate? lying? inadequate?) language.

It was really my fault, because he whole-heartedly wanted to marry me, he was *sure,* however foolish this turned out to be, and I did not, I always held back, I always knew I should not have done it.

I married because I was a woman, to get it over with, to stop thinking about whether to marry or not, or what, to know where I was. And then I didn't like where I was, which I should have known if I had had any sense, so it is *all my fault*. I can't write that, for every reason.

We might have worked something out, all the same, if . . .

He was never at home.

What sort of whingeing complaint is that?

I was locked up with his womenfolk, like Mariana in the Moated Grange, but worse.

I can't write this *stuff*. Every ink-blob destroys a bit more of the truthful balanced memory I am trying to hang on to, of a sort of unspoken justice, of a kind of saving not-looking-but-knowing about the whole knotty mess of the experience.

She writes: "Shit." "Fuck." She crosses them out.

I could write it if it was a parody of this sort of document, a work of art or fiction *pretending to be* one of these.

I married him because I was beglamoured by Margaret Schlegel, because I was a reader, dear Reader.

I married him because my sister was dead and he comforted me.

This piece of paper is not about why I married him. It is about what he did, those actions of his, that offer me a way out of the decision I took.

I write things so that someone can sit in judgement on him, and I sit in judgement on myself, the one entails the other; they are both, I was going to say intolerable, but what I mean is, very nasty.

She turns to her lecture. She will work a little on that, and then take another run at the dreadful catalogue.

Howards End, Ch. 22

Margaret greeted her lord with peculiar tenderness on the morrow. Mature as he was, she might yet be able to help him to the building of the rainbow bridge that should connect the prose in us with the passion. Without it we are meaningless fragments, half monks, half beasts, unconnected arches that have never

joined into a man. With it love is born, and alights on the highest cur[v]
ing against the grey, sober against the fire. Happy the man who sees fr[o]
aspect the glory of these outspread wings. The roads of his soul lie cle[a]
and his friends shall find easy going.

It was hard going in the roads of Mr. Wilcox's soul. From boyhood he had
neglected them. "I am not a fellow who bothers about my own inside." Outwardly he was cheerful, reliable and brave; but within, all had reverted to chaos,
ruled, as far as it was ruled at all, by an incomplete asceticism. Whether as boy,
husband or widower, he had always the sneaking belief that bodily passion is
bad, a belief that is desirable only when held passionately. Religion had con-
firmed him. The words that were read aloud on Sunday to him and to other respectable men were the words that had once kindled the souls of St. Catherine
and St. Francis into a white-hot hatred of the carnal. He could not be as the
saints and love the Infinite with a seraphic ardour, but he could be a little
ashamed of loving a wife. "Amabat; amare timebat." And it was here that Margaret hoped to help him.

It did not seem so difficult. She need trouble him with no gift of her own.
She would only point out the salvation that was latent in his own soul, and in
the soul of every man. Only connect! That was the whole of her sermon. Only
connect the prose and the passion and both will be exalted, and human love will
be seen to be at its height. Live in fragments no longer. Only connect, and the
beast and the monk, robbed of the isolation that is life to either, will die. . . .

But she failed. For there was one quality in Henry for which she was never
prepared, however much she reminded herself of it: his obtuseness. He simply
did not notice things, and there was no more to be said.

Women in Love, Ch. 13

"What I want is a strange conjunction with you—" he said quietly; "—not
meeting and mingling;—you are quite right:—but an equilibrium, a pure balance of two single beings:—as the stars balance each other."

She looked at him. He was very earnest, and earnestness was always rather
ridiculous, commonplace, to her. It made her feel unfree and uncomfortable.
But why drag in the stars.

Ch. 27

This marriage with her was his resurrection and his life.

All this she could not know. She wanted to be made much of, to be adored.
There were infinite distances of silence between them. How could he tell her of

the immanence of her beauty, that was not form, or weight, or colour, but something like a strange golden light! How could he know himself what her beauty lay in, for him. He said "Your nose is beautiful, your chin is adorable." But it sounded like lies, and she was disappointed, hurt. Even when he said, whispering with truth, "I love you, I love you," it was not the real truth. It was something beyond love, such a gladness of having surpassed oneself, of having transcended the old existence. How could he say "I" when he was something new and unknown, not himself at all? This I, this old formula of the age, was a dead letter.

In the new, superfine bliss, a peace superseding knowledge, there was no I and you, there was only the third, unrealised wonder, the wonder of existing not as oneself, but in a consummation of my being and her being in a new one, a new paradisal unit regained from the duality. Nor can I say "I love you" when I have ceased to be, and you have ceased to be: we are both caught up and transcended into a new oneness where everything is silent, because there is nothing to answer, all is perfect and at one. Speech travels between the separate parts. But in the perfect One there is perfect silence of bliss.

They were married by law on the next day, and she did as he bade her, she wrote to her mother and father.

Frederica thinks hard about these passages. There are complicated connections between literature and life. She may have chosen to lecture on love and marriage in Forster and Lawrence because she is snarled in the death of marriage and the end of love: but the marriage was partly a product of the power of these books. Part of Nigel's attraction was Forster's incantation "Only connect." He had Mr. Wilcox's attraction of otherness, but was not, is not, obtuse.

Both characters, both novelists, so passionately desire *connection*. They want to experience an undifferentiated All, a Oneness, body and mind, self and world, male and female. Frederica has tried to want this. Exhortations to want it have permeated her reading. When she was very little she tried to believe in God. She looked at the stars and tried to *think* Someone intelligent, loving, caring, out there, and could not. Forcing herself hurt her head behind her eyes: she remembers the sensation precisely, and it is repeated as she remembers it, and as she tries to desire connection and Oneness. Thinking of her own infantile efforts to believe causes her to think again about something she has noticed in both pieces of writing. They are sustained by what were surely archaisms in their own time, phrases harking back, yearning, for earlier modes of expression.

"Her lord" . . . "the morrow" . . . "Happy the man who sees the glory of those outspread wings." . . . "Only connect the prose and the passion and both will be exalted."

"This marriage was his resurrection and his life." . . . "In the perfect One there is perfect silence of bliss."

And "she did as he bade her," Lawrence's wife echoing the ironic "her lord" of Forster's Margaret, archaic both.

Forster was uneasily mocking, whereas Lawrence was in deadly earnest, thinks Frederica, but both are *imbued* with religious language. Ursula's beauty is "immanent" like a strange golden light. Forster makes love incarnate "the salvation that was latent in his own soul," connecting beast and monk. Sexual love for Lawrence confuses and abolishes grammatical categories, no I and you, no subject and object, but "my" and "her" in a paradisal One "where everything is silent," where language is unnecessary and defeated, thinks Frederica.

She writes:

It is not so simple as supposing that sexual love replaced for the Moderns the mystical experience of the Christian religion. It is more that the narrative of the Novel, in its high days, was built on, out of, and in opposition to the narrative of the one Book, the source of all Books, the Bible. Both Forster and Lawrence use for the joining of lovers the old biblical symbol of God's covenant between Heaven and Earth, the rainbow, even though Forster's rainbow is also a simulacrum of the rainbow bridge built by Wagner's all-too-human deities between earth and Walhalla.

Why bring in the stars? Ursula asks. D. H. Lawrence said the novel is the one bright book of Life. In the one bright book you have to have it all, the Word made flesh, the rainbow, the stars, the One.

Why, thinks Frederica, does it seem so impossible, so far away, so *finished,* this Oneness, Love, the Novel?

Those archaisms were a way of containing and continuing—*just*— the past of the monks, the mystics, the preachers. Now, it can't be done.

Or perhaps, it's only me who can't do it.

Frederica looks at her markings on her dreadful catalogue of Nigel's sins, or offences, her partial, her lying, summing up of her own story, and asks herself what she thinks about love.

Does the word mean anything?
Did I love Nigel?
He taught me desire.
That destroyed something in me: a separateness that was a strength.
But I did want to *know.*
To know, yes, but not to be *fused* with someone else. The idea is, and was, a little sickening. I am a separate being.

Before Nigel, the men I loved were Alexander and Raphael. They were like unfinished rainbows, they were like Birkin's stars in the sky, they were beautiful and untouchable, and I *liked them that way,* I could put energy into trying to change them, to make them desiring and desirable, but they weren't *for that.* They were what I loved, as paintings are shining. They were the same as each other.

Stephanie and Daniel were part of each other, I think. She knew. He knew. I have had my moments, lately, of desiring Daniel, of imagining his touch, because he knows what it is about.
I don't. I betrayed Nigel because I can't do it.

I recognise John Ottokar. He is *charged,* the way Nigel was, and unknown, in an interesting way.
We could hurt each other. I know that. I am older now.

She thinks: If I don't want Oneness, what is it I want?

She remembers a day, long ago, on the Goathland moors, when a word hit her as a description of a possible way of survival. Laminations. She had been young, and greedy, and acting Princess Elizabeth, the Virgin in Alexander's play, who had had the wit to stay separate, to declare, "I will not bleed," to hang on to her autonomy. And she, Frederica, had had a vision of being able to be all the things she was: language, sex, friendship, thought, just as long as these were kept scrupulously separate, *laminated,* like geological strata, not seeping and flowing into each other like organic cells boiling to join and divide and join in a seething Oneness. Things were best cool, and clear, and fragmented, if fragmented was what they were.

"Only connect," the "new paradisal unit" of "Oneness," these were myths of desire, the desire and pursuit of the Whole.

And if one accepts fragments, layers, tesserae of mosaic, particles.

There is an art form in that, too. Things juxtaposed but divided, not yearning for fusion.

What is really fused is the sperm and the ovum in the zygote, Frederica thought with a certain intellectual rigour. Not man and woman, but cells. Language fails man and woman trying to transcend it and themselves. But the genes go coiling, spiralling, joining, building sentences and phrases of life with their primeval alphabet. Two halves become One.

She remembers her son, who has been suspiciously silent during all this thinking and writing and failing to write. And all the thinking is undone. For it is clear what love is. This flesh which is and is not her own, which was and is not part of her, which completes the circle of the arms.

"Leo. *Where the hell are you?* Leo! Leo! *Where are you?*"

Frederica never invades Agatha Mond's space, but Leo does. Less often, Saskia Mond comes down to play with Leo, to eat supper when her mother is out. So now Frederica goes upstairs, in search of her son. There is no sound of movement, no shrill voices. She turns a corner, and hears Agatha's voice, quiet and dramatic.

" 'It's a house on fire.'

" 'There aren't any houses in this wilderness.'

" 'It's a camp-fire. Soldiers perhaps. Looking for us, perhaps.'

" 'We should hide.'

" 'No, it's a bush, on fire. It's a great thorn bush, burning all by itself on the moor.'

" 'Let's look,' said Mark, who was always impetuous. 'Who could have set a bush on fire?'

" 'Lightning, maybe,' said Dol Throstle.

" 'We should go and see,' said Artegall.

"So the four of them walked over to the burning bush, which could be heard crackling and smelled singeing from a great distance. When they came near it the air was visibly shivering in the heat, and full of flying black specks of burned matter. There was no sign of any human presence, no footprints, no broken stems.

" 'Just a bush, burning,' said Claus.

" 'All the nests,' said Dol Throstle. 'All the young birds will be burned.'

" 'They may well be flown,' said Artegall. 'It is late in the year for them to be still in the nest.'

"He remembered his huge leather books, with page after page of drawings of eggs, speckled and mottled, of nestlings and fledglings, of plumage and claws.

" 'There's something moving in there,' said Dol Throstle.

"The four travellers peered into the smoke. Deep in the heart of the burning bush something stirred and writhed in the heat.

" 'It's a bird burned naked,' said Claus. 'A very big bird.'

" 'It's not a bird,' said Dol Throstle. 'I can see its beaky mouth. It's got teeth.'

" 'It's a snake, a nasty snake,' said Mark.

" 'We must rescue it,' said Artegall.

" 'It's just a nasty snake,' said Mark. 'And badly burned I should think. Better leave it. Rescued snakes always bite you. I read stories too.'

"The two boys, prince and page, glared at each other with brief anger. Then Artegall drew his sword and moved towards the bush. The heat flared in his face: he could smell his own hair burning. He cut away a few branches, in order to get nearer. He was afraid of trying to hook the snake: a sword was not the best implement for that purpose, and if he pushed wrongly the snake might fall from the branch it was on, into the roaring bonfire beneath it. Wrapping his cloak about his face, Artegall pushed nearer to the bush, and pushed his sword under the whole body of the snake, which, to his surprise, seemed to have strength and intelligence enough to coil and cling to the blade.

" 'You've skewered it,' said Mark.

" 'Hold on!' said Artegall to the snake.

"He withdrew the sword and its burden, steel and sinuous flesh, carefully through the flames and smoke. His own hand was scorched, and his sleeve black.

" 'It's *roasted*,' said Mark.

"The snake was very large, and mostly blackish in colour, with a weaving pattern of gold spirals and coins visible under the smoke. Its belly was pale golden, and it had horned eyebrows above a diamond-shaped head. It lay limp for a little time, like a piece of rope, and then a ripple of life ran along its body and it coiled itself, painfully it appeared, raised its head, and opened two great eyes like carbuncles, fiery and burning with inner light."

"What's a carbuncle?" says Leo.

"A big red jewel," says Agatha. "A big fiery-red jewel. Sometimes also a painful bump on your skin, which can also be red and shiny."

"I don't like snakes," says Saskia.

"You don't know any," says Agatha. "But most people don't." She is sitting on the sofa, with Leo on one side and Saskia on the other. Frederica sits down on the floor.

"Go on," she says.

"And then the snake spoke. It spoke with a kind of hissing, sibilant voice, a voice like leaves rustling, and silk being pulled swiftly through a ring or a buckle, a voice dry and yet sharp and swift. It said, 'I am the Horned Viper, the King of the snakes in this country, and I was thrown into that bush by an angry soldier who set it on fire. I have it in my power to make you able to hear the speech of the creatures that have speech: the birds, and the running and creeping things with legs, and the flying things, and the things that tunnel and burrow. But only you can hear, because only you held out your hand through the flames.'

" 'I didn't believe the creatures talked,' said Artegall. 'I have read it, of course—'

" 'It wasn't exactly talk, in the beginning. Once, we were all one thing, and could hear each other's nature well enough if we *listened*, with no need for speech. And then men made words, and used words for mastery, and we also spoke out what once we had heard and known in our heads, and understood. There have always been a few Men who can hear, or remember in their blood, the old speech—'

" 'And will everything speak to me?' said Artegall.

" 'Why are you talking to it?' said Mark. 'It can't answer.'

" 'No, of course not,' said the snake. 'Most things won't want to go any-where near you, and most will pretend to be dumb, even if you challenge them. We do not love you. But you may *overhear* things that are useful, even in the gossip of woodlice or the chatter of starlings.'

" 'I should go mad,' whispered Artegall to the King Snake, 'if I could hear everything's voice all the time.'

" 'Well you won't hear it, unless you *listen*,' said the snake. 'And then only if you are patient and persistent. Now I shall go.' And suddenly, like the crack of a whip, he was away, across the heather, and pouring himself into a crack between two great granite boulders.

" 'Did it speak to you?' said Dol Throstle.

" 'I thought so,' said Artegall.

" 'I've heard of that,' said Dol Throstle. 'I couldn't hear it.'

" 'I don't believe it said *anything*,' said Mark."

"Mark is very silly," says Leo.

"No, he's not," says Agatha. "You'll see. He's just a bit cross, at the moment, because he was only a page and a whipping-boy before they escaped, and after the escape he thought that Artegall would be helpless and useless because he'd never come out of his tower. . . . But he'll change. People change."

"Good," says Saskia. "I don't like people who are always cross."

"What are you telling them?" says Frederica to Agatha.

"It's my story," says Saskia.

"I can hear it too," says Leo. "It's all right, Agatha says I can hear."

"You're very welcome," says Agatha.

During the next weeks, Frederica joins the others at the story-telling sessions. She gets a *frisson* of ancient pleasure from watching Leo and Saskia lost in another world; from time to time she is lost herself, for the story is intricate, and Agatha tells it with conviction, inhabits it herself. It is the tale of a prince, Artegall, who wakes one morning in the sunlit tower overlooking a harbour, and finds that everyone has gone. He has spent his whole life in this tower, because his country is at war with neighbouring powers; the town is empty because an enemy fleet has landed. Artegall is rescued by a cook's maid, Dol Throstle, a palace guard, Claus, and his page and whipping-boy, Mark, with whom he has practised soldierly arts, fencing, wrestling, archery. The four escape in a wagon, in disguise, and undertake a journey north, in search of Artegall's dangerous uncle, Ragna, who is neither friend nor enemy. They are pursued by various forces. Artegall is believed by everyone to be useless and simply a parcel, but turns out, despite his incarceration, to be a skilled tracker of game and finder of paths, simply because a princely education has included endless large leather books on venery, woodcraft, geography, navigation and so on. Mark, the page, assumes that he will now assert the superiority denied him by Artegall's position, but Artegall proves "I am *someone,* not just a prince." As they go north, Agatha tells Frederica, the landscape becomes alive: creatures are met that are magical, or from other worlds, and speak other languages.

She says, "I wrote it for bookish children. Like myself, like you. For children despised because they read. To say, you can *learn to live* from books. Not didactically. But the obvious thing would have been to make Mark, the ordinary boy, triumphant. Whereas I think princes and princesses are what we all are in our minds—to be a prince *is* to be ordinary in a fairytale—"

"Isn't it too old for Leo and Saskia?"

"Would it have been too old for you?"

"No. I'd have loved it. I'd have devoured it."

"Well, then. They listen. They ask about the words. I don't know what some of the teachers on our committee would say."

Frederica tells Agatha about her difficulties with the dreadful catalogue. She has been writing a quite different kind of fantasy tale, she tells Agatha, grimacing. Agatha looks darkly composed, and says it must be most disagreeable. She listens, she is sympathetic, but she offers no confidences in return. Frederica wonders from time to time who is Saskia's father. Agatha has visitors: married couples, single friends from Oxford days, male and female, members of the committee, Civil Servants. She cooks elegant little dinners, to which Frederica is sometimes invited. These are the great days of the marathon home-cooked meal, the five-course delicious gourmandising, *pâtés* and prawns in cream, delicate soups and imaginative *hors d'oeuvres*, followed by *estouffades* and *boeuf en croûte*, by *gigot* and ducklings in cider, by stuffed carp and *paupiettes* of sole, followed by delicious salads of endive and oranges, watercress and cucumber, followed by home-made tarts and soufflés, followed by a rich cheese board and possibly devils on horseback. Agatha serves, always, an avocado salad, a roast chicken with garlic, a tart from a French pâtisserie. Three courses, one cooked. The conversation is civilised and quiet. Agatha appears to have no attachments. Frederica notices at one of these dinners that Alexander is interested in Agatha. She notices the warmth with which he looks forward to a Bristol school visit on which he will go with Agatha, whilst Frederica takes care of Saskia and Leo. She thinks: They could do well together. She wonders what she means by this, and decides that she supposes they both have no need of violence. She thinks of Alexander sharing a house with Agatha, quiet and civilised, never quarrelling, never, she supposes, trembling with passion of any kind. She thinks, she does not know Agatha well enough to make any such supposition about her, however well she knows Alexander, by now. Agatha does not want to be known, and some people, Frederica can see, find this quality rebarbative, call her, in their own minds, cold. She is composed, Frederica thinks. She does everything carefully, just so.

She *likes* to live in that story.

But she's not retreating into her childhood, she's grown up. She seems to me much more grown up than I imagine I seem to her.

Frederica feels safe, telling things to Agatha. She trusts her completely, not to gossip, and also not to distort or *seethe* what she's told, in her mind. Because Agatha never reciprocates with confidences, Frederica only tells her things in a slightly ironic, impersonal tone, even if they are very personal and hurtful things, such as how to describe having an axe thrown at her, even, what to say about discovering you have a sexually transmitted disease. Agatha listens, and makes one or two precise remarks about the etymology of "venereal." You can confuse Venus the hot and hurtful with the vernal airs of spring, she says. They seem to go together because of Botticelli's Venus landing in Paphos covered with flowers. But really it isn't that. You must just find some exact words.

"I could leave it out," says Frederica.

"You could," says Agatha. "But it might be very important, as proof of something. What matters is what's evidence. That is."

"It's just the life of some bacteria, really. I feel it's a sort of violation, but really it isn't, really I *don't care* what he did when I wasn't there."

"You might, if you cared more altogether."

"I don't think I care about anything," says Frederica. "Except Leo."

"I expect you will," says Agatha.

Frederica looks at Agatha's neatly drawn face, its clear, elegant proportions. She wants to ask What do you care about? And dare not.

XI

❧❧❧❧❧

Arnold Begbie has converted Frederica's pitiful narrative into a Petition for Divorce.

In the High Court of Justice
Probate, Divorce and Admiralty Division
(Divorce)
To the High Court of Justice
Dated the 1st of April 1965

The petition of Frederica Reiver showeth:—

(1) That on October 19th 1959 the petitioner, Frederica Reiver, then Frederica Potter, was lawfully married to Nigel Reiver (hereinafter called "the respondent") at the Parish Church, Spessendborough, in the County of Herefordshire.

(2) That after the said marriage the petitioner and the respondent lived and cohabited at divers addresses and finally at Bran House, Longbarrow, in the County of Herefordshire.

(3) That there is one child of the petitioner and the respondent now living, namely Leo Alexander, born on the 14th of July 1960.

(4) That the petitioner proposes the following arrangements for support, care and upbringing of the said Leo Alexander. He will live with the petitioner at 42 Hamelin Square, London SE11, a house shared with Miss Agatha Mond and her daughter, Saskia Felicity Mond. He will start school in September at the William Blake Primary School, Lebanon Grove, London SE11, in company with the said Saskia Felicity Mond; the petitioner intends to apply for maintenance as hereinafter set out.

(5) That since the celebration of the said marriage the respondent has treated the petitioner with cruelty.

(6) That the respondent, who is a man of violent temper, has frequently nagged, sworn at, shouted at and struck the petitioner.

(7) That on September 28th 1964 the respondent attacked the petitioner with several blows to the head, ribs and back; that when she sought refuge in the bathroom, he turned off the mains-electricity to the house, in order to frighten her, and kept her imprisoned therein for several hours.

(8) That on Sunday 4th October 1964 the respondent again attacked the petitioner in her bedroom, so that she ran out of the house in fear and hid in the stables. That when she came out of hiding, the respondent was waiting with an axe, with which he threatened her; that when she ran out into the fields he pursued her, abusing her verbally, and threw the axe, wounding her in the hip.

(9) That before the specific acts of cruelty set out above the respondent treated the petitioner with neglect, spending most of his time away from home, in the company of business friends, beyond the reasonable requirements of the pursuit of his business. That he insisted that the petitioner and child remain at all times in Bran House. That he treated visiting friends of the petitioner with rudeness, and unreasonably refused ever to entertain them or to allow his wife to see them.

(10) That there is reason to believe that the respondent has committed adultery, since the petitioner was diagnosed in November 1964 as having contracted a venereal disease. The petitioner has sworn an affidavit that the disease could have been communicated by no one but the respondent.

(11) That the petitioner discovered a large collection of lewd and filthy publications in the respondent's wardrobe.

(12) That the petitioner has not in any way been accessory to or connived at or condoned the adultery hereinbefore alleged and that she has not condoned the cruelty hereinbefore alleged.

(13) That this petition is not presented or prosecuted in collusion with the respondent.

Frederica considers this document: another narrative of her marriage. She says, "He won't like this."

Begbie smiles. "He cannot be expected to like it."

Frederica tries to cast an analytic look over it.

"You haven't written that he stopped me from *working*."

"I didn't think it was wise."

"In fact that was the most cruel thing." Frederica's tone is small and dry. "It stopped me from being *myself*."

"Marriage is expected to have that effect," says Begbie.

"And you have written that I am asking for maintenance. I don't want it. I can work. I want to keep myself."

"You are asking for custody of your son. And for care and control of him. The Court is not necessarily going to look favourably on you as a parent if you put too much stress on your desire to work, if you display too much personal ambition."

"If I were a man—"

"You have a good chance of custody because you are a woman. Women are presumed to wish to stay at home and care for children. Your sex is your principal advantage, if I may put it so. Your husband, as you have described him, has all the other advantages, in the Court's eyes—a beautiful home, several other devoted women who know the boy intimately, the capacity to pay fees at a good boarding school. You will not appear in a good light if you put your own pride before your son's comfort. And if your husband has treated you as cruelly as you claim he has, you must surely wish him to pay you the support to which you are entitled."

"It isn't like that. *I don't* want his money. I don't want a quarrel and a battle. I want Leo, and to be myself, and to work."

"In the adversarial system, both of the British law, and of the marriage relation, I fear a battle is what you must be resigned to. May I ask if your husband has ever been violent towards his son?"

"No. Not really. It counts as violence to Leo to hurt me, I think. It hurts Leo. But no."

"Only towards yourself?"

"Everyone else worships him. Yes, only towards me."

"A pity. A pity." He sits back in his chair, contemplating the disadvantages of Nigel Reiver's lack of cruelty towards his son.

He explains to Frederica that the petition will be served by post; that it will be filed in the Divorce Registry, and that the respondent must enter an appearance in the Divorce Registry if he intends either to contest the divorce, or to cross-petition. If he does not intend to defend the divorce, he must return an acknowledgement to the petitioner's solicitor. He asks Frederica what she thinks her husband will do.

Frederica tries to think. She imagines Nigel's dark face, looking down on the foolscap pages. The blows, the axe, the lewd and filthy pictures. She imagines rage. Nigel's face becomes that of a blue-black demon. She crosses her own arms defensively across her breasts.

"He won't let it pass. He'll fight, and he'll want Leo."

"Then we will fight. We will fight resourcefully. We shall need witnesses to the acts of cruelty—a Court does not always accept the unsupported evidence of an aggrieved spouse. Doctors, family, friends who saw the injuries? It would be a great advantage to be able to prove adultery, which we should be able to do if your account of your—infection—is accurate (and again supported by medical evidence). Are you sure you have no idea where your husband went on his journeys, whom he saw, what he did?"

"I didn't ask. I didn't mind, much. What I wanted was a life of my own. He went around with Pijnakker and Shah, doing business with his shipping, I think. They belonged to a lot of clubs in London, where I certainly wouldn't want to go. There was one called the Honeypot, I remember. And one called Tips and Tassels. I saw a brochure for that once. Oriental waitresses in belly-dancing silk trousers and bras. With tassels. I think Shah had a financial interest in that, I think I heard them saying."

"I know those places," says Begbie, with a note of satisfaction. Frederica watches him sharply. "I know who goes to those places," says Begbie, looking at Frederica. Frederica says nothing. "High-class call girls and tarts," says Begbie. Frederica thinks that she knows this, and has not thought about it, because it was nothing to do with her. She wonders what she meant by "nothing to do with her." She means that she has no proprietary interest in Nigel's body, she thinks to herself in legal words in the lawyer's office. She wants *her own life*. She would not, in theory, mind if he had his, if hers were not house and confinement. Is this so? She remembers her shamed disgust over the filthy pictures. She did not find them amusing. It is very possible that she would not find the Honeypot, or Tips and Tassels, amusing if she were there. Arnold Begbie appears to be hearing her thoughts.

"Evidence of filthy literature in the respondent's possession is admissible as evidence for adultery to be inferred," he says. "If a woman visits a brothel, that is taken as conclusive proof of her adultery. In the case of a man, such a visit provides strong evidence of adultery against him, but is not conclusive."

"Interesting," says Frederica, drily.

She has the impression that Begbie is taking some sort of pleasure in her general discomfiture, which for him is somehow to do with the imagination of the actions of human bodies, and for her is to do with the discrepancy between what caused her pain and what must be adduced as evidence in order legally to end it. If I had cared more about the Honeypot and so on, she thinks, I might not now be here, because I might have cared more *altogether,* and then things would have come out differently.

"If the divorce is defended," says Begbie, "we need to consider the bars to dissolution of marriage. You must consider: denial of the charge, connivance, condonation and collusion. Your attitude to your husband's extra-marital activities could well be taken as condonation, if you are not careful. Then there are the discretionary bars. The ones you must consider here are the petitioner's own adultery or cruelty. Any adultery of your own—I am required by law to put to you— should be recorded in a sealed discretion statement, which will go before the Court."

"I haven't," says Frederica. "I haven't—committed—"

"Both the other side and the Court are likely to wonder whether your relationship with Mr. Thomas Poole was entirely . . ."

"Well, it was. It was for convenience. He had children, and a flat, and a job. We shared baby-sitting. He was a friend and colleague of—*of my father's,*" says Frederica, avoiding Alexander, genuinely indignant.

"Good, good. And now you live with another woman. Good. Are you sure there is no one else? If the other side decide to contest the divorce they will seek to know . . ."

"No."

"And your friends, to whom your husband objected. Were they men, or women friends?"

"Men."

"But he had no cause to be jealous or suspicious?"

"None. They were *my friends.*"

"And always were?"

"Not always, not all. I—slept with some men, at Cambridge."

"Of course. Pre-nuptial incontinence does not come into the domain of public morals. But it may lead to a presumption that you had no objections to sleeping with more than one man: it might lead to questioning about your subsequent conduct."

"I haven't slept with anyone else," says Frederica. It is curious that although this is true, she feels that she is lying and will be found out. This is possibly because Begbie, who is *her* solicitor, is disinclined to believe her. Again, he reads her thoughts.

"Lawyers are temperamentally inclined to question people's statements," he says. "Of course I accept that you have been faithful to your husband."

"It isn't a question of 'being faithful,' " says Frederica. "I'm not sure I know what 'faithful' means. But I haven't slept with anyone else."

"Very good."

Frederica still has the feeling that her solicitor dislikes her. There is something she is not doing or saying that she should be doing or saying. Weeping, perhaps? Lately, any emotion has driven her to dryness. When she was younger, she could scream and weep. But now, she needs to hold herself together. She needs to be competent. And yet she feels that Arnold Begbie does not entirely approve of her dryness and competence.

Out in the square, she sees the same women and children playing on the grass inside the iron railings with their locked gates. They have shocking-pink knitted hats, warm coats, and near-naked legs and thighs. They pursue a shiny pink-and-blue plastic ball into the bushes. The children laugh and hurtle: the women, in their childish garments, admonish them to "be careful." Frederica sees herself as a caged or netted beast. She sees something limp and snarling in a barred cage on wheels, in a hunter's net suspended from a bough. The net is not made by Nigel, who ran after her, panting, in hot blood; and hurled an axe at her, letting her own blood out of her haunch. The net is made by words which do not describe what she feels is happening: *adultery, connivance, pre-nuptial incontinence, petitioner, respondent.* She tries to think out these words. *Adultery* has connotations of impurity (adulterated butter, adulterated white flour) or perhaps of theft? *Incontinence* somehow equates sexual pleasure with lack of muscular control of bowels or bladder: The proper use of the sphincter is to contain, thinks Frederica. These legal words carry with them the whole history of a society in which a woman was a man's property, and also a part of his flesh, not to be contaminated. And behind *continence* and *incontinence* is the alien, ancient, and powerful history of Christian morals. In Cambridge sex was freedom, was individuality, was a gleeful assertion of self-determination, of energy, of choice, however accompanied by an undercurrent of biological terror. We were all cheerfully in revolt, in those days, thinks Frederica, against convention, against bourgeois prudery and caution, against *our parents* essentially, whom for that purpose, the purpose of necessary revolt, we identified with prudery, coldness, respectability. This language is something quite different from prudery and respectability. It is the harsh language of "the domain of public morals." It judges me as a member of society, even whilst offering me a way out of the mess I have got myself into by *joining* society, by getting casually married, because it solved the problem of whether to get married.

This is the day of the extra-mural class at Our Lady of the Sorrows. Frederica goes back to Hamelin Square, where Leo is having tea with Saskia and the surrogate grandmother, Mrs. Alma Birdseye. Agatha too comes in during this meal. The evening darkens; a gang of children scrabble briefly at the basement window and run away; Agatha and Frederica draw the curtains and let down the blinds, making a softly lit warm space inside. Agatha reads from her story. The travellers have been led into a deep thicket by a muddy imp called Yallery Brown, and it is beginning to snow, great slushy flakes which put out their fire, leaving them in the dark, the *real dark,* with a thick blanket of wet cloud between them and the moon and the stars. Artegall hears the speech of shrews and rats in the undergrowth, and of owls staring and listening from thorny branches. He hears the voice of slow worms, beneath the wet leaves, beneath the humus, beneath the earth. The shrews and rats listen for the worms, the owls listen for the shrews and rats, the children in the warm room listen and shiver and imagine the fear of the dark. The creatures speak of hunger, and imagine food. The owls do not like the smell of the humans. Suddenly Dol Throstle sees the glimmer of a cold light, far away in a tangle of brambles and bent thorn-branches . . .

"Go *on,*" says Leo.

"I can't," says Agatha. "There isn't any more, I haven't written any more."

"But you know it," says Leo.

"Not exactly," says Agatha. "Anything could happen."

"Why is the dark?" says Saskia.

"Because we are on the earth, which rolls round and round and at the same time makes great circles round the sun, so that when it is dark we are on the side facing away from the hot sun, which is a great fiery ball—"

"Why?" says Saskia.

"I don't know," says Agatha.

"I'm not afraid of the dark," says Leo, resting his red head on Frederica's knee.

Frederica is afraid. She is afraid of the thicket she is in, of what might happen, of losing Leo, of hurting Leo. These things are in the domain of public morals, now. Someone, somewhere, will judge her. She holds on to Leo.

She arrives at Our Lady of the Sorrows clutching her lecture on Love and Marriage in Forster and Lawrence. She is consoled by the journey on the Underground. There are so many people, so many faces, so many possible lives going on. People who are real, despite the prevalent fashion for looking like round-eyed pale-faced dolls with shining mouths. People with bald crowns and beehive hair, with flowing locks and bristling fans of curls, with Beatle caps and plastic rainhats, semi-circles of transparent plastic, spotted and dotted with crimson and emerald, purple and orange discs, tied with ribbons over grey curls under folding chins. She is safe and anonymous here, and everyone is *interesting*. This is the glory of London, her present London, which is several small worlds, Daniel's church, Hugh Pink's flat, Rupert Parrott's dusty office, the house in Hamelin Square, the staff room, the great studios of the Samuel Palmer School, Arnold Begbie's office and the extra-mural class.

There is a new whiff, amongst the old cabbage and chalk, on the turning of the stair, a rich, rotten whiff which she recognises without naming it. When she arrives in her classroom, she sees what it was: Jude Mason is sitting isolated in the front row, wearing his filthy blue velvet skirted coat and what appears to be a policeman's cape. His iron-grey locks spread over the shoulders of this garment, oiled and gleaming. The other members of the group are talking to each other, and not looking at him.

"I am a vagrant," he tells Frederica. "Come in literally out of the cold. It is cold in my living place, as I have no cash for the meter. It is cold in the streets. Would it inconvenience you if I took refuge here? The British Library also is closed."

"You are not to interrupt everyone," says Frederica.

"Or disrupt, or corrupt. I will say nothing at all, if you let me sit quietly in this corner and listen to you."

Frederica says to the class, "This is Jude Mason. He works at the Art School. He has written a book which is coming out in a few months."

They nod, peacefully. Frederica takes out her notes, and begins to speak of Lawrence and Forster. She speaks of what they have in common: a desire for some kind of whole life, unified experience, complete presence in or on the earth. A dislike for mechanised life, for cities, for fragmentation and dissolution. She speaks of the lost Paradises that haunt Forster's Sussex and Lawrence's Nottinghamshire, that send the one in search of wych elms with pig's teeth, and the other in search of communities of like souls in hot, sunny, "untouched" places. She tries to connect this with the passionate desires of their intelligent women, Margaret and Helen Schlegel, Ursula and Gudrun Brangwen, for liberty and subjection, for thought and instinct.

She scans the class. One of the art students, in a skinny black jumper, a skinny black mini-skirt, thick black tights and laced granny shoes, said to her last week, "We have to be different, we are art students, we have to dress differently." Her friends, all in black on black on black, all with burgundy lips and pale faces, indicated agreement. They are uniformly different. The extra-mural class is heterogeneous. Rosemary Bell has a scarlet woollen shirt and a grey jacket and trousers. Dorothy Brittain has a billowing smock in Liberty wool, patterned with little red and black eyes on fawn. Humphrey Maggs has a collar and tie (white and navy) neatly inside his blue jumper. Amanda Harvill has a long-sleeved, high-necked cream woollen Courrèges-style tunic, stopping well above the knees. She has several gold bracelets on her thin, tanned wrists. Her eyelids today are shining bluebell-blue spangled with gold dust. Ronald Moxon, the taxi-driver, has a donkey jacket over an Aran sweater; Ibrahim Mustafa wears a Beatle-like collarless jacket, navy piped with green, over not quite harmonious grey flannels; Lina Nussbaum has a turquoise long-haired sweater with a cowl neck, Sister Perpetua is black and veiled, Ghislaine Todd has a bottle-green polo-neck under an embroidered waistcoat, Alice Somerville and Audrey Mortimer wear tweed suits over blouses, Una Winterson wears a rust-coloured corduroy shirt-waist dress, and Godfrey Mortimer and George Murphy wear dark suits. Frederica is interested in how much more interesting she finds the suits than the art students' customary solemn black, and looks for the third suit, which is usually John Ottokar.

He is not wearing a suit. He is wearing a rainbow-coloured sweater, made of knitted triangles of every bright colour: violet, purple, crimson, orange, yellow, grass green, bottle green, sky blue, dark blue. It is a beautiful, expansive, expensive sweater, with navy ribbing holding it together at collar and cuffs and welt. In his suit he always appeared contained, discreet, smooth, a little paradoxical under the weight of his beautiful bright sculpted golden hair. Now, to go with the sweater, the hair appears to be looser and livelier, very slightly dishevelled at the edges. His body is at ease in this brilliant jerkin: his large face smiles amiably at the room; his blue eyes, under his broad brow, meet Frederica's fiercely when her look crosses his. He is in a corner, a bright patch, a surprise.

She remembers he said: I want you.

He smiles at her.

She looks at his field of triangles and at Jude's blue velvet, and thinks of dominos, masks, bright disguises. The art students are dressed as art students. The people here are "ordinary people," that is to say, separate and heterogeneous people, all already in some sense acting a part, the part of a child or a student, on a junior chair behind a desk, listening to Frederica talking about Lawrence and Forster and sex and death and the earth. Who is John Ottokar? A computer programmer, a man in a suit, a man who doesn't speak language, a bright patch of triangles? Who is Jude, under his ostentatious disguise? Who is Ghislaine Todd, so neat, so limitedly flamboyant in her flowered waistcoat—a psychoanalyst who hears people's lives in their total disconnected dullness and their total dreamed coherence; is this person, thinking about Lawrence and Forster and marriage, the same, or another? What is her face like, sitting invisible behind her patient? The same? Which is her "real" face? What is the difference between Humphrey Maggs's speedwell blue and John Ottokar's harlequin triangles? Both are brightly *not* their working uniforms. But the speedwell blue breathes allotments and public libraries, whilst the harlequin is dangerous . . . But it is not "dressed up" as Jude is dressed up. Or, for that matter, as Sister Perpetua is dressed up, with a starched white band across her forehead and folds of black veiling around her face and shoulders.

The discussion is wide-ranging. Frederica thinks that an extra-mural class is carried on in the lingua franca, the Common Tongue, it is truly extra-mural, outside the enclosures of academies, disciplines, sects, factions. What the class speaks is gossip at one extreme and precise philosophical discrimination at the other, and the thread of the language they have to construct to speak to each other connects both extremes with a web of knots and separations. These grown-up human beings speak wisely and foolishly of other human beings:

Margaret and Ursula, Forster and Lawrence, Birkin and Mr. Wilcox, as though they were (as they are) people they know (and don't know). They know perfectly well, if reminded, that four of these six beings are actually made of words, are capering word-puppets, not flesh and blood. Godfrey Mortimer, when Frederica makes this point, makes the point that as far as the class is concerned, Lawrence and Forster are also made only of words: they cannot be touched or tasted, the evidence for their thoughts is considerably more suspect and partial than the evidence for those of Margaret and Ursula. They can talk, they do talk, of what Margaret and Ursula "really wanted" or "should have done" or "might have become," which Frederica knows to be critically illegitimate and guesses also to be what Lawrence and Forster "might have wanted" their readers to discuss. So we learn to understand. So, to quote Forster and Margaret, we "connect" the prose and the passion, in linguistic and imagining eddies of speculation and comment, understanding and bafflement. The class bring themselves to the text. Amanda Harvill, with a moue and a shudder, opines that the Schlegels are "not real women." Sister Perpetua says that on the contrary, they *are* real women, women driven by beliefs about sex and relationships that form and distort their responses. They are not *sexually intelligent* women, says Sister Perpetua, unlike Ursula Brangwen, who understands the language of the body and how it connects to the language of the mind. It doesn't always, says Jude Mason, in a three-word intervention unusual, for him, in its brevity. Sister Perpetua says she *knows* it doesn't always. (Later, she tells Frederica she told Jude to take a bath, as she thought no one else would. "What did he say?" said Frederica. "He said, 'I like my pungency, it's a form of fastidiousness, I keep the People distant,' " says Sister Perpetua. "So affected, you can do nothing with those people, there are many at the back door of our convent.")

The conversation circles round. George Murphy brings up again the question of the novel and the job. During the earlier discussions of "post-war British fiction" Murphy has sardonically pointed out the limitations of most novelists' knowledge of most people's work. Novels, he says, are obsessed with sex and love and God and food, which is fine by him, most people are obsessed by sex and love and God and food. But most people are also obsessed, says George Murphy, by work, by commodities and machines and property, which they do not regard with the contempt and loathing most novelists lavish on these things, but with fascination, obsession, intelligence. Most people, says George Murphy, have relations with groups of people with whom they work, which are not necessarily obsessed with sex and love, though these things come into it. He is interested in Forster's Mr. Wilcox, who is meant to represent the world of work and money— "along with Leonard Bast," says Sister Perpetua—and is a crude and villainous fool, however Forster tries to make him interesting or mysterious. And look at Birkin and Ursula, says Murphy. What do they do, the moment they fall in love? They give up their jobs and look for a pre-lapsarian pastoral existence. As though, says George Murphy, the human ingenuity behind machines and institutions was all evil and destructive. No novelist can know me, says George Murphy. They don't know what I think about all the time.

"They know what you think about in bed," says Amanda Harvill, who clearly finds Murphy attractive. "No, they don't," says Murphy. "I can have the most luscious bird in my arms and be completely *fired up* and part of my mind will be worrying away about share prices and coffee crops and board politics. And the novelist will get the bird right, perhaps, and not have a clue about all the other pockets."

The discussion moves to the Goat and Compasses. Jude Mason continues to accompany the class. They find a long table against a wall, and occupy all of it. George Murphy sits between Amanda Harvill and Rosemary Bell, the hospital almoner, who is a Marxist, and tends to involve herself in ideological conflict with Ghislaine Todd, the psychoanalyst. On this occasion, Rosemary and Ghislaine are almost in alliance against George and his views on life and work. Both are sympathetic, for quite different reasons, to the desire for wholeness and self-identity Frederica has diagnosed in Birkin, Ursula, Helen and Margaret; both are much more ready to accept Mr. Wilcox's complacent stupidity and Lawrence's beetle-miners' animal degradation as truths. George smiles with irritating superiority and says they are utopian pastoralists, the pair of them. His dark suit is well cut but crumpled a little at the waist and inside the elbows. Amanda Harvill stares at him with faded blue eyes under bright blue starry eyelids. Frederica can see her thin hand, caged in its gold circles, resting on Murphy's knees. Jude's smell rises richly from his trousers and his coat-skirts and the lank locks of his grey hair. He is next to Frederica. Opposite them, leaning back into a dark corner, is John Ottokar in his bright domino.

Frederica says to Jude, "Sister Perpetua had a point."

"My *mana?*" says Jude. "I use the flesh against the flesh. I am undesirable and without desire, a good state."

Frederica shifts in her seat.

"Shall I go further away?"

His smell has elements of bacon and elements of rancid butter, elements of sweat and elements of stale beer, though she has never seen him drink, and he is now sipping a grapefruit juice.

"No. I can put up with you. So I might as well."

He considers Frederica. "*You* are not without desire."

"That's my business."

"Not here. You stand up before us, and we watch you, we scan, we surmise."

"I am without desire, because I have to be," says Frederica. "I am required by law to be without desire until I can get divorced." Her eyes lift and meet those of John Ottokar in his bright plumage. It is like being blinded by a torchbeam. She drops her eyes. Jude shifts in his garments, wafting his air around her. She says to John Ottokar, "I like your jumper. A new departure."

"I couldn't resist the principle of its construction."

"Does it have one?"

"Haven't you worked it out? It's the perfect combination of order and chaos. Every *other* triangle—reaching round and round or up and down—is in the strict order of the spectrum, from violet to dark red. And between the building-blocks of order, everything is random, yellow and orange and pink and green in any order, as they come. I like that. When I worked it out, I liked it. I couldn't afford it, but I bought it."

He does not take his eyes off Frederica.

"Frederica is required by law to be without desire," Jude tells John Ottokar.

"Difficult," says John Ottokar, smiling.

"Likely to provoke the opposite reaction, all things considered," says Jude. "Like most things prescribed and required. We want the opposite."

John Ottokar smiles. Frederica stares into her wineglass, slightly flushed, and remembers *Babbletower.* Jude knows about desire and its quirks. She looks at John Ottokar's triangles and tries to imagine him under them. He must not be desired, and Frederica has always wanted what she cannot have. His skin is taut and his shaved moustache glints gold. His eyes are kind, she thinks, but is not sure. She says, "Do you think about your work all the time, like George?"

"It haunts my dreams. I am writing a programme for oil tankers. I plot their courses round the world and work out the optimal deployment of the fleet. My machine speaks to me. Off the coast of Nigeria, I put in a ship and my machine prints out WHAT SHIP. THERE IS NO SHIP. I dream about other things, too," says John Ottokar, looking at Frederica.

"My work is gone from me," says Jude. "Rupert Parrott has my work and I am bereft. I sit in the British Museum, reading about the perfectibility of mankind. It is chastening, chastening."

At closing time, they all go into the street. Frederica sets off for the Northern Line on the Underground. John Ottokar, his radiance concealed under a black PVC raincoat, accompanies her. So does Jude.

"Shall I see you home?" says John Ottokar. Frederica stands on the pavement next to him and finds she is very slightly trembling. "I will see you home, too," says Jude. "I live your way. I live in Stockwell. We will go home together."

"I never knew where you lived," says Frederica to Jude, looking at John Ottokar.

"No one does," says Jude. He says, "I'm not much protection for a lady on the Underground. They attack me, the louts, when they've drunk a little, they take exception to my nature. You, on the other hand, you two, would be protection for me, as far as you go."

John Ottokar says, "Do you look like that because you *want* to be attacked?"

"I look like this because I must. It is my nature to look like this, this is my self-identity and true nature, this is my Birkin-in-Mexico, my costume for crossing the Rainbow Bridge, connecting the prose and the passion, and if I am despised and rejected of men, I must e'en bear it. I cannot *wear a mask,*" says Jude, leering at John Ottokar in his shiny surcoat and his many-coloured jumper.

"And you are asking me to come home with you as protection?"

"No, no, as protection for Frederica. You may leave me to my fate in the Oval. I go down to the end of the black line on my own. But you could significantly reduce the odds in favour of my being stripped and whipped, wounded and set upon."

They travel together in silence. John Ottokar gets out, with Frederica, at the Oval, abandoning Jude to his possible fate: they see his grey face impassive at the window as the lighted carriages whisk into the dark. Being forced up against Jude's scent in a crowded carriage has an anaphrodisiac effect on the other two: they walk, apart, through the dark streets, into Hamelin Square, and turn, still apart, on the doorstep. Frederica does not invite John Ottokar in. The street lamps make rivulets of golden and silver light on the planes and creases of the PVC.

"I'll give you a ring," says John Ottokar. "If that's OK." His voice is casual.

"That's OK," says Frederica. She goes in, out of the dark. A step has been taken.

But he does not phone, and the next week he is not in the class.

Arnold Begbie receives a reply from Nigel Reiver's solicitor. This states that his client intends to defend the divorce, denies the matrimonial offences with which he is charged, and requests immediate discussions in the matter of access to his son, Leo Alexander. Frederica says she does not want to see Nigel; she is afraid of him, and she does not want to upset Leo. Begbie says she will strengthen her case if she appears to be reasonable, unless she expects Nigel to treat either her or her child with violence. Not Leo, says Frederica. He loves Leo. Images of Nigel and Leo float before her mind's eye; Nigel blown up like a demon, roaring and fire-eyed, blue-black and electric. Leo with her hair and Nigel's eyes, her mouth and Nigel's stocky shoulder-set, with his own white, intent, frightened face. Some small, rigid sense of justice in her points out that a child has only one father, whom it is almost always better to know than to imagine. She agrees to see Nigel, in Arnold Begbie's office.

She expects him to glower with rage and hatred. He sits there in Begbie's chair, with the lattice shadows across his dark face, the set of his body hidden inside his dark suit, and gives her an intent, business-like look. He is a whole, living, complicated human being, not a demon. She does not know him. She remembers the fierce and delightful movements of his naked body. He says, "Of course, I still hope that you will come back to me."

"Why? We weren't happy. I drove you mad. You expected me to be something I wasn't."

"We have Leo," says Nigel, using an unfair verb. "We could try."

"I can't," says Frederica.

They stare at each other.

"Let me see Leo. Anyway. Let him come home for a holiday."

"Home."

"Back to where he was born, then, where he grew up, if you want to be pedantic. Let him run in the country. Let me see him. He's my son. I love him. You can't deny that, you're too straight to deny that."

"I know you love him. He loves you."

"There is no need to hide him from me. I promise not to upset him."

"Mrs. Reiver," says Begbie, "is afraid you will not return the boy at the agreed time."

"I shall not want to return him, of course. But I am not fool enough to suppose I shan't do myself a lot of harm by hanging on to him. And I am not monster enough—whatever Frederica thinks—to hang on to a boy who wants to be somewhere else."

Frederica is not sure that the last remark is true. But it sounds very reasonable.

"Give me Leo for a month in the summer."

"It's too long. He'll worry."

"Three weeks. If I promise never to discuss—what will ultimately happen—and not to try and persuade him to stay for ever. Let him ride Sooty and run in the fields. He'll be happy. He'll think things are better. He must miss Bran House a bit. It will be his, one day."

"OK," says Frederica. "Three weeks." She knows so little about children, so little even about Leo. She has made some sort of instinctive judgement about how long Leo will be happy to revisit his old places before he becomes either afraid of losing her, or afraid of losing his old life again—which, which? *What is best for Leo?*

"If he doesn't want to come at all, you must accept that. I promise to try and make it seem easy for him to come."

"I trust you," says Nigel. Then with a flash of anger. "I don't know why I should, I don't know why I should ever trust you with anything again." And then he bites back the anger and is a mildly smiling man in a suit.

Frederica speaks to Leo. She asks him, would he like to go back to Bran House for three weeks in the summer? With you, he says immediately, as she knew he would. No, she says, with Daddy. Who wants to see you. Very much. She continues doggedly. All over England she imagines people grinding out these sad sentences. We can't get on together any more but we both love you, we both want to see you. Leo pinches his lips together and considers. He closes his face and excludes her from his considerations. She thinks of her nephew, Will, who will not forgive his father. How can Leo forgive her? How long is three weeks? asks Leo, unanswerably, since she cannot return to the imagination of stretches of time in a small child's mind. I shall miss you, in three weeks, she says, drily, casually, desperately. It is in answer to this remark that Leo informs her, equally drily and casually, that he thinks it might be quite nice to go.

He goes in July. He will spend his fifth birthday at Bran House. By then the extra-mural classes are closed for the summer, and the art students are undergoing their final assessments. There are few books, if any, for review, and Frederica's income is reduced to the small sums she is paid by Rupert Parrott for reading his slush heap. Agatha is preoccupied: she is writing the first draft of the Report of the Steerforth Committee. Frederica goes upstairs as usual to prepare Saskia's tea, on the next day when it is her turn to prepare Saskia's tea. Agatha comes home to find her friend and lodger reading Tolkien to Saskia on the sofa where the readings take place. Saskia scrambles down from the sofa and runs to her mother, who gathers her up in her arms. Frederica begins to weep. Her face spreads with salt water. Agatha sits next to her and strokes her hair, puts an arm round her thin shoulders. Saskia touches her wet cheeks. Frederica weeps. She wants to tell Agatha: I have ruined Leo's life. But cannot, in front of Saskia. Agatha gives her coffee, and biscuits with chocolate icing, and suggests that Frederica take a holiday. "Saskia and I are going away, too," says Agatha, not saying where they are going. "So you are free. Eat some more biscuits. You need blood sugar. No one is perfect. Human beings survive. Leo loves you and you love Leo."

"It isn't enough."

"It has to be."

Later, Frederica wonders again about Saskia's father. Are they going to a secret rendezvous with this unknown person? Agatha appears to have solved the problem of the second parent by annihilating him.

XII

꧁꧂꧁꧂꧁꧂

When Agatha and Saskia have gone, Frederica is alone in the house. It seems to expand and float, it is full of scattering bright air. London summers are dry and dusty, but inside the white-painted basement Frederica experiences a giddiness, a sense that she is blowing away like an untethered balloon. She cannot sleep. She is racked by desire—for Leo, for whom she weeps, for work (what has happened to her huge ambitions?), for love (there has always been *someone,* Alexander, Raphael Faber, to whom the threads of love could be hooked and pulled taut). She tries to think of work—what does she want to do, to make? She thinks, Perhaps I shall go back to Cambridge and talk to Raphael about doing my Ph.D. after all. Perhaps I will go back into the British Museum and start reading about Milton and metaphor. The moment she has this thought, *Paradise Lost* invades her mind in bright apparitions: Adam and Eve entertaining the angel made of translucent air in the bowery, blossoming, fruitful garden, Satan and Beelzebub floating dull and fiery on the dark infernal lake, the glistening glossy snake wreathing and coiling its sinister way across the enamelled paradisal lawns. This is what it is to be human, thinks Frederica, more than a little mad—to entertain such guests, such mythic beings made of language and light.

All the same, somehow, the idea of Raphael and Cambridge is not entirely delightful. There is something "bygone" about the Cambridge lawns and the Cambridge cloisters, the teacups and the tobacco.

What do I really want? Frederica asks herself, with her blood beating in her empty head in her empty room. And cannot answer. Solitary Frederica is an unreal being, because Leo exists.

She decides to telephone Leo. It is the second day of his absence. She is afraid to hear Bran House on the end of the line, afraid of all the people there, except Leo, afraid too of what Leo may have become, may think of her.

"Bran House," says the telephone, in a female voice, comfortable, that she cannot place. It is Pippy Mammott.

Frederica says, "Could I speak to Leo, please?"

A silence. Frederica can hear the polished hall, the muted heavy doors.

"I should like to speak to Leo," says Frederica, rather relieved that she does not have to name herself.

"I shouldn't think so," says the voice, answering her first remark.

"I just want to say hullo to him. To keep in touch."

"So did others."

"I know." She does not want to expatiate, or to plead with Pippy. Who also loves Leo. "Is he there?"

"I shouldn't think so."

"Could you look?"

Another silence.

"No, he isn't there. He's out."

"Will you tell him I called? Could he call back?"

"I shouldn't think so."

"He might want to," says Frederica, unable to say "*Please*" to Pippy Mammott.

"He might not," says Pippy. "Best not to disturb, if you want my opinion, as I'm sure you don't."

Frederica, hearing hatred, puts the phone down, carefully. She is shaking. Tears brim.

She decides to call round her friends. She speaks to Hugh, to Alan, to Tony, to Alexander, to Daniel, to Edmund Wilkie. She decides to have a party. She speaks to Desmond Bull and to Rupert Parrott. Rupert has a wife Frederica has never met, Melissa. He asks if she may come to the party. Tony too has now a girlfriend, Penny Komuves. He will bring Penny. Wilkie is back with his old girlfriend, Caroline, of the *Astraea* days. They have both been involved with others, and have now returned. They will all bring bottles, as Frederica has no money. Tony Watson says he has rediscovered Owen Griffiths, who used to love Frederica in Cambridge and is now working in the Labour Party's research department. Frederica decides against inviting Thomas Poole, perhaps out of fear of "the public domain," perhaps out of fear of complications. She does not think of inviting Jude Mason, but is unsurprised when he appears with Daniel, to whom he has attached himself.

It is a good party. The voices mix, mingle and oppose.

"Did you get to the poetry festival at the Albert Hall?"

"No, but some friends did. They said it was wild."

"The audience howled and hooted. And bayed. It was pandemonium."

"It was Nüremberg at times. I was there."

"Jeff Nuttall and John Latham were painted blue. They were dressed as books, which they destroyed. Everyone danced."

"They were all high, they were all spaced out. Adrian Mitchell read a poem about Vietnam."

"It was full of enthusiasm and incredibly tedious."

"The Americans have dropped paratroops in Vietnam. They are on the offensive. It's their war now."

"Wilson should speak against them."

"How can he? Our welfare state is funded by American handouts and subventions."

"They want him to send troops. They urge him to send troops."

"He's cunning. He won't. He won't give them more than words."

"He had no majority in the Commons on the corporation tax. He can't hang on. There'll have to be an election."

"We shall have Reggie Maudling as Prime Minister. He'll succeed Alec Douglas-Home."

"We shan't win the next election. We'll have the Tories back."

"I wouldn't write Wilson off. He's cunning."

"Is it true he's ruled by someone called Marcia Williams?"

"Not ruled. He trusts her."

"Kitchen cabinet . . ."

"Ah, Daniel. Just the man. My theological novelist is trying to take her book back again. First she wanted it back because her husband wouldn't like it. Now she wants it back because he does. He says it's a wonderful picture of the Death of God in our society. He sees the stabbed selfish husband as the sacrificial lamb, I think. He wrote me a

340

letter, saying that when the clergyman loses his faith he *is* the Death of God, and when his wife stabs him, his death opens the way for the Presence of God to be restored, since his Death is incarnate in his doubt."

"It sounds very contemporary."

"Phyllis Pratt says God will be more thoroughly annihilated if she withdraws the book. She's writing another, though. It's got a title. 'Grind His Bones.' It's another theological thriller, she says, about a sexton who composts the vicar and his curate. I can never tell when she's joking. I won't withdraw the book. It's got a cover with a Magritte-like loaf, bleeding gouts of blood."

"Dreadful."

"Saleable, in the present climate. You wouldn't talk to Mrs. Pratt about her theological doubts?"

"I'd rather not."

"*I'll* talk to her."

"Did you hear Patrick Heron at the ICA? He was attacking the Americans. He accused them of cultural imperialism. He thinks it's a kind of chauvinist modishness, all the critics who go round saying everything good comes out of America."

"What he is doing himself," says Hugh Pink, "is incredibly beautiful. All these floating discs and brilliant fields of saturated colour. It's like seeing the elements of creation, it's like seeing angels, except you shouldn't use analogies for it, it simply *is*. It makes me feel ill."

"Ill, Hugh? Why?"

"Because it makes me want to write, as though that was the only sensible thing to do. But I hate poems about paintings, I hate the second-hand. I want to do *something like that* with words, and there isn't anything, or if there is, I don't have access to it."

"How are you, Jude?"

"Ill. Impatient. Lost."

"The printers are trying to bowdlerise your book. They have queried many of your words in red ink."

"I will not have my words touched or changed."

"We'll run it past a lawyer, of course."

"I will not be bowdlerised."

"Don't worry. Your book will either offend, or not, as a whole. There isn't any point in chopping off a few warts."

"You console me."

"I don't mean to, necessarily. Are you writing another?"

"I am too nervous. It is appalling, not to be writing. I have no life. I am no one. So I go to gatherings to which I am not invited."

"I would have invited you if I knew where you lived."

"I can find my way *by other means,* as you see. I like your underground home. You would not like mine."

"What are you doing, Frederica?"

"Nothing much. My son is away. I teach, but the teaching's seasonal. I am trying to get unmarried."

"I can't think why you ever got married. I could find you some work researching at the TV centre. Would you like that? What are you going to do in the long run?"

"I don't know. This morning I thought, I might go back to a Ph.D. I've discovered I can teach."

"Difficult to imagine."

"I *can.*"

"OK. You can. Those that can't, teach. What is it you can't do?"

"Write a novel? Don't be nasty, Wilkie. I *like* teaching. It matters. Ask Alexander."

"What does he know?"

"He's on a royal commission on teaching. He goes in and out of schools."

"Hmm. That might make a good programme. How they learn? What they learn. There are people up in North Yorkshire looking at what the brain does when we learn. Are we a computer, or a jellyfish, or a computing jellyfish? I'm a jellyfish man myself, I think we're made of flesh and blood and neurones *in jelly,* but it's not fashionable. It's all algorithms. Algorithms. Everything analysed into binary dichotomies. Either/or. Whereas you and I know it's both-and, and a few more things as well. Now *there's* something useful to do, study the memory."

"Marcus is doing that."

"So he is. He's turned out well. Surprising."

Tony Watson's new girlfriend, Penny Komuves, is a lecturer at the LSE, daughter of a Hungarian-Jewish economist whose ideas are current in Harold Wilson's Treasury thinking. She and the cheerful Owen Griffiths chatter away about Wilson's kitchen cabinet, to which both have an ancillary access; they gossip about Mrs. Wilson's discomfort in Number 10 and the influence of Marcia Williams. Penny Komuves is short and dark and solid, with a Vidal Sassoon haircut, which suits her. Owen tells stories of George Brown's drinking. Desmond Bull and Hugh Pink discuss Patrick Heron's anti-American aesthetic manifesto as though it was at least as important as Ian Smith's threatened declaration of Rhodesian independence from Britain. Rupert Parrott is different in the company of his wife, who is a rather County girl with a fine-boned face amongst a curtain of silver-blond hair, and angles—rather pretty angles—where less well-bred women have curves. She says almost nothing all evening, turning her head with polite interest from face to face as people speak. The other person who doesn't speak is Daniel, who had hoped to see Agatha, whom he likes; he mentions this to Alexander, who says he had also hoped to see Agatha. "I think she went to Yorkshire," says Daniel. "She said she might see me there, if I go up to see Will and Mary."

"She didn't tell me she was going," says Alexander, with pleasurable sadness. "She sent me a draft of two chapters of our report. She writes very clearly."

Frederica chops up dark bread and French bread and celery and chunks of cheese. Jude Mason looms up behind her.

"You do not appear to be happy. Will you trust me to hand that round?"

"I am not happy; I think that's the first personal remark you've ever made to me."

"I am in your house."

"So you feel you should take an interest in me?"

"No. I feel able to diagnose. You have too many ties. You could have lived as I do, without desire, and then you could have been—"

"What, Jude?" Frederica is slightly drunk. Jude's steely face goes in and out of focus.

"Single-minded. You dissipate yourself. On affections and concerns. Daniel is single-minded. *Tollit peccata mundi,* to speak blasphemously. I prophesy. You will not be what you have the possibility of being."

"That's cruel."

"I am not concerned with kindness. Draw in your tentacles, young woman, all this is trivial, all this chatter. Our deity—I call it Time, Time rules sublunary beings—our deity does not forgive an addiction to the trivial."

"You are pompous. And I am not addicted to it. I am stuck in it. And it isn't trivial altogether. It's like cells breeding, it is *what is*."

She sees the faces and chatter in her room as a warm brew of potential life and form, infinitely interesting, if only she could find her own proper, her own *real* relation to it. What is "real"?

"I am repelled by cells breeding."

"Your bad luck."

Jude sways. "I have seen things you can't imagine. Horrors that are nothing."

He sits down heavily in Frederica's desk chair, breaking a glass of red wine on the desk, dropping the breadboard on the carpet. Wine drips. Daniel fetches a floorcloth. Jude closes his eyes. "Stoned," says Desmond Bull. Jude falls forward on the desk amongst his grey hair.

"He can't stay here," says Frederica.

"I'll take him away," says Daniel. "I'll stow him in the church."

"I'll help," says Rupert Parrott. "I feel responsible for him, now." Melissa Parrott stands up.

"Get on with it, then. I'll go out and look for a taxi. If we are responsible, do let's get on with it."

"I can manage," says Daniel.

"Rupert says he's responsible. So let's *get on with it*."

"Masochist," says Jude, through loose damp lips, opening one reptilian eye and closing it again.

The friends go home. Frederica stands on the doorstep and watches them go. The yellow light spills on to the step. Her friends make off towards the Tube, except for Rupert, Melissa, Daniel and the inert Jude, who depart in a black cab. As Frederica turns to close the door, a figure steps out of the shadows of the next doorway, a figure that makes a faint crackling sound. Frederica takes in a gasp of breath and steps up into her own doorway. She cannot see a face: the man wears a soft, wide-brimmed hat, pulled down. She has seen this figure in this hat and the glistening, crackling PVC across the mud-circle a few nights ago, and again, standing motionless on a corner of the square, perhaps a week before.

"Don't be afraid. I wanted to see you."

The blond face turns up into the yellow light.

"I was having a party. You should have come."

"I didn't want to. Intrude. Be at a party. I wanted to see you."

"You'd better come in."

She is afraid, even now she knows it is John Ottokar. He comes up the steps behind her. A car engine in the street coughs into life, and then dies again. Frederica closes them in.

"Come down, have a coffee."

"I don't know."

"Why have you come?"

"You know why."

He takes his hat off; his arms crackle on the way up, and on the way down. There is the thick, yellow hair, lying glossy and bright.

Frederica cannot answer him: she knows, and does not know, and will not say she knows.

"I've been watching your house," he says. His voice is lowered and conspiratorial, although the house is empty. He is a lover, not a thief, yet Frederica is reluctant to tell him the house is empty. He says, "If I can't have—what I want—I shall lose what I have."

Frederica could say, "No, you won't." Or she could ask, "What do you want." She knows what he wants. She asks, "What do you want?"

"You," he says intently. "You are what I want. It's terrible to want anything so much."

"Come in," says Frederica. "You can't stand here—we can't stand here—in the entrance."

They go down the stairs into the basement. His feet are heavy. His face is heavy. In the class, in the pub, it has always been alert, mildly curious and pleased, responsive. Now it is set into an effort of mindless will. Frederica wants to laugh, and cannot. The tension in his body crosses the air between them. They sit down, on the edges of armchairs, staring across the room.

"You didn't come, for weeks. I thought you'd given us up."

"My brother was ill. I had to see to some things. I saw to them. It was a bad time. I could only think about you." He hesitates. "When things went wrong, it became clear to me that I had to—come to you—I'm not making sense." He hesitates again. "I told you, I'm no good at language. I—I have a picture in my mind of you *understanding* it all—"

"All?"

He bows his head.

"My—history. Two people in a room. Bodies and histories."

Frederica has been thinking about his body, though not about his history, which she cannot imagine. She thinks of all the bodies that have just stumbled and strolled and hurried out of this room: Hugh Pink, white and gingery; Alexander, long and bending; Owen Griffiths, bustling; Tony, brisk, and Alan, elegant; Daniel, solid as a rock and jutting with energy; Rupert Parrott, pinkly gleaming; Edmund Wilkie, fin-de-siècle pale, with heavy dark-rimmed glasses; Desmond Bull, muscular and chemical-tinged; the repugnant Jude, grey and scaley. She likes John Ottokar's shoulders. She likes his wide mouth. He is a shape she likes. His skin and hair have for her a kind of delineating glitter of interest and electricity, a field, almost, of force, an almost visible aura of movement in the air.

She says, "I don't know your history."

"No."

He stares at the ground. He does not tell her his history. He lifts his head and stares silently at her. Frederica stares back. The looks are like touching each other; they shock. She says, "I must clear up all this mess." She does not move.

"Later," he says. "Not now."

He stands up. He crosses the carpet, which seems suddenly to be an immense desert space. He puts a hand on the nape of her neck. She thinks, Do I want this? and raises her face to his. He stares down at her and brings down his mouth like a gold bird striking. But gentle. At the moment of touch, gentle.

Frederica thinks: Do I want this, do I want this? John Ottokar touches her face, her hair, her long haunches, her small breasts. He touches lightly, lightly, so that her skin begins to desire, half-irritated, half-compelled, to be touched more violently. She puts her own hands on his shoulders. He kisses her face, again, and his fingers question her clothes, a button, a zip, a strap, so that inside these the naked woman is defined and comes to life. And her mind does not cease: Do I want this, do I want this? She stares out of the basement window at the cone of light falling from the street lamp, frowning slightly, lips nevertheless parted with mindless pleasure, and thinks: Do I want this? She remembers her own young greed, and her need to know—about her body, about sex, about male bodies—her indiscriminate clutchings and searchings and muddles and laughter and disgust. She is afraid now, as she was not, then. Her body is used, not furiously ready. She remembers her childish attempts to attract Alexander's attention and make him want her. She thinks of them as childish now, she thinks of herself as old, on the edge of being undesirable. She thinks that she wanted Alexander because he was remote, the teacher, her father's friend, tabu. And now, she thinks, there is the same thrill: I am the teacher, I am wanted because I am separate and looked at, there is a boundary of the forbidden to cross. She thinks all this whilst she stands there on her carpet in the lamplight, and her clothes fall slowly around her as John Ottokar's fingers find their fastenings and make her into a woman, a woman he wants, and has imagined, and has not seen, and now sees. I am thin, thinks Frederica. I have no breasts to speak of, despite Leo. John Ottokar reaches the warm triangle of her pants, slips a large hand inside them, and takes them gently down to her knees, and then, kneeling, below. Frederica puts a hand over the red-gold triangle of hair, and John Ottokar kisses the hand, and the hair, softly.

He is still wearing all his clothes, including the PVC raincoat. When he moves to kiss her, kneeling before her, his outer casing crackles and whispers loudly, whilst his hair against her hand is sleek and thick and soft and yellow. Frederica is still *thinking*: she makes an effort not to think of Leo and Nigel, who become immediately present in the room. Her nostrils remember the smell of Leo's hair: the closest, the most powerful, the most loved smell of all. She kneels down next to John Ottokar and buries her face in his gold; its smell is good, and alien, and wholesome like bread. She begins to tremble. John Ottokar is shrugging off the PVC skin: inside is a flowered shirt, a shirt like a garden of green chrysanthemums and blue roses, a busy Paradise but well cut, a shirt to go inside a suit, a respectable-shaped shirt but burgeoning with brilliance. Frederica puts timid fingers to its mother-of-pearl buttons. Do I want this? Do I want this? Neither of them speaks. They are separate, and yet intent on connection. The struggle with his shoes is ungainly: Frederica looks modestly away. His trousers are quick, a snakeskin sloughed. His prick is grand and blond and sure of itself. Frederica laughs when it is revealed. They fall together, warm flesh on warm flesh. Do I want this? I want this. I think I want this. I.

They roll laughing on the carpet, near Jude Mason's still damp winestain: they clutch, they touch; it takes its way: it is good. No one speaks, but Frederica hears his voice in a drowse, a series of soft meaningless syllables, full of *z*s and *s*s, a rush of stuttering *t*s, a dreamy hum, and then a final strange whistling, like the sharp thin cry of a bird. She swallows her own cry; she will not let go so far; she keeps her pleasure, which is intense, partly secret.

In the morning, the two wake naked in Frederica's narrow bed. When, finally, they get up, still almost without speaking, John begins to clear away Frederica's party, still naked, padding in and out of the kitchen with dirty glasses and empty bottles. Frederica sees the bottles and ashtrays and Leo's toys, a tank, a mechanical dinosaur, an articulated wooden snake.

"I can't stay here," she says. "By myself. I can't stay here."

"We could go somewhere else."

"I was thinking of going up to Yorkshire. To see my family."

"We could go to Yorkshire. I don't know Yorkshire. I'm on holiday."

"We can't both go to see my family."

"You could see them—after—when I have to be back. We could have a few days, by ourselves. We could."

"We could just get dressed and lock the house, and go north."

"I've got a car. I could drive you."

"Why not?"

"It is all right, isn't it?"

"It is all right."

Her body hums with happiness. Her mind surveys the place where she lives: books, toys, typewriter, Rupert Parrott's typescripts.

"Let's go *quickly*," she says.

XIII

There is a moment on the road north when red-brick houses give way to grey stone, and grey stone walls make their appearance. The colour of the sky and the grass changes in relation to these stones: the sky is a bluer blue, the grass a bluer green, and the whole world, to the eyes of a northerner returning, both more solid and more potentially liquid, more serious, less friendly, more real. Frederica sits beside John Ottokar as his dark blue car eats the miles of road, and is surprised by the violence of her sense of homecoming. Most of the houses they see are not particularly beautiful; they are dour enough, though sometimes softened by creepers or climbing roses; the nineteenth-century ones have an air, she thinks, of civic and non-conformist confidence. She remarks on this to John Ottokar, who replies that he grew up in Milton Alfrivers, a twentieth-century Garden City planned by Quaker philanthropists in Essex. "Toy houses in toy closes," he says, "we said they were, in the 1950s. Solid though, with pretty gardens. We wanted to get out."

Frederica, who wanted to leave the north for London, and who likes London, who likes her various displaced London lives, cannot quite describe her sense of belonging to this grey and blue and green, so lapses into silence. They drive into the Dales, and the grey-green hillsides slope up and away from the road to the sky, crazily divided into uneven patchworks by the industrious and energetic dry-stone walls, long snakes of skilfully layered dark flat stones, occasionally staked with bare wooden poles. These craftsmen are my people, thinks Frederica, and then reprimands herself for sentimentality. But the walls are beautiful. "Such skill, such precision," says John Ottokar, looking at the orderly human rearrangement of rocks and stones. "That's what my father always used to say," says Frederica. "I used to wait for him to say it, as he always did. Now I look at the walls, and that's what I think. Such skill."

They are not going to Freyasgarth. They have booked in at the inn at Goathland, where they arrive in the thick blue evening, where the light on the moors is like water or suspended powder. They sign themselves in: Mr. and Mrs. John Ottokar. It is a fantasy, a fiction: Frederica feels freed by it. She is *not* Mrs. Ottokar; nobody here knows who she is. They go up a creaking black wooden stair to a low-ceilinged bedroom with a sprigged wallpaper and a sprigged bedspread. They embrace: John Ottokar's large body is interestingly strange still, and yet warm, and yet connected to hers. They go out of the door and watch the last light flicker and fade over the bowl of hills: they watch the early stars in patches, and the fast rags of cloud blown in darker patches between the starclusters. They hold hands. His fingers are warm; she has the idea that his fingertips make little shocks against her own.

Inside, there is a warren of dark bars, a smell of rich beer, a smell of wine, a smell of paraffin. They eat in a restaurant with peach-painted rough-plastered walls, and have a candle between them in a cobalt-blue pot. They eat roast beef and Yorkshire pudding and are formal with each other, suddenly. They share their histories, or parts of their histories. Frederica describes Bill and Winifred (non-conformism, teaching, common sense), Stephanie (good, clever, dead), Marcus (mathematical, brilliant, difficult), Blesford Ride and Blesford Girls' Grammar (a) liberal and b) stifling and boring). John Ottokar tells of a childhood amongst pacifist Quakers; his father, now retired, was production manager in a chocolate factory, imprisoned during the war for conscientious objection. He describes his mother, but Frederica fails to imagine her, although it is clear that she too is a Quaker and a pacifist. "We went to the local Grammar School in Milton Alfrivers," says John Ottokar. "It was OK. We went to Bristol and did maths. They thought we ought to be separated, so one of us started in Bristol and one in Liverpool, but it didn't work out, so we both went to Bristol."

"Which were you?"

"I was the Bristol one."

"Did *you* think you ought to be separated?"

Frederica is making conversation.

"Yes and no," says John Ottokar, evenly. "I could see why they thought what they did, but it didn't work out."

Frederica thinks of asking, "Why didn't it work out?" and finds she cannot: she is somehow forbidden. There is a silence. He is working out what to say.

"At first we weren't doing the same course at Bristol, but by the end we were, we were doing the same pure maths course." He stops again, and starts again. "Living in the same digs. Solving the same problems the same way."

"Happy?" asks Frederica, who now realises that all this is somehow dangerous ground. There is a long silence. John Ottokar eats and frowns. She remembers him saying that he came to the extra-mural class to learn language.

"Very happy in one way," he says, finally. "I mean, that is, we *knew* each other, you know. That was all we did know. And because— because we were together—we—didn't get to know anything else. We didn't have—friends of our own—that is to say, we did have some friends, we had friends of both of us, and we liked those friends because we were like each other, but we needed—I needed—I needed, I thought, a life of my own, so to speak." He gives a snort of painful laughter. "A girl of my own, for instance. Opinions of my own, I sometimes thought, though an opinion is an opinion, if you happen to share one *genuinely* you can't pretend you don't, that's silly. We were very involved in the CND marches—the whole Aldermaston thing. We marched with our parents and all the Quaker Meeting from Milton Alfrivers. We played in a band. We were part of something much larger than ourselves. That was good." He thinks again. "If you can say terror is good."

"Terror?"

"You march and march, you sing, you link arms, human *solidarity,* but you're doing it out of terror at what some fool can do to the world—of what can't be imagined, but *must.* Every now and then you *do* imagine it. You know? Marching is what you can do, but every now and then you know—that marching might achieve nothing."

Frederica has thought about the Bomb. But, either from self-preservative insensitivity, or from a possibly ill-founded faith in human reasonableness in the last resort, or from individualistic foolish courage, she has always turned away from being obsessed by it. She has a distaste for mass emotion, which she does not admire in herself, but does acknowledge and respect. She has absolutely no desire to spend time demonstrating, and thus is sceptical about the value of demonstrations. She is not sure she wants to involve herself with "all that," though well enough disposed towards it. She takes an internal step back from John Ottokar, and looks sharply at his outer self, across the table. His head is bent over his apple crumble: he is frowning. When he feels her look, he lifts his head, and smiles at her. The smile is full of light and of bright warmth. Frederica is dazzled and touched. She smiles back, a wide smile.

She wants to ask him if, and how, and when, he found a girl of his own, and dare not.

The love-making is more inventive, more collusive, less startled, than the night before. He learns quickly what Frederica does and doesn't like; he stirs her body, he keeps it singing, he is pleased with himself, she is humming with pleasure, with pleasure, with pleasure. They sleep, and wake, and turn to each other and touch hands and faces. Frederica is drowsily alive; she breathes in the air he breathes out and the intimacy is acceptable, is delightful. He speaks in her ear, *tesh, teran, azma,* unknown syllables. And again, softly past her ears, that strange, low whistling note of triumph and ending. He falls asleep quickly and heavily and she raises herself to look at his sleeping face in the moonlight, intimate and strange, a still, sculpted, empty face, fair and beautiful, closed to her. Do I want this? says the insistent serpentine voice. She extends her thin body the length of his, skin to skin, in the fading warmth of their pleasure and each other.

In the morning they eat breakfast in the pink restaurant, now looking out at the moor. There are other guests: a family, a married couple, a solitary spectacled man reading *Lady Chatterley's Lover.* They ask the inn for sandwiches, and set out to walk on the moors. They stride out: their steps go together. The rhythm of the striding, the warmth of her lively skin, bring poems into Frederica's mind, poems she learned when her body ached to be touched, and was not.

> "Love, do I love? I walk
>   Within the brilliance of another's thought
>   As in a glory. I was dark before
>   As Venus' chapel in the black of night:

> *But there was something holy in the darkness*
> *Softer and not so thick as otherwhere*
> *And as rich moonlight may be to the blind*
> *Unconsciously consoling. Then love came*
> *Like the out-bursting of a trodden star . . ."*

She thinks of saying this to John Ottokar, and dare not. As a girl she said it to her mirror, conjuring a non-existent face: and now his face, more or less, shines in that space, but the poem is still her secret, is private. I was looking for you, she wants to say to him, and says instead, "Did you find her, the girl of your own?"

"The girl?"

"Never mind."

"Oh, the girl of my own. Oh yes. I found her. She was a French girl. It was—difficult." He pauses. "It was dreadful."

A long silence. Frederica says she is sorry. They walk on. John Ottokar says, "I don't want to—spoil this—by bringing in all that. It's past. It's a—a bad story. Funny and bad.

"When I saw her, Marie-Madeleine, I thought she was beautiful. She was staying in the house we were lodging in: she was a *lectrice* at a school. She wasn't happy. She was out of place. I didn't tell anyone— not anyone—what I felt. I thought about her. I wondered how I could—speak to her. Finally, I went up to her as she was coming back from work—near the school, not near our house—and I said, I wanted to get to know her, to talk a bit. She said, 'Which one are you?' That was the first thing she said. She couldn't tell us apart, then. So I said I was John, and asked her to the cinema. I thought it was dark and secret. We went to see Cocteau's *La Belle et la Bête,* I think. We sat down in the dark. After a bit I had a funny feeling—I knew before I saw—I saw my brother had come in, and was sitting on the other side of her. So when the lights went up, she saw both of us. She had very good manners, she discussed the film with both of us. We went out to coffee, and talked. About CND, about jazz, about the film. She smiled at both of us.

"So then we went out several times, the three of us. I knew what he was thinking, he didn't have to say. He knew what I felt, I wanted Marie-Madeleine, *I wanted her.*

"I don't think he *wanted her,* exactly. He wanted *what I wanted.*

"I told him, I must be alone with her. I told him, we had to separate a little, we had to have individual lives, we had to be two.

353

"I told her I wanted her. She let me kiss her. And then other things. I could speak to her that way, she knew what I felt.

"But he wouldn't let it be."

"What did he do?"

"He haunted us, at first. He always knew where we were going and turned up, by accident on purpose. One day, Marie-Madeleine told him we wanted to be alone together. She said, nicely, that he should find a girl of his own. He punished her."

"How?"

"He pretended to be me. She couldn't tell us apart. He took my clothes, and took her out, and made love to her, and then mocked her, because she couldn't tell us apart. She went home, she said the situation was too much for her. She was humiliated. And frightened. I shouldn't tell you all this."

"I want to know."

Frederica is greedy to know. She is intrigued. The story is dramatic. They stride companionably along sheep tracks. She says, "You said, when you came, that you brought your history."

"So much of it is *our* history."

"What did you do, when she left, when Marie-Madeleine left?"

She has a very clear mind-picture of Marie-Madeleine, a thin dark French girl with tendrils of ragged curls, downcast eyes and a secretive pointed mouth. Nothing, probably, to do with the real Marie-Madeleine.

"I was furious. I told him *we had to separate.* I said I was going to get an ordinary job and live an ordinary life, on my own, like any other single person, any individual, I was going to make my own life. He couldn't bear it. He—he *pleaded.* He apologised. I packed up in the night, and he crept into my room when I was packing. I said no doubt he knew which train I was leaving on, but I didn't want him on it, he wasn't to come. He said he would make her come back. I said that wasn't the point. I left the house to get in the cab to the station, the next morning, and he came out, he was going to get in, he took hold of me. I stood in the street and shouted. I—I hit him, once, he sat down on the pavement. I went."

The words come awkwardly and painfully. The clouds race in the blue sky: there is a lot of wind, blowing the words into the heather. Frederica imagines the scene. She sees John Ottokar, stiff with grief and rage, closing the cab door. She sees the figure sitting on the pavement, with the breath knocked out of him. She sees this figure from the back, a figure in a space, "he."

"And then?"

"The next I heard, was a phone call from Marie-Madeleine, in Caen. She was desperate. He'd gone there, he was sitting on her doorstep, begging her to come back to me, acting the fool, serenading her with a guitar and a trumpet—he's the musical one—in the small hours.

"I went and brought him back. He had—a sort of breakdown. She said she couldn't take it, she never wanted to see either of us ever again. He's in therapy, now. I—tried that, but I didn't like it, I quit. He—depends on his therapist. He lives in a sort of commune, I think. He was in hospital for a bit. I got my job and my flat.

"If—you and I—go on—you need to know these things."

"It's all *interesting*."

"That isn't the word I'd use," says John Ottokar.

Frederica is a clever woman, but she is not a woman with an unusually quick imagination. It is not until the two are in bed that night that her imagination really begins to work on the other, the absent brother. She wonders, as she smells the particular smell of his hair, of his chest shining with sweat, of his sex, what it could really be like to make love to another man, indistinguishable from this one, "identical." She measures the length of his arm-bones with the span of her hand, she studies the whorl and spiral of his ears, she touches and tastes their interior with her tongue. Could there be another, the same, who punished Marie-Madeleine through *trompe-l'oeil* and humiliation? The essence of love is that the beloved appears to be unique—*more unique,* thinks Frederica, in whom was instilled (by her father) the knowledge that "unique" is an adjective that cannot be qualified. She tries to imagine another Frederica and her mind shies away in panic.

They set out to walk across the moors to the Falling Foss; they leave the car at Sleights, and walk through Ugglebarnby, Iburndale, Little Beck. The names on the map are ancient and full of life: Hemp Syke, Soulsgrave, Foul Syke, Old Mary Beck, High Bride Stones. At the edge of some woodland they see splashes of scarlet and blue and gold: two people are moving slowly along the hedgerow, pausing and bending; the colour is their thermos flasks, plastic boxes and canvas knapsacks. As Frederica and John Ottokar pass they straighten up and recognise her. They are Jacqueline Winwar and Luk Lysgaard-Peacock. Frederica, held in a kind of glass globe of touch and tension with John, does not want to stop and speak. She wants to greet these two marginal persons and pass on. Luk Lysgaard-Peacock appears to expect this: he inclines his head and returns to his contemplation of the damp grass and the roots of bushes. But Jacqueline greets her warmly and asks if she is on her way to Freyasgarth. She offers coffee from the scarlet flask and John Ottokar accepts. They sit down on large scattered stones, each holding a different brightly coloured plastic beaker. From where they are they can see the new Early Warning System on Fylingdales Moor, three pure white spheres, huge and perfectly round against the sky with its bright blue and slow-moving shifting fluffy clouds, like sheep slowly metamorphosing into cotton-wool, or octopods, or feather beds, or chariots.

Jacqueline asks Frederica if she is on her way to Freyasgarth. Frederica says she does not know: she is taking a few days off on impulse. Jacqueline's bright brown eyes consider John Ottokar. She tells Frederica that Marcus would be pleased to see her. There is something intimate and very slightly proprietorial in her tone: Frederica wonders, as she has wondered on other occasions, exactly what is the relation between those two. Daniel will be pleased to see Frederica, too, says Jacqueline, if she comes. Frederica says she did not know Daniel was there. No reason why she should, she adds. And Agatha will be very surprised, says Jacqueline. She is bringing Saskia to meet Will and Mary. We are all looking forward to her visit. Oh, says Frederica, put out. Jacqueline smiles. We are looking forward to meeting Agatha, she says.

John Ottokar is staring at the three great spheres. It is almost as though they were in another dimension, he says, another reality. Their size is incommensurate with the moorland, their scale is in another world. They are beautiful and sinister. They are so beautiful and simple it is not easy to see them as man-made, and thus they do not seem to spoil the wild landscape as they might be expected to. They are huge yet unobtrusive.

They are monuments to human power, though, says Luk Lysgaard-Peacock. They are listening for the sound of Armageddon. We have built engines that can destroy the world, and we have built these huge, inhuman domes, that watch and listen for the approaching doom. He laughs drily. "I do not suppose they are a very adequate defence," he says, "despite their scale, despite their grace."

No one present can remember how many minutes' warning the radomes give of the approaching cataclysm: four minutes, six? twelve? Prepare to meet thy doom, says Frederica. We shall melt in a flash. Not necessarily, says Luk Lysgaard-Peacock. Death can fall through the air and melt silently and invisibly into grass, into milk, into our teeth and our bones. Though it need not come flying in over the North Sea from Siberia. A local accident is just as sure. There was an accident in Cumberland not long ago; it was hushed up; but the strontium is in the bones of children who were under the blowing cloud. I measure it, in the shells of snails, he says. He shows John and Frederica a box of striped snail shells. In certain snail populations, he says, a band of strontium can be detected in the shells. He has a friend who studied much larger snails—*Partula suturalis,* on the Mooréa atoll, near where the French explode their test bombs. He was using bands of strontium to measure the growth of the shells, and was expelled by the French when this came to their attention. "I've found concentrations of it in Lancashire populations," he says. "You take the shell, and embed it in a transparent gel, and cut it vertically with a fine diamond saw, so that you have a beautiful spiral—a Fibonacci spiral—and you can date events on the spiral, by measuring minerals . . ."

John Ottokar asks about Lysgaard-Peacock's work. He is studying population genetics, he tells them: several populations of the striped snails, *Helix hortensis* (or later *Cepaea hortensis*) and *Helix* or *Cepaea nemoralis* were studied in the 1920s and 1930s to record the predominance or rarity of certain patterns—variations in stripes, their number and thickness, their absence, their colour. "If we look at them now, we hope to see Darwinian selection in action," he says. "We have populations in various habitats—hedgerows and roadsides, various woods, beech, oak, and mixed—and we look for changes in snails with changes in environment. Some are pink, some are yellow, and there is evidence that unbanded snails are more numerous in beechwoods, and striped snails in hedgerows, where they may be disguised from thrushes. We came here because there is a thrush's anvil here where we collect the broken shells—as you see—and count the numbers, and their changes in pattern."

There is indeed a large stone in the roadside verge surrounded by smashed fragments of shell, some open and showing the spiral column, gleaming in the centre, some like crushed eggs.

"But the thrushes are diminishing," says Jacqueline. "Several of the anvils are abandoned: the thrushes have been killed by the pesticides in the food chain, we think; they eat fat shiny worms full of parathion or dieldrin, or heptachlor, and if they are not poisoned they can become infertile, or produce monstrosities, the poisons damage the DNA, change their genes as surely as radiation does—the thrushes we study here are still here and still singing and still breaking snails on the anvil—but in many places they are gone. And then we expect to find changes in the snail populations."

Frederica shivers: there is something uncanny in this conversation about man-made death falling silently through air and water and matter, through leaves and fur and flesh and bones and bony shells, here in the moorland air, face to face with the silent vision of the watching, listening, towering white spheres. John Ottokar and Jacqueline Winwar talk to each other with the indignant fear of their generation, with the wrath against their elders that they are still young enough to feel.

Frederica turns over the shells collected by Luk Lysgaard-Peacock. She looks at the lovely coils and spirals, the helical houses of the vanished creeping creatures, horned, slimy, glistening, seven-thousand-toothed. Lysgaard-Peacock shows them to her—pink and yellow, single-banded and multi-striped. *Helix hortensis,* he tells her, has a white lip—"a lovely, ivory-white, gleaming lip," he says poetically, whilst *Helix nemoralis* can be distinguished by a jet-black lip, "a glossy black." From his chosen language she can see that he loves the creatures he studies.

"They carry their history on their outsides," he says, "on their backs you can read their genetic make-up."

"And you can read that Darwin was right, that natural selection changes the genes of the population?"

"Not exactly," says Luk. "There are puzzling things. If strict Darwinian theory was true, populations under the same selective pressures should become more and more genetically homogeneous—but this isn't so. They show a surprising genetic polymorphism. All sorts of forms persist when strict theory might suggest that they should have vanished. There are fossil populations of *Cepaea nemoralis* tens of thousands of years old with just as much variety of shell colour and banding patterns as we find today."

"Perhaps there are different selective pressures—"

"I like to quote Bacon," says Luk Lysgaard-Peacock. "On diversity, I like to quote Bacon. I try to read the language of the DNA on the backs of my snails, and I think of what he said. 'It is the common wonder of all men, how among so many millions of faces, there should be none alike: now, contrary, I wonder as much, how there should be any. He that shall consider how many thousand several words have been carelessly and without study composed out of 24 letters; withal how many hundred lines there are to be drawn in the Fabrick of one man, shall find this variety is necessary.' The alphabet of the DNA has only four letters, but they can produce an apparently infinite variety. Even in snails."

Frederica considers Lysgaard-Peacock's own face. His beard is very strong and stiff and russet, cut neatly and full of vigour. His mouth amongst the red spikes and spines is soft and secret. His eyes are deep-set. His ears are pointed. He is foxy. He is not unlike herself, in that, and his colouring is roughly related to her own—people might suppose, wrongly, seeing the four human beings together, that these two were related, she thinks. She smiles at him, and he smiles back, not wholly present in his smile, thinking about snails and the DNA. Frederica's glance slides on to John Ottokar, with his wide brow, his shining head, his spine, known and touched vertebra by vertebra. She says to Luk, "Some faces are alike. John has an identical twin. I don't know him."

Lysgaard-Peacock hands her two shells, both yellowish-green and unmarked.

"Geneticists love twins," he says. "Most particularly twins with different histories."

"You must ask him," says Frederica.

"I may," says Luk. He hands her another shell, this one boldly divided by spiral dark stripes on a pale ground. "A present," he says.

John and Frederica come back to Goathland in the evening. They walk in the dusk through the village, where the black-faced sheep stare with yellow, inhuman eyes. Something tugs at Frederica's memory. She came here once, in a bus, on a trip, and had what she has now docketed as an interesting and instructive experience with a traveller in dolls. The sight of a sheep and a thorn bush brings back this person, Ed, in his interesting and repelling fleshiness, but it also brings back a thought. It was a thought about her own separateness, and the power that was possibly inherent in keeping things *separate*— sex and language, she thinks, ambition and marriage, *what* was I thinking? She remembers she was thinking about Racine, and the rhythmic movement of her feet, comfortably in time with the rhythmic movement of the feet of John Ottokar, brings back the couplet in the landscape to which it was wholly irrelevant then, and for *that* reason interesting, for *that* reason compelling:

> Ce n'est pas une ardeur dans mes veines cachée
> C'est Vénus toute entière à sa proie attachée

She remembers, and with it her delight in the balance of the lines, the way they pivot on the caesura and are both separated and joined by the rhyme. She says the verse out loud, and John Ottokar puts his hand over her buttocks, lovingly, and laughs, and says, "Precisely." Frederica stops in her tracks, dizzy with sex, and puts her arms tightly round him: watched by sheep, and by the man who was reading *Lady Chatterley* in the rosy restaurant, they embrace, they kiss, they walk on. They lean together. Frederica's mind, a dark snake burrowing in darkness, looks for a word which then seemed the key to power and safety. She remembers her distress that Stephanie had apparently found happiness with Daniel. She thinks of Forster and Lawrence, only connect, the mystic Oneness, and her word comes back to her again, more insistently: *laminations.* Laminations. Keeping things separate. Not linked by metaphor or sex or desire, but separate objects of knowledge, systems of work, or discovery. In her pocket her fingers touch Luk Lysgaard-Peacock's snail shells, two greenish and one striped. Are the stripes laminations, or organic growths? The layer of strontium, exposed by the diamond saw in the spiral form, is a *layer*—an accident in Cumberland, a time of fall-out in the air—what is she saying? Partly that even fear of death in the air is not all-consuming or all-pervading. She has the first vague premonition of an art-form of fragments, juxtaposed, not interwoven, not "organically" spiralling up like a tree or a shell, but constructed brick by brick, layer by layer, like the Post Office Tower. The radomes are on the moor and are seen amongst the heather and the neolithic stones and barrows, but their beauty is in the difference as well as in the simultaneity of the vision.

She is feeling for something, and doesn't know what it is, cannot push the thought further. Laminations. Separation. I was thinking about the Virgin Queen, and the power of her solitude and her separation, the fact that her power and her intelligence were dependent upon her solitude and her separation.

"What are you thinking?" says John Ottokar, and takes her shoulders, and turns her face to his. "You've gone away from me. Where? What are you thinking?"

Desire moves round the column of Frederica's spine like the spiral of a helter-skelter, round which she spins screaming with fear and delight.

"I had an idea for a book called *Laminations*."

"Why *Laminations*?" he says later, in the bedroom. At the time, he simply smiled and nodded.

"I haven't thought it out. It's to do with what was in the lectures, the Romantic desire for everything to be *One*—lovers, body and mind, life and work. I thought it might be interesting to be interested in keeping things separate."

"I know about that," he says, sitting naked on the edge of the bed. The lights are out, but the room is full of pale moonlight. "I know what it is like to be afraid of being two separate creatures confined in one skin."

They are naked and cool in the night, sitting companionably on the edge of the bed. On an impulse she touches his sex, the two balls moving loose and separate inside the cool bag of skin. The penis shrinks like a soft curled snail, and then swings out blindly, a lumbering and supple serpent becoming a rod or a branch. Two in one, thinks Frederica, as his arms go round her. You might think, she thinks, as their bodies join, that here are two beings striving to lose themselves in each other, to become one. The growing heat, the wetness, the rhythmic movements, the hot breath, the slippery skins, inside and out, are one, are part of one thing. But we both need to be separate, she thinks. I *lend myself* to this, the language in her head goes on, with its own rhythm, I *lose myself,* it remarks with gleeful breathlessness, I *am not,* I come, I come to the point of crossing over, of not being, and then I fall away, I am myself again, only more so, more so. His face, *post coitum,* is calm like an Apollonian statue. There is no clue to what is inside his brain-box. I love that, says Frederica's chatty linguistic self, I love not knowing, I love it that I don't know him.

Daniel sits companionably with his father-in-law on the Freyasgarth lawn, making a daisy-chain for his daughter. The fat pink-tipped flowers are scattered across his black thighs, where she has strewn them. The two men sit in deckchairs on the grass and watch the young girl, barefoot in a sky-blue dress, strut and pirouette and swoop in front of them. Her reddish-gold hair falls in a silky curtain about her calm, round face. There are two ways of making daisy-chains. One is to pierce the end of each stalk, and thread the next flower through the green until its head catches. The other is to select a tough daisy with a powerful stalk and thread it through the heads of several others, piercing each at the nape and pushing up through the golden pollen circle, making a thicker, more luscious petalled rod, all pink and white and feathery. Daniel made a bracelet by this method, but Mary exclaimed at the cruelty and extravagance, and he is now making a long green garland, studded intermittently with florets. It goes slowly: split stems curl back and are discarded. Mary runs up and down, bringing handfuls of flowers. Bill says she is denuding his lawn and making it look conventional and respectable.

"There'll be new ones tomorrow," says Mary. "There always are. The more you pick, the more they come."

The blue dress is no more than a floating triangle of cotton, held on by shoe-string straps. Her skin is freckled and new and lovely. She bends down, and straightens. Bill says to Daniel, "She reminds me. She is very like, very like."

"The movements of the neck. The wrists."

The dead woman is dreadfully present. The two men measure each other's apprehension of her absence. Mary jumps high, fluttering her flying feet. They applaud Mary. Bill says, "When you do dance, I wish you / A wave o'th' sea, that you might ever do / Nothing but that, move still, still so—"

"What is that?" says Daniel.

"Nothing," says Bill. "A play I used not to like. I begin to see the point of it."

Mary's dance brings her past in a rush, feet thudding on the grass. She says, "There's a car coming."

Daniel thinks it will be Agatha Mond and Saskia. But it is not. Winifred brings the visitors out: it is Frederica, completely unexpected, and a blond man, completely unknown. Frederica considers Mary, who is slightly out of breath, and looks at Daniel, seeing the same ghost. Their faces twist, and then are stoical.

Daniel sees that Frederica is shining with sex like a sunbather rubbed with butter. Her sharp face has its old edge, a keenness, a glitter, which makes him see that he preferred the recent, more battered, subdued Frederica. He sees a kind of black space walking in the garden, which is his absent wife. Frederica says, "Jacqueline Winwar tells me you are entertaining Agatha here."

"She is visiting Professor Wijnnobel about her committee. She suggested coming over, so Saskia could meet Mary."

Frederica prickles. "It's odd she didn't say anything. To me."

"Is it?"

"It's *my* family. I feel it's odd. I suppose it doesn't matter."

"You are here, now, anyway," says Daniel, equably.

He is being disingenuous. He has noticed, now and then, a speculative gentleness in the way Agatha Mond looks at him. He has thought he noticed (and then dismissed the idea) a particular carefulness of intention when she handed him a plate, or a glass of wine. Nothing much. He likes Agatha Mond. He was, he realises, looking forward to a quiet talk with her in the sunshine, in the north, a step or two forward in discovery. She is a secret woman. He was looking forward to finding out a few things. This—apart from his feelings about Mary and Will (who has gone off on a hike with the local scouts)—is the first *personal* feeling he has had, the first mild *wish* he has formulated, since . . . And now Frederica is here in a great cloud of sex and self-importance like a swarm of bees and a too-sweet smell of honey. Winifred is offering tea to John Ottokar, who is praising the landscape, shyly. He does not look entirely happy. He is standing apart from the family group.

Agatha and Saskia arrive in a hired Mini, a yellow Mini with black trimmings. Agatha is surprised to see Frederica but apparently delighted. She is wearing a woven straw hat and a shift with big, innocent white daisies on a navy ground. Her skin has gone browner in the few days she has been away from London. Her arms are smooth and bare: Daniel wonders what it would be like to run his lips over them, and says, "I'm glad you could make it. Would Saskia like juice? Mary has been dancing."

"I dance," says Saskia.

"It's such a pity Leo isn't here," says Winifred. "On his birthday, too."

Frederica has said nothing about Leo's birthday. She has been trying not to think of it, of him, of what he will be doing. Everyone looks at her, and looks away. John Ottokar wanders off and looks at a rosebush, very intently, as though none of this is to do with him.

Agatha turns to Bill and says that she is in the north because she is drafting the Report of the Steerforth Committee, and has been discussing the technical chapter, the controversial chapter, on grammar, with Professor Wijnnobel. She says she has read the evidence Bill submitted to the committee, with great interest. She would like to talk to him about the relations between reading literature and the new stress on the children's own writing, " 'creative' writing, only I do shy away from that word, I do dislike it."

"Usage will sanctify it," says Bill, "if your Professor Wijnnobel is to be believed. Why do you balk at it?"

"Daniel might agree. It feels blasphemous, it has a faint tainted air of blasphemy hanging around it. I notice you use a religious metaphor, 'sanctify.' "

"On purpose," says Bill, delighted.

"Of course. What do you think, Daniel?"

"Creative? It doesn't seem blasphemous to me. Ugly, though. It makes me think of white elephants at jumble sales, raffia lampshades and pottery rabbits and paper flowers."

They laugh.

Marcus arrives, with Jacqueline. They fetch chairs and make a tea party on the lawn. Birds can be heard, and the hum of bees. John Ottokar is ill at ease. Jacqueline brings Marcus to him, introduces them, says that they have artificial intelligence in common, since Marcus is mapping algorithms in the brain and John is mapping them in shipping traffic. The two men begin to speak of computer languages and their relative strengths and weaknesses. John Ottokar relaxes; he becomes a professional man at a family tea party. Frederica is regretting having come. She had formed some demonic image of Agatha Mond invading her own world, the world of her origins, and this is hard to square with the calm figure discussing teaching methods with Bill Potter, discussing the interesting split in the committee between supporters of Will to Power, and supporters of Eros. "All they are united in," says Agatha Mond, "is opposition to Mickey Impey, who wants to 'liven up the Report' by writing little gnomic epigrams for every chapter." She gives an example:

> *"A tender love of spit and spot*
> *And mopping up of shit and snot*
> *Is what most teachers have not got."*

"True enough, as far as it goes," says Bill.

"But not verse to be *prima donnaish* about," says Agatha Mond.

"He is threatening to lampoon us in the Sunday papers and on the television if we don't print his contribution. He could, too. He could make us look ridiculous in exactly the places we can't afford to look ridiculous in."

It is all very civilised. Daniel notices that Agatha does not address any remarks particularly to himself until Frederica goes away into the kitchen with Jacqueline. She does then turn to him, her face shadowed under her hat, against the red and white stripes of her deckchair.

"I am glad . . . ," she says. "I wanted . . . I was looking forward to seeing you."

"So was I," says Daniel. The two little girls are doing something together at the edge of the garden: Mary, four years older, is showing Saskia something growing, or nesting, between the stones. "They get on," he says, thinking immediately that this remark is fatuous, since there is no real evidence either way. They are not apparently fighting.

"That's good," says Agatha. "I'd like it if . . ."

Frederica returns. Daniel sees her against the sky, so that her hair is brighter and lighter in the sunlight. She looks across at the two little girls, and says to Agatha, "Mary is quite incredibly like her mother."

"Like her father, too," says Agatha. "I think."

"Oh, do you?" says Frederica. "I've never seen that."

"The set of the mouth," says Agatha. "A determined chin. Can a chin be determined? The way it is held, anyway."

"Stephanie's mouth was like that. Mary's mouth is exactly like Stephanie's mouth."

"Married couples resemble each other," says Jacqueline. "Statistically, genetically."

Daniel is deeply annoyed to find that Frederica's voice has come to resemble her sister's. Featureless against the sun, she too is a walking *memento mori,* at least from certain angles; blurred in the light, her edges softened.

"Excuse me," he says, and rises, and walks away into the house.

Frederica and John say good-bye to everyone and drive off. No explanation of John has been offered or asked for. Bill says to his daughter, vaguely, "Be careful," and neither Bill nor Winifred suggests that John Ottokar might come again. They are pessimistic, Daniel thinks, about Frederica's chances of conducting herself sensibly. With reason, he thinks, cross with Frederica almost in the old way. Agatha Mond and Saskia too depart, returning to the Vice-Chancellor's lodgings in Long Royston. Agatha puts out her hand to Daniel: he takes it: there is no *frisson*. Something has not happened. It might not have happened even without Frederica. But Daniel is irritated and feels low.

He is approached by Jacqueline, who asks about his work, and tells him about Ruth, who is becoming more and more involved in Gideon Farrar's Children of Joy. The Children of Joy are a rapidly growing movement in the Church of England. Gideon conducts weekend retreats in seaside barns and country houses, where the Children dance, sing, shout and encounter each other's bodies in loving exploration, acting out infant joys and terrors, anger and tenderness, birth and death. They eat paschal meals, feeding each other around a communal altar table with home-baked breads and home-brewed wines. There are posters of Gideon's benign gold-bearded face above a drawing of robed arms enfolding a flock of naked and aspirant adolescent bodies, a pastoral *couvade*. Daniel does not like either Gideon or the Children of Joy, but is suspicious of his own reasons for this dislike: his is far too inhibited a being, he recognises, ever to be able to sing and shout in communal joy. He asks Jacqueline if Ruth is happy.

"Ecstatically," says Jacqueline.

"I used to think Marcus was in love with her."

"He was. Is, perhaps. I don't understand it. There was a time when they used to make love. Marcus never told me that: she did. She felt she ought to, because he wanted it so much. She said. Then she felt she ought not to, because it was giving off bad messages in the meetings of the Children. They believe they mustn't hide anything. They had a kind of what I call 'emotional stripping session' and someone claimed they could smell bad odours on her body or in her breath or something—I know the phrase 'bad odours' was used. So she gave it up. She thinks she ought to be able to make him go to the Children and she feels she's failed because he doesn't. They still see each other."

Daniel stares over the wall of the garden at the wild land. Jacqueline says, "I know you don't like Marcus."

"That isn't true. I think that isn't true. We've known bad things together and no good ones." He considers Jacqueline. "You like him. That's good."

Jacqueline stands a little more upright.

"I love him. I don't know why. I just one day noticed that I did, that he was *it, the one,* I was even almost annoyed, because you can't say he's a sensible sort of person to fall in love with. Now, Luk Lysgaard-Peacock—he wants to marry me, I think, and he knows what he wants in life—he's ambitious—and kind, and has a first-rate mind, and respects mine. And Marcus is vague and not-quite-there a lot of the time, and doesn't know what he wants, except he wants Ruth, in a funny way, but I think that's because she doesn't *talk,* she's a kind of non-person. I've always just supposed if I waited, he would see I was there, one of these days, and change. You know? In a flash of light, *see* me?"

"It does happen."

"And we were only kids, and he was much more of a kid than I was, and—and I see that *I am* ambitious, too, and I quite like waiting and waiting to be seen, because I can get on with my work while I'm waiting—I've had an idea about neurons and memory—about the nature of learning—a *real idea*—I always talk too much to you, don't I?"

"It's my job."

"I hope not only that. But it does mean I go on at you as I would at no one else—I've *never talked to anyone* about Marcus, I just had it all fitted out in my mind—"

"If I say what I think, you'll be annoyed."

"Say it, all the same."

"I think you should look at Luk Lysgaard-Peacock. In a different way."

"You don't really think that. You know better."

"I have to go on believing in sense, in the possibility of good sense prevailing."

"Not much evidence of *that,* in the world we live in."

"Not much evidence. I agree."

"Whereas love is all over."

Daniel laughs. "All over." He says, "If you are going to work on learning—"

"It's all biochemistry. Love, learning, the lot. Whatever else it is. And don't say knowing that—seeing it that way—doesn't change anything—because actually, it does. It does."

Frederica goes to Paddington. She stands under the Departures and Arrivals. Her mouth is dry, her heart bangs audibly, her blood fizzes.

She is alone. Her brown shoulder-bag hangs below the hem of her bright green cotton shift, which hugs her buttocks. Her long, thin legs tremble visibly. Her eyes are made up like does' eyes. She has had her hair cut, finally: it is a shining bronze cap, or helmet, with pointed tongues licking her cheekbones. At night, in the basement flat, waiting for John Ottokar, she is alive with apprehension, but not like this. This is so extreme, it is abject.

The train comes in. She makes her legs move towards the barrier. It is a very long train, and has come a long way. She jostles for position, she stares. The crowd hurries from the train. From far back she sees the red head bobbing and darting; she hears the running feet scurry and thud; she sees the stout figure weaving its slower way after him. He is wearing a new jacket she does not know, and new, polished shoes. He reaches her; his head butts her crotch; his grasping hands go out and clutch her backside; she bends down; they clutch, they cling, they grip, the small body tries to batter its way back into the thin one it came from. He kicks her legs, he pulls at her neckline, he dislodges her handbag. She kneels on the dirty concrete to contain and support him. He is crying out: she understands the words.

"I hate it. You've cut your hair, I hate it. You *didn't tell me,* I hate you. It's horrible, I think it's horrible, I hate it."

The two small hands scrabble in the smooth cap, dishevelling it, bushing it, tugging, twisting. It is so well cut it falls, raggedly, more or less back into place.

Pippy Mammott arrives, out of breath, with Leo's satchel and suitcase, which she dumps in front of Frederica. She stands and puffs, solid in a red-white-and-blue-checked shirtwaist dress and Clark's sandals. She doesn't speak to Frederica. She says, "Well, good-bye, Leo. Come back soon. We'll miss you."

Leo turns round, still clenching a handful of Frederica's hair, and holds up his face to be kissed. Pippy Mammott bends to kiss him. Her face is very close to Frederica's. She purses her mouth, and Frederica thinks for one dreadful moment that she is going to spit on her. Pippy Mammott's eyes are full of tears. As she kisses Leo, these begin to run out violently, and splash on his small, freckled cheeks.

"We had a good time," says Pippy Mammott to Leo Reiver.

"A *very* good time," says Leo. "Tell Sooty I'm coming back."

He twists his hand, still full of Frederica's hair, to wipe his cheek. He hurts her.

"Thank you," says Frederica to Pippy.

"Don't. Don't thank me," says Pippy. "If I had my way." She does not finish this sentence.

"Come on, Leo," says Frederica. "Let's go home."

Her own tears have come from nowhere and are now falling heavily, dripping from her chin on to Leo's shoulder. She could not find a word for why she is weeping. She cannot control it. Her hands remember Leo's chest, his waist, his weight.

The two women weep, angrily and helplessly. The little boy looks from one to the other, and transfers his attention to a pigeon, swooping in the station canopy, with the light on its wings.

XIV

In September, Leo and Saskia go to school. Both Agatha and Frederica accompany the two, who walk stolidly, hand in hand, through the grey, dusty Kennington streets. The William Blake School has been chosen by Agatha after careful consultation with the school inspectors with whom she works. Lebanon Grove is a treeless crescent of little shops, in the centre of which is the school, a high, gloomy red-brick cube with dusty, barred windows, inside which can vaguely be seen dangling paper parrots and chickens, poppies and clouds. There is a large asphalt playground behind a high, spiked, barred railing, and three entrances—churchy openings with Gothic stone arches and heavy-hasped doors, over which, carved in the stone, are the legends BOYS, GIRLS and MIXED INFANTS. Despite its grim Victorian look, the school has a reputation, Agatha assures Frederica, for progressiveness and innovation. The two women are seized with terror. The two children clasp each other: yesterday Leo said, "The good thing about Hansel and Gretel was that there were *two* of them, I think. They were all right because they were two." Larger children rush in past the smaller ones; pushing, shoving, calling. The children are mixed: black, brown, white, and mixtures of these. The Reception teacher meets the two on the doorstep of MIXED INFANTS and takes their hands. She is a slip of a girl in a strawberry-coloured mini-skirt and high black patent boots. Her hair is dandelion-coloured, her lips painted a ghostly pale cream, her eyes black-rimmed, with false lashes. She resembles a large doll. Frederica had expected a motherly body and sees a child amongst children. Miss Nightingale's voice is kind and sensible. She leads them into the cloakroom, where each child has a hook with an animal and his or her name. Leo's hook has a lion, and the legend: *Leo. Lion*. Miss Nightingale tells him his name means lion, and he says, "I know," and Miss Nightingale says she is pleased. Saskia's hook has a fluffy kitten and says: *Saskia. Cat*. Saskia says she does not want a cat, she does not like cats. Miss Nightingale looks around and offers her a camel or a sheep. Saskia chooses the camel. "They *spit*," Saskia tells Miss Nightingale, who says, "I know. I've seen them. They are very contrary."

Agatha and Frederica say good-bye. They walk out into the street, bumping against hurtling children. Agatha says it is a good school: the buildings may be grotty, but the children's work is displayed along every corridor; there is a frieze of *The Hobbit,* made by a whole class, with the travelling dwarves with their coloured hoods, Bilbo the Hobbit with his pipe and his furry feet, Gandalf the wizard with his flowing white beard and flaming staff, a mountainous background with peering orcs in cave-mouths and wolves on the skyline, a wood full of fat black spiders and carefully constructed webs, and at the very end, Smaug the dragon in his cave, made out of shining milk-bottle tops for scales, and lying on a treasure made of coloured sweet wrappings and tiny plastic beads. The collage is excellent: Agatha tells Frederica to observe that the children have had to consider how trees grow and spider-webs are woven, to think about perspective and be inventive with materials. On the corridor above this, illustrations to William Blake's poems "The Lamb," "The Tiger," "The Little Boy Lost," "The Clod and the Pebble" celebrate the school's name. There was nothing like this in the schools of Frederica's youth. She finds it exciting and invigorating. But she does not know how Leo will survive group life. In the tiled corridors the shrill voices echo and bay. Frederica was a child pushed aside by, hunted by, other children. A solitary, angry child. Does this hand on? She says to Agatha, "I was no good at group life. I hated school."

"Me too. It seemed eternal. It dragged so. I say to myself, Where are they now, the ones who were so successful, so popular as children?"

At home Frederica has another long, legal envelope. This contains a letter from Arnold Begbie, and encloses, he says, the Respondent's Answer to Frederica's petition. As you will see, says Begbie, the respondent denies all the material facts alleged in our petition. His solicitor has written a letter, of which I enclose a copy, urging you to meet him with a view to reconciliation and restitution of conjugal rights. He also claims custody of your child.

Frederica reads the Answer, on its heavy foolscap paper.

The respondent, Nigel Reiver, by Messrs. Tiger and Pelt, his solicitors, in answer to the petition filed in this suit, says:

(1)   That he is not guilty of cruelty as alleged in the said petition.

(2)   That he is not guilty of adultery, as alleged in the said petition.

(3)   That he claims custody of the child, Leo Alexander, mentioned in the said petition, and proposes the following arrangements for his care and upbringing:—

That he should live with the respondent in the family home, Bran House, Longbarrow, where he will be cared for by the housekeeper, Miss Philippa Mammott, who has cared for him from birth, and by his two aunts, Miss Rosalind and Miss Olive Reiver.

That he should go to Brock's Preparatory School, for which he is entered, and to which his father went, and subsequently to Swineburn School in Cumberland, for which he is also entered.

That he should visit his mother regularly in the holidays and that she should visit him when she wishes to do so, at the family home, Bran House.

Frederica goes to see her solicitor. She sits in the barred light, and hears her own voice, a pleading voice, a panicky voice.

"He can't take him, can he?"

"It would be very unusual for the court to award custody of so small a child away from the mother. Very unusual. Very bad luck. We must ensure it doesn't happen. We must fight. Since your husband clearly intends to fight, we must fight back. I had imagined he might at least have admitted the adultery—if we would drop the cruelty—that would have been civilised, though we would always have to be careful about appearing to collude, or connive at such adultery. For our legal system is oppositional, Mrs. Reiver—the law requires that there be a guilty party and an innocent party, and is hostile to any appearance of *agreement* to divorce, seeks zealously for evidence of manufactured evidence, or lax moral attitudes suddenly conveniently tightened. Not that that appears to be the case here. Your husband is loving and forbearing—"

"Furious and pig-headed."

"As you please. He will say he is loving and forbearing. He condones desertion. He wants you back. You must *prove* that he treated you badly enough for divorce to be a reasonable requirement. I shall instruct Griffith Goatley. He fights like a bull terrier. We need witnesses to the cruelty, and witnesses to his behaviour when away from you. You would not consider instructing an enquiry agent?"

"No. That's a horrible idea. And besides, I can't afford it, I can't afford *anything*."

"I will ask about those clubs. The Honeypot. Tips and Tassels. There may be a doorman. A barman. An ex-doorman, an ex-barman. They are reluctant to be witnesses. It is not good for their employment. They may know a young woman who may be prepared to say something. It is worth a try. We must have a case."

"He threw an axe at me."

Begbie looks mournful. "We need to *prove* it."

"I have a huge scar. Pink. It throbs in rainy weather."

"We need to be able to *show* what caused it."

"I don't want Leo in a dormitory in a prep school. It's horrible, it's unnatural, I can't bear to think of it—he's *little*—"

"Lots of little boys survive quite adequately." A pause. "I did." Another pause. "The judge probably did."

His face is lugubrious, frowning with what might be anxiety and might be a kind of professional *Schadenfreude*.

"He'd *hate* it."

"We must hope it doesn't come to that. It shouldn't. I'll get Goatley. Meanwhile, think of *anyone* who can describe your husband's unreasonable, cruel, or aggressive behaviour. Maids? We must get on to the doctors. Your friends?"

"They didn't *see* him hurt me. They saw me shortly after."

"Hearsay evidence is not admissible."

"He *can't have* Leo."

Daniel keeps watch in the dark in St. Simeon's Church. Orange street light glares through the jumbled stained glass of the windows, producing a muted glare of acid colours on stone, which occasionally flare differently as headlights pass in the street. He sits in the shadow, behind a Victorian pillar, looking at the faded reproductions of Rubens's *Deposition* and Holbein's *Dead Christ* which Canon Holly has hung over the altar. It is October 28th and Daniel wishes to give thanks for, to contemplate, the ending of an evil. On this day the House of Commons, in a free vote, has passed the Murder (Abolition of the Death Penalty) Bill. Daniel sits in the presence of whatever haunts the dark stone and meditates on the panoply, the grisly ceremony, the ghoulish cruelty, of what has just been done away with. What he has felt, all his life since he first became aware of the pain of death, is not, mostly, a sympathetic identification with the sufferer, though that is part of it. He has seen and he has imagined the man or woman in the dock seeing the judge's black cap, hearing the sentence pronounced, having to do things that belong to the still living, walk back to the cell, eat, speak, defecate, breathe, as a human being certainly dead, a human being whose existence is the knowledge that in ten days, nine, eight, seven, six, five, four, three, two, one day, ten hours, nine, eight, seven, six, five, four, three, two, one, ten minutes, nine, eight, seven, six, five, four, three, two, one, they will come with the hood and ropes, and the dead legs must walk to the gallows and the trap. A death is a death, and this death is a peculiarly horrible death, because of its certainty, because of its public enactment, because it is unnatural, as many other murders are not unnatural. But a death is a death, Daniel knows. Many wait in pain. All human beings come there. What horrifies him about the infliction of capital punishment is the horror it spreads into the whole society which enacts it, connives at it, decrees it. The breath of evil in the court officials, the policemen and -women, the counsel at the bar, the judge, who together must enact the sick drama that leads to the killing. The evil that can be smelled in the cells and in the warders and in the other prisoners who witness the agony, with furtive glee or sick horror. The pleasure in pain that thrills in the press and in the sickened, the profoundly infected, imagination of the people as they imagine what can't be imagined, whether with a murderous delight, or a bloody righteous wrath, or with the unwilling, terrified, *damaged* identification with the sufferer's terror, which was his own response as a child. In Calverley he had met a blabbering man, a shaking man, who was a priest who had attended executions in Calverley Gaol, and had lost his mind in a mixture of guilt, terror and revulsion. A society that can make these mechanisms, Daniel believes, is a sick society, and if it cannot be called an inhuman society, it is only because cruelty is human, cruelty is part of our nature, as it is part of the nature of no other creature. (The warmongering chimpanzee is a discovery of the future.)

Daniel sits in the church and destroys in his mind, one by one, the elements of the narrative and the drama. He thinks of them all soberly, gagging as he always gags as he pronounces in his head "to be hanged by the neck until you are dead. And may God have mercy on your soul." He imagines the black cap and the posy on the judge's desk, the condemned cell and the last walk as Saint Ignatius Loyola taught his followers to picture and meditate on the Stations of the Cross, bringing the agony of the God-Man vividly to life, step by step in the dark-room of the brain, blood, sweat, broken bones, the stink, the roar, the failing muscles, the spitting crowd, the piercing thorns, the failing thighs and knees, the crunching shock of the nails. These things are obscene, and the obscenity is not in the murderous impulse, but in the ingenuity that devised and devises the long-drawn-out agony, the spectacle, the complicity of participants and passers-by. He cannot really see, in the dark, either the heavy, pearly, meat-stiff fall of Rubens's painted flesh, or the grim, stretched, leathery cadaver of the Holbein. Those two knew what flesh was, its beauty and intricacy, its mixtures of rose and wax, blue and grey, shadow and fatty sheen. They painted it at the moment of its dissolution, with aesthetic pleasure in their own power, love of the flesh as it was and would not be, alive in their steady contemplation of death. This is Christ, the divine man, a man tortured and executed, and perhaps, Daniel thinks, it is right after all to find God here, where human ingenuity in evil is most crassly lively and most disingenuously self-righteous. And it is good to thank whatever is for the end of evil, at least in this time and in this place. In later years, when the freedom of the 1960s is spoken of, Daniel will always think of this quiet dark night, when he cleared his imagination's charnel-house and torture-chamber of their gibbering ghosts, and ended sitting in a dark blue silent dome of night darkness, soft and cool and still.

A week before, exactly a week before the Murder (Abolition of the Death Penalty) Bill, in Hyde, in Cheshire, Ian Brady, twenty-six, a stock clerk, and Myra Hindley, twenty-three, a shorthand-typist, were charged with murdering Lesley Ann Downey, aged ten, whose body had been found buried in peat in the Pennine moors six days earlier. Brady was also charged with the murder of Edward Evans, aged seventeen. If the chronology had been a little different, Daniel will think, often, would he have had his quiet night?

Agatha Mond comes down to Frederica's basement to collect Leo for school. It is her day. She has Frederica's post in her hand. There are two fat foolscap envelopes, a small brown one, and one covered with small "Victorian scraps"—angels' heads and bullfinches, a lily and a rose. Leo is struggling with the zip of his anorak, with which he refuses to accept any help. He frowns. Frederica mimes distress and fury over his head to her friend, opens the foolscap letters rapidly, not because she is eager to know their contents, but because she dreads them, and formless dread is always worse than the known and delimited. A letter from Nigel's solicitor, Guy Tiger, is enclosed in a letter from her own solicitor, Arnold Begbie. The letter is about Leo. It is not the first. Nigel has taken to dispatching a steady stream of these legal documents. He does not write letters himself: language is not his medium. He has never written letters to Frederica. She has no box of dead love-letters to consider with incredulity or regret. Begbie's covering note says that the present letter requires careful thought. Frederica, unable to speak because of Leo, snatches up the dressmaking shears with which she has been making chains of paper men for her son, holds up the letter to Agatha, and mimes its destruction.

"Comes the blind Fury with th'abhorred shears," says Agatha. They grin. The quotation makes them both feel better. They do not question why this should be so: they are women who share a certain culture.

"Blind Fury is about right," says Frederica savagely.

"*Courage,*" says Agatha.

Leo zizzes his zip to a triumphant snap. He and Saskia and Agatha depart.

Frederica reads the letter again.

Dear Mrs. Reiver,

I am instructed by my client, Mr. Nigel Reiver, to put to you, through your solicitors, Messrs. Begbie, Merle and Schloss, some considered proposals for the welfare of your son, Leo Alexander Reiver.

My client wishes me to state clearly that the present separation between you is not of his seeking, and that his urgent wish is that you should return, with your son, to the matrimonial home and seek a reconciliation. He rejects entirely the imputations of cruelty and adultery set out in your Petition for Divorce, and seeks earnestly to prove to you that he is prepared to forgive your own desertion, which was entirely without cause, and without any previous warning, discussion or attempt to settle your supposed differences reasonably and amicably.

My client particularly and with great sorrow regrets your unprovoked and unconsidered decision to take with you his and your son, the said Leo Alexander Reiver. He believes that this action was not in the best interests of his son, who was a happy child, living in a cheerful and stable household, in which there were several relatives and a very loving housekeeper prepared to care for him and bring him up in the world into which he was born and where he will, in due course, take his rightful place as owner of Bran House.

My client is informed that you have taken the child to live in a deprived and socially unstable area of London. He is informed that you inhabit a basement flat in what could be described as a near-slum; that you arrange constantly changing and intermittent care for the boy whilst you absent yourself to earn money by part-time employments of various seasonal kinds. My client does not feel that this way of life is in the interests of his son. He has proposed, very generously, paying you a reasonable sum of money as maintenance for his son and yourself, so that whilst the said Leo Alexander is in your care you would be able to devote your full attention to him. My client believes that, if your abrupt departure from the matrimonial home was, as you have stated, to seek employment, your own priorities make you less fit to have the care and control of so small a child than those women who could give him their complete attention, in the comfortable home and healthy country surroundings where he grew up. My client believes that the boy's interests would best be served by his immediate return to the home he has known since birth. He would, of course, if you persist in your present way of life, grant you generous access to the boy, and would always make you welcome at Bran House, as its mistress, or as a visitor, as you may choose.

My client is also extremely concerned and distressed by the provisions you have made, without consulting him, for his son's education. On social and educational grounds, and with the welfare of the child uppermost in his mind, he begs you to reconsider your decision to send the boy to the William Blake School in Kennington, which he does not consider a suitable environment for a boy born into his family, or with Leo's expectations. The sons of the Reiver family have for the past three generations attended Brock's Preparatory School in Herefordshire and Swineburn School in Cumberland. It is my client's heartfelt hope and expectation that he will be able to give his son the excellent education he himself had, and that Leo may be educated amongst his peers, including several of his second and third cousins already at the schools.

In the present circumstances, my client proposes that his son be sent forthwith to Brock's School, where we have ascertained that a place will be held for him. As you are aware, my client will sue for custody of his son if and when your Petition for Divorce reaches the courts. He still earnestly hopes to avoid this eventuality by persuading you to return to the matrimonial home. In the interim, he suggests that it will be the fairest, most appropriate, and most beneficial arrangement if Leo is moved immediately to Brock's Preparatory School, where both his parents will be free to visit him on equal terms. His request is both reasonable and generous, and he hopes that you will give it your immediate and sympathetic attention . . .

She reads the second legal letter, which tells her that the fixing of a date for the hearing of her divorce has been deferred, since the Respondent has asked for time to prepare his case. She opens the brown letter, which contains a very small cheque from the Crabb Robinson Institute, and the one with stickers, which is an invitation to "A Studio Debauchery" from Desmond Bull. Bull has become interested in *collage,* of which the cherubs and lilies are an outpost. He is making a large picture of layers of faces, from past and present, newspapers and paintings, with Robespierre's eyes in Marilyn Monroe's face above Bronzino's Fraud's scaly tail, or with Roosevelt's seated figure cut into Titian's seated Pope. This work is at a chaotic stage, and varies from the banal to the suddenly witty and shocking. Desmond Bull is cheerfully certain that any day now Frederica will join him on his studio mattress. She likes his paintings: she likes him: what follows is obvious. Frederica, because of John Ottokar, cannot claim that she is prejudicing her legal freedom by this move, and is even tempted to make love to Bull to reassure herself that she is not tied to John Ottokar. Because of John Ottokar, she has started to take the Pill, which is making her heavy and bad-tempered, unless it is life that is making her heavy and bad-tempered. She has eaten two packets of pills now, day by day, one in September and one in October, and John Ottokar has vanished for almost exactly that period of time. Desmond Bull's blatant campaign has its attractions for that reason too: it gives the Pills some *point.*

She has not told Arnold Begbie about John Ottokar. There are various reasons for this, involved and at cross-purposes. Begbie will think she was lying when she said she had not committed adultery or incontinence or whatever the law calls it. This matters because she feels judged by Begbie, which ought to be nonsense, but is not. And then, to tell Begbie about John Ottokar is to make the relations with John Ottokar more solid, more real, than either she or John Ottokar wants to think they are. They are not adultery, which is serious: they are just sex. "Just sex" does not stand the glare of legal light upon it. It is as partial a description as "incontinence" or "adultery": it is provisional and does not bear looking at. There *are no words* with which Frederica feels able to explain her relations with John Ottokar to Arnold Begbie.

Frederica feels wild and oppressed. She takes the sharp shears and slices Guy Tiger's letter in two, vertically, and then again horizontally, and then again, until she has a handful of rectangular segments. This will not get rid of it, she reflects gloomily. More copies can endlessly be quartered, like the heads of the hydra. She picks up the pieces and lays them out on the desk. "A happy child living in Brock's School." The art students are excited by William Burroughs and his cut-ups. Frederica rearranges Tiger's letter into a kind of consequential structure. So.

A happy child living in Brock's School where there were several relations held for him prepared to care for him and will sue for custody of his son which he was born and when Petition for Divorce reaches the rightful place as owner of Bran hopes to avoid this eventuality my client is informed return to the matrimonial home, a deprived and socially unstable environment, suggests that it will be best that you inhabit a basement, the most beneficial arrangement a near-slum; that you arrange immediately to Brock's preparatory intermediate care for the boy, parents will be free to earn money part-time. His request is both kinds. My client does not care for the boy and he hopes that you in the interests of his son immediate and sympathetic paying you a reasonable would best be served by persist in your present way devote your full attention that if your abrupt access to the boy and would always find the matrimonial home as House or as its mistress or as a employment less fit to have the small child who was extremely concerned and distressed by their complete attention without consulting him, for his stable household, in sending the boy to the William Blake relatives and a very loving housekeeper into his family or bring him into the world into the Reiver family he will in due course have taken the child to live in Cumberland it is my client's area of London. he is informed he himself had what could be described as his peers including several constantly changing and sins already at the schools whilst you absent yourself his son be sent forthwith employments of various seasonal proposals for the welfare of Messrs Begbie, Merle and Schloss we have ascertained that the present separation is between his urgent wish for imputations of cruelty in the matrimonial home in the Interim to forgive your own desertion to settle your supposed differences and decision to take with you Alexander Reiver with great sorrow regrets persuading you to return to Swineburn School and to women who could give care and control of so heartfelt hope and expectation may be educated among money as maintenance in the comfortable home environment for a boy born your own priorities make departure from the welfare of the child.

Lawyers are concerned to make unambiguous statements with unquestionable conclusions; Frederica's cut-up has therefore less beauty than a cut-up of some richer text might have, but it does approximate to a satisfactory representation of her confusion, of her distress, of her sense that the apparent irrefutable clarity of Nigel's solicitor's arguments is a nonsense in her world. She considers it. She finds the Burroughs a student has pressed upon her—"*This* is the voice of now, *this* is where it was going, fragments shored against my ruin and all that, just try this, this is the voice of now, this is *release,* this is the ultimate."

"Cut-ups are for everyone. Anybody can make cut-ups. It is experimental in the sense of being *something to do.* Right here write now. Not something to talk and argue about."

"All writing is in fact cut-ups. A collage of words read overheard. What else? Use of scissors renders the process explicit and subject to extension and variation. Clear classical prose can be composed entirely of re-arranged cut-ups. Cutting and re-arranging a page of written words introduces a new dimension into writing enabling the writer to turn images in cinematic variation. Images shift sense under the scissors smell images to sound sight to sound sound to kinesthetic. This is where Rimbaud was going with his colour of vowels. And his 'systematic derangement of the sense.' The place of mescaline hallucination: seeing colours tasting sounds smelling forms."

Frederica considers this. It is both attractive and repellent as a way of seeing, as a way of acting. Frederica is an intellectual, driven by curiosity, by a pleasure in coherence, by making connections. Frederica is an intellectual at large in a world where most intellectuals are proclaiming the death of coherence, the illusory nature of orders, which are perceived to be man-made, provisional and unstable. Frederica is a woman whose life appears to be flying apart into unrelated fragments: an attempt to tear free from the life of country houses and families; a person who for two months has been a female body chemically protected from the haunting fear of conception; an angular female body symbiotically tied to a rushing, small, male red-headed energy, whose absence itself is sensed as a presence and as a claim; a mind coming to grips with the fact that English literature is a structure half connected to and half cut off from a European literature which was transfigured by Nietzsche and Freud; a person in a basement with not enough money; a memory containing most of Shakespeare, much of seventeenth-century poetry, much, too, of Forster, Lawrence, T. S. Eliot and the Romantics, a chancy baggage which once seemed a universal, reasonable necessity; a Petitioner in a Divorce Court; a wanderer in studios; a judge of the works of such as Phyllis Pratt and Richmond Bly. Frederica is a woman who sits at her desk and re-arranges unrelated scraps of languages, from apparently wholly discrete vocabularies: legal letters, letters about the Initial Teaching Alphabet from Leo's school; Leo's first written words, which are BUS and MAN; the literary texts and the quite other texts that dissect these texts; her reviews, her readers' reports, which do not use the critical vocabulary she has acquired, for this is useless in three-hundred-word segments. She is a being capable of turning her attention from a recipe for an *omelette aux fines herbes* to the *Tractatus,* from Dr. Spock to the Bible to *Justine.* Language rustles around her with many voices, none of them hers, all of them hers.

Like many human beings who feel that they are exploding with grief, confusion, or anger, Frederica has thought of controlling or venting (both contradictory verbs are appropriate) her pains by writing. She has even bought an exercise book in which to record what she feels, in which, she told herself in the stationer's shop, to reduce the lawyers' language to plain expressive English. The exercise book is golden in colour, with a laminated plastic cover, on which is a purple design of geometric flowers, like those we learn to make in school, with overlapping swoops of the compass, shifting the centre and the circumference to make petal in petal, half-moon meeting half-moon. Inside, it Frederica has written a first sentence.

"Much of the problem appears to be one of vocabulary." Which led to no sequel. As far as it goes, this sentence is acceptable, but there is no vocabulary to provide the next sentence. A week later, like a terrier shaking a rat, Frederica wrote:

"There is no vocabulary to provide the next sentence."

A month later, she wrote:

"Try simplicity. Try describing a day."

I woke up too slowly. My tongue was furry. There was a taste of—what? Metal, decay, old wine. I want to write "death" but that's exaggerating. I got up. I went to the bathroom. I did the things you do in the bathroom, piss, shit, replace the death-taste with an alien taste of nasty (?artificial) mint. I hate mint. I have always hated mint but I go on putting it in my mouth. I know I ought in this style to write about the pleasure and relief of pissing and shitting but I don't want to. It is ordinary and satisfactory and writing about it would be shocking, would look as if it were meant to be shocking, which would be the opposite of what I am trying to do. Do I know what I am trying to do? I am not enjoying writing in this style. When I had come out of the bathroom I went to wake Leo. His face was buried in the pillow: it was pink and sweaty where it touched it: it was dry and warm on top. I kissed it. Leo's smell—all his smells—are the best thing I know. I find I don't want to go into what they are like or why they are the best thing. This style won't do that, although it leads you in that direction, it makes you think, aha, yes, now I describe Leo's smell. Keep going. We had breakfast. We had boiled eggs and toast. The bread was a bit old. It always is. I like fresh bread but not enough to go out and get it. If I wrote about the pleasures of fresh bread in this style for long enough I might entice myself to go out and get some, but probably not. We had the usual fight about who ties Leo's shoes because we are late. The usual fight. Describe it. Come on. I can't. This style fills me with a dreadful nausea. People write whole books like this. It looks so clever and it's a cop-out. I wanted to try and think about what had gone wrong and *what I am for* and it is nothing to do with furry mouths or one-verb sentences or noticing things you notice all the time *gracefully,* but as though they hadn't been noticed before, as though they were shocking or surprising. At this rate I could write hundreds of thousands of words and get further and further away from thinking anything out.

Tonight I am teaching *Madame Bovary.* The thing about Madame Bovary was, she didn't teach *Madame Bovary.*

That's banal too. Writing things down makes everything *slightly worse.* Slightly worse, what a fate. Writing is compulsive. And useless. Stop writing.

Frederica considers these abortive beginnings. The desire to write something is still there, accompanied by the nausea. Once, after John Ottokar had made love to her and slept, she had tried to write what she felt about him, about lying with the blond head breathing on her breasts, about wondering whether he would come again, or stay, or settle, or vanish, about whether she herself could bear to hold herself open to him, or would close, would turn her face away, would retreat in a flurry of ink like a cuttlefish (her habitual metaphor for this manoeuvre). Do I love him, she had made herself write, a real question, but the sight of it, and the sight of the rows of sentences beginning with the first person singular had filled her with such distaste that quickly, quickly she had torn the pages out of the book, ripped them into scraps and flakes, and ground them down amongst tea-leaves and sprout-peelings in the bucket under the sink.

"I hate I," she had written in the notebook. This was the most interesting sentence she had written yet. She added the intellectual's question. "Why?" And an answer.

I hate "I" because when I write, "I love him," or "I am afraid of being confined by him," the "I" is a character I am inventing who/which in some sense drains life from me ME into artifice and enclosedness. The *real* "I" is the first I of "I hate I"—the *watcher*—though only until I write that, once I have noticed that, that I who hates "I" is a real I, it becomes in its turn an artificial I, and the one who notices that that "I" was artificial too becomes "real" (what is real) and so *ad infinitum,* like great fleas with lesser fleas upon their backs to bite 'em. Is the lesson, don't write? It is certainly, don't write "I."

This page had not been torn out. Frederica finds it faintly nauseating, but interesting.

She thinks, perhaps cut-ups. She has a vision of controlling the miseries of the divorce and its dragging negotiations by cutting it all up into a kind of nonsense-diary, which produces occasional gems of scrying, like "my client does not care for the boy," though Frederica's innate fairness cannot find much satisfaction in that. The problem is that Mr. Tiger's client *does* care for the boy. That is the problem. And beyond that how anyone as clever as she, Frederica Potter, once was could have got herself into the present mess. She gives a little laugh, rummages through her cyclostyled lecture-notes, and comes up with the quotations about wholeness from Forster and Lawrence. She cuts them away from her text, and slices them up in approved Burroughs-mode. A vertical snip, a horizontal snip, re-arrange. This method produces something interesting and loosely rhapsodic from the Lawrence:

She wanted to be made much of the age, was a dead distance of silence between the immanence of her peace superseding knowledge, height or colour, but something was only the third, unrealized could he know himself what not as oneself, but said "Your nose is beautiful being in a new one, a new, sounded like lies, and she was the duality. How can I say "I," he said, whispering with truth to be, and you have ceased to the real truth. It was transcended into a new oneness of having surpassed one because there is nothing to answer, old existence. How could travels between the separate new and unknown, not him, there is perfect silence of self at all. This I, this old letter.

In the new, superfine bliss she could not know there was no I and you, there to be adored. There were wonder, the wonder of existing between them. How could he tell summation of my being and of beauty, that was not form, or paradisal unit regained from the strange golden light. How love you, when I have ceased, her beauty lay in, for him. We are both caught up and your chin is adorable. But where everything is silent, disappointed, hurt. Even when all is perfect and at one. Speech "I love you, I love you," it was parts. But in the perfect Oneself, of having transcended the bliss.

Which says more or less what it was originally saying, with more or less the same rhythm, as though all the breathings of all the words were interchangeable. The Forster, more tightly constructed, will not deconstruct until cut into considerably smaller segments, when a certain effective contrast of high and low, abstract and solid words begins to work.

Outwardly he was cheerful, could only point out the salvation, all had reverted to chaos and in the soul of every man. By an incomplete ascetic whole of her sermon, only connect husband or widower, he had always, and both will be exalted, passion is bad a belief that is at its highest. Live in fragments passionately. Religion had connect, and the beast and the monk were read aloud on Sunday, life to either, will die. No gift of her own she would only connect! That was the form of a "good talking." The prose and the passion would be built and span their human love which she was never prepared to give. Only connect his obtuseness robbed of the isolation that there was no more to give. It need not take the souls quiet indications the bridge a white-hot hatred lives with beauty. One quality in Henry saints and love the Infinite, however much she reminded could be a little ashamed simply did not notice things she said. He never noticed bothers about my own inside, the sneaking belief that bodily desirable only when held respectable.

She pastes the three cut-ups, the solicitor's letter, the adjuration to connect, the ode to Oneness, next to each other in the notebook.

She thinks: I am being unjust. I am not thinking clearly. I am accusing Forster and Lawrence of making me marry Nigel, out of some desire for Union of Opposites, of Only Connecting the Prose and the Passion. Whereas in fact, at least in part, I married him for exactly the opposite reason, because I wanted to keep things separate. I thought the sex was good, was satisfactory, which is better than good, and I think I thought that because he was rich, I wouldn't have to be a housewife like my mother. I thought all the other parts of myself could go on being what they were, and marrying Nigel would deal with negotiating sex, and with not being a housewife. I deserved what I got, whatever that was: it includes Leo, who is not a question of what I deserve, but of *his own life*.

But the desire to Only Connect, the romantic bit, that was there *too*, we are a mixture of impulses. Here I go again, connecting to John Ottokar, disconnected from him.

She writes a word, underlining it, as a title. *Laminations*. She senses the shape of a possible form, a space where a form will be, that is not yet there to be apprehended. *Laminations*. Cut-ups are part of it. It is a form that is made partly by cutting up, breaking up, rearranging things that already exist. "All writing is in fact cut-ups. A collage of words read overheard." These sentences of Burroughs's sent a spiky thrill of recognition through her brain. *The point of words is that they have to have already been used, they have not to be new, they have to be only re-arrangements, in order to have meaning.* If you write "ragdon" or "persent" those are nothing, but write "dragon" and "serpent" and the thoughts and stories and fears and inventions and colours and stinks and softnesses and violence of human beings everywhere drag and float at the end of them like giant kites sailing from thin strings or monsters of the deep caught on fishermen's lines. Where the cut-ups go wrong is in an over-valuation of the purely random, a too great reliance on the human capacity to insist on finding meaning in the trivial, the flotsam and jetsam of the brain's tick and tock, messages on scraps of paper with one word on. Anything is a message if you are looking for a message. But the glare of an eye looking for a message anywhere and everywhere can be a mad glare, a pointless glare.

She writes down, slowly, under *Laminations*:

> I found my own growing inclination, which I discovered was not mine alone, to look upon all life as a cultural product taking the form of mythic clichés, and to prefer quotations to independent invention. (Thomas Mann, *Die Entstehung des Dr. Faustus*)

Quotation is another form of cut-up; it gives a kind of papery vitality and independence to, precisely, cultural clichés cut free from the web of language that gives them precise meaning. The Mann quotation looks solemn and academic compared to the cut-ups, but it has more life in it. Or a different life. "Only connect" is a cliché, and so is Lawrence's Oneness; also they are ambiguous words of power. You could quote other things, Frederica thinks, as the beginning of the form of what will be *Laminations* goes in and out of focus in her mind's eye. You could quote newspapers. Dostoevski made his novels from the clichés and the reported facts that are newspapers. In this context even the *faux-naïf* style of "I did the things you do in the bathroom" would be one cliché amongst the rustling others, and therefore admissible, contained, laminated. She thinks: I need a card index, not a notebook, I need to shuffle. You could quote your own life. Lawyer's letters amongst lectures on Mann and Kafka. Raw material, worked motifs.

That week, she adds:

> James told of how, when walking on a summer evening in the park alone, watching the couples make love, he suddenly began to feel a tremendous oneness with the whole world, with the skies and trees and flowers and grass—with the lovers too. He ran home in panic and immersed himself in his books. He told himself he had no right to this experience, but more than that, he was terrified at the threatened loss of identity involved in this merging and fusion of his self with the whole world. He knew of no half-way stage between radical isolation in self-absorption or complete absorption into all there was. He was afraid of being absorbed into Nature, engulfed by her, with irrevocable loss of his self; yet what he most dreaded, that also he most longed for. Mortal beauty, so Gerard Manley Hopkins said, is dangerous. If such individuals could take his advice to meet it, then let it alone, things would be easier. But it is just this which they cannot do. (R. D. Laing, *Divided Self,* p. 91)

To this she adds:

> The god ascends the stage in the likeness of a striving and suffering individual. That he can *appear* at all with this clarity and precision is due to dream interpreter Apollo, who projects before the chorus its Dionysiac condition in this analogical figure. Yet in truth that hero is the suffering Dionysos of the mysteries. He of whom the wonderful myth relates that as a child he was dismembered by Titans now experiences in his own person the pains of individuation, and in this condition is worshipped as Zagreus. We have here

an indication that dismemberment—the truly Dionysiac suffering—was like a separation into air, water, earth and fire, and that individuation should be regarded as the source of all suffering, and
rejected. (Nietzsche, *Birth of Tragedy*, p. 66)

And:

> World declaration hot peace shower! Earth's grass is
> free! Cosmic poetry Visitation accidentally happening
> carnally! Spontaneous planet-chant Carnival! Mental
> Cosmonaut poet-epiphany, immaculate supranational
> Poesy insemination!
>
> Skullbody love-congress Annunciation,
> duende concordium, effendi tovarisch illumination,
> Now! Sigmatic New Departures Residu of Better
> Books & Moving Times in obscenely New Directions!
> Soul revolution City Lights Olympian lamb-blast!
> Castalia centrum new consciousness hungry
> generation Movement roundhouse 42 beat
> apocalypse energy-triumph!
>
> You are not alone!
> Miraculous assumption! O Sacred Heart invisible
> insurrection! Albion! awake! awake! awake! O
> shameless bandwagon! Self-evident for real naked
> come the Words! Global synthesis habitual for this
> Eternity! Nobody's Crazy Immortals Forever!
>
> Esam, Fainlight, Ferlinghetti, Fernandez, Ginsberg,
> Paolo Lionni, Daniel Richter, Trocchi, Simon Vinkendog,
> Horovitz. Invocation to First International Poetry
> Incarnation at Albert Hall.

And:

Vladimir:	Rather they whisper.
Estragon:	They rustle.
V.	They murmur.
E.	They rustle.
	Silence
V.	What do they say?

E.	They talk about their lives.
V.	To have lived is not enough for them.
E.	They have to talk about it.
V.	To be dead is not enough for them.
E.	It is not sufficient.
	Silence
V.	They make a noise like feathers.
E.	Like leaves.
V.	Like ashes.
E.	Like leaves.

(*Waiting for Godot,* p. 63)

And:

The head Sublime, the heart Pathos, the genitals Beauty, the hands & feet Proportion.

As the air to a bird or the sea to a fish, so is contempt to the contemptible.

The crow wish'd every thing was black, the owl that every thing was white.

Exuberance is Beauty.

If the lion was advised by the fox, he would be cunning.

Improvement makes straight roads; but the crooked roads without Improvement are the roads of Genius.

Sooner murder an infant in its cradle than nurse unacted desires.

Where man is not, nature is barren.

Truth can never be told so as to be understood, and not be believ'd.

Enough! or Too much.

(Blake, *Marriage of Heaven and Hell,* Plate 10)

It is like any student's commonplace book. It rustles with uneasy energies. One night, on an impulse, Frederica adds an anecdote.

After the extra-mural class, in the pub, Humphrey Maggs told us the story of a friend of his whose mother died and left her nothing but debts and a bacon-slicer. She had had a shop which had gone bust, and all that was left was a bacon-slicer. She took it into the cold store of the butcher's shop, which was empty and about to be sold, and tried to slice her wrists with it. It was hard to get her wrists near the blade, and it was too cold in there for her to go on trying: she collapsed in there, in a mess of blood, "a welter of gore, you could say," he said. The cold stopped the blood running and "they" found her and took her to hospital. They tied her up and stitched her up. She liked it there. She became a hospital orderly and after a bit trained as a nurse. She works in an operating theatre. She likes that. She feels needed. No, I don't know what became of the bacon-slicer, he said when I asked him. I expect she sold it. I expect it's slicing bacon somewhere, doing what it was designed for.

This story is interesting because of the words bacon-slicer, and for that matter the thing to which they refer, a whirring blade with a precise function which is not self-slaughter. It is a tale of congruities and incongruities, perhaps spoiled by this excrescent commentary which I may learn to omit.

Two days later, she adds another.

A woman is sitting in Vidal Sassoon's salon, the Bond Street one. She is having her long hair, which she has always had, shorn into one of those smooth, swinging cuts, like blades in their precise edges and points. Two young men are working together on the nape of her neck. Her feet are surrounded by shanks and coils and wisps and tendrils of what until recently was her body. It sifts, it is soft, it pricks between her collar and her skin. One man leans over her and holds the two points of her new hair down, dragged down, to her jaw. He hurts her. If she tries to look up, he gives her a little push down again, which hurts her. The other works above the vertebrae of her naked nape with his pointed shears. She can hear the sound of hair on blade: a silky rasping. He nicks her skin with his points. He hurts her. She is almost sure that the small hurts are deliberately inflicted. Over her neck the two talk. "Look at that one then, look at her strut, she thinks she's the *bee's knees,* the *cat's whiskers* and she's a walking *disaster,* look at that clump he's done at the back, like a great *bubo* all bulging and she can't see it, she can't see it jiggle and wiggle as she walks, she thinks she looks *delicious,* he told her so, he held the mirror at the right angle, so she couldn't see what a godawful *mess* he had made, cutting higher and higher trying to make it better and now there's nothing left to cut, only a gob on the back of her *lumpy head*." They laugh. The woman under their hands tries to look up and is jerked down. She thinks, I will always remember this, but doesn't know why; there are many humiliations, many disasters, why will she always remember this one? They let her head up. She sees her face through tears. The line is like a knife along her jaw. They tell her she looks lovely. All the women in the room have the same cut and all look lovely in the same way, except those who don't. When she moves her head, the curtain of her hair swings and re-forms into its perfect edge. Her neck is naked. She gives the two a tip, though she would like not to. Her hair looks good. Does she?

This is a distinct improvement on "I went to the bathroom": it has no "I" although it is a true story, and a story about Frederica. It gives her a quite disproportionate aesthetic pleasure, both because the words do not immediately nauseate her, and because she has somehow *got it right,* has pinned something down. (As the young men had her pinned down, she thinks, wondering if this is part of the pleasure.) The incident had rankled in her memory but is now pleasing and shapely. It gains something from being next to, but not part of, the cut-ups, the bacon-slicer, Nietzsche, Blake, and *The Divided Self.*

XV

❧❧❧❧❧

October 1965

The extra-mural class is in full swing. Frederica is teaching Dostoevski and Thomas Mann, Kafka and Sartre. John Ottokar has not signed up for the current session, nor has he said anything to Frederica about this. Most of the rest of the class are there, at ease with each other now, knowing where to look for a response. Couples have formed, jealousies have deepened. Jude Mason has not returned, though his hippopotamus-grey skin can be seen shining under the red lights of the life-class studio at the Samuel Palmer School, and postcards with Nietzschean quotations appear in Frederica's pigeonhole there. Leo has made a friend at school who also lives in the square: a tall black boy with a broad gentle face, whose name is Clement Agyepong; he has a brother called Athanasius, a mother who is a nurse on night duty, and an occasional father, who "sells things." The Agyepongs are second-generation English, whose parents came from Ghana. Frederica likes Clement. Clement belongs to a gang of small boys who race around the square and are suspected of ringing door bells and running away, of twisting off windscreen wipers, nicking milk bottles and vandalising the window-boxes which are beginning to appear on the more gentrified houses, which have new white paint and new brass knockers, which are occasionally unscrewed. Frederica feels an emotion about Clement that she dare not describe to anyone. She is pleased that he and Leo *really like each other,* two boys playing and talking together. She is pleased that she herself likes Clement so much, laughs at his jokes, listens to his stories. She is pleased that her son has a black friend who is *a friend*. She is also pleased because before Clement was

391

Leo's friend, Leo had been knocked over by-accident-on-purpose once or twice, playing in the square. Dinky cars had gone out and had not come back. His tricycle disappeared and mysteriously re-appeared, without its bell, without the rubber treads on its pedals. These things worry Frederica. She fought her own battles at school, was bashed, bitten, tripped and torn. This is normal. But she always felt safe walking to school in the village as a small child, or riding into Blesford on the bus as a larger one. She wants to see Hamelin Square as an urban village, but it is not. It is less safe. She has not begun to imagine how much less safe she is—along with her contemporaries—going to feel it is. Urban fear in 1965 is a sprout, no more. She is more afraid of Nigel's solicitors finding out about the bicycle and the Dinky toys. Her bruised and tearful son, she thinks, wiping eyes and knees, could be cantering in the paddock on Sooty. Or being tortured by horrid sprogs in shorts in some prep school locker-room, she thinks, more darkly, offering home-made scones and jam to Clement, and reading *The Tale of Mr. Tod* to both boys.

Clement is collecting wood for the bonfire. It is traditional to have a Guy Fawkes bonfire on the earthy tip in the middle of Hamelin Square. The boys rush around to local shops, cadging vegetable crates and broken chairs. Too much cardboard is bad, Clement tells Agatha and Frederica, it flares up and flakes all over, you need wood that will burn steady. Nothing like car-seats that will stink, either, he says, good wood. The fathers, middle-class and working-class, bring contributions. One night the whole collection is stolen in the small hours, and never recovered, though expeditionary forces are sent out to inspect rival bonfires on local bombed sites and football fields. The collecting starts again and guards are mounted, little boys in the daytime, the odd lounging man in the dark. Leo is excited. He does not know what the bonfire will be but it fills his imagination with light on the night sky. He is desolated to find that the great day occurs in fact in the middle of one of his now regular weekend visits to Bran House. He tells Frederica he won't go. This is the first time he has made any demur about his movements between his parents. He comes back from Bran House white-faced and solemn, and says nothing of what he has done or said there. Frederica never asks him, and hopes that those in Bran House maintain the same discretion. She does not like to imagine Pippy Mammott or Olive and Rosalind asking probing questions about the William Blake School, or Clement, or John Ottokar, who has not been introduced to Leo, but has been seen by him, once or twice, sitting with Frederica—only sitting—after Leo has been safely tucked up in bed. Frederica *does not want to know* what Leo is being asked, and this deep desire for ignorance keeps her quiet. But she imagines, and is afraid. Out of what Leo might inadvertently say could be made the evidence on which he will be taken from her.

Leo says: I won't go there when it's the bonfire. *I won't.* Frederica says: You must. Leo says: I won't. I will see this bonfire, I *will be there.* Frederica says she expects there will be a bonfire at Bran House he can see. Leo works himself up into a breathless rage, wheezing and squealing, reminding Frederica of her father and herself. She says, "I *can't* ask your father." Leo says, "You can. You just won't." "Daren't," says Frederica. "You hate me, you don't love me, you don't want me," shrieks her son in his wrath. Frederica telephones Arnold Begbie, who replies, after an exchange of letters, that he is told there will be an excellent bonfire, a positive beacon, in Herefordshire. Leo has another tantrum and ceases to speak. He does not speak for twenty-four hours. The next evening, Frederica comes in with his supper to hear him speaking on the telephone.

"You told me. *You* told me how to make the number. In case I ever wanted you, you said, and I do want you. I want to go the bonfire *here* in vis square. We're building it."

He listens.

"No, Mummy doesn't *want* me to stay here, she says I can't, she says she doesn't want me."

He listens.

"I know. It would be nice there, too. But I've *set my heart* on vis bonfire."

Frederica admires his phrase. I've set my heart.

"I told you, she doesn't want me to stay. Otherwise, I wouldn't need to telephone, would I? She isn't *reasonable,* you know she isn't. She doesn't understand how much I *really need to* see vis bonfire with my friends. She thinks you won't understand I only want to see vis bonfire, but I know you will understand. You do, don't you?"

He listens.

"So I can stay? *Thank you.* I knew you'd understand. I'll find her. You'll talk to her, you'll *tell* her. Just *tell* her. Here she is."

"Frederica?"

"Yes."

"What is all this? What have you been doing to him? Why can't he see this bonfire he's set his heart on?"

"I thought you would want to hold to your weekend."

"And have him think I'm a tyrant. Weekends can be changed, can't they? If he wants something so much, he ought to be able to ask for it, without you riding roughshod over him. *Can't* you have him, or something? What are you doing?"

"Of course I can have him. I can always have him. I just—"

"I expect you had something else on. As far as I'm concerned, he's welcome to stay for the bonfire. I'll have him the weekend before, that suits me quite well, I've got things in Holland . . . Never mind that. Same arrangement, weekend earlier. Put him back on."

"Thank you," says Leo. "I knew you'd make it all right."

The phone makes a gratified quacking.

Frederica goes crossly into the kitchen.

Leo comes back from his next visit to Bran House with his red hair shorn and shaved, so that his pale crown shows through. Frederica is horrified. She catches him up in her arms—he clings, as he always does, tight, choking tight. She says, "Oh, what have they done to you?"

"Pippy said I looked like a little girl. Like a fairy, she said, or one of those hippies. She said she'd make a little man of me."

"Do you like it?"

"Not much. I feel a bit cold. I fink I look a bit silly. Clement's hair's short, though. His is curly. Mine was all floppy. I ought to have gone to the hairdresser, Pippy said."

"You don't like the hairdresser."

"No. I don't like those clipper things on my neck. Pippy did it with scissors and a razor. She said, 'Admire my handiwork.' Everyone did admire it. But it is a bit cold and I look a bit sort of skull-like. But it'll grow, won't it?"

"It will."

Clement and Athanasius, known as Thano, have also made a Guy, which they push around the local streets in a broken pushchair. "Penny for the Guy," they say at the mouth of the local Tube, at the entry to Hamelin Square. The body of the Guy is made from an old stained, tea-leaf-coloured pillow, clothed in a green-and-orange shirt covered with parrots and palm trees. It has a limp pair of pink rubber gloves pinned to its "shoulders," and a pair of diminutive infant's plimsolls, cracked and holed, propped at the base of its lolling trunk. It has a paper mask-face, done on bright orange shiny paper with black felt-tips, round eyes with long, spiky cartoon lashes, a bravado curly moustache. This is tied to a punctured football, on top of which sits an old baseball cap, with the legend SUNRISE RISE AND SHINE! on its brow. Agatha, confronted by this vision at the mouth of the Tube, studies it critically.

"OK, I'll give you a sixpence, because you have done some work. Someone tried to get money out of me for a Daz box with a smiley-face drawn on it. But I can't bear your Guy's horrible armlessness and leglessness. Bring him round this evening and we'll see what we can do." Clement and Thano duly appear with their creaking conveyance, and Agatha helps them to stuff and stitch old tights with waste paper—the Guy's new legs have a certain androgynous curvaceousness, and his arms are plump and solid. Agatha tells Frederica that she was filled with pity and terror at the sight of the dangling gloves, "like parody thalidomide sufferers." She hates the whole business of Guys, she says, the whole idea of celebrating the burning of a minor conspirator, all those centuries ago. I know, says Frederica, but I remember what fun it all was, after the war, when I was little, when we had fireworks again. I don't want them *not* to have what we had. And then you think, how dreadful, a man's fingers and innards all bursting and sizzling, the *pain,* how can we? I know, says Agatha.

The characters of *Flight North* have reached what appears to be an impassable wall of icy rock, sheer, glassy, frozen, louring. They are based in the Last Village, a tiny community which lives in ice huts around a very small geyser in a very small lake in the midst of a frozen waste. In the depths of the lake, in the warm waters, swim shoals of coral-coloured shrimp and steel-blue darting fish, which the people eat sparingly, on certain feast days only. They are globular people, with lovely bracelets of shining fat round their wrists and elbows and knees; they have rose-red faces with round apple cheeks, framed in furry hoods made from the skins of bears and foxes and martens; they look cheerful, but are not. The company of travellers or fugitives has been augmented considerably: they have acquired an ancient, draggled Thrush, who speaks when he chooses, which is not often; a Crow, whose speech is understood only by Artegall, who does not entirely trust it; a strange hound, grey and frequently invisible, which Saskia believes will turn out to be a Wolf; and a strange creature found by Mark in a cave on a moor, which some-times appears to be a squat toad-like minor dragon, and sometimes is clearly only a lump of flinty stone with glinting silica in the ledges under what appear to be its "brows." It is about the size of a large tom-cat, and in its stony form heavy. Mark, who mostly has to carry it, is often ready to abandon it, but the Thrush says its moment will come, and it has various useful gifts, like the power to start fires in wet wood. The most recent recruit is called Fraxinius, and moves in and out of resembling a human being as Dracosilex moves from stone to reptile. Fraxinius is one and a half times as tall as the men of the party, and skeletally thin and gangling. Everything about him is pale buffs and browns and straw colours—his eyes, his caramel-coloured teeth, his ivory lips, his bushy hay-coloured brows, his barley-sugar smoking eyes, his shoulder-length, knotted, mud-coloured hair "like a hillside which has lain under snow." He can appear to resemble a broom, or a besom, or a clothes pole, and moves, when he can be seen to move, slow and creaking, but when he is not watched, or seen out of the corner of an eye, he appears to bundle along weightlessly, like tangled straw on the wind. The Last Village suits neither Fraxinius nor Dracosilex. Fraxinius spends his time slumped like a broken ladder in a corner of a hut, growing paler and drier in the smoke from the perpetual central hearth. Dra-cosilex squats like a boring stone. The Thrush has its head under its wing. The Crow reports that the inhabitants of the Last Village are building a great fire on the mountain ledge near the black ice-wall of the escarpment.

Clement and Thano have taken to listening to the story. Saskia origi-nally objected to this but has come round—they share not her private night-time narration but a kind of bumper recapitulation and—almost always—dramatic Shock—which is narrated on Sunday afternoons. Agatha says that the requirement of the Sunday Shock is formally very satisfying, no doubt like constructing episodes of novels like *The Idiot* or *Dombey and Son*. The story does not usually have anything to do with the daily lives of its narrator or listeners, but in this case the Bale Fire has been growing *pari passu* with the bonfire in the mud in the centre of Hamelin Square.

Agatha sits on the sofa, in a black velvet top like a mediaeval page's surcoat, and a pair of silvery knitted trousers. Her dark hair is loose and falls about her face. Saskia is curled up against her. Clement and

Thano sit side by side on the floor by the fire. Frederica and Leo are in an armchair.

"Mark and Artegall offered to help with the collection of wood, but the villagers refused sullenly, saying their fire was their own handiwork. They travelled long distances in search of the wood, which had to be dead and dry; they dragged it back on rough sledges they made from poles tied together with hide. There were not many trees on the Grüner Waste; what there were were stunted thorn bushes, tenacious of life, leaning along the wind which always blew through their fingers, full of ice crystals, which settled there like an encrustation of diamonds.

"Dol Throstle made friends with an old village woman called Throgga, who lay muffled and wheezing in a heap of skins by the fire, toasting fragments of goat-cheese in its embers, or drowsing. None of the villagers talked to Throgga; they brought her beakers of water, and sometimes the leg of a roasted rat or rabbit, but they treated her otherwise as if she was not there. For this reason, perhaps, she was glad to talk to Dol Throstle, and told her tales about the Bale Fire.

" 'It is always set alight an hour before midnight on the Longest Night,' said the old woman. 'In good years, we cook a feast of roots and baked scones and roast ptarmigan in its embers at dawn. If it burns very bright, it is a sign that there will be Spring. We do not have Spring every year here, you must understand. Some of the young things cannot remember Spring. But in *good years* Spring comes and the sun is hot and golden for a day, or a few days, or even a few weeks, and all sorts of herbs and flowers and bushes spring out of the ice, which runs away in little rushing rivers full of cresses—and the sky is the colour of a thrush's egg, not the iron colour it is now.'

" 'It will be hard for the fire to burn at all this year,' says Dol Throstle. 'Out there there is nothing but sleet, icy rain, cold and running and freezing when it gets darker.'

" 'They cover the Wood with skins,' says Throgga. 'But the damp gets in, and a wet wind can prevent the fire from taking hold.' "

There are steps on the stairs. A head comes round the door, blond, smiling a little. It is John Ottokar.

"I knocked," he says. "No one answered."

"We are listening to this story," says Leo, reproving.

John Ottokar takes off his duffel coat. He is wearing his brilliant patchwork sweater. He takes a step into the circle.

"Can I stay and listen?" he says. "Don't mind me. I'll just sit here. Is that all right?"

He is courteous, he looks tentatively at Agatha, he sits down on the carpet beside Frederica's armchair. Her dangling hand brushes the thick pale hair. Agatha is mildly put out. She flushes. I don't know, she says. *Go on,* say Saskia, Leo and Clement. Agatha shrugs and goes on. Throgga tells how the young men must leap the burning fire. The higher it is when they leap it, the brighter the coming year will be. The weather deteriorates.

"Never had the travellers seen such rain, a rain of ice, of hailstones, of sheets of frozen slush, which turned the walls of the snow-huts to dripping glaciers in the brief daytime and to casques of ice at night, which burned any unwary finger that came near their surfaces. The villagers began to look unpleasantly at the Company: they began to say they had brought ill luck and that the Fire would never light whilst they were there. Throgga told Dol Throstle there was secret talk of driving them away, back into the Grüner Waste. Or worse, Throgga said, but would not say what 'worse' was."

John Ottokar sighs, an exhausted sigh, and leans his head back against the arm of Frederica's chair. The story moves on: the villagers mutter, and when the day for the Bale Fire comes, their tinder is wet and the brands they try to take from the huts to the high ledge with the fire on it, sputter and die in the wet wind. The Crow tells Artegall that Dracosilex can light the Bale Fire, and Artegall replies testily that no doubt he could, if he were in his reptile form, but he is a stone and nothing but a stone, and there is no art to revive him.

" 'There is a way,' said the Crow. 'You must take him to the geyser and bathe him in its warm waters, and wash him, and turn him, and he will become flesh again. For he is a salamander and salamanders are at home in the hot depths of geysers: they become lively, there.'

"So the two boys carried the heavy stone down to the geyser lake and plunged their arms into its warm, bubbling depths, holding the stone being very carefully, and lapping the water round him. And their fingers felt the cold stone quicken, and become rough skin, and twitch, and they felt a heartbeat, and the thrum of blood, and the stone toad put out thrusting little legs, and a stubby tail, which had never previously manifested itself, and it twisted out of their clutching hands and pushed off purposefully into the depths.

"There was a long silence, broken only by the bubbling of the geyser in the pool.

" 'He likes it down there,' Mark said. 'It makes him lively. I expect he'll stay for ever and eat shrimps.'

"Artegall hung over the pool, staring down through steam and troubled water and saw two bright golden eyes staring up at him.

" 'Dracosilex, Dracosilex, come up and help us light the fire.'

"And slowly the beast returned to them, lithe now and shining, fiery-crested and gleaming olive-gold. Artegall received him in his arms and wrapped him in his own coat, and hurried across the icy scrub and up the mountain, steaming from exertion and because of the heat of the wet creature in his wet coat in his arms.

"The villagers were gathered in the driving sleet, staring at the great beacon of wood, which was well built, but soaked through in its upper layers. One of the men said that never, even in the worst year in human memory, had the fire refused to light at all. One said that there should be seven different kinds of wood in the fire, and only six were certainly there, with a doubtful twig or two that might or might not be the seventh, horn-wood, a wood of a forest tree rarely found and susceptible to frosts. Artegall came forward and said that if it was permitted for him to intervene, he had a way to light the Bale Fire. One old man said it could only ever be lit by a brand from the ashes of the fire which had been lit last year from the ashes of last year's Bale Fire. One old woman asked Artegall, what was his way, and he opened his jacket, which smelled slightly scorched, and there was the lively creature, glowing red and gold like coals under his craggy grey-green skin. And the old woman said the dragon was a Sending, a magic gift that should be accepted, and the old man said it was dangerous magic which would threaten their traditional ways. But the people were cold and despondent in the rain and snow, and perhaps for that reason the old woman's enthusiasm prevailed over the natural sluggishness of the villagers. So Artegall was permitted to put Dracosilex on the stone ledge near the fire, and he set him down, and asked him to do what he could, to help if he might, and stepped back. And Dracosilex squatted there, glowing on the iron earth, and swayed a little, and opened his mouth, and sighed a great sigh. And out of his mouth, like the tongue of a chameleon, came a sin-uous noose of what seemed to be liquid flame, which wrapped itself round the Bale Fire, and again, and again, three times, in a coil. And Dracosilex closed his mouth again, but the liquid thread of flame hung there on the wet wood, and there was a spitting and hissing and a steaming and a sizzling, and the wood began to sprout buds and shoots of flames, which crackled and caught. And soon the whole fire was roaring and blazing so that no force on earth could have stopped it.

"Never was seen such a fire! The villagers roasted meats and made lardy cakes of fat and flour in its outreaches, and from its summit great blades of flame, red and yellow shot with emerald and bright blue, painted the dark sky and flickered bravely in the diminishing sleet, and wrinkled and waved in the wind. All night they danced, and when it was still quite high, towards dawn, the young men began to leap the flames, dropping pebbles, some black, some white, into the embers as they leaped. And some of the women and girls leaped, too—they all wore trousers, in that country, for the cold made nonsense of skirts—and the watching crowd began a growling, rolling kind of song, to a small drum and a bone pipe, as the leaping grew faster and more furious, and a kind of stamping dance took up the new rhythm. And one hot girl took Mark's hand, and made him jump with her; he was afraid, high above the heat, with the tongues of flame reaching up for him from the cauldron of coals, and he came through with singed eyebrows, and smoky lashes, and tears in his eyes. And Artegall took a little run, and leaped, just high enough, and landed in ash, spraying himself with sparking cinders. And two great men lifted Dol Throstle high in the air as though she was an inflated skin bottle, and she closed her eyes, and felt the heat, and opened them, and saw the cold black night glistening against the firelight. And then two of the young men appeared, when everyone had jumped, half-leading, half-dragging, half-carrying the fragile fawn body of Fraxinius. Dol Throstle stepped forward then, and said that it wasn't right to make the creature jump; he wasn't well, as could be seen, and was dry as tinder, and not part of the community. But they said he must jump, he was the last, he must go over. He stood there, drowsed or dazed it seemed, with his knotty locks hanging on his shoulders, and his thin arms dangling at his side. And then he said, in his strange whistling voice, 'I am agreeable.'

" 'We'll drag you out, if you fall,' said the village lads, not too pleasantly, for everyone had in their mind a vision of the conflagration that would follow if this desiccated being were to tumble on hot coals. And Dol Throstle said again, 'He's so dry, he'll *attract* the fire, the flames'll go for him.'

"And the old woman said, 'The flames only go for whom they choose. They will let him pass, unless they choose him.'

" 'I am agreeable,' said the thin creature again, and he shook off the hands of those who held him, and set off in an ungainly shamble towards the Bale Fire.

"And when he came to it, he took a leap, and rose high, high, like a dry leaf in the current of an updraught, and seemed to float and sail against the night sky, which was now paler, deep blue, not black. He hung above the burning logs like a great bat or owl, and they all cried out, at his lightness, at

400

his ease, at his weightlessness. And then he came eddying down, not on the other side, but on to the coals, into the very heart of the fire. And the fire took hold of him greedily, and took energy from him. He blazed—hair, hands, arms—and a wild smoke enveloped his blazing form. Dol Throstle began to weep, and Mark set forward to rescue him, calling for help. But Fraxinius stood there and blazed, and as he blazed, he changed beneath their eyes, drawing energy and form from the flames, which drew energy and form from him. In the red light he became green; his muddy hair became a curtain of new tendrils and new leaves; his outstretched twiggy arms put out shoots of green and his legs became thick, green, living trunks, upholding a body pliable and liquid, emerald and mossy, above which was a smiling green-gold mask from the eyes and mouth of which sprouted young green shoots, and above which twined a crown of shining leaves. And when he was fully grown, he strode out of the fire, with long, sure steps, a tall shimmering green figure with a mane of emerald hair, who wore a cloak of flames which enveloped him and floated after him in the air. And he strode away from the company and away from the folk of the Last Village, and came to the impassable rock face, and put his hand against it. And where he put his hand there was a rushing of green flaming water and melted ice, and thaw of molten rock, which ran away like lava. And the rock face dissolved, or split, into a high, narrow passage, inside which granite steps led into a tunnel apparently walled with thick pillars and, as it were, twisted hanks or root masses all made of green, green ice that gave off light in sparkings as he came near it, and reflected the movement of his flaming leaves as he passed. And he went into the roots of the mountain, and they saw his bright conflagration wink and diminish as he went on into the depths, shining and striding.

"And when he had gone, the fire was dimmed, and the sky was fiery with the dawn, and the crack in the mountain was dark and dangerous, but it was not closed."

Agatha invites everyone to Sunday brunch. John Ottokar says he would love to stay; he and Agatha smile at each other. Frederica is partly pleased—she would like John Ottokar to know Leo in a quiet and uncomplicated and uncompromised way. She is grateful to Agatha. She sees that John Ottokar sees that Agatha is beautiful. She gets up to help Agatha to make the impromptu meal. She herself could not provide one: she has eggs, a little cheese, fruit, two pieces of chicken. Agatha makes a large salad, with fish, and beans, and eggs, and green things and tomatoes. Clement and Thano say they have to go home. They have to go to church, they say vaguely. They are

Catholics, but not Catholics who abjure Guy Fawkes Day. Agatha says she will make pancakes to follow the salad. Frederica beats the batter. Agatha says: "He seems to be a nice young man."

"He comes and goes."

"That's OK, isn't it?"

"I don't know when he will come or go."

"Do you want to?"

"I don't *want to* want to. I don't want him to matter that much, too much. I can't afford . . ." She doesn't finish that sentence. She starts another. "But it isn't very *convenient,* not knowing from one day to the next, whether someone will come or not."

"Can't you ask?"

"I don't think so." She thinks. "I don't know that any answer I'd get would mean anything."

"Things you don't know," says Agatha, "take up energy, they rankle in the mind. Best not to let them. A counsel of perfection, I do know."

"He's nice, though."

"He's certainly beautiful. And seems nice enough, yes."

Frederica thinks that Agatha never has any men visiting, young or old. You would think, she thinks, that Saskia had been produced by parthenogenesis. But that can't be. There is, or was, someone, somewhere. Will she ever be told? Frederica is beginning to doubt it.

In Agatha's sitting-room, John Ottokar is teaching Leo and Saskia a game. Scissors, paper, stone. "You put out your hands together," he says. "*Simultaneously,*" Leo says. "Simultaneously," John Ottokar agrees. His smooth gold hair falls forwards over his brow. He shows them. A flat hand, paper. Forked fingers, scissors. A clenched fist, stone. Scissors cut paper, stone blunts scissors, paper wraps stone. The children are entranced. They play quite differently. Leo changes his shape at each game: he is stone scissors stone paper scissors paper stone paper. Saskia holds on to one form patiently: paper paper paper paper, then suddenly scissors, then stone stone stone stone stone, scissors. John Ottokar laughs and keeps the score. "I played this when I was your age," he tells them. "With my brother."

"Who won?" says Leo.

"No one," says John Ottokar. "We always put out the same thing. Identical. Two scissors, two stones, two papers."

"Boring," says Leo.

"Not exactly. Frustrating, though. Not exactly *playing*."

"Like when Leo and me make the same noise on the recorder 'cause we only know C and B," says Saskia.

"A bit like that," says John Ottokar. "We used to play the recorder, too."

He stays and plays, quietly, all afternoon. He cuts out newspaper trees with scissors, he glues cut-out dinosaurs in a book, he talks easily to Agatha and Frederica. He stays to supper and helps put Leo to bed, sitting in the corner of Leo's bedroom, out of the light, and listening whilst Frederica reads about Moldy Warp and Fuzzypeg and the old Roman coin. When Leo is tucked in bed, he follows Frederica into her own room, draws the blind, and touches her on the shoulder. Frederica, preoccupied, turns to face him. He puts a hand on her neck, sure, and a hand on her buttocks, sure, and his mouth on hers, gathering her body into his. His skin warms hers and sets it alight. Shafts of lightning run up her spine. She leans back releasing her mouth, to say thickly, "It isn't *fair*."

"What is? What isn't, what's worrying you, nothing must, nothing must."

He is doing what he can to make their clothed bodies one.

"We *can't*. Leo. Leo. I can't. You can't just."

"OK. Just sit down and keep still with me then. Keep still."

They subside on to the couch. Unsatisfied desire has its own *frisson*, its own bliss. They enjoy it. They do not undress, they do not make love. So that when Leo wanders vaguely in, saying he cannot sleep, there is nothing untoward, no whiff of salt, no exposed organs he should not see, but a large man smiling in a jester's sweater, and a thin red-headed woman in a chocolate-brown shirt over lilac velvet pants.

They do not talk, much. They sit, next to each other. At midnight, John Ottokar leaves. At the foot of the area steps Frederica says, "Leo will be away next weekend. You could come here . . ."

"I can't." At first it seems that he is going to leave it at that. Then he says, "I've got to go on a kind of religious retreat. There's a group. Some of them Quakers, some of them from Ceylon, and some doctors. Some doctors. It's a new thing. I—I go sometimes. I'm expected. Next weekend, I'm expected."

"Where?" says Frederica, who dares not say "Why?"

"Does it matter? There's a kind of Retreat House called Tanglewood, in a Quaker village in Bucks, called Four Pence. I know it sounds dreadfully twee. Names don't matter, words don't matter, if they do, you can change them. I'd tell you about it, but I rather suspect you won't like it, you won't want to know. Religion isn't your thing."

"I'm not *hostile* to religion."

"Aren't you? Think about it, and tell me next time, what you think about religion. I'm hostile to it myself, half the time. But it's there, you can't deny it's there."

"I don't try to."

He looks at her as though she is the world's greatest nay-sayer. He says, "I know I ought not to tell you. I'm under instructions not to—"

"John!"

"You see. You don't like it."

"How do I know what I—? When you don't?"

"We shouldn't have started this conversation. My fault. Come here. Hold on to me. Don't talk. That's better. Now, *this* is real, whatever *that* is. *This* is real."

Her alarmed body does not tingle as it did. He strokes her spine and the flame lies low, flickers sullenly. He puts his warm, mute hand suddenly, swiftly, between her legs, holds her gently, waits for the shift in her pulse, the very slight relaxation of her tense muscles, and says, "This is real. Remember. Now I'm going."

He goes.

Frederica is on the whole pleased that John Ottokar has met Leo in this public, uncompromised way. This is more because she does not enjoy the fact that her relations with John Ottokar have a clandestine and furtive aspect than because she wants to establish any *particular* rapport between son and lover. She does not want to include John Ottokar in any tentative trio, man, woman, child. Nobody wants that. She wants things to be easy and friendly. So she is pleased when John returns once or twice more when Leo and Saskia and Agatha are there. They go once, even, to the Natural History Museum, two women, John Ottokar, the boy, the dark little girl. She feels something discreet and stable and mature is being set up. One evening, over supper, she says to Leo, "Shall we ask John Ottokar to the bonfire?"

Leo says, "No. I don't like John Ottokar."

"Oh, Leo. Why? He taught you scissors, paper, stone—"

"He makes horrible scary faces at me when no one's looking."

"He doesn't—"

"Through the window. Bits of him go white. Sneery faces."

"Why should he do that?"

"And I don't like his smell. He has a bad smell."

"Leo!"

"You asked me. You did ask me. If you want him at ve bonfire, you ask him. I expect the smell won't be too bad out there, not with all the smoke and stuff."

"I won't ask him, if you feel like that."

"I don't feel like anything. I just told you. I just told you, *he stinks.*"

Frederica wonders about discussing with Agatha the possibility that Leo is reacting to herself, John Ottokar, and the smell of sex, even though they have been so careful. Or maybe he simply said the worst thing he could think of—which has certainly been effective, if he did, for Frederica now never thinks of John Ottokar without wondering about the smell, real or fantasised, and of *what*?

Bonfire Night arrives. Agatha and Frederica have been visited by Giles and Victoria Ampleforth, the owners of the pretty white-painted corner-house in Hamelin Square with its vandalised window-boxes, its renovated Georgian shutters, its polished brass knocker. Giles and Victoria want to join in the fun, want to contribute, do not want to be rejected by the other inhabitants of the square, for they know they represent gentrification, which the local Labour Party vociferously opposes, though its councillors, or some of them, and even some Labour MPs are "doing up" the pretty terraced houses in the sallow and sullen squares of south-east London. Giles is an architect, lean and apologetic; his dusty thatched head and horn-rimmed stare do in fact cover a resolute intention to restore, beautify, *save* all the houses in Hamelin Square. Victoria is the proprietor of a children's boutique, Rags, Tags and Velvet Gowns, which sits oddly in the local row of shops between a ferocious Cockney greengrocer and a Pakistani chemist's shop. She sells fancy dresses and sweaters, and a stock of fat and grinning stuffed lions and tigers and polar bears, home-made and full of bounce. Giles wants to be friends with the Agyepongs and the Utters, a huge matriarchal society of the unemployed, who live behind grimy brocade curtains in Number 17, apparently with no furniture and no carpets, though occasional chairs are hurled through windows, some of which now form part of the base of the bonfire. Victoria has made bowls full of hot cider with bobbing frothy apples in it, and trays of dark, burned, sticky toffee. She is afraid it will be rejected, does not want to bring it out. Agatha says, Nothing venture, nothing win, and, Everybody *always* likes toffee. But the middle-class households lurk behind their shutters until the festivities have started, which they do when Kieran Utter sets light to the petrol-soaked brown paper at the centre of the pyre, and a roar of flame leaps upwards. Rockets go up from various areas, and patches of red sizzling light, green fountains of sparks, silver geysers, hiss and flare and vanish into black velvet. Frederica and Leo bring out Leo's box of Roman candles and Vesuvius fountains and peacocks. Leo and Saskia hold sparklers, and wave them solemnly. Someone screams; something hisses. The fire catches and begins to crack and gleam. People come out and stand and stare into it; children run squealing, hide behind cars; Victoria Ampleforth picks up courage and goes round the square with a tray of toffee which everyone accepts happily. She picks up more courage and brings out a stout folding table, behind which she sets up her stall with her hot cider and a collection of Polish enamelled mugs, scarlet and green and blue. The sky is full of puce rain, it is full of silver arrows falling, it is full of humming blue flies. The Guy—Clement and Thano's Guy—has been built into the pyre in a rotting wicker chair, to which he is tied with string and old knitting wool. "Like a Druid sacrifice," Agatha says; he lolls and smiles, the flames not yet near him. "It's a good thing there's no wind," says Giles Ampleforth. "This thing is far too big for this square. We ought to have water buckets around."

"Mrs. Kennet has got her hose attached in her kitchen," says Carole Utter. "As per usual." She takes a swig from a beer bottle. "Two kids got their hair burned last year, and a car got its paint blasted."

"I don't know whose that little Austin is," says Victoria. "It's always parked here, but it doesn't belong to any of the residents."

Frederica brings out a basket of oven-roasted chestnuts, which are also acceptable to everyone. Leo says he wants a banger, and Frederica tells him he doesn't.

The sky is a gold meadow full of crimson serpents; it is a huge fan of silver fronds; it is indigo lit with orange and sepia and hot yellow and scarlet.

They drink hot cider, plastic cups of red wine from a box with a spigot, bottles of ale, Tizer by mistake, Coke and rum, sweet sherry, advocaat. Clement and Thano have got strings of Chinese firecrackers; Brian Utter attaches one to the branch of a tree near the little Austin, where it bangs and splutters and crackles and twists, causing Leo to burst into tears, and a small bald-headed man with a moustache to cry out, "Mind my car!"

The fire is now producing clouds of smoke. It is difficult to see across the square. People are linking arms and singing—"Oh my darling Clementine," the only song the English can ever get very far with. Across the square, through the smoke, Frederica sees John Ottokar, in his many-coloured patchwork jumper; he is bending to set light to something; he straightens up, and waves at her through the grey billows. She makes her way round to him, with smarting eyes. Whatever he has lit does not rush into the air or explode into shimmers of light. It burns sullenly, a tallish thing, producing a blue flame like a cowl around it.

"Skoob," says John Ottokar. It is a new art-form. Book-burning. "Books" backwards. Frederica does not like it. The books are lurid paperbacks. The top one has a pair of breasts bursting out of black lace and a vanishing face above them. The next one down, however, is Tillich's *The Ground of Our Being* and below that, Bishop Robinson's *Honest to God*.

"I don't like book-burning," says Frederica.

"That's why Skoob," says John Ottokar. "No point burning things nobody cares about."

He raises a glass of ink-dark wine to the Guy.

"Here's to him. He had the right idea. Explode it all. From underneath. Then there's a chance of living a real life. Up in flames. Theophany."

"You're drunk."

"Oh no. You may be. Let's dance."

He links arms with a swaying line of residents, and pushes his other arm through Frederica's. She smells his armpits, acrid, sour, and another smell, thick incense, musky, sweet, sweet. She tries to pull away, and he pulls her tightly to him, his head back, his lovely face ruddy in the reflected flames.

"Let's dance."

Through the smoke, on the other side of the bonfire, she sees John Ottokar in his multi-coloured sweater.

She has failed a test she was waiting for.

Little black boys, little white boys with sooty faces, rush like imps, widdershins, as John Ottokar comes round and links arms with Frederica on his left, and the population of Hamelin Square sway, amiably drunken, and sing. "We'll take a cup of kindness yet/For the sake of Auld Lang Syne."

XVI

 Towards midday on the second day, the Lady Roseace and the young Narcisse paused in their headlong flight to allow their horses to breathe, and to give some relief to their own bodies. It was a late spring day, full of hope; they had come through the neck of the mountain pass, and were on a fair plain, where delicious little bosky groves mixed with springing cornfields and hay meadows. In every tree the birds sang as though their tiny throats would burst with the passage of the trills and whistles and gobblings and gurglings of their invariant musical phrases. Butterflies fluttered from flower to flower, or floated along the meadow borders. Crickets rubbed their dry legs monotonously against their thoraxes. The travellers found a stone basin, into which a fountain ran between mossy stones, and a wild cherry tree, full of fruit, with which Narcisse filled his hat, whilst the Lady Roseace brought out the wine and water flasks, their stock of biscuits and sausages and dried cheese. They were out of the environs of La Tour Bruyarde. They were free, and expected their free food to taste delectable, and so it did. They were free, and so they looked at each other with a new curiosity, dusty and travel-stained as they necessarily were. In the old days, the young Narcisse's face had been almost too extravagantly lovely, a gold-skinned shield-shape surrounded by luxuriant blue-black curls like clustering grapes. His huge dark eyes, too, had been like grapes, with those long, glistening lashes and perfectly curved wine-dark brows which many women would give much, in cash or kind, to have naturally, and which are almost always the prerogative of the male sex. His cheeks were lovely planes and his chin a perfect, gravely pretty triangle, above which, in the old days, his mouth had had a suspicion of a sulky swelling, a youthful push of a pout. But hard experience had ironed out the roundnesses and plumpnesses and soft dimple-pits of that boyish beauty and replaced it with a melancholy gentleness, a droop of the upper lip, a tension in the lower, that the Lady Roseace found more interesting and more attractive than his primitive self-conscious loveliness. His teeth, as he bit into his biscuit, were as white and even as they had ever been. His neck was strong now; there were muscles under the skin, like a young stag rather than the soft fawn or silken porcelet he had then resembled.

As for the lady herself, she had worn less well, and kept her face in the shadow of her hood, and her back to the sun as she ate. Her flesh, too, had tightened and pulled, in the curious and wonderful and terrible days of La Tour Bruyarde, and she had visible tendons and moving muscles where no woman was expected to have them who had been properly nurtured in milk and silk; she had lines on the surface that were more *indecent*, that is to say, *improper*, than the exposure of pretty nipples or a round white belly would have been, for youth is and was a woman's best ornament, and this should never be forgotten, particularly by women no longer young. And those pretty nipples, to tell the truth, those rosy buttons of bliss, were not now what they had been, but had slipped, so to speak, down the slopes of the blue-veined alabaster mounds of her breasts, which had themselves slipped, slipped, so that there were fissures and tiny ravines, declines and cuts and crackings in the heaving surface, which was now more like chamois leather (a pretty substance) than heaped snow, or ripe peaches, or whatever other delicate simile excites my reader. But under her travelling gown, her corset gave a youthful apple-shape to these hidden blown roses, and her waist was wonderfully trim, and her thighs, too lean perhaps for the taste of that time, promised for that reason a performative agility, a delectable grip and spring. So thought Narcisse, considering what he could see, and imagining amiably (and generously) what he could not.

"We shall come to look back on these past days as a bad dream," said the Lady Roseace, nibbling a sausage, toying with a cherry.

"We must not forget them, ever," said the young Narcisse. "For there is a lesson to be learned—about excess, about the metamorphosis of freedom into humiliation and slavery. We must go into the world and preach moderation in all things."

"As for me," said the Lady Roseace, "I mean to become a Quietist, a Retired Person in a rosy cottage far from the rut and muck of human conflict. You may preach if you will, but I shall abstain, from everything, *everything*, including preaching."

"You are too lovely to abstain from *everything*," said the young Narcisse, congratulating himself on abstaining from the treacherous phrase "*still* too lovely."

The Lady Roseace met his eye sadly and sweetly.

"Truly *everything*," she said with her lips, and who knows, with her will too, but the young Narcisse read a different message in the disposition of her limbs on the grassy bank where she sat. And he rose up, and went off into the wood, to relieve his bladder and prepare his instrument for singleness of purpose.

And the Lady Roseace lay back peacefully in the grassy hammock and thought she heard laughter in the air. She thought she heard a kind of yelping laughter, and the babble of many excited voices, and a kind of interwoven music of song and cry and howl. And the clear note, liquid and clamant, of a horn. And she thought, lying there, It is the lord of these fields, out hunting for his pleasure. And she knew it was not. And she hoped, as the excited babble grew nearer, that it would pass by the grove where she was partly hidden. And she knew it would not.

When Culvert rode into the clearing the Lady Roseace's dress was covered with the bloody slaver of the hounds' jowls, and her sleeve was torn and bloody where she had fought them off, and her dress too was torn, between her bubs, to her crotch. And she tried to hold it together, and he said, "I have seen you, more than enough, there is no need for modesty. Let it flap."

"Not modesty. Decency," said the Lady Roseace.

"You have no right to be decent, and no need, where you are going, which is where you have come from, where the idea of *decency* was long ago done away with."

And the Lady Roseace said, "My dear friend Culvert, whom once I loved as I love my own skin, to save whom I would once gladly have died and thought my life well given, why do you seek to prevent me from leaving La Tour Bruyarde? I am not going to your enemies, for your enemies are my enemies, and if they find me, they will do to me what they would do to you, for we were once one, as you well know. I am going merely because I feel myself old and tired, my sweet friend, and unable any longer to play my part in your grand design of free life within the walls of La Tour Bruyarde. My idealism is quenched, dear heart, but not my sympathy—I desire only to live

411

alone in a country cottage and think of our great hopes, and our great days—and your great achievements in the world you have created. Others can play the part you projected for me, others with stronger hearts and stronger limbs and steadier visions. I am a spent force, Culvert, and not worthy to be in your company. But I remember how in the old days you said—when we planned our freedom in hiding from the Revolutionary Armies—you said that the true principle of our new society should be perfect liberty, to fulfil in harmony every least desire, of body or soul. And now, my dear lord, every least desire of my body and my soul is renunciation. I desire solitude, poverty, inertia, quotidian boredom, things we mocked and despised in our high days, but things which now I believe have a certain value for such as myself, wrung out like old cloths, cracked like dry posts. O Culvert, O magnanimous, subtle Culvert, liberty must include the *freedom to leave the group*, harmony of desires must include the desire to abstain from desiring? Let me go now, and the people will praise your wisdom and gentleness for generations."

"This is simply flattery," said Culvert then, staring down from his shifting horse, which danced uneasily, and which he controlled completely with the iron resolve in his grim knees. "You should hear yourself, your weak, lying, flattering voice, saying what you do not believe, to save your skin, which is no longer worth saving, which disgusts me. You do not think me magnanimous or wise. You do not think what I have made in La Tour Bruyarde is just or beautiful. You have murmured against me and despised our work; you have sneered and doubted and made our path difficult from the very outset of our Project. We cannot afford to let you go loose and tell lies about us to the weak, unstable outside world. We cannot afford to let you weaken our resolve by opening chinks in our defence, to let you water the strong wine of our purpose with the spittle of fear and indecision and vacillation. Where one weak link parts, the whole chain springs loose and the other links rattle to the ground. No, you must return, foolish woman, and meet the punishment I have designed for you.

"Where is that young fool, Narcisse?"

"He is gone. We quarrelled and parted. He is far away."

So spoke the Lady Roseace, in her despair, to give the young man a chance.

Now Narcisse in the deep thicket was frozen in mid-piss, his organ in his hand, scarce daring to breathe or move, lest he discover himself. And when he heard her thus attempt to save him, he debated with himself whether he should sally out of the thicket to defend her (which was not very possible, with the hound pack and the huntsmen still gathering) or whether he should stay where he was and accept her gift of hiding. But he might have saved his moral niceties, for the hounds picked up his scent and followed him into the brush, where they leaped up at his unbuttoned garments and tore viciously at those parts over which he held his lovely hands, and at the hands too, so that both were mangled to shreds of dangling flesh. And then Culvert came and took him, and bound him upright in his saddle, all bleeding as he was now, and bound the Lady Roseace also, with her torn clothes, and so they rode back to La Tour Bruyarde.

"We might try to save her," said Turdus Cantor to Colonel Grim.

"We must do what is possible," said Colonel Grim, "which might barely include saving ourselves."

"She will be better out of this," said Samson Origen. "Provided it is quick."

It was not quick . . .

"And now," said Culvert to his captive lady, "I shall show you the machine I have prepared for you. I shall explain its intricacies and its sinuosities and its delectable and devilish resorts and triggers, one by one."

And he clapped his hands, and a trolley was wheeled on to the stage, on which stood a small, shining, pointed tower or turret, a conical affair, perfectly plain on the surface. And from its base, like the elastic of a dunce's cap, dangled a leather string, with stirrups.

"Now," said Culvert, "when the leather tongues at the base of this ingenious turret are pulled tight in their eyelets round your ankles and securely spiked on their steel prongs; when the tip of the turret has been inserted into that soft place it is designed for, then this smooth cone will open a myriad tiny mouths, from which will issue a myriad tiny tongues, that will lap and lick and titillate, but which are also made of fine steel and tempered blades, and will shave and slice and carve and work, bit by bit, inch by inch." And Culvert explained to Roseace that this instrument was designed to enter her, and to expand inside her, and blossom at its summit and along its sides with an ingenious series, a veritable forest, of little brushes and soft, probing glove-fingers, which would give intense pleasure, and then of little penknives, and forks, and tweezers, and scissors, and revolving cheese-wires, and whisks, and pincers and probes, which would be triggered by motions, and fluids, and belches, and each other . . .

"We shall take notes," he said, "on the variables, the optimal applications of pleasure and pain, the alternations of each, whether pleasure is involuntary in the presence of fear, as some have argued, whether in death, the female orgasm is as violent as that of a hanged man . . ."

The Lady Roseace had heard and read of the great courage of heroes and heroines in the face of unbearable pain. She believed, rightly, that such courage cannot be maintained if its opponents are truly determined it shall not. She believed, rightly, that she had perhaps one more chance to speak before, in some sense, she ceased to be, although *something*—which she devoutly hoped would not much resemble Roseace—would in some sense live through the attentions and ministrations of the instrument. She said, "This is a most ingenious device."

"I think so. I have given it much thought."

"It must have taken ingenuity and practice."

"Even so. I have laboured."

"You must have planned the Instrument, from the earliest days of our coming here, or even from before . . ."

"It has always been in my mind, yes."

"Tell me, Culvert, was it designed in the abstract? Or always for me—"

"Always for you. Its proportions are constructed to fit the proportions of your interior cavities, as I have often and often measured them."

"So when we came, you knew it would end here?"

"It has not ended," said Culvert. "But you will end here, yes. Unless my machine is defective. Which I am very sure it is not."

"Irony is a useless weapon against Projectors," said Colonel Grim.

"Irony is a useless weapon when they are inserting a biting and scratching and sawing metal device into your cunt," said Turdus Cantor.

"Irony is the last satisfaction," said Samson Origen. "Before death. Death will be very satisfactory to that poor lady. But her death will not, I think, be as satisfying to our Projector as he supposed it would when he projected it. And I do not know if he is clever enough to see that the satisfaction will not be greatly—if at all—increased by constant repetition of the experiment. It is time to prepare our own evasion. Would you not say? With a little more cunning and a little more aggression than those two innocents?"

"I thought," said Colonel Grim, "that you believed it was best not to have been born, and next best to die quickly. I can't see why you would want to stir from this Tower, where your second-best fate impends even more insistently."

"I abstain from sexual bliss myself," said Samson Origen. "And I would rather not die as part of another man's desperate search for its vanishing lineaments in my pain or anyone else's. I think we will find a way of gratifying our Projector and pleasing ourselves."

"You will act against your principles."

"But not against yours, mon Colonel. So you must be active in this."

Babbletower has a cover with a black tower on the midnight-blue sky, with a white moon riding on one of the rather Disneyish turrets, and white arched windows winking in its gloom. A trail of scantily clad people, mostly women with flowing hair and exposed breasts in Empire-line clinging dresses, winds its spiral way round the lower levels of the mass, and vanishes through a heavy doorway. The people bear some resemblance—partly owing to the way their diaphanous clothing clings to their limbs—to Samuel Palmer's churchgoers winding their way to Evensong in a Kentish vale. Only three colours have been used in the printing: cobalt blue, black, and pink. The lettering is black and Gothick. BABBLETOWER, by Jude Mason. Inside, the title page says "*Babbletower: A Tale for the Children of Our Time. By Jude Mason.*" The book appears in March 1966. Frederica receives two copies, one from Rupert Parrott ("Thank you for bringing this book to my attention. I am sure it is worth publishing it. We must hope it will do well.") and one from Jude, inscribed "For Frederica, who thought I couldn't, and then decided that I could. In one of the most improbable interpretations of that phrase the Onlie Begetter. I babble. I salute you. Jude."

Frederica finds the cover passable, no more. It is striking. But simple. And has a misleading Tolkienish-science-fictionish look.

She notices a few reviews. The *Daily Telegraph* (brought home from the Ministry by Agatha) has a headline A FURTHER SYMPTOM OF OUR DECADENCE, and says that the book, occasionally quite powerful, reflects the sensationalism, desire for perverse stimulation of jaded palates, determination to shock at all costs a cynical public increasingly difficult to shock or to rouse except by extreme crude measures. "We are a sick society, in which apparently anything goes, in books, in behaviour, in style of dress, in pointless posturing. In a more robust society, this book would not have been published, for the publisher would have had convictions, and the courage of those convictions. In the present climate of slimy liberalism, anything is allowed to creep out from under a stone and preen itself in the common sun."

The *Guardian* headline is THE WOUNDED SURGEON PLIES THE STEEL and its critic concludes that we live in a sick society and the only way to confront our sickness is to explore, to inhabit, to hunt out every last hiding place of our shames and our subterfuge, our divided and blunted consciousness, working our way bravely through disgust to a new understanding. We are in a state of breakdown, and only by breaking down all inhibitions will we come to see our sick selves as we really are, and embark on the difficult and dangerous project of re-integration. "*We must accept that we are loathsome,*" says this critic, "and Jude Mason has taken a fearless step forward on all our behalfs."

In *Encounter* there is a long article by Marie-France Smith, who is described in the Contributors' Notes as "Carlyle Professor of Comparative Literature at Prince Albert College in London University." Professor Smith is learned, and treats *Babbletower* as a learned treatise, exploring the explorations of liberty and license of those post-revolutionary French thinkers Charles Fourier and the Marquis de Sade, "who urged on the crowd that besieged the Bastille where he was imprisoned, through a speaking trumpet made out of the fall-pipe of his latrine." "There is considerable interest amongst current French thinkers, the heirs of surrealism and anarchism, both in Fourier's gentle belief that indulgence of every natural (i.e., every possible) human desire could be harmoniously ordered into a new paradise, a new Jerusalem, and in the darker belief, of Sade, who also believed all existing natural passions should be admitted and permitted by the state, but had a further belief in the *unnatural act* which could be an instrument of power over Nature and a deep insight into her ways. Sade's philosophical interest in transgression may be related to that of Nietzsche, who remarks that the wisdom of Oedipus and the understanding of Hamlet are bought by *unnatural acts . . .*"

Frederica encounters Jude himself outside the male lavatories in the Samuel Palmer School. He is wearing his blue velvet Caroline coat, which looks as though clouds of greasy dust would rise from it if he were tapped with a carpet beater. His hair swings and swings, iron-grey and knotted and gleaming with its own ancient oils, ending at the hem of his coat-skirts. It has pale flecks like a small flock of clothes moths on it, minute shredded scraps of pink lavatory tissue, improbably electrified. He is preceded by his own rancid smell, and succeeded by the wafted air of the latrine. Frederica thanks him for the book, congratulates him on it, and asks if he is happy with the reviews.

Jude's long grey face folds lugubriously. He pulls a sheaf of reviews from his pocket and begins to read.

"How can I be pleased," he says, "when I am treated as a *symptom* of other people's swinish *malaise*? I am *myself*, I hope, and my book is mine, and a work of art, I do believe and maintain, contrary to their insulting insinuations."

"At least they're talking about it. If they think it's a symptom, they'll talk about it a lot. Come away from the loo, Jude, and tell me what you think about Marie-France Smith."

"A cold philosopher who would unravel the rainbow. Nowhere in her whole disquisition on Sade and Fourier and *les philosophes* does she use an active verb of my people, my personae. *Nowhere* does Culvert *do* or Samson Origen *think* or Turdus Cantor *speak*. It is as though we *were not*. All of us, who peopled my poor skull and rode across its plains and savaged each other so incessantly and ingeniously, *we are nothing*, Frederica, but a few concepts. We are Liberty and the Id, we are the fraying backcloth of the Theatre of Cruelty."

"For God's sake, Jude Mason, are you trying to say the critics should have discussed your characters *as though they were real people?*"

"As though they were *real characters*, my sweet. A lot more real than Mr. Philip Toynbee or Mr. Cyril Connolly or Professor Marie-France Smith."

"You are an ungrateful sod. They've done you proud."

"Not a sod. A total abstainer. In mourning for a world."

Frederica understands. She says, "You miss them. You've lost them. Are you writing anything else?"

She is dragging him by the elbow up the stairs out of the basement, away from the lavatories.

417

"Hush. Tell no one. I'm thinking of a story of Artists. And a lot of poisonously fatal Young Things. But artists disgust me, rather. They're too simple. Soldiers, now. I might write a tale set in a barracks. A fortified barracks under siege, no ingress nor egress."

"Like *Babbletower*."

"In no way. On the shore of a salt sea, with a desert behind its back, defending a space where life may not flourish. That's promising. I've thought of that just talking to you, here, now. But in truth, my angel, I am flummoxed and bereft. I am a *one-man* wake and I am lost. I am to be interviewed by the *Evening Standard* tomorrow. I have no opinions to offer their young woman."

"You have lots."

"Just as bad. They want one or two simple ones. A line. I am not a line. I am a tangle."

Frederica asks whether Rupert Parrott is happy with the book's reception. This evokes further plaints.

"I had *supposed* that some festivity would have been forthcoming. A few glasses of champers, which of course I don't *drink* but I do like to look at the bubbles going up, and some *canapés*. You know, when I first read about a party with *canapés* I was in my *indigenous French* phase—so imagined a *Roman orgy* where everyone lay around on *canapés,* couches, all different colours, salmon pink and sky blue and bronze—a delectable rolling-around on sofas, an ogling. I do feel I might have had a minor or minimal orgy for my debut, even if the *canapés* were all bite-sized, and made for teeth and gullet rather than fundament."

"We could all go to the pub today and drink to *Babbletower*," says Frederica. "Alan and Desmond Bull and you and me and a few others. No *canapés* in pubs, but we could raise a glass to you."

"Conciliating your Eeyore with burst balloons in honey-pots," says Jude, revealing an unusual aspect of his reading. "Very well, I will permit you to console me, we will take a *jar* together."

He does not take a jar, when the celebratory group is gathered in the local, which is a rather opulent scarlet-leather-and-gleaming-brass-and-engraved-mirrors-and-fat-frilled-glass-lampshades place called the Griffin. He takes "a Bloody Mary without the Mary, *all blood,* dear, with several shakes of that dark brown fluid which I believe is made like the Roman *liquamen* from rotted fish." He is high on excitement; his smell is hotter and ranker than its usual cold dustbin air.

The party consists of several painters and a few art historians and some students, as well as Frederica, Alan, and Desmond Bull. They all inspect the book and deprecate the cover. Gareth Larkin, who teaches graphics, says he will set Jude's book as a project for his second-year students—"and that way you'll have twenty or thirty alternatives to choose from. I like to give them something to bite into, in the second year, something real."

"Jude could pose for the torture scenes," says one of the female students, who is wearing a purple shirt with a frilled high collar, scattered with sprigs of daisies, above a black hobble skirt and laced granny boots.

"You'd enjoy that," says Jude, automatically. His face is a mask, a skin stretched over something; he is *going on rather*, today, Frederica thinks, wondering what he is "really" thinking or feeling.

Later, when the artists have drunk a large number of pints, and Jude has imbibed several more "simply Bloodies, thank you, dear," there is a potential moment of ugliness when it becomes clear that there is a feeling that Jude should buy a round of drinks. It is not clear to Frederica whether Jude is aware of the muttering and growling. Someone says *sotto voce* that having a sold book in the hand is worth a studio of unsold canvasses when it comes to the liquid. Jude goes to the lavatory and Frederica offers to buy the round; these are the days before the women's movement, when it is still quite difficult, though not impossible, for a woman to buy a round in a pub. Alan helps her to carry and offers to help her to pay. She refuses the offer, and becomes irrationally annoyed with Jude herself, as he re-arranges his coatskirts on the tubby red stool he is occupying. Fourteen pints and a simply Bloody makes quite a hole in her own small resources.

The interview in the *Evening Standard* is conducted by an up-and-coming trendy young journalist (these are the freshly shining, newly hitched days of the word "trendy") called Marianna Toogood.

Jude Mason insisted on being interviewed in a Soho teashop: La Pâtisserie de Nanette, a tiny cubby-hole of a café, behind thick lace curtains, where there are three little round tables with white lace cloths flung over dark red plastic cloths, and rickety little bentwood chairs. It seemed an odd place to meet the author of "a tale for the children of our time," which has been described as disgusting, sadistic, pornographic, intellectual, profound and "a mirror of our present disorders."

419

I did not know what to expect, and at first took my interviewee for a tramp who had wandered in by mistake, an impression I am sure he meant me to have. He wears his hair very long; it is dark grey and centrally parted; his clothes, a sort of velvet frock-coat which was once pale blue, and velvet britches, could charitably be described as well worn. There are holes in his shoes. His face is long, his bones prominent, his eyes hooded. He could do with a wash, but has a certain fancy-dress *panache*. He is a fairytale figure, a cross between Captain Hook, Gollum, and the Marquis de Sade, from whom he claims to have learned his craft.

He is difficult to interview, since he answers most conventional questions with a simple "no" or a resolute silence. He prefers not to divulge where he was born, where he was educated, where he lives, or whether he has any family or friends. His voice is extremely "cultivated," with a clipped twang which is more BBC than the BBC, a Brideshead bray. He did reveal that he had run away from school—a boarding school, one assumes, since he said "I absconded in the deep darkness"—to sit at the feet of the surrealists and anarchists, and of the playwright Jean Genet, who he says is "the Master" but not a model for his own way of life. "Genet believes that stealing is a good and easy way of encouraging the flow of goods in a community: since I have and want no possessions I neither steal nor am stolen from."

He earns his living, he tells me, as an employee in an art school. When asked what he does there he is surprisingly forthcoming. "I offer myself. I display my puny musculature. I let them trace the lineaments of my absence of desire." He has an affinity for the art students, perhaps? He tells me he read his book *Babbletower* aloud to selected groups of them, during which he was overheard and "discovered" by "someone" who showed his manuscript to his publisher, Rupert Parrott, of Bowers and Eden.

Parrott obviously has an eye for the *risqué* and unlikely success—he published Phyllis Pratt's *Daily Bread,* the best-selling story of stabbings and *crises de foie* amongst the rural clergy.

He has ordered several *pâtisseries,* which he consumes with greedy deliberation, biting into them with long yellow teeth. During the interview he devours a meringue swan, biting off its head with a decisive snap, a kind of choux pastry called a *religieuse* (a nun) which has a chocolate-veiled "head" on a fat, cream-filled body, and two *feuilles de palmier.* He says he does not often get the chance to eat *pâtisseries.* He likes eating, but does little of it—"indigence is a great staver-off of *embonpoint.*" He does not drink, or smoke. I wonder whether this is because, like Timothy Leary, he believes psychedelic drugs to be healthier than the normal psyche-deadeners of our society, alcohol and nicotine. This suggestion makes him indignant. He remarks oddly that he needs "neither

mind-expanders nor chest-expanders nor sock-suspenders nor a trouser press."
I get the feeling that he considers me to be intellectually so far beneath him that
it is not worth giving serious answers to my questions.

Many of the reviews of *Babbletower* have suggested that it is likely to become
cult reading among the young and turned on, the disciples of Artaud and Peter
Brooke, *Gormenghast* and Burroughs. He is, I suggest, a proto-hippy or Flower
Person. He repudiates this, quoting Peter Pan about being a little chicken
sprung from the egg. "I am what I am and was, my hair is what it was and is, my
book is my book and sprang from my head fully armed, *sui generis*."

But he likes the art students? I would like him to like *something* besides de-
capitated sugar swans and nuns.

"They are revolting," he says. He corrects himself. "They are in revolt. They
are breaking their chains. They will not submit to be made to crassly imitate or
even look at the drawings of Michelangelo or the techniques of Ruskin. They
will all be original in their own ways, which are all new and unsullied by contact with the boring and *complicated* past, and which therefore all resemble each
other in their freshness and innocence and simplicity." He appears to mean what
he says, but it is hard to be sure.

I ask him if he thinks *Babbletower* will attract a large following. Yes, he says,
he should think so. I ask him why, what about his book will attract them?

"Oh," he says, "the world is full of people doing horrible things to other
people for love, and people love to read about people doing horrible things to
other people because they want to learn how to do horrible things themselves
to the people they love and they want to learn to write about that, naturally, it
is part of it, writing it down. It keeps the world going, like Genet's movement
of goods from place to place."

He bites into a great pastry cabbage and smiles at me through spurts of cream.

Rupert Parrott, when he sees this, shouts at Hugh Pink. His shouting
always has a breathy quality, as though the shouter himself is trying to
suppress it. He shouts that Mason must be prevented from giving any
more interviews. He is making them all look ridiculous. Hugh Pink
replies pacifically that the chances are that he gave a perfectly reasonable interview, but that the journalist took against him, or against the
cake shop, or something. Or against his smell, says Hugh Pink, which
she did have the good grace not to mention, though it can't have
gone down very well with the meringue. Hugh says he supposes the
interview will be good for sales, which it is. *Babbletower* passes three
thousand and continues to sell.

Frederica is stopped by Jude outside her office. He pulls out the growing sheaf of reviews from his inner pocket and peels off the interview. He is outraged. He is particularly outraged by Marianna Toogood's reporting of "*crises de foie*" in the novel of Phyllis Pratt. "They are illiterate, these young *things*," he says. "*Crise de foi*, sans *e*, crisis of the Faith; crise de foie, *with* an *e*, *liver attack*, as in foie gras, *fat liver*. Pig-ignorant."

"It could be a joke. A pun."

"Don't be silly. She's not capable of any such refinement. Pure pig-ignorance. Look what she did with my remarks about the revolting students' revolting reluctance to learn the rudiments or study the great who have gone their way. She can't recognise *irony*."

"Journalists never can. Most people can't. Rule One. As she should have known, since you can't see it's *her* joke about the *crise de foie* or *foi*."

"She made me look a fool. She didn't report any of the things I actually *did* say about my book, about my people, about my meaning. Only made animadversions on my teeth."

"You do ask for it, you know."

"Ask for what? I ask for nothing."

Frederica catches sight of another, newer review.

"Is that Anthony Burgess? Can I look?"

Burgess's review opens with a disquisition on evil. He quotes Golding's oracular saying "Man produces evil as a bee produces honey." He suggests that the English have always been uneasy with evil—"They don't go beyond right and wrong, they lean naturally towards the comedy of manners, where virtue is inextricably entangled with Class, whereas on the Catholic and Calvinist continent, writers are not afraid to acknowledge the whiff of sulphur from the Pit, the eternal confrontation between Good and Evil." He cites Al Alvarez's rousing introduction to his anthology of modern poetry prepared to measure up to the horrors of our history (the Holocaust, the Bomb): "Beyond the Gentility Principle."

Jude Mason, says Burgess, is far out beyond the Gentility Principle. In the battle between Saint Augustine, the Bishop of Hippo, who believed that fallen man was naturally evil, and Pelagius, the hopeful Hibernian heretic, who believed that man could by free will and reasonable exercise of virtue achieve salvation, who, asked Burgess, is not instinctively on the side of Pelagius? And who, who ponders long and deeply, does not come to fear, to accept, that the grim Bishop was nevertheless in the right of it, that there is some quasi-mechanical system of destructiveness, betrayal, cruelty, in which we are entrapped, however we struggle?

Jude Mason, says Burgess, is that new kind of 1960s artist, the Fabulator. His Fable enacts the battle between Augustine and Pelagius but in a society more like the post-Revolutionary France, where the sardonic Marquis de Sade promulgated his theories of freedom and terror, a renegade Augustinian, whereas the "sweetly dotty" Charles Fourier constructed a Utopian vision of Harmony where the stars would sing together because human passional and sexual freedom and bliss had heated the universe and changed the music of the spheres, had turned the oceans to a kind of agreeable lemonade, sharks to supertankers and supertigers to supertransport. Jude Mason's people, says Burgess, are trapped in their Projector's Fourierist utopian project, which is a mechanical conveyor-belt to Sadeian subways and dungeons.

This book, says Burgess, portentously, mischievously, is in great danger of being prosecuted for obscenity, for a "tendency to deprave and corrupt." Can it be acquitted on that account? True pornography, he says, is *kinetic,* it moves to action, it titillates, it irritates and excites flesh and spirit to seek relief. It does not follow that because a writer's concern is deeply moral, deeply concerned with right and wrong, that what he writes will necessarily lack this *kinetic* quality. "The value of art is always diminished by the presence of elements that move to action: the pornographic and the didactic are, in a purely aesthetic judgement, equally to be condemned." Jude Mason is both didactic and pornographic: it is to be supposed that he believes his own stance to be that of his creation Samson Origen, who professes a Nietzschean eschewal of the libido and all its works. But he has chosen to construct his fable, his *machine,* his clockwork, in parody of the drives and devices it criticises, the sado-masochistic panoply of straps and knives, the pornographic relish of human surfaces and orgiastic contortions. Does his titillation titillate? Do his switches set in motion cogs which turn on switches which set imitation in motion? The greatest works of art are not kinetic but static. *Ulysses, Lady Chatterley's Lover, The Rainbow* "discharge their emotions inside the book itself, producing the catharsis of art." Jude Mason, though he has considerable talent and ingenuity, is working in a more dubious and dangerous mode. Freud and Mephistopheles might smile mockingly at this Projector as he smiles mockingly at his own Culvert.

Babbletower appears in March 1966. In April Harold Wilson wins a General Election with a greatly increased effective majority of ninety-seven. *Babbletower* has now sold six thousand copies and aroused much discussion. Alexander Wedderburn reports to Frederica that Naomi Lurie, the Oxford don on the Steerforth Committee, has told him in confidence that the Director of Public Prosecutions has asked her to read and report on *Babbletower,* to give an opinion on whether a prosecution under the 1959 Obscene Publications Act would be appropriate, and whether expert opinion would be heavily in favour of the book. Dr. Lurie, says Alexander, doesn't like the book but believes it can be argued to have literary merit, and should be in print.

One of the new Labour MPs in the new Parliament is Dr. Hermia Cross, a physician and Methodist Lay Reader whose Liverpool constituency contains both a smart suburb and a racially pullulating series of council estates. Dr. Cross, surprisingly, asks the Attorney-General in the House whether he intends to take any steps about a dangerous and disgusting book which has received misguided praise in some quarters. The Attorney-General, Sir Mervyn Bates, replies that he believes that the peak of the book's sales is past, that it is priced too high to be widely circulated, and that Literary Criticism, on the whole, appeared to believe the work had some merit. Dr. Cross retorts that she believes the book presents acts of cruelty in a seductive light, and that we are living through a time of horror when it is unfortunately clear that literary works *can* influence minds predisposed to evil to commit acts of cruelty and degradation. The trial of Ian Brady and Myra Hindley is being heard as she speaks, though she makes no direct reference to it. She is backed up by Sir Evelyn Maiden, a Tory MP from Suffolk, who says he has seen the book, "and it is filthy, filthy, filthy muck." She is also backed up by other Tory backbenchers. In the Sunday papers that weekend there are articles mocking the protesting MPs, and a cartoon of Dr. Cross dressed as a governess brandishing a whip over a crawling bare-arsed figure who is presumably Rupert Parrott, since it is clearly not Jude Mason. There is also an article entitled "Sticks and Stones May Break Your Bones" by Roger Magog, which argues hotly and passionately that it is always wrong to restrict the written or the spoken word, "because precisely, *words cannot hurt you,* every man has the right and the freedom to make up his own mind how to react to incitements and temptations and actions of whatever kind, and what we should do for the weak and wrong-headed is *educate them to judge better,* not suppress other's freedoms. We must be vigilant, but not repressive . . ." On the following Monday, Dr. Cross announces that if the DPP will not act as it should, she will take out a private prosecution against the publishers and author of *Babbletower* under Section 3 of the 1959 Act. This—and the unfortunate coincidence of the Moors Murders trial—brings about a change of heart in the DPP, which announces that it now intends to bring a prosecution against the book.

Frederica hears this news from Rupert Parrott himself. She goes round to Elderflower Court with a heap of reports, and a basket to carry away further books. Parrott is sitting behind his desk. He says, "Now see what you have brought upon me!" and hands Frederica the official letter. "They have seized my stock," he says. His round cheeks are pink, his eyes glittering. "We shall fight," he says. "We shall fight, no matter what the cost, no matter what the pain. It is a matter of principle, of freedom of conscience, of the right to free speech. If people like this are allowed to win, we shall be back in a society where burning books is a step on the way to burning people."

He looks an unlikely martyr for free speech, with his little curls, his mustard-coloured waistcoat and his tartan tie. Frederica says, "What will you do?"

"Elect for trial by jury when we come before the magistrates. Assemble a team of expert witnesses who will make it once and for all impossible to attack literary works. Demolish Mrs. Whitehouse and Dr. Cross and their pro-censorship movements. Start a Defence Fund with appeals to other publishers for solidarity. Bear witness."

"What does Jude say?"

"To tell you the truth, I could do without Jude. He is our weak link. He will make a dreadful impression on a jury. Apart from the way he looks, he has a tendency to counter-productive frivolity. I count on you, Frederica, to keep him in order, that is, to make him see sense. We must have a good Brief. I thought of Augustine Weighall. We must talk to the solicitors. We must explore *every possibility.* There can be no question of losing. We cannot afford to lose."

He purses his mouth and looks directly at Frederica. "We need all the help we can get."

"I'll do what I can," says Frederica, not sure what that is, what role she can have.

"But screw your courage to the sticking-place," says Rupert Parrott, "and we'll not fail. Who said that?"

"Lady Macbeth, I think."

"Ah," says Rupert Parrott. He laughs, a warm, rueful laugh. "Not a good choice. I must be careful. You can't make mistakes like that, under cross-examination."

"She didn't exactly *fail*."

"In the long run she did. She got damned spots on her hands and died in a nightmare. I intend to *win this case* and die contented in my bed."

Frederica in the first part of 1966 has her own problems. Her divorce is apparently no nearer being heard, and she is besieged by a long series of letters from Nigel's solicitors about Leo's education. "If the boy is to go to Swineburn, as is to be hoped, or to some other Public School, he should already be studying Latin and French, in order eventually to be prepared to sit the Common Entrance examination. Mr. Tiger's client is reliably informed that no such preparation is or will be available at the William Blake Elementary School. He is perfectly prepared to pay his son's fees at a local Preparatory School to be agreed, and would be glad to be informed as expeditiously as possible of any arrangements that could be made for his satisfaction in this regard." Frederica snips and pastes these messages into her *Laminations*—"French facilities Latin elementary all confusion opportunity languages"—and sends off spirited messages to Mr. Begbie, who translates them into lawyers' *lingua franca*.

"Tell him that as far as I know he himself never passed an exam, doesn't speak any languages and never reads a book, whereas I have distinctions in four languages at A Level and a First Class English degree from Cambridge, and share a house with a Principal in the Ministry of Education, so might be thought to have my son's educational interests at heart. Tell him my father is a distinguished schoolmaster and no one could care more than we do about education and civilisation, neither of which are my husband's *strong points*. Thank you."

She describes this situation with indignation to Alan Melville and Tony Watson, the chameleon and the fake of her Cambridge days. Alan, the chameleon, whose elegant manner covers a ferociously competitive struggle to break out of a Glaswegian working-class world, wonders whether Leo might not be quite happy in a boarding school in the country, "with educational *standards*" and civilised boys. Tony, who is the son of a rich socialist man of letters and was sent to prep school and public school, who pretends to be a working-class chap, with woollen shirts and donkey jackets, is all for leaving Leo where he is. "If they bash him in the playground, you'll see. If he isn't learning anything, you'll notice. Alan doesn't know what he's talking about. Thirty little boys in a locker-room, all of them wanting to cry for their mummies in bed at night, is nevertheless like a crocodile pond, with jaws snapping and the fattest getting fatter. And you just don't know what sort of pervert's putting your son to bed at night. I do."

"You survived," says Alan.

"So did you, all your wasteland gangs and playground battles."

"Some don't," says Alan.

"I know," says Tony, who is reporting the Moors Murders trial, and living in a hotel in Chester. The discussion of where Leo will be least vulnerable has a new edge because of the fates of Lesley Ann Downey and John Kilbride, whose ordinary, gentle, childish, vanished faces appear daily in softened grey newsprint everywhere. Tony has heard the home-made tapes of the little girl crying out to be released, to go home to her mother, saying that she is frightened, being told to shut up and keep still. At the end of these tapes are children's voices singing Christmas music. On the reverse, Tony tells Frederica and Alan, is the crazy humour of the "Goon Show." Don't tell me, says Alan. I don't want to know any more. I don't myself, says Tony. I don't want to go back there, I don't want to be a reporter, I don't want to know. Frederica, her heart thumping, her gorge rising, distressed by the juxtaposition of this and Leo, by fear of losing him, by fear, by fear, finds she is weeping. Alan and Tony put their arms around her as she sobs. A car coughs in the street. Tony puts down the blind.

Frederica has also received several visits from Paul Ottokar. John Ottokar appears less frequently, and never telephones. So that when Frederica sees the blond face with its sweep of gold hair at the basement window, or the figure standing waiting in a black PVC mackintosh when she comes home from her shopping, she learns to assume it will be Paul, who, unlike John, has no regular job to go to. Even so, it is difficult to tell. They hunch their shoulders the same way. They

427

stand with their feet at the same angle. Their grave, tentative, charming smile is the same smile.

"I thought I'd drop in. I hope you don't mind. I'm at a loose end."

"I don't mind, no. But I've got a lot of work to do. Essays to correct. Some writing. Have a cup of coffee."

"Thank you. I will."

He does not keep still. He prowls around her basement room, taking books out of the bookshelves, putting them back differently. He picks up paperweights and balances them, and makes a feint of dropping them, and smiles, and restores them. He says, "Where's your record-player? Where's your music? Let's put on some music."

"I don't have a record-player. I'm tone-deaf. I like silence. I can't think in music."

"You won't get very far in swinging London. You'll need to know about music to know my brother. We've always had music. We played in a group, did he tell you? We played in the Aldermaston marches. He plays the horn and I play the clarinet. We're good. I'm forming a new group. I want him to come and play. Neither of us is *really* good without the other. We anticipate. We hear each other's thoughts. It's got a lovely name, my new group."

"Has it?"

"It's called Zag and the Ziggy-Ziggy Zy-Goats. Clever, don't you think?"

He prowls.

"You should come and hear us. When we play, we're good together. Other times, we aren't. I took it hard, Frederica, that my brother should have signed up for all your book classes without so much as a word to me. I took it hard, but I understood it. Both of us feel both things, you know, the need to be *two,* and the need to be *one.* We don't always feel them simultaneously. I read all your books from your class, when I was in the—when I was in retreat. *Dr. Faustus* and *Death in Venice, The Castle* and *The Idiot, The Birth of Tragedy from the Spirit of Music,* I read all that. I made sure you'd be interested in music."

"No. It's been left out of me."

"I'll play to you, one day. We'll play to you. *Everyone* now, *all the time,* understands the world through music. Books are like little scratches on the window. Inside, your soul spreads out in music. Music is wiser than *pyramids* of books."

"Sit down, you're making me nervous."

"I'm nervous myself. I'm intruding. I'm being rude, I'm doing what John won't like. Forgive me."

"Sit down."

"If there was any music, I could keep still and listen."

"There isn't."

"I'm making you angry. Look into my eyes. I am the one you haven't kissed, the body you don't know. Is it delectable or terrible to look at the *same thing* and know you don't know it, although you do?"

"I think you'd better go. I have things to do."

"Aren't you curious to see if it's the same, or different? Same face, same voice. Same kiss? Shall I kiss you, so you *know* whether it's the same, or different?"

Frederica sits and sips Nescafé out of a black mug with a rose-pink lining, salvaged from Cambridge, retrieved from Freyasgarth. What is disturbing is the sameness, not the difference. John Ottokar can be still and gentle, like a great lazy cat, and this one cannot, his fingers move nervously on his knees, which tremble together; his head tosses imperceptibly to some tune that twangs in his brain. But the smile is John's smile, and the eyes are John's eyes, and the fingers are John's fingers, and the voice, with its clarity and warmth, the voice is John's voice.

She says, "I don't want to know. I think you ought to go. I'll work out what I feel about John *with John,* if that's what he wants."

"He won't mind, if you kiss me. He'll expect it. We come as two sides of one coin, two faces of one herm. He knows that. Dear frowning Frederica, his kiss is not *complete* without my kiss, either for him, or for you, and he knows that. Don't be cross. Kiss me. He knows I am here, now, he *knows I am here,* he expects this. We always know. Take one, take both. He *knows I will be here.* Reject one, reject both. It might be better. We might be too much for you."

"You might," says Frederica. "You well might. But I'll discuss that with John."

"When I'm gone," he says, rising abruptly, "you'll be sorry, you'll desperately want to know what I'm like, you'll *ache.*"

"I'll take my chance."

"You don't take chances. You're cold, you're canny, you'll never hold him with that grismal frown. You'll bore the pants off him."

"I really do think you'd better go."

He goes.

Next time he comes, it is as if this conversation had never taken place. The figure waiting by the steps of Number 42 is sober-suited, in one of those collarless suits made fashionable by the Beatles, but in sober midnight-blue, over a white polo neck. Frederica, at the same instant, experiences a lurch of sexual delight, and makes an intellectual observation that this is almost certainly Paul.

"I'm sorry to bother you," he says. "I'm sorry to intrude, but I should be grateful for some professional advice, if you could spare me a moment or two."

"Come in," says Frederica.

"The thing is," says Paul Ottokar, once they are well in the basement, resuming his prowling, "the thing is, that the little group I belong to—not Zag and the Zy-Goats, which doesn't interest you, because you aren't musical, but the little spiritual splinter-group or spearhead—we are having a Poetry Weekend, and as my brother has no doubt told you, we—he and I—are dreadfully ill-read animals, and I don't know where to start my reading for this weekend. We are going to be called the Spirits' Tigers, I think, and someone called Richmond Bly is going to come and talk to us about 'The Visionary Aspects of English Romanticism.' Now I haven't the *vaguest idea* what all that is—but I do pick things up very quickly, as you may have observed—I got a lot out of *The Birth of Tragedy from the Spirit of Music*, I nicked dear John's copy—*he knows,* of course, I expect he *felt* it rising off his desk and going into my satchel, we're like that, we have kinetic knowledge of each other. So I thought I'd come to you for a reading list of *essential* English Romanticism for this weekend. So I can surprise Elvet Gander—I *love* surprising Elvet—there will be a poet there called Fainlight, I think, and a performance artist called Silo, who plays the drums with Zag and the Zy-Goats. Is it an impossible request? Can you make me a shopping list or batting order of English Romanticism? It will be good for my rather unenlightened soul."

"I could do that," says Frederica.

"I can't make head or tail of the *Visions of the Daughters of Albion*, I thought of *chanting* them. Like mantras. With bells and a drum and a wailing of thin horn music."

Frederica sits and writes. She writes down "Kubla Khan," *The Ancient Mariner,* "The Immortality Ode," "The Death of Hyperion." Paul Ottokar says, "I hope I wasn't offensive, last time. I was high. If I was offensive, please don't be offended. I should like us to be friends. In a minor key."

"Do you want a list of criticisms, or just of texts?"

"Whatever *you* think. I am in *your* hands."

Frederica writes. She wants to ask: And will John be coming to your Poetry Weekend? She does not ask.

"I'll make you a cup of coffee, whilst you write," says Paul Ottokar. He finds her kettle, her coffee, her cups, her milk, without hesitation. He finds Leo's biscuits iced with smiley faces, cherry-coloured, lemon-coloured, coffee-coloured, chocolate. He puts them out on a plate with Peter Rabbit and Benjamin Bunny. Frederica writes: Thomas de Quincey: *Confessions of an English Opium-Eater,* and accepts her own smiley biscuit, on her own plate, from the gently courteous intruder. She feels like crying.

John Ottokar telephones. He sounds strained. He talks about nothing much for a good five minutes and then says, "Can I come and see you?"

"When?" says Frederica.

"Over the weekend," says John Ottokar.

"Leo is going to his father this weekend."

"Then I'll come," says John Ottokar.

Frederica does not say then: "But there is a Poetry Weekend in Four Pence." She feels wise, and restrained, not to say this. She washes her hair, and makes the bed with clean sheets, and buys supper, supper that won't spoil, smoked trout and salad, a lemon tart. When John Ottokar arrives he is wearing his Liberty shirt with the green chrysanthemums and a collarless jacket in green baize, bottle-green, bound in dark blue. He has, despite these bright garments, a faded look to Frederica's eye. As though the other were brighter, sharper, clearer, more extreme than this one. Frederica searches his face for differences, and he sits there, over the dinner table, a little stony, a little guarded, undergoing her scrutiny as though it was exactly what he expected. He speaks rather doggedly of events in his world of work: Tony Benn's policy on North Sea oil, the balance-of-payments problems that loom. He looks around the basement room and says, "It's good to be here."

"I thought you would be busy with a Poetry Weekend."

"Ah," says John Ottokar. He puts down his knife and fork. He stands up and goes over to the basement window and looks out at the dark well.

"I think, Frederica, it might save us all a lot of pain and trouble if I were to put on my coat now, and go, and never come back. The alternative is pretty dreadful for both of us. It starts here. Either I ask you—what's he been saying, what's he been doing, what did you answer, what did you do?—or I don't, I keep quiet, and *both of us imagine*—you and me, that is—and he becomes a huge—a huge—a *demon* between us. I know now, you aren't looking at me—not *me*—you're looking at both of us, comparing, wondering. Your memories are all mixed up—which one smiled *that* smile, which one liked that poem, perhaps. Probably both did. Tearing ourselves apart is an act of violence, Frederica, an *unnatural* act in a sort of a way. You don't want all that. And I want you to myself, or not at all."

"What does he want?"

"To have what I have."

"At the same time as you, or instead of you?"

"That's a good question. At the same time, but *better*. He'd like both of us to make love to you, and he would be the one to do it *better*."

"And none of that is up to me?"

"Oh, some of it is, yes. But some of it isn't. I thought I would get away—from him—and I *can't*—there are reasons why I can't—good reasons—but I want my own life."

"Can't he get a girl of his own?"

"He wants mine. Whoever she is. And I—don't want that. That is between us, that *is* a difference."

Frederica says, "You can't just let him win. That isn't good for either of you."

"But you must see—as for *you*—I want *you*—and what I don't want, is for you to have to fight him—or be fought over—or *have anything to do with all that*. I want you to be you—as I first saw you—all thin and nervy standing there talking about the 'form of consecutive prose' wasn't it, with your eyes lit up, and your mind following a thread with a kind of *single-minded glee*—I thought, if I could get her to look at me, like that, to think about me with that sort of concentration."

"I do. I am. I do."

"You might have done."

"I do."

She stands behind him, and puts her arms round him. He is trembling.

"I won't be beaten," she says, "I'm a fighter, you know that. We can't be beaten. We must think our way *through* all this. I can lock him out."

He trembles more violently. "No," he says, "that won't work."

"*You*," says Frederica furiously, "*you* have got to know where I stand. *You* have got to stop being gloomy, and fight. You can't just walk out on me, having just walked in, because he's trying to walk in too. Did you let him have everything he was trying to take, when you were little? The cake, the tricycle, the little knife?"

"Oh yes. I always let him. There was always another, somewhere, I could have, until he came and wanted it."

"Well, *there isn't another Frederica Potter.* There is one of me and one only. I am I, and inseparable from myself, and indivisible into equal or unequal halves. And at the moment I want *you,* and you are what I want, unless you go on being gloomy and renunciatory, in which case I shall get depressed—but then *he* won't get me, John Ottokar, *neither of you will.* It's up to you. Only, I warn you, I warn you, I will not be a soft ball you toss between you, I will not be talked about or shared out in my absence, I will live my own life, which, just at the moment, I choose shall include *you.* End of speech."

John Ottokar turns away from the window and takes her in his arms. He sighs.

"Come to bed," says Frederica. She turns to pull down the blind and for a moment thinks she sees a blond figure in a dark PVC raincoat standing patiently outside the window. She puts her face to the glass, and there is nothing. She pulls down the blind, and holds out her arms. Whoever wants to see two merged shadows on the translucent cloth can see them. She begins to unbutton John Ottokar's shirt.

They make love. Most of that night, and most of the next day, with the blind drawn down, they make love. They make love in deepening silence, broken only by the odd squeak and suck of skin, the odd bird-like cry, the odd rustle of hair on cotton sheet, of finger- and toenails braced against flesh and bedclothes. They explore each other's bodies, diligently, companionably, leisurely, with little fits of

reciprocal fury, with slow, slow holdings back and rapid provoca-
tions. She learns his many tastes, his dryness and damp, his sleekest
surfaces and his roughest. She learns him as though he were inside
her skin, as though she were inside his. No two can be closer, no two
assemblies of living cells can be so confounded, so intertwined: they
wind sinuously about each other like snakes, they buck like goats,
they swallow like silent fish in the deep, they follow delectable rancid scents like cats in the jungle. They eat, are eaten, fling back free
a while and separate on drenched bedclothes. Both the body's hope
and the mind's fear of the fusion of cells somewhere in there, in the
pulling and gripping dark, are absent: they may do as they please,
only to please, because they are protected by the Pill. What Frederica delights in most is the warmth of flat belly against flat belly, the
push of pelvis against pelvis. When they pull away in the morning
light, she touches his skin and finds it is bloody; she touches her own,
and her fingertip is scarlet. "Look at us," she says. They are like
painted savages, streaked and smeared with warm and drying blood,
spread thin like ruddy paint, in whorls and runnels, palm-prints and
traced loin-cloths, which reflect each other, body and body. It is her
own blood, the blood of the seeping, "break-through" bleeding produced by the Pill in odd gouts and sprinklings, nothing to do with
the old rhythms of fertility. Frederica looks to see if John Ottokar
feels distaste for this body-paint, but he is tracing its contours with
his own finger, smiling.

"Signed in blood," he says. "You can read me on you and you on
me."

"Like savages. A rite of passage."

"Does it hurt?"

"No. It's lovely. It's warm. A glow."

They are whispering. Above their heads, Saskia's footsteps trot and
stop: Agatha calls out, the words inaudible.

"I've marked you," he says. "We've marked each other."

"Let's never move," she says, but this is an artificial note, this breaks
the spell, for in the end they must move, and they know it.

"Are you happy?" she says, like all lovers, and he answers, "Completely," one lovely hand heavy on the sharp edge of her haunch.

For whatever reason, this visit of John's puts an end to the visits of
Paul, at least for a time. Frederica wonders if Paul *knows*, in some way,
and the knowledge keeps him away. Knows what? she wonders, a

week or two later, when the red glow has been washed off her skin and has cooled and faded a little—only a little—in her memory. For she does not know, she does not exactly want, or need, to know, what she and John Ottokar intend, or desire. Frederica has told no one but Agatha about John Ottokar, and Agatha very little. John Ottokar as a secret, as a hidden pleasure, is nothing to do with her and Leo's future. But she is not free, as once she was, to feel her way in and out of loves and likings. For Leo watches her, calculating, jealous, wondering what she wants, what she plans, and his watching, like Paul's quite different watching, weighs on her. And although in the early summer Frederica does not see Paul, she realises that Leo does, or has.

"I smelt that bad smell of that smiley man again today," says Leo. And, "That man with the smell came by and looked in."

She cannot mention this to John. She does not know what to make of it. She is nervous.

She dreams she is in bed with two men, one red, one white, made of hot stone, with stone erections tipped with drops of blood (the white man) and white drops of semen (the red one). They turn to her, they lay their heavy arms across her chest, crushing her. They mount half of her, a thigh one side, a thigh the other. They are heavy, they crush her, she cannot cry out. She wakes. She is afraid. She is rather pleased with the energy and simplicity of the dream-forms, as though they were a work of art she had deliberately constructed.

XVII

❧❧❧❧❧❧

Dear John,

I write this letter only after much deliberation. There is a convention amongst psychoanalysts to put it at its lowest—in certain circumstances it bears a resemblance to a TABOO—there is a convention that it is "not done," may be injurious, to approach the relatives and lovers and associates of any "patient," with or without that "patient's" consent. Conventional psychoanalytic treatment is a relationship between two people, analyst and analysand—other relationships are worked out within that framework.

As you know, and as I know you know, I am "treating" your brother for what have been diagnosed as "manic-depressive episodes." As I believe you also know, I am in considerable sympathy with those new, and I believe promising, I will go so far as to say *exciting* ideas, thought-patterns, hypotheses, which suggest that we should look on unusual manifestations of the psyche not as aberrations from a specified *norm* (What is normal? Who dictates what we shall take as our *norm*?) but as ways of exploring the spirit, of exploring the pain, the Experience of the soul in a damaged and damaging environment. I do not, in other words, see your brother as a "sick man" in need of a "cure." But he is undoubtedly a perturbed spirit, undergoing, passing through, a kind of psychic electrical storm, in which great bolts of lightning "all sweating, tilt about the watery heaven," and he could be empowered or destroyed by these fiery currents.

I was pleased—pleased is a trivial word, I mean to say, and *should* say, *joyful,* to find Paul, or Zag as he prefers to be known, as a participant in the Meetings of the Spirits' Tigers. The good old Quaker word "Meeting" does suggest what these gatherings are meant to be, and one of the purposes of the Meetings is to restore to the spiritual group the energy, the *violence* even, which, as Christopher Levenson said in his poem from which we took our name, has

436

slowly over the centuries leached away from the original Pentecostal waitings on the Inner Light. The Quakers no longer quake: the disciples no longer speak with tongues: the Inner Light is dimmed: "the Spirits' Tigers are grown tame." It is entirely good that we few should come together to reverse this entry, to generate energy, heat and light, to make each other as far as possible *whole* in the spirit, at least to *empower* those of us who are lost, or wandering, or crashed. I believe Zag's choice to make one in these Many is a wise choice and to be supported. I believe the group—the Meeting—has been constituted by a wisdom and a purpose beyond the random needs of its individual members.

Now, what has this to do with me? you will ask. Or you will not ask, you will despise my rhetorical attributed question, for you know very well in part—*but not I think, in its wholeness*—what I am going to say to you, to request of you, to lay on you, in the vulgar tongue of our times.

As I was delighted to see Zag bathed in the light of the silence of the Tigers, so I was, on the two brief occasions when we met, overjoyed to see you. Your presence relaxed and calmed him; you brought a serenity to the Meeting which was good for others besides Zag; I think maybe the depth of the silent contemplation did you some good too, or so it appeared.

But you have not come to the last few meetings, and you have not answered the letters that have been sent to you. Zag says he believes you have "given up on him" and also "given up on the Tigers."

I have been a cabin attendant on Zag's spiritual voyage long enough to know that he believes it is your wish to put a distance between you. This is a sane wish, worthy of respect. There are three things I would nevertheless say to you—after great deliberation, as I say.

1. Your retreat is directly endangering Zag's progress—he feels bereft, he feels angry, he feels many many negative things, which he turns against himself, like a child who cuts his own skin. When he does not see you you become in his mind a fantasy spectre or emanation, powerful, to be fought. When he does see you, he sees that you are a complex, separate human being, with *real* needs and a *real* life with which he can come to terms.

From Zag's point of view, steady contact with you—above all, perhaps, in the sane and controlled emotional "field" of the Spirits' Tigers—is necessary for the preservation of some sense of "reality." And however much I may believe that "reality" is not the same thing as common-sense *convention* or *normality,* I do believe it exists. There is a real world—even if infinite—and there is an unreal world, and Zag is in great danger of being trapped in the latter.

2. Your retreat is, I suspect, endangering you, John. For you are *part of* Zag, and the separation must be a subtle unravelling, not a brutal and bloody teasing. You know that in your heart of hearts. Your "dailiness" you cling to is

437

an unreality as dangerous as Zag's bad trips to the Aurora Borealis. If I over-step the mark, burn this letter. If I speak to any flicker of recognition in any anxiety anywhere in your head or your heart, consider further, come and talk to me, come back to the Spirits' Tigers and bring the problem into the white light of our joint watchfulness and dreamy unknowing.

3. The world is changing before our eyes. Consciousness is changing. We can move into a state where *we do not hurt each other*. You were drawn to the Spirits' Tigers for reasons beyond even your mysterious positive and negative charge to and from your brother. We can say these things, these days, without sounding mad, or cranky, but soberly and truthfully.

Again, if this says nothing to you, burn this letter, forget you received it.

With best wishes.

Yours very sincerely,

Elvet Gander

John Ottokar shows this letter dumbly to Frederica. He holds it out, over the table in a coffee bar where they are meeting in his lunch-break. He is wearing his suit, and a blue-and-white-striped shirt, and a dark blue tie with small emerald spots on it. Frederica is irritated by his portentous and apprehensive expression. She is more irritated by the content of the letter.

"*His* problem," she pronounces, "is logorrhea. Some of those sentences mean almost nothing."

"It's partly a question of religious language," says John Ottokar. "It tends to be kind of portmanteau and empty at the same time. I do rather hate it. The Quakers avoid it if they can."

"He's meant to be a psychoanalyst."

"It's not exclusive. You can be both."

They are bickering about language, in order to avoid discussing the letter.

"What do you think?" says John Ottokar.

"It's nothing to do with me," says Frederica. "It's *your* letter, and *your* brother, and *your* Quakers and *your* Tigers. And *your* psycho-analyst."

"I see."

He stares gloomily at the tablecloth. He puts together his papers, as though he is about to leave.

"I'm sorry. I sound spiteful. I don't mean to be. It scares me. All these things you seem to be involved in, to *belong to*."

"I don't say that. The point is, I haven't gone to the Spirits' Tigers, not since . . . not since we . . . I know you don't like it. I want—I want to give—what *we* have—a chance."

"If you think I think I've got any right—am in any position—to stop you being a spiritual Tiger—please reconsider. I don't have any such right—I'm not asking for it."

"I know."

And don't look gloomy and submissive, Frederica wants to cry out; what I liked was your independent *prowling*. John Ottokar says mildly, "Elvet Gander has got a point. He won't say Paul is sick, because he doesn't like the word, but Paul is whatever Paul was when everyone said he was sick. He can't cope with normal life, I do know. And I do know that I could help. He's right there. I know."

"Well then, you must help him."

"But if I help him at the expense of my own life—if I get all *snarled*—"

Frederica feels she ought to say, "We'll deal with this together, we'll see it through, don't worry." Those are the lines that are written into the script, but she doesn't want to say them. She doesn't know where she and John Ottokar would or would not be going *without* Paul/Zag and Elvet Gander and the Spiritual Tigers.

"I don't want to bore you," says John Ottokar, responding accurately to this unspoken communication.

Frederica laughs.

"I don't see how anyone could find all this *boring*," she says. "Frightening, yes. What will you do?"

"I shan't go to the Tigers. I do want peace and quiet—the normal. I find them *heady* and—and intensely satisfying. But I ought perhaps to write to Gander and try and say what I feel, why I don't think it's a good idea. And I don't want to write, I hate writing, I hate putting things down, it's all lies, it's all *approximate* . . ."

"I'm going to meet Gander myself," says Frederica. "Rupert Parrott's having a meeting 'In Defence of *Babbletower*.' He's asked all his trendy authors—Gander, and Canon Holly and Phyllis Pratt. He's asked me, because he says I can make Jude behave better. He says a recent graduate gave evidence in the *Lady Chatterley* case, just a young girl, to show she was unsullied. I can't see me making a good impression in the witness box as an unsullied young girl who had read *Babbletower* and was still unsullied. He's terribly worked up. In a crusading sort of way. Whereas Jude is terribly worked up in a *personal* sort of way, and doesn't look well."

The June end-of-the-year exhibition at the Samuel Palmer School is still known as the Dip Show, though the students are now taking a degree, not a diploma. This is why they must pass a literature exam, and why Frederica has been working hard, invigilating and marking papers. Frederica and Agatha go to the Dip Show together, on a sunny Sunday afternoon. Leo and Saskia go with them, and Clement and Thano attach themselves to the party. So does John Ottokar, who turns up "for the fairy story," and stays to lunch, as he sometimes does.

Frederica enjoys the atmosphere. The great studios are divided into spaces, and there are abrupt changes of identity from space to space. A series of stormily menacing rural landscapes is juxtaposed with a box containing brilliant demi-lunes and diamonds of purple and yellow spots and stripes. This is next to a series of collages—balloon-breasted bearded men in fishnet tights and stilettos wrestling or embracing giant carrots and stuffed rabbits, which is in turn next to a painterly series of portraits of men and women in the act of peeling soft plastic masks off their faces. Frederica now knows enough about painting to see that what makes these interesting is the virtuosity and variety of the troughs and channels and folds and texture of the different surfaces, the perspectives of the doubled eyes and twisted sockets. She can also see that the student (Susie Blair) has been taught by Desmond Bull. Susie Blair writes decorous little essays for Frederica on "Show the different methods by which Jane Austen invites and discourages the reader's sympathy for Emma Woodhouse and/or Fanny Price"—these essays show no sign of the savage intelligence that imitates flesh and plastic in oil paint. Frederica enjoys the gaps between the painters' writings and their inventions, which she could never have thought up, or begun to imagine, even the weakest. In the next cubicle are a series of dream-worlds somewhere between Claude and Arthur Rackham, entitled *Faery Lands Forlorn*. They ought to be kitsch, and are not, not quite. Saskia says, "Look at the little greeny lights."

The painters are dispensing red and white wine in crinkling plastic beakers; everything is spread with a faint dust of trodden potato-crisps. The party hurry past a room with nothing in it but a red canvas, a white canvas and a blue canvas, with the predictable rubric "United?" They come to the graphics department, where everything is display-conscious. Here they discover that the design teacher has been as good as his word, and has set *Babbletower* as an exercise in jacket design and poster production. Here too they find Jude himself, patrolling the display like an Ancient Mariner ready to pounce and expound. He hurries up to Frederica, John and Agatha.

"Here you have the Artwork for a work of art *temporarily,* we hope, suppressed. What is your opinion of all this? Who carries away the palm for *suggestiveness*?"

"Vis man," says Leo to Saskia, *sotto voce,* "is ve *other* smelly man. My mum knows lots of really *stinking* men."

"This one *pongs,*" agrees Clement, equably.

"Be quiet," says Jude. "Little children should speak when spoken to, you must know that. How fortunate that you are all too short to see my collection of turrets. Go over there, where a well-meaning young woman has done a pretty Perrault and give me your opinion of her Puss-in-Boots and her Little Red Riding Hood. Marks out of ten, please."

Some of the *Babbletower* covers are banal. Others are clever and suggestive. One has Hockneyish drawings of a man in a wig and a woman in hoops, leering at each other half-heartedly. Two or three have Disneyish Germanic castles. One has a long procession of maggot-like infants, carrying rose branches, passing under a portcullis into blackness. One has three Blake-like Elders or Wise Men standing on a battlement amongst flocks of big black birds. One has Brueghel's beautiful painting of the unfinished, crumbling, weed-ridden Tower of Babel, with brilliant little droplets, or tongues of scarlet shiny blood dripping out of its orifices and down its ledges. Jude points this one out with approval. "The lettering is a bit fancy," he says. "If you look closely you can see it's made of needles and pins, I don't like that. But it's better than these dreadful *people* who aren't my people, who stop you *seeing* the people in the book, who *interfere.*"

"This one's clever," says Agatha.

It is semi-abstract and very bright—a tomato-coloured double-apple-cheeked fruit, with a serpentine pointed conical tube in very bright green, coiled round it and penetrating it.

"I hate it," says Jude.

"It's a good joke," says Agatha, in her mild, dark voice. "Cul-vert. Rose-Arse. It's all there, in *purely visual language.*"

"I can see that. I hate it."

Agatha considers.

"I might hate it, if I were you. But since I'm not, I find it very witty. I hope it got a good mark."

"It did," says Jude.

He takes them "to see my glory and my shame." He hurries them down flights of stairs and into the refectory, where there is a display of the Foundation Course Life Studies, which include Jude naked, in chalk, in charcoal, in pastel, in gouache, in pencil, in acrylic, in oil. He is a faceless skinny length of bone in a tent of hair, he is meticulously delineated nipples and prick in bronze and green on grey paper, he is soft, soft lead, uncannily recalling the exact tone of his hippo-grey skin, sitting regally in a gilt chair, lying foetally coiled on plumped and depressed cushions. He is tendons and knobby knees and chilblains and scraggy neck; he is aquiline disdain; he is gloom with downcast eyes. The three little boys go from image to image; they do not say so, but everyone can see they are comparing the depictions of his genitals. Leo points and whispers: Clement nods.

"I am instructive," says Jude.

"Do you *enjoy* seeing these?" says Agatha.

"It convinces me I exist, I suppose. And that we do not see ourselves as others see us, which I know. And that my shins are not proportionate—at some moment, from some angles—with each other or with other parts of my anatomy."

Far away, in the bowels of the building, they hear music. It is a jazz clarinet, wooden and liquid, a clear long, long wail, a run of chords, a desolate repeated complaint. They wander in its direction. One or two canted notices, hung on door-knobs, say in red letters on white card: PERFORMANCE THIS WAY. Performance art is not—not yet—really on the agenda of the Samuel Palmer School. Not many people are following the signs, but the children pull the adults along. In a sculpture storeroom, abutting the garages and car park, a small dais has been set up. It is shrouded in black velvet, hazed with chalk dust. Behind it is a long and welded sculpture, painted in pillar-box red, with a series of blade-like forms suspended from a series of ladder-like forms. To its right is a huddled crowd of chipped and cheesy-surfaced classical plaster casts: a bland Apollo tipped off-balance against a smiling, hoofed Pan, a headless Athena with her Gorgon breastplate, a horsehead, a very small centaur. On the left of the dais is Paul Ottokar, in tailcoat and white tie (he looks classically beautiful), playing the clarinet, with his music propped before him on a very pretty gilt stand. On the right is a kind of cage-like edifice made from multi-coloured playstraws, inside which is a human being dressed like a large bird, with a bright yellow bulging rump, a feathered tail, wrinkled yellow tights, large clawed feet constructed from wire, insulating tape and putty, a tarred and feathered torso, and a head crested with green feathers, masked like an American Indian bird-man, over which is strapped an aluminium contraption with a very long, proboscis-like stabbing beak with a strip of Day-Glo-pink fluorescent paint running its whole length.

With this he monotonously taps a large metal plate, painted with a black-and-white spiral pattern, at his feet. The tapping is not in synch with the clarinet music. At irregular intervals the bird-man raises and lets fall his wings/arms in an impotent way. When he does this, a rattle whirs briefly. Saskia says, "It is the Dong with the luminous nose." Leo says, "It is *ve other* smelly man, ve *other* John." He looks at John, to make sure there are two. Frederica looks at John, to see what they should do. John stands in the shadow of the plaster casts and smiles slightly, listening. The only other person in the room is Desmond Bull, who kisses Frederica and smiles at Jude.

Paul Ottokar pauses in his playing, without acknowledging his audience. His companion does not pause in his manic tapping. Paul Ottokar bows, sits down, and begins to play the Adagio from Mozart's Clarinet Concerto. The man-bird taps, mechanically. The beautiful sounds bubble and flow. The beak stabs and taps. Frederica tries to shut out the tapping and cannot. The bird-man raises his wings and whirs. The music gathers power. The bird-man ceases to tap and for a moment a small trill is alone in the silence. Then the bird-man begins a virtuoso imitation of a hen laying an egg. The children laugh. It is a very good imitation. The music sings away. The bird-man taps again. He stops. He makes a series of sounds which can be interpreted as a hen trying frantically to escape pursuit, failing, and having its neck wrung. He strangles, he gags, he croaks. The lovely music runs on. Frederica thinks: There is *not enough point* to all this, or else I am missing something. It is a thought she is often to have, in those years.

When the music has come to an end, Paul Ottokar closes his music book, folds his music stand, takes out a box of matches and sets fire to the straw cage.

"Watch it!" says Bull.

The base flares, blackens and dies. The structure collapses. Clarinet player and bird take a bow. They step off the dais. "Is vat all?" says Leo.

"That is all," says Paul Ottokar, unsmiling.

"It was *quite* funny," says Clement judiciously.

"It gives a headache," says Saskia, more musical than Frederica and Leo.

The brothers are side by side.

"You burned the cage," says Leo. "How can you start again?"

"We aren't going to," says the bird-man, with a Liverpudlian voice under his mask. "We've done that, now. We're going for a spaghetti. It's the end of the day. Anyone coming?"

"Yes," says John Ottokar. "That would be a good idea. Anyone else?"

Everyone goes to the Spaghetti House around the corner. It seems quite natural, quite ordinary, two brothers have met by accident, a group of friends have decided to have spaghetti after a Dip Show.

The bird-man is introduced as Silo. Under his aluminium dong-beak and his formal mask he is pale, scrawny-necked and bespectacled. Frederica asks John Ottokar, who appears to know him, if Silo is anything to do with Silence. John says no, his name is Sidney Lowe, it's the first syllable of his names. Paul Ottokar says, "You could take it as a sign, though, that the syllables come out like that. It might have a meaning."

"Most syllables can be made to mean *something*," says John.

"Empiricist, nationalist," says Paul, as though these words were delicate insults.

The meal goes well. The Spaghetti House is made with barn-like booths and red-checked tablecloths; all the booths are full of celebrating art students drinking Chianti. The children become restive, waiting for their dishes of carbonara and bolognese, and John Ottokar organises a kind of round-table serial game of scissors-paper-stone. Leo says, "Is it *true,* what you said, you two always put out ve *same thing,* always?"

Paul smiles at John. "Did you tell him that?"

"It was true, then."

"And now? Try now?"

It is like arm-wrestling, a trial of strength in a pub; it is amiable, but tense. John and Paul are sitting opposite each other. They put out a hand each. Flat, both. Paper, paper. Again. Clenched fists. Stone, stone. Stone, stone. Stone, stone. Scissors, scissors. Paper, paper. Scissors, scissors. Stone, stone. Stone, stone. Frederica watches with alarm. Bull says, "This is nothing to do with the law of averages." Silo says, "Do you read each other's minds?"

"No, no," says Paul. "We just *know*. Quick as a flash, we *know*."

Scissors, scissors. Paper, paper. Stone, stone.

They look pleased with themselves. Paul says, "Do you remember, we used to sing?" He hums. "Anything *you* can do, I can do *better*. I can do *anything*, *bet*ter than you." John joins in.

"No you can't." "Yes, I can." "No you can't." "Yes, I can."

"It was true and not true," says Paul.

Frederica has not seen them together since the bonfire night. Leo and Clement and Thano start singing. "Anything *you* can do, *I* can do *bet*ter." Frederica thinks: I thought the problem was, the two of them, fighting over *me*. She has the sexual self-confidence, over-confidence perhaps, of her curious historical position, brief and anomalous, a Cambridge woman when there were eleven men for every woman. They were princesses, those women, though ordinary enough, in fact. Now she sees that it is not that, not so much that, that is the problem. She is in competition with each brother for the attention of the other, and must lose. They sit at ease, smiling at each other, thrusting out their identical fists, paper, scissors, stone, with no winner, no loser, no difference.

She thinks: They are like the two blades of a pair of scissors. She thinks: If we are two, we are two so, as stiff twin compasses are two. She thinks, with an internal mad laughter, "Those whom God hath joined together let no woman put asunder." She has a brief memory of their joined bloody bodies, John's and hers. She feels Desmond Bull's hand, making a firm secret curl behind her buttocks, strong, steady. She does not push it away.

They sing another song. Everyone joins in.

> "I'll sing you one-oh.
> *Green grow the rushes-oh.*
> *What is your one-oh?*

Saskia and Agatha raise clear voices. Thano sings strongly. It is a good, friendly party. "I'll sing you two-oh. Two, two, the lily-white boys, clothed all in green-oh. One is one and all alone, and ever more shall be so. I'll sing you three-oh. Green grow the rushes-oh. What are your three-oh? Three, three, the Rivals."

"You're out of tune, Frederica."

"I expect I am, Paul. I always am. I told you, I'm not musical. I'm tone-deaf."

"We could teach you. You probably aren't *really* tone-deaf. Almost no one really is incurably tone-deaf. You could learn."

"No, I couldn't. I can't. I'll shut up, since my singing offends you. I'll be the audience."

Desmond Bull's fingers wrinkling the cloth on her buttocks. The two faces opposite, both with eyebrows quizzically and ruefully raised, the charming expression identical, *the same.*

"Go *on,*" says Leo, crossly.

"Three, three, the Rivals. Two, two, the lily-white boys, clothed all in green-oh. One is one and all alone and ever more shall be so."

Laminations

Instructions for use. Your Pills are presented in separated bubble-strips, clearly marked with the days of the week. Press each pill out of its bubble and swallow it with water at the same time each day. It is important not to miss a day: if you do, you may not be fully protected. When you have taken three weeks' supply of pills, you must take none for the next week, during which bleeding may occur. This bleeding may be scanty, though occasionally it may be copious, more than your usual menstrual bleedings. This bleeding is break-through bleeding, and cleanses the womb: it is not a "period," and should cause you no discomfort. If heavy bleeding occurs and persists after several cycles of the Pill you should see your doctor, who may prescribe an alternative dosage.

The herald brought the little glass slipper to the house of the three sisters, and there was great excitement there. The eldest stepsister claimed that the slipper was hers, and would fit her; the stepmother measured her foot against the delicate shell and declared that it would never go in. "It is a small price to pay for the hand of a Prince and half a kingdom," said the stepmother then. "Be resolute, and I will take a slice from your heel with this knife, and the foot will slide in." So they did as she suggested, and the eldest sister came before the herald and the young Prince and stretched out her fat leg proudly and turned her foot in the shining shoe. But the herald observed that gouts of dark blood were welling up inside it and brimming over, and he asked the sister to take off the shoe again, and she did so, and her wound was visible to all, and she was shamed and disgraced. Then the second sister, no whit discouraged by her sister's failure, tried to force the pretty shoe over her knobby foot, but it would not go, no matter how she struggled and shoved. So her mother took the little axe with which they killed the hens, and quick as a flash chopped off her big toe, and bandaged it, and then they were able to force the foot in, and the second sister hobbled proudly into the presence of the Prince. But the brown bird in the tree that flowered on Cinderella's mother's grave called out, "There is blood in the shoe, there is blood in the shoe," and when the herald came near he saw that the shoe was full of blood and the second sister was faint with pain. So she too was disgraced, and went away to weep and sulk. And the herald asked, "Are there no more young women in the house?" And the stepmother said, no, but the father said, "There is only Cinderella, in the ashes, in the kitchens." So Cinderella was sent for, and she came, and stretched out her pretty little foot, all grimed as it was with ashes, in its cheap stocking, and the shoe fitted exactly, like a glove. And when the Prince saw that the shoe fitted exactly, he recognised his beautiful dancing partner in the little skivvy, and said, "What was lost is found, and this is the bride my heart is sworn to." And they both rode away together, past the brown bird singing in the weeping tree.

Quaere. Who cleaned the coagulated blood out of the shoe, twice over, before Cinderella inserted her virginal toes?

> *Under a Tree I saw a Virgin sit*
> *The red and white rose quartered in her face.*

> *Just at the stroke when my veins start and spread*
> *Set on my neck an everlasting Head.*

"I take no such pleasure in life that I should much wish it, nor conceive such horror in death that I should greatly fear it; and yet I say not, but if the stroke were coming, perchance flesh and blood would be moved with it and seek to shun it." (Elizabeth I)

"You had a conversation with Gran, did you not?"

"No, she shouted down: 'What is all the noise?' I said: 'It is just the dog barking'—not that the tape-recorder had dropped on my toes as was alleged I had said."

"But this was during the shouting?"

"No, it wasn't."

"It is very odd that she should ask the question after the noise had ceased."

"No; she was probably awakened from her sleep and had got out of bed to come to the bedroom door."

"You were quite determined that the old lady should not interfere?"

"Yes, I shouted up so that she would not come down. If she had come down she might well have dropped dead with shock."

"There were spots of blood on your shoes?"

"Yes. It was probably splashed on. Possibly because the shoes had been left in the living-room. I had been out in my high-heeled shoes."

"The trial is now in its eleventh day. Have we heard this suggestion before, that the shoes were in the room, and that you were not wearing them that night?"

"No."

"Let me see the shoes, please. Is there any trace of blood inside those shoes, as far as you know?"

"No."

"Your feet were inside the shoes and your feet were taking whatever blood fell upon that area?"

"No."

"Are you now wearing the high-heeled shoes you were wearing that night?"

"Yes."

"May I see one of them, please?" (*Shoe handed to the Attorney-General*). "Is that the shoe you were wearing to go on the moors?"

"Yes, I went in the car. I always wear high-heels outside. We were not going to walk on the moors. We were just going to park."

The Story of Stone

Peter Stone, a sculptor, a student at the Samuel Palmer School. A slight, bowed young man, with a pitted, ashy skin, loose lips, and a shock of colourless hair always full of stone-dust. He was working, I was later told and shown, on a kind of minor marble menhir, white with pinkish veinings, which was in the Dip Show, or Degree Show. It was an erect cylindrical form, with a gently rounded top, which had been chipped and worked into a crazed, dimpled, sinewy surface, so that the marble glittered here and there, and did not have the smoothness one easily associates with marble. It was not very big; three feet perhaps. Having learned to look for subversion and opposition in new works of art, I decided that this was an act of defiance against the welded metal or moulded plastic and fibre-glass sculptures: Stone's carving was the only *carved* work in the Show, that year.

I invigilated the final examination he took: final in every sense. He must have been sitting in about the third row back: one of the big studios had been set out with temporary desks. He came in smiling broadly, and sat down staring around, and writing nothing. He was twitching and fidgeting. He began to write. His handwriting was very large and vacant. He kept coming up to the front for more paper. He asked to be excused, left the room briefly, came back and wrote a few more large words, asked for more paper, rushed out to be excused, dust falling from his hair, came back, wrote more words. Because they were all art students, no one paid much attention to this behaviour. Finally he reached a point where he was writing one large, childishly formed word per sheet, rushing back and forwards, writing another. A sheaf of paper rose in front of him. Finally he rushed out and did not return. "Stoned," one of the other students said. We laughed, and finished our work. I gathered up his papers at the end of the exam. He had written only one sentence, over and over, in huge round letters. YOU CAN'T GET BLOOD OUT OF A STONE.

Later we discovered that he had run down the Holborn up escalator, on to the Central Line platform, and had opened his arms and jumped into the path of an approaching train. He was killed, instantly they said, as they always do. Perhaps he thought he could fly. Perhaps he was in despair over his exams. No one knew. There must have been a great deal of blood. The train driver collapsed and has been unable to start work again. This story is almost too neat, as though the language had constructed it, not it the language, blood and stones, but it is a true story, a story of our times, uncanny only because of the too great, glittering precision of the language.

Why a Tongue impressed with honey from every wind?
Why an Ear, a whirlpool fierce to draw creations in?
Why a Nostril wide inhaling terror, trembling and affright?

449

Why a tender curb on the youthful burning boy?
Why a little curtain of flesh on the bed of our desire?

The Virgin started from her seat, and with a shriek
Fled back unhindered till she came into the vales of Har.

But Shelob was not as dragons are, no softer spot had she save only her eyes. Knobbed and pitted with corruption was her age-old hide, but ever thickened from within with layer on layer of evil growth. The blade scored it with a dreadful gash, but those hideous folds could not be pierced by any strength of man, not though Elf or Dwarf should fuse the steel or the hand of Beren or of Túrin wield it. She yielded to the stroke, and then heaved up the great bag of her belly high above Sam's head. Poison frothed and bubbled from the wound. Now splaying her legs she drove the huge bulk down on him again. Too soon. For Sam still stood upon his feet, and dropping his own sword, with both hands he held the elven-blade point upwards, fending off that ghastly roof; and so Shelob, with the driving force of her own cruel will, with strength greater than any warrior's hand, thrust herself upon a bitter spike. Deep, deep it pricked, as Sam was crushed slowly to the ground.

No such anguish had Shelob ever known, or dreamed of knowing, in all her long world of wickedness. Not the doughtiest soldier of old Gondor, nor the most savage Orc entrapped, had ever thus endured her, or set blade to her beloved flesh.

Observer May 8th, 1966 (Maurice Richardson)

"If those two were sane they'd have gone mad long ago." I was rather impressed by this comment—by a local hall porter—on the psychology of Ian Brady and Myra Hindley. Behaviour so atrocious can only be described in terms of Irish or Hegelian logic, the logic of contradictions. How does one begin to explain it?

It is all very well to say that we were all once polymorph—perverse infants, and that Mr. Everyman's unconscious teems with sado-masochistic impulses. True, of course. But there is nothing impulsive about their dreadful calculated performances and the elaborate decoying that must have preceded them. I find it less difficult to empathise with Jack the Ripper than with these two. Odd how one always calls them Brady and Myra.

The other peculiar feature here is the dual element. *Folie à deux* in which two people go mad together is not unknown. An hysteric who falls in love with a psychotic will share the psychotic's delusions as long as they are together. Separate them, and the hysteric recovers, while the psychotic remains insane. And according to Freud hysterical women may share the perversions of their lovers. . . .

In the dock: Brady is thin, bony, rather gangling. Lean face with straight nose jutting out under his rather flat forehead. His dark brown hair is neat and tidy, yet looks faintly dusty. His clothes—grey suit, pale blue shirt, ultramarine, mildly artistic tie—are dateless, not like those of David Smith, who goes in for the gear. One of the first things you notice about him is his bad colour: pale mud. He really does look terribly sick.

Myra by contrast is blooming. Her hair, naturally brown, has been changing colour from week to week. First silver-lilac, then bright canary blonde. She is a big girl with a striking face: fine straight nose, thinnish curved lips, rather hefty chin, blue eyes. Full face she is almost a beauty. The Victorians would have admired her.

She wears a black-and-white speckled coat and skirt and a pale blue shirt open at the neck: it matches Brady's. I suspect she imitates everything he does, even to always keeping her handkerchief neatly folded. At a glance she looks as smartly turned out as a duchess, but when you look closer you see at once that this is mass-produced supermarket chic: there is an ambience of bubblegum and candyfloss.

Both take copious notes and lean over the front of the dock to prod their solicitor, the eupeptic Mr. Fitzpatrick, with a pencil. Occasionally they offer each other a packet of mints. Once during David Smith's evidence Myra flashes Brady a quick bright smile. When he goes into the witness box she gazes at him. When it is her turn, he draws faces on his scribbling pad.

Tea—yes—with some of the hosts of detectives working on this case. We talked about modern youth, violence, censorship, permissiveness and all that. One of them, who is a bit of a sociologist and has a highly specialised knowledge of swinging Manchester, thought there was a dangerous current of perversion in the air. "Kinky" had become a household word. He'd seen a shop advertising: NEW LINE IN KINKY RAINCOATS. Why, he said, don't they label them raincoats for sexual perverts and be done with it? He said it twice over. This may be an unduly puritan reaction: it is quite a common one. We shall encounter it more often as a result of this case. . . .

I haven't myself dreamed about the case at all, but occasionally in court towards the end of the afternoon I've caught myself lapsing into fantasies. These have taken the form of carrying out vengeance on the accused, which shows how careful you have to be. Once, I said to myself: If I were to put on Batman's gear, swoop down on the dock, which I could easily do from my seat in the gallery, what would the *News of the World* pay for my life story?

I lie awake at 2 a.m. because some race-going son of Belial—there are night clubs now even in Chester—has jammed the horn of his car. I try to find a suitable text in Sartre's *Saint Genet* which a kind local friend has lent me: he thinks that Brady might conceivably turn into his opposite. I'm afraid he has a long way to go, and he lacks Genet's talent. How about this?

"Thus the evil doer is the Other. Evil—fleeting, artful, marginal evil—can be seen only out of the corner of one's eye and in others . . . The Enemy is our twin brother, our image in the mirror . . . For peace-time Society has in its wisdom created what might be called professional evil doers.

"These evil men are as necessary to good men as whores are to decent women. They are fixation abscesses. For a single sadist there is any number of appeased, clarified, relaxed consciousnesses. They are therefore very carefully recruited. They must be bad by birth and without hope of change."

H'm. I think I know what Mr. Justice Fenton Atkinson would say to that. And I rather think I agree with him. We've had rather a surfeit of evil up here.

The summer holidays return. Leo will go to stay at Bran House; it is as though there were a regular pattern of life, and Frederica half-hopes that Leo thinks there is, but it is no such thing, it is all provisional and full of violence and threats of violence. The lawyers' letters fly. She cuts them up and pastes them into *Laminations*. She considers her own summer plans. Perhaps she will go back to Yorkshire.

Whilst she is thinking this out, John Ottokar telephones. He is at work; she has never seen where he works or where he lives, which she believes is somewhere in Earls Court. She imagines his place of work as a large space full of huge, clean, quietly humming machines, with walls of glimmering blue-grey screens showing graphs, and the columns of the strange binary language they print out on interleaved concertinas of pristine paper. She imagines him surrounded by other decorous, suited people, some of them—she is not sure about this—in surgical white coats. She imagines cool, metal venetian blinds, and shining steel furniture. It is probably nothing like this, but this is what she imagines. He says, "Can you come out to dinner with me?"

"I should think so. I can get a baby-sitter. Agatha's working late, I know. I can ask a student."

"Chez Victor," he says. "Eight o'clock."

Frederica likes Chez Victor. It is small, and dark, and simple and sophisticated, and truly French; the food is French French food and reminds her, amongst dark green paint and etched glass, of the heat of Provence, M. et Mme. Grimaud, wine and garlic. She wears a black linen shift, well above her knees, and a silk shawl, black, embroidered with creamy cabbagey roses and golden lilies, with a long, shimmering fringe. She has learned to line her eyes with a black, surprised stare, and to lengthen her lashes; nothing can make her angular quickness look doll-like, but this is as near as she will ever get. She has painted her wide mouth creamy-brown, a pale colour, which does not wholly suit her. John Ottokar is wearing his suit. Frederica loves to see him in his suit. She is afraid of having to live her life amongst the unkempt, the meagrely bearded, the sagging and woolly, the deliberately ill-defined. She likes edge. John Ottokar in his suit, with his long, blond, well-cut hair, has edge. He looks good in Chez Victor: a serious man eating a serious meal. They have *pâté, soupe de poissons,* skate in black butter, an *entrecôte sauce béarnaise, pommes dauphinoises,* an excellent salad, a perfect *tarte au citron.* They discuss the coming summer.

"I am thinking of going back to Freyasgarth."

"It is beautiful, up there."

"We had a good few days in Goathland."

"More than good."

There is a constraint in him.

"Do you want to come for a bit? Do you have any holiday?"

She never invites him: she always waits for him to move. This time, she has exposed herself.

"Of course I want to come. Of course I do."

"But?"

"I have ten days owing to me."

"But?"

"You *know* what the 'but' is, Frederica. The Spirits' Tigers are having a month-long Retreat, at Four Pence. They've got people coming from Timothy Leary's League for Spiritual Discovery. And some

Buddhists. And Elvet Gander. And of course Paul. He wants me to come. Gander's writing again."

He looks at the starched white tablecloth. He does not look at Frederica. He says, "Paul asked me to ask you if you'd come."

"God, no," says Frederica, quick as a flash, with automatic revulsion. She looks at his brooding face, turned down, lit a little by the shine of the clean cloth in the dark green room. "I'm sorry, John. I don't mean to sound nasty. But I'm not religious and I *hate group things,* I hate them, I hate pressure on me to lose myself, I can't bear it, I won't."

"I told him you wouldn't. I told him why. I told him what you've just said."

"And?"

"He said, that's exactly why she *ought* to come, she doesn't know what she doesn't know."

"Probably he's right. But I'll go on not knowing, if you don't mind. I'll put a lot of books in a bag, and go north, and read and write, and be part of my family, which is a group I've got no choice about belonging to."

"I shall lose you."

"Who can tell? We have to decide what's important. I can't imagine *you*—not the you I know—in some sort of ecstatic group love-in, all moaning and humming and confessing, if you want to know. But everybody has all sorts of sides to them. There are things about me *you* can't possibly imagine."

"It isn't like that. It isn't moaning and humming."

"I know. I'm unfair. I think we ought to stop talking about it."

"The Quaker silence," says John Ottokar, and does not finish the sentence.

"The Quaker silence?" says Frederica.

"When I was a boy, the silence made other people bearable for me. And more than that. You could sit there—they were all quite ordinary—and after a time, after a time of silence—everyone was quiet— you lost—not your *self* exactly—but all the mess of—the *fuss* of your life—you were all quiet together. It wasn't that everyone became one, or anything—I couldn't bear that any more than you could. It was just that they were *true*—*truer*—than before—to be truthful, I don't really want them to be Tigers—I just liked the quiet, the truth. Look, Frederica, this really is a thing words can't deal with. I keep saying

454

'true' and you don't know what I'm talking about, it doesn't *represent* what I'm talking about."

"Perhaps I do."

"It's something I can't really do without, anyway. Not having known it. I don't think there'll be much of it—if any—at Four Pence this summer. But there's the other thing too, I've got to look after Paul, that's how it is."

"I understand all that."

At this moment, she loves him, she would use the word "love," for what she feels about his careful truthfulness.

"I shall lose you," he says.

"I don't know," she says, trying to be as honest as he is. "I shouldn't have sounded so nasty, but it is true, I can't really bear it, all that, Tigers and chemical ecstasy and hugging-encounters, I really feel—"

"Repelled."

"Yes."

"So do I. Really. I shouldn't go. For myself. Only Paul—"

"You wanted to be separate."

"I do. But *really*. Sometimes I think Gander could help us through."

"Do you?"

"Not with much conviction. I don't know *what* I think. The trouble with Paul is, he does. I'm the tough one, in one sense, but he's the one with convictions, and feelings, he *dives*—"

"I can't cope with both of you."

"Fair enough. I shall lose you."

He stares at the tablecloth. Frederica bites lemon tart. Her tongue tastes sweetness and sharpness. She has no need of any chemical: the tart is sweet, is sour, is unforgettable.

"It is up to you," she says.

He lifts his head.

"I shall come with you. I won't lose you. It matters to me. We'll make our own quiet, up there on the moors."

His hand moves to touch hers, on the white cloth. She has a moment of fear—has she promised more than she can give, has she *taken on* the complicated coils of the brotherhood?

"No promises," he says, hearing this thought in the silence. "Just a summer holiday. A good one."

She takes hold of his hand. His skin is dry, and warm, and good. They get the bill, and go on the Underground, back to Kennington.

When they come back to Hamelin Square, there are more people than usual on the pavements. The Agyepongs are out, and also the Utters, and the small man with the little Austin is standing behind it. The door of Number 42 is open—not the area door, but the upper door, and framed in it are Leo, Saskia and their substitute-granny, peering anxiously out. As John Ottokar and Frederica emerge from the pan-handle, so to speak, of the square, into the frying-pan itself, a golden figure leaps up the area steps, three at a time, and crosses to the central mud patch in three long balletic, scissor-like jumps. This figure has flying gold hair and a long, shimmering, shining robe, a kind of sleeved gown in transparent plastic shot with rainbow colours, like oil spilled in a puddle on the road. The plastic makes a hissing and swishing noise. The figure's arms are full of something which he places carefully in the old chair which lolls against the broken bed-stead on the mud, where the bonfire's charred traces can still be seen. He bends over the chair, and Hamelin Square is suddenly full of music, not pop music but Brunnhilde's fire music from the end of *The Valkyrie*. It is not clear why no one moves forward, but no one does. He produces a straw-cased Chianti bottle, from which he pours libations into the chair, and then, sweeping in a great circle round the edge of the mud patch, over various towers of books, which can now be seen to ring the whole circle. He is singing, or humming, not Wagner, but some ecstatic blending moan. He dances, extending his arms in the light of the street lamps. It becomes clear that inside his plastic robe he is naked except for a swirling design of gold and bur-gundy body paint, spiralling round his arms and legs, making targets of his nipples, crossing in arching branches over his belly under his erect cock in its golden bush. As they watch, he produces a cigarette lighter and sets fire to the skoob turrets, of which there are seven, all of them quite high. His face too is painted, a snarling cat mask under the blond flying hair. He skips from burning books to burning books, making obeisances, mopping and mowing. He sings, he dances. "Ite Bacchae. Io Zagreus." It is absurd and frightening. The books flare and then burn sullenly, smelling bad and smoking. He returns, pour-ing more paraffin from the Chianti bottle. Frederica, at first paralysed like everyone else by the noise and the flickering flames and the strangeness, is suddenly galvanised by a dreadful fear. She pulls her hand away from John's and runs forward, kicking at the nearest skoob tower, to demolish it. The books are somehow fused together, and fall together, a falling tower, spitting sparks. Frederica can read their spines. They are her books, and not only her books, but part of herself, the books she has been teaching to her civilised extramural class. *The Castle, The Trial, The Idiot, Madame Bovary, Anna Karenina, Mansfield Park, La Chute, The Age of Reason, Lord of the Flies, Free Fall, Women in Love, Howards End.*

Rage takes hold of Frederica, rage unreasoning and wild, rage all too reasoning and justified, for all her notes, all her work, are written into the flyleaves of these burning books. She tries to kick the books apart to extinguish the flames, she rushes to the next tower—*Paradise Lost, Euripides, Dr. Faustus*—and the cloaked figure swoops at her from behind the bedstead, *yowling,* as she puts it to herself, finding *le mot juste* even in the conflagration.

"*I'll kill you,*" she howls at Paul-Zag, "let me get at you, *I'll kill you*—"

"I can't be killed," he intones. "I am born from the flames I don't burn I am not consumed."

"Rubbish," says Frederica. *"You will pay for this*—"

She tries to grasp him: his skin is hot and slippery under her hands, which are now smeared with gold and wine-dark grease. She grabs hold of the flying plastic, which is now very hot and limp and feels as though it will melt. He leaps back towards the centre of the square, and sets light to the old chair, in which is the Chianti bottle, which explodes, sending a tower of flame at the dark sky, singeing the blond locks badly and melting one side of the robe, which, as plastic does, shrivels and shrinks in the heat, producing its own stink and its own thick smoke. Frederica is divided between murderous rage and the desire to retrieve, to extinguish, to protect her books. She moves towards the next tower and is forestalled by Paul-Zag, who dances forwards, bends down, and before her horrified eyes clasps the whole structure protectively to his breast. There is now a terrible smell of burned flesh, as well as burned plastic and burned books. Paul falls over backwards in the mud. Frederica kicks her sullenly smouldering books away from his charred breast and belly. John Ottokar—too late, weeping—arrives at Frederica's side. Paul lies on his back and looks up at the haze of streetlight, the black-let-down-with-orange-and-sodium-silver sky, the very distant, diminished stars. He is not yet in pain; that will come. Marie Agyepong appears with a pot of zinc-and-castor-oil ointment. Paul looks at Frederica out of sly and inhuman eyes, their lashes painted and weeping black and red tears on his gilded cheeks. The sky, he announces, is full of great spiders spinning, it is swarming with octopods in every colour, it is thick with crawling worms and maggots who eat flesh and spit blood, they must all hide, but there is nowhere to hide. Brunnhilde shrieks defiance and submission. Frederica thinks she can see her enemy summing up, cannily, the effect of his pronouncements on the assembled company, all now creeping up on the mud patch. "He is high," says Marie Agyepong, "that's most of it, he's on a bad trip."

"I am high," says Paul. "I am in a high place, I shall leap down and my angels will hold me up, you'll see, I am on a bad trip and the spiders are coming after me, I shall fall and great will be the fall thereof and when I fall it will all fall, all that's holding it *up* will drag it *down,* you'll see, whether you want to or not, you'll have to see."

"It *hurts,*" he says suddenly, and begins to moan frantically.

"I sent for an ambulance," says Marie Agyepong. "He's burned quite bad, they'll have to take him to the burns unit in Roehampton."

And indeed, the sirens can be heard, coming round the corner, into the square.

John Ottokar says he will go with his brother, in the ambulance.

Frederica, having comforted Leo, spends the night sorting the burned books from the almost intact, the black paper from the scorched brown and yellow, the ashes from the written words. She weeps quietly, once the kindly neighbours have gone home. John Ottokar does not ring from the hospital. He does not ring the next day, either.

XVIII

After Paul-Zag's demonstration, there is no further word from the Ottokars. Frederica listens for the telephone for a day or two, and then flares into something resembling her old anger. She goes to visit Desmond Bull, in his studio. She admires the masks and the collaged staring eyes; she drinks beakers of Bull's Blood, she falls, queasy with red wine, turpentine and anger, into the arms of Bull on the mattress on the studio floor. Bull is a no-nonsense lover, like a steam-hammer, she thinks, which is what she needs. A bang, a bonk, abandon. She bites his shoulder, she scratches his ribs and buttocks, she urges him on, like a wild woman. She is under the protection of the Pill; they meet, theoretically, as equals. No finesse, no holding back, no exploration, no discovery. But a reasonable amount of pleasure, a not unpleasant throbbing and bruising, a salutary moment or two of oblivion. Followed, in due course, by a meal of pasta asciutta, rigatoni seeping hot tomato and melted creamy cheese, and a heated discussion of Patrick Heron's striped paintings. It is equality, possibly, Frederica thinks, pushing the twins back into her mind's caverns. She wonders if she is behaving like a man. She can feel the marks of her own teeth in her lips; she can feel the swelling where his cheekbone has ground on hers. The lineaments of satisfied desire, she does not say. Desmond Bull asks after Jude Mason and his book. It has gone quiet, Frederica says, it's the fallow season for lawyers.

She goes north, alone. She is fretting; she does not know what to do, with her summer, or with her life. She misses Leo, and yet, guiltily, feels free without him; she will not think about the Ottokars, and has nothing to do with her freedom. It is a warm summer: she sits on the

459

lawn behind the Freyasgarth house, looking onto the moors, and reading novels for review (there are not many, the supply dries up in the summer) and the texts for her next year's teaching. *Death in Venice* and *Daniel Deronda*. It takes her a day or two to realise how much older her father looks; he is becoming a little deaf, his steps are careful, even tentative, his opinions are advanced, also, more tentatively. Daniel arrives, two days after Frederica, to see Will and Mary, to rest for a few days. He too thinks Bill looks older.

A drama is going on which neither of them quite understands, since it is largely kept from them when its actors are present in Freyasgarth, and much of it takes place at Long Royston or in Calverley. It is to do with Marcus and his two friends, Ruth and Jacqueline. Frederica, lying in her deckchair on the lawn, watches these three pass, in twos, in threes, in fours—sometimes including Luk Lysgaard-Peacock—arguing, vehemently or gloomily, staring at the ground or gesturing, frozen into silence by Frederica's look. Once, Frederica comes upon Marcus and Jacqueline, standing by the gate. Jacqueline, brown, determined, severe, is berating Marcus.

"You've *got* to. Only you can do anything to stop this wickedness. You know it's wickedness, and you know *you* can do something. Why are you so *wet*?"

"It isn't any of my business. And I wouldn't change anything. Only make it worse."

"But it's *horrible,* Marcus."

"Possibly. Possibly."

They see Frederica, and freeze into silence. She broods for a moment, and returns to the intricacies of Thomas Mann's vision of liveliness and decay in Venice.

Marcus and Jacqueline come to Sunday lunch at Freyasgarth. It is not clear to Frederica whether or not they come as a couple; she even goes so far as to ask Daniel, who says he has no idea, but rather thinks it alternates, on-off, "to everyone's dissatisfaction." Winifred makes a good lunch, a roast, a salad, a raspberry soufflé. Afterwards, they have coffee in the garden. A figure approaches the group from the house; the door bell has not rung. It is Ruth, the nurse, with her pale plait hanging between her shoulders, wearing a cotton gingham dress, blue-checked with a crisp white collar. She looks very young. She says to Winifred, "Please forgive me for intruding, please forgive me for coming in without knocking. I've come to say good-bye to you. I'm leaving Calverley—I've resigned my job, I'm going away."

"I'm so sorry," says Winifred. "I hope you'll be happy. Where are you going?"

"You said you hadn't decided," says Marcus. "You said you were thinking."

"Well, I've thought. And I've prayed. And it has all become quite clear. Quite clear. And once it was clear, there wasn't a moment to lose. So I've given in my notice, and packed things, and here I am to say good-bye."

She continues to smile brightly at Winifred. She does not look at either Marcus or Jacqueline. Daniel says, "Where are you going, Ruth?"

"I'm going to take vows. Oh, nothing like the old nunneries, nothing enclosed like that. But the Children of Joy are forming a little residential community—the Joyful Companions—and I'm to be one of the first Companions. I'm suitable, I have skills I can bring to the work."

She smiles her little white, composed smile. Daniel offers her his chair, which she accepts, still not looking at Jacqueline or Marcus.

"It is a wonderful opportunity," she says, in her clear, composed little voice. She folds her hands in her lap, and looks down at them.

"Is this to do with Gideon Farrar?" asks Daniel.

"Of course. The community will begin in Gideon's vicarage near Bolton. It is ideally situated, there is plenty of quiet country round, and the parish is a country parish, but we will be able to receive— guests, people in need—from the industrial cities—we will be able to go out and find them . . ."

Marcus says, "You were doing good where you were, in the children's ward."

"Oh yes, but that is a place of death and despair. A terrible place, where I couldn't go out. With the help of the Children I can be much *more* use—we can help each other, and the sick and the unhappy, we can *show* people. We can heal. Gideon can heal. I've seen him. We can work together."

"Vows?" says Daniel.

"Oh, not like vows used to be. New vows. I can't tell you them, but they're simple, fidelity to the community, perpetual watchfulness, complete trust."

Jacqueline says, explosively, "You can't do this, Ruthie. It's dangerous. You *can't*."

"It isn't dangerous. It's saving. I knew you wouldn't understand."

"Gideon Farrar may have charisma, but *you know*, Ruthie, he's dangerous—*you know* and I know you know."

Ruth rises to her feet again, and smooths the gingham dress carefully.

"I knew you'd be like that. I won't let you upset me. I know you don't understand. I know—I'm afraid—you won't understand. That's why I came—now—to say good-bye—where everyone could see—so you couldn't—make it hard. You don't understand and I know you don't understand."

"Nor do I," says Marcus.

"I know. I thought you might. You so easily could. But you don't. I think I'll go now. There's no point in letting anyone upset me."

She stands. She shakes hands with Bill, who looks gloomy, and Winifred, who smiles mildly. She tries to kiss Jacqueline, who turns away, kisses Daniel, who says, "Look after yourself, Ruthie," and attempts to kiss Marcus, who suddenly takes hold of her wrist.

"Don't go, Ruthie." It is not clear what he means, don't leave now, or don't go to the Children of Joy.

She pulls her hand away. She walks quickly away, into the house. Her head is bowed. It is possible she is crying. Marcus goes after her. She begins to run. They both disappear into the house. Jacqueline stands up, sets off, thinks better of it. Luk Lysgaard-Peacock appears at the back gate, from the moor, dressed for walking. Jacqueline pays no attention. She says to Daniel, "*You* know Gideon Farrar. *You* know what he does. Stop her."

"I can't. What do you know about the Children of Joy?"

"Nothing. The whole thing is entirely distasteful. But I do know Gideon, and where Gideon is, love means sex. He *uses* his—his *presence*—his separateness—all those young girls—*he works them up*—I've been there, I know—"

"Does he hurt them?"

Jacqueline thinks about this. She says, "I think so, yes. I think he makes a kind of horrible fantasy of sacrifice and communion and really it's just lust—"

"Those are all just words."

"Are you trying to excuse him?"

"No. I know him, as you say. I think your words are accurate words."

"Well, then, stop Ruth."

"It's hard. She's grown up. She's made a choice."

Marcus reappears. He walks past his family, past Luk, out on to the moors. He begins to walk away, fast. Jacqueline stands up and runs after him. She catches him up at some distance; they can be seen as they embrace. Marcus bows his head on her shoulder, they walk on, arms entwined.

Luk Lysgaard-Peacock comes into the garden and is offered coffee, which he accepts.

Frederica and Luk Lysgaard-Peacock find themselves alone in the garden. Bill has gone to sleep; Marcus and Jacqueline have vanished; Daniel is taking Will to visit a friend, and Mary has gone along for the ride. Winifred is stacking dishes. Luk Lysgaard-Peacock does not ask about the drama, but Frederica tells him, briefly.

"Ruth came in and announced she is going off to live in a holy community and take vows. They are all upset. Jacqueline went off to cheer up Marcus, or vice-versa."

"In that case, I will save my own news."

"Your own news?"

"I have been invited to be head of a research institute in Copenhagen. It's an honour."

"So you're going?"

"I'm thinking. There are reasons for and against."

He considers the now empty moor beyond. Frederica has seen him look at Jacqueline. She wants to tell him, waiting never works. This would be impertinent. So she says, "Are there *Helix hortensis*—or should I say *Helices hortensis*—over there?"

"I imagine so. Not the particular population I am studying. And not my two slug populations on the moors, which are so strangely different."

Frederica becomes mildly interested in both Lysgaard-Peacock and his snails. She is interested because she suspects him of being another laminated being, a creature capable both of giving his entire attention to small, pearly, convoluted crawling lives, of thinking thoughts about genes and DNA of which she has no conception, and of furious but not incapacitating sexual devotion. She is trying to turn the jottings of her own *Laminations* into a coherently incoherent work. She has had the idea that she is many women in one—a mother, a wife, a lover, a watcher, and that it might be possible to construct a kind of plait of voices, with different rhythms and vocabularies. But it will not work. The story of Stone is one thing. The legal cut-ups are quirky new *objects.* But the moment she tries to write anything tinged with her own *feelings,* she is disgusted, as though she had touched slime, a metaphor she undoubtedly finds because of her temporary contact with *Helix hortensis.* If she writes what she feels truly—Leo's strangling arms, the memory of Nigel's blows, John Ottokar's blood-stained belly, disgust overcomes her at its falsity; it is false because it is *banal,* a cliché. She looks again at Luk Lysgaard-Peacock. He is a watcher, a collector, a thinker, a walker—he is "in love" with a brown girl who is "in love" with her brother, Marcus—inexplicably, to Frederica's mind—and this love makes him, too, more banal, more ordinary. She dare not speak these thoughts to him—he has a great deal of reserved dignity. But she does observe that the sex lives of the snails are no doubt less complicated, less anguished than those of human beings. She says she believes snails are hermaphrodite, and can manage the whole business by themselves. Lysgaard-Peacock replies that there is still some dispute about whether they do, in fact, ever keep themselves to themselves. The general belief is that they require another snail to reproduce— there is, as he puts it, some courteous dispute and jostling about who shall put what where. Snails, he says, are equipped with a curious organ, known as a *gypsobelum,* or love-dart, with which they apparently excite each other. Indeed, the differences between these organs are one of the clear ways of distinguishing *Helix hortensis* from *Helix nemoralis.* He describes the work he has done on two populations of large slugs, *Arion ater,* one on the moorlands and one from the valley lower down. These creatures, he says, are interesting because the moorland population, although identical in appearance to those of the valley, are self-fertilising, and genetically identical, whereas the valley slugs are sexually propagated, and genetically diverse. Odd, he says, that the upland, hermaphrodite, celibate slugs have preserved, over presumably thousands of years of disuse, enormous genitalia. Not in line with Darwin. Frederica asks him whether all this genetic science has changed his attitude to human behaviour. He thinks.

"I was going to say, no. But I think, yes, when I think about it. Love, and all that, is human, like language, which is purely human. I've never liked the idea of teaching apes human language—it diminishes them, in some way, like putting them in knickers and bonnets. But when you begin to understand how we are all constructed by the coded sequences of the DNA—hermaphrodite slugs, sexed slugs,

Cepaea hortensis and ourselves—when you realise all the things that go on busily in your cells all the time with which your language-consciousness appears to have nothing to do—I think it does change you, yes. I think it does diminish your sense of your own importance rather comfortably. Love is love, and all that, but sex is a blind drive, like—oh—antibodies breeding round diseased cells, or viruses hurrying along our blood."

"I thought that might be comforting."

"Oh well. At times. To the head."

"Perhaps one has to make do with that?"

"Ah, but the *luck*, if one didn't, if things went well."

"In my experience," says Frederica, "they *don't* go well. Or not for long."

"Are you trying to tell me something?"

"No. Well, no, not really."

"Nothing I don't know."

Frederica copies part of an article lent by Luk Lysgaard-Peacock into her *Laminations*, partly because she likes the idea of the snails wearing their genetic code for all to read on the spiral of their shells. She also copies out a description of the love-dart of *Helix hortensis* and its difference from that of *Helix nemoralis*.

Laminations

Habits and habitats. Helix hortensis is described as a somewhat indolent yet moderately sensitive animal, carrying its shell obliquely upright when crawling. It is less nocturnal in habit than its congener, though said by Nagel to be deeply skioptic or responsive to shade, and does not conceal itself so deeply and carefully during the day.

Diagnosis. H. hortensis is distinguished from *H. nemoralis* by its smaller size, more globose shape, white aperture and thinner and more glossy shell; moreover there is much less band variation, there is a larger proportion of bandless and 5-banded shells, and the commonness or rarity of the band formulae is quite different in the two species.

Internally, the differences are striking, the chief divergence being the structure of the gypsobelum or "love-dart" which in place of presenting the four simple longitudinal blades with connecting crescentic films, as in *H. nemoralis,* has the four blades deeply cleft and widely reflected along their entire length, forming thus eight sharp, divaricating blades; there are also no crescentic films between the blades, which terminate abruptly at the base, and not gradually, as in *H. nemoralis*; the vaginal mucus glands are also usually more branched than in *nemoralis,* and instead of being simply and uniformly digitate, are swollen or sacculate at the extremities.

Frederica cuts Luk Lysgaard-Peacock's information into her reading of the documents of the counter-culture.

Timothy Leary, *The Molecular Revolution,* lecture delivered at LSD conference sponsored by the University of California. Extracts.

Lecturing to a Turned-On Audience

If any of you have smoked marijuana in the last two hours, you are listening not just to my symbols. Your sense organs have been intensified and enhanced, and you are also aware of the play of light, the tone of voice. You are aware of many sensory cues beyond the tidy sequence of subjects and predicates which I am laying out in the air. And there may even be some of you in the audience who decided that you'd put over your eyes that more powerful microscope and find out, "Well, where is this fellow at, anyway?" Perhaps you have taken LSD tonight, in which case my task is not to wake you up but rather *not to pull you down.* I have often had the experience in lecturing to psychedelic audiences of having my eyes wander around the room and suddenly be fixed by two orbs, two deep, dark, pools, and realise that I am looking into someone's genetic code, that I have to make sense, not to a symbolic human mind, not to a complicated series of sense organs, but I have to make sense to many evolutionary forms of life—an amoeba, a madman, a mediaeval saint.

Iron wheels revolved there endlessly, and hammers thudded. At night plumes of vapour steamed from the vents, lit from beneath with red light, or blue, or venomous green.

There stood a tower of marvellous shape. It was fashioned by the builders of old, and yet it seemed a thing not made by the craft of Men, but riven from the bones of the earth in the ancient torment of the hills. There upon a floor of polished stone, written with strange signs, a man might stand five hundred feet above the plain. This was Orthanc, the citadel of Saruman, the name of which had (by design or chance) a twofold meaning; for in the Elvish speech *orthanc* signifies Mount Fang, but in the language of the Mark of old, the Cunning Mind.

Helix hortensis—Scalariform and sinistral monstrosities
Irregularly grown and anomalous shells.
Helix hortensis monst. scalare Ferussac [picture]
Shell with elevated spine and partially dislocated whorls.
Monst. sinistrorsum Ferussac
Shell reversed or sinistral in coiling.

We must realise that evolution is not through, that man is not a final product, and just as there are many species of primate, there may be just as many
species evolving from what we now call man, *Homo sapiens.* It may well be
that we'll have two species. One species, which is the machine species, will
like to live in metal buildings, and skyscrapers, and will get their kicks by just
becoming part of a machine. That species of man will become an unnecessary, easily worn-out part of the whole technological machinery. In that
case, man will become anonymous—just like the anthill or the beehive. Sex
will become very depersonalized. It will become very promiscuous. You
won't care who you make love to because they're all just replaceable parts.
You know, she's the new pretty blond girl who runs the electronic typewriter; so that we may well get a new species who will be technological. But
I do know that our seed-flown species will continue. And we may hang out
in new pockets of disease which the machine people haven't cleaned up
with their antiseptics. And we'll be somewhere out in the marshes, or somewhere out in the woods, laughing at the machine and enjoying our senses
and having ecstasies and remembering where we came from and teaching
our children that, believe it or not, we're not machines, and we weren't designed to make machines, and we weren't designed to run machines. I think
you have to be a very holy man to appreciate and understand and run a machine because the machine is a beautiful yoga and a beautiful ecstasy. I've
nothing against machines; it's just incredible that the DNA could produce
us and then produce those machines.

(Timothy Leary, *Soul Session,* p. 221)

Frederica's thoughts run uneasily on genetic similarities and differences, machine-men and seed-flower species, stones, paper and scissors. She thinks that the DNA which is the fetish of the turned-on
has probably very little, though not nothing, to do with the DNA of
Helix hortensis, in the food-processor, on the slides, under the microscope, of Luk Lysgaard-Peacock. She would rather know what
Lysgaard-Peacock knows, but is closer, even when trying to understand the snails, to the language of Leary.

Long legal envelopes continue to arrive, even in the summer, even in Freyasgarth. Frederica opens one and finds a thick document, with a covering letter from Arnold Begbie, who says, with studied neutrality, that it appears that, upon reflection, "your husband, the respondent" has decided to add to his Answer, already filed, "a prayer for counter-relief" on the grounds of desertion, mental cruelty and frequent adultery. The respondent has applied to the registrar for leave to amend his answer and to enter the cross-petition, and this leave has been granted.

Mr. Begbie says that he wishes to point out to his client that her husband is required to make specific allegations of her own misconduct, but is not required to divulge the evidence upon which he will rely to prove this misconduct. The question of desertion is clear, and the question of mental cruelty is related to this and to the removal of the child, Leo Alexander. The allegations of adultery are numerous and precise. Mrs. Reiver has not elected to include a discretion statement in her own petition, and has assured Mr. Begbie that the question did not arise. He would therefore be grateful to know how she would like him to proceed. She will note that the new prayer for counter-relief does include a prayer for the court's discretion in the matter of the cross-petitioner's own adultery.

Mr. Begbie also wishes to inform Mrs. Reiver that all the persons cited in the cross-petition's allegations of adultery must be named as co-respondents and served personally with notices of the petition; they may then choose whether to enter an appearance, if they wish to defend the proceedings, or take part in any other way. If these persons do not wish to contest the proceedings, they need do nothing.

Mr. Begbie will be grateful to receive Mrs. Reiver's further instruction as soon as possible.

Frederica looks at the counter-petition. It is long, and detailed. It is fact and fiction. It names Thomas Poole, Hugh Pink, John Ottokar, Paul Ottokar and Desmond Bull, and speaks of acts of intimacy, public embraces, and nights spent under the same roof. It claims custody of the child of the marriage, Leo Alexander. It is a snake of black language, tied with red tape in an impeccable bow. Frederica's first, easiest, simplest emotion is that she has made a fool of herself in not *telling* Arnold Begbie about what she calls, to herself, "the end of my celibacy." Her second is rage that Begbie, whom she neither really likes nor really trusts, should need to know where she has lain down, whose skin she has touched, by whom she has been penetrated. It is *private,* she thinks. She then takes in the implications of the serving of the petitions on Thomas Poole (who may simply be ruefully sensible) and on the Ottokars. Can Nigel claim damages against John Ottokar? Can Paul be called to give evidence? They have vanished into the Spirits' Tigers: she cannot see John wanting to maintain their uncertain, delicate, tentative love or liking in a witness box before a judge. He is not ready, and may never be, and she may not want him to be, now, or yet, or ever, how can she tell, but the law and Nigel will make it be solid, be cut and dried—*cut,* and *dried*—gone . . . And some, though not all, of this, is true, and will the court, whose ways are not her ways, suppose she is a woman sensible enough to keep Leo? It is the Swinging Sixties, but the courts are run by old men in eighteenth-century wigs, with nineteenth-century outward morals, and she will be pulped, mashed, humiliated, *destroyed.*

She has taken the horrid envelope to her bedroom, to read in peace. She cannot speak of this to her parents. She begins to weep, blindly, uselessly, furiously. The door opens. It is Daniel.

"What is it, Frederica?"

"Look!"

He looks.

"Half of it's lies. *Lies.*"

"You'll get your divorce, one way or the other."

"Yes, but *Leo.* Who will get Leo?"

Daniel sits on the bed.

"They usually give the child to the mother."

"But I look *horrible* in that document, feckless and frightful. And they've got everything, the pony, the Right School . . ."

"But you want him with you?"

"It isn't a question of want or not want. We *have* to be together. He saw that. I thought I could leave him, but I couldn't, I couldn't have, not ever—"

She thinks of Daniel, a good man, as she is not a good woman, walking away from Will and Mary. She has always wondered how he could have done that, and has not asked, and will not ask. But she looks at him, red-eyed, stricken with guilt.

"Oh, Daniel."

He holds her. She lies on his shoulder and weeps, with more and more abandon. He strokes her hair, his mouth set grimly. They hear Mary pass, singing, singing in tune and clearly, as no Potter ever has.

"Your daughter can sing in tune."

"My dad could. He used to sing th' *Messiah*, in the big choirs."

"She sounds happy."

"Human beings are tough."

THE COUNCIL OF THE WISE (1)

Frederica finds herself, almost by accident, at a meeting in the offices of Bowers and Eden in Elderflower Court to discuss the organisation of the defence of *Babbletower*. Rupert Parrott's solicitor is a cautious small man called Martin Fisher; another solicitor has been found to represent Jude, also a small man, called Duncan Raby. Martin Fisher is dapper and silvery; Duncan Raby is sleek and dark and can bend his fingers backwards, which he does, with little cracks, in moments of agitation. Godfrey Hefferson-Brough, QC, is to lead for Parrott's defence; Samuel Oliphant, QC, has been retained to represent Jude. Hefferson-Brough is large and craggy, with tree-trunk bones and red-veined cheeks and sharp eyes under tangled eyebrows. Samuel Oliphant is one of those whippet-like lawyers who look as though they are on the scent of a fine point even in repose; he has colourless, apologetic hair, and fine bones which are transformed by a wig into blades and edges. These four and their clerks are present at this meeting—other lawyers will come and go from time to time during the succeeding months. When Frederica arrives at Bowers and Eden with a heap of annotated manuscripts from the slush heap, she finds Jude in the entrance lobby, surrounded by his miasma, asserting in his sawing voice that decisions are being made without him, behind his back, undercover. Parrott is protesting, pink-faced and tense, that Jude would not be here if things were being hidden from him. The sawing voice rises: "I overheard your *secretary*, Parrott, saying to *someone*, it would be *easier* without the *author present*, he can be very *temperamental*, very *difficult*—"

Frederica says, "Oh, shut up, Jude. You are having your cake and eating it. If ever you do overhear things like that it's your *civilised duty* to ignore them, and anyway, you know in your terms it's a compliment, you *like* to be thought temperamental and difficult. Everyone's doing their best."

"What do *you* know about it?" says Jude, still truculent, but milder.

"I know you," says Frederica. "I know how much Rupert has done for you. I think you should shut up."

"We are having a Council of the Wise," says Parrott. "I think you should join us. I think your advice would be of help. This is just a little preliminary gathering—some experts, mostly Bowers and Eden authors—Professor Marie-France Smith has agreed to come along, and Roger Magog. They wrote well of the book, very well, they will advise us. And I've persuaded Phyllis Pratt to give us her thoughts, yes. You are a part of our deliberations, and you brought both Mrs. Pratt and Jude to our attention. You could come and help on the Eng. lit. front."

They sit round a shiny oval mahogany table in an upper room Frederica had not even known about; it smells musty and unused, but with an overtone of past nuts, and old apples. Rupert Parrott sits at one end, flanked by pairs of lawyers. Frederica and Jude sit at the other. Also present are Canon Holly, representing the Church, Elvet Gander, representing mental health and the sciences of the soul, Marie-France Smith and Roger Magog, and a squat person with red ringlets and a red beard, both mildly matted, with merry blue eyes behind gold-rimmed glasses and an open-necked madras-checked shirt, who is introduced as Avram Snitkin, an ethnomethodologist. Jude lays his long grey hands on the mahogany and asks earnestly, "What is an ethnomethodologist?"

"That is hard to say," Snitkin replies cheerfully, "since no two ethnomethodologists can agree on a definition of ethnomethodology. We have very beautiful conferences, discussing the meaning of the term 'ethnomethodology.'"

"And you can't give me a working definition?" says Jude. "A court will require a working definition."

"We study what people actually think they are doing when they are in the process of doing whatever they do. As opposed to the things sociologists think that people think they do when they perform acts already classified and categorised by sociologists, in certain ways."

"You are sociologists?"

"Many of us, most of us, spring from that discipline. The classic ethnomethodological study was the bugging of a jury room in order to observe, without any interference in the data by *overt* observers, what function jury members believe themselves to be performing *in qua* jurors—what jurors think jurors are. Do I make you any wiser?"

"Oh yes," says Jude.

"And where did you 'bug' this jury room?" asks Samuel Oliphant, articulating the inverted commas.

"In California, don't worry," says Snitkin, smilingly.

"Dr. Snitkin has made a study of the uses that people—men— make of—of *risky* published material," says Rupert Parrott. "That is why I invited him to this gathering. He believes that pornography performs a useful social function. That it, so to speak, *siphons off*—"

"An unfortunate metaphor," says Jude. "Very. I must point out that my book is not pornographic. It is in that context *emetic*. It will be better if we do not use the word 'pornographic' about it."

"Let me call this meeting to order," says Parrott. "The idea of this meeting is to exchange ideas between lawyers and persons who might be thought to be experts, in the new fields of 'expertise' in the literary and social value of works of art which are supposed to 'tend to deprave and corrupt' the general public. When *Lady Chatterley* was triumphantly acquitted, the defence produced an impressive file of the great and the good, poets, professors, bishops and one young girl, to say that the book was full of tenderness and sweetness and light and advocation of married fidelity. The prosecution relied on reading aloud 'bouts' of explicit sexual description, and rhetorically and famously asking 'Is this a book you would allow your wife and daughters, or your servants, to read?' It is my opinion, and the opinion of the legal advisers who are here today, that the prosecution of *Babbletower* will be different from the prosecution of *Lady Chatterley*, because the book is different, but not only for that reason. There is scope for 'experts' who are not simply literary critics or respected public figures. I won't go on, now, but will hand over the conduct of proceedings to those who will guide us."

Frederica looks round the table. Marie-France Smith is a surprise; she is a tall, slender, blond, elegant woman, with a strikingly beautiful face, long hair tied back with a black velvet bow, and an expression of gentleness and wary tension combined. Phyllis Pratt, the novelist, is the shape of the cottage loaf she described in her novel, *Daily Bread;* she has little fat curls, dark and silver, on her ample head, smile-lines moving up into round cheeks from soft mouth and eye-corners; she wears a serviceable jersey trouser suit in bottle green with a flowered Liberty shirt under it, sprinkled with honeysuckle. Canon Holly's ragged silver mane and his smoke-stained, lupine teeth she knows well. Magog is meaty and energetic and restless. Elvet Gander has a bald head and a precise, distinguished, long-nosed, carved-looking face, with a wide, controlled mouth and deep-set dark grey eyes above high, clean-cut cheekbones. His head is the head of a tall man, a grandee, though when he stands, his body is surprisingly short and slightly bowed, with long hanging arms and bowed legs. His skin has a grey cast—not an unhealthy putty-grey, like Jude's, but a polished granite, stony.

The subsequent conversation is conducted by the two solicitors with occasional comments from the two silks. Preliminary discussions are held of lines of argument in defence of *Babbletower*: psychological, political, literary merit, usefulness as emetic, religious depth. One of the lawyers—Raby—says he feels clergymen can "backfire" as witnesses. It might be possible to agree with the other side not to call clergymen. Canon Holly says that would be a pity, since there is great and genuine theological suffering and profundity in the work. "Convince me," says Samuel Oliphant, mildly, enticingly, dangerously. "There was a Bishop in the *Chatterley* case," says Hefferson-Brough. "Got rather mangled. Said the book promulgated marriage. Got reprimanded by the Archbish, I hear. Cantuor. Not a good precedent, on balance." Canon Holly says he knows a better Bishop, a radio Bishop with a large following, who might appear, who has thought much about the experience of pain and desolation. Raby says he is against bishops. Martin Fisher says, if they have a Bishop, we should have a Bishop. Jude says bishops are sods and buggers like everyone else. Phyllis Pratt tells Jude that the assembled company is trying to *help* him; her tone is that of the chairman of the Mothers' Union (this is before chairwomen and before personified Chairs). Jude says, "I simply thought—" Phyllis Pratt says, "Don't. Don't simply think. You have a task to perform, part of which is not to make things difficult for your friends." Jude says, "Who is my friend, when all men are against me?" "And *folie de grandeur,* dear," says Phyllis Pratt, "and premature martyrdom, are both *unhelpful.*"

Hefferson-Brough says, "Naturally, your appearance will have to be regularised."

"Regularised?"

"You will have to be tidied up. Short back and sides. Suit. Tie. A good wash. *Sine qua non.*"

"Oh no," says Jude. "I am a poor bare forked thing, and such as I am, I am, and as such you must e'en take me, for a man and his clothes are *one flesh* and cannot be parted. I have as it were and to my own secret deities *vowed* that neither hair of my head nor nail of my feet and fingers shall I wilfully cut with scissors or injure with files and this state I propose to maintain come hell come high water."

"Short back and sides," says Hefferson-Brough.

"It might be best," says Oliphant, "not to call you into the witness box at all. It might be the most advisable course."

"It would be extremely foolish not to call me," says Jude. "I will speak. I will appear and expound and defend my book."

"I can tell you now," says Hefferson-Brough, "that if you insist on going into the box looking like that, we may as well go home now. That is what I have to say."

Duncan Raby changes the subject. He asks about witnesses to literary merit. It is agreed that Anthony Burgess shall be sounded out, since he wrote well of the book. Also Professor Frank Kermode, Professor Barbara Hardy, Professor Christopher Ricks, William Golding, Angus Wilson, Una Ellis-Fermor, and "that chap at Cambridge," says Hefferson-Brough, "that chap everyone's always talking about." "Dr. Leavis," says Frederica. "Him, yes." "He wouldn't appear for *Lady Chatterley*," says Martin Fisher. "Although he's a Lawrence man. I can't see him liking *Babbletower*."

"I was his student," says Magog. "As a postgraduate. He is cranky and paranoid, though undoubtedly a genius. I think I myself will better represent his critical approach. He is not easy to deal with, and I don't think he'd agree."

"We are glad of your support," says Martin Fisher.

"You represent the teaching profession also," says Duncan Raby, bending back his fingers.

"I want to put the case that *nothing* should be suppressed, that censorship is ludicrous and unworkable."

"Here you must argue for the merits of *Babbletower,* as an expert on its merits, literary or social," says Raby.

Magog does not answer this remark. It occurs to Frederica that he has not actually read *Babbletower*: as a teacher, she is now experienced in the eye-movements, the judicious nod, of those who have not read something they claim to have read. Magog says there are writers on the Steerforth Committee of Enquiry who might have the requisite *gravitas.* Alexander Wedderburn, for instance. He himself thinks there is little merit in Wedderburn's *writings* but Wedderburn has a good presence and is taught at O Level and A Level, he will impress. Hefferson-Brough says he is exactly the sort of chap who will go down well with a jury.

Tea is served, by Rupert Parrott's secretary, from a silver teapot into pretty little Crown Derby china teacups. A plate of biscuits is handed round: bourbons, custard creams, squashed flies. Avram Snitkin, sitting next to Frederica, murmurs, "Fascinating."

"What is?"

"Your British rituals of decision-making. Tea and biscuits. I am thinking of writing a study of the compiling of lists. Who compiled the list of the people who are here to compile the list of the people who will be invited to give evidence for *Babbletower*? How far is this list a ritual list of people who must be asked but won't appear? And so on."

"I suppose an ethnomethodologist would be interested in what happens to a person who defines himself for the duration as an expert witness for the defence of a book, of this book?"

"Indeed. Including an ethnomethodologist."

On the way out of the publishing house, Frederica finds herself between Jude and Elvet Gander. Jude is morose and unusually silent. Gander says to Frederica, "We have not officially met, I believe, but I know *of* you."

"What do you know *of* me?" Frederica asks, truculent and rattled. Nothing has been heard of John Ottokar since the service of the counter-petition and prayer for relief. He has vanished from her life as though he had never been. A date has been set for the divorce hearing in November. She is afraid.

"Nothing but good," says Gander, in reply to her question. "You were much in question at a difficult series of sessions in Four Pence this summer. I break no confidences if I say so, I think, and I assume that you too find your situation, shall we say, *difficult*? Forgive me if I speak out of turn."

"Perhaps you do. I don't know that I want to think or talk about—about *them,* about all that."

"One of the two brothers took the same line. The other was voluble. I attempted to mediate—to make the silent speak, and the roarer be still. The results were unfortunate."

Frederica is silent.

"Midnight arson," says Gander. "Midnight arson, minor explosions, damage to property."

"The path of excess leads to the palace of wisdom."

"You mock. I do believe there is much truth in that. I would like to help you, but you are not ready to let me. You think I am a charlatan."

"I don't." He waits. "Perhaps I do."

"You don't know."

"I don't know that I *want* to know."

"You may suddenly, quite suddenly, decide that you need me. I am here, if you do. You interest me."

"Don't listen to the tempter," says Jude. "He'll blow your mind."

This is an un-Jude-like phrase, in an un-Jude-like vocabulary. It sounds different. It evokes small mines, arson again, explosions.

Gander laughs. "Fair is foul and foul is fair. You do right to mistrust the chance-met. We shall meet again, in easier circumstances. As for you, Jude Mason, I would like to say, this process, this legal process, is going to be a severe test of your exiguous survival machinery. If you need help, I am here."

"You will help the whole world," says Jude. "Indiscriminately."

"No, no. We meet those who need us. We gravitate to them. Karma brings us where they are. We three are walking along this road together for a reason. Or, if we were not, we now are. So I tell you what I see in your face and your stars and your body language, in case that may be the reason. If not, no harm done, forget it."

As the divorce hearing approaches, Frederica grows thinner and sharper. She is obsessed by the fear of losing Leo, a person who makes her life difficult at every turn, who appears sometimes to be *eating* her life and drinking her life-blood, a person who fits into no pattern of social behaviour or ordering of thought that she would ever have chosen for herself freely—and yet, the one creature to whose movements of body and emotions all her own nerves, all her own antennae, are fine-tuned, the person whose approach along a pavement, stamping angrily, running eagerly, lifts her heart, the person whose smile fills her with warmth like a solid and gleaming fire, the person whose sleeping face moves her to tears, to catch the imperceptible air of whose sleeping breath she will crouch, breathless herself, for timeless moments in the half-dark.

She thinks, perhaps, she might be able to talk to Agatha about this terror, but Agatha is preoccupied and evasive, is uncharacteristically short with her. Frederica takes note of her own friends, her particular old friends, Daniel and Alexander, going up Agatha's stairs, rather than down to her own basement, and tells herself it is natural, Agatha is beautiful and clever, Alexander has always been easy prey for mysterious silence, Daniel needs to get out of himself. Agatha is "working late" a lot, too, which Frederica, asked to baby-sit, regards with sour suspicion. One evening she is baby-sitting when Agatha is still out and Alexander arrives. He comes down to talk to Frederica— "*faute de mieux,*" Frederica says, jokingly to him, and crossly to herself. Alexander accepts a cup of coffee and tells Frederica what he sees she needs to know and has not bothered to discover, that Agatha is strained to breaking by the practical and political difficulties of the drafting of the Steerforth Report.

Agatha does not discuss her work with Frederica. Frederica does, or did, discuss hers with Agatha—it interests both of them. Alexander leans back on Frederica's sofa and talks about the committee.

"It's very difficult for a *group* to write something. It's quite interesting to see what kinds of manoeuvres we go through to get it done. We've got two people in overall charge of the writing—Agatha and myself—we co-ordinate what will be the chapters. Then we've got little sub-groups, working together on different areas—we've got a group on 'Spoken and Written English,' and one on 'Classroom Conduct—Love and/or Authority,' and one on 'The Class Problem in the Class—the Question of What Is "Correct" and What Should Be *Corrected*,' and one on 'The Principles of Education—Is It Child-Centred or Community-Oriented, and Can It Be Both?' And one on what sort of grammar to teach, and how much, and why. And that one has a sub-heading, language as an *object of study,* like zoology, or mathematics. It's amazing what terrible passions it all arouses—real, important passions, mind you, about real, important things. You get evidence in from schoolteachers saying they want to create 'whole personalities,' 'friendly atmospheres,' 'full and satisfying lives,' 'full development of potentialities,' 'satisfaction of curiosity,' 'confidence,' 'growth,' 'perseverance,' 'alertness,' and that sort of thing—and when you actually start looking at what they do, how they behave, what they *mean* by these phrases, you find that the words are like sand slipping through your fingers, you feel you're staring through a microscope at a lot of life-forms that suddenly look like great thick snakes curling round and *biting* each other. We're writing about teaching language and the language we write about teaching language won't stick to the thing we're writing about. Won't describe it. Steerforth himself said almost nothing for months of our deliberations and then suddenly made a little speech about how profoundly *resistant* the mind was to studying its own operations. He and Hans Richter and Wijnnobel are writing a kind of preface pointing out how 'children' and 'language' have both been profoundly changed in our time by becoming objects of intense study, of focused attention."

"Agatha never talks about all this. It's fascinating. Go on."

Alexander goes on. He describes the drafting groups, and the unexpected alliances, oppositions and alignments. The journalist, Malcolm Friend, who has contributed almost nothing to the debate, turns out to be a brilliant drafter of pellucid paragraphs and is in charge of the "child-centred, community-oriented?" debate. The teachers are divided on the question of classroom authority—some oppose learning anything by rote, and are in favour of the child "discovering naturally when he needs to," using the model of language acquisition by untutored two-year-olds. Some believe equally strongly that children *need* to know things they are reluctant to learn, as a store for when they will be glad of them, or because "society" needs them to know these things. The word "society" is not yet the problem it will become, but it is a problem. A majority of the committee, probably, dislike grammar and teaching grammar: the minority in favour of it are ferociously moved by its order, its beauty, its complexity. Emily Perfitt believes in learning poetry, but in eschewing grammar, which she defines as "mental cruelty," quite simply— an *interesting locution,* according to Wijnnobel, Alexander says. He describes how Agatha keeps the drafting groups in order by threatening to second Magog and Mickey Impey to join them. These two are part of no group and act as ambassadors "from one to another."

Frederica says she met Magog at Bowers and Eden. She recounts the meeting of that committee. She says the lawyers were endlessly qualificatory and endlessly subtle about the nature of expert witnesses. She says life is full of lawyers and committees defining the indefinable, like childhood, tendencies to deprave and corrupt, language, pre-nuptial incontinence, adultery, guilt. She says she feels terribly guilty towards Nigel, because she should not have married him, but that she is not technically guilty of most of the things of which she now stands accused. Some, yes, she says. But it's *nobody else's business.*

Alexander says he knew before he joined the committee that there would be one lucid moment when he *knew* what teaching was, and children were, and language did, and that this knowledge would disappear in a welter of study and definition and complexity. He says it has happened exactly so, and that the complexities are real and substantial. He says that the good teachers they have observed *know,* as he knew then, what teaching and children and language are, and act on their knowledge.

He says he is sorry Frederica feels guilty but he is sure she will soon be able to put it all behind her.

Frederica tries to say: I am afraid of losing Leo. She is so afraid of losing Leo, that she cannot utter the sentence.

So she says, "They were discussing asking you to give evidence for Jude."

"Do I want to?"

"You ought to. He'll *die* if they condemn his book."

"I don't like it."

"No. But you don't want it suppressed."

"I suppose I don't."

They hear Agatha come in. "Well," says Frederica. "Off to your drafting then."

Laminations

My mother groan'd! my father wept.
Into the dangerous world I leapt:
Helpless, naked, piping loud:
Like a fiend hid in a cloud.

Struggling in my father's hands,
Striving against my swadling bands,
Bound and weary I thought best
To sulk upon my mother's breast.

William Blake,
Songs of Experience

Our work has been concerned with two things, or concepts, which have in recent history become both absorbing subjects of study, and *problems,* as perhaps they were not in the past. We refer to "the child" and "language." Before the nineteenth century the child was either an infant or a small adult, wearing the same clothes as his parents, subject to the same legal penalties, including hanging by the neck, and controlled by the same moral codes. Now we take account of the length of time it takes a human creature to become an independent, responsible being, both physically and mentally. We take an intricate interest in the processes—including the learning of language—by which such independence and responsibility are achieved.

Language, too, has become, not merely the glass through which we see "the world outside" but the instrument with which we shape and limit our purposes and our apprehensions. Our philosophy is a philosophy of language: Wittgenstein sees philosophy, indeed, as "language-games" which are "forms of life," whereas the school of "Language, Truth and Logic" sees linguistic forms as productive of both facts and fictions about the nature of things. There is a growing belief in some schools of thought that "language is divorced from the world," that it is perhaps simply a partial system which best describes only its own interrelations and structure. At the same time, there is a proper and increasing interest in language as an instrument of power, of subjection and manipulation, and a concomitant belief that even young children should be familiarised with and alerted to language's manipulative potentialities. There is, in this context, the vexed question of the relation of such political uses of language to the ingrained British habit of defining "correct" speech and writing in terms partly of the speech habits and linguistic structures of a particular group or class, of identifying the "rules" of grammar with the rules, both helpful and restrictive, of prevailing interests and power-structures.

(Draft, subsequently heavily revised, of the Introduction to the Report of the Steerforth Committee of Enquiry on the Teaching of the English Language)

We are likely to withdraw our willingness to listen when we are told that infantile sexuality is polymorphously perverse. And Freud must mean that polymorphous perversity is the pattern of our deepest desires. How can this proposition be taken seriously?

If we divest ourselves of the prejudice surrounding the "perverse," if we try to be objective and analyse what infantile sexuality is in itself, we must return again to the definition. Infantile sexuality is the pursuit of pleasure obtained through the activity of any and all organs of the human body. That this is Freud's notion becomes abundantly clear if we examine the specific nature of the "perverse" components in infantile sexuality. They include the pleasure of touching, of seeing, of muscular activity, and even the passion for pain.

Freud and Blake are asserting that the ultimate essence of our being remains in our unconscious secretly faithful to the principle of pleasure, or, as Blake calls it, delight.

In man the dialectical unity between union and separateness, between interdependence and independence, between species and individual—in short, between life and death—is broken. The break occurs in infancy, and it is the consequence of the institution of the human family. The institution of the family means the prolonged maintenance of human children in a condition of helpless dependence. Parental care makes childhood a period of privileged freedom from the domination of the reality-principle, thus permitting and promoting the early blossoming, in an unreal atmosphere, of infantile sexuality and the pleasure-principle. Thus sheltered from reality by parental care, infantile sexuality—Eros or the life instinct—conceives the dream of narcissistic omnipotence in a world of love and pleasure.

But if the institution of the family gives the human infant a subjective experience of freedom unknown to any other species of animal, it does so by holding the human infant in a condition of objective dependence on parental care to a degree unknown to any other species of animal. Objective dependence on parental care creates in the child a passive, dependent need to be loved, which is just the opposite of his dream of narcissistic omnipotence. Thus the institution of the family shapes human desire in two contradictory directions, and it is the dialectic generated by the contradiction which produces what Freud calls the conflict of ambivalence.

But the contradiction in the human psyche established by the family is the contradiction between the life and death instincts as previously defined.

(Norman O. Brown, "Death and Childhood,"
Life Against Death, p. 113)

When they finally woke, it was already dark night. Gretel began to weep, and said, "How are we now to get out of the Forest?" Hansel, however, comforted her: "Wait a little while, till the moon has risen, and then we will find out our way." And when the full moon was up, Hansel took his little sister by the hand and they followed the flinty pebbles, which glittered like newly minted groats, and showed them the way. They went on all night and at daybreak came to their father's house.

> *Other echoes*
> *Inhabit the garden. Shall we follow?*
> *Quick, said the bird, find them, find them,*
> *Round the corner. Through the first gate,*
> *Into our first world, shall we follow*
> *The deception of the thrush? Into our first world . . .*

Go, said the bird, for the leaves were full of children,
Hidden excitedly, containing laughter.
Go, go, go, said the bird: human kind
Cannot bear very much reality.

T. S. Eliot, *Four Quartets,*
"Burnt Norton"

A Dream

A woman, waiting for a divorce hearing, finds herself on the banks of a quick little stream, very English, overhung by trees, with sun and shadow chasing each other along it, and a breeze, too, stirring the leaves and the water. She is walking in a meadow in long grasses, by this stream, wearing her engagement ring, which is a row of alternating blue and white stones, sapphires and moonstones. The clasps of the setting spring open and the stones of the ring fall and roll in the grass, blue and white stones rolling everywhere, tiny and glittering, more than the ring ever contained. She tries to gather them up: they slip like drops of water through her fingers and bounce, as tears bounce when wept with great force. The dreamer, who is not the woman now, "sees" the woman's face with empty eyeholes like the empty sockets of the ring, and blue and white stony tears pouring down her cheeks.

In the river, hidden under the bank, are "water-babies" wrapped like caddis-grubs in shreds of old leaves and broken snail shells, glued into a housing; they peer out, they hang in the current which rushes and bubbles past them but does not detach them.

The tears and stones trickle into the river and melt like waterdrops on water.

The thought of our past years in me doth breed
Perpetual benediction: not indeed
For that which is most worthy to be blest—
Delight and liberty, the simple creed
Of Childhood, whether busy or at rest,
With new-fledged hope still fluttering in his breast:—
Not for these I raise
The song of thanks and praise;
But for those obstinate questionings
Of sense and outward things,
Fallings from us, vanishings;

From the moment of birth, when the stone-age baby confronts the twentieth-century mother, the baby is the subject of violence, called love, as its mother and father have been and their parents before them . . . We are effectively destroying ourselves by violence masquerading as love.

(R. D. Laing)

At least 83 people, mostly children, are dead, and 46 were still entombed early today on the hillside at Aberfan, near Merthyr Tydfil, after a rain-soaked coal-tip avalanched on Pantglas Infants' School, a farm and a row of houses yesterday morning. Eighty-eight children are safe and 36 are in hospital.

Mr. S. O. Davies, Labour MP for Merthyr Tydfil, said that debris from a local colliery was still being tipped on the slag heap when the disaster happened . . .

Among those brought out alive and taken to hospital was the headmistress, Miss Ann Jennings, 64. The body of the deputy head-teacher, Mr. D. Beynon, was found, with five little children in his arms, all dead . . .

. . . Because of early morning fog, 50 children from the neighbouring village of Mount Pleasant escaped the tragedy. Their school bus was delayed and they arrived at the school 10 minutes late, and just after the landslide had occurred. The mother of one of them, Mrs. Olwyn Morris, said, "If there had been no fog, my boy, Joel, 14, would have been in the school. He ran home crying and told me what had happened."

XIX

꙰ꙮꙮꙮꙮꙮ꙰

"Put your coat on, Leo, hurry up."

"I don't go to school today."

"Oh yes, you do. Agatha and Saskia are waiting."

"But we are being divorced today. I am coming to be divorced."

Frederica has said nothing to Leo about this event.

"You can't come," she says. "Little boys don't go to the divorce courts."

"*I* do."

"No, you don't. You must go to school."

He holds her dressing-gown: she means to change for her court appearance when he is gone. He stamps. He shrieks. "I will, I will, I will."

"You won't," says Frederica, raising her voice to match his. Both are near tears, white with anxiety.

"I am coming with you."

Agatha appears in the doorway.

"We are going to be divorced," says Leo.

"You aren't. You are going to school, with me. Don't upset your mother."

Leo glances from one woman to the other, weighs up the effect of further demonstration, and takes Agatha's hand, refusing to meet Frederica's eye.

"See you later," says Frederica, adding "alligator," on an uncertain, quavering false note.

Leo does not reply. He stomps off with Agatha. It is a bad beginning.

Frederica puts on a black dress. It is a black wool crepe shift with a pointed shirt-collar and buttoned cuffs at the end of long sleeves. She looks at her face in the mirror and thinks she looks respectable and urban. She thinks about make-up, sees that she would be better without it, fox-faced and clean-cut between the knife-blades of red hair. She applies the make-up nevertheless, to mark the occasion, perhaps, to hide behind it, perhaps, because the natural look of unmade-up skin has not yet come in, perhaps. As she always does on important occasions, she makes a dab with the mascara brush at her red-pale eyebrows, which normally she never touches, and as she always does, botches and blotches it, leaving gouts of black in the ginger, scrubbing them out, raising red welts. She wonders about relieving the black with a necklace or a brooch—she is not given to wearing jewellery—but the only thing she can find is a pretty Indian string of garnet and pearl beads, given to her by Nigel, which seems tactless.

She has refused offers to accompany her to the Court. She has tried not to think about it too much—she is not, she thinks, afraid of appearing in public, even in the witness box, for is she not a good public speaker, a charismatic teacher, an articulate person? She has been afraid of losing Leo, but not of losing him because of anything she may say or do. She has her confidence. She puts on a pair of black, shiny high-heeled shoes, slings her bag on her shoulder, and sets off for the Underground. The time ahead is a kind of blank. But at the end of it, something will be over, will be settled. She will be—not free, the word is beginning to be meaningless—but responsible for herself to herself again. The inside of her mouth is dry.

Inside the Court building she meets Arnold Begbie, who has with him her Counsel, Mr. Griffith Goatley, holding her brief and a whole heap of other briefs. Mr. Goatley is a blond, clean-cut, fastidious-looking person, with a beautiful pale skin and beautifully manicured hands. He tells Frederica not to be nervous, and she says she is not. He tells her to speak out, and to say everything she has to say, clearly—"Even what you may find it distasteful to say, Mrs. Reiver, just speak out." He says that she is the only witness he will be calling, in her own suit. "We have signed affidavits from your doctor, in the matter of the little infection you unfortunately had, and from a barmaid at the Tips and

Tassels Club, and from a waitress and the doorman at the Honeypot, in the matter of your husband's probable adultery. This should be quite enough—would certainly have been quite enough—had the counter-petition not been brought. My colleague Laurence Ounce, who is appearing for the opposition, seems to be calling a considerable number of witnesses in person. Only one of the persons named as co-respondents has entered an appearance—"

"Who?"

"Mr. Thomas Poole."

"There was nothing wrong—that is, there was *nothing*—he will say so—"

"Of course. That is Mr. Ounce, over there, with your ex-husband, I assume—"

Frederica gazes distractedly around the stony corridor she is standing in. There is Nigel, stocky, fierce, in his dark suit and a blood-red tie, with the faint hint of blue on his strong chin, even at this time in the morning. There too are both Olive and Rosalind, in tweed suits, one honey-coloured, one green-and-mauve, both slightly seated, over sensible flanged suede shoes, and there is Pippy Mammott in rust, with her face scrubbed pink and shining and her hair full of iron pins.

There is Mr. Ounce, and Nigel's solicitor, Mr. Tiger. Mr. Ounce is portly and billowing, with vinous cheeks and a mouth with all sorts of fluent and savorous curves in it; he has not got much hair, a struggling dark, thinning thatch, but that will vanish under the wig. He is wearing his gown, which billows about his billows. He laughs, and Nigel laughs with him. The three women ostentatiously do not see Frederica. Nigel genuinely does not.

It is like waiting in an examination hall. A clock ticks, somewhere. Dust motes are suspended in long tubes of pale November light. Frederica thinks: I am too thin to be convincing. It is an odd thought, not real, a product of unreal air, full of old pain, old terror, old triumphs and despair, old dust.

And then suddenly they are all in the Court, and there is the judge, Mr. Justice Hector Plumb, under his wig, a man not plummy but the opposite, chalky, with a yellow note to the chalk, a man with a thin, semi-transparent hooked nose and deep-etched lines running down and down in papery skin to a folded neck under his bands, a man whose hands, lifted to cover his mouth as he coughs, show bones through softly folded, shimmering, ancient skin above thick pale nails. A man with glaucous eyes under extravagant white eyebrows, a man patently not well, saving his strength, watching from inside the bright cocoon of his purple robes.

Griffith Goatley explains, in a melodious and pleasant voice, that the two suits, between Frederica Reiver and Nigel Reiver, and between Nigel Reiver and Frederica Reiver, have been consolidated and are to be heard together. "I appear for the wife, Frederica Reiver, and my learned friend, Laurence Ounce, appears for the husband. The petition of Frederica Reiver, being the leading suit, is to be heard first."

Frederica's petition, with its charges of cruelty, mental cruelty, adultery, is read out. She is called to the witness box, and finds herself standing looking out over the court, where she sees Nigel, Arnold Begbie, a spattering of complete strangers.

Griffith Goatley takes Frederica through her marriage. He addresses her courteously, as though she was a very young woman who had found herself in a world that turned out to be unpredictable and dangerous.

Q. And in the beginning, your marriage, this marriage which you say you made after reflection and after some three years of acquaintance, your marriage was happy?

A. Yes. In many ways, yes. It was not quite what I expected.

Q. What did you expect?

A. I thought he liked me for what I was. But afterwards, he seemed to want me to stay in his house and never to go anywhere, or see any of my old friends. Or work.

Q. You have a first class degree from Cambridge University?

A. Yes.

Q. And you were a popular and successful undergraduate?

A. Yes. I think so. I am an intellectual. I intended to go on and do a Ph.D.

Q. Your husband knew of this ambition?

A. I believe so. He often said he admired me for my independence, for my self-reliance, things like that.

Q. But when you were married, this changed?

A. Yes. When my son was born, of course, it was more reasonable to expect me to stay at home, perhaps.

Q. Did you feel that your husband's attitude to your independence was only because he felt you should look after your son?

A. No. I felt he was jealous. I felt he felt I should stay put, in the house, where I was. I felt he felt that that was what women did.

Frederica hears her voice. It is not her voice, it is the voice of a quiet young woman, acting out the lives, making the plaints, of intelligent women everywhere.

Q. Was there any lack of help in the house?

A. No.

Q. Would it have been possible for you to see your friends, to work on a thesis, perhaps, without harming your son, or your marriage?

A. I think so, yes. My husband is very well off, and there were many people looking after Leo, anyway.

Griffith Goatley's gentle, reasonable questions continue. He takes Frederica through her shock that her letters were being opened, through Nigel's telephone insults to her friends. He takes her also through Nigel's increasingly lengthy absences.

Q. You felt he was neglecting you?

A. You could put it that way, yes. I felt he thought I was shut up there, now, that part of his life, the wooing, was finished. He went back to his world, but I couldn't, I mustn't.

Q. Would you say your marriage was sexually happy?

A. At first, yes. Very. (A pause.) That was the best thing . . . the language that worked . . .

Q. Did that change, in later times?

A. Yes.

Q. Can you tell us why?

A.   Partly, I think, because I withdrew. I began to see I ought not to have got married.

Q.   And was there anything in your husband's behaviour that led you to reconsider your marriage?

A.   He became increasingly violent.

Q.   When you say, increasingly violent, do you mean as a lover, or as a jealous and unreasonable husband, Mrs. Reiver?

A.   I mean both. He began to hurt me. In bed. And then he began to attack me. Out of bed.

Q.   I believe on one occasion, you looked into his boxes in his cupboard, when he was away.

A.   Yes. I did.

Q.   Can you tell us why you did this?

A.   He had stolen one of my letters. From my brother-in-law, who is a clergyman, and had written to cheer me up. I was trying to find it.

Q.   And what did you find?

A.   A collection of—of pornographic pictures. Dirty magazines.

Q.   You were shocked?

A.   It was very interesting. I was horribly shocked. I felt—quite ill. I felt—*dirtied*. I was surprised to feel so bad.

Q.   Can you say what the pictures were like?

A.   They were sado-masochistic. (Frederica senses that this precise technical term was not what was required.) There were women being tortured and made filthy. Chains and leather and knives. And lots of flesh. I felt dirtied. I was surprised.

Q.   And did your husband ever attack you? Physically?

A.   He began to, yes.

Griffith Goatley takes Frederica blow by blow through the battery, the ridiculous confinement in the lavatory, the chase through the stables, the axe, the wound. The healing.

Q. And did you, at any time, tell anyone else that this wound had been caused in this way?

A. No, I was ashamed.

Q. What had you to be ashamed of?

A. I think people are often ashamed of being hurt. Of having got themselves into a position where . . . anyone should want to hurt them so much.

Q. And what was your husband's attitude?

A. He was very affectionate.

Q. He was remorseful?

A. He was sorry, yes. But he was excited by the—the drama. I knew it would happen again.

Q. So you decided to leave?

A. I thought I would have to. I was very disturbed. I was afraid. It was out of control. I thought I would get away and think things out.

Griffith Goatley takes his witness through her flight in the woods, through her search for somewhere for herself and her son to live, through her decision not to return. He asks her if during her marriage she believed her husband to have been faithful, and she says that, on reflection, she sees she did not, that she had not wanted to understand his prolonged absences, his visits to clubs "with topless waitresses" with "business associates." Griffith Goatley refers to signed affidavits from the barmaid at the Tips and Tassels, from the doorman at the Honeypot, which state that Nigel Reiver has been seen leaving with certain women, whose profession is to "entertain men all night." "The doorman, as you will see," says Griffith Goatley, "deposes that Mr. Reiver is a well-known customer of the club, who enjoys the shows and the ladies. The doorman says," reports Griffith Goatley, "that Mr. Reiver's tastes are well known, slap more than tickle, so to speak, not averse to a few risks."

Q. Do you know what the doorman may mean by that, Mrs. Reiver?

A. No. Not exactly.

Q. Are you surprised by this evidence?

A. No. Well, yes, in a way, I didn't know. But no, on the other hand, I did know there was something and was trying not to. I don't know how much such things matter.

Q. They may matter very much. I will turn, if I may, and I apologise for speaking frankly, to the evidence of your doctor. On two occasions in November 1964 you were treated at the Middlesex Clinic for sexually transmitted diseases.

A. I was.

Griffith Goatley goes through the medical evidence.

Q. And how do you believe you came by this infection?

A. From my husband.

Q. You are sure of this?

A. Quite sure. He was the only person I slept with, between marrying him and leaving him. I was furious.

Q. Furious?

A. Well, I know now, it could have hurt—the baby, it could have—hurt his eyesight. *Or his brain.* I ought to have been told.

Judge. Are you offering this evidence in support of a charge of adultery, or of cruelty?

Griffith Goatley cites several precedents for both.

He concludes his examination of Frederica with a few questions about her present way of life, her home, Leo's school, his friends. He sits down. He has told the story of an intelligent, perhaps over-confident, perhaps over-educated young woman, who has found herself in deep water, socially and sexually, who may have provoked reasonable irritation but has been attacked and abused out of all proportion to her faults.

Laurence Ounce asks if he may put a few questions to this witness at this point, on behalf of his client, in answer to her petition. The judge gives him leave to proceed.

Q. Tell me, Frederica Reiver, why did you marry Nigel Reiver?

A. Why?

Q. Yes, why. You are a clever woman, you had a life-plan of sorts, you had known your husband some time—known in every sense I believe—before you decided to marry him. You were not, I take it, swept away by sudden passion. So why?

A. He wouldn't take no for an answer.

Q. But you are a very strong young woman, strong-willed, clever, we are always being told how clever you are. I am sure you have given no for an answer to several other young men?

A. Yes. I have.

Q. So why were you suddenly ready to marry this one? You were already sleeping together, I believe?

A. Yes. As I said, that worked. That was the thing I was sure about. I thought all the rest would follow.

Q. An odd view, for an "intellectual," as you labelled yourself.

A. Not really. All intellectuals these days read D. H. Lawrence, who says we should listen to—to our passions—to our bodies. To our feelings. I had strong feelings. Good ones.

There was nothing but cool respect in Griffith Goatley's eliciting of information. Laurence Ounce meets Frederica's eye with sexual intelligence; he implies, with a twist of his clever lip, with a cock of his large head, that they understand each other.

Q. Ah, D. H. Lawrence. The immemorial magnificence of mystic, palpable, real otherness. You felt *that*.

A. I don't know why you're asking. But yes, in a way. The prose is dreadful. But why not? Yes, that. It did seem to work.

Q. You married for good sex. Despite the fact that Mr. Reiver in no way shares your intellectual tastes, may never have opened Lawrence?

A. It was the attraction of opposites. I didn't know anything about him. He seemed—you quoted it—*other*. I liked that. I thought he was more—more self-sufficient and grown up than most of the men I knew.

Q.   And you knew a great many?

A.   I was in a position to.

Q.   An odd phrase. You refer, no doubt, to the privileged position of Cambridge women. You were not sexually inexperienced when you married Nigel Reiver?

Griffith Goatley objects. Pre-marital incontinence is inadmissible as evidence in a divorce suit. The judge over-rules him, when Ounce explains that he is seeking to establish how likely or unlikely Mrs. Reiver was to have been surprised by "sexual peccadilloes and so on, on a husband's part."

"You may answer," says the judge.

"You knew quite a lot about men, when you married," says Ounce, wrinkling his eyes at Frederica, waiting to re-establish the fleeting sexual connection between them.

"Yes," says Frederica.

"How many men had you slept with?"

Goatley objects; his objection is sustained; the judge and the Court have seen Frederica hesitate, not knowing the answer.

"Moving on," says Ounce, "moving on to the question of these feelthy pictures. Do you not think—as a sophisticated woman, as you are, that you may have been exaggerating your reaction to them? You have a degree in English literature, a good degree. You must have discussed Shakespeare's bawdy, Chaucer's naughty tales, Rochester's lyrics, with aplomb, in your day, I imagine. Are you really shocked by a few filthy pictures, however deplorable—are they not an unfortunate phenomenon like smoking-room songs, like the lavatory jokes indulged in by all little boys, including your own son, I have no doubt."

"I can only say I was terribly shocked. It does interest me that it was such a blow. I agree, if you'd *told* me I'd react like that, I'd have said I probably wouldn't. But they made me sick."

"A real foray into Bluebeard's cupboard. Perhaps best to leave cupboards shut, you might think. All marriages need private places, private cupboards, you may think. The pictures were not forced on you, were not left about to upset you?"

"Oh no."

"Going back to your evidence. My learned friend asked you why your sexual happiness changed. I believe he expected you to reply, 'Because my husband neglected me and was cruel to me' or some such answer. But I wrote down what you did say. It was 'I think it went wrong because I withdrew. I began to see I ought not to have got married.' Would you care to comment on that observation, Mrs. Reiver?"

Frederica looks down at her hands. She cannot quite speak. He has heard her thoughts. She knows the answer, and knows she should not give it, and cannot speak.

"Come, Mrs. Reiver, you are usually so articulate, so clear. It is a simple question. 'I began to see I ought not to have got married.'"

"I began to see I had promised something I couldn't give," says Frederica, temporarily relieved by having at last said what is in her mind. She pauses again.

"You had married in bad faith?"

"Not exactly."

"Not exactly. But it might look like that. You might be thinking, I have made a mistake, maybe even, a dreadful mistake, and a sensitive man, even if not the most articulate man, might become irascible, sensing this reserve, might have fits of blind irritability, in response to this withdrawal."

"I didn't withdraw."

"Forgive me, Mrs. Reiver. It is the word you used."

"*Withdrawing* doesn't excuse axe-throwing."

"It does not. But we do not admit that an axe was ever thrown. Tell me again, Mrs. Reiver, why you married Nigel Reiver."

"I have told you. Sex. Sexual happiness, that is. And persistence. His persistence."

"The fact that he was very rich had nothing to do with it?"

"Almost nothing. I like—I liked—good restaurants. But it was more the glamour of the opposite, of the unknown, how the other half live. Bad faith, again. I am not asking for maintenance, not for myself. I hope I am allowed to make that clear at this point. I didn't marry for money. A bit for the glamour of the difference."

"You *are* very articulate," says Laurence Ounce, somehow diminishing Frederica.

Q. If we may turn to your precipitate flight from Bran House, for a moment. It was very convenient, was it not, that your friends, a group of male friends, were visiting at the time, were able to hang around with a Land Rover and wait for you?

A. They were not welcome. They might never have come again. I was very frightened. It seemed like then or never. At the time.

Q. And how did you prepare your son for this midnight exodus? Did you tell him you were leaving Bran House, his father, who loved him, his aunts, the housekeeper who had been responsible for his upbringing, his pony, to whom he was so attached? Did he come willingly?

A. (The witness is visibly shocked by this question.) He decided himself.

Q. What do you mean? You put it to him, to a little boy in his bedroom, a *very small* boy—you asked him to decide between his parents?

A. No. I would never do that. No. I didn't tell him. I didn't wake him. I didn't think I could. I didn't think it was fair. I didn't mean to go for long, for ever, then, at that moment. I felt he was better where he was.

Q. You felt he was better where he was.

A. Well, then, in a sense, obviously, yes, he was.

Q. How did he come to go with you, then?

A. He ran after me. He said he was coming. He seemed to know I was going.

Q. He wanted you to stay?

A. No. He said he was coming. I would have gone back in with him, and stayed. But he said he was coming.

Q. He was a desperate, confused little boy, in the middle of the night?

A. Yes. But he was determined. You don't know him. He has a strong will.

Q. You are not going to tell me that a little boy of—four years old—has a will strong enough, in the middle of the night, to impose a decision on a loving mother who has—with some self-renunciation it would appear—decided that *he was better where he was?* Was it not rather, Mrs. Reiver, the case that a little boy, whom you had been content to leave in his bed, sensed inconveniently that you were leaving him, and came out to remonstrate, to plead? And you, fearing that your rendezvous with your young men would be missed, snatched up this little boy, *as an afterthought,* and carried him away as an unplanned piece of luggage?

(The witness is silent.)

Q. Would you not say it was more or less like that?

A. (In a whisper) No. It was not like that. I love my son.

Her voice is small and dry. She cannot utter, she cannot speak. She licks her lips, a nervous gesture which the Court notes.

Griffith Goatley asks his client a few calm questions after this. He then produces signed affidavits from Bill Potter and Daniel Orton, describing violent assaults made upon them by Nigel Reiver on two occasions after his wife's departure.

Laurence Ounce's first witness is Miss Olive Reiver. He establishes that she is the unmarried sister of Nigel Reiver and lives in the family home, Bran House. He takes her through her brother's marriage.

Q. Were you surprised when he married Frederica Potter?

A. Not by then, no. She had often been staying with us. They were obviously very much in love. I was happy to see Nigel so happy.

Q. And Frederica. Was she happy?

A. It was hard to tell. She didn't find it easy to fit in to our way of life. She wasn't from our sort of background.

Q. Do you think she found you intimidating—the close family— the lifestyle of the country, to which she was not used?

A. Oh no. I think perhaps she rather despised us. She thought we were a bit slow and boring, I think. She lived for the moment when Nigel was there. She didn't try too hard with the rest of us.

Q.   She perhaps missed her old friends?

A.   I wouldn't say that. She had lots of visitors. All the visitors she wanted. Mostly young men from London. We made them welcome, of course; that was good manners.

Q.   Was any attempt made to prevent her friends from coming, or to discourage communication with them?

A.   Oh no. We keep open house. I think they found us a bit stick in the mud. Tweedy types. (Laughs.)

Q.   And when your nephew was born—young Leo—did she seem more settled?

A.   Oh no. Perhaps the reverse. She began to seem quite sulky and unhappy. We couldn't cheer her up. She took to sitting in her room.

Q.   She was depressed?

A.   You could call it that. It was a good thing there were so many of us to give a hand with the baby.

Q.   But she loved the baby?

A.   Oh, I think so. But I don't think she's the sort to whom looking after a baby comes naturally. She didn't hold him naturally, you know, she was kind of awkward. *Reserved* with him.

The evidence moves on to the alleged acts of cruelty.

Q.   Did you ever see your brother express anger towards his wife?

A.   They had the odd row. They both gave as good as they got. Shouting matches on the stairs. Kiss and make up, I've seen it several times. Normal, I'd say. She did sulk rather a lot, and that provoked him. But they were happy after their rows, all smiles and hugs.

Q.   Did you ever see your brother strike his wife?

A.   No. Never.

Q. But he might have done?

A. I don't know what went on in their private quarters. But I wouldn't think it was like him. We'd have seen, if she'd been bruised, and she wasn't.

Q. On a certain occasion, in 1964, the doctor was called to dress an extensive gash in your sister-in-law's thigh?

A. She told us she'd tripped over the barbed wire in the paddock field, going about to look at the moon.

Q. Did that strike you as an odd story?

A. Not really. She was always running around at night and wandering off. She was bored, poor thing.

Q. And the injuries were consistent with the barbed-wire story?

A. The rips in her trousers were. I didn't get a close look at her leg. That wasn't my concern.

Q. The wound didn't happen when she was wearing a nightdress?

A. I know nothing about a nightdress. I never saw a nightdress. I did see trousers with bloodstains and barbed-wire rips.

Q. Did you ever think your brother might have caused the injury?

A. No. I'm surprised to hear it suggested. He loves her—well, anyway, he loved her. He was very tolerant of her ways, in my opinion, and has made great efforts to get her to come back and live in the family home, with the little boy. It's not surprising he got a bit irritable—she made him look a bit of a fool, you might think, just going off like that in the middle of the night, with a pack of arty types from London. But he wouldn't *hurt* her. What good would that do?

Q. And what do you think should happen now, after she has stayed away for three years?

A. I don't approve of divorce. I'm a regular churchgoer, I know the Church's teaching is that marriage is once and permanent. I think a child should live in the family home with both his parents. But if she won't come back and try again, try a bit harder, I think she should let Leo come back to us, to the home he grew up in and will inherit, where he's loved and safe.

Laurence Ounce calls Rosalind Reiver. The witnesses have not been in the courtroom before they give evidence. Rosalind Reiver too reports that Frederica had frequent visitors, made no attempt to settle in Bran House, "sulked" and enjoyed quarrelling with her husband. She also states that the wound in Frederica's thigh was said at the time to be caused by barbed wire, and that she has seen ripped trousers with bloodstains consistent with this story. She too knows nothing of a nightdress.

The two sisters are impressive because of their solid, unimaginative ordinariness. They are reasonable, circumscribed, English country gentry. They frown as they appear to try to be fair to their errant sister-in-law. They make it clear that they are devoted to Leo; their heavy mouths smile, their dark eyes open with love when he is mentioned. Rosalind adds to Olive's evidence a moving image of the two of them teaching the enthusiastic little boy to ride Sooty, of the mother refusing to come out and watch his exploits, "reading a book" all the time, when he has learned to post at the trot. She too thinks Nigel has been very patient.

Laurence Ounce calls Pippy Mammott. Pippy's face is pink and shining with generous indignation. She is a more volatile witness than the stolid sisters, in that she has an air of having worked herself up to make an appearance, state a position, fight for a cause. Pins are working their way out of her head: now and then, during her evidence, she puts up her hands to put them back, looking as though she is trying to hold her head together. Ounce puts to her much the same series of preliminary questions as he put to the sisters, about the early days of the marriage, about Frederica's friends, or lack of friends, about their way of life, about Leo.

Q.   She seemed happy to be pregnant?

A.   I wouldn't say that, no. Oh no. I would say it came as a blow to her.

Q.   It wasn't a planned pregnancy?

A.   I overheard her talking to one of her friends on the telephone. She was always talking away on the telephone, all the time. She said, "Guess what, I'm preggers, it's an absolute disaster, it ruins absolutely everything, my life is in ruins."

Q.   Are you sure these were her words? Or is that just the drift of what she was saying?

A.   I was dreadfully shocked to hear her. It was a terrible thing to say. So naturally I remember it.

Q.   But perhaps when the baby was born she felt different? Many women are shocked to find themselves pregnant, but love their child when he comes.

A.   I don't think she felt any different. She wasn't natural with him. I tried to show her little things—how to soothe him, how to do his little nappies, how to get him to take his milk, but she was very irritable, very sulky, very sluggish, she didn't want to know. I caught her looking at him as though she wished he weren't there.

Q.   That was your interpretation.

A.   I know who did everything for that child. I know who put plasters on his knees and who he turned to when his guinea-pig died. I know who knew how he liked his eggs and his toasted soldiers . . .

Q.   Perhaps she felt *de trop*?

A.   What did you say?

Q.   Perhaps she felt you looked after him so well, she was super-fluous?

A.   I don't think that was so, not at all. She plain *wasn't interested*. She was always *reading a book* when she wasn't walking *by herself* or phoning her friends. I've seen her feeding the little boy with one hand and holding up some book with the other, and her eyes were on the book, I can tell you, not on the baby. I've heard him howl his little heart out, and I've run and run to see what the matter was, and he's been hurt with a penknife, and there she was upstairs, *reading a book,* and didn't seem to hear a squeak. Not a squeak.

Q. But the boy loved his mother?

A. Naturally he did. He was always trying to get her attention. Mostly he failed. But I was there—his Pippy—and his aunts were there, and so he was well looked after.

On the question of Nigel's attacks on his wife, on the question of the trousers, the imaginary nightdress, the nature of the wound, Pippy's witness coincides precisely with that of Olive and Rosalind. It goes further.

Q. Did you see the wound in question?

A. Naturally I did. If there's anything to be dressed, or cleaned, or tended, I'm the one—even when it's her.

Q. How would you describe the wound?

A. Very jagged, very uneven. Typical barbed-wire, like you see in hunting. Dr. Roylance said so immediately. Typical barbed wire, he said. Silly girl tried to scramble over a hedge without seeing there was wire the other side, and fell. She doesn't have country instincts. We all knew the hedge was wired. Nigel was very upset. He sat with her all day, soothing her, and chatting.

Frederica writes a note to Goatley. "She's lying. They're all *lying*."

"Exaggerating?" he writes back.

"No, *lying*. Flat, magniloquent *lies*."

"Perhaps she believes herself?"

"She *can't*—none of it was *like that*."

"The judge might notice she's full of animosity. It does come through. But it's hard to credit her with the imagination to lie on a large scale."

"But she *is*—"

"Ah, yes, but what does the court believe?"

Ounce does not ask Pippy, as he asked Olive and Rosalind, what she thinks should happen now. He does say, "Do you think there is any hope of reconciliation after three years' absence?"

"As to that, I couldn't say. I know Nigel wanted things to be as they were and should have been. Families should be together. But I say, if she won't do as she should, the little boy should come back where he's at home, and happy, and loved. There's an abundance of love, a *sufficiency* of love, I do want to make that clear. She could see him all she wants, she knows she could, but he needs his proper things in the proper place. He can't be happy in a basement in *south London,* he's a country child, born and bred . . ."

The court is adjourned for lunch after Pippy's evidence. Frederica drinks a half-pint of shandy. She cannot eat. She does not like beer, but needs alcohol and is thirsty. She tries to joke; she says to Arnold Begbie, "I feel I'm on trial for reading books."

"You are. Partly."

"I wouldn't be if I were a man."

"Perhaps not. I know a couple—early thirties, can't have children, desperate to adopt. The social worker concerned in vetting them sent in a report saying, 'Plausible couple, well-intentioned. Too many books in the house. Wife reads.' "

The next witness after lunch says his name is Theobald Drossel, known as Theo. He is very small; only his head can be seen above the box; he is almost entirely bald and his skin is unhealthy. His face is long and lugubrious. He wears a brown suit and a checked shirt. Frederica finds him faintly familiar, and then, as he says what his profession is, recognises him in the same instant. He is the little man from Hamelin Square, whose Austin coughs continuously. He says he is the director of the Sharp Inquiry Company.

"I watch people. I find things out. Anything, really. I find out. I do mostly marital work. In the nature of things."

Q. You have been in the employment of Mr. Nigel Reiver?

A. Yes. Since December 1964.

Q. What were you asked to do?

A. Follow that lady. Mr. Reiver's wife, see where she went, what she did. See what the little boy did.

Q. And where was Mrs. Reiver living from October 1964?

A. She was living in Bloomsbury, in a mansion flat owned by a Mr. Thomas Poole. I watched her go in and out of the flats, and I watched her go to work with Mr. Poole and come back with him. In the nature of things, I did not gain access to the flat to see what went on there.

Q. Did you form any impression of the relationship between Mr. Poole and Mrs. Reiver?

A. It was very loving, very affectionate. I saw them kiss and cuddle on various occasions, when they separated in the street, and so on. I saw them go shopping with all the kids, his and hers. They was very like a married couple, you know, easy with each other, very affectionate.

   I engaged their *au pair* girl in conversation on two occasions. I pretended to be a neighbour who wanted to borrow a drill. I find a drill is a more plausible thing to try and borrow than sugar. Lots of people don't have drills. The young woman— very prudently—wouldn't let me into the flat, so I couldn't ascertain the sleeping arrangements. I pretended to think that Mrs. Reiver was, so to speak, Mrs. Poole, and the young woman in question, Miss Röhde, (referring to his notebook) enlightened me, as she thought, as to the real situation, but said she supposed they would soon marry, *everything pointed that way,* she said, they would make a lovely family.

Q. Later, Mrs. Reiver moved house?

A. Yes. She went to live in Hamelin Square, Number 42, with a Miss Agatha Mond and her little girl. Miss Mond appears to be unmarried and to have few visitors.

Q. And Mrs. Reiver? Did she have few visitors?

A. No. She had a great many. She had many male visitors, both single ones and in large groups. I kept a record, the days I was there—I wasn't always on this job, you must understand, I had other commissions, there are gaps in my information. I counted about seven or eight very regular male visitors, to whom she was very affectionate, kissing and hugging and stroking.

The witness reads out a list: Tony Watson, Hugh Pink, Edmund Wilkie, Alexander Wedderburn, Daniel Orton, Desmond Bull, Jude Mason. He reads out a rough count of observed visits, singly and in groups. Frederica stares. Her private life is a spectacle for this little man in an Austin. He describes her friendly evenings as "wild parties—the neighbours used to *murmur* about them as they passed my car. She was felt to be a bit outrageous, in the square."

Q. Did you feel that any of these visitors were more than simply intimate friends?

A. I followed the lady on various occasions when she visited Mr. Desmond Bull in Eagle Lane, Clerkenwell. I got friendly with his landlady, who is rather proud of having a Bohemian painter lodging in her house. This landlady—Mrs. Annabel Patten—told me—he reads from his notebook—"he has a mattress in his studio where he screws his models and students and women who come." It was her opinion that Mr. Bull was "an insatiable sex maniac." I do not think she meant by that that he was mad or perverted, merely that he enjoyed sex. She herself took a vicarious pleasure in his activities, and . . .

The judge points out that what the landlady said is inadmissible, since it is hearsay. Ounce asks his witness if he himself observed anything in Mrs. Patten's house.

A. I was able to gain her confidence enough on July 28th, 1966, to be allowed to peep in through a glass panel—one of those frosted things—on Mr. Bull's door. There I observed Mrs. Reiver holding a glass of wine in a state of undress.

Q. Undress?

A. Stark naked. Very much at her ease.

Q. Perhaps she was modelling for Mr. Bull.

A. If she was, that was not all, because I saw Mr. Bull, also stark naked, with his member erect, walk towards her and push her down. On his mattress, you see, the one on his studio floor. I was able to persuade Mrs. Patten to sign a statement as to what we had witnessed—she said she didn't mind, as Mr. Bull "doesn't give a fuck who knows what he does, he's proud of it."

Judge. Mr. Bull has made no answer to the service of the Petition naming him as co-respondent.

Clerk. No, my lord.

Judge. He has not put in an appearance.

Clerk. No, my lord.

Judge.   He is content to let this matter go forward and not to contest it.

Q.   Are there other men with whom you observed Mrs. Reiver to be on intimate terms?

A.   There is Mr. John Ottokar.

Q.   When did you first see Mr. Ottokar?

A.   That must have been in May or June 1965. He used to come regularly to the square and stare at her lighted windows like a love-sick male dog. At first I thought he might be a burglar—I was sitting quiet in my car, quite unobtrusive—I sit for hours, often, sometimes I read a bit, by torchlight—but I saw his look, the way he looked. And one night she let him in. So I crept across the square and looked down into the basement. She sleeps in the basement. Often she doesn't draw the curtains. Even when she does, since it's a fairly thin blind, you can see quite clearly from the shadows what she is doing, what anyone else in there is doing. I was able to satisfy myself that intercourse had taken place. I saw it take place again on July 5th and July 14th and on at least fourteen subsequent occasions.

Q.   And did you observe Mrs. Reiver with Mr. Ottokar anywhere else?

A.   I followed them to Yorkshire in the summer of 1965, where they signed into a hotel under the names of Mr. and Mrs. John Ottokar.

Judge.   Was that necessary, given how much you said you had seen?

A.   Oh, I think so, my lord: I was able to obtain signed affidavits from the hotel staff there, and also my brief was to follow her everywhere she went, not to lose sight of her.

Ounce.   Are there more men you have seen with Mrs. Reiver in compromising situations?

A.   There is Mr. Paul Ottokar.

Q.   Mr. Paul Ottokar.

A.   The problem with Mr. Paul Ottokar is that he is Mr. John Ottokar's twin. His identical twin. I did not realise at first that there were two young men of this description—blond young men with long hair—so to speak *haunting* Hamelin Square, because you don't expect it, do you, you don't expect two vagrants hanging around in the small hours to be watching the same window and look alike. But on one occasion I have observed one brother to be watching from the basement area from which I have watched myself on occasion when Mrs. Reiver was so to speak amorously engaged within with the other brother, so I did a bit of thinking and realised there were two. Mr. John Ottokar works for the Eurobore Systems Analysis Centre. Mr. Paul Ottokar is a pop singer called Zag who sings with a group called Zag and the Szyzgy Zy-Goats. S-z-y-z-g-y, my lord. Pronounced "Ziggy."

Judge. Say that again.

Witness. Zag and the Ziggy Zy-Goats.

Judge. Clever. Very clever.

Witness. My lord?

Judge. Continue. So you found two brothers, twin brothers, taking an interest in Mrs. Reiver?

Witness. Yes, my lord. It is more difficult to tell them apart than you might think. For sometimes both of them wear respectable suits, and sometimes both of them wear, kind of *costumes*—harlequin things, and shiny cloaks and stuff, and painted bodies. And when they watch at night, they wear black PVC raincoats, and it's beyond me to know which one is inside and which is out watching.

Judge. What do you mean, painted bodies?

Witness. Well. They go in for very weird behaviour, very ostentatious, self-advertising kind of stuff. There was one night, one of them set fire to a lot of books, with paraffin, on the bit of waste ground in the middle of the square. He was wearing nothing but a long glittery plastic cloak and he was painted all over in all sorts of colours on his naked body. I formed the opinion he was under the influence of some sort of drugs. Mrs. Reiver had a battle with him over the fires. It was her books he was burning, I think, perhaps. They wrestled, and he fell in the fire, and got quite burned. They called an ambulance. She was holding on to his naked body and screaming and crying.

Ounce. Was Mrs. Reiver's son in the company of these painted young men?

A.   Often and often, both when she was there and when she wasn't. He plays a lot with a gang of little black kids that run around in the street doing silly things like steal milk and ring people's door bells, and one of the brothers encouraged them to set firecrackers under my little car. It did quite a lot of damage.

Q.   Is there anything that leads you to feel certain that Mrs. Reiver did have intercourse with both brothers, and not only with Mr. John Ottokar?

A.   Well. Once I could see they were arguing and so I crept up and listened. No one can see you in the area outside the basement window if you keep in the shadow of the steps. And he was shouting at her, he was telling her they both always shared women, that he was the *real* one and his brother was "the shadow" and a lot of stuff like that. I wrote one phrase down. "This is the real flesh you have imagined." He seemed to be trying to say the experience wasn't complete without both of them, so to speak.

Q.   And what was her response?

A.   I saw them lying on the bed. I saw him undressing her, before I had to run, because I heard Miss Mond coming home.

Part of the Evidence of Thomas Poole, examined by Laurence Ounce.

Q.   And why did you invite Mrs. Reiver to share your flat?

A.   Because I was sorry for her—she had been very frightened, was at a loss, and needed, she believed, to hide from her violent husband. It seemed a sensible arrangement. We were both single parents, with the care of children, who needed to work for our livings. I was able to help her find work. We were able to share housekeeping and baby-sitting.

Q.   And you enjoyed having her?

A. Very much. We knew each other well. I was a colleague of her father, as a schoolmaster, at Blesford Ride School.

Q. So you were *in loco parentis*?

A. To an extent.

Q. Although your children were the same age. Or almost.

A. There are more generations than two.

Q. Indeed there are. You are not old enough to be her father. Did you find her—do you find her—attractive?

A. Yes. She is an attractive woman.

Q. Did it occur to you that things might work out very well if you married, if you worked together, harmoniously, and shared your lives as you were, in fact, already doing?

A. It did occur to me, yes.

Q. Would you have liked to marry Mrs. Reiver, had she been free?

A. The question is purely hypothetical.

Q. Would you?

A. Yes. I would. I admire her greatly and feel love for her.

Q. To the point of making love to her, in earnest of your hopes, when she was in your flat?

A. No. She didn't want it. She had been much hurt. She needed peace, and a time to reflect. I tried to give her that.

Q. Why did she leave, Mr. Poole?

A. Because she decided to ask for a divorce, and felt that our co-habitation might compromise her. She may have been right. I am very sorry it had to be so.

Q. Perhaps she left you for younger men, and a racier life?

A. Perhaps. She was determined to divorce her husband and take charge of her own life. I don't think she would do anything to jeopardise that.

Q.   Would it surprise you to learn that she has been reported as giving "wild parties" and entertaining a pop singer called Zag?

A.   Nothing would surprise me about Frederica. She has a streak of recklessness. But she is also an adult, and an intelligent woman, who made a mistake she is paying for.

Q.   You refer to her marriage as "a mistake."

A.   She was much cast down by the sudden death of her sister. I think she married whilst deeply involved in that grief, that terrible pain. I think she should not have made any decision, in that state. But there it is.

Nigel Reiver is the last to give evidence. He stands in the witness box, watchful but relaxed, his face a mask of courteous attention, his body "ready to spring," is the phrase that comes into Frederica's head. he does not look at her, either with defiance or with regret. His hair is smooth and longer than it used to be; he too is entering the Swinging Sixties.

Frederica is suddenly invaded by a total memory of the first time they made love, in his bachelor flat amongst the dust and dirty shirts; she remembers his body above hers, and his intent face, looking darkly down; she remembers her surprise at the vanishing of her own habitual detachment, the surprise of her hot pleasure, her complete presence in his hands, under his weight. From time to time, with other men, inconveniently, she has been visited by the ghost of this completely unghostly moment of life, this excess of delight. Now is a bad moment to remember it; she looks down, and feels the hot blood running up her neck. All these words, all these lies and equivocations and painful approximations and truths are to do with this, which cannot be described.

She listens to him describing their marriage, in his usual blocked, cautious words. He is not indignant, as his sisters were on his behalf. On his own, he might not move an arbiter to think him greatly wronged. Frederica is moved.

Q.   Your wife has complained that you were absent for unreasonable periods, that you prevented her from having a life of her own.

A. I expected her to be my wife. Her idea of what that meant and mine weren't the same. With hindsight, I think both of us could have given way a little.

Q. You were surprised when she suddenly left.

A. Very. I didn't think things were that bad. I knew she was a bit upset. I thought she'd come back.

Q. You hadn't hurt her, or frightened her?

A. I lost my temper, once or twice. I was worried. Normally, I pride myself on keeping my temper. So when I do shout and hit, it frightens people, it frightened her perhaps, more than it ought.

Q. You say you shouted. Did you hit her?

A. I pushed her about a bit once in the bedroom. She provoked me.

Q. Provoked you?

A. I got the sense she wasn't *with me* and didn't want to be. Her thoughts were somewhere else. It was like living with a—with a—with a walking corpse. That isn't what I mean. She was there, but there wasn't anyone there. I wanted to shake her, to get her attention back, and once or twice I did, that's all.

Q. Did you ever throw an axe at her?

A. No.

Q. She has claimed you did. Can you remember any episode which she might be referring to?

A. No. (Pause.) She must have just made it up. She's got the imagination.
    (He gives the impression that he has not.)

Q. When your wife left, did you hope she would come back?

A. Of course. I thought it was a silly misunderstanding.

Q. Did you make any efforts to get her back?

A. Yes. I looked everywhere I could think of. I went to see people—friends—and family. She hid from me. When I found her, she'd clearly decided to live in a different style.

Q. But you still wanted her back?

A. I believe in marriage. We have a child. A woman's place is with her husband and child. She wouldn't talk, she wouldn't discuss, she wouldn't entertain the idea. I'm not a saint, I'm a reasonable being. I've waited and hoped. Now, I think I give up. I'd like to remake my life: but I do want my son. I love my son, he's happy at home, where he belongs.

Griffith Goatley questions Nigel about the obscene pictures, about the Tips and Tassels, about the Honeypot. Nigel replies that the pictures were given to him by a schoolfriend who thought "they were a good joke." "I put them with my rugger things and forgot them. I expect they're still there." He is open about the Tips and Tassels and the Honeypot.

A. Certain sorts of business entertaining does go on in places like that. With foreigners, you know, people who expect this kind of thing. It doesn't mean much to me, either way, but I go along with it. I admit once or twice I did go off with women from there. It isn't very nice, I see, but it isn't what I think of as "adultery"—

Q. It *is* adultery.

A. Here it is, it's named so. It is, I see that. But it's just horsing around, you know, naughtiness. I never thought of it as anything to do with my marriage. It's not like paying serious attention to another real woman.

Q. Real?

A. Woman out of one's own class, one's own world, who might make claims, distract your *feelings* . . . (He stops, apparently at a loss for words. He says) I don't think all that has anything to do with why she left me. I don't think it was important.

Goatley. She may hold a different view on that.

A. I bet she doesn't. *That* isn't what's at stake. It's her idea of her independence, that's what's the real issue here. I give in on that now, I'm asking for a divorce, being a wife isn't her idea of how to live, I accept that now. If we'd both been a bit wiser in the beginning, it would have saved a lot of tears. But we do have a son, and for his sake I would try to keep it up, I would have tried, because I think he comes first and he will be best in Bran House, in his own place. I wanted her to stay, but she went off with all these men, and a man can only take so much of that.

Laurence Ounce produces a signed affidavit from Nigel's doctor, Dr. Andrew Roylance, who says that he has never at any time treated Mr. Reiver for any venereal infection, and that he remembers the occasion of Mrs. Reiver's flesh wound, which he was told was, and which was in his opinion consistent with, a tear caused by falling on barbed wire scrambling over a wall or hedge with a concealed strip of the wire.

Frederica is recalled to the stand, and examined by Laurence Ounce about the evidence of Theobald Drossel.

He takes her through the evidence about Thomas Poole, and through Thomas Poole's own evidence. Frederica replies confidently enough that she lived chastely at Poole's flat, and adds tartly, "I would have had to in any case, even if I had not wanted to, since I had caught the infection."

Q.   If you had not had the infection, you might have slept with Mr. Poole.

A.   I do not think I would, no. I am just pointing out, it was out of the question.

Q.   But you *thought* about it being out of the question.

A.   Mr. Poole has said that he himself thought we might consider—a closer relationship. I didn't. He says I didn't. He is quite clear.

Q.   So it matters to you to be thought chaste, to be a woman who does not sleep with all and sundry?

A.   I have never done that, and don't intend to.

Q.   What are your relations with Mr. John Ottokar?

A.   Private, I hoped. I have made love to him. I admit that. On several occasions, more or less as Mr. Drossel says.

Q. Do you love Mr. Ottokar?

A. I don't know what that word means, any more. I don't know how to tell a Court what I feel about him. I think I do feel— have felt—love for him. Yes. It is—it was—a serious relationship.

Q. It is—it was? How do things stand at present?

A. I don't know. I haven't seen him since the summer.

Q. I believe he is your student.

A. Was my student.

Q. You were, as it were, in a position of responsibility towards him?

A. Hardly. He comes to an *adult* class I teach. We are all grown-up people, in that class.

Q. And sleep with each other?

A. No. This is different.

Q. Mr. Ottokar is not here today. He has been served with a petition, and has not entered an appearance.

A. That is so.

Q. Was there, is there, any question of your eventually marrying Mr. Ottokar?

A. None that I know of. None, that is. All this—these proceedings—have probably put an end to it. I mean to the relationship, not to the idea of marriage, which never arose, until you mentioned it.

Q. Never arose. Never arose. It was simply an affair, under your son's nose, but not serious.

A. It was serious. It was not frivolous. I tried to see him without upsetting or involving Leo.

Q. And his brother?

A. I have never slept with his brother.

Q. What is your relationship with his brother?

513

A. I should like to say, none. His brother—his brother—he invades my flat, without my consent. He invades his brother's relationships. It is hard to explain briefly.

Q. Mr. Drossel describes a scene in which he claims one Mr. Ottokar burned your books whilst under the influence of drugs.

A. I think he was. Yes, he did. It was Paul and I tried to stop him. I don't want him in my house, or near my son. It is all very unfortunate.

Q. It is all very unfortunate. Very unfortunate, I would agree. You feel a little out of control of these brothers and their passions and their way of life?

A. I may never see them again. I haven't seen them, either of them, for months. It's past.

Q. But you feel love for Mr. Paul—I'm sorry—for *Mr. John* Ottokar.

A. I did. I don't know what I feel now. I *don't know.*

Q. And Mr. Desmond Bull. You heard Mr. Drossel's evidence.

A. That was the only time.

Q. The only time?

A. The only time I made love to Desmond Bull.

Q. But you go there often?

A. He is a colleague. I like his pictures.

Q. But the only time you made love to him on his mattress, to which he invites many women, was the time when Mr. Drossel happened to have his eye to the etched window?

A. Yes. That one time.

Q. We may find that hard to believe. Why did you break your rule, if it exists, on that one occasion?

A. I needed comfort. I was in a great rage, after Paul Ottokar's skoob activities.

Q. Skoob?

A. Books, backwards. Towers of burned books. A new art-form.

Q. So one artist burns your books and your natural reaction is to make love to another because you "needed comfort," because you were "in a great rage."

A. Yes.

Q. And that is what you normally do, when you are in need of comfort, make love to some man?

A. No.

Q. You say you have never made love to Mr. Hugh Pink?

A. No.

Q. Nor to Mr. Tony Watson nor to Mr. Alan Melville?

A. No. That is, no, not since I was married.

Q. And Mr. Edmund Wilkie?

A. Not since 1954. A long time ago.

Q. Tell me, Mrs. Reiver, do you think the act of sex is sacred, or just a kind of quick source of comfort or assuagement of rage?

A. "Sacred" is a word that isn't in my vocabulary. I think sex varies with people and times. I think it can be very serious— very important—and now and then not important, just something that happens. One should never hurt or cheat people. This isn't a good answer, I know, when I'm in this court, which calls sex adultery, and sees every man as a potential husband and father. But the truth is, *I was faithful to my husband until I left him*—as he was not, even if it was only tips and tassels and honeypots, so to speak. *Sex isn't*—

Q. Sex isn't?

A. It doesn't matter.

Q. You were going to say?

A. Sex isn't the root of the matter. The root is unkindness and cruelty.

Q. You will have read Sigmund Freud, being so clever. Everything has a sexual element, according to him. Unkindness and cruelty may spring from the sexual insecurity of a man denied and at some deep level rejected, frustrated, trivialised?

A. (Silence.)

Q. You have no response to that?

A. It wasn't a question. It was a statement.

Q. A statement on which you don't wish to comment.

A. No. I think not. No.

The lawyers make their final speeches. Griffith Goatley speaks first. He presents his client as a brilliant and generous young woman—he emphasises the "*young*"—who married in good faith someone not from her own background, someone socially more privileged, from a class with very well-defined ways and expectations, into which she was expected to fit—to fit gratefully, he might suggest, as might be clear from the evidence of her sisters-in-law and housekeeper. There was no suggestion of compromise, says Mr. Goatley. "From the moment of marriage this young woman's husband treated her primarily as a fourth member of his household of adoring women. The reasonable expectations she might have had of any continuance of the friendships or conversations she valued in her own world were disappointed. Her husband's absences were longer and longer, and as he himself has admitted, concerned not only with business, but at least as much with convivial pleasures, and more reprehensible activities— some of which endangered his young wife's health, and, as she has pointed out, might well have endangered the health of their unborn child. She felt herself unwanted and superfluous in this apparently idyllic home—and whatever Your Lordship may make of the factual side of the evidence of the Misses Reiver and Miss Mammott, it seems abundantly clear that there was never either liking or sympathy or understanding shown towards my client."

Griffith Goatley, with clarity and reasonable precision, sums up Frederica's tale of violence—the blow to the spine, the terror in the lavatory, the axe-throwing. "Her husband and his family deny that any of this took place: they have closed ranks: their evidence, you may think, is almost remarkably consistent and homogeneous. My client is, as she has been throughout her married life, isolated and unsupported." Frederica is not, he says, a saint or a heroine—"she is a young wife who got out of her depth—both as to social class, and, you may think, despite some juvenile peccadilloes, as to sexual cruelty, as to the interest in hurting and humiliating women represented by the nature of the pornographic material she discovered, and by the kind of entertainment provided at least by the Honeypot, and by precise services offered by the particular call girl, Myra Thanopoulos, with whom Mr. Reiver does not deny that he has associated."

He asks that Frederica Reiver be granted a divorce on grounds of cruelty, both mental and physical, and on grounds of adultery.

Laurence Ounce describes his client as a serious, dynamic young man—much involved in his business, but this is normal, is not a fault or a sin, who has married a girl met whilst she was a Cambridge undergraduate, happy and flourishing amongst the admiration lavished on her in this world of young men. He was aware of her reputation as a sophisticated and *experienced* young woman—though not, perhaps, of the extent, or, one might say, the indiscriminate nature of this sophistication and experience.

He felt, perhaps, that he had carried away the princess for the ball under the eyes of the suitors. He believed, perhaps, the story of the fairytale—"The most surprising people do believe it, my lord, and act upon it, and learn to adjust their naïve expectations with good and bad humour as the case may be." He believed that they would marry and live happy ever after, that the princess would become lady of the manor and live as her predecessors had lived. But she did not want to, had no intention of being happy ever after. Adjustment was certainly required on both sides—when was it ever not? But Mrs. Reiver would not adjust—she needed her court of young men, her "career," her books, her "independence," just as though her marriage vows had never been made, and even though she has a small son who might be thought to be enough occupation for the next few years of the happy ever after. She has admitted, strikingly, that she "withdrew" and "realised she should never have married." She puts this realisation as *preceding* the cruelty she claims her husband exercised—she is involuntarily honest, even though unstable. She invents a story, of acts of violence committed by her husband. Of acts so suddenly cruel, out of the blue, that she is forced to make a dramatic midnight flight through the woods—"The story is now Bluebeard's Castle, and the grisly exhibits have been duly viewed in the cupboard"—snatching up her son *as an afterthought* "although she thought he would be better where he was." What are we to make of this tale? It is confidently rejected by my client, by the Misses Reiver, by Miss Philippa Mammott. Mrs. Reiver has a first class degree in English. She is an expert in the European novel, on which she has been lecturing with some success, it appears, to Mr. John Ottokar, amongst others enchanted by her rhetoric. She is at home in Dostoevski, Stendhal and Sir Walter Scott. She knows all about axes and women in white robes fleeing through the woods in the dark. My client's sisters, more prosaic, see *trousers* with hedge-tears typical of barbed wire's jagged ripping. Are we to believe that these taciturn, churchgoing ladies—"tweedy and boring" as they put it themselves, got together and concocted a foolproof coherent story? And that they then suborned the excellent Dr. Roylance to commit perjury? This is not feudal England, and he is not a retainer. No, the unstable, creative imagination, the *literary cleverness,* is all Mrs. Reiver's." Mr. Ounce submits that Mr. Reiver has no case to answer as to the alleged cruelty. Look at these two, he says, and decide who it is safe to believe. In all marital problems there is a balance of right and wrong and it is very rarely all on one side. But in this case it is clear where the guilt lies, as it is clear from Mrs. Reiver's subsequent behaviour what sort of lifestyle she would naturally choose, left to herself.

When the judge begins to speak, Frederica thinks again: I am too thin. She *has not enough weight.* She is nothing. The things she knows she cannot say and the things she says are not descriptions of what she thinks was and is what happened or is happening. He has not heard her. He will find against her. He looks down from his height, sourly she thinks, wet buried eyes in a sick skin.

He says:

"We old men have to remember that marriages change, that social customs change, that expectations change. You are here in a Divorce Court, in a Christian country where the established Church, to which one of you belongs, believes marriage is for ever and indissoluble. You both desire divorce, although our law requires that you must neither connive nor collude in seeking it, but show cause why you should be divorced, give evidence of matrimonial offences which are sufficient reason for divorce. Mrs. Frederica Reiver, the wife, first sought relief alleging cruelty and adultery. Mr. Nigel Reiver was for some time long-suffering, sought restoration of his conjugal rights in the matrimonial home, and has now, perhaps for sufficient reasons, decided that his patience will lead nowhere, that his hopes are unrealistic, that his best help is to accept the situation with a good grace.

"I have carefully considered the evidence set before me. Mr. Reiver admits to the adultery of which he is accused, but denies the charges of cruelty. The major charges—the blows and the story of the axe-attack—depend entirely on Mrs. Reiver's own uncorroborated account. She appears to have complained to no one about this alleged attack within the time which is allowed to make this complaint admissible as evidence of the attack. She appears not to have complained specifically of this attack to the shadowy young men who waited for her in the Land Rover after her flight, though we do have the affidavit of Mr. Hugh Pink that he was told—*eleven days* later—that an axe had been thrown. This evidence we must weigh against the very clear evidence of the Misses Reiver and Miss Mammott, and whilst it is not beyond the bounds of credibility that these respectable bodies should have agreed a story to support their brother and employer, it is my belief that the balance of probability is against it. The same balance of uncertainties applies to the sorry tale of the venereal infection. Mrs. Reiver claims that she could have caught it only from her husband. He does not deny that he has consorted with women from whom he *could* have caught such an infection, but he presented medical evidence that he did not. Mrs. Reiver claims to have seen no friends, male or female, since her marriage, until she ran away. This is contradicted by the evidence of the Misses Reiver and Miss Mammott. Her recent behaviour does not suggest that physical chastity is high enough on her scale of values to render it entirely improbable that she could have contracted the infection elsewhere.

"Her own adultery—subsequent to her desertion, which she does not deny—is amply witnessed and supported. She denies several counts and admits others. We need not go into the truth, or lack of truth of the contested allegations, since what is admitted is enough to show the nature of the case.

"I have some sympathy with both parties to this divorce. Both misunderstood the nature of each other's commitment, though this might have been more easily remedied than Mrs. Reiver's petition melodramatically assumes. Mr. Reiver expected to find a wife who behaved like a wife and accepted the constraints upon her freedom inevitably incurred by becoming a wife. Mrs. Reiver assumed that Mr. Reiver admired her as she was, for her intellectual virtues perhaps, and would allow her a latitude he was far from admitting. The higher education of women has in many ways, I have observed, been very hard upon both men and women. It has encouraged skills and raised expectations which society as it is at present constituted is incapable of fulfilling or satisfying—skills and expectations perhaps incompatible with the fulfilled life of wife and mother. Other women, faced with the realisation of this problem, have perhaps been more patient, more tractable, more resourceful. Mrs. Reiver was young and volatile. She chose to run away.

"Much turns on the alleged axe attack, which is the only substantial act of cruelty alleged. I feel that it is unsafe to accept Mrs. Reiver's evidence on this point—the balance of probability, which this court is allowed to consider to be adequate—lies with the husband's account, and the evidence of his household. Mrs. Reiver's desertion is undeniable.

"Mr. Reiver's attempts to persuade her to return are well documented and wholly convincing. Both parties have committed adultery: neither has any prospect, apparently, of a second marriage, which might offer a family to the little boy.

"I find for the husband, whose prayer for counter-relief the Court accepts. He is granted a decree nisi. The wife's petition is rejected.

"In the matter of custody of the son, Leo Alexander. The Court will institute custody proceedings as soon as is reasonably possible. The Court Welfare Officer will visit both parties, and both houses, and will also talk to the boy himself, who is, I understand, articulate and bright. I should like to be able to institute the custody hearing before Christmas, but the Clerk fears that because of pressure of cases this may not be practicable. The Court directs that for the present the child shall stay where he is, with his mother, to disrupt his life as little as possible. Since it is clear that he has been happily travelling between households, the Court also directs that he spend Christmas with his father, arriving on December 24th, returning to his mother on December 27th promptly."

Frederica stands outside the courtroom in her little black dress. Her visible knees beneath its high hem tremble and knock together. She feels she has been watching a film about a woman whom she rather despises, a silly woman who has been judged and found wanting. On top of this, she feels obscurely, the story of her life has been changed by the way it has been told today—both the true bits, and the velleities, and the flat lies, one part of a new fiction, a new story, in which she—who is she, does she exist?—is entangled as in a fine, voluminous net. She thinks she does not care who wins the divorce, as long as the divorce happens. She thinks that the story that was told is the story of a woman unfit to have charge of a small boy, whom she does not love enough. She feels she has stepped into a world where the codes, the rules, are different: reading is wicked, is neglect, a movement of love or comfort to one man is simply defined as depriving another of his *rights.* She stands by herself and her knees knock. Words come into her head. "Who is it that can tell me who I am?" Who said that?

Someone comes up behind her and puts an arm round her shoulders. "That was pretty dreadful. Are you OK?" It is Nigel. She flinches, and then turns to meet his eye: he too is involved in this linguistic net laid over bare limbs in a bed, over the axe, over the little boy sleeping, over what can't be named or defined or understood.

"I'm shaking," she says.

"You know you don't have to worry about costs. I'll pay."

"Thank you."

"We'll talk about Christmas."

"We will."

"All's fair in love and war, heh?"

"No. It isn't. It isn't. Some things aren't. Lies aren't."

"I want my son, Frederica."

"So do I. So do I."

"I don't think you do, not really, not deep down. That's what all this is about. That's what I'm fighting for."

He is telling the truth. She bows her head.

"We'll see," she says, in a small voice.

"We will. If he comes home, you can come whenever you want, you can take him on holidays, we'll make it *good,* we won't exclude you."

"He wants to stay with me."

"We'll see about that."

He pats her shoulder again, and again she has the double movement of flinching and turning to him.

That night, she dreams. She is outside a high gate, with barbed wire wreathing its top. The weather is darkly hot and stormy. She is not tall enough to peer in through the keyhole, which is high above her head and massive. She knows no one will come. She looks around for something to stand on, to see in, and finds a kind of rolling platform on wheels, which she knows, as dreamers know, is what is used to roll condemned men, unable to walk, close enough to the hangman. She pushes it towards the keyhole. Its wheels are wooden, and crank and grumble. She mounts the steps and grips the bar in front of her. She can see in. The keyhole is like a long telescopic tunnel. Dark. Beyond is a garden. It is in many ways the Long Royston garden where she played the young Virgin Queen in Alexander's *Astraea*. It has wide lawns, with croquet hoops and rose trees, and is bordered by a forest of dark boughs, with beautiful ashy black leaves, and golden fruit covered with soot, so that the gold shines dimly, fitfully, through the black dust.

Over the lawns pad great cats. Lions, tigers, black panthers, with gold eyes, with green eyes, with blood on their white fangs, silent and pacing. She knows she has to try and let them out, and that if she lets them out, they will devour her. There is no key. She has the idea that she can pour herself through the keyhole, but this is nonsense. A voice in the head says, "You are thin, you are thin." She sees that she is indeed thin, she is two-dimensional, a paper woman, a cardboard woman. She watches herself insert herself between the great gates, insubstantial inch by inch, and float above the garden like a kite. At the end of the garden is a kind of shrine, a cave with a stone bed in it, on which is a stone lion, a small lion, which emits a kind of pulsing light, a hot, bright glow. She manages to alight on the grass, and walks towards this creature. All the other great beasts pad behind her. She is in a dress made of red and white paper, which shreds and falls in drifts like petals as she goes forward. She is as she was the young Elizabeth, pursued with scissors by her stepmother, Catherine Parr, and her stepmother's jocular, amorous husband, Thomas Seymour, intent on shredding her petticoats for fun, or so it was said in Seymour's trial for treason, for which he lost his head. He lost his head, the voice says in her head, as the grass becomes full of floating red and white fragments between the croquet hoops. Her dress is no longer a dress, it is a paper band round her waist from which hang red and white ribbons, which do not cover the ruddy triangle of her pubic hair. Now, as in the play, she cries out the line of the beggarwoman in the ballad whose red flannel petticoat was cut away—"Lawks a mussy on me, this is none of I." Figures are hurtling after her, large stone women, red women, white women, howling, "Off with her head." If she can reach the stone lion she is safe. The garden grows as she runs. She trips on the hoops, her feet bleed. A red woman pronounces, She thinks she is Una with the lion, but everyone knows that is a lie, a whopper, a terrible tarradiddle, Una was a virgin and virgins don't have lions.

Virgins have stone lions, she says. That isn't right. They don't. The stone lion snarls and begins to grow a stone pelt, bristling. Its eyes are red. It yawns. She must reach it.

She isn't a virgin, say the pursuing three. They are all red now, all three, and she is white with fear, with cold, she shivers in the cool evening in the garden and tries to cover her nakedness with her hands. They have the faces of Easter Island gods, carved in red stone, in bloodstone, in carnelian. They say, She can't do anything, she's made of paper, she's cardboard, she's just cardboard, she's thin, she's a line.

Paper wraps stone, she says, falling towards the glowing creature couched on the stone bed. And everything falls, showers of red and white paper roses, showers of cards, the heavy stone figures. Everything falls, and she is under, and the stone lion is under her.

She wakes.

XX

"Members of the jury," says the Clerk of the Court, "the prisoners at the bar, Bowers and Eden Limited, and Mr. Jude Mason, are charged that on the 13th day of March last, they published an obscene article, to wit, a book entitled *Babbletower: A Tale for the Children of Our Time.* To this indictment they have pleaded not guilty and it is your charge to say, having heard the evidence, whether they be guilty or not."

There is only one prisoner at the bar. He is wearing a charcoal-grey flannel suit, a white shirt, and a neatly knotted dull-crimson tie. His hair is a smooth skullcap of iron grey shot with silver; his face is gaunt, his eyes downcast. He has the look of someone released from confinement, a rehabilitated prisoner, a monk returned from contemplation to the "real" world. His clothes, precisely observed, fit very well; nevertheless, at first glance, they have a look of hanging on him, a suggestion of the clothes hanger, the scarecrow. His neck is thin and grey inside his collar. His bones have a mediaeval look, the cheekbones high and carved, the nose prominent, the eyes half-shut, a little sunk.

Frederica is in Court, with Daniel. She does not at first recognise the prisoner, although she has been part of the meeting which argued for his transformation, and indeed produced the argument that prevailed.

"It's only a *mask,* Jude, for God's sake. A court trial is a fiction, we play parts, it's a game of chess. You have to play the White Knight, you have to *look like* a respectable member of society, as the court will think one ought to look, that's what matters, you have to *look right,* it's part of it."

524

"It isn't a fiction. It's a truth. I am on trial and I am as I am. My appearance is a true statement of what I am."

"*I don't* know what your appearance states," said Duncan Raby, Jude's solicitor.

"You are not skilled in the semiotics of clothes," said Jude. "My coat is sky blue, the colour of truth, and it is the dress at once of the Enlightenment philosophers and the licentious beaux of the courts. My coat is sullied, as truth is sullied. My hair is nature, untended. As is my skin."

"That's nice to know," said Raby. "But it won't cut any ice with Mr. Justice Gordale Balafray and it's a tactical disaster."

"Come on, Jude," said Frederica. "You must wear the mask appropriate to the rite you find yourself in. You must play their game. You must look respectable. Hair grows and a coat can be put in a cupboard. You expose your naked body happily enough for gain—"

"That is also a form of integrity."

"Do you want to win this case?" cried Rupert Parrott. *"Or not?"*

But Frederica is shocked to see the prisoner at the bar. He does have a look, she thinks, of the virtue having gone out of him. He looks ill.

The jury sits in its box. There was some discussion, before it was empanelled, about whether it should be an all-male jury, as used to be customary in obscenity cases. The judge declared himself possibly in favour of such a jury: both Counsel for the Prosecution and Counsel for the Defence were agreed that there was no necessity for such a ruling in their view, and that the presence of one or more women on the jury would make it more representative of the public opinion, the community at large of right-thinking persons, which is represented. As a result there are three women on the jury, none of them young, one the owner of a beauty salon and a widow, one a retired physical training instructor from the Women's Royal Navy, and one a housewife. The men are all middle-aged except one, a swarthy young man in a leather jacket who owns a gramophone record shop. There are a bank manager, an accountant, a swimming-pool manager, a technical college lecturer (in physics), an electrician, a restaurant owner, a tailor and a teacher from a comprehensive school. Most of them read the oath with no stumbling; the tailor is Jewish, wears a skull cap, and swears by the Old Testament.

Some procedural discussion takes place. It is agreed that, following the precedent of the *Lady Chatterley* trial in 1960, the jury shall hear the

speeches both for the Prosecution and for the Defence before they retire to read the book itself: this provision was then made because it was
felt to be unjust that they should read it having heard only one side,
with the Prosecution's comments sharp in their minds. Mr. Justice
Gordale Balafray is a very large man, long-faced, darkly handsome
under his white wig, which therefore shines whiter. He has a reputation for fairness both to barristers and to witnesses. He has a reputation
for liking the arts, too.

It is also agreed, that since the witnesses both for the Prosecution
and for the Defence are "expert witnesses," they have the right to remain in the Court during the trial and not be excluded.

Sir Augustine Weighall, QC, begins his case.

"If Your Lordship pleases. Members of the jury, I appear with my
learned friend Mr. Benedict Scaling to prosecute in this case. The defendant company, Bowers and Eden Ltd., is represented by my
learned friends Mr. Godfrey Hefferson-Brough and Mr. Peregrine
Swift; the defendant Mr. Jude Mason is represented by Mr. Samuel
Oliphant and Mr. Merlyn Wren."

Sir Augustine has a pleasant, aquiline face, with a thin mouth
shrewdly pursed when he is in repose. He has the gift of keeping still
when he is speaking, looking attentively and considerately at the jury,
meeting eye after eye, impartially, with concern. He speaks clearly,
unemphatically, practically. He tells the jury that they are here to decide whether the book *Babbletower: A Tale for the Children of Our Time*
is an obscene book within the meaning of the Obscene Publications
Act, 1959. The word "obscene," he tells the jury, is defined by the
Oxford English Dictionary as "offensive to modesty or decency; expressing or suggesting unchaste or lustful ideas; impure, indecent,
lewd." It has other meanings, including "lack of perspicuity in language; uncertainty of meaning; unintelligibleness," and it is the case
that the previous law against "obscene libel" did perhaps lack perspicuity, and was uncertain in its meaning. The 1959 Act elucidates
the matter in Section 1(A)1, where it defines "obscenity" as follows:

"For the purposes of this Act an article shall be deemed to be obscene if its effect . . . is, taken as a whole, such as to tend to deprave
and corrupt persons who are likely, in all circumstances, to read, see,
or hear the matter contained or embodied in it."

"This elucidation provides other problems of perspicuity in language, meaning, and intelligibleness. You may think you need guid-

ance on the precise force and meaning to attribute to the words 'deprave' and 'corrupt.' The same dictionary gives as the current sense of 'deprave': 'To make morally bad; to pervert, debase, or corrupt morally.' The definition of 'corrupt' is longer and more complex. The 1959 Act no doubt intends the third meaning of the verb as given: 'To render morally unsound or rotten; to destroy the moral purity or chastity of; to pervert or ruin (a good quality); to debase, defile.' "

In practice, Sir Augustine tells the jury, the phrase "deprave and corrupt" has been taken to mean "to cause to behave badly," to incite to actions which are contrary to the law, to ideas of decency or propriety which are generally current in the community. He gives precedents for this understanding. He goes on to quote Mr. Justice Stable, who exhorted a jury to "remember that the charge is a charge that the tendency of the book is to corrupt and deprave. The charge is not that the tendency of the book is either to shock or to disgust. That is not a criminal offence."

Counsel in past cases have rightly emphasised this, and have said to the jury, as he himself is now saying, that the fact that they find a book unpleasant, or shocking, or disgusting, is not in itself a reason to consider it "obscene." But he believes that the phrasing "*tend to* deprave and corrupt" does give the jury the right, and possibly the duty, to consider the effect of the book on the soul, if that word is permissible, on the state of mind and health of the spirit, of those who may read it, whether or not it may lead directly to action which is depraved, corrupted, or unlawful.

He tells the jury that they are the only judges of whether or not the book is obscene. Evidence will be led from expert witnesses, by both the Defence and the Prosecution, as to the nature of the work in question, and as to whether it has any literary or other merit. But the opinion of these witnesses will be relevant only as to the merits and demerits of the book, not as to the point of obscenity, on which their opinion should not be asked; if they offer opinions on whether the book is obscene, the jury should disregard them. The matter of obscenity, of whether the book tends to deprave and corrupt, is for the twelve men and women in the jury box, representing humane and civilised society and common sense, to decide.

When they have decided that, and only then, the question of the literary or other merits of the book may arise. Section 4(2) of the Obscene Publications Act entitles the defendant to an acquittal if the jury is satisfied that notwithstanding the obscenity of an article, its publication is justified as being for the public good in the interests of "science, literature, art or learning, or of other objects of general concern." The Defence have given notice that they intend to raise the Section 4(2) defence and prove it through the testimony of experts. They will argue that the book has literary merits and other important values—social, psychological—which justify its publication in the public interest. "You will make up your own minds as to that, on hearing their evidence. His Lordship has ruled that, exceptionally, the Defence witnesses should be heard first in this case, so that the Prosecution will know upon what grounds they defend the book before calling witnesses in rebuttal."

Sir Augustine tells the jury that Mr. Justice Byrne, in the case of *R. v. Penguin Books,* the *Lady Chatterley* trial, ruled that the prosecuting counsel should not read out passages of the book before the jury themselves had read the whole of the book. Mr. Gerald Gardiner, QC, in his objection on that occasion said, "I am not objecting to my learned friend putting before the jury the nature of the story, or the grounds on which the Prosecution contends it is obscene. . . . I submit the Prosecution are not entitled to try to prejudice the jury's mind as to particular passages before they have read the book as a whole."

Sir Augustine says that he will therefore summarise his case against the book at this point, and examine particular passages later. In the old days when books were tried for "obscene libel" and there was no defence of literary merit, or public interest, it was often sufficient for "purple passages" to be read out and to be found unacceptable, to secure a conviction. Here, it is the whole book which is on trial and must be judged, as to whether it tends to deprave and corrupt. Sir Augustine says he is very happy to accept this ruling, since, although *Babbletower* contains many very explicit descriptions of lewd actions, of explicit sex, of unnatural acts, and most gravely, detailed and superfluous descriptions of cruelty and torture, it is the tendency of the book itself that is in his view finally obscene, corrupt, that is, rotten, and depraved, that is, unnatural and degrading. He believes that the jury will find that such literary merit as it has—and he does not intend to deny that it has some—does not outweigh the unpleasantness, the perversity, of its actions and its conclusion.

"It has been said," says Sir Augustine, "that in the trial of D. H. Lawrence's *Lady Chatterley's Lover* it was Lady Chatterley herself who was on trial, for her adultery, for the fact of her sexuality. In the case of *Babbletower* it is the prisoner in the dock who is on trial, his imagination, the world he created, the tendency of the messages he offers. *Babbletower* is a book without hope. Its slender narrative turns on the decision of a group of people with vaguely French names to go and found a community in 'freedom'—'freedom' in this case meaning complete freedom of sexual expression, no matter how disgusting or perverted that expression may be. This 'freedom' degenerates into licence and into cruelty, madness and destruction. The tortures and humiliation—not only of grown men and women, but of little children—that follow, are described in lurid and superfluous detail. The word 'pornography' is derived from two Greek words, *porno*, a prostitute, and *graphein*, to write. It has been defined as writings about whorehouses and prostitution. It has also been defined as 'the writings of prostitutes.' You may think, when you have read *Babbletower*, that it is simply the product of a depraved and dirty imagination. You will be told, I am sure, by the Defence, that it is a very *moral* book, showing that licence leads to cruelty and repression. You will make up your own minds about this. You may come to the conclusion that the so-called 'moral story' is no more than a thread on which to hang writings that titillate, that exacerbate, the darker and nastier imaginations of men. You may be told the story is tragic and terrible; you may wish to retort that it completely lacks what Aristotle called *catharsis*, the purging of pity and terror. It is a book that begins, and remains, merely nasty and disturbing. In the opinion of the Prosecution, it arouses unpleasant, worse than unpleasant, feelings—it stirs up the worst instincts of men, where the sexual urge meets the urge to be cruel. You will hear psychological evidence from both sides about this matter. I will say no more now.

"*Lady Chatterley's Lover*, ladies and gentlemen, was felt to be an offence to public decency because it described sexual acts explicitly, and because it used four-lettered words which are felt to be part of a vocabulary proscribed by our society as a whole. It was mixed up with feelings about class and the nature of marriage. Many eminent witnesses argued that it was tender—"

Mr. Hefferson-Brough objects. Comparisons as to obscenity between one book and another are not admissible.

The judge says they are admissible if the point in question is one of literary merit, and not simply of comparative obscenity.

Sir Augustine says that in practice this is a very fine tightrope to tread. He says that he wished merely to observe that the kind of problem raised by *Babbletower* was different from the problems of love, marriage and language raised by *Lady Chatterley,* who was acquitted. It was a problem of cruelty and perversion. He will move on to his next point, which is one concerning the possible or probable readers of the text. The Act speaks of "persons who are likely, in all the circumstances to read, see or hear the matter contained or embodied in it."

He reminds the Court that the country has just lived through the trial of the Moors Murderers. He asks the jury, when they listen to the arguments that they will undoubtedly hear about literature, about fiction, not inciting readers in general to bad acts, to remember the library of Ian Brady, to remember Myra Hindley's participation—learned from Brady, who learned it from books, at least in part—in acts derived imaginatively from books, from *The Scourge of the Swastika* and from the Marquis de Sade. Myra Hindley was possibly a normal young woman before this relationship. The works of the Marquis de Sade are certainly in Mr. Jude Mason's library. His *Babbletower,* his isolated "Tour Bruyarde," is plagiarised from the terrible Marquis's Château de Silling in *The 120 Days of Sodom.* "Do not think, ever, ladies and gentlemen, 'Well, it is only a book.' Men and women are greatly moved by books, their lives may be enriched, changed, or ruined by books. Dictators seize and burn books, because books are dangerous. That fact too will be advanced, no doubt, as a reason for not condemning *Babbletower.* But they are right, the dictators. Good books are dangerous to bad men, and by the same token, bad books are dangerous to good men."

Godfrey Hefferson-Brough rises to open the case for the defence of Bowers and Eden. He is a fleshy man, a red man, a hairy man under his false hair. He is not humorous, he is not beguiling, he has a tendency to thunder. He appears throughout the proceedings to be a prosecuting counsel who has strayed into the realm of defence, and is happiest attacking the opposition. Augustine Weighall's style is sweetly reasonable and understated: Hefferson-Brough would like to make rhetorical flights. It is significant that he, like Martin Fisher, the Bowers and Eden solicitor, is an "Erstwhile Hog," which is the arcane term for an Old Swineburnian. Rupert Parrott, too, as we have seen, is an Erstwhile Hog.

He speaks a panegyric about Bowers and Eden. They are an old firm, a respectable firm, dating back to the old days of John Murray, John Blackwell, and George Smith. A specialist firm, whose field has always been religion, theology, social thought, with a lighter section of belles lettres and fiction, fiction appropriate to the *gravitas* of the house, not salacious fiction, not avant-garde fiction, not shockers and penny dreadfuls. A few donnish detective stories, with perhaps an inquisitive vicar, or vicar's lady, as the sleuth, a few novels lately like Mrs. Phyllis Pratt's excellent *Daily Bread* about the daily lives of the clergy. Mr. Rupert Parrott, the recently appointed managing director of this small firm, is young, but old for his years, a churchgoing Christian, a happily married husband and father, the dynamic successor to a perhaps dozy, perhaps out-of-touch board of directors. He has tried to expand his list to include burning concerns of the moment, things nowadays hotly debated, new strains of theology, works on the Holocaust and its causes, works on the Samaritans, on new forms of social help for the despairing, works also on psychoanalysis and psychiatry, on sociology and philosophy, on the pros and cons of new things like psychedelics and pop music, serious analyses of these things, up-to-date and responsible.

Babbletower and its author came to Mr. Parrott's attention through a literary friend who read for him, and whose judgement he trusted. He saw immediately that it was a controversial book, a book that would arouse strong feelings, a book that was strong meat, yes, very strong meat for readers to digest. But he formed the view—"and it is a view I believe you will share, ladies and gentlemen, when you have read the book"—that it was a powerful and original work, a satirical work about the follies of utopian projectors, and about sexual optimists who believe anything goes and all is permitted. He formed the view that it was—despite its frankness, its full-blooded depiction of the consequences of folly and wrong thinking—he formed the view that it was an *intensely moral* work, a work attacking just those aspects of our society which the 1959 Obscene Publications Act is itself designed to attack, the vacuously pornographic, the licentious, the depraved and the corrupt. For the depraved and the corrupt in *Babbletower,* as you will see, ladies and gentlemen, receive short shrift, they meet a terrible reckoning. This is a book designed to bring home to you the disgusting nature of the world of the depraved and the corrupt in our own society—in all societies—and if you are disgusted, the book has worked its work, for it is not designed to give you a warm and comfortable glow of pleasure. No, it is designed to warn, to alarm, to *avert*. There are episodes, there are tendencies in our society which it is needful for wise men to know about, shun, and do away with, and it is the knowledge of these tendencies—and a righteous horror—that *Babbletower* promulgates.

Hefferson-Brough, like Sir Augustine, discourses on the meaning of "tend to deprave and corrupt." The Act, he says, was designed to stop pornography, the filth dirty old men use to masturbate with, the slime oozing from the gutters of brothels, the puerile jokes about torture which we all know, and which the author and publisher of this book abominate as much as you do, ladies and gentlemen. The Act was not designed to stop works of literature—even *daring* works of literature that take a fearless look at a real social problem, the decay of social and sexual controls that leads precisely to a flood of true pornography, trivial, rotten and rotting to the fibres of our community. The Act was designed to make it possible for works of literature to be published in freedom and without fear of prurient attacks. We shall lead evidence to show that there is overwhelming support for the literary, psychological and social importance of *Babbletower*. Bad books do hurt good men, as my learned friend wisely said. But good works hurt nothing but bad books.

"As good almost kill a man as kill a good book; who kills a man kills a reasonable creature, God's image; but he who destroys a good book, kills reason itself, kills the image of God, as it were in the eye."

Frederica wonders if this quotation is not excessive. She looks at the jury to see how many of them react to *Areopagitica*; one man frowns with recognition, one woman gives a beatific smile of assent and nods; most others stare, puzzled and stolid, into space.

Samuel Oliphant, QC, then speaks on behalf of Jude Mason. He says that his client is a young man, an artist, who lives in poverty in order to practise his art. He is not a pornographer, and in his view *Babbletower* is a complex work of art, the subject of which is the relation between erotic freedom and community, between repression and cruelty. His work is, and will be shown to be, in a great European tradition of satirical flouting, of moral outrage working *through* the outrageous. In cases where a work of art is being prosecuted as an obscene publication, it has been held—he cites precedents—that the *intentions* of the author or publisher are irrelevant to the jury's decision as to whether the book is obscene. In other cases—he cites other precedents—it has been held that in the case of literary merit, intention can and must be discussed. "In the *Lady Chatterley* trial, D. H. Lawrence's intentions invariably and inevitably came into the evidence and the debate. It was suggested by many Defence witnesses that Lawrence was a Puritan. He had written a frank book about sex, but his intentions were puritanical. The same, ladies and gentlemen, could be argued of my client. One of his characters—perhaps the only wholly sympathetic character in the whole tale of excess and punishment—is a figure with the strange name of Samson Origen, who preaches abstemiousness, indeed abstention from all activity, a kind of asceticism. Strange though it may appear, in a book so full of plain-speaking sexual descriptions and even orgiastic behaviour, the ruling atmosphere is one of asceticism and abstemiousness. There is a certain humour, a certain irony, in Mr. Mason's work, which is on the side of Samson Origen. It would be possible to miss this humour, this irony, particularly when you are reading with an eye to looking for depravation and corruption: I therefore bring it to your attention as perhaps the saving grace of this sorry tale. Mr. Mason's intentions are to mock folly, and worse than folly, through exposing and depicting it mercilessly. This is an art as old as time, and as honourable as any other."

During these speeches, Frederica is aware of a strange whirring and clicking coming from behind, or under her seat. As the judge says, "The next question, is it not, is to arrange for the reading of the book?" she turns, and sees the gingery hairy face of Avram Snitkin behind her, bright blue eyes peering between sandy lashes.

Mr. Justice Gordale Balafray asks what arrangements can be made for the jury to read *Babbletower*. How long should be set aside? Where should the reading take place?

Frederica whispers, "Are you recording this on your tape-recorder?"
   "Of course."
   "Is it allowed?"
   "I've got permission from the Court. I didn't say it was ethno-methodological research. I said it was for the publisher's records. I'm baffled they don't use it for the official records but they don't—there's their shorthand writer, over there, with a *pen.* But they don't mind me making a recording; they say that's fine."
   She hears the snake of tape rustle on its reels, digesting the words.
   The barristers and the judge discuss the reading. Samuel Oliphant says that the book could be taken home and read in quiet domestic

surroundings, at a reasonable speed. Hefferson-Brough says that for *Lady Chatterley* a special room was found at the Old Bailey, with arm-chairs. Juries have been known to retire to hotels. The jury foreman reports that the chairs in the jury room are hard. The judge seems decided by this last complaint; he retorts that they are the chairs in the jury room, where the jurors are doing the work they have been called to do. We have all sat on hard chairs, in our time, says he, in schools, in libraries, and been none the worse for it. Indeed, he himself finds himself more alert, sitting on a good solid hard chair, than sunk on cushions. No, the jury-room chairs must suffice, will suffice.

The jury set off to read the book at two-fifteen. The Court waits. Elvet Gander says to Adelbert Holly and Avram Snitkin that perhaps the judge is a person with sadistic inclinations. That could, of course, go either way, for or against *Babbletower.* Frederica thinks of going to speak to Jude, but he has disappeared, apparently into the belly of the Old Bailey. Rupert Parrott repeats several times that the Counsel for the Prosecution is formidable. Parrott's face is pink and shining. He is wearing a peacock-blue waistcoat under a fine blue-grey worsted suit.

At four-fifteen the judge sends to enquire of the jury how much longer they will need to read the book. Three or four claim to have finished it already. The foreman—the swimming-pool manager—says that he has been asked to request a dictionary—a *large* dictionary, my lord, and also, if it's not too much trouble, a *French* dictionary, as well as the English one, that is. Several more jurymen say they will soon be through. Hefferson-Brough asks that the jury be told to read the book carefully and thoroughly, or alternatively be dismissed and replaced. The jury returns to its room and its hard chairs, and its copies of *Babbletower* with the black, pink and cobalt covers. Twelve men and women, twelve readings, or skimmings, or stumblings, or approximate scannings. One woman takes the book home to bed, reaches the death of Roseace, and wakes her husband, gagging. This is later known, because her husband is "in the Print," a member of a print trade union, and tells a journalist on the *News of the World,* who prints this information when the trial is over.

The Court reassembles the next day. The first witness for the Defence is called. He says he is Alexander Wedderburn. His profession, he says, is that of a playwright. He is a member of the Steerforth Committee Enquiry into the teaching of the English language. He has worked in cultural radio—the Third Programme—and educational television. He has been a schoolmaster in a boys' boarding school. His plays are set texts at O Level. He is described in the Press as "a very handsome public figure, wearing a well-cut corduroy suit in a dark green, with a lemon-coloured shirt and a blue tie with green carnations on it. He has a mane of silvering hair, a pleasant tenor voice, and an expression of cautious courtesy and helpfulness which never failed, even under pressure."

His evidence lasts three hours, and is solid and, on the surface, calm. Hefferson-Brough takes him through the text of *Babbletower*, reading out long passages—mostly not sexual, and none of them cruel—asking him if he feels these passages have literary merit as pieces of English prose, if he thinks the characterisation is subtle, if he thinks the content is serious. Alexander says that *Babbletower* is not part of a genre that requires subtle characterisation. Hefferson-Brough asks him to explain "genre" to those members of the jury "who do not know any technical literary terms." He reminds his witness "not to be technical if you can help it." Alexander says that the point about the characters in *Babbletower* is that they are *types,* like the characters in an allegory, or a satire, or a comedy of manners. They don't need depth. Their actions are what is important. He is asked to explain "allegory," "satire," "comedy of manners." He is asked to say that to say that characters are "types" is not to say that they are vulgar or crude. He replies, "Of course not," and hears a ripple of laughter, laughter against either him or Hefferson-Brough, with whom he is meant to be agreeing. They *represent qualities,* says Alexander. Good qualities? Not necessarily. Many qualities. As in life.

The trial is to be characterised by Hefferson-Brough's paucity of vocabulary for discussing literary merit. Alexander thinks at first that this is due to an excessive concern for the jury's sensibilities as common readers, or "ordinary men and women," whatever those are. But his experience of Hefferson-Brough's questions, which is very similar to that of the specifically *literary* experts who follow him, is of struggling through a suffocating cloud of wool, trying to find air, trying to find light, trying to make a precise sentence and being told again and again that his vocabulary—his expert vocabulary—is inadmissible in this place, must be rephrased. Scrupulously Alexander tries to say that one passage is more successful than another, that one scene is almost tragic whereas another is merely blackly comic, Grand Guignol. "And what do you mean by Grand Guignol, Mr. Wedderburn? Tell us in

English, please, tell us what that is, so we may share your thought."
And of the scenes that Alexander says are "less good than others,"
Hefferson-Brough immediately asks, "But would you say that this
scene is well-written? Does it have literary merit? Is it good, or is it
not?" And Alexander says again and again, because he must, that it is
good. *Babbletower* is flattened in his hearers' minds to a series of
"good" passages.

In answer to Samuel Oliphant he reiterates that *Babbletower* is a serious work, by a promising young writer, with a moral purpose.

Sir Augustine Weighall then cross-examines.

Q. Mr. Wedderburn. You are a man of very wide reading, a man
whose life has been devoted to great writing. Your own verse
drama gives me intense pleasure, I may say, on the page as on
the stage. I do not flatter: I am glad to take this opportunity of
speaking of your "lovely inchanting language." I want to ask
you a simple question. Did you *enjoy* reading *Babbletower*?

A. Enjoy? Yes, and no.

Q. Let us discuss both halves of that entirely comprehensible answer. Let us start with the "yes." *What* did you enjoy?

A. Vivid descriptions. The successful depiction of a world part
fairytale, part dystopia.

Q. Dystopia?

A. Anti-utopia. Depiction of a not-ideal world. Good writing.
The sentences are lively. The atmosphere is brooding.

Q. Did the book—I know you will answer clearly, for you are a
thoughtful man and a writer yourself—did the book give you
any *sexual* pleasure?

A. (After some thought) Some, occasionally. Not much. All writing is connected with sexual pleasure. Wordsworth said the
rhythms of language are the rhythms of the human body, of
"the grand principle of pleasure in which we live and move
and have our being."

Q. That is very interesting. The rhythms of all writing are in your
view connected to sexual pleasure. That is indeed very inter-

esting and illuminating. Did the book give you any more specific sexual pleasure—such as you might feel looking at an erotic painting, for instance?

A.   Not much.

Q.   Yet you said it was well written, and "vivid," you said, and "lively." A very large proportion of this book is descriptions of sexual acts, of naked bodies. Yet they gave you no pleasure?

A.   Not much.

Q.   Are you perhaps denying the pleasure, out of a desire to defend the book?

A.   I don't think so. I think the author meant me to experience only a limited pleasure. Meant me to imagine pleasure, and then to find he had cut it off, so to speak.

Q.   He tried to disgust you?

A.   That is the *unpleasant* side. He had good reasons.

Q.   He may well have had. So, in so far as you responded sexually to his writing, it was with disgust?

A.   It is more complex than that.

Q.   More complex. Perhaps the writing was meant to have an *emetic* effect, to disgust you with the world and action of the book?

A.   It is more complex than that, too.

Q.   It seems to be very complex. The only certain thing is that you are resolute to deny that he meant you to experience any pleasure in the infliction of pain, any reprehensible pleasure in the infliction of pain?

A.   I did not say that.

Q.   And you do not think that?

A.   You have me in a grammatical snarl.

Q.   But you know what I am asking?

A.   I do not think that the intention of the author was to make me feel reprehensible pleasure in the infliction of pain.

Q. And you did not feel any?

A. No. Or almost none.

Q. You are a man who has to be truthful, I see, Mr. Wedderburn. Not none. *Almost* none.

Tell me, as to the question of literary merit. *How good* do you think *Babbletower* is, in literary terms? We are not allowed to compare books as to relative obscenity, but we are allowed to make comparisons of *literary merit*. D. H. Lawrence, when *Lady Chatterley* was tried, was taught in many university courses, throughout the world, as was abundantly testified. My learned friend Gerald Gardiner, on that occasion, made the point that some of the early works of Chaucer might be thought to be risqué without that great name attached to them. Tell me, Mr. Wedderburn—as a teacher, as a writer— *how good* is Mr. Jude Mason? As good as D. H. Lawrence? As good as William Burroughs? As good as Mickey Spillane?

A. It is his first book. It is a serious literary book. It is not a shocker, like Mickey Spillane, who is unreadable, in my view. It is well written and seriously meant. You can't really come to any conclusions about the final status of living writers at the outset of their careers.

Q. You can't really come to any conclusions about the literary merit of young living writers at the outset of their careers?

A. I said "final status."

Q. But judgements of literary merit are *provisional* in this kind of case, as opposed to that of D. H. Lawrence.

Samuel Oliphant objects. The judge overrules him. Alexander says they are of course provisional, compared to D. H. Lawrence, but that does not mean they cannot be made.

The next witness to be called is Dr. Naomi Lurie, Reader in English Literature in Oxford University, and a Fellow of Somerville College. She says that she is the author of various books, including *Dissociated Sensibility, Myth or History?* (1960). She says she is in charge of the studies of many young women, and would be quite happy for them to read *Babbletower*. She would, she says when pressed, encourage them to do so. No, she would not positively *teach* the book. She is opposed to the teaching of contemporary writing; Oxford University until very recently taught *nothing* written later than 1830.

She is a dark-haired woman in serviceable tweed, in her mid-fifties. Hefferson-Brough says to her, "You are a maiden lady, living in an exclusively female college, and you write on devotional poetry. But you admire this book, you have said, you have said you believe it has literary merit?"

Dr. Lurie says, "I am certainly unmarried, and I certainly teach women. I don't believe women make any different literary judgements from men."

There is a ripple of laughter in the Court. Dr. Lurie smiles primly.

Sir Augustine tempts Dr. Lurie into the statement that Swift's *Modest Proposal* for solving the Irish problem by roasting and stewing the infant Irish is shocking in the same way as *Babbletower*. "Or worse." He asks Dr. Lurie if Swift makes the prospective taste, "the culinary delights," of the broiled babies attractive. No, says Dr. Lurie. And the loathsome practices in *Babbletower*, the sodomy, the torture, the orgies, says Sir Augustine. "They are unattractive in the same way?"

"I think so," says Dr. Lurie. Sir Augustine's fine face takes on an ironic smile, which he turns on the jury.

"You find the descriptions of Narcisse's juvenile peccadilloes, of Damian's love-making with Roseace, as repugnant as Swift's broiled babies?"

"I do not say that. Swift is a pure satirist. He writes with *saeva indignatio*."

"Savage indignation," Sir Augustine translates kindly for the jury.

"Whereas it is part of Mr. Mason's plan to, so to speak, put the reader through the pleasures of the *Babbletower*."

"To *put the reader through*. Not to stir, not to titillate, not to seduce? Your verb is austere and pedagogic."

"He does wish to titillate, at the time, of course. But temporarily."

"He turns titillation on and off, like a tap."

"If you like," says Dr. Lurie.

Anthony Burgess is the next witness. His face is craggy; his voice is round and beautifully produced. He praises *Babbletower* in musical terms: *brio, appassionata, fugue*. He says in answer to Hefferson-Brough

539

that he believes that *Babbletower* is a deeply moral, almost too moral, book.

Q.   How can a book be too moral, Mr. Burgess?

A.   Well, as I have said before from time to time, the value of art is always diminished by the presence of elements that move to action. This book is didactic. The didactic is lesser than the purely aesthetic. It has *designs on you*. Never trust a book that has designs on you.

Q.   *Babbletower* has moral designs on you?

A.   Yes. It moves by disgusting and frightening you.

Q.   But it is a work of literature.

A.   I don't know what you mean by "but." It *is* a work of literature. It is a very promising, serious piece of writing. It ought to be praised. It isn't *Ulysses* or *The Rainbow* but it ought to be read, it ought to be discussed.

Sir Augustine rises to cross-examine. He measures the novelist with his eye.

Q.   You quoted yourself just now. You said that the book was a lesser art-form than the purely aesthetic because it had designs on you, it moved to action.

A.   It is didactic, yes.

Q.   In your review—your very perceptive and brilliant review of the book—you do not only say that the book moves to action because it is *didactic*. You associate the didactic and the pornographic as "moving to action." You associate them *in this book*.

A.   That is so. You have understood the review.

Q.   So the book is pornographic as well as didactic.

A.   It is not high art, in which everything is resolved in a balance, a form that can be contemplated with aesthetic pleasure. It is a mixed form, a hybrid form, which makes its effect by moving to action. That does not mean it is not a work of art, or that it should not be published. We can't suppress every book that isn't as good as *Ulysses*. Or *The Rainbow*.

Judge. Indeed not. I must remind the jury that the opinion of literary experts on whether or not the book is obscene should not be taken into account.

Q. Mr. Burgess, I am going to ask you, as I have asked others, whether the book gave you any sexual pleasure? Moved you sexually?

A. Oh yes. It did. It's a good book, it does its work. It stirs you up. Most good books do. Reading and sexual excitement are intimately connected.

Q. Except in *Ulysses*?

A. In *Ulysses* of course, too. That's an unworthy question. But differently.

Q. Differently?

A. It's rawer, here. In *Babbletower*.

Q. Mr. Burgess, you are a writer. A daring writer, you take risks. When you write about sexual excitement, or even more, about cruelty, do you imagine your reader as you write?

A. Yes.

Q. How do you imagine him or her?

A. As like myself. Excited when I am. Detached as I am.

Q. Do you imagine the effects of your writings on the less educated, the more imaginatively restricted persons who may also read your books?

A. That is harder. It would be silly to pretend everyone reads in the same way. It would be silly to pretend one could gauge the effect of a piece of writing on all its potential readers.

Q. Do you feel responsible for the weak, the uninstructed, the excitable readers of your books?

A. You can't be, wholly, responsible for all readers. But up to a point, yes, I do. And, in answer to your unspoken hint or

541

question, I am quite sure that Jude Mason is not trying to *work up* ignorant readers into a state of irresponsible excitement. But you can't predict that that will never happen.

Q.   You can't predict that that will never happen.

The next witness is a novelist too, who is also lead reviewer for a serious Sunday newspaper. He is a dapper, pretty man called Douglas Corbie; he is little, with a melodious but insistent voice, and time is beginning to etch nutcracker lines in his cheeks. His hair is the cream colour of metallic blond hair going white. He has written many thick and well-received novels—*A Pernicious Influence, Hengist's Horse, The Voice of the Mock Turtle, Life in a Glass House*—and has sat on the committee of the Society of Authors and the Literature Panel of the Arts Council. He is examined by Samuel Oliphant. Douglas Corbie agrees that he is himself a novelist of some importance, that he is a leading critic, that he has read *Babbletower,* and admires it.

Q.   It is a serious work of literature, in your opinion.

A.   Without any doubt. The young man is extremely promising. He has much to learn but he is extremely promising. He should be encouraged; young writers should be encouraged, as I know to my cost, having found the going hard.

Q.   Can you say why it is a serious work of literature?

A.   Oh yes. Because it treats of evil. We don't consider evil, in our society, you know. We are English and *ever so nice* and we are obsessed with problems of right and wrong *manners,* with little details of social correctness, yes, with silly things like fish-forks and *placements,* and whether people have the right *accent,* or whether their shoes are or aren't nasty. And this in the time of Auschwitz and Hiroshima, so shaming in many ways, all our fuss about flowerbeds and whether white flowers ought to be in herbaceous borders, or whether they are vulgar, you know?

Q.   But does Jude Mason tackle the problem of evil?

A.   Oh, well, yes, he does, *indeed he does,* and with gusto, with such gusto almost *too* enthusiastically, all those Gothic chains and dungeons, a bit bathetic, in a way, but very effective, very effective, no doubt. William Golding has treated evil. *Lord of the Flies,* a book about the evil of schoolboys let loose, very revealing. Mr. Mason's dormitory life in *Babbletower* is the evil of schoolboys let loose too, a Grand Guignol version. *I myself* prefer to embed my depiction of evil in the day-to-day, in drawing-rooms and theatre bars and suburban kitchens and school staffrooms, I prefer to embed it in *felt life,* as James said, yes, to notice the social detail. As Auden said, "A crack in the teacup opens / A lane to the land of the dead." Teacups will suffice, though Mr. Mason appears to think not, he chooses the full panoply, beatings and hangings, a more *dangerous* way, difficult to bring off—he *does* bring it off, very largely, of course—but *I myself* believe the study of evil is more effectively embedded in *felt life.* The people at Auschwitz, you know, the torturers, they went home at night to suburban kitchens and pink lampshades and knuckles of pork, all that stuff, you can do it through lampshades and pork, you don't need . . .

Q. What do you say of Mr. Mason's book? Is it serious? Is it good?

A. Oh yes, as I said, he's good, he's learning, he will be very good, it's important to let him keep trying, very important. Yes.

Sir Augustine says, "No questions, my lord."

The next witness is Professor Marie-France Smith, from Prince Albert College. She wears an elegant suit, in fine black wool piped in white.

Hefferson-Brough is gallant with this witness, who is both lovely and fragile. His gallantry rattles Professor Smith, who is trying to produce a dry, scholarly account of what she believes to be the intellectual background of *Babbletower.* Hefferson-Brough takes her through her *Encounter* review of *Babbletower* step by step.

Q. You say in this article, Professor Smith, that this book which the ladies and gentlemen of the jury have just read is "in the mainstream tradition of European intellectual history and philosophical debate." That is a large claim.

A. I could prove critically, I think, that the author has a very wide acquaintance with French thought, with French controversy, at the time of the Revolution and later, about how far human beings should be free and how far it was necessary for them to be restrained.

Q.   You mention the names of certain thinkers in your review. A certain Charles Fourier, for example. Can you tell us about his thought, and about how it is to be found in this book?

A.   Fourier was a gentle and eccentric thinker who like many thinkers at the end of the eighteenth and the beginning of the nineteenth centuries believed that a revolution in human feelings and lifestyles could introduce an age of Harmony. He believed "civilisation" (the last few centuries) was evil, repressive and decadent. He believed human harmony could be achieved by indulging all human passions and desires, of which he identified, I think, 810. He believed "civilised," decadent men thought all human beings were roughly the same, but that in fact they differed greatly. He felt that lesbians, sodomites, flagellants, fetishists, nymphomaniacs and so on could and should be accommodated rather than punished. He wrote a *Nouveau Monde Amoureux* which depicts the journey of a group of colonists to Cnidus in Asia Minor, where they found a community, a *phalanx* of erotic freedom. They organise sexual orgies, and also gastronomic orgies—Fourier saw warfare, in Harmony, as a civilised contest between chefs as to the making of little pastries, of which he was very fond. He liked inventing hierarchies—he had a court of love with high priests, pontiffs, matrons, confessors, fakirs, fairies, bacchantes . . .

Q.   And all this, you say, was very gentle?

A.   Oh, wholly, yes. It was like Watteau's *Embarkation for Cytherea,* a dream world with a serious political imagination behind it. Fourier *really believed* that the Terror in the French Revolution might, pushed a little further, have ushered in one desirable further breaking down of rules and conventions—the abolition of marriage, which made almost everyone, in his view, unhappy. "In Harmony," he wrote, "every mature man and woman must be granted a satisfying minimum of sexual pleasure."

Q. And you see *Babbletower* as in that tradition?

A. The first part, yes. The characters are setting off to found a Nouveau Monde Amoureux, a New World of Love. What happens owes as much to de Sade as to Fourier.

Q. Tell us about de Sade. You take him seriously as a thinker?

A. You must. He is important. He represents the line from the Enlightenment philosophers who extol human reason and free will, in its cynical vein. He asks, If we are free to follow our passions, who can prevent us from following our desire to hurt others, to kill, to rape, to torture? Those are, he says, human passions; they are *natural*. Voltaire, Rousseau, Diderot, the freethinkers, lead, according to one view, to the guillotine and the Sadeian *boudoir*. Mr. Mason has understood this. He has shown it.

The prisoner looks at his hands. He does not look at Professor Smith. Some of the jury notice this.

Q. What is your evidence for this diagnosis?

A. Well, let us start with the title. *La Tour Bruyarde* translates as the noisy, or shouting, or howling tower—the word "bruyard" suggests the noise made by hound dogs. It is an image of the Tower of Babel, which was constructed to displace God from Heaven, and was punished for its presumption by having a spirit of discord sent amongst its members, so that their languages were confused, they could no longer understand each other. It is a communal enterprise, set against the Authority of God. The *Babbletower* community is Fourier's Nouveau Monde Amoureux. It is also Sade's Château de Silling, where the libertines cut the bridge that connects them to the outer world so as to perform their terrible deeds.

Hefferson-Brough thanks Professor Smith for her clear exposition of the *gravitas* of *Babbletower*. He sits down. The prosecutor rises.

Q. Thank you for your charming lecture, Professor Smith. You have painted a very convincing picture of a very French intel-

lectual document, a philosophical dialogue called *La Tour Bru-*
yarde. These books you speak of, de Sade, Fourier, they are in
print in France?

A.   Yes.

Q.   Freely available?

A.   Yes. Not all of Fourier. Much was never edited, the
        manuscripts are in the Bibliothèque Nationale.

Q.   These preoccupations are very *French* preoccupations, are they
        not? Your country has always given more latitude to sexual
        freedom?

A.   In some ways.

Q.   English people have had to go to France and buy books
        thought unsuitable for English readers, to see the Folies
        Bergères, and so on. Some people think it is a good thing to
        have these latitudes. Some believe that our greater care for our
        own public morals, our greater concern for restraint of the
        things M. Fourier was so anxious to promulgate, has something
        to be said for it. Those who drafted the British Act of Parlia-
        ment according to which this case is being tried might have
        been of the second party, you may think.

Samuel Oliphant rises to object that this is a statement, not a question.

Q.   Tell me, Professor Smith—you have spoken with such cool
        clarity, such French analytic vigour, both of de Sade and of
        Babbletower. You do not, if I may say so, *seem* like a natural de-
        voted reader of the lucubrations of the satanic Marquis. Do
        you *enjoy* de Sade?

A.   Enjoy? No, I do not. (This is clearly a true statement of revul-
        sion.)

Q.   But you read him because you think you should?

A.   Yes. As I said, he is important. I prefer Fourier.

Q.   The gentle, the dotty, the permissive Fourier. The verbal Wat-
        teau of fairies and flagellants. And *Babbletower*, Professor Smith.
        Did you *enjoy* Babbletower?

A. No. I admired it.

Q. But the author would have liked you to enjoy it?

Both the beautiful professor and the prisoner at the bar cast down their eyes, flushed.

A. We are taught, these days, that authorial intention is something we cannot know, and is irrelevant to our critical judgement.

Q. And—forgive me—you felt no *frisson* of sexual pleasure during your reading?

A. (Very flushed) I may have. I do not remember. It was neither my primary nor my predominant response.

Q. Thank you, Professor Smith.

The next witness is a theatrical director, Fausto Gemelli, who has worked with Peter Brook and Charles Marowitz, who speaks with enthusiasm of Edward Bond's *Saved,* which presents the murder of a baby in a pram as an acting out of Blake's "sooner murder an infant in its cradle than arouse unacted desires." He speaks of Genet's *Maids* and *Balcony,* of Artaud's Theatre of Cruelty, which aims to be, in Artaud's words, "like victims burned at the stake, signalling through the flames." Samuel Oliphant asks him if, in the time of Genet, Bond, Artaud, the *Marat-Sade* and Peter Brook's *Lear,* he finds anything culturally out of bounds in *Babbletower.* He replies that he does not. He is passionately enthusiastic, gesturing, crying from a cloud of long black hair. Sir Augustine says, "No questions," judging perhaps that Mr. Gemelli speaks to his own audience and alienates others in about equal proportions.

The trial is now in its third day. The Defence calls Elvet Gander, who says he is a medical doctor, a psychiatrist, and a psychoanalyst. He agrees that he works with schizophrenics, with disturbed adolescents, and that he writes general books on language and society, on the psychic health and sickness of the community in which he lives. He agrees that he is the author of *Language Our Straitjacket, The Oppressor's Tongue, Am I My Brother's Keeper?,* and that he has a particular interest in the links between language and repression ("and *expression,* of course," he adds).

Elvet Gander in the witness box has a hardness and polished look. His skull shines, his nose shines, his long teeth shine brightly. His eyes are huge, sculpted and hooded; he speaks, as he gives his evidence, in an increasingly incantatory flow, even, towards the end, swaying slightly like a snake-charmer, and tapping gently with his hand on the ledge of the box. He wears a crumpled corduroy jacket—black—over an off-white polo-necked jumper and cord trousers. Frederica sees him, fancifully, as polished ivory, polished creamy marble. Hefferson-Brough asks him a series of questions designed to establish that he believes *Babbletower* to be important as a depiction of *private psychic disintegration* and of a more important malaise in society at large.

Gander speaks at length, plangently, musically, weaving his audience briefly into an assenting union, although afterwards many, most of them, cannot remember all he said, cannot, some of them, remember almost anything. He says human beings are divided creatures, more and more divided, more and more cut off from each other and from any sense of themselves and their identity. He says that *Babbletower* reflects both dividedness and a deep desire for unity of self and of community, as indeed does the original myth of the Tower of Babel. He says that human beings experience themselves as projections of other people's ideas (primarily their families'), or of their own fears and hidden wishes. He says that we live in a world where we are labelled, judged and punished as criminal, madman, pervert, sadist, when other words might apply as well, or better: desperate, affectionate, logical, confused. Language destroys us as language creates us—Lady Chatterley was condemned for honest no-nonsense four-letter *words* describing bodily functions we have erected a whole cage of euphemisms and evasions to avoid naming, so dividing ourselves from ourselves. There are physical ailments—Tourette's disease—where the body, the nerves, involuntarily ejaculate the unspeakable, "fuck," "shit," "piss." He does not apologise to the Court for the use of these words. They are nocturnal emissions of the human corpus, to be wiped away like stains, like the *ejaculations* they are in truth. Yes, we muck about with the language of our bodily selves at our peril, and Jude Mason has shown us the consequences, the leather tongues and steel tools we make when we are forbidden to use tongues and tools.

Godfrey Hefferson-Brough, faint but pursuing, tries both to stem the flow and to concentrate his witness's attention on "the book in hand, so to speak." This coincides with Gander's intent and rapturous comparison of dialogue to coition and masturbation to interior monologue. "There is evidence that the sexual discharge in male onanism is greater than it is in intercourse."

"Is this relevant?" asks Mr. Justice Gordale Balafray. "How does this connect to the matter in hand, to the question of the subject-matter of this book?"

"I am saying it is onanistic babble, consciously and conscientiously *exposed,* my lord. I am saying it is a product of isolation and a sense of unreality."

He rushes on. He talks of the community of *Babbletower,* La Tour Bruyarde, in search of a lost primeval unity. "An *impossible* identity, polymorphously perverse, *one.* I could quote Rilke, my lord, who prays to be made a self-sufficient hermaphrodite."

"Does he indeed?"

> *"Mach Einen herrlich, Herr, mach Einen gross,*
> *bau seinem Leben einen schönen Schoss,*
> *und seine Scham errichte wie ein Tor*
> *in einem blonden Wald von jungen Haaren."*

"I do not know," says the judge, "whether I want to ask you to translate that for the benefit of the jury, Mr. Gander, or whether I want to ask that it be struck from the record as irrelevant. My German is a little rusty. In so far as I can follow your quotation it seems a little—a little—well. Perhaps Mr. Hefferson-Brough can enlighten us on whether we should ask for a translation."

Mr. Hefferson-Brough says that the general argument was, if he has understood Mr. Gander correctly—Mr. Gander's enthusiasm, though infectious, has carried him away perhaps—the point appeared to be that the community was sick and that it desired, and failed to achieve, unity.

Judge. What has this to do with "onanistic babble" and quotations from Rilke?

Gander. May I answer? D. H. Lawrence said he would make his world—his novel's world—healthy, by inviting into it every little black snake that coils and curls at the edges of the marshes of the unconscious. The French surrealist Leiris said, "Masochism, sadism, almost all vices in fact, are only ways of feeling more human." I am saying Culvert, the hero of *Babbletower,* like Fourier, as Professor Smith has pointed out, sets out to *include everything* in his Tower, in his community, so there shall be no lost soul, no sour rejected creature prowling, but *all shall be one.* It doesn't work, of course, in his book, but the desire is noble, is noble, is sane and healthy. I offered Rilke's metaphor because it amused me, as an image of wholeness—of the impossibly yearned-for hermaphroditic polymorphously perverse beautiful self-satisfying *wholeness.*

Judge.   I am not sure I ought to; we may be wasting the Court's time, but I am going to ask you to translate it.

Gander.   Thank you, my lord. It goes—let me see—it goes

> *Make* One *beautiful one, Lord, make One big one,*
> *build a beautiful womb inside for its Life,*
> *and erect its Shame like a Pillar,*
> *in a blond forest of young hairs.*

Judge.   Thank you. Thank you very much. I am sure the jury would rather know that that was what it said than not know.

Gander.   It is very strong. Very beautiful.

Judge.   It may be. It sounds better in German, it is true. Mr. Hefferson-Brough, I do think we should return to the *gravamen* of this matter.

Hefferson-Brough.   Certainly, my lord. Mr. Gander—can you say, in your own words, what you think are the purposes and effects of what have been called the—the sado-masochistic passages that become more frequent as the story becomes, so to speak, *darker.*

Gander.   Certainly, I can. They have been well defined as degradation ceremonies. I would refer the jurors to an article by H. Garfinkel in the *American Journal of Sociology* LXI (1956) on "Conditions of Successful Degradation Ceremonies." In modern society these ceremonies are part of our alienation and take place in all our institutions—R. D. Laing in his article in a book called *Ritualisa-*

tion of Behaviour in Animals and Men—a Royal Society publication—defines many modern psychiatric diagnoses as ceremonials of alienation, degradation ceremonies precisely. Some public confessionals are the same thing. I think the institutions of the confessional and the theatre in *Babbletower* function as degradation ceremonies. You could compare them to the rituals enacted in certain brothels where men are compelled to dress up as naughty children or martyrs in chains and *be degraded*. As Genet has shown, people also need to enact the masters of ceremony, degraders, judges and bishops and generals, yes. In brothels as in real life. A movement of violence, of bloody revolt, is often necessary to pierce through to our authenticity.

Judge.   I am not quite sure I understand you. You are saying that courts and psychiatric hospitals and perhaps the Church are designed to degrade people? You are saying that Mr. Mason says this?

Gander.   No, no. Only that from certain angles such institutions can be *perceived as* degrading, and *Babbletower* deals, profoundly, brilliantly, *fluently,* with the riddles and ambiguities of our degradation of each other. You could say, my lord, that the desire to degrade is an aspect of Original Sin, an aspect of that force of *division of people* which is represented by the Lord God in the Bible smiting the presumption of the original inhabitants of Babel.

Judge.   Your own expressions are precise and convoluted, Mr. Gander. Do I understand you to be accusing the Lord God of a kind of sin in dividing people by smiting them?

Gander.   The Lord God is a human myth, a human projection, so yes.

Judge.   You were sworn in, I must remind you, on the Bible.

Gander.   I said, I swear by Almighty God. I did. I do. But that God is a force of unity, a field of light, of beauty, not a harsh judge smiting people.

Judge.   You enlighten me.

Gander.   I have a quotation, my lord, from Simone de Beauvoir on Sade which makes quite clear what I am saying.

Hefferson-Brough. It may be that we can dispense with this quotation, and return to *Babbletower* and its depiction of cruelty, which, you were saying, I think, is a profound study of human misery, *malaise,* you said, exactly, a French word, meaning sickness or misery.

Gander. But my quotation does just that, it explains Sade and also Jude Mason. Listen. Simone de Beauvoir is very clear. She is a major writer, a respected thinker. She says: "To sympathise with Sade too readily is to betray him. For it is our misery, subjection and death that he desires; and every time we side with a child whose throat has been slit by a sex-maniac, we take a stand against him. Nor does he forbid us to defend ourselves. He allows that a father may revenge or prevent, even by murder, the rape of his child. What he demands is that, in the struggle between irreconcilable existences, each one engages himself concretely in the name of his own existence. He approves of the vendetta, but not of the courts. We may kill, but we may not judge. The pretensions of the judge are more arrogant than those of the tyrant; for the tyrant confines himself to being himself, whereas the judge tries to erect his opinions into universal laws. His effort is based upon a lie. For every person is imprisoned in his own skin, and cannot become the mediator between separate persons from whom he himself is separated."

Hefferson-Brough. You are not saying, Mr. Gander, that Mr. Mason is arguing that "we may kill, but we may not judge."

Gander. Oh no. He *rejects* de Sade, he *rejects* him. But he gives the argument a run for its money. We live in a free society, a serious argument has a right to a run for its money.

Judge. A serious argument. "He believes in the vendetta, but not in the courts."

Gander. It is an argument. You are a wise man, this is a wise Court, you must see—I am sorry, I put that badly—*I know you know* that is a serious argument. You, and Jude Mason, must both reject it. Even I, with all my scepticism about judgements, labelling, projections, emanations, spectres—even I prefer *this Court* to a vendetta, to a simple killing. I reject Sade. But I

recognise his profound importance. You cannot *ban* him. Or
Jude Mason.

Judge.   Very well, Mr. Gander. Very well. Mr. Hefferson-Brough,
your witness has taken us into deep water.

Hefferson-Brough.   It is clear that we are speaking of a deep novel,
my lord. Not a pleasant novel, but not a trivial one. One that
goes deep.

Sir Augustine asks Elvet Gander whether there are *any* books he
would suppress, if it were up to him. The witness replies that he
would suppress the novels of Barbara Cartland, which are lies, and
bring untold misery to those who believe them. Sir Augustine says
that even these are surely evidence of some human velleities, some
mind-set worthy of serious study. Gander smiles and agrees. "I was
hasty. I was making a rhetorical point. You are right. There is no
good reason for suppressing anything at all."

Q.   Anything goes, in the end?

A.   Oh yes, I think so. Anything goes.

Q.   No further questions, my lord.

Godfrey Hefferson-Brough is beginning to look red and heavy. He
consults with his junior and with Rupert Parrott, obviously in doubt
about further witnesses. Nevertheless, he calls Avram Snitkin, who
entrusts his tape-recorder to Frederica for the duration of his evidence.

Snitkin has been called, essentially, to describe various pieces of so-
ciological research which claim to show that those with a propensity
to offend, sexually, are less, rather than more, likely to do so if they
have access to "explicit literature." He is a bad witness, because he
can hardly bear to make a statement without enclosing it in a cocoon
of "on the one hand" and "on the other hand," and "so to speak"
and "in some very precisely delineated circumstances." He is also a
bad witness because it is easy for the Prosecution to enquire whether
the writings used in the experiments referred to were classifiable as
"pornography." Snitkin speaks for a long time about this, saying at
vast length that the term depends on the definition of the word
"pornography," which itself depends on the uses to which the mate-

rial described is put by the people whose habits in the context of the use of what might be defined as pornography are being studied . . .

The judge cuts him short, perhaps already rendered irritable by the jousting behaviour of Elvet Gander.

Snitkin also argues that there are studies that have shown that obscenity is traditionally a weapon of the alienated and frustrated. He is prevented by the judge, and by Hefferson-Brough, from defining "obscenity," "alienated" and "frustrated" at great length. He describes the beliefs of "the young, the idealistic who hope to remake our society." He says:

"If anarchy is an essential precursor to the creation of an alternative society, so the deflowering of language, rendering it obscene and useless, is part of the process of structuring a new one."

Sir Augustine asks him if he is saying *Babbletower* IS "obscene."

Hefferson-Brough objects—the witness's opinion as to the obscenity of the book is inadmissible.

The objection is sustained.

Sir Augustine asks him if he considers *Babbletower* an example of the "deflowering of language desiderated by the young."

Snitkin says no, not at all, quite the opposite. It's *against* the deflowering of language, it's hyper-articulate. It's *literary*. "I was simply saying," he says, "that we live in a climate of opinion where it's not particularly shocking. That's what I'm saying."

Sir Augustine. Some of us live in such a climate. Some of us try
    not to.

The next witness is Canon Adelbert Holly, white mane flowing, nicotined fingers gesticulating, dog-collar shining. He is identified as a Canon of St. Paul's, a writer on theology and psychology, a trained "sexual therapist" and the director of a charity which mans telephone lines to provide help to the despairing.

Hefferson-Brough asks him if he finds *Babbletower* to be a well-written book with a moral message. Canon Holly agrees that it is both well written and moral.

Q.   You would, in your capacity as a Christian pastor, encourage
      people to read this book?

A.   Oh yes. It is a deeply, a profoundly Christian book.

Q.   Can you tell us why you are able to describe it in this way?

A.   It is a book about suffering and the infliction of suffering. Suffering and the infliction of suffering are at the centre of the Christian religion. We venerate the dead body of a man who has been whipped, tortured, crowned with thorns, pierced by a sword and hung by his hands, pierced with nails, until he is dead. We claim, moreover, that our God exacted all this suffering from this Man—who was part of Himself, who was Himself—as payment for our sins. Our God is a cruel God and a jealous God. The Bible tells us so persistently. Cruelty and suffering are *at the centre* of our creed and our ritual. The Christian religion is an expression of the perception that what we now call sado-masochism is a central truth of our existence.

Judge.   You are telling us that you, a Christian priest, believe that God is essentially cruel, and that this book says so?

A.   *Part* of what we used to call God is cruel. The other part is Human, is Christ. I am with William Blake, who wrote, in his *Vision of the Last Judgement,* "Thinking as I do that the Creator of this World is a very Cruel Being, and being a Worshipper of Christ, I cannot help saying: 'The Son, O how unlike the Father!' First God Almighty comes with a Thump on the Head. Then Jesus Christ comes with a balm to heal it." We must worship Christ's Humanity. We must eat his battered body and drink his spilt blood in remembrance of Him, as he adjured us to do.

Hefferson-Brough leads, or attempts to lead, his witness back to a moral analysis of some of the events in *Babbletower,* the hunting of children, the death of Roseace. He attempts to get his witness to say that these episodes are morally shocking, not sexually titillating. He does not quite succeed, as Canon Holly's responses to his questions are rapturous and wild—"Oh, *superbly* horrible, *brilliantly* effective, *beautifully* dreadful." Canon Holly divagates into general reflections on children and death, drawn, according to him, from the profound psychoanalytic insights of Norman O. Brown. *Babbletower,* the Bible, and the works of Norman O. Brown, cries Canon Holly, deal with the generation of love and death in the human community. Neither the germ cell nor the One Spirit of the human community know death, says Canon Holly.

Death comes with individuation, when the infant is separated from the breast that suckles it and becomes a separate sexual being—at the moment when, within the family, the individual *separates* and starts a *new* nuclear *family,* death is born—when the Son becomes the Father, the Father can die, must die. "The human family is created by an intense mode of love and creates an intenser mode of death, that's what Brown says, my lord, that's what Jude Mason demonstrates."

Judge. Is it? You have lost me, Canon, I fear. I can understand your individual sentences, but your general drift I find hard to follow.

Holly. I can clarify.

Judge. No, don't. I trust the jury to have understood as much as they need. I trust the members of the jury to see whether this theological interpretation concurs with their reading of the book in question.

Samuel Oliphant questions the Canon on behalf of the author.

Q. You are acquainted with Jude Mason?

A. I have known him some little time.

Q. How would you describe him? Is he a serious writer?

A. He is a very gifted young man, with very severe difficulties, as the very gifted often have. His relations with society have not always been easy, and his living is hard, but he struggles to communicate his messages, to create his art.

Q. He has persisted with his writing despite severe personal difficulties?

A. He has lived on the edges, at extremes, in poverty. His attitude is a symptom of a sickness—he has been socially persecuted and derided, he is a scapegoat and a victim.

Mr. Oliphant, who has not quite expected this answer, hesitates, and then decides that to go on is better than to go back.

Q. You are saying he lives in difficulties, and knows the pain of modern life?

A. I always think of him as a kind of Holy Fool, like Jean-Paul Sartre's Saint Genet, in his book of that name. Or Dostoevski's Idiot, an innocent at large in a cruel world. Sartre sees Genet as a *shaman,* he is dismembered, chopped to bits, by the spirits in death and is reborn, wise. Jude Mason has the wisdom of the resurrected. His life has been hard, but he has been reborn, renewed, in his work.

Jude Mason does not look grateful for this odd encomium. The Defence barristers look intensely embarrassed. Sir Augustine rises to cross-examine.

Q. I am interested in your observations on Christianity and sado-masochism. Are you saying that the tortures in *Babbletower* are presented as a religious experience of the cruelty of the world, or of its Creator?

A. I am, yes. I am. I do believe it is so.

Q. You think that the motive for describing these explicit sexual cruelties is one of pure religious fervour, a desire to bring the reader to know every depth of degradation of pain, of sexual pain?

A. The divine Man knew every depth—he died in pain—and we need to know.

Q. He was not, I think, subjected to sexual degradation.

A. *All* degradation is sexual. He was a Man; he suffered as a Man.

Q. And you think the reading of this book—with its recondite sexual horrors—is in some—distant, perhaps—some way *related* to the Passion of Jesus Christ?

A. I cannot think we are not meant to know what is *possible* in this world.

Q. Let us be quite clear—you think it a *Christian act* to encourage the reading of this book?

A. I would quote John Milton's *Areopagitica:* "I cannot praise a fugitive and cloistered virtue, unexercised and unbreathed, that never sallies out and sees her adversary, but slinks out of the race, where that immortal garland is to be run for, not without dust and heat."

Q.   But did not Our Lord Himself say, and tell us to pray, "Lead us not into temptation"?

A.   The translation has altered. We say now—"Do not put us to the test."

Q.   Do we indeed? No further questions, my lord.

Frederica misses several further witnesses, as she has to spend time with the Court Welfare Officer, who comes to interview her before the custody hearing. The Court Welfare Officer is a Mrs. Anthea Barlow, a middle-aged lady in a Persian lamb coat, with a fur hat and bright, wide-apart eyes. She has greyish fair hair and a slightly ecstatic expression, which does not inspire confidence in Frederica, who sees her as the same sort of churchy woman as Charity Farrar, the wife of Gideon, who has founded The Children of Joy. Mrs. Barlow asks sensible enough questions in her light, rushing voice. Has Frederica thought that Leo might be happier in Bran House, in the fields, in the paddocks and orchards? Frederica says yes. She says she nearly left him behind, for those reasons. Mrs. Barlow asks why she did not?

"Because *he* wanted to come, and for the first time really I saw he was *mine,* my child, I am the mother he *has,* his genes are *mine,* not Pippy Mammott's, he needs *me* with all my imperfections, we look at each other with the same look."

"And his father?"

"Him too. That's the disaster. But he is a *little boy,* and a clever boy, and a sharp-willed boy, and he does know what he wants."

"Do you love him?"

"More than anything else, including myself, including my books, whether I want to or not. It's just the nature of things. It's a ridiculous question."

"I know. I just like to see what sort of answer I get to it. You'd be surprised what some people say. They make it a function of a battle, or they say, 'I've got to, haven't I?' "

"Well, I have got to, haven't I? It's part of my biology."

"I have no doubt that you love him."

"What will happen?"

"It's not in my hands. I must talk to his father, and his aunts. I must talk to him. May I talk to him alone?"

"If he wants to."

"I'm experienced in talking to children. I won't worry him."

"He's a bit on edge. I want to say—I don't approve of sending little boys away to school, I think it's dangerous and horrible, such *little boys*—but he's like me, he's a loner, he needs to run his own life, *he'd hate it*. Please understand that. *He'd hate it*. I hope I don't sound shrill."

"No. Reasonable. Can you look after him?"

"I've got all these good arrangements. I've got Agatha and Saskia. And a good school."

"It is. I know it."

"What will happen?"

"There is always a predisposition in favour of the mother. Less, maybe, with boys. But judges tend to assume women will care better for little children. Rightly, in my view."

"There are a lot of other women, in his case. But I am his mother."

"You are. And I do see how much you care."

Back in Court, Hefferson-Brough has called Rupert Parrott to the stand. Parrott says he is proud to have published *Babbletower,* that it is an important, if controversial, book, that its message is deeply moral, and is a message for our times. He speaks in a light, pleasant, very slightly pompous voice, with exaggerated courtesy, a little old-fashioned. His blue eyes shine, his round cheeks are flushed and shining, the attention he gives to his questioners is just too intense, too considered. Hefferson-Brough asks him if he thought the book ran any risk of being thought outrageous, unacceptable, obscene, when he took it on.

A.   Well, yes, naturally. It's strong meat, it's strong stuff, it doesn't pull its punches. But I was quite confident that the reading public, *and* the authorities, would take it for what it was—a serious and ambitious literary work. I felt its moment had come, and that I was there to bring it into the world. It says things about our society that need saying, need bringing into the light.

Q.   What sorts of things are these?

A.   Much has been made, by the Prosecution, of the scenes of sadistic treatment of little children in the dormitories. Those are in fact one of the things that made me recognise that the book had to be published. I recognised the dormitories and the tortures from my own schooldays—

Q. You are an Erstwhile Hog? That is to say, an old boy of Swineburn School.

A. Yes, I am. As you are yourself, I believe, and as is Jude Mason, the author of *Babbletower*. There are many fine things in *Babbletower*, but one of the finest is the depiction of what went on routinely in the dormitories of big schools—almost certainly still goes on.

Q. Let me be clear. You are not claiming that murder took place in the dormitories of Swineburn?

A. No, but almost, and nobody said anything. There is a conspiracy of silence. A climate of acceptance. Boys are thought to be nice, and teachers are supposed to be kind and considerate. This book tells the truth. It seems like wild fantasy but quite large chunks of it *that I know about* are sober fact. That is why I was so struck by it, initially. Later, I understood its other great merits. But it has an element of sober realism people lucky enough not to be Erstwhile Hogs may not assess properly.

Q. You believe it is for the public good to know that things happen in real life which are not very far from the fantastic events depicted in *Babbletower*?

A. On balance, yes, I do. I mean, I think public innocence about such things is no longer possible. Anyone who heard Fausto Gemelli's evidence will agree that we live in a moral climate now where things are pretty generally discussed rather than hidden. We are less easily shocked—as a nation—than we were in the days of Christine Keeler and Mandy Rice-Davies. I think there are good and bad aspects to all this—I think Press reports can upset certain people, vulnerable people, almost certainly much more than imaginative works like *Babbletower*. Sir Augustine mentioned the Moors Murders. I think the reporting of them was terrifying and disturbing in a way this literary work isn't. But I think we admit generally *now* that certain things go on that we once used—as a public community—to pretend didn't exist. When Oscar Wilde was sent to prison the judge said, "It is the worst case I have ever tried," and claimed that Wilde's crime was "so bad" that he had to put "stern restraint" on himself to suppress the language he would rather not use, "which must rise to the breast of every man of honour who has heard the details of these two terrible trials." There was one lone voice in the Press then that said the judge must have tried worse crimes, murders and extortions, and that society was guilty of hypocrisy. "Why does not the Crown prosecute every boy at a public or private school, or half the men in the Universities? In the latter places 'coederism' is as common as fornication, and everyone knows it." There is a gap between what many or most people now *know* about human nature and what we are allowed to say. Those of us who suffered at school—as I did, and as I can see Jude Mason did—suffered also from the little boys' normal conspiracy of silence. I think the public conspiracy of silence is as bad as the frightened conspiracy of little boys in dorms. We are grown-up men now. We live in a grown-up time. We have a right to responsible grown-up descriptions of the actions of which we are capable.

(Scattered applause in the Court.) The judge asks for silence and requests that the interruption not be repeated.

Sir Augustine asks Rupert Parrott only a few questions.

Q. Mr. Parrott—you are a generally respected publisher. You have a reputation for being intellectually up-to-date, even *avant-garde*.

A. I would say so, yes.

Q. You publish Elvet Gander, who has enlightened the Court about degradation ceremonies and polymorphous perversity.

A. You need not sneer at him. He is a serious thinker, much respected and admired, and I am proud to publish him. (Scattered local applause.)

Q. I hope I was not sneering. You publish also Canon Adelbert Holly, who has told us that the essence of Christianity is masochism and the suffering and infliction of pain?

A. I do. And am proud to publish him. I do not agree with all his points of emphasis. But he is a daring and a subtle theologian.

Q. No doubt. No doubt. You feel a considerable sense of mission about *Babbletower*, do you not? You feel it represents a blow for sexual freedom, fearless, explicit description of hidden vices and horrors, do you not?

A. I do. You try to make these feelings sound misguided or absurd, but they are not. It is a serious and beautiful and courageous book, confronting the dark fearlessly. I am, as I said, proud to be associated with it.

Q. You feel also a sense of mission, I sense, about the revelation of the squalid school secrets you shared with Jude Mason and perhaps with that other Erstwhile Hog, my learned friend, the Counsel for the Defence.

A. To an extent, yes.

Q. To an extent. You do not think your judgement of *Babbletower* is perhaps twisted, perhaps vitiated, by your recognition of your schooldays in parts of it, in the dorms of La Tour Bruyarde? As Dr. Gander has reminded us, childhood wounds lie deep and fester. Might they not cloud your judgement?

A. I don't think so. I think they reinforce it. I would like to do away with the hypocrisy which made those sufferings possible and prolonged.

The next witness for the Defence is the accused in the dock, Jude Mason himself. He stands in the box, eyes downcast at first, holding his fists close together in front of him; Frederica suddenly intuits that he is wearing imaginary manacles. She looks at his thin face and his eye-hollows and imagines the fall of his hair as it used to be before he was sanitised and tidied. He looks insubstantial, grey-skinned after his publisher's pink, bony and brittle. Frederica wonders what has become of his smell, the frying grease, the rancid sweat, the body fluids. Does he now emit carbolic soap or Old Spice? Her nostrils imagine the sniff of fresh newsprint. She smiles. Samuel Oliphant rises to examine his client.

Q.   Tell us your name.

A.   Jude Mason.

Q.   Is that your real name?

A.   Yes. It is not the name my parents gave me.

Q.   What was that?

A.   Julian Guy Monckton-Pardew. (A ripple of laughter in the Court.)

Q.   You changed your name?

A.   Many people do. I changed my name, and my life.

Q.   What sort of a family do you come from?

A.   I have none. They have cast me off. My father made a lot of money selling pork and veal pies to pubs. I am a vegetarian. Not out of virtue or anything. Out of squeamishness. My mother was a photographic model. Her name was Poppy. I called them Poppy and Pappy. We lived in Wiltshire. They had enough money to pay nannies and nurses and send me away to prep school at five and to Swineburn at thirteen so I can't be said to have known them very well before we mutually cast each other off. I don't know if they're alive or dead. They don't know if I am. That suits all of us.

The sawing voice is monotonous but conveys an uneasy urgency: these are things the speaker has rehearsed and wants to say, not things reluctantly drawn from him.

Oliphant.   Mr. Parrott has already spoken about your experiences at Swineburn. Were you happy there?

Jude.   Oh, from time to time, blissfully and disastrously happy. It was those times that ruined my character and my life. Mostly I was miserable, frequently I was terrified. There was a great deal of refined cruelty in that school, as has already been suggested. A great deal.

Oliphant.   Cruelty exercised by whom?

Jude.   Oh, routinely by the masters. We were whipped all sorts of
ways by all sorts of men, for all sorts of reasons. You survived
better if you developed a taste for it, if you learned to cater to
those who had a taste for it. Also the boys were cruel, in
thumping, bashing ways and in subtle, teasing, nasty ways, as is
no doubt normal everywhere. I imagine it was all quite *normal.*

Oliphant.   Did you survive?

Jude.   No. In short, no. Contrary to appearances, I have no taste for
being hurt, just a lot of enforced experience of it. I did think it
was inevitable and immutable and eternal, as little children do,
and most adults conveniently forget.

Oliphant.   Were you a good student?

Jude.   I believe so. I was very good at languages. Poppy-mommy,
my sweet mother, glimpsed perhaps half a dozen times a year,
was, or is, I am told, partly *French.* She modelled rather *naughty*
clothes sometimes. My French was good.

Oliphant.   And English literature and language?

Jude.   Ah. When I was a *little boy* the English master predicted a
glorious future for me. Scholarships, university, poetry of the
profounder kind. I was a *stellar student* in my early days. I was
the star in all the plays, you know, in all the Shakespeare
plays.

Oliphant.   What parts did you play?

Jude.   I was a delicious squeaking Cleopatra. The English master,
Dr. Grisman Gould, was good enough to say that he had
never seen a better one. I believed him at the time. Later, I
took to doing *friends.* Horatio, you know, Kent, steady souls.
I'd have liked to do Iago, but you don't get school productions of *Othello.*

Judge.   Where is all this questioning leading, Mr. Oliphant?

Oliphant.   I am hoping to establish Mr. Mason's literary background. As a help with the question of the literary merits of
his book.

Judge.   I see.

Oliphant.   And my learned friend Mr. Hefferson-Brough has already linked Mr. Mason's experiences at school with the seriousness of his purpose as a writer.

Judge.   Your client's *intentions* are not relevant as to the question of obscenity.

Oliphant.   I understand that, my lord. But they are relevant as to *literary merit,* and the two are linked here, are very much linked, in the formative years of my client's mind.

Judge.   Very well. But I do not think we need to examine closely all his lessons or amateur dramatic performances. He obviously enjoyed his dramatic performances.

Jude.   Not always, my lord.

Judge.   Indeed? Not always. Continue, if you please, Mr. Oliphant.

Oliphant.   You did not go to university, Mr. Mason?

Jude.   No.

Oliphant.   Although you might have been expected to?

Jude.   I was very unhappy. I ran away from the school. I ran away rather classically, or perhaps romantically would be a better word, in the middle of the night. I stole a bicycle and went all the way to Harwich. I got on a boat and went to Amsterdam. I messed around there a bit and then someone took me to Paris.

Oliphant.   You were sixteen?

Jude.   Yes. I don't think my parents looked for me. I never heard of it if they did. I sent a postcard from Paris with a Poste Restante address and got a postcard back saying they didn't want to know.

Judge.   Are we really to believe that is all the contact you had?

Jude.   I don't know why you shouldn't believe it. It's true. It's quite easy to stay hidden, my lord, if people have no real desire to find you. I was a disappointment, it has to be admitted. Poppy said continually I was a disappointment. She said it on the postcard. She can't spell. She wrote it with one *p.* I probably

sent a disappointing postcard. It had a sphinx on it, by Gustave
Moreau. They were afraid I was decadent.

Judge.   So you sent the postcard to provoke them?

Jude.   It wasn't *much* of a provocation, my lord, from a sixteen-year-
old boy who had been living pretty rough for six months.

Judge.   That is as may be. I am interested in your veracity, you see.

Jude.   I am telling the truth, and nothing but the truth.

Judge.   But not the whole truth?

Jude.   You can't tell the whole truth in one-line answers, my lord. I
don't think you'd like the whole truth if I told it. I really
don't. It isn't very nice. But I haven't told you anything untrue. I swore not to.

Judge.   Mr. Oliphant, please continue your questioning.

Oliphant.   In Paris, did you attempt to continue your studies?

Jude.   I decided to get a ticket to the Bibliothèque Nationale. I
made various friends—various people looked after me a bit—I
talked to people in cafés—I worked a bit in theatres and cine-
mas, showing people their seats. I got interested in French literature. A man I met told me about Fourier. He seemed odd,
you know, and interesting, so I said I was working on him and
went to the library and did work on him, and got interested. I
am an auto-didact. I believe in auto-didacticism. Auto-didacts
tend to study one thing at once, study it to death. I did
Fourier, and then I went on to Nietzsche.

Oliphant.   And when did you start your own writing?

Jude.   There was never a time when I was not writing. I was writing when I was a very little boy, and before that I was telling
stories to myself. I used to dress up in front of the mirror and
act the stories. Once I acted a whole pantomime for Poppy
and Pappy—it was *Cinderella,* I made all the costumes and
played all the parts, I didn't have any friends, though I did have
a Nanny at that point who acted the Fairy Godmother and the
Narrator. They clapped a bit, but they had to go out before I
got to the glass slipper. I'm sorry, I see I'm boring you and

being irrelevant, but you did ask for the whole truth and that was my first bit of writing. I've never ever told anyone all this before—not ever having been under oath—except one person. And *that* was a mistake.

Oliphant.   When did you start writing *seriously*?

Jude.   All that was serious. It was deadly serious. It was my real life. Much more real than the horrible school *cells* and *teams.*

Oliphant.   When did you start writing *Babbletower*?

Jude.   Well, in a way, then, when I was a little boy. Who was it said there are only five or six good plots? Anyway, I was always writing the same story. The story about the *group of friends* who *run away* to a *better place* and make a better life, a more beautiful life, a freer life, where they can do what they want. It's the story of *Cinderella* and the story of *Pilgrim's Progress* and the story of *The Coral Island,* I suppose. Getting out of the dungeon and the cinders and going to the ball or to heaven and sleeping in feather beds and eating off gold plates. Only as I got older and more suspicious I saw that the place you make might turn out to be much like the place you ran away from.

He is now, Frederica thinks, acting the great writer accounting for his great talent, modestly. Oliphant says firmly,

Oliphant.   But *Babbletower* is a grown-up book, not a childish fantasy.

Jude.   It is a grim grown-up book about childish fantasy. And about grown-up fantasy. It is also a grown-up fantasy itself, I have to admit. That's not wicked. Fantasy is natural to human beings as honey is to bees. People are always saying things are as natural as honey, these days. Now what was . . .

Oliphant.   You have heard the very clear evidence of Professor Marie-France Smith. What did you make of her arguments?

Jude.   (The sawing note more pronounced.) Professor Smith is an *academic* and her account *smells of the lamp,* as they say, I believe. She makes my book sound all cut and dried, a trussed-up little plump *thesis* waiting to be roasted and consumed. I don't recognise the terrible passions of my book in Professor Smith's arid little "explanation." *I lived that story, Mr. Oliphant, I have lived through all those things—*

It is at this point that the first fleck of white foam, or crust, appears in the corner of Jude's mouth. He pokes at it nervously, with the tip of his tongue.

Oliphant. Well, you may dislike the emphases. But you did read Fourier, you say yourself, and you do maintain that *Babbletower* has a serious moral point, do you not?

Jude. Does art ever have a "serious moral point"? It moves, it appals, it makes you chuckle, it delights, it despairs. All right, you don't like my answers. You are right not to. I am behaving stupidly. I can't help myself. But my book is not a stupid book, it is a good book, and is meant to enlighten and to move, not to harm and disgust. Those who cannot see that can't read properly.

For several more repetitive minutes, Jude and his Counsel joust around the ostensible "purpose" of *Babbletower.* Oliphant is patient with his client's natural tendency to contradict, for rhetorical effect, points that are designed to help him. Jude is got to agree that his vision of human nature is "dark" and "pessimistic," but not "perverted," not "twisted." He complains briefly about meaningless adjectives and is brought again to the point. He says that like Nietzsche he desires a "strong" pessimism, a "gay" despair. He asks if he may quote Nietzsche and is told to go ahead.

Jude. He says: "Whenever anyone speaks, without bitterness, rather innocuously, of man as a belly with two needs and a head with one; whenever anyone sees, seeks and *wants* to see only hunger, sexual desire and vanity, as though these were the actual and sole motives of human actions; in brief, whenever anyone speaks '*badly*' of man—but does not speak ill of him—the lover of knowledge should listen carefully and with diligence, and he should in general lend an ear whenever anyone speaks without indignation. For the indignant man, and whoever is constantly tearing and rending himself with his teeth (or instead of himself, the world, or God, or Society), may indeed morally speaking stand higher than the laughing and self-satisfied satyr, but in every other sense he is the more commonplace, less interesting, less instructive case. And no one *lies* so much as the indignant man."

May I say, my lord, that the "English vice" is not what it is always said to be, but precisely *indignation*. We get furiously upset about everything—the price of stamps, the state of public lavatories, the behaviour of schoolboys and politicians, the weather, books that are written with the heart's blood and fuelled by real passion. It is *indignation* that has put my book on trial, seeing things that are not there, making hypotheses about its effect that are *quite unjustified*. My book thinks badly of man, but so do quite a lot of other writers, including Saint Augustine. *Indignation* is prurient and suspect, my lord, it is unworthy to be heard. Do not hear it.

Judge. You should perhaps have read for the Bar, Mr. Mason, instead of devoting your time to Fourier and Sade.

Godfrey Hefferson-Brough, perhaps wisely, asks the defendant very few questions about *Babbletower.* He returns almost compulsively to the state of affairs at Swineburn School in the late 1940s. Later, the Press is to remark that just as it began to appear that Lady Chatterley herself was on trial for adultery in the trial of Penguin Books, so it seems, from time to time, in the *Babbletower* case, that the real defendants are the masters and boys of Swineburn, the Erstwhile Hogs and the erstwhile Swineherds. One journalist, asking why Hefferson-Brough returned so compulsively to the charge, to the school, when the advantage to his client was, to put it nicely, dubious, will conclude that he was compelled to do so by some unresolved business of his own. "Everything in England," this journalist writes, "comes back to the inextricable links between our educational system, privilege, or lack of it, and sex. De Sade was abused by the Jesuits, but Fourier was sublimely innocent of the snares and puerile disasters of the Public School dorm."

Q. You say, Mr. Mason, that you were taught by Dr. Grisman Gould.

A. That is so.

Q.   He was a good teacher?

A.   In his way, sublime.

Q.   So I believe. He had favourites?

A.   Not *obviously*. But yes. He singled out particular boys. He gave them an extra-curricular literary education. He disabused their innocence, you might say.

Q.   Were you one of his favourites?

A.   For a time. Later, I was not. That was a normal pattern. First he loved you. Then you "disappointed" him. Then he began to find fault. Then he destroyed you.

Q.   That's a strong word. "Destroyed."

A.   Most of his favourites came to grief. There were scandals. They were said to have cheated. Or were caught in the lats with little boys. Or got drunk. Or killed himself, one. They were going to be wonders and something always happened.

Q.   Were you yourself involved in any scandal?

Judge.   Where is this line of questioning leading, Mr. Hefferson-Brough?

Hefferson-Brough.   It is all to do with the realism of the subject-matter of this apparent fantasy, my lord.

Judge.   It is hard to see how.

Jude.   I don't mind answering. I am telling everything, today.

Judge.   That is for me to decide. Continue, Mr. Hefferson-Brough.

Hefferson-Brough.   Does the question stand, my lord?

Judge.   I think not. I think Mr. Mason need not answer that question.

Jude.   I don't mind.

Judge.   You must speak when you are asked to.

Jude.   How can I explain, if I may not speak?

Judge.   You are not here to explain your life, but to defend your book. Mr. Hefferson-Brough.

Q. Did Dr. Grisman Gould ever interfere with you, Mr. Mason?

A. I wouldn't call it *interfering*. That is quite the wrong verb. He was a person of infinite subtlety and charm. Oh dear, yes.

Q. Are you aware of the Erstwhile Hogs' Round Robin, Mr. Mason?

A. No. Tell me. I should like to know what that was.

Q. Do you know what became of Dr. Grisman Gould?

A. I think he is dead. I am not sorry if he is.

Q. He committed suicide in 1952, Mr. Mason. He was dismissed from the school, dishonourably, after the composition of the Round Robin.

A. How?

Q. How?

A. How did he kill himself?

Q. He slit his wrists in a hot bath.

Judge. I do not think you can pursue this topic further, Mr. Heffer-son-Brough. The witness has said he knows nothing of these facts.

Hefferson-Brough. Certainly, my lord. I would like to ask Mr. Mason if he believes that Dr. Grisman Gould was a corrupter of youth, the centre of a circle of corruption and perversion at Swineburn in the 1940s and early '50s.

A. Not a circle. It was never more than one at once I think. That's how he kept going. Each one thought he was the first and only. And his successor thought the predecessor was a *disappointment,* as Dr. Gould said he was. He looked like the Archangel Michael, you know. Austere, pure, golden. I suppose you knew him, too. I don't like to think of him bleeding in a bath. Ugly. Better than a bullet in the brain, but ugly.

Q. Mr. Mason, is it from Dr. Grisman Gould that you first learned of the—the sado-masochistic practices described in *Babbletower*?

A. It may well be. He gave me Rousseau's *Confessions.* Rousseau couldn't reach orgasm without being whipped. The things in my book happen everywhere. Dr. Grisman Gould's speciality was *confession* afterwards. Verbal recapitulation.

Q. Indeed. Are we to recognise the model for your Projector, Culvert, in Dr. Grisman Gould?

A. Not *culvert,* Mr. Hefferson-Brough, as in the English *drainage system.* Cul-vert, as in French, green or verdant cul or—orifice. Hmm. Do you know, I had never thought about whether Culvert was Dr. Grisman Gould. He is so many, Prince Charming, the Scarlet Pimpernel, Rousseau, Charles II, James I, Fourier, myself—I think he may also be Dr. Grisman Gould. Dr. Gould might have acknowledged him as Prospero acknowledged Caliban, to whom he taught language. "This thing of darkness I acknowledge mine." I could have confessed *for hours,* having invented Culvert. You distress me. I did not invent Culvert to propitiate Dr. Grisman Gould.

It can be seen that the defendant is trembling. The crumb of white in the corner of his mouth is extending into a fine white crust that runs along his lips. From this point on in his evidence his words are accompanied by the sound of a fluttering or beating, which is his knees knocking gently and rapidly against the wooden box, which is his hands playing on the bar before him. It is like a wing-beat, or a heartbeat, not quite regular, but persistent. His answers, written down, may seem jaunty, foolhardy, but to those in the Court the plangent voice had also a fixed, raucous note which is disturbing and irritating.

Sir Augustine Weighall rises to cross-examine. He rearranges his gown with care. His face is grave, concerned and almost friendly.

Q. You have told my learned friend that you were christened Julian Guy Monckton-Pardew. Did you give up that name as a rejection of your parents, or as a rejection of the connotations of the name itself?

A. Both.

Q. What do you dislike about the name?

A. Every aspect of it. The pretentious double-barrel. The romanticism in Guy is all crusaders and Old England (or Old Norman Conquest) and Julian is a name no pretty boy should be asked to bear. Also, I have to tell you, my parents made it up. He was Monckton, and she was Pardew; it comes from the French, Pardieu, I suppose. It's a burdensome sort of name. Like a plaster imitation of an effigy in a church.

Q. That is a very articulate rebuttal. And the name you chose has its own romantic poetry, too, in opposition, I take it. Would I be wrong in suggesting that you chose Jude as a tribute to Thomas Hardy's hero Jude the Obscure?

A. You would not be wrong. I meant to be obscure. I am obscure.

Q. Hardy's Jude was an auto-didact, a workman, an intellectual excluded from the inner circle of university life?

A. He was. It seemed appropriate. Romantic, as you say. There's nothing wrong in romanticism.

Q. Indeed there is not. Hardy's Jude was called Jude Fawley, as I recall. But you chose the name Mason. Hardy's Jude was a mason, a stonemason by trade, I believe.

A. He was. He was an honest craftsman, and he saw the poetry in stones. I believe art is craft first. I meant always to be an artist. "Mason" seemed a good place to start.

Q. Your name is indeed precisely crafted. I believe *Jude the Obscure* was received with considerable criticism when it first appeared?

A. With vituperation. It was burned by a bishop. Hardy said the general idea was "We Britons hate ideas, and we are going to live up to that privilege of our native country. Your picture may not show the untrue, or the uncommon, or even be contrary to the canons of art; but it is not the view of life that we who thrive on conventions can permit to be painted."

Q. You have that by heart. It obviously means a great deal to you. How long have you had that by heart?

A. Since my schooldays.

Q. So you chose your name, long before the writing of *Babbletower,* for its associations with an obscure auto-didact and an unconventional, rejected book?

A.   That is so. There is nothing wrong with that.

Q.   Was it Dr. Grisman Gould who drew your attention to *Jude the Obscure*?

A.   Indeed it was not. I found it quite by myself. Quite by myself. He did not like Hardy. He found him heavy-handed and im-probable. His tastes ran to poetry.

Q.   Can you tell us which poetry?

A.   Shakespeare. The sonnets. The early poems. *Venus and Adonis. The Rape of Lucrece.* He was very subtle on lacerated skin. He had his little games with rosy cheeks and threads of blood. We knew all about the dirty Dark Lady and the fair young man. He was good on paintings of martyrs, too. Crawshaw. Oscar Wilde, by extension. *The Ballad of Reading Gaol.* "Each man kills the thing he loves." He knew about that. When you knew him very well, he would read you Bosie's sonnets about Shame.

> "*I am Shame*
> *That walks with Love, I am most wise and turn*
> *Cold lips and limbs to fire . . .*"

"I am the Love that dare not speak its name." Bosie was a dreadful poet. Dreadful. I nearly gave Grisman Gould up when he started on that stuff.

Q.   Bosie was Lord Alfred Douglas?

A.   Yes.

Q.   To whom Oscar Wilde addressed passionate letters?

A.   Yes. They were silly letters, badly written.

Q.   You admire Wilde?

A.   As a writer, in moderation. As a man, no. He was a fool. A snob. He made a fool of himself over worse fools.

Q.   Dr. Grisman Gould admired Oscar Wilde?

Q. A. In moderation, too. Why are you going on about Oscar Wilde? Are you trying to draw an analogy?

Q. Do you accept an analogy?

Samuel Oliphant objects and his objection is sustained. Sir Augustine turns to another line of questioning.

Q. How do you make your living, Mr. Mason?

A. With great difficulty. I expose my body in public places. I achieve sempiternity in charcoal, in acrylic paint, in oils. In short, I model in art colleges. It is an honest trade, and humbling.

Frederica can hear this roll off Jude's tongue: it is his practised party piece.

Q. And did you pursue this trade in Paris?

A. No. I did not know how to set about it. I did not think of it.

Q. So how did you live?

A. I made myself useful to various people. I was a *protégé,* from time to time. People took an interest in my career, in my mind, in my future.

Q. Where did you live?

A. In many places. Backstage. Under bars.

Q. With the kindly protectors?

A. No. As a matter of fact, no. If you mean, was I a kept boy, no. *I was not.* Never again. No.

Q. Never again?

A. I sleep by myself. I live by myself. I am a private person. I do not see how this is relevant to your enquiries, or whatever the phrase is, *but I have no sex life.* It is over-valued. Sex is better in the head, *pace* D. H. Lawrence, who knew a lot less than he thought he did about a lot of things.

Q. Are you saying, Mr. Mason, that after your schooldays you have lived chastely and written vivid sexual fantasies, for choice?

A. Not always, and not entirely. But that has been the general idea, the ideal state of affairs, yes. Nietzsche said philosophers were always "irritable and rancorous" towards their senses. He said sex was very damaging to spiritual and artistic preparation. "Those with the greatest powers do not need to learn this from experience, from unfortunate experience." He was right.

Q. Let us turn to your writing, Mr. Mason, now we understand a little better what you believe in. Despite your admiration for Nietzsche, you were a little unhappy with Professor Smith's definition of your book as a philosophical exploration of freedom and restraint?

A. She was *so dry.* So *logical.* A book is a passionate thing, it is made of experience, it is lived as it is written, it is more immediate than reality.

Q. More immediate than reality.

A. I think if most people were honest, they would admit that imaginary experiences are more real than actual ones. It is like the smell of coffee—the thing itself is never so good, it is always a bit musty. I began to write to avoid life as it is lived, and found I had found it more abundantly.

Q. Life. You are quoting the Bible there, Mr. Mason, as you are no doubt well aware. But the life *you* offer your readers is not a very usual life—it is, as has already *abundantly* appeared in evidence, a life of manacles and ingenious tortures, pederasty, orgies, coprophilia, flagellation and slow murder for pleasure. What do you wish to do to your readers, Mr. Mason? Do you wish to make them take pleasure in the images of these horrors? To make them shun them? To incite them to copy them?

Jude is silent. He is silent for some time, licking the crust round his dry lips. He says, finally,

A. I don't know. I don't consider readers, particular readers. I write what I have to, what I see. These are the fantasies people have, some people live by. This is how people are, more people than you think. I don't know *why* people need fantasies, any more than I know *why* they dream. I only know, if you stop a man dreaming, you destroy his mind. If you shut off his fantasies, I think, you make him dangerous.

Q. But Culvert *indulges* his fantasies and becomes a killer.

A. It does him no good.

Q. It does his victims no good. Did you take pleasure in the death of Roseace, Mr. Mason? In the writing of that death?

A. Pleasure?

Q. Do not stall, Mr. Mason. It is a simple question. Did you take pleasure in the slow death by sexual torture of the Lady Roseace?

A. Did Shakespeare take pleasure in Cornwall's pleasure in the putting-out of Gloucester's eyes? Did he mean to incite Elizabethan noblemen to go about putting out people's eyes? They did, and enjoyed it. Now we don't, much. He put us off the idea, I believe.

Q. *King Lear* is a great and terrible tragedy. Are you comparing *Babbletower* to that kind of work?

A. No. Oh no. I am a mere Marsyas. A minor artist, a pipe-player who was flayed by Apollo.

Q. Explain your reference.

A. He was a goat-foot, a satyr, who challenged Apollo to a musical contest. He lost, and Apollo flayed him alive. He pulled him, Dante says, out of the scabbard of his limbs, "*della vagina delle membre sue.*" He had no more song, after that. Oscar Wilde says that modern art is the cry of Marsyas, bitter and plaintive and sad. Not tragic. Tortured but not tragic. Tragedy is past.

Q. So your art is not tragic, it is a satiric piping. You wish to blow a raspberry at convention?

A. Raspberry? I don't understand raspberry.

Q. Come, Mr. Mason. You must have heard the term. A rude noise.

A. Don't say "Come" to me in that tone of voice. I don't see why a rude noise is called a raspberry. For the little rosette of anal veins around a fart, perhaps?

(Some laughter, some irritable restiveness in the courtroom.)

Q. Would you accept, Mr. Mason, that it is difficult in some ways to reconcile the savagery of many of the comments in *Babbletower* with some of your own attitudes and statements during the course of your evidence?

A. I do find it difficult myself. Giving evidence is much less pleasant than writing. You are not in control, giving evidence. You are tempted into saying silly things.

Q. You have, so to speak, "presented" yourself to the Court. You pose as an unsophisticated auto-didact, a victim of the public school system. You are constructed of literary images, references—Hardy, Wilde, Marsyas. It is as though you were self-designed as a player in a drama where you were a victim, unjustly accused of writing a corrupt book—long before this trial ever took place, or this action was brought. You are a bit of a *poseur,* Mr. Mason.

A. Is that a question? (The witness is shaking so much that his answer is croaked.)

Q. I am trying to get to the bottom of the purpose and nature of the book you have written. Mr. Avram Snitkin, a witness called by the Defence, has talked about the modern desire to shock, to break taboos, to use "bad" words to create anarchy—

A. I reject all that. I am not interested in anarchy. I am an artist. A lot of nonsense is talked about those words, those words you don't use—you can't do *anything* with those words, it's like studding your pages with gobs of exudations—*those two words,* "gobs" and "exudations," are better words than "shit" and "snot," they're words you *react to.* If I want to upset you I can write in perfectly legitimate words a description of bliss, or hurt, or evacuation, which will leave a trace on your memory as though a knife had slid across your brain; I can leave a *trace* of these that won't go. Poor old Lawrence tried to accommodate and tame those words, like old copper coins with the faces

578

rubbed off, bum pennies for bun pennies. It won't work because they only exist to shock. And no, I don't write to pose
or to shock, Mr. Weighall, *I don't.*

Q. You don't. You write to hurt—to slice our brains and our
memories—

A. That is not illegitimate.

Q. Let me finish. You said earlier, and I quote: "I write what I
have to, what I see. These are the fantasies people have . . ."
You write the kinds of fantasies that are enacted in brothels and
written down badly in dirty books in brown wrappers, Mr.
Mason, but you write them in better words and make them
more powerful. Do you not agree that they might hurt people
just as much as these other pornographic works?

A. Hurt? Hurt? I don't think those other things *hurt,* Mr.
Weighall. I have been in those places, and I know, I have
been amongst the incense and the poppies and the tawdry
bits of silk and satin and tulle. I have seen grown men making
fools of themselves in nappies with bottles, or loaded with
heavy chains. I have seen judges pretending to be housemaids
in frilly aprons and black stockings and I've seen postmen
pretending to be judges and an eminent surgeon pretending
to be a fire that could only be put out in a particularly disgusting way. If I wrote you a scientific treatise on these
things, you *couldn't touch me*—but I am an artist—meretrix,
meretricious I may have been as a boy, porno-grapher I am
not, *I am an artist.*

Q. You protest eloquently. You have not answered my question
about your readers, Mr. Mason. You have not answered it. I
put it to you that when you were a boy, Dr. Grisman Gould
hurt your body and depraved your mind with a mixture of literature and cruelty—and that you are intent on passing on that
hurt to the world, to your readers, to the possible victims of
those of your readers who resemble your own betrayer.

A. You understand nothing. I loved him. He was not a tawdry
Svengali. He was—he was—he is dead, it doesn't matter what
he was, he is not on trial, though he appears to be. He is dead,
and I loved him, and I have not loved since, and shan't.

Q.   You have not answered my question. Hurt was done, you were depraved and corrupted, and you are *passing that hurt on*.

Jude.   (to judge) Do I have to answer that? It—isn't—a question. This is all nonsense.

Judge.   It is a question of opinion. You need not answer it.

Jude.   He need not have asked it.

Judge.   The jury will please ignore the question.

Snitkin's tape-recorder whirs. Augustine Weighall says he has no further questions, thus leaving the deleted question, the struck question, the non-question, indelibly engraved on the jurors' minds as the climax of his case against Jude Mason.

Frederica leaves the court during the evidence of the next witness, a schoolmaster who confirms the stories of excesses at Swineburn, and asserts that he would have no objection to his charges reading *Babbletower*. She meets Alexander Wedderburn, wandering along the corridors. Alexander thinks the case is going badly for the Defence. He says that Augustine Weighall is much cleverer than Godfrey Heffersen-Brough. "He must have known something about Jude's history," says Alexander. "More than his own people did."

"Probably met him in some brothel in Piccadilly," says Frederica tartly. "They all dress up and *port about,* as my father used to say. Jude is an idiot. Why must he *show off*?"

"He said. He's an artist."

"So are you. You don't."

"The dreadful thing is, he's potentially a better one. And they might put him in prison. He's got no common sense. That's his tragedy. I have. Abundantly. That's mine."

"Don't you start talking in cheap epigrams. I *hate* Oscar Wilde."

"So does Jude."

"With the hate that dare not tell its name, I guess. Now I'm doing it."

"You're worried."

"I never thought I'd say it, but I've got kind of *attached* to Jude. I never thought I'd agree with Canon Holly, but he is a kind of holy fool, a real *idiot*."

The Defence's final witness is the novelist Phyllis Pratt, Bowers and Eden's only bestseller. Mrs. Pratt is wearing a pink suit over a floral shirt, and an amethyst cross on a silver chain. She addresses both the Counsel for the Defence, and later Sir Augustine, in a sensible, complicit, lemon-and-honey voice, tart and warm. She states that she has much enjoyed *Babbletower*—"quite a *satisfactory* experience, like a fairy story, with the punishment of folly and a few thrills to it, but never real enough to *alarm* anyone." She says that as a vicar's wife she has met "many tortured souls who have harmed others, or who would have liked to harm others" and believes that reading *Babbletower* would "on the whole, merely cheer such people up. That somebody knew, and could make fairytales out of it. Fairy stories and detective stories do much less harm than real reports of what went on in concentration camps, I think you'll find. They put a kind of pink glow round it all, that takes it out of the sordid real world."

Would she, Hefferson-Brough asks her, give it to her children to read?

"Any mother knows that some children can take *anything* and some cry and cry over the death of a seal or a Bambi and never quite recover. I think Mr. Mason made a little mistake calling his work a tale for children. It isn't. Children don't like explicit sex. They like dirty noses and dirty bottoms, not genitalia doing what genitalia are made for, or can be contorted to do. No, I'd be careful who I *recommended* it to. But one must be sensible, that goes for every grown-up book."

Sir Augustine asks her, as he has asked all the defence witnesses, whether she was sexually moved by the book.

A. Of course I was. He's a clever writer. I was moved by the bits that appealed to my particular fantasies, as I expect you were, and I laughed at some of the others, and I skipped some of the others, as I expect you would in normal circumstances.

Q. It can't be normal reading for you, Mrs. Pratt. Your own books are grounded in realism, in village life, in domesticity, in the Church.

A. I heard you grilling Mr. Mason about fantasies. The heroine of my first book stabbed her husband in a real *welter of gore* when he pushed her too far. That was a fantasy, Sir Augustine, which would perhaps have become a fact, if it hadn't got out on paper and cheered up a multitude of other vicars' wives and other women indulging similar fantasies. What Mr. Mason said about fantasies and dreams was very wise. They save us, they save us from action.

Q. Even the warning dreams, the premonitory dreams, of murderers?

A. Come, come, Sir Augustine. You are not going to tell me that anything as accomplished and fastidious and in places downright *funny* as *Babbletower* bears any relation to the deranged vision of murderers? Or that poor Mr. Mason wants *to kill someone*? He is a good writer, and he's half-dead with anxiety, and I think it's a pity.

Augustine Weighall has considered other obscenity trials, and believes that previous prosecution witnesses have been ill chosen. He has decided, also, that his witnesses, coming after the long file of defence luminaries, must be succinct and convincing, carry weight. In the event, he calls five: Hermia Cross, who began the public agitation against *Babbletower,* a chief superintendent from Staffordshire, a suffragan bishop from a difficult part of Birmingham, Roger Magog and Professor Efraim Ziz, a historian of Judaism.

Hermia Cross is disturbingly sensible. She is an MP, has been a local councillor, has worked with recidivist adolescents and with the Marriage Guidance Council, is a Methodist lay preacher and a school governor. She is solid and stolid, with dark straight hair and a firm straight mouth, short but full of presence. She says that she agrees that *Babbletower* is better written than most pornography, but doesn't believe it is literature. Literature, she says, is complex and varied. *Babbletower,* like all pornography, is simple and repetitive—"like a good wank, if you'll forgive the expression." It repeats pain and hurt, and is offensive because it puts ideas into the heads of those who like hurting children. "A good wank is one thing, my lord. Hurting children's another. We live in the permissive society, I'm told. We see where that leads. It leads to Brady and Hindley hurting children. Killing children. All the rest is trappings. This book is offensive and dangerous."

Asked whether she agrees with Phyllis Pratt that fantasy might provide a beneficent release, she says she does not. "Not in my experience, it doesn't. I think that's *her* fantasy, if I may say so. Airy-fairy. I think it does more good to watch and pray, if you feel temptations, than to set pen to paper and indulge your imagination. Watch and pray." Asked by Oliphant if she believes that this goes for stabbing people with bread-knives too, she replies that that is not the issue in question. "But yes, quite probably. Watch and pray. Somebody somewhere may wield a bread-knife in earnest, as a result of reading about one." The Court stirs: they are Phyllis Pratt fans. Samuel Oliphant pushes his advantage.

"You are not a great reader, Miss Cross? You do not have a passion for literature?"

"No. I don't. I think a lot of time is wasted by a lot of people, reading rubbish, and talking rubbish about books. But I *do* know the difference, I think, between a book that is just nasty and a book that is positively hurtful."

"How do you know?"

"I know quite a lot—pragmatically—about the sort of people who are vulnerable to that sort of book. It's common sense."

"And do you consider *yourself* depraved and corrupted by *Babbletower.*"

"Sickened. Disgusted."

"That is not what I asked."

"No. But I am not its expected audience. I watch and pray."

Superintendent Wren is a large, ferociously groomed wax-skinned man, with a surprisingly light voice. His evidence is dull and cumulative, a list of cases in which it is his understanding that crimes were incited, or suggested, by reading matter. "Those that are content with reading," he says, "don't stay content, they start thinking, Why *not,* and then they go on to try it out. Like Ian Brady. They try it out." One of his examples is a man who, hearing *The Brothers Karamazov* read on the wireless, was suddenly seized with an impulse, snatched up an axe from his coalshed, and murdered his mother-in-law in her bed.

Augustine Weighall, to pre-empt the Defence, asks him, "You are not suggesting that *The Brothers Karamazov* should be banned."

"No, sir. I am not. I am just explaining, that those vulnerable to suggestion, do act on it. Now this book is not like *The Brothers Karamazov,* a difficult book, that makes you think, a human book, that makes you feel. It is a book in which nothing happens except sex and death, a typical pornographer's book—"

"Objection. The witness's opinion as to whether the book is pornographic is inadmissible."

"Objection sustained."

The suffragan bishop's name is Humphrey Swan. He is thin and sad and bespectacled and insubstantial. He says that *Babbletower* is evil, and far from presenting a Christian view of the world, as Canon Holly has argued, is quite possibly open to prosecution for blasphemy in connection with its dubious presentation of Our Lord's sufferings. He expatiates on this at some length. He says that the book *does* lead the weak into temptation, temptation to great evil.

Asked by Hefferson-Brough if he considers that he himself has been depraved and corrupted by the book, he replies that he has been dragged through dirt and made to see horrors.

Q.   I did not ask if you felt disgusted. I asked if you felt you had been depraved and corrupted.

A.   If I must answer that question, yes or no, I must answer yes. I am a worse man, a sicker soul, for having read that book. I shall take time, I shall need effort, to recover from the experience. An element of good in my soul has been slaughtered and is festering.

Q.   That is strong language, Bishop.

A.   So is the disgusting language of that book, sir. Strong and bad. Worse than bad, because it is *truly* tempting in its sensuousness. Evil. Evil.

Rupert Parrott's face is red with fury when he sees the jaunty figure of Roger Magog in the witness box. He says in a stage whisper to his solicitor, "He thought there was more attention in it for him, this way." The judge stares reprovingly. Magog states that he is an educator, a writer on matters social, literary and educational. He states that he is a member of the Steerforth Committee of Enquiry. He is wearing a red bow-tie and a kind of navy blazer. He smiles around the court, including Parrott in his benignity.

Weighall.   People may be surprised to see you in this court, Mr. Magog, appearing as a witness for the prosecution. You have,

I believe, a reputation as a liberal thinker, a defender of our liberties?

Magog.   Indeed I have. I am proud of it. I have written essays on freedom of speech. I spoke in favour of *Lady Chatterley.* I wrote articles in support of the Sexual Offences Bill, which is, as we speak, before the House of Commons, and will, I trust, reach the Statute Book this summer.

Weighall.   You wrote an article in the *Guardian,* I believe, when *Babbletower* was first published.

Magog.   I did.

Weighall.   Tell the Court about this article.

Magog.   It was called "Sticks and Stones May Break Your Bones." It argued that the written word could harm no one—no adult—and that there should not be any prohibition of any written text depicting any lawful act, as it is impossible in practice to distinguish pornography from literature, and it is more important that literature not be repressed than that pornography is *suppressed.*

Weighall.   Admirable sentiments, you may think. Yet you are prepared, now, to argue before this Court, that the tendency of *Babbletower* IS to deprave and corrupt those who may read it?

Magog.   (very firmly) I am.

Weighall.   What brought about this change?

Magog.   It was quite simple. I read the book. (Gales of laughter in court.) I knew you would laugh. You may laugh, you may all laugh, you have a right to laugh. I made a fool of myself, but I have learned something. When I wrote the article I genuinely believed *no book* could harm someone like me, someone normal and sensible and well read. It was a matter of principle. Then I read the book. It was a dreadful experience. I know now what it is to feel depraved and corrupted. This book—you may laugh—revealed things to me about myself that horrified me—that if I were a weaker man, if I were some of the unfortunate children I have taught—might have tempted me. In short—I saw the light. I deliberately use the religious language of a conversion experience. It was a sign. It is better *not* to live in a society which indulges and admires depictions of cruelty. I was made deeply uncomfortable by the *Marat-Sade,* I was disgusted and dirtied, but I believed it was for the good of my soul to see those horrors. I am told there is a writer who has made what he believes is art out of *enacting* the horrors of the Moors Murders for audiences. I am told he claims he is taking "crucial anxiety" and "turning it upside-down in creative play." I have heard that they are arguing that they should have access to corpses and disembowel them in Harrods' windows—artists have as much right as anatomists to corpses, they say. I have no doubt Mason would find it easy to justify the horrors of *Babbletower* on the same grounds. But I do not want to live in a society that can find anything—*anything at all*—playful or creative in these horrors. I have come to believe they should be—not swept under the carpet—but incinerated. Burned with flames of fire. I have had enough of the Permissive Society and before long those who advocate more and more of it will come to feel as I do, to weep for their lost cleanliness and innocence. True freedom is not freedom to hurt others.

Samuel Oliphant takes up this phrase in cross-examination.

Q. Mr. Magog. You said, "True freedom is not the freedom to hurt others."

A. I did. It isn't a fashionable thought, these days. I stand by it.

Q. But, Mr. Magog, is not that—according to Professor Smith, according to Dr. Gander, according to Mr. Wedderburn—is not that the central message of *Babbletower* itself?

A. *Babbletower* is a text that twists round and round itself like the snake round the tree. What *is* its true message? We have heard that the Marquis de Sade felt we should be free to murder and rape. The devil can dress his texts with a little morality. The message I get from *Babbletower* is Sade's message, the modish message of the moment. The author kills off his murderous hero to give his readers another sadistic kick. It is clever and disgusting and infectious.

Sir Augustine's last witness comes into the witness box slowly, and when he is there, is hardly visible above its rim. He is tiny, old and frail; he has a sweet, small face, with a parchment-coloured skin traced like an ancient map with fine lines and the brown islands of age; he wears gold-rimmed spectacles on a beaked nose, and a black silk skull cap above a fringe of baby-fine bright white hair. He wears a loose black jacket, under which his spine is humped and twisted; his hands are twigs, claws, knots of bone and vein, which grip the bar in front of him. He says that he is Professor Efraim Ziz, and teaches in Cambridge. He is an expert on Jewish history and rabbinical writings. He is a survivor of the Treblinka death camp, where he lost his wife, his children and his sisters. He is the author of *Babel and Silence,* and of *The Tongues of Men and of Angels,* studies of Jewish mystical histories of language and silence, of a book on Kafka and the German language, and of *A Private Place.* This last, he explains in a small, clear, precise voice, is an account of that sense of "an inner private, silent place" which made possible the survival of some "fortunate or unfortunate inmates of those places."

He is asked by Sir Augustine if he has read *Babbletower.*

A.   I have.

Q.   Can you give us your opinion of it.

A.   It is written by a writer of talent. It is a clever and tormented book. In the last resort, it is pornography, not literature.

Q.   Can you justify that opinion? So that the jury may understand how you arrived at it?

A.   Pornography is confined to certain aspects of human nature; it is to do with one person's power over another person's body. It reduces human beings to bodily functions—certain repetitive, emphasised, selected functions which are made public without any remnants of privacy, or secrecy (the places of imagination, gentleness, the unspoken, kindness and delight). Pornography tears away veils from shames which then fester and destroy. It diminishes humanity.

Q.   You have written about these matters, I believe.

A.   I have. I should like, if I may, to quote a passage from Maurice Girodias's *Olympia Reader,* which I criticised in my book.

      "Moral censorship was an inheritance from the past, deriving from centuries of domination by the Christian clergy. Now that it is practically over, we may expect literature to be transformed by the advent of freedom. Not freedom in its negative aspects, but as the means of exploring all the positive aspects of the human mind, which are all more or less related to, or generated by, sex."

      This is obviously a foolish statement, an exaggeration. But it is an exaggeration of a position which is taken by respectable people, including those who have eloquently defended *Babbletower.* Nothing should be hidden, nothing should be silent, nothing should be unspoken. And what should be spoken is sex, is the body *as body.* A society with no religious beliefs may reach this position logically. Nietzsche, to whom Mr. Mason is so attached, wrote, "Once Spirit was God, then it became man, now it is becoming mob." Mob is public man as pure animal, as pure body. I have seen the power of totalitarian states; I have seen the power of those who had total freedom—total *permission*—to do as they pleased with the bodies of others. There are limits to this power. There are *not so many things* you can do to bodies. But those who "enjoy" this freedom—in all senses of the word "enjoy"—resemble each other.

It is not only—perhaps not mostly—what Efraim Ziz says that has its effect on the crowded courtroom, perhaps on the jury. It is his physical presence, his frailty, his age, his survival, his gentleness, his sweet seriousness. Samuel Oliphant rises to ask him, as he has asked Magog, whether he cannot accept that *Babbletower* is on his side, is making his own points, is "opposed to total or totalitarian freedom."

Ziz replies:

"Mr. Mason has used the myth of the Tower of Babel, which is a myth about language and God, to make a modern point about the human body and its freedom and its sufferings. There is a long tradition of rabbinical commentary on the fact that the inhabitants of the Tower were not all destroyed, as the inhabitants of Sodom and Gomorrah were, or the whole generation before the Flood. And this

was, according to Rabbi Juda ha Nassa, because they loved each other. They worked together. After their presumption they were not destroyed, but were taught eighty languages by the eighty angels around the throne of God. Speech and writing were made *more difficult* for them, but they were saved. Whereas Mr. Mason's people are not saved, because there is nothing but total freedom and the body in his book. They are not dignified. There is no hope."

Q. You sound as though you are describing a pessimistic book, but a work of literary merit?

A. I do not say there is no literary merit. I say there is not enough. Not enough to save the book from doing more harm than good to those who read it.

Q. Your view is that of a religious teacher?

A. Yes. And it is that of an expert in pain, who wishes to see less of it in the world.

The barristers make their final speeches. Sir Augustine is clear and on the whole unemotional. He reiterates the point that *Babbletower* is repetitive and constricted in its subject matter; he quotes one or two of the most distressing passages; he quotes also a passage from Sade.

Is murder a crime in the eyes of Nature? Doubtless we will humiliate man's pride in reducing him to the ranks of other productions of Nature, but nevertheless he is merely an animal like any other, and in the eyes of Nature his death is no more important than that of a fly or an ox. . . . Destruction is Nature's method of progress, and she prompts the murderer to destruction, so that his action shall be the same as plague or famine. . . . In a word, murder is a horror, but a horror often necessary, never criminal, and essential to tolerate in a republic.

Who, he asks, copied out and studied this passage? Who referred to the innocent victims of his sadistic crimes as animals? Ian Brady, the murderer, who shared his reading matter and the nihilism, the desperate vision derived from it, with his dazzled victim and fellow criminal, Myra Hindley. "Do not believe, members of the jury," says Sir Augustine, "that cruel acts and cruel visions cannot be passed on, from one human being to another. The well-intentioned 'experts' who have amused and bemused us with their academic dissertations on the harmless pleasures of sado-masochism and their determined cheerful *liberal* willingness to say that 'everything goes,' refused, almost to a man and woman, to admit that they were sexually or viscerally stirred by the excesses of *Babbletower*. They refused to admit that their flesh tingled or crawled when they read of the torture of little Felicitas or the ingenious death of the Lady Roseace. They are expert witnesses, they are specialist witnesses. Professor Marie-France Smith is a beautiful woman, a cool Frenchwoman, who, for reasons best known to herself, chooses to spend her time studying the sexual dottiness of M. Fourier and the nasty doctrines of the evil Marquis. Canon Holly, a Christian clergyman, is willing to equate the most grotesque fancies of Jude Mason with the sufferings of his Lord. Dr. Gander is harder to follow, but it is clear that his normal responses to depictions of pain, of sexual excitement, of the desire to hurt, are hopelessly entangled in abstract words to which he can give any meaning he chooses—words like 'liberation,' words like 'freedom,' words like 'oppression'—words which can only have the odd meanings they have for him because in fact he lives in a decent society where he is free to say what he pleases because his rights are protected by the vigilance of courts like this, and juries composed of sensible people such as yourselves.

"You have read the book, members of the jury. I do not know how you responded to it. You may have been disgusted, you may have been sickened, you may have been stirred in ways that disturbed you. Your flesh may have crawled, as mine did. I have appeared in many obscenity cases, ladies and gentlemen, and I can tell you that most pornography is sickening in quite a different way from *Babbletower*. It is sickening because it is boring, it is grotesque, not threatening, it is against life because it appeals from dead imaginations to dull imaginations. I will grant that *Babbletower* is better written than the trash which normally, in horrible bulk, appears before the courts. It is more disturbing for that reason. It is more potent. The expert witnesses have told you at some length that this is because of its literary merit. They have also told you that it is hard to assess the literary merit of contemporary works. They have told you their reasons for wanting this book published, and they have told you—most of them—that it has not stirred them up. I think you know better than that, members of the jury. I think your responses are simpler and more honest, not tied up in abstract languages and doctrinaire beliefs. I think you are better judges of what Ian Brady and Myra Hindley might make of *Babbletower*—and not only them, but smaller sadists, ready to do smaller hurts that are nevertheless hurts.

"I believe that Mr. Parrott is a good man, an honest man, a well-intentioned man, and a slightly foolish man, who has been misled by modish rhetoric and mistaken libertarian idealism to take risks that he would have been better to have turned away from. I believe Mr. Mason is a man whose mind and body were depraved and corrupted in his youth—even in his childhood—and I feel a great deal of sympathy for him. My learned friend Mr. Hefferson-Brough obviously feels personal sympathy for the sufferings of this Erstwhile Hog, and I extend mine to him. I believe that Mr. Mason's early experiences did lead directly to his later way of life, his acquaintance with the seamier aspects of our society, and to the form and content of *Babbletower* itself. I believe you may have read, as I have, that it is an accepted understanding, nowadays, that child-beaters have been beaten children, and that those who exploit innocent children sexually have themselves, often, been so exploited as children themselves. It is known as a circle of deprivation—or perhaps a circle of depravity—and it is our duty, as responsible human beings, to break it. Mr. Mason has been hurt, and he is trying—perhaps even unconsciously—to hurt others.

"You have been told—and I tell you again—that discussion of motive, of intention, is irrelevant in deciding whether a work has a tendency to deprave and corrupt. Mr. Parrott may be a good man, and Mr. Mason may believe he is a serious artist, but the first question for you is whether *Babbletower* has a tendency to deprave and corrupt—to deprave and corrupt not *literary experts,* but ordinary men and women, trying to live their lives, men and women who can be tempted or crushed by despair. If you decide that the book has such a tendency, you must then consider whether it has sufficient literary or other merit—sufficient gravity, grace, seriousness, beauty—to outweigh the detrimental effects of this tendency on ordinary readers. Whose testimony will you trust in this? Those long-winded experts, who see the whole thing through a cloud of their own complex terms and good intentions, or the wise Professor Ziz, who believes the book is a dangerous book, is 'pornography not literature' and is himself 'an expert in pain who wishes to see less of it in the world.' "

Hefferson-Brough's speech is longer, noisier, and more repetitive than Sir Augustine's. He says frequently that "in this day and age" much is acceptable that would once have been thought obscene libel, and does not give the impression that he is sure that this is for the best. He says that it is right to publish serious studies of sadism and masochism, and it is right also to make serious literary representations of them. He speaks passionately, and at too great length, in the general perception, of the harm done by secrecy and silence at places like Swineburn, by people like Dr. Grisman Gould. He uses tired words—"brilliant," "outstanding," "promising," "talented"—of Jude Mason, and speaks warmly of the responsibility of Rupert Parrott, of the unlikelihood of Bowers and Eden being found in the position of publishing anything that tends to deprave and corrupt. He praises the good sense of Alexander Wedderburn and Phyllis Pratt; he demolishes Roger Magog with his only literary reference.

"Mr. Facing-both-ways was a character in *Pilgrim's Progress*. Mr. Magog likes to pronounce upon issues of the day. No doubt you will find him pronouncing in favour of *Babbletower* at some point in the future, as he pronounced in favour of it last week." Of Efraim Ziz's evidence he says, perhaps unfortunately, that concentration camp guards can no more be thought of as typical probable readers than can Ian Brady or Myra Hindley. "Ordinary, responsible English people are not like that, ladies and gentlemen. They are like you and me. They can take these things in their stride. If we are to ban all books that might encourage monsters to be monstrous we should start with the Brothers Grimm and the giant who cries fee-fi-fo-fum, I smell the blood of an Englishman. Because some people in some places have ground up bones and made bread we mustn't forbid fairytales. And the eminently sensible Mrs. Pratt has told us that that is what *Babbletower* is—a fairytale."

Samuel Oliphant reads out various passages of *Babbletower*, none of them sexual or sadistic: the descriptions of the woods, the remarks of Samson Origen, the descriptions of the tower and its daily life. He reads well. He says, "Is this depraving or corrupting? Or is it good writing, by a young man whose career stands in danger of being mined by the enthusiasm of moral zealots, out of touch with the times. A young man whose life has been hard, but who has, in circumstances of pain and difficulty, written a brilliant, daring and moving book, for which he should be being rewarded, rather than castigated and punished? A young man, who, far from being a seducer and a tempter, is a stern moralist and a tragic poet."

The jury look at their hands, at the ceiling, at the prisoner in the dock.

Mr. Justice Gordale Balafray sums up. His summing up is dry, and he thanks the jury for their patience, giving the impression that his own has sometimes been tested. He tells them that they are to decide the question of obscenity—of whether the book, as a whole, has a tendency to deprave and corrupt. If, and only if, they come to the conclusion that it has, they must decide on whether the work has sufficient literary merit—or other quality of value to society—to outweigh the tendency to deprave and corrupt. "The Defence has raised a defence under Section 4, which entails, as we have seen, the calling of expert witnesses. As we are all aware, the world these days is a world of specialised knowledge and is full of experts on everything under the sun. But English criminal law is based upon the view that a jury takes of the facts and not upon the view that experts may have. You, ladies and gentlemen of the jury, are the sole judges of the facts in this case. It is my place to put the law to you, but the facts—both as to the tendency to deprave and corrupt, and as to the literary or other arguments which may outweigh that tendency—are yours and yours alone to decide. You have heard the dictionary definitions of the words 'deprave' and 'corrupt.' I do not know if I can improve on those definitions, or elaborate on the meaning of the word 'tendency.' "

The judge goes on to recapitulate the evidence. On the whole, he is fair and appears to lean to neither side, though he becomes testy when faced with the evidence of Canon Holly and Elvet Gander, and says, "You may think that the Prosecution has a point when it refers to the obfuscating language of some of the so-called experts, their use of words in ways contrary to commonsense interpretations of those words, and so on. You are here to uphold the commonsense virtues, to represent ordinary men and women." He remarks, also, that in Canada only five witnesses may appear for each side, and states that "there is some attraction in this restriction, you may think, in this concentration of witness."

He speaks of the jury's solemn duty to balance the decision as to whether the book is obscene against the difficult assessment—"more difficult, as both sides admit, in the case of a new book, by a living author—of its literary or other merit." He reiterates, "You, the jury, are to be the sole judges of these things. You are to decide, on the basis of what you have read and heard, whether this book is obscene, and, if it is, whether its merits outweigh this obscenity sufficiently for the publication of the book to be in the public interest."

The jury retires. The Bowers and Eden people discuss whether or not the judge's summing up was hostile or friendly: the fact that they cannot decide is felt to be on the whole a good sign. Canon Holly ventures the opinion that they have put up a strong fight, and Rupert Parrott says, "Shut up," and then apologises. The judge sentences some prisoners who are already convicted. Jude Mason has disappeared somewhere. Frederica cannot imagine his feelings. Avram Snitkin tells her that no jury will convict for obscenity "in this day and age." Frederica snaps, "I don't want to hear that phrase again." "Why?" says Snitkin. "It's a pompous cliché." "Its got a precise meaning." "Its connotations are horrid. Anyway you're wrong. I've been looking at their faces. They hated Canon Holly. They thought Jude was putting them down. They didn't like him." "Juries don't work on 'like' and 'not like,' you know. They take their duties very seriously. They aren't coming back."

After three hours, the jury return to enquire whether they have to decide the question of obscenity separately from, and before, the question of literary merit. The judge tells them that this is indeed so. The foreman says that this is difficult, given that they have, so to speak, heard everything at once, both sides of the matter. The judge agrees that it is difficult, and says he wishes he could help them further.

After five hours, they return. Jude Mason returns to the dock. The clerk speaks into the silence.

Members of the jury, are you agreed upon a verdict?

Foreman. We are.

Clerk. Do you find that Bowers and Eden are guilty or not guilty of publishing an obscene article?

Foreman. Guilty.

Clerk. Do you find that Jude Mason is guilty or not guilty of publishing an obscene article?

Foreman. Guilty.

There is a general hesitation in the Court. The judge says, "Let us be quite clear. You find the publishers and the author guilty of publishing an obscene article. A defence has been raised under Section Four of the Obscene Publications Act, arguing that the book has literary and other merits that outweigh the alleged obscenity of the book. Do you find such merits in the book in question?"

Foreman.   No, my lord. We do not.

Clerk.   And that is the verdict of you all?

Foreman.   It is.

Frederica finds she is weeping. Rupert Parrott listens white-faced to the judge, who says that the book has been published in good faith by an honourable firm, imposes a small fine (£500) and orders all copies of the book to be seized. The judge then turns to Jude.

"It is possible for me to impose a sentence of imprisonment upon you, but it seems to me that it would be wrong to do so. Evidence has been given, including your own, that you see your work as a serious work of art, although the jury has found otherwise. I shall impose a fine of fifty pounds, having regard to your clear lack of means to pay any greater fine."

"I knew you were all against me," says Jude.

XXI

Rupert Parrott declares his intention to appeal. The lawyers advise against it, on grounds of expense, of the unlikelihood of success, of waste of time and effort. It will take a long time, they say, and a great deal of money, to acquire the court records, which are in any case only selective. Parrott says that he has a complete record of his own, recorded by the diligent Avram Snitkin, and sets his secretary to the transcribing of this document. He speaks of engaging a new barrister, since Hefferson-Brough is firmly set against going any further. Mention is made of John Mortimer, a young playwright and divorce lawyer who is also having some success in this field. A correspondence of some acrimony begins in *The Times* about jurors, and exactly what, or who, the commonsense common man is whom they are supposed to represent. A fund is started for the Defence of the Arts against legal onslaughts from the Establishment. It is not very well subscribed. Samuel Oliphant is more in favour of an appeal than Godfrey Hefferson-Brough, and spends some time perusing the typescript of Snitkin's tapes as it piles up in Miss Patty Stott's out-tray. There is a snag. His client has disappeared. He went to the lavatory whilst Parrott was making statements to the Press at the end of the trial, and has not been seen since. Letters to his convenience address remain unanswered. His slots before the art students are filled by an ex-boxer, chocolate-coloured and muscular.

Frederica does not really listen to Parrott's troubles about the loss of Jude, because she has troubles of her own. The custody hearing approaches, and Jude's trial has made Frederica even more despondent than she would have been. She feels that both she and Jude are naughty children whose naughtinesses have found them out, have been judged by the inscrutable rules of the inscrutable grown-up world to be not naughtiness but grave crimes. She feels too, as children do feel, that what she thought was the grown-up world, and believed to operate by logic, operates in fact according to the system created out of its own prejudices and emotions, which cannot be second-guessed. She and Jude have been made to recite travesties of their life stories, in language they would never have chosen for themselves. They have been judged and found wanting. In a sense, it does not matter. Who cares, Frederica thinks, what those twelve stolid and baffled people think of *Babbletower,* what His Honour Judge Plumb makes of educated women or sex after the Pill? But these things do matter. Jude's book will not be read, and worse, worse, Leo will be taken from her.

At first she draws comfort from the frequent visits and reassurances of Anthea Barlow, who exclaims brightly that she has established a real *rapport* with little Leo, who is "wise for his years," who is "a constant surprise to me"—"You must be so proud of him, Mrs. Reiver." Later Frederica begins to feel irritation with Mrs. Barlow's over-frequent quotations from Julian of Norwich. "All shall be well, and all shall be well, and all manner of thing shall be well, Mrs. Reiver."

"You don't *know* that."

"I believe it. Dame Julian was talking of the long term, of course. You don't have any religious beliefs, Mrs. Reiver?"

"No," says Frederica, reflecting that even here, where she is simply being intellectually truthful, she is open to judgement, judgement which may take her child from her. "My brother-in-law is a clergyman," says Frederica lamely.

"All shall be well and all shall be well and all manner of thing shall be well. By the purification of the motive in the ground of our beseeching. That's how Dame Julian goes on. By the purification of the motive."

"I'm not quite sure what you mean."

"Oh, I'm just chattering. You must want what's best for Leo, for dear Leo, Mrs. Reiver."

Frederica has a vision of fields and paddocks, of woods and hills, an English vision. She sees Sooty's stolid black figure swishing through meadow grass in a slight drizzle.

"Nothing is altogether best," she says. "It's not black and white. It's a mess. Most of life is. Courts don't seem to know that."

"Oh, of course they do. They don't see life at those rare moments when it isn't a mess, you must remember. Mess is their business. You must have faith."

"They believed all those lies those women told. Olive and Rosalind and Pippy Mammott."

"It may not be the same judge, Mrs. Reiver. Have faith."

But it is the same judge. The custody hearing takes place before His Honour Judge Plumb. This time Leo is taken to the courtroom, and sits with Mrs. Barlow whilst his parents tell the judge what arrangements they have made for his welfare. Nigel's barrister has brought photographs, of Bran House, of the orchard, of Leo's room; he has also brought photographs of the pile of bed-heads and rotting chairs in Hamelin Square, luridly lit by the bonfire, in whose shadows the black children dance. He explains that Leo's place is assured at Brock's and Swineburn. "I need not assure Your Honour that the Swineburn of the 1960s is a very different place from the Swineburn that has been so much in the press since the *Babbletower* case. It is a traditional but forward-looking school, with high standards and a kindly regime." He explains that the three women of Bran House are in the Court and ready to speak, or to give any help they can to describe the loving home that awaits Leo—as it always has—since he was snatched away from it.

Nigel speaks. He is brief, he is sensible. He says his son is his son and he is fortunate enough to be able to provide for his security and loving care. He says he does not doubt that his ex-wife loves the boy in her way, but he does not think she is the type to be interested in kids, not really, and she will find she can do very well by visiting and so forth, which she will be free to do. He says he doesn't like the look of the place where she is living or the kinds of friends she has, and he doesn't want Leo to grow up there. He speaks brusquely, man to man, looking the judge in the eye, confident but anxious *enough*.

Pippy Mammott speaks. She says that the boy's mother has never loved him, that she isn't maternal, that she only wants the boy to spite his family, that she herself is his real mother, has looked after his sicknesses, taught him to tie his little shoes, done *everything* whilst "she" looked on, or "sulked," or "read books."

Frederica speaks. Or tries to speak. She is inaudible. The judge peers down at her, his long white face creased into a frown.

"Speak up."

"I'm sorry. I wanted to say, the square isn't like that, now. It's gentrified. We've got a circular lawn, with a yin-yang pattern in bricks. The dump's gone. We all contributed."

"I see."

"It's important not to make it look worse than it is. Because any arrangements I make can't compete with Bran House. I wouldn't want Leo not to go there. But he wants to be with me, and my arrangements are good, and will work—though it is harder for a woman to work, and look after a child, than a man. But we are two women, two responsible women, Your Honour, two efficient women. I know the Bran House people love Leo—he loves them—but I too have feelings about tradition and family. My family is a bookish family, a *thinking* family—it matters as much to me that Leo should grow up in a house *full of books,* as it does to his father that there should be a pony and woods. And I care about schools and I happen to think it's *wicked* to send away little boys to sleep in dormitories when they could be at home with their mothers. You may not agree, but it is a belief I do hold, and Leo is my son. My father was a schoolmaster in a boarding school, a very liberal one, so I know what I'm talking about.

"I know I've been criticised. You criticised me, when you heard the divorce. Some of the evidence you heard was lies, but that's over, that's done. It isn't ideal to have to try to earn your living and bring up a son—and I won't take maintenance for me, I don't want it—it isn't ideal, but it can be done. If I were the person they say I am, I wouldn't even be *trying* to keep Leo. When you heard the divorce, you asked if I meant to take him when I left. I said I thought of leaving him because it would be better for him, but he insisted on coming. Please understand—*that is what happened.* I thought of leaving him, and he came, and—he's a little boy, but he knows what he's doing. I wouldn't think of it again. Unless he asked."

Judge Plumb says: And if he asked?

Frederica: I'd listen, I suppose. He's his own—

She cannot speak.

Judge Plumb asks to speak to Mrs. Barlow, alone. Mrs. Barlow comes out of the Court and says the judge wants to see Leo, who has been taken away to "play" somewhere else. There is a long wait. Then all the parties file back into the Court. Frederica feels ill. Her life has passed, in this moment, entirely out of her control. She was proud and fierce and independent: she was clever and free and wild. And now she is in a room full of people all of whom exercise control, influence, over her future, because of the existence of an absent small boy whose rights and desires are more important to her than her own. She thinks, briefly, that sex made Leo, and remembers pleasure with Nigel, which seems to have nothing to do with Leo. She feels emptied, and knows that everything will be taken from her. She does not even hear the beginning of the judge's remarks.

". . . there had to be substantial doubt in this case whether the very strong presumption in the favour of the mother, the biological presumption that she would care for the child, that the child needed her physical presence, at least in the early years, would apply. Mrs. Reiver has been described—by those unfriendly to her—as 'not the maternal type,' and it is true that she is not an archetypal mother-figure. But few real women are, yet most bring up children. Miss Mammott is extremely motherly, and whereas Mrs. Reiver showed no signs of resentment towards Miss Mammott for her role in the little boy's upbringing, Miss Mammott displayed a spitefulness towards Mrs. Reiver, a possessiveness about the boy, which I did not find wholly encouraging. It has been eloquently argued, on Mr. Reiver's behalf, that his family is old and has traditions his son may inherit. I was however struck by Mrs. Reiver's argument that her own more modest family also has traditions, which she may reasonably expect her son to adhere to. It takes all sorts to make a world, the sporting and the bookish, the entrepreneurial and the intellectual.

"I am entirely convinced that both parents love Leo very deeply, and are primarily interested in his welfare. In this he is a fortunate little boy, compared to many who appear before me. It is clear that he would be less comfortable living with his mother than with his father, but comfort is not everything. And as an old boy of a particularly spartan prep school and public school I am inclined—which may surprise her—to agree with Mrs. Reiver that little boys, at least, are best at home, with those who love them.

"I have been very impressed with the clarity and perceptiveness of Mrs. Barlow's accounts of her conversations with both the father and the mother, the people at Bran House and the people in Hamelin Square. She herself is very impressed with the intelligence of the little boy, and after speaking to her, I have myself spoken this morning to Leo. I always take off my robes on such occasions, so as not to frighten the children more than can be helped. It is quite clear to me from talking to Leo—and, indeed, from what Mrs. Barlow reports—that he wishes to stay with his mother. He does not wish to lose contact with his father or his old home but he fears the loss of his mother as the worst thing—"the *bad thing*" that could happen to him. Mrs. Barlow has suggested that there may be an element of fear *that his mother would leave him,* in his fear that he will be taken from her. These are deep waters. They need not concern this Court, since it is quite clear what the boy wants, and he is able to state his wishes fearlessly, and in the expectation of being listened to—on which his parents are to be congratulated.

"I therefore award joint custody of the boy to his father and his mother—with an expressed wish that his mother's wishes should prevail on his early schooling at least. I award care and control of the boy to his mother, Frederica Reiver."

Outside the court again, Frederica stands giddy, looking round for Leo. There is a scuffling sound, and a shrill cry, and she feels a violent pain on the right side of her head. Pippy Mammott has rushed up and swung her heavy handbag at Frederica's face. The sharp clasp cuts her eye-corner: her cheek begins to swell into a grazed, bleeding bruise. The Bran House people gather round Pippy, who is crying hysterically, and pull and hustle her away. Nigel stops to study Frederica, but Mrs. Barlow has taken Frederica in charge, has a Persian lamb arm round her shoulder—she smells of Je Reviens—and is drawing her away down a corridor. In some curious way, this moment of violence is a release. Nigel calls, "I'll see you," Frederica nods, her head bowed over a bloodied handkerchief. Heels tap on stone: the opponents hurry apart. In a kind of antechamber Frederica finds Leo. She begins to cry. Anthea Barlow brings a bowl of warm water, with cotton wool, and dabs at Frederica's cheek. Tears run into the water. Leo sits beside her, his body pushed against hers. Frederica smells disinfectant, Je Reviens, and Leo's hair, Leo's warm red hair. He does not discuss his experiences. He does not ask how she hurt herself. He winds his fingers in hers, and says, "When can we go home?"

Spring 1967 runs into summer. The gentrification of Hamelin Square continues: tubs of geraniums and tiny cypresses appear and are stolen, more windows are painted white, a park bench appears on the grass, is stolen, and is replaced with a more stolid one, bolted to the earth, with a bright green waste bin, also bolted to the earth, next to it. Homosexual behaviour (in private) and abortion are made legal. The world explodes in colour: the Beatles produce *Sergeant Pepper's Lonely*

Hearts Club Band, with its Peter Blake cover on which the four moustachioed majordomos in brilliant satin uniforms stand beside their suited waxwork selves of 1963, under the cardboard eyes of Karl Marx, Laurel and Hardy, Alistair Crowley, Cassius Clay, Mona Lisa, W. C. Fields and Tarzan. The songs are full of brilliance, "Lucy in the Sky with Diamonds," tangerine trees and marmalade skies. BBC2 begins to transmit in colour. Frederica has a colour TV because she has acquired a small TV column in a women's magazine which flares briefly under the name of *Boadicea,* with mini-skirted, glacé-booted, gold-macintoshed career women striding through it. She cannot stop watching, and neither can Leo. The colours are rich, are jewelled, are electric and psychedelic after the small grainy grey worlds of *Muffin the Mule, The Virginian* and *Batman.* An orange cut in half is a glistening revelation, an open rose is a visual drama, the Queen's pink and blue and green and yellow outfits seem absurd and inappropriate, as they did not in mere black and white. The *Report of the Steerforth Committee* is published. It is a fat document in two volumes and arouses a storm of protest—*Charter for Permissiveness, The Beginning of the Age of Ignorance, Fetter Our Children with Rote Learning, Why Do They Not Realise That Education Is Oppression, Out of Touch Committee, Committee Unacceptably Child-Centred, Where Are Our Verbs and Conjunctions, Participles Depart* and so on. Roger Magog adds a note of protest saying that the committee has failed to understand the need for partnership and trust between pupils and teachers. Guy Croom adds a dry note predicting that certain skills are about to disappear for ever. No journalist reads the document through, and its conclusions are often stated to be the opposite of what their authors believe they are. Alexander commissions a series of modern-dress Shakespeare scenes for educational television, and thinks of writing a Brechtian play about the French Revolution.

Cassius Clay tears up his draft papers and refuses to join the war against the coloured people of Asia in Vietnam. In June the Israelis win an efficient and passionate Six-Day War against the Egyptians and the Jordanians: they take possession of Jerusalem, and process to the Wailing Wall, despite booby-trap bombs which explode amongst the trumpets.

In July the Round House is given over to a Congress on the Dialectics of Liberation, which is addressed by anti-psychiatrists who believe that the human race is being destroyed by illusion and mystification; by

Stokely Carmichael, who believes the Third World and the American blacks must get the guns from the white man and use them; by Herbert Marcuse, who is happy to see flowers and believes in a Marxian liberation of the instinctual self from technology. Violent attacks are made, verbally, on mass suicide and mass murder, and David Cooper sums up, calling his summing up *Beyond Words,* calling for an end to "the opposition between subject-object, white-black; oppressor-oppressed one; colonizer-colonized; torturer-tortured; murderer-murdered one; psychiatrist-patient; teacher-taught; keeper-kept; the cannibal-the one who is eaten up; the fucker-the fucked; the shitter-the shitted upon." There is an orchestra of piano frame, metal pipes, milk crates, tin cans. There are flowers everywhere, blooming and wilting.

Plans proceed to appeal against the *Babbletower* decision. There is concern over the non-appearance of Jude Mason; there is a theory that he has fled to Paris again and an underlying, suppressed fear that he may be dead. Another person who has not been seen is John Ottokar, who has made no sign of life since he was called a co-respondent. Frederica has given him up; she is proud, she will not telephone his place of work; if he does not want to see her, she has other things to do. She goes back once or twice to Desmond Bull's studio, goes dancing with Hugh Pink, who dances badly, but has sold a volume of poems—*Orpheus Underground*—to Rupert Parrott. It is a strange, hectic time. It will come to seem much longer in memory than it is, as though Flower Power went on and on. To most people the noise, the smells, the brilliance, are peripheral, are words only, go past whilst they cook or push pushchairs or nurse the elderly, or work in shops and banks and laboratories, wandering into clubs or festivals, once, or twice, or more often. In June 1967 the "spontaneous underground" UFO sprouts the Electric Garden in Covent Garden, which opens with a fight between supporters of Yoko Ono and the Exploding Galaxy. Avram Snitkin is now conducting ethnomethodological research into flower people, electric gardens, Technicolor dreams and alchemical weddings. He has taken a fancy to Frederica and invites her to come along with him from time to time, but she does not go until August, when the Electric Garden has folded and re-opened as the Middle-Earth.

In July Leo is seven and Frederica is summoned to see his teacher at a parents' evening. She sits with Agatha in the school hall, under a dangling forest of paper streamers of paper flowers, pinned to cotton threads attached to the paint with blue-tack and drawing-pins. They wait in line, until the teacher—a young woman in a kind of suede tunic, with long hair like Minnehaha's and eyes painted round in black—can give them their ten minutes. Frederica sits, when her moment comes, hunched over the low desk.

"He's doing just fine, Mrs. Reiver. Such a bright little boy."

"He is, isn't he?"

"His relationships with the others are good, no problems there, he has lots of friends."

"I'm so glad."

"He hasn't started reading independently yet, of course, he's a bit late with that. I expect he's a slow developer."

"What?"

"I expect he's a slow developer. As far as reading goes."

"There must be some mistake. He has an enormous vocabulary. He said 'incandescent' the other day. He talks about 'prototype' jets and 'machinations.' "

"I expect he does. He probably doesn't have the motor skills. Don't worry."

"Listen—he can read *all Beatrix Potter*. He reads them *to me*."

"Reads, or recites, Mrs. Reiver? He's probably too clever for his own good, for his reading, that is."

"He reads them to Saskia."

"Saskia is a fast reader. Don't worry, Mrs. Reiver, all children develop at different speeds. He'll learn."

"But my family is a reading family—"

"I expect you put him off. A bit, you know. Too much emphasis, too many expectations. Go easy on him."

"But if he *can't read*—he can't learn *anything*—"

"Don't worry, Mrs. Reiver."

She looks at her watch.

Frederica talks to Agatha. She says, "He can't read, I didn't *notice,* he talks all the time, I'm dreadful—"

"I did wonder," says Agatha. "I tried him out once or twice. Saskia's quick. He's impatient. He can't be bothered with the little words, and he can't run at the big ones. They teach them with all sorts of methods, look-and-say, ITA, all sorts of experiments, some of which work with some children, some of which don't. Don't worry. There are people I know who can help. It's early days."

Frederica is desolate. She says nothing to Leo. She listens to him "read" *The Tale of Mr. Tod* and feels, when he goes to Bran House for his summer holiday, that she deserves to lose him. It has not occurred to her that Leo could be *her son* and not read.

August comes. The Beatles go to meditate with the Maharishi and Brian Epstein kills himself. The Beatles return. They say the Maharishi has told them not to mourn. Jude Mason is still lost, and Frederica, restless and lonely, goes to the Middle Earth with Avram Snitkin. Avram Snitkin is observing, not dancing. He has brought with him a notebook with an *art nouveau* cover in purple and gold and silver, and a paper bag full of fudge. He takes out the pieces of fudge and arranges them in a row on the edge of the table in front of him. "Have some," he says. "It's hashish fudge, it's a good recipe, it'll do you good." His eyes are moist with happiness, his hair floats gingery towards his shoulders, his beard bunches, his bare crown gleams purple and green, orange and rose, yellow and crimson, in the strobe lighting. He squats like a stolid dwarf in a corner and smokes his own rolled cigarettes, reaching out meditatively from time to time and ingesting the hashish fudge. Frederica wants to take a piece, and does not. She is a northern Puritan, getting back control of her own life. She has a little flowered shift, with cut-away armpits, a little girl's shift, covered with great innocent white daisies and brilliant blue convolvulus, on a black ground. The points of her red helmet of hair lick her white cheeks.

"Do dance," says Avram Snitkin, "if you feel like it." He takes another chunk of fudge. Frederica looks around. The place is like a warehouse, or a hangar. It is concrete, coloured only by the moving lights, which weave and dance and swirl, giddy and violent. It is full of scented smoke; the smoke changes the light, thickening it, filtering it, catching it and twisting it. The noise threads through the light. Somewhere, a long way away, a band is playing, a group is singing. Avram Snitkin likes to be marginal; they are in an alcove, round a corner, they cannot see the players.

Frederica is not musical. She is a not a child of her time in this. She is torn apart by the noise. By the amplification of the throb, by the howl, by the blast. By the thrum, by the beat, by the rhythm, by the reprise, by the clash. It gives her no pleasure. It explodes the blood in her ears, it appears to be jabbing through her kidneys, it is pain, it is pain, it is pain.

They are dancing. They are gyrating, dreamily, in their conical witch-shifts, in their elven robes, in their falling black layers of cheesecloth, in their silver-and-white net, in their *fleurs du mal,* purple and black, in their white roses and moonflowers. They sway like snakes piped to, they twist and turn slowly, they move all together to the rhythm, smiling slightly, intent in their incantations and evocations. They are all dancing together, but there are no couples. Frederica is good at jiving—she can twist and turn at the end of a man's arm, spiral away and stamp and laugh and come back. Jive is sex, jive is a swing, jive leaves you laughing and breathless. These creatures—most of them are girls—are like mushrooms, like twining flowers, they go round and back, all together, all separate, a group, no individuals, no pairs.

"I do empathise with these people," says Avram Snitkin. He pops in another cube of fudge. His smile is beatific. "I do empathise with these people." Frederica looks at his notebook. He has written, "I do empathise with these people," drawn a smiley-face, added a copperplate alphabet and a series of loops followed by another, round which he has drawn a snake.

He repeats, "I do empathise with these people."

Frederica gets up and walks carefully round the dancers, looking for the loo. The noise increases. It is a not-unsubtle noise, turned up to a howl, to a screech, to a scream. She catches a glimpse of the group that is playing. The lead singer has a loose coat of multi-coloured satin patches with huge silver cuffs and lapels. His trousers are white satin and he wears a kind of Augustus John hat in white satin. He is waving a white stick wound round with flowers and ribbons. His head is thrown back, his throat throbs with his ululations, his face is John Ottokar's face.

Frederica turns round and starts walking back again. She thinks she must go home. Her teeth are blue, her hands are green, her hair is murky purple. She sifts smoke, she slides between dreaming figures.

She makes her way back to Avram Snitkin, who says or shouts, "I do empathise with these people."

Frederica cannot speak. Two lines of Herbert come into her head.

> *Thus thinne and leane, without a fence or friend*
> *I was blown through, with ev'ry storm and winde.*

She begins to say them to herself like a mantra. Later, whenever anyone says "the sixties," this is what she will think of, Zag and the Szyzgy (Ziggy) Zy-Goats singing in the Middle-Earth, the hum become a howl, the maze of light, the crowd of single dancers. Thus thinne and leane, without a fence or friend, *I do empathise with these people,* I was blown through, by every wand'ring wind. Blown through, blown through, blown through.

"We need Jude to sign the appeal form," says Rupert Parrott. "Frederica, you were always our lead to him. Can't you find him?"

"There's not been a squeak out of him. All the Press fuss, no one has had any idea."

"You don't think he's jumped in the river?"

"I would have thought," says Samuel Oliphant, "that he'd have made sure we saw him jump, or at least found his floating body."

"I thought that at first. I'm not so sure now. Don't we know *any-one* who might know where he is?"

"Daniel," says Frederica. "He used to phone Daniel, in that crypt. Daniel and Canon Holly."

Frederica and Rupert Parrott go round to St. Simeon's. Daniel is sitting in his egg-box cubicle, talking to a schoolboy who has failed his A-levels and taken six codeine pills. He is persuading him to go to a hospital. After a bit the boy puts the phone down, whether because he is bored or because he is sleepy or because he has despaired is not quite clear. Daniel writes up the conversation, ending, "I think he knew six codeines won't kill him but I may be wrong." He says, "What brings you here?"

"Jude. We can't find Jude. We need him to sign the appeal form. And we're worried about him, of course. We'd like to be sure he's all right. Obviously we would."

"He hasn't been here."

"Has he called?" says Frederica.

"That would be confidential, if he had. But he hasn't, no."

"Do you have *any idea* of where he lived?"

"Not really. South London, I had the impression, I don't know why."

"He came 'home' on the Tube with me once."

"South London's very big," says Rupert. "And he might have gone elsewhere. Anywhere else, except he had no money."

"No bank account?"

"No. He took postal orders. Or cash."

Daniel turns over the log of the early days, when Jude Mason was the anonymous and irritating Steelwire. Whilst they are doing this research, Ginnie Greenhill comes in, offers tea, and asks what they are doing.

"I remember something," she says. "I do remember something." She thinks.

"I almost had a conversation with him once, when Daniel was away, in Yorkshire. He talked about living at the top of a tower."

"That was his book."

"No, no. He said, 'No one wants to live where I live because a child fell from here, from the top of the tower.' "

"That was *his book,*" says Rupert Parrott. "A child fell from the top of Babbletower."

"Well, perhaps he put the fall in his book," says Ginnie Greenhill, who has not read the book.

"He says all sorts of things," says Daniel.

"We could try," says Ginnie Greenhill. "We could ask the local newspapers and the social services about children who fell from the tops of towers. In South London."

This search takes time. More children have fallen than they expected, from towers in Rotherhithe, in Brixton, in Peckham, in Stockwell. They ask the councils who lives in the flats from which the children fell, and find no one resembling Jude Mason. The most hopeful is the Wastwater Tower in Stockwell, on an estate called the Wordsworth Estate, where all the towers are mysteriously and perversely named after lakes—Grasmere, Derwent, Ullswater. A small girl did fall from the top of this tower in 1962; she was two years old, the daughter of a seventeen-year-old mother who was accused and acquitted of pushing her. Her name was Diamond Bates. This is all anyone knows. The flat is now occupied by an unemployed man—"a bit simple," called Ben

Leppard. Frederica frowns in thought. She says "Monckton-Pardew. Benedictine Pards. It could be him." "He's lived there since 1962," says the council official they are talking to. "Let's try it," says Daniel.

The Wordsworth Estate has, though it is already unfashionable to say so, a certain presence, a certain style. Its concrete towers are uncompromising and erect; wide open spaces spread between them. There are little balconies and the windows vary in form—some are circular, some are small rectangles, some are large. Their frames were once painted pale blue, but are now smeared and peeling. The idea of the architect was to expose the natural materials, the concrete, the metal, so they would weather as granite weathers. But concrete does not weather as granite weathers, and the smears and stains on the tower-surfaces look like great expanses of splashed and drained dirty dishwater. The space between the towers, which on the maquette was green, with bushes and trees, is cracked asphalt, with the odd spike of a ripped-off sapling, dying in its round hole; there is green between the cracks, where the earth bulges, the green of moss, green of algae. It is a grey day in early autumn when Daniel and Frederica arrive. The wind blows fish-and-chip papers across the asphalt. The entry to Wastwater Tower stinks of urine and is stained with smeared faeces. These are clichés, and like clichés, are depressing most of all because they are commonplace and inescapable. It would be nice if the lift worked, but it does not. Frederica skips up several floors, and then, the hare to the tortoise, waits for the steadily toiling Daniel. They are both completely out of breath when they reach the thirteenth floor. Frederica's lungs are bursting, her heart is hammering. Daniel wipes his face with a handkerchief.

They are in a bare concrete landing outside a blue door with peeling paint. On the landing is a plate with a chicken bone (the rib cage) and a smear of tomato ketchup. They knock. No one answers. They knock.

A voice from the floor below says, "Ben doesn't come out."

A girl is standing there, neatly dressed in a pleated skirt, a jumper, and white school socks. She is perhaps ten years old, round-faced, and has a mixed inheritance, wiry African hair, dark red in colour, dusky cheeks, a large mouth.

"Do you know him?"

"We feed him. Mum does. We put his food, and he fetches it in when we aren't looking. He doesn't like to come out. Mum says he's a bit simple."

"What does he look like?"

"We haven't seen him for yonks. He used to be a weirdo. A long-hair. He used to get beat up. Now he don't go out."

"Can we get to see him?"

"Not if he don't answer."

"Has nobody got a key?"

"It isn't locked. No one wants to go in there. It stinks something dreadful."

Daniel tries the door. The hall is empty, the floorboards bare. There is a smell. A decaying version of Jude's lively odour. They go through a dark passageway into a largish room, which has a whole wall of glass, and is therefore full of grey light, which shows old wall-paper covered with autumn leaves, stained and sprouting salt and fungi. There is almost no furniture. A mattress, with a heap of blankets, in one corner. A table, with a row of coloured ink bottles and a pot of calligraphic pens. A Baby Belling, on the floor, encrusted with layer upon layer of burned food like the crust of an extinct volcano, black, mouldy, verdigris, soot-brown.

In another corner is a very neat heap of books, arranged in several flat towers, by size.

There is someone curled in the blankets, but he does not move.

"Jude," says Frederica.

"Out," says the ghost of the sawing voice.

"It's us. Frederica and Daniel. Your friends, we hope. We want to talk to you."

"Out."

Daniel advances and turns back the blankets. Jude is lying there in the respectable shirt he wore to the trial, which looks as though it has never subsequently been taken off. His hair is growing—it is tousled and filthy, but it is a good nest of grey wires, not a grey skull cap. Daniel sees that Jude is dangerously thin. He says, "We'll have to get you out of here. You'll have to come with us. I could get you into a hospital."

"You—need not strive. Officiously. To keep alive."

Frederica says, "They need your signature. For the appeal."

"There is no need. They will lose."

"Jude—come on—you used to *fight,* in your way—"

"And now I am dying in my way. Go away."

In the end, they carry Jude, more or less, down the twisting stairs of the tower, and into a taxi, whose driver sniffs Jude's smell, thinks of rejecting him, looks at Daniel, and accepts. Jude begins to cry when Daniel suggests a hospital. In the end they take him to Daniel's own bedsitter, which is in Clerkenwell, and is spartan in a more cluttered way than Jude's echoing eyrie, is small, and overfurnished. Jude is bathed, by both Daniel and Frederica, moaning a little. His hair is washed, and becomes oddly floating and electric, giving him the air of a Blakean sage. He closes his eyes throughout the operations, and is dressed in Daniel's pyjamas, and put into Daniel's bed. Daniel will sleep on the sofa. "Not for the first or the last time," says Daniel. Frederica says she would have Jude, but there is Leo, there is Agatha, there is Saskia. "No," says Daniel, "he's my job. For the present."

"He's got to sign the appeal form."

Jude opens his eyes. "If you keep them from me, I will sign it." He closes them. He opens them again. "I wonder, did you find my original garments?"

"No," says Daniel.

"They were in a paper box somewhere there. They are all I have."

"You want me to go and look for them?"

"I have no others. Yours will not do for me, and you would not care to lend them. Thank you."

He closes his eyes again, and settles back into Daniel's pillow. He murmurs, "You are a man of God." There is a note of satisfaction in his voice.

Daniel lets Frederica out. He says, "I wonder how long I've got *him* for."

Frederica says, "You're both as tough as old boots. You'll get him out, when the time's right."

"Aye," says Daniel. "I will."

The Space is mysteriously hung with silken draperies, painted with symbols, cups and swords, suns and moons, sunflowers and compasses, crowns and chains. It is lit by glancing rays of coloured lights, and scented with strange smoky perfumes. Two parties of travellers advance across it and meet. One party are fair tall folk, cloaked in shimmering grey cloaks over flowing green robes belted with silver belts wrought of leaf-shapes and clasped with emeralds. All wear crystal wings that flash in the changing light and silver bands in their flowing hair, from which simple jewels hang to rest on their brows. They are led by a white-robed figure, hooded, with a tall stave in his hand, and they are singing quietly.

A Elbereth Gilthoniel
Silivren penna miriel
O menel aglar elennath!

Their feet are sandalled or shod with fine boots in pale leather.

The second party are white-robed and masked with sun and moon masks in silver and gold. They are crowned with mistletoe, and in their midst are figures partly naked, but with bright metallic sunbursts and crescents covering their sex. They are led by a Bard who introduces them:

> *These, the Twenty-four in whom the Divine Family*
> *Appear'd; and they were One in Him. A Human Vision!*
> *Human Divine, Jesus the Saviour, blessed for ever and ever.*
> *Selsey true friend, who afterwards submitted to be devour'd*
> *By the waves of Despair, whose Emanation rose above*
> *The flood, and was nam'd Chichester, lovely, mild & gentle! Lo!*
> *Her lambs bleat to the sea-fowls' cry, lamenting still for Albion.*
> *Submitting to be call'd the son of Los, and his Emanations*
> *Submitting to be call'd Enitharmon's daughters and be born*
> *In vegetable mould, created by the Hammer and Loom*
> *In Bowlahoola & Allamanda where the Dead wail night & day.*
> *I call them by their English names: English, the rough basement,*
> *Los built the stubborn structure of the Language, acting against*
> *Albion's melancholy, who must else have been a Dumb despair.*

The Bard steps forward. He says:

"Let us celebrate the mythopoeic imagination of Albion. Let us celebrate the Makers, who made systems and were not enslaved by those of other men, but broke through to the Vision of what lies beyond Language, to the eternal symbols and the unchanging Light. Let us celebrate the sevenfold vision of William Blake and the true Jerusalem; let us celebrate also J. R. R. Tolkien, who single-handed forged the Elvish languages and the myths of Middle-Earth and the lands beyond the Western Sea. What you are about to see is a Rite and an Invocation, a Calling and a Dance, and who knows what shadowy forms, or creatures of light, may not come into our ken as we weave together these two powerful nests of language, text and textures, into the warp and woof of a new Cloth of Dreams . . ."

The figures on the stage begin to chant, and to pass long, shining threads from one to the other. The Elves sing of Earendil and Luvah. The Bard describes the work of the Emanations.

> The Feminine separates from the Masculine and both from Man
> Ceasing to be his Emanations, Life to themselves assuming:
> And while they circumscribe his Brain and while they circumscribe
> His Heart and while they circumscribe his Loins, a Veil and Net
> Of Veins of red Blood grows around them like a scarlet robe.

The threads are now mixed with red threads, and one of the Bards is turning in the weaving like a bobbin.

> Covering them from the sight of Man, like the woven veil of Sleep
> Such as the Flowers of Beulah weave to be their Funeral Mantles;
> But dark, opaque, tender to touch, and painful and agonising
> To the embrace of love and the mingling of soft fibres
> Of tender affection, that no more the Masculine mingles
> With the Feminine, but the Sublime is shut out from the Pathos
> In howling torment, to build stone walls of separation, compelling
> The Pathos to weave curtains of hiding secrecy from the torment.

The Elves sing of the terrors of Orthanc and Minas Morgul; of the web of Shelob and the Eye in Barad-dur. A soft voice sings of the hope of severing the bonds, breaking the bounds, making a bridge of rainbow light.

Happenings are happening all over London. Frederica has come to this one with Alan Melville. The Bard is Richmond Bly, and Alan and Frederica are present out of morbid curiosity. It is hard to see what is happening as the stage is full of smoke and threads of silk and swirling garments and weaving, and it is hard to hear, as there is an accompaniment of breathy flute music, pan-pipes and tinkling bells. There is also a vague noise of disturbance from outside, from the car park which adjoins the theatre-department building where Richmond Bly's Rite is being performed. It is a noise of motor bikes revving, and drumming, African drumming, Frederica thinks vaguely, and gongs, and tambourines, and cymbals. This noise swells. The mythopoeic celebrants of Albion dance meditatively on. A voice says, "I am the Lady Galadriel, I wear the Ring of Water." The noise from the car park has diminished, and appears to have gone away, but then returns in a much louder burst. It is clear that the noisemakers have left the car park and entered the building through the basement. A kind of rhythmic drumming and stamping begins to mount from the depths. Alan Melville says, "I knew we ought to come, I knew it would be interesting." Frederica says, "Interesting might be the wrong word."

The invaders swarm through the theatre. Many of them are naked, painted with flame-shapes in red lipstick, or corkscrew patterns in what looks like woad. They are carrying posters on sticks, most of which depict the Buddhist monk who immolated himself by fire in Vietnam, a cross-legged seated body clothed in saffron, clothed in flame, clothed in smoke, keeling over on stone. Others are carrying stout staves on which are impaled pigs' heads, sliced in half, showing teeth and vertebrae and brains. They run up to the stage. They are many, they are male and female. The drumming intensifies. They fight with the robed figures. They seize the pipes and little bells, they play their own rhythm. A figure in black, a kind of blond demon, leaps to the front of the stage, swaying to the drumming, and takes the microphone from its place beside the Bard. "Let's have a poem," says the poet. It is Mickey Impey. "Let's have a poem! Zag is coming! Let's have a proper poem." He begins to chant:

> *The Zy-Goats dance*
> *To the ziggurat*
> *They dance and prance*
> *For the Cat in the Hat*
> *The great gold Cat*
> *In his shiny Hat*
> *In his super-sleek sanguine*
> *Shiny Hat.*
> *By the light of the skoobs*
> *They waggle their boobs*
> *Wiggle their pubes*
> *Snort in their tubes*
> *For the glittering Cat*
> *By the ziggurat.*
>
> *Goat and compasses*
> *Cat and fiddle*

Lush farrago and Tarradiddle.
Amphisbæna
And alley-cat
What's the meaning
Of this and that?
Scallywags
And Pleiades
Orthoptera
Helicoptera
THE BEES THE BEES THE BEES KNEES.

Spirally spirally spirally twirl
Widdershins widdershins widdershins whirl
Coil recoil
Trouble and toil
The cosmic pot on the cosmic boil.
Shimmy your pelvis
Twirl your toes
Rotate the honey pot
Roger the rose.
Come and dance
Dance and prance
To the ziggurat
And the great gold Cat
In his super-sleek sanguine
Shiny Hat.

The audience laugh and chant with him. Paul–Zag in his white satin trousers and jester's jacket comes through the audience, unsmiling and beautiful. He steps up on to the stage. He is followed by his Group, all in white satin, carrying baby-baths, pink plastic baby-baths full of something dark and slopping. Richmond Bly, masked and robed, steps forward to confront the intruder, tripping over the microphone wire attached to Mickey Impey, recovering himself.

"Excuse me," says Richmond Bly, behind his sun mask. "This is a serious Rite."

"I know," says Paul–Zag. "It's a Happening, It's all happening. You're happening, I'm happening, we're happening, it's really happy. Take delight in the unforeseen. Allow me to make you an honorary member of Zag and the Szyzgy (Ziggy) Zy-Goats."

He waves forward his followers. The stage is crowded with grinning half-pigs'-heads on sticks, with burning monks, with singing and dancing.

"You are a jolly goodfellow," says Zag to Richmond Bly. "And I am a jolly goodfellow. Let us be joined."

A young woman wearing a dead poppy and a few feathers dips her arms into the baby-bath, which is full of pale intestines in dark blood. Zag lifts a string of them above his head and winds them round the neck of Richmond Bly, round his own neck. The red runs down their white clothes, both their white clothes.

"No," says Richmond Bly. "I always—faint at the sight of blood."

"Loss of consciousness is good for you," says Mickey Impey. "Dissolve the one in the many."

"No, really," says Richmond Bly, plucking at his fleshy necklace without being able to bring himself to touch it.

"You are not the Wizard of Oz," says Mickey Impey, snatching off Bly's sun mask. Paul Ottokar stands smiling, grave and lovely, dripping blood.

The followers are stuffing their trousers with offal, with intestines, and drawing them dripping out through their flies.

Richmond Bly's heavy face goes lemon-coloured, goes candlewax. He falls heavily forward, fulfilling his word. His face slides in pigs' blood. Some of the audience laugh. The drummers drum. The drummers drum. The drumming makes it better, increases the laughter.

"Make things *happen*," cries Mickey Impey. "Happenings don't have *audiences*. We are all *actors*. Move, you tubs of lard, get off your bums, come and dance."

"All the same," says Frederica. It's not *real*."

"The pigs' heads are real," says Alan. "And the monk was real."

"Oh hell," says Frederica. "I'm going home. I've got to relieve the baby-sitter. No one in the future will think there was anyone who had to leave a Happening to relieve a baby-sitter."

A smell of burning begins to mix with the smells of butchery and incense. A smell of burning paint. There is the soft sound of an explosion. Someone begins to call out, "Clear the theatre. Fire! Fire!" People push and cry. The drums drum. It turns out later that someone has set fire to various small skoob towers in the corners of the studios, and that a can of acrylic paint has exploded. Frederica hurries down the stairs amongst clouds of smoke through a river of foam. She does not wait to see whether the building will burn down—the baby-sitter is waiting. She goes down into the Underground, on the long, plunging escalator down which the sculptor Stone wandered wildly to his death.

The escalators are crowded. Frederica sometimes studies every face, looking for the differences, the similarities, the thoughts, and sometimes glides past, seeing all the white spaces as identical. Tonight she sees nothing, no faces, a white procession. A voice cries, from below, "Frederica!"

She sees his face coming up to her from the dark. Clean-cut, well-groomed, blond over a black suit and a black plastic raincoat, John Ottokar. As they pass, she shouts, truculent, "What have you got to say for yourself?"

"I was scared."

"No excuse."

"But true. Wait for me."

"No, I won't." She is enraged. But when she reaches the bottom she regrets this. She hesitates, turns, runs round, and gets on to the up escalator. She meets John Ottokar, again about half-way, coming down.

He says, "I said Wait!"

"And I said No. And then I changed my mind."

They pass and sail on. They are very long escalators, the longest in the Underground. She thinks she hears him call "Wait" again, and does wait, stands at the head of the escalator, looking down at the faces coming up, all different in the unearthly lights, none of them his. After a long time she makes her way down again. He is not at the foot of the escalator either. And the baby-sitter is waiting. She walks through arches, she gives a coin to a singer who is softly asking, "Where have all the flowers gone?" She waits on the platform, looking under the dark arch, smelling old, old soot, thinking of the dead Stone and the living Ottokar.

There are plenty of seats in the train. She sits by herself, thinking that this is not her time, she did not enjoy the Happening, though it had its interest. She looks at her shadowy face in the dark window. White, staring, with dark eyes, darker than they are, smudged with exhaustion. A transparent paleface, a ghost, more elegant than the real flesh in a shining mirror. She meets her own eyes and catches the look of someone standing, farther along, someone reflected, by an angle of the light, two or three or four times, his face upon his face upon his face, like fine paper masks, but really only one, one face, John Ottokar. She smiles tentatively at him in the dark glass. His mouth lifts in an equally tentative smile. She moves her head, fractionally, the ghost-light in the red hair, and he nods. She hears the rustle of PVC, she smells, amongst the soot and cigarette smoke, faintly, the blond hair, the presence. She does not look round. She says to the glass, "I've learned to do without you."

"I never doubted that. The question is, Can you be doing *with* me?"

"I might."

"That's good."

They touch hands, and smile at each other's shadow in the glass.

After all the trouble, the announcement in the Press in December is curt.

Babbletower wins appeal. Judge misdirected jury. He dropped them in at the deep end and left them to swim with no directions.

"The appeal judges found in favour of the publishers Bowers and Eden, and of Jude Mason, author of *Babbletower: A Story for the Children of Our Time*. The publishers had appealed on eleven grounds. The appeal judges dismissed most of these, but agreed that the trial judge had been unnecessarily disparaging of 'expert' witnesses, and had not given the jury sufficient direction concerning the defence of literary merit, 'dropping them in at the deep end and leaving them to swim as best they could' in the words of one of the appeal judges."

There are photographs of Rupert Parrott, drinking champagne with his legal advisers. There are only old photographs of Jude Mason. Daniel brings these newspapers to Jude, who is still lying in Daniel's bed. He is less skeletal and is wearing new pyjamas, provided by Ginnie Greenhill. Jude sits up and scrutinises the papers expressionlessly.

"So that's all right," says Daniel. "You can get up now, and make a lot of money, and be famous."

"No. I want none of it. They've picked me clean, I want none of it."

"You've been justified."

"Some said one thing. Some more have said another. It is not good to be *talked over,* picked over."

"Well, however that may be, my friend, you've got to get up now, and go elsewhere."

"You should have thought of that before you brought me here."

"I did. I said you could stay until you were better. Now, I think you'd better go."

"I may not be better."

"That's a risk we've got to take. You can get up and buy me a drink."

"I might," says Jude. "I'll think about it."

 The three friends looked at the heap of bones, white bones, fresh bones, skulls and ribs and shins and carpals and tarsals chucked together, with a rag of cooked flesh here and there upon them.

"The Krebs have come, and gone," said Samson Origen.

"We must not touch these," said Colonel Grim. "In case they return, and learn we are still alive."

"Let us go away from here," said Turdus Cantor. A beast began to howl somewhere far away in the forest, and a great bird turned and turned above them in a hot blue sky. So the three old men began to walk away across the valley, looking back from time to time at the Tower, and the grim mound at its foot, until it was so far away that its human origin could not be distinguished, and it looked like a chance heap of rocks, sprouting green here and there, with what might be shells or pebbles clustered palely at its foot. And they went on walking, and if the Krebs did not catch up with them, they are walking still. ∾

Help call in church basement. Hugh
Fredrika + son + Hugh   Sex + the Rig. p. 25